Anonymous

Semi-Tropic California

Anonymous

Semi-Tropic California

ISBN/EAN: 9783337405588

Printed in Europe, USA, Canada, Australia, Japan

Cover: Foto ©Andreas Hilbeck / pixelio.de

More available books at **www.hansebooks.com**

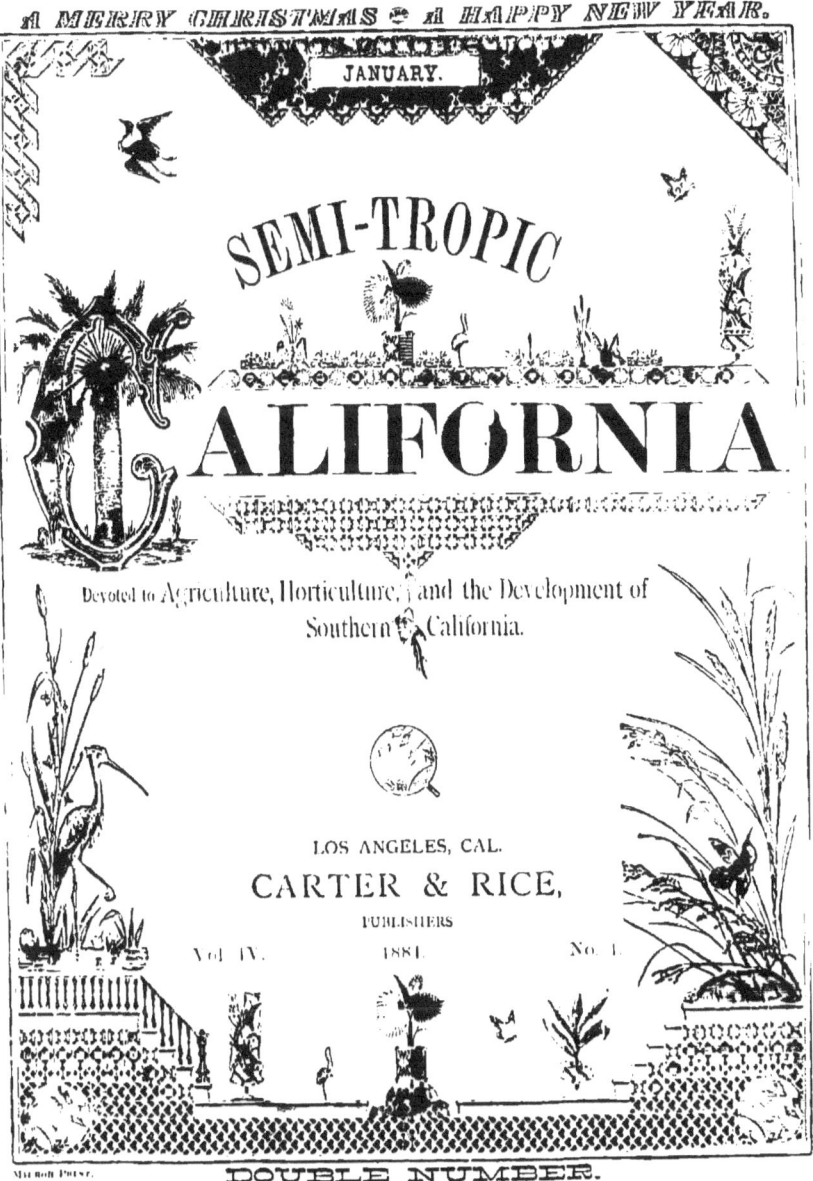

A MERRY CHRISTMAS & A HAPPY NEW YEAR.

JANUARY.

SEMI-TROPIC

CALIFORNIA

Devoted to Agriculture, Horticulture, and the Development of Southern California.

LOS ANGELES, CAL.

CARTER & RICE,

PUBLISHERS

Vol. IV.   1881.   No. 1.

DOUBLE NUMBER.

SOUTHERN CALIFORNIA HORTICULTURIST.

VOL. IV.   LOS ANGELES, CAL., JANUARY, 1881.   No. 1.

THE OLIVE.

BY C. J. KENWORTHY, IN THE "FLORIDA DISPATCH."

Botanists maintain that the olive—*olea Europæa*—is indigenous to the southeastern countries of the Mediterranean, and to have spread westward at a very early period. The traveler who visits the central Riviera from the west observes the increase in the size of the olive trees as the train carries him to the east. At Beaulieu there is an ancient olive tree which measures 23 feet in circumference at four feet from the ground. It is said to have yielded 375 pounds of oil annually. Some estimates its age at 1,000 years. Very large and aged trees are only to be found in the warmest and most sheltered parts of the Riviera, owing to the severe frosts which at times destroyed whole districts of olive yards. Great damage resulted from the frosts of 1709–1788, and large numbers were destroyed in the severe winters of 1820, 1829 and 1839. The olive appears to be unable to resist a temperature below 21 or 22 degrees.

The varieties of the olive are numerous. Risso describes forty varieties of the *O. Europæa*, and the *Hortus Judaicus* mentions fifteen varieties as cultivated in France. The variety most generally cultivated in the maritime Alps is that known as the *olevier pleureur*. It reaches a height of over thirty feet, and gives a full crop every two years. Its oil is good, and keeps well and long. At Cannes the "pleureur" is exclusively cultivated. At Carnoules a variety with upright habit and dark green leaves is generally grown. At points the following varieties are cultivated near the sea: *O. plynale, O. rostrata,* and *O. longifolia*; in the valleys, *O. renaria, O. rimoana,* and *O. rubra* succeed the best; on the hills, *O. pleureur, O. regalis,* and *O. caucifoli* flourish, and on the highest and most exposed points, *O. minima, O. subterra,* and *O. precosa* are planted, because of their power to resist low thermometric ranges.

This tree will grow in any but very damp soils. The soil best adapted to its cultivation is a stiff soil, though it is stated that the best oil is produced on a moderately light soil. The trees are planted about 20 feet apart. Owing to their slow growth they are propagated by planting small branches, or rooted suckers, which spring up around the trunk of an adult tree. The stock thus obtained is generally grafted in May with the particular variety which the grower wishes to cultivate. Raised in this

way, the olive grows about half a crop at the age of twenty years, and at forty years if raised from seed.

Where the olive is grown as in some parts of the Riviera, on the hillsides, the ground is terraced; each terrace is faced with a stone wall, and keeping these in repair is an important item of expense. The olive blossoms on the Mediterranean from April to June. The berries ripen and the harvest is collected from November to May. The fruit grown on the small trees of Provence are gathered by hand. On the Riviera the laborers knock them down by means of long sticks, or by shaking the branches. If the trees are very large, men ascend them and shake the berries off the branches. The fallen berries are generally collected from the ground by females. It is interesting to notice that this custom of beating the olives is expressly mentioned in the Old Testament, Deuteronomy, xxiv, 20: "When thou beatest thine olive trees, thou shalt not go over the boughs again." The olives are collected from the ground and transported to the mills; some are worked by water power and some by oxen. The mills are the property of private individuals, who supply everything necessary for the extraction of the oil, and only require a small reward for the workmen, and the *reseva*, or residue of the olive paste after the first and second qualities have been extracted, as fuel for the use of necessary appliances.

The mills are usually two stories, the lower containing the mill and presses for the best qualities of oil, and in the upper story the mill in which the *reseva* is reground. The mills and presses are of the most primitive description, and do not appear to have been improved for a century. When ground, the material is placed in *sportini*. The *sportini* are made of hemp, like an archery target. Let the reader imagine two archery targets sewed together at their margins, with a round hole in the center of each. The section of such a bag, filled with paste, forms an oval receptacle. Twelve *sportini* are placed one above the other in the press, and the oil which runs out is the *huile a manges*—"cold drawn" oil. The second quality oil is extracted by impressing the paste with boiling water, which is poured over the *sportini* as the press descends. The residue is the *reseva*, the miller's perquisite, which contains about one third of the oil. The residue is treated with hot water in the press; the oil and water is run into a trough, agitated by a water-wheel, and then into a series of square stone reservoirs, each lower than the other, so that but the surface water can

pass from one to the next. In these troughs the residue gradually deposits, and the oil rises to the surface. Fermentation is set up in the deposit, and more oil is liberated. Finally the residue is dried and cut in lumps about a foot square, and used as fuel or manure.

The miller prepares two qualities of oil from his residue. That which results from the first pressing is named *huile de reseva,* and that which results from fermentation in the reservoirs is called *huile d'enfer.* The quantity of virgin oil used by one hundred pounds of good quality berries is about twelve pounds, and of *reseva* oil about four pounds. The mills and processes are very primitive, and American ingenuity could improve upon them.

On the Mediterranean the olive crop is an uncertain one, owing to late spring frosts and dry seasons. The rule is, in average periods, for one year to give no crops at all, the next a limited crop, and the third a full one, followed by the cycle of three again. On the continent the olive is subject to two diseases. The *tephritis olivæ* deposits its eggs in the berry in the early stages of its growth, resulting in the destruction of the fruit attacked. A fungus, *demetium monophyllum,* attacks the leaves and buds and the trees look as though they were covered with fine soot. But the fungoid disease is principally met with in damp localities and in continental valleys. Owing to the fact that a large portion of the oil exported from the Mediterranean consists of cotton-seed oil, as the vine is being destroyed by the phylloxera in a large portion of the Riviera, the orange and lemon cannot be successfully grown, and it would appear that a large number of the residents of that country will be compelled to immigrate. Owing to the high price of wool, and its great consumption at the health resorts and the large cities, olive trees are being annually destroyed to meet the demand.

We very readily appreciate virtue in others, but the appreciation is hardly ever strong enough to make us imitate it.

We make solemn promises to be awfully good when we are in danger of death, but when we begin to get well we forget all about them.

One feels complimented if you tell him that he has a heart of oak, but if you carry the simile still further, and tell him that he has a wooden head also, he is apt to feel that you are carrying the joke a little too far.

SEMI-TROPIC
CALIFORNIA,
— AN —
ILLUSTRATED MONTHLY.

Devoted to Agriculture, Horticulture, and the Development of Southern California.

Terms: $1.50 per Annum, in Advance.

• Office, Rooms 1 & 58, Baker Block.

Address, - - Geo. Rice, Los Angeles, Cal.

GEORGE RICE,
Secretary S. California Horticultural Soc'y,
Editor and Manager.

With this number we commence our fourth volume, assured by the past that our future is a bright one.

During the past year we have done double duty—first, as an organ of the Immigration Bureau, and second, in the interest of horticulture in Southern California.

We name horticulture second for the reason that The Semi-Tropic was originally intended to do a strictly immigration work, and it was a secondary consideration that we absorbed the *Southern California Horticulturist*.

The demands on us for a horticultural or an agricultural paper are so imperative that we shall devote considerable space and time to these topics hereafter.

We have made arrangements with many of the foremost and most practical men and women of Southern California to write articles for our pages—articles from a practical standpoint, containing information acquired by years of experience on the Pacific coast.

Is there a farmer, large or small, in Southern California but can be benefited by the experience of others?

We are sure every one should be a subscriber to a paper that is intended for him, and we ask every reader whose eyes fall upon this article to subscribe, and to persuade his neighbor to do likewise.

Help increase the circulation of the Semi-Tropic, and so increase its power of benefitting you.

Subscribe *now*.

See the special offer in next column to subscribers. Attend to it at once, and get your neighbor to do likewise.

OUR GREETING.

We wish our readers a merry Christmas and a happy New Year! Three years ago the *Horticulturist* came into existence; one year ago it was merged into the Semi-Tropic California; to-day we feel the pleasant privilege of being a welcome guest in many a household, and that our cordial good will is responded to by many who bear towards us sentiments of real gratuity.

Many are they who have left the cold and bleak North and East to enjoy our beautiful climate, and who have made homes among us. In these homes we are assured of a hearty response to our Christmas greetings.

It is very encouraging to have so many congratulations from our horticulturists for the work we have done in pointing out the most successful methods, as well as the mistakes made, in agriculture and horticulture.

The coming year is destined to be one of unusual prosperity. The tide of immigration is setting in; our seasons have been good, and we look forward to a year of "peace and plenty."

"Hard times" will be the refrain of the "hard cases" who refuses to labor, and can not always eat the bread of idleness; while the true energetic American citizen, who uses his talents, will of necessity prosper.

So once more, with oft repeated wishes for your prosperity and happiness, and with our warm assurances of good will and happily cheer, we wish our patrons, friends, and everybody, a merry Christmas and a happy New Year.

SPECIAL GRAND OFFER.

We have bought and paid for one hundred dollars' worth of garden and flower seeds, from the Mohawk Valley seed gardens, of which we will give *one dollar's worth* to each of the first one hundred subscribers who remit us $1.50. We will also give our premium map (retail price $1.50) to each subscriber. To sum up, we will give

The Semi-Tropic Cal., 1 year, . . . $1.50
Map of Cal., Nev., Arizona, etc., . .   1.50
Seeds (your choice from Catalogue, .   1.00

Total, ... $4.00

All for ($1.50) one dollar and fifty cents.
Call on or address,

                         GEO. RICE,
                    Los Angeles, Cal.
(Room 1, Baker Block.)

Answers to correspondence will be one of the features of our paper hereafter. Send in your questions.

SIXTH DISTRICT AGRICULTURAL ASSOCIATION.

Under the able management of Messrs. J. E. Hollenbeck, Gov. Downey, O. W. Childs, J. F. Barretto and L. J. Rose, of the Board of Directors, the Sixth District Agricultural Association is a success. The Society owns the beautiful Agricultural Park, worth at least $20,000, and freed from all incumbrance, besides cash on hand for contingencies and premiums at future fairs. That the Society's affairs will be judiciously managed by the above named gentlemen no one will doubt. The remaining members of the Board, residing at a distance, cannot, of course, give much time to the local management of the affairs of the Society. We believe the interests of Southern California can best be served by the harmonious working of the two Societies (the Agricultural and Horticultural).

The Agricultural Society should do as it did last year—make an exhibit of fine stock, and, by the proper use of the finest race track in the State, encourage the raising of thoroughbred and fast horses in our own locality.

There is abundant field of usefulness for both Societies, which, in our opinion, would be cramped and hindered were the two united.

LOCAL HORTICULTURAL SOCIETIES.

We consider a local society a necessity in every neighborhood that would make progress in its work. It is at the meetings of such organizations that an exchange of experiences benefits each member. The active, energetic Fruit Growers' Association of Riverside is the foundation of the peculiar success of that locality. It is through the influence of these societies that people are educated to important methods of action. There is no need of any man losing his identity as a fruit grower by having common methods of action with others. One thing is certain, we cannot exterminate any common pest that may attack our fruit growing interests without united action, and this may be best secured by means of local societies.

We venture the assertion that no man is so thoroughly well posted in his farming operations but that he can learn new and advantageous things from such a society. Many new men in the business are planting orchards and vineyards, and they should have the benefit of the experience of those who have been fruit growers for years.

It is the experience of every man who

by ... a member of such a society, that ... time and money well spent to attend ... meetings.

By the united action of a society a pressure can be brought to bear that cannot be withstood, be it in marketing their products, or asking a law to protect.

SEASON HINTS.

It is time to make arrangements for planting trees, to be looking around for grape cuttings, to be getting your orders ready for new and choice varieties of fruits —large and small.

Trees by the roadside should be planted by every farmer or owner of a lot. The eucalyptus and pepper tree will grow almost without irrigation, if planted early, so as to get a good start from the late rains.

Blue-grass plats can be started by sowing the seed during the rains. How beautiful a plat of grass is, and how easy it is to have one. The ground should be well broke and pulverized, and after sowing the seed, covered with well-rotted straw and manure. A sprinkling of the seed over the plat, during the late rains, will insure a good set.

If the plat to be planted is exposed to the sun, sow wheat or barley with the first sowing of blue-grass seed—this forms a sod and protects the young grass. Cut the barley before it ripens, and water the plat well and often until well set.

The planting of cereals should receive the prompt attention of every farmer who intends to sow this season. Don't put it off too long.

Plants by mail is a branch of business that is rapidly increasing in importance each year. It is an excellent way for us here on the Pacific coast to get the choice varieties of small fruits that the Eastern nurserymen have brought to such a high standard. Strawberries, raspberries, currants, gooseberries, cuttings of fruits, grapes, etc., etc. For obtaining small quantities of new and choice varieties of fruits, it also proves a very cheap method for those nearer by, as quite a large number or variety of plants can be mailed for fifty cents or one dollar's worth of postage. The cost is equally low for postage, whether sending 3,000 miles away, or only a score or two.

We hope many of our horticulturists will take our advice and do something more in small fruits than they have done heretofore. We have a large list of catalogues from nurserymen all over the country, that can be consulted by calling at this office.

STRAWBERRIES.

No farm or garden should be without a strawberry bed. The farmer who of all others should have an abundance, so generally has no strawberries. We put in our plea for his family, and insist that he shall provide them with this excellent fruit—not only a few as a luxury, but an abundance. The time is near at hand for the setting of the plants, and it is time to look round for the choicest specimens. A fine variety requires no more ground or attention than a poor kind, and we advise every one who intends to grow this luscious fruit to be careful to get the best, even if the first cost is much more than for an inferior quality. Much that has been said about strawberry culture has conveyed the impression that it is a great deal of trouble; that runners have to be cut off and much care given otherwise, while in fact it is no more trouble to raise strawberries than it is to grow carrots. But the cost is very little—nothing compared with the result in fruit. One can begin as small as he pleases; if he cannot afford the outlay for a large bed, let him buy enough for a start and raise his own plants. It makes no difference where the farmer may live, he can get plants by mail by the hundred. Some of the choice kinds they are raising East—the Mt. Vernon or others—will do well here.

It is the first step which tells. While we have in view especially the family comfort, it may be well to consider that in most localities enough berries can be sold from the first crop to pay for the whole outlay only don't sell and let the family go without, but have enough for both demands.

How many shall I plant? will be one of the first questions to decide. An ordinary family should have at least two hundred plants, and generally four hundred will not be found too many, if the fruit is used freely. It is better to provide for an abundance.

What kinds? If restricted to one kind, we have no hesitation in saying Charles Downing. If there are successful strawberry-growers in the vicinity, find what does best with them, and plant the same kind. If 400 plants are set there may safely be four kinds. Charles Downing, Monarch of the West, Champion and Sharpless would be a good selection, but it may be varied and not go amiss. The Wilson is a good market berry, is easily grown; is firm as I ship well, and is large in quality we do not consider it as good as any as named above.

How to plant: Select a good bit of soil,

all the better if it was in potatoes last year, and if practicable, within sight of the house, and prepare it just as you would for a good crop of cabbages; this means an abundance of the best manure well worked in. Mark out the rows two feet apart, three if a cultivator is to be used, and set the plants one foot apart in the row, using a trowel to open the ground, and when the plant is put in, crowd the soil down firmly over the roots with both hands. Thereafter run the cultivator, hoe, or rake, often enough to make the soil mellow and keep down the weeds. The plants will by and by throw out runners. Turn them into the row and let them take root. For the after treatment of the bed, consult "Notes about Work" at the proper season.

Raising plants: If it is preferred to buy a few plants to start with, and raise a stock to put out next year, set these two feet apart each way, and let runners form. Ashes are very useful to promote the growth of runners.

Finally, plant strawberries, and do it this spring.

Get ready for the Citrus Fair, March 14th, at the Pavilion. Selected oranges can be forwarded in their growth by thinning out and only leaving a few on a branch. Partially girdling small branches with one or more oranges will also increase the size.

Remember that this fair will be of great importance to Southern California. The premium list will be large and complete, and all premiums guaranteed.

Defiance and Champlain Wheats.— A. M. Southworth in Herald. In March, 1879, I obtained from Messrs. B. K. Bliss & Sons, of New York, one pound each of Defiance and Champlain wheats. The end of the second harvest with this seed gives a net result from the pound of Defiance wheat, 308 lbs., with a volunteer crop of 200 lbs. the second year, or at the rate of 80 and 28 cents to the acre. From the pound of Champlain wheat, 325 lbs. the first year, and a volunteer crop of 300 lbs. the second year, or at the rate of 82 and 25 cents per acre. Total result of second year's crop from two pounds of wheat, 1,800 lbs. of grain and 500 tons of hay. This was grown on a rich, sandy loam of bottom land, about six ft. to water, and two miles south of west side of rare track. I sowed four acres of White Australian on the same kind of land, and it rusted to be worthless.

Some men grumble because they have no opportunity, while other men go to work to make opportunities for themselves.

It is a curious fact that from vice to ruin the road is a long and hard one, while from virtue to vice the road is very short.

LOS ANGELES.

COUNTY AND CITY.

ONE HUNDRED years ago the fourth of September next, the order was issued from Mission San Gabriel, by the then Governor of California, Felipe de Neve, directing the establishment of the Pueblo of Los Angeles.

(And here we would suggest that the event should be celebrated, and that there could be no more appropriate manner of celebration than by an exposition of the products of our soil, our improvements in stock-raising, our advancement in floriculture, and last but not least, by an enthusiastic gathering of robust, comfortable, healthy people, such as no other part of the earth can bring together.)

water taken from the river for irrigation purposes.

The first houses were adobes, similar to those now standing. We believe many of the buildings now standing in Sonora town were among the first built.

THE MISSIONS.

Sixteen years after the founding of Los Angeles, the third and last Los Angeles county mission, San Fernando, was established in the valley which bears its name. The oldest of these missions, San Antonio, was founded July 11, 1771, the second, San Gabriel, Sept. 8, the same year. The Priests were the power; and the government of the county, as well as of the State, was practically in the hands of the missions.

for some time thereafter Los Angeles the nominal seat of the Territorial Government. First Echendia, and afterward Pio Pico [now a citizen of this city], were appointed Governors by the Mexican authorities.

The early history of the county is exceedingly interesting—a portion of it as thrilling as a romance.

It would appear, to the casual observer of our history, that Los Angeles is an old settled country, when in fact it is a new country, open for a tide of industrious immigrants.

Los Angeles may be said to have sprung into life with the tide of emigration which set in for Southern California since the war. Practically speaking, So uth ern California, with her grape vines over one hundred

RESIDENCE OF J. E. HOLLENBECK, LOS ANGELES.

The first settlement was composed of forty-six persons, twenty of whom were children under ten years of age. Of the twelve adult males, two were Spaniards, one a native of China, the other nine of some one of the following places: Sinaloa, Sonora, or Lower California.

For the center of the town, a parallelogram was laid out as a public square, and is now our plaza, opposite the Cathedral "Church of the Lady of our Angels." Dwellings were built on three sides of this plaza; half the remaining side was designed for public buildings, and the other half for an open space.

At a short distance from the plaza, and on the low grounds along the river, thirty fields were laid out for cultivation, and

The first vineyard planted in San Gabriel contained 3,000 vines. It was called *Viña Madre*, "Mother Vineyard," and from it sprang the many vineyards throughout the State.

Padre José María Salvedea brought this mission to the zenith of its prosperity. He instituted a thorough system of improvement and ornamentation. Everything under his rule was organized, and this organization was sustained by compulsion. His vigorous rule resulted in the production of large orchards and vineyards, and the exercise of almost every useful industry. His discipline was excessively severe, the lashing a common mode of its expression.

In January, 1833, Don Manuel Victoria, then Governor of California, abdicated, and

years old, and her missions crumbling into decay with old age, is yet a new country, with hardly one fourth of the tillable lands occupied.

THE ANGELES.

Nues t ra Señora Reina de Los Angeles, "Our Lady, Queen of the Angels," the county seat of the county, the metropolis of Southern California, the railroad center of the State, has a population of 1,800, which will be more than doubled in the next decade. The city is lighted with gas; has an abundant system of water works and irrigating ditches, has three lines of street railroad in operation, has an efficient fire department, a well regulated police force, and all the machinery of a well regulated city.

EDUCATIONAL.

In educational matters this city ranks second to none in the State, and California bears the enviable reputation of having one of the best public school systems in the United States, and the administration of the system is highly satisfactory. In addition to our complete system of city schools (to which we shall devote more time in a future issue), we have a number of other schools that take high rank in educational matters. St. Vincent College, Sisters' school, and a number of private schools; the University of Southern California, of which we give an engraving on another page, all speak well of the attention paid to the present and future educational wants of the city. Southern California should now have a Normal School, and it is believed that the coming Legislature will locate one here.

We have a Public Library Association, with well appointed rooms, a large library of books, and all the leading magazines and papers of the country; an institution that would do honor to a city of many times the population of this.

We have a full representation of churches, and a number of fine church buildings, and it is easy for any new-comer to find a church with which to identify himself.

Benevolent institutions take care of the unfortunate, with a provident bounty that is not excelled by any city in the country.

The societies of Masons, Odd Fellows, Good Templars, etc., etc., are all well represented.

RAILROADS.

From this city the steel tracks for the iron horse to traverse, extend their arms like the spokes from the hub of a wheel. Extending to the north, connecting with San Francisco, Sacramento, and the cities of the Alta California, and thence across the mountains and plains to Omaha, making connection with the great roads to all parts of the continent. A road extends to the East through Arizona (which is pouring her wealth into this city), through New Mexico (another new field for us), to Kansas City, connecting with the railroad center of the Mississippi, and bringing us twisted three days nearer the eastern world.

Roads also extend west to Santa Monica; south to Wilmington and the harbor of San Pedro, connecting with the Pacific Steam Ship Company's line of steamers.

Another goes to the southeast through rich valleys to Anaheim and Santa Ana, and is soon to be extended to San Diego.

Inside of two years, yet another arm will reach in to us from the East, and engine and cars, bearing the talismanic letters, A. T. & S. F. R. R., will come thundering into the gates of our city.

And here we make the prediction that Los Angeles will be a city of over 30,000 at the taking of the next census.

MANUFACTURES.

Are represented by a woolen mill that has been somewhat cramped for want of means and proper water privileges, but is now in the hands of Mr. B. F. Coulter, a gentleman of ample means, and if our city will do its Southern California alone, if properly understood

RESIDENCE OF WM H PERRY, LOS ANGELES.

the right thing as to water-power will make the woolen factory an institution of the city.

Two breweries furnish the city and county, and are extending their trade into Arizona.

The planing mills of Perry, Woodworth & Co. do an immense business in connection with their extensive lumberyards.

A number of other manufacturing enterprises will claim our attention at another time.

BANKS.

The city is represented by three banks, each of which have ample capital, and are well managed, taking rank with the best financial concerns of the country.

HEALTH.

As a health resort, Southern California is considered the great sanitarium for persons with lung affections, throat or bronchial troubles.

Persons who have traveled the world over in search of relief for consumptive tendencies, only found relief when they came here. Members of royal families of the old world have come here, and, in one instance, they have been so greatly benefited that a book was published, illustrating and telling of our wonderful country. It seems that it was time to drop the worn-out, hackneyed subject of "climate and resources," said we, go to work. But it is a fact, nevertheless, that the climate of Southern California alone, if properly understood by the outside world, would give us a population of wealthy people, who would come here to enjoy living, and gain a new lease of life, and would make this the great winter resort of the United States, and even of portions of the old world.

When that time shall come, our city will be the home of families of wealth, fine residences will be erected, employment for the poor, a home market for our luxuries that can and will be produced in profusion as soon as the demand is created.

CONCLUSION.

Los Angeles has everything to make her a great city. She already is the railroad center, has a shipping port, an extensive agricultural country surrounding, as rich as the valleys of the Nile; the great mineral regions of Southern California, Arizona, Mexico, and New Mexico, at our doors to buy of us everything we can produce, to buy of our wholesale houses, to ship their ores here for reduction as soon as smelting and reduction works shall be erected, and capital will soon find that here is the place to buy and another treasure.

We call attention to a brief review of a number of our most enterprising men and firms in another place in this paper.

SUBSCRIBE FOR THE SEMI-TROPIC CALIFORNIA. It will only cost you $1.50 for the year, and save you many times that amount.

THE SEMI-TROPIC is the only agricultural and horticultural paper in Southern Cal.

Semi-Tropical Fruits

CITRUS CULTURE

GENERAL SUGGESTIONS AND THOUGHTS ON CITRUS CULTURE, INCLUDING OUR ORANGE TRADE, PAST, PRESENT, AND PROSPECTIVE

Continued

WHEN competing railroads shall have been completed spanning the continent below the snow belt, then a new era will dawn upon us, and our noble fruit will rapidly find its way and be introduced to all portions of our country; and the day is not far distant which our orders will come from across the waters of our oceans for whole cargoes of our oranges.

We also enjoy a decided advantage for the Tahiti, and all other oranges except those grown in California, must be picked green, or in a semi-green condition, to be carried successfully to distant markets. The truth is, our oranges keep sound when, under the same circumstances, theirs would decay. Ours can be ripened on the trees, and will then keep for months, while from other orange growing districts they must be shipped almost in a green condition, or not at all.

When an orange is picked green, or only partially ripened, it is at the expense of its flavor. When picked unripe they are tough and stringy, or become sour, accompanied with a flat, insipid taste, as is always prevalent in the Tahiti oranges in our markets.

The peculiarities of our climate—the nights always cool, the absence of rain for about nine months of the year, and the general dryness of our atmosphere, prepare our oranges by a gradual and natural process, while yet on the tree, for great keeping and shipping qualities.

And then again, in the event of an emergency in the future when prices may ruin too low, all our surplus can be most profitably converted into orange wine and brandy, for which there would be an unlimited demand.

As corroborative of these statements in regard to the extraordinary keeping qualities of our oranges, and other points, I now quote from Mr. J. De Barth Shorb, of San Gabriel, Los Angeles county, an extensive pomologist. He says:

"The area up to which this culture can be once safely followed is not nearly limited, the population and consumption of the State and adjoining Territories is rapidly increasing each year; new markets are opened up to us through the energy of the Southern and Central Pacific Railways directory in extending their lines, and therefore I think the consumption will keep pace with the production and sustain the present market price. Another and most important reason to sustain this opinion rests in the fact that on this coast the oranges remain for a period of at least four to six months on the trees after they are matured without decay, thus giving us that period to ship them, while other orange producing countries cannot. To ship their fruit as soon as it is matured, and very often before; hence the demoralized condition of the orange market in our Eastern cities at certain seasons. While other countries are compelled to gather their entire crop in a very limited time, we can supply the market only as fast as the consumption warrants. Our oranges are remarkable for their good keeping qualities when packed for market. I am indebted to Mr. Wm. Pridham, agent of Wells, Fargo & Co. at Los Angeles for the following statement establishing this fact: 'Eight boxes of oranges were gathered and shipped from my orchard about the last of March, 1875, to Wells, Fargo & Co.'s agent at Portland, Maine; thence shipped to San Francisco by steamer, thence overland to New York, and from thence by steamer to Europe, where they arrived in perfect order and condition, not one being decayed; a year such trial and satisfaction that another shipment be made soon to a different destination. I have not space to give the particulars.'"

RESIDENCE OF I. W. HELLMAN, LOS ANGELES

the successful marketing of our oranges not enjoyed by other citrus producing countries of the world, in the peculiar and unparalleled keeping qualities of our fruit, and also in the great length of time from the commencement of their ripening to their full maturity. Our oranges commence to ripen and are marketable in December, and they continue to grow richer and more delicious until May, allowing fully six months to market our crops. This is a peculiarity and advantage not enjoyed, I believe, by any other known orange growing country of the world. Our oranges can become fully matured before picking from the tree, and still be in perfect condition in every respect, and when picked ripe will keep long enough for transportation to the most remote markets of the world. The Havana, the Florida,

by Mr. Shaw, of this county, to England, and after a passage of seven weeks' duration were found to be in perfect condition, though they had been open and used from during the passage through the tropics.

A San Francisco paper says: "The Tahiti orange crop is later in market than the Los Angeles crop, and arrives at San Francisco in hot weather, in a damaged condition. The business has become quite unprofitable, so much so that California importers propose to abandon the trade. This change in commercial affairs will open the market for about 3,000,000 more oranges from Los Angeles."

there has been much of trial and disappointment, but now that the causes for failure have been clearly ascertained, the outlook for the future is very bright. Wild land, adapted to the orange, costs $10 to $50 per acre; then it has to be cleared. Seedling trees cost from ten cents to $1 each, according to size. The entire cost of bringing an acre into bearing, placed at a very low estimate, is $400. An orange grove requires as much cultivation, and more than a crop of corn, and as much fertilizing every year as any crop grown. A grove in bearing is a grand good thing. At various points along the St. John's are es-

and most profitable industry in the State."

Now, for our own benefit, let us draw some inferences from the foregoing. With all labor hired, it costs us less than $ but an acre to buy land and bring our orchards into bearing. As most of us do our own ranch work, we reduce the expense materially below these figures. They who have visited Florida, and are in a position to judge, affirm that our orchards receive much stricter care, etc.; also that our trees are freer from disease. Our good groves will produce over 50,000 oranges per acre. Some sections of California are beginning to find to their cost that the whole State is not

RESIDENCE OF N. R. VAIL, LOS ANGELES

The New York *Observer* of May 8th has an article on "Orange Culture in Florida," in the course of which some facts and figures are put forth that should contain crumbs of comfort for the weak-kneed of our brethren—those who are nervous on the score of over production. This article was in the form of a letter from an old resident of the State, now living at San Mateo, on the St. John's river. I call a few of the items, though, did not want of space forbid, the entire letter were well worth reproducing:

"In the history of the past fifteen years

tablished packing houses, whose business is to collect the fruit from the orchardists, box it, and ship it to Northern markets. These packing firms generally buy the fruit on the trees and pick for themselves. At San Mateo they have paid for the fruit on the tree $15 per thousand. A good grove produces 50,000 oranges per acre—profits $630. The Florida orchardists anticipate a never a lack of market. The culture of oranges in Florida has already increased the value of real estate by many millions, and it bids fair to be the leading

suitable for orange growing. The superior keeping qualities, and the fact that our oranges will stand shipment better than the Florida fruit, are well known. Through the nearing completion of the southern route a vast market is opening to us. The great Mississippi basin, teeming with inhabitants, presents a fair field and small competition.

In regard to prices obtained for our oranges for a series of years, I again quote from Mr. Shaw:

"By very careful estimates made in 1874, of the crops on an orchard of 400 trees,

309 of which were twelve years old from the seed (the balance being too young to bear), I obtained as a net result, over and above cost of transportation to San Francisco, commissions on sales, etc., $20.50 per tree, or an average of $1,135 per acre.

"I do not claim this amount as an average crop or result, but I do think that with proper care and attention, the average can be made equal to $1,000 per acre on trees of twelve years of age. I have seen trees on our property that have yielded over 3,000 per tree, which sold at $20 per thousand, would give, per acre, a result of $1,140. The average price for the past five years throughout the county, to those who

tween 1874 and 1880 the price has never averaged less than the above figures, except the season of 1878-9, when prices ruled lower, mainly owing to the smallness of the oranges, caused principally by over bearing.

Mr. Shorb, at the Citrus Fair held in February, 1880, at the thriving colony of Riverside, San Bernardino county, said "As to profits in the year 1877-8, my own were upwards of $1,000 per acre." This present year, 1879-80, prices range from $10 to $50 per thousand, governed by the quality of the fruit, bringing the average price fully up to prices obtained in 1874.

In conclusion, I will say: Nature has

without the expense of fencing. Our market prices unbounded, at remunerative prices. What more could we ask, and to what object can our Eastern brethren or our far off friends emigrate where the inducements are more inviting, and the chances of success more abundant, than here in the sunset land of beautiful California?

Hundreds of thousands of dollars will soon be necessary to bring in exchange for our products. We shall then be a prosperous and wealthy people, and our riches will be permanent—better than bank stock, it being as United States interest bearing bonds, producing wealth and

BAKER BLOCK, LOS ANGELES

have shipped their fruit, has been between $20 and $25 per thousand, and the present year the average will likely exceed this sum. I see no reason to doubt but that the market will remain the same for many years to come."

This statement shows what oranges brought in 1874. Mr. Shorb's prediction that the market would remain the same for many years to come has thus far been fully realized and proven. I find from a careful examination of San Francisco prices current for the season of 1877-8, that the average price for Los Angeles oranges has been $22.50 per thousand. In the interim be-

done all that could be asked for California in preparing the best conditions for orange growing. Our soil is rich and deep, and easily tilled. It is naturally underlaid, and has but little hardpan to contend with; the trees to remove, no brush or under growth to clear away, and nothing to drain but clean as a prairie, and ready for the plow. Our trees are healthy and vigorous, our fruit of superb quality and good keeping, our trees productive and long lived, our climate healthy and amply temperate for the most perfect success of the business. Then, our lands are cheap at present. The herd law protects our orchards,

independence to the frugal, industrious, and enterprising of our people.

It is of use to have too many irons in the fire. When a man tries to catch two rabbits, most needs lose one, and is apt to lose both.

When a man invited a large but very brawny laborer's son at the wedding, said he stuck him by weight and didn't care for the workmanship.

Start out at once for the Santa Teresa, California, once $1.50 per year

Southern California.

TUSTIN CITY.

A THRIVING SETTLEMENT IN THE SANTA ANA VALLEY.

The town-site of Tustin was formerly owned by Mr. C. Tustin, an enterprising and liberal gentleman who, about six years ago, decided to sub-divide and sell it in small lots to settlers who wished to engage in semi-tropical fruit culture. The land proved to be well adapted for this purpose, and was speedily purchased by a class of people who developed the resources of the large portion of their means in laying out their places, and worked almost incessantly, but during a recent visit to some twenty places we failed to find one discontented person.

THE SOIL AND PRODUCTIONS.

The soil is generally a rich loam; but in some places clay predominates. Little irrigation is a tonity required; but most of the settlers irrigate to a greater or less degree. Every variety of fruit known in temperate and semi-tropical regions thrives luxuriantly, and some of the finest specimens of corn, potatoes, and roots on exhibition at the Los Angeles fair came from Tustin.

quinces and lemons, from H. Maxy; oranges and lemon lemons, from Mr. Wilson, the largest orange ever grown in Los Angeles county, from Mr. Preble, corn, from Messrs. Snow & Adams and several other parties. There was here a general assortment of fruits, grains, beans, etc., showing the capability of the soil for the production of these articles. The credit of hosting the exhibits belongs to Mr. H. K. Snow, who spent several days in boxing and shipping them.

CLIMATE AND LOCATION OF TUSTIN.

Tustin is really a portion of Santa Ana, and does not boast of any extensive mer-

TEMPLE BLOCK, LOS ANGELES

rich valley in a manner which astonished the old settlers who would probably have told you that the land was only fit for grazing. But the new-comers thought otherwise, and ploughed deep and cultivated thoroughly, planted orchards and vineyards, erected handsome cottages, fine residences, church and school buildings, and to-day there is no portion of our county which presents greater attractions, or has a more promising future than Tustin.

To accomplish anything on a barren twenty-acre tract in Tustin, or any other portion of Los Angeles county, requires money and hard work for several years. The settlers expended, in many cases, a

The whole exhibit from this section was highly creditable, and surprised and delighted visitors. Judge McKee, of the Supreme Court of California, said in the presence of the writer that when he had inspected the region which could produce such a magnificent variety of fruits and cereals; and many other distinguished visitors expressed themselves in a similar manner. The principal articles on exhibition were as follows: pumpkins, grapes, and apples, from Snow & Adams, grapes and apples, from P. Potts, apples, from L. J. Collis; a branch of fine Naval oranges, from J. Lyons, apples, from Homer Jul-

cantile establishments, hotels, or other adjuncts of a town. There are, however, two stores, school houses, and a post-office. It is probable that it will have a railroad station shortly, as at present writing it seems likely that the Southern Pacific railroad will be extended from its present terminus at Santa Ana to San Diego, passing near the heart of the settlement.

The climate of Tustin is healthy and agreeable the greater portion of the year; but in the fall and spring there are a few days during which a violent wind sweeps through the Santa Ana valley, at times doing considerable damage. A system of wind-breaks in the shape of trees of the

no means permanent. The most experienced of our orchardists inform us that by taking precautions early in the season they greatly modified the effect of the cold blast. A bandage of cornstalks or sacks, bound firmly around the trunks, is of great service, and many ranches, protected by thick rows of eucalyptus and pepper trees, seem to have escaped entirely.

Mr. G. Howland, who resides south of the city, has a piece of land which was formerly strongly impregnated with alkali. He at first believed that it was worthless, but decided to experiment with it. Bearing in mind the fact that soda and potash, when exposed to sunshine and air, lose much of their power, at the commencement of the dry season two years ago he plowed it up and left it to the sun and wind. Just before the rains set in last winter he sowed the whole tract with barley, and was gratified to find that this cereal flourished on the supposed worthless land. He obtained a fine crop, and believes that he has solved the problem of how to treat our alkali lands.

Wilmington during the past four years has had a steady prosperity. The harbor will soon become a priceless boon to our county, and the town a thriving business center.

No one should leave Los Angeles before visiting Santa Ana and its thriving neighboring settlements. The southern end of Los Angeles county is improving with marvelous rapidity.

proper varieties, planted close together, will in time greatly modify this evil.

TUSTIN'S FUTURE PROSPECTS.

Tustin does not aspire to become a bustling town, but the people believe that they have one of the pleasantest locations for homes to be found in the world. They are not anxious to receive large accessions to their population, but will welcome all deserving new-comers who may desire to cast their lot among them. They are at present a thrifty, enterprising class, who succeed in nearly everything they undertake.

                J. C. P.

COUNTY NOTES.

Downey farmers have a bonanza in their poultry yards and dairies.

The cheese-makers at Compton are developing a valuable industry. As a dairy country Compton cannot be excelled.

Some of the finest wheat ever grown in Los Angeles county was produced on the ranch of Mr. David Cole, at Cahuenga, during the past season.

Anaheim wines are steadily gaining in popularity in the East. A letter from a leading merchant of Chicago, in our possession, states that all wines from California had a steadily improving market.

The frosts which have occurred since November 1st have undoubtedly done some damage to our young orange orchards in certain localities, though the injury is by

C. W. GIBBS, 13 AND 15 SPRING STREET, LOS ANGELES.

THE GOLDEN FUTURE.

BY R. M. WIDNEY.

IN February, 1868, the writer, then a resident of one of the middle counties, called upon a merchant from Los Angeles who was on business in San Francisco. The object of the call was to ascertain facts as to the then condition of Los Angeles county, and its future. The picture painted by that merchant, though an old resident, was uninviting in the extreme. Said he, "It is a small place, mostly hills, very little pasture, dry ground only fit for stock, and hardly fit for that; no cultivation except on one or two small places of two or

see how the country was. Riding out from the seaport, Wilmington, I found that the country consisted of table, or mesa land, undulating hills, level valley and high, rugged mountains in the distance. There were about 500,000 acres of table land and undulating hills; about 160,000 of valley lands. These lands were covered with a rank, rich growth of wild clover, alfilaria, malva and mustard. The crop would have averaged, over the 800,000 acres, at least two tons to the acre. The clover and alfilaria were over two feet high; the mustard from ten feet to fifteen feet high. The soil was a deep, rich, sandy loam; the warm sun from a cloudless sky, sent its

rains; but this does not often occur." I said to him. "Here is the rank growth of this year; there stand the dead stalks of an equally rich growth of last year; there, in broken fragments, lie the stalks of a similar growth of the preceding year; and over the ground under these is the decomposing matter from the previous years; and that wash, out to the depth of several feet, is exposed the decomposed vegetable matter, mixed with earth, showing that for ages centuries past nature has been growing luxuriant crops of vegetation. Where nature can raise such magnificent crops of weeds, man can raise any crop of grain which has in it an much more water per ton of

LUMBER YARD OF JACKSON, KELLOGG & CLOSER, LOS ANGELES

three hundred acres where water can be had for irrigation. The water is all taken up, and no more land can be irrigated. The place is overdone and will go down again. A few oranges are raised in the city, but they cannot be raised any other place. Dry years kill off all the stock, and the place is of no account."

Such I found to be the general opinion of Los Angeles in 1868. However, I took the steamer, and, passing Los Angeles, went to San Diego. There was no town there; it was before the excitement arose as to that place. Returning, I ventured to stop in Los Angeles to look around and

life-giving rays upon the landscape of semi-tropical luxuriance. "This is a grand country, this is the finest and richest acre body of land I have ever seen, the agricultural possibilities of this place are grand," I exclaimed to the person with me, who was then a resident of several years in the county.

With a look of surprise, incredulity, and pity, mixed, he said: "This is not an agricultural country, farmers cannot do anything here. This is a dry place; nothing can be raised here without irrigation; farmers would starve to death; this year there is a rank growth on account of heavy

green growth thru the weeds, provided man puts in the grain under the same favorable circumstances that nature puts in the seed of the weeds, that is he must plant the seed before the rain fall. Get eastern farmers in here, and see what can be done." "Well, maybe there is something in that," he replied.

At that time Los Angeles county imported from San Francisco all of its butter, breadstuffs, vegetables, and fruit; also, nearly all of its grain, cured meats, and eggs.

Outside of live stock and wool, the

county comes to a hny loaded one train a year with produce. The inhabitants, some higher in number, bewailed the general dilapidation, and helplessly did nothing.

Such was the past. A new class of men came upon the scene—men who knew how to handle the rich virgin soil. Twelve years have gone by, and over twenty towns and villages dot the plains, all within an area of forty miles square. A thousand farms and orchards cover the valley and hills. Without irrigation, a large part of the farmers are harvesting luxuriant crops of small grain and corn from land that in 1868 was supposed to be unfit for farming, simply because a river of water could not be run over it.

Railroads extend from Los Angeles city through the fertile portions of the county, connecting with the commerce of the nations over the ocean, and connecting with the commerce of the United States by two lines of railroad. This system of transportation makes us a commercial center, and furnishes a market for all our products. During the year 1880 Arizona consumed nearly the entire produce of this county. Over $50,000 per month in agricultural products were shipped to that market. These mining regions are rapidly developing, and a vast population is settling, for mining purposes, in the barren mountains of Arizona and New Mexico. This increasing population will consume all of our surplus products. Last year the people of Los Angeles received San Fran-

Santa Barbara counties, and then did not have enough. This establishment produced such a fine quality of hams and other meat that it could not supply the demand, and was compelled to stop for want of material.

To sum up the whole financial situation in a few words, the producer can realize heavier yields per acre, with less cost of production, with a better market, at good or higher prices than any other place in the United States.

In education, the common schools are well supplied with fine teachers. The University of Southern California, opened in October last, is prepared to give as complete an education as can be had.

The Churches are well represented with

UNIVERSITY OF SOUTHERN CALIFORNIA, LOS ANGELES.

west 16 miles to Santa Monica, on the ocean shore; south 21 miles to Wilmington harbor; southeast 40 miles to Santa Ana; north 396 miles to San Francisco, there connecting with all the railroads of California; and, by means of the Central and Union Pacific Railroads, with the railroad system of the United States. The Southern Pacific Railroad extends East from Los Angeles through Arizona and New Mexico, and connects with the Atchison and Topeka Railroad making connection below the snow belt with all the railroads of the Southern and Northern States. It will be seen that five railroads radiate from Los

cisco prices for all products, at their doors. The debts of the people were reduced over one half on the average, and large numbers paid out entirely.

While in 1868 one train of cars could have carried our surplus agricultural products, in 1880 from two to three trains per day were largely loaded with the rewards of agriculture.

All grain, from barley, wheat, and corn, up to the northern fruits and semi-tropical fruits, grow here. A pork packing establishment, last year and this, purchased and used all the hogs raised in Los Angeles, San Diego, San Bernardino, Ventura, and

good congregations and suitable places of worship.

Socially, there is to be found here as refined and cultured a class of people as are in any part of the country. In fact, for a few years past the most energetic and intelligent people from other localities have been coming here in large numbers, they will bring the fine future prosperity. One thing is certain that society here will go far above the average in most other places.

As to health, any person who comes here in a condition of health not beyond recovery will build up as fast as the recuperative power in him will act, while all can have a new lease of life, shorter or longer, as their individual cases may be. All must die. No here all sooner or later must pay the debt of nature. But of this place it can be said that the day of demise is carried far each further into the future.

There is no rigor of climate either of cold or heat. The vital forces are not consumed in a struggle with the external circumstances.

Fig. 1.—Young Plant.

cumstances. This leaves the vital energy of each person to be consumed in mental and physical labor. My observation has been that each person accomplishes from ten to twenty per cent. more in results, by

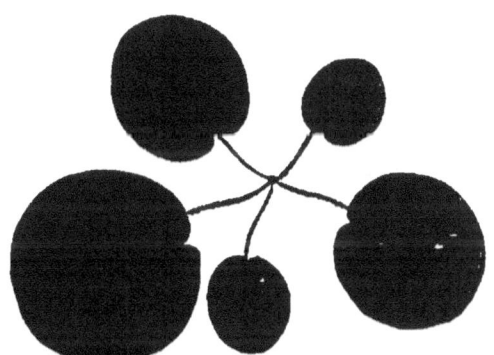

Fig. 2.—Young Plant at the Completion of Second Cycle of Growth of Five Leaves.

Fig. 3.—Opening Bud and Young Leaves.

reason of this condition of climate, here than in any other place.

The outlook for the future of Los Angeles was never more flattering, and never had a firmer foundation for permanence.

To all who contemplate a change of residence I would say, come and see. If, after looking over the situation, you are not satisfied, then do not stay here, but pass on to the place that suits you best, for you will most likely fail in any place where you do not see success.

VICTORIA REGIA.

GROWING ALONG OF WATER LILY HOUSE, GOLDEN GATE PARK, SAN FRANCISCO, CAL.

IN this number of the Semi Tropic California, we present our readers with a description and illustrations of the most beautiful and rare of all aquatic plants.

It is exceedingly difficult of cultivation, and even in its home seems to find few congenial localities; at least it is so seldom seen that travelers are often compelled to go hundreds of miles out of their course to see it in its native habitat.

The first plant grown in the United

States was produced at Springbrook, near Philadelphia, by Mr. Caleb Cope, in 1851. Since that time many attempts have been made to grow it, but without success. The fine plant now in this country is the Water Lily House, at Golden Gate Park, at San Francisco. While in bloom several months ago it was one of the most delightful flowers known of in society.

The Victoria Regia is a native of South America, and was first seen by a Spanish botanist, in 1801, while on a river in a tributary of the Amazon. Its peculiar natural home is directly under the equator, and is as much a tropical one as almost anywhere found, it lies within three degrees on each side of the equator and from east to west a distance of about thirty-five degrees of longitude, from the Atlantic through the Andes

Fig. 4.—Full Bloom.

RAIN SIGNS.

[Los Angeles Republican.]

Having been in the country over twenty years, and been as observant as others of the signs of the times, we think our opinion is as good as any man's, and as other prophets don't seem to hit it very correctly, we have thought it best to relieve the overstrained anxiety of the general public and make a few statements in our own way for the benefit of those who wish to plan and sow. So then, firstly, when clouds begin to gather, rain may be looked for. We have history for this. It was so in the days of Noah. Secondly, should rain fall on or before the fifth of any month, it will certainly be known on or before the tenth of the same month. Thirdly, if the season has been a remarkably dry one, and the evaporation been great, and if rain didn't occur in October, November, December, or January, it may be looked for (anxiously) in the same months of the following year. We place great confidence in this latter rule, as we have watched closely since 1856, and in all the years intervening between then and now we have had one kind of weather or another. Fourthly, if the rainfall of any season has been successively large, and the moisture was as two is to three or more, and the showers continued to fall damply for a month later than usual, and the barley bulged and cooled, and the corn grew rank and tall, and the streets got dusty after the rain quit, rain may be reasonably expected on or about the fourth Tuesday in January following the first Monday in December, sooner or later. A 'fifer gave us this latter receipt. He mixed on the Xalba, and damned it many a time because of the small superabundance of water that came, like the wind, "when it listeth." Now the farmer can tell when to plow and sow.

Messrs. McKinley Bros., who have an extensive and thriving nursery south of the city, have received a letter from Jno. Britton, a box manufacturer of San José, stating that the pear crop of that section was last season almost totally destroyed by the coddling moth. Our fruit-growers must bestir themselves, and not let this pest spread throughout Los Angeles county.

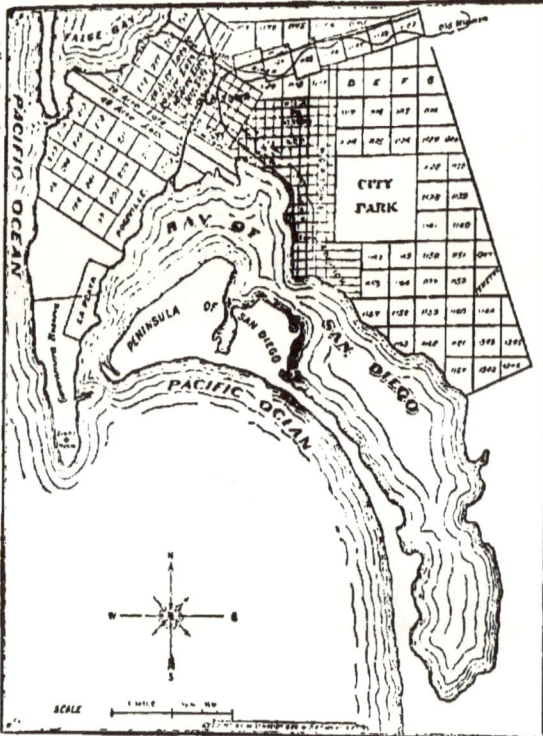

SAN DIEGO, CALIFORNIA.

Sixty-one thousand three hundred and twelve emigrants landed at Castle Garden, New York, during the month of October.

NADU'S WAREHOUSE, LOS ANGELES.

Mr. C. R. Workman, who resides on Lemon street, presented us recently with several of his Eureka lemons, grown from imported stock. The fruit seems excellent, has a thin rind, with no perceptibly bitter taste, and it will undoubtedly become a very popular variety with those who are about to set out semi-tropical orchards.

You can generally tell by the looks of a man's place whether he takes SEMI-TROPIC CALIFORNIA or any other good horticultural or agricultural magazine. If the weeds are two feet high in his front yard, the fences in ruins, his fruit trees unpruned and uncared for, and his children clad in rags, you may safely conclude—nay, you can positively assert—that he believes that it does not pay to read. If his place is in good order, and he his a neat bank account, you will find his table well stocked with papers, his children well educated, and a general air of prosperity over all his possessions.

The Vineyard.

COST OF A VINEYARD.

San Marino, Dec. 6, 1880.

Editors Semi-Tropic: In answering your inquiry as to the cost of establishing a vineyard I shall endeavor to give you in detail such estimates as may be relied on where the work is to be done by contract.

Plowing twice before planting, at $2 per acre $4 00
Harrowing and pulverizing the same 50
Cuttings (1,000 vines, 6 feet apart) per acre 5 00
Planting, per acre 2 00
Two plowings after planting, at $1 50 per acre 3 00
Cultivation and final pulverization 50 cts. per acre 50

Total cost, end of the first year $15 00

tivation, etc., plus the cost of picking and delivering the grapes. This cost, of such ing the grapes, per acre, can scarcely be approximately given with any degree of exactness, as I find this charge varies continually from year to year, according to the quantity of grapes produced.

In Napa and Sonoma counties contracts have been let some years ago at a price of $25 per acre, covering the entire cost of pruning, cultivation, picking, and delivering the grapes at convenient distances from the vineyards. I can see no reason why this price cannot be always assumed as the total cost all over the State where all the conditions are similar to our own.

You will observe I have made no estimate for the cost of irrigation, as the charge again will vary so widely, according to character of soil and price of water, that

The ancients used to say of a certain kind of man that he was a man of mettle. The expression left the matter a little indefinite, as no one could tell exactly what metal was meant. The moderns are a lot more explicit, and say clearly that a certain man is a man of brass.

One of the gentlemen who purchased a medical certificate of "Dr." Buchanan declared, after a three months' course, that he was quite able to cure a child of any disease, and that in three months more he hoped to be able to do the same for a full-grown man.

Mr. T. E. Walker, lately of Arizona, has purchased twenty acres of Capt. Stanley's ranch, south of the city. He is making ex-

Horton House, San Diego, Cal.

Second Year.

Pruning, per acre 1 00
Plowing twice, $1 50 per acre each 3 00
Cultivation twice 50 cts per acre each.... 1 00
Hoeing near the vine, $1 per acre 1 00

Total cost, second year ... $6 00

Third Year.

Pruning the vines and removing wood, $2 50 per acre 2 50
Plowing twice, $1 50 per acre each ... 3 00
Cultivation twice, 50 cts. per acre each 1 00
Hoeing near the vine, $1 50 per acre 1 50

Total cost, third year ... $8 00

In the fourth year the expenses of pruning and removing the wood from the vineyard will be increased one dollar more, or to $3 50 per acre, all the other expenses remaining the same as during the third year.

From the fourth year on the expenses will be as charged to the fourth year's cul-

it would be difficult, if not impossible, to give any reliable figures thereon.

It should always be borne in mind, in making estimates of the cost of cultivation of all the different productions of our country, that the character of the soil is always an important factor in increasing or lessening such costs. Every practical man who has handled a plow, or who has carefully observed others plowing, knows that the mechanical construction of soil, on which its friability or toughness depends, often times makes a difference in the cost of cultivation of from 50 to 100 per cent.

I believe this answers all the questions you have asked, but should I have omitted anything, will cheerfully supply the omissions. Respectfully yours,

J. DE BARTH SHORB.

tensive improvements, and in time will have one of the pleasantest homesteads in the ——

Mr. J. R. Millard, who resides on the mesa land bordering on Date street, finds that plateau well adapted to the growth of tropical fruits. His orange trees, although entirely unprotected, escaped all injury, and even the tender lime was spared.

Subscribe for the Semi-Tropic Californ-ist. It will only cost you $1 50 for the year, and save you many times that amount.

The Semi-Tropic is the only agricultural and horticultural paper in Southern Cal.

SEMI TROPIC CALIFORNIA'S

Map

OF PORTIONS OF THE COUNTIES OF

Los Angeles,

SAN BERNARDINO

AND

SAN DIEGO,

CAL.

W. F. Willmore, Compiler.
Carter & Rice, Pub.

Department.

N. C. CARTER, · · · · MANAGER.

THE immigration work so successfully carried on by the SEMI-TROPIC last year, will be one of the special features of our paper during 1881. N. C. Carter will have charge of this department, and that means business, as every one knows Carter is heart and soul in favor of settling up our vacant lands, that he knows how to bring people out here by fair representations, and that the people he does induce to make their homes with us will be honorable and respected citizens among us.

We bespeak the continued co operation of our citizens, knowing that the work done so far shows for itself, and that our future depends upon the cultivation of the fertile lands now laying idle in Southern California.

AT HOME.

One year ago, when we commenced the publication of the SEMI-TROPIC, we were compelled to go to San Francisco to do our printing, the facilities at home not being adequate.

To-day we are at home, this number being printed and finished complete by the enterprising printing house of Messrs. Varnell, Caystile & Mathes, and shows for itself what can be done in the art preservative.

This number contains more fine wood engravings than ever before contained in any magazine or paper published and printed on this coast.

To print wood cuts in an artistic manner requires special facilities and fine work that few printing establishments in the United States even attempt. It certainly speaks well for the enterprise of our home printers of the *Mirror* that they are able to produce so fine a work as we present this month.

Mr. C. H. Edwards, the pressman on this issue, earns the reputation of an artistic printer. The work of printing engravings is considered the graduating point of every accomplished pressman, and Mr. Edwards shows he is master of his trade.

"You can never wear those boots out," said a shoemaker. "Then I don't want them," replied the customer, "do you suppose I want boots to wear in the house?"

Since Mr. Stanford, of the Central and Southern Pacific Railways, was before the Railroad Commissioners, and assumed that the roads he represented were chartered by the United States Government, and were therefore not subject to State control, and hence that the Railroad Commissioners had no right or power to establish for them a schedule of freights and fares, the San Francisco *Chronicle* has been going for him and his roads. The *Chronicle* says "Mr. Stanford's statement is at variance with the almost universal opinion of the public as to invest with great interest anything shedding such light as will be regarded as primitive or conclusive upon that subject. The provision in the present Constitution making it mandatory upon the Commissioners to adopt such a schedule leaves these officers no discretion in the matter. Under their oath, they must obey the plain and explicit requirements of the fundamental law. They must adopt a schedule, and the well-known demands of the people require at the hands of the Commissioners a heavy reduction from the present exorbitant rates. To this feeling more than to all other causes is attributable the heavy majority by which the new Constitution was adopted at the polls. It was this potential and prominent feature of that instrument which caused the railroads to present a combined resistance against its adoption which menaced its success. The people had for years complained of the oppressions and exactions of the railroads. Time after time they had, without success, appealed to their representatives in the Legislature for redress. Bill after bill had been defeated by means at once humiliating to the people and disgraceful to the corporations. Finally, despairing of removing these oppressive monopolies from the position of master of the people to the proper one of servant, the people determined to create, through the fundamental law, a Commission springing directly from themselves, and clothed with plenary power to do what their representatives in the Legislature had constantly failed to perform—reduce the tariff on freights and fares on the various railroads of the State to such an extent as to make production to the interior profitable to the producer, instead of permitting the transporter to swallow up all the profits in carrying the produce to market. It was this feeling among the people which inserted the provision for a Railroad Commission in the Constitution, and it was the spirit of defied and insulted justice which made that fiat irrevocable through the mandate of fundamental law. Being thus mandatory, the Commission must obey it. To fail to do so would not only clothe Commissioners with the foul taint of dishonor which even hangs, and will forever hang, over the names of legislators who proved recreant to their pledges made to the people, but would

probably eventuate in an impeachment which, because of the failure of the Commission to perform a plain and compulsory duty, could not fail to be successful and work their removal. It is not for the Commissioners to consider or determine whether or not these railroads are subject to the State or United States control. Their duty is to comply with their oaths by obeying the law."

The *Chronicle* also publishes the articles of association of these roads, wherein they say: "On the 19th day of August, a D 1872, was duly incorporated and organized under the laws of the State of California" etc. The *Chronicle* has the documents, and the Railroad Company had better come down without shouting, unless two of the Commissioners are solid for the railroads. We know General Stoneman, one of the Commissioners, is solid for the law and the people.

THE correspondence of the SEMI-TROPIC for 1880, including requests for sample copies, amounts to 3250 letters and postal cards. It has required a great deal of work and a great amount of postage stamps to answer so many inquiries.

We will answer as far as possible all communications hereafter through this column, the others to be answered by letter, consequently the correspondence department of our paper for 1881 will be a prominent feature. Send in your questions.

FINE CHICKENS.

Chas. P. Jillson's pen of Plymouth Rocks, headed by the champion cockerel, "Los Angeles Chief," an importation from the yards of Keefer, Chicago, Ill., are fine birds. The latter was the winner of the first prizes at the great poultry show in Chicago last year, and is believed to be by far the finest cockerel on this coast, and not excelled in the United States. Mr. Jillson paid over $100 for him, and he ought to be a nice fellow. Jillson's brown Leghorns are said to be the finest in the country. We know from experience that his word about his stock and eggs for hatching is always true, more than can be said of another chicken dealer and a thousand miles away. Mr. Jillson can be relied upon to fill any and every order given him according to the golden rule. See his advertisement, which reads like business, and means just what he says.

Plants grown in the dark become colorless and weak, and while they have plenty of light and little air they would be slender and sickly, even though they have their natural color. The lesson we learn from this teaches us to always give, not only sunlight, but also fresh air at every possible opportunity.

The Climate.

SOME RANDOM REFLECTIONS UPON THE WEATHER.

BY GEO. C. SWAN, SAN DIEGO.

Now that Zero has been been felt, and the gentle zephyrs have been blowing—storms, gales, and destruction on the other side of the Rockies—your correspondent feels like making, for your Christmas number, a thanksgiving theme of the mild and genial season Southern California has enjoyed.

With the exception of one or two cold waves during the winter, nipping tender shoots and trees in some sections, and a wind storm or two, prostrating a few trees, in the vicinity of Anaheim, we cannot chronicle any further damage or disturbance during the entire year. The lowest

ern States in regard to thunder storms and tornadoes. Only those who have witnessed the storms of Florida and the lower Mississippi can testify to the fearfulness of their thunder storms.

We thank Dr. Griggs, in his able article recently published in your monthly, for calling attention to the fact of our exemption from such storms, and regret that he did not emphasize it more strongly. We do not wonder at the remark of one who had witnessed such storms in all their severity—the late Prof. Agassiz. When speaking to the people here, he said that "they ought to lift up both hands and thank God for being in the zone of calms." He struck a key note for Southern California which should resound throughout the length and breadth of the land. Read the accounts of the storms, hurricanes, and tornadoes ranging from Maine to Florida, and from Minnesota to Louisiana, as published in the Eastern papers. Look at the long

have spent some part of it out of doors. The nights are cool, requiring warm blankets to sleep in comfort, and not one night can be mentioned during the whole year but that one or two blankets were necessary, and during a residence of over seven years only one night has been found when one blanket was uncomfortable—a ratio of one to 2,600. What a luxury some of those nights would have been to a Cincinnatian, a Louisvillian, or a citizen of St. Louis, where we have known thirty nights in succession with the thermometer in the nineties.

To-day—a fair sample of December's early-winter day—with coat off, we have picked olives from a tree in the garden. Part of this article has been written with the door and window open, and the thermometer 65 in the shade.

A letter from one of Ohio's favorite sons last season, dated at Paris, who had previously spent a winter in Southern Califor-

LANPHERE'S BLOCK, LOS ANGELES.

point indicated here by the signal service thermometer was 32°.

If we were all, like Macaulay, of remarkable memory and large experience, it would not be necessary to make a comparison of our delightful seasons, but while ninety-nine one-hundredths of us are like little children, requiring "line upon line and precept on precept," governed somewhat by the feelings of the moment, it becomes proper to remind those of us who have been croaking about our weather to bear in mind that although the season was almost cool, Southern California was better off than say last year than the much celebrated winter resorts of Southern Europe; thirty-six times better off, as regards storms, than all the balance of the United States; thirty times better off than a portion of the Southern States and all the Northern States in regard to cold and wind storms, and infinitely better off than the warmer South-

list of shipwrecks along the whole coast of the Atlantic. See the unprecedented number of disasters upon Lakes Erie and Michigan, not only once, but once a month for two months in succession. Then say if this remark of Prof. Agassiz should not be emblazoned along the highways and posted over the doors of every house in the land!

A zone of calms! Think of it, ye dwellers in the paths where tornadoes laugh at overturned houses, uprooted trees, and fields devastated!

A zone of mild weather! The highest point reached, as reported by the signal service, 84°! Think of it, ye denizens of a frozen zone, imprisoned within walls of wood, brick and stone, rebreathing the fetid atmosphere of depleted oxygen!

We have been complaining of the slight cool weather which we have experienced, and yet my memory fails to recall a whole day but that a convalescing invalid might

nia, and whose family desired to see Europe, reported the winter resorts of Southern Europe so cold that the whole party were obliged to go to Africa to get warm. One of Chicago's prominent men said, last winter when complaints of cold weather were being made, "This is delightful; if you have no colder weather than this I shall be satisfied." He returned home, but two invalid members of his family remain, and are doing well.

Two prominent railroad men spending part of last winter here, who had wintered in Southern Europe, preferred Southern California.

By as much as the climate of Southern California is preferable in a normal condition, when floods, snow, and storms abound elsewhere, by so much more will it be preferable in an abnormal condition, when general disturbances occur, when the planets

RESIDENCE OF WINTER'S HOME, LOS A...

make a near approach, and when sun spots portend unusual limitation.

We wonder why so many living in the cold of the north, who are able to make the trip, prefer to remain housed up during the winter, when the genial sunshine of this section is broad enough to afford warmth and health to every one.

And now that the route below the snow

WOOL

There would be a ...on wool if there were ... product in ... market ... ... many. There, perhaps, ... branch ... agricultural industry that is likely to ... well for at least the next decade is woo growing. For the coming season the p ces are assur... All over the ... country ... manufacturers are ... ... prices later ... With th ... and the present y ... ... home production, all rates ... ... n

line will soon be completed, and, we trust, a lower rate of fare inaugurated, a n w era will dawn upon our favored sec ion, where the snow-bound citizen of the Eastern States may make the trip in comfort, view new scenes, and be refreshed an i invigor ated by the breezes of the grand Old Pa cific.

CENTRAL BLOCK, LOS ANGELES

GROCERIES

The Climate.

SOME RANDOM REFLECTIONS UPON THE WEATHER.

BY GEO. C. SWAN, SAN DIEGO.

Now that Zero has been keen felt, and the gentle zephyrs have been blowing—storms, gales, and destruction on the other side of the Rockies—your correspondent feels like making, for your Christmas number, a thanksgiving theme of the mild and genial season Southern California has enjoyed.

With the exception of one or two cold waves during the winter, nipping tender shoots and trees in some sections, and a wind storm or two, prostrating a few trees, in the vicinity of Anaheim, we cannot chronicle any further damage or disturbance during the entire year. The lowest

ern States in regard to thunder storms and tornadoes. Only those who have witnessed the storms of Florida and the lower Mississippi can testify to the fearfulness of their thunder storms.

We thank Dr. Gregg, in his able article recently published in your monthly, for calling attention to the fact of our exemption from such storms, and regret that he did not emphasize it more strongly. We do not wonder at the remark of one who had witnessed such storms in all their serenity — the late Prof. Agassiz. When speaking to the people here, he said that "they ought to lift up both hands and thank God for being in the zone of calms." He struck a key note for Southern California which should resound throughout the length and breadth of the land. Read the accounts of the storms, hurricanes, and tornadoes ranging from Maine to Florida, and from Minnesota to Louisiana, as published in the Eastern papers. Look at the long

have spent some part of it out of doors. The nights are cool, requiring warm blankets to sleep in comfort, and not one night can be mentioned during the whole year, but that one or two blankets were necessary, and during a residence of over seven years only one night has been found when one blanket was uncomfortable—a ratio of one to 2,600. What a luxury some of those nights would have been to a Cincinnatian, a Louisvillian, or a citizen of St. Louis, where we have known thirty nights in succession with the thermometer in the nineties.

To-day—a fair sample of December's early-winter day—with coat off, we have picked olives from a tree in the garden. Part of this article has been written with door and window open, and the thermometer 65 in the shade.

A letter from one of Ohio's favorite sons last season, dated at Paris, who had previously spent a winter in Southern Califor-

LANFRANCO BLOCK, LOS ANGELES.

point indicated here by the signal service thermometer was 32°.

If we were all, like Macaulay, of remarkable memory and large experience, it would not be necessary to make a comparison of our delightful seasons; but while ninety nine one hundredths of us are like little children, requiring "line upon line and precept on precept," governed somewhat by the feelings of the moment, it becomes proper to remind those of us who have been croaking about our weather to bear in mind that although the season way about real, Southern California was better off during last year than the much celebrated winter resorts of Southern Europe; thirty six times better off, as regards storms, than all the balance of the United States; thirty times better off than a portion of the Southern States and all the Northern States in regard to cold and wind storms, and infinitely better off than the warmer South-

list of shipwrecks along the whole coast of the Atlantic Sea the unprecedented number of disasters upon Lakes Erie and Michigan, not only once, but once a month for two months in succession. Then say if this remark of Prof. Agassiz should not be embalmed along the highways and posted over the doors of every house in the land?

A zone of calms! Think of it, ye dwellers in the paths where tornadoes laugh at overturned houses, uprooted trees, and fair fields devastated!

A zone of mild weather! The highest point reached, as reported by the signal service, 96°! Think of it, ye denizens of a frozen zone, imprisoned within walls of wood, brick and stone, rebreathing the fetid atmosphere of depleted oxygen!

We have been complaining of the slight cool weather which we have experienced, and yet my memory fails to recall a whole day but that a convalescing invalid might

nia, and whose family desired to see Europe, reported the winter resorts of Southern Europe so cold that the whole party were obliged to go to Africa to get warm. One of Chicago's prominent men said, last winter when complaints of cold weather were being made, "This is delightful; if you have no colder weather than this I shall be satisfied." He returned home, but two invalid members of his family remain, and are doing well.

Two prominent railroad men spending part of last winter here, who had wintered in Southern Europe, preferred Southern California.

By as much as the climate of Southern California is preferable in a normal condition, when floods, snow, and storms abound elsewhere, by as much more will it be preferable in an abnormal condition, when general disturbances occur, when the planets

RESIDENCE OF WALTER S. MOORE, LOS ...

make a near approach, and when sun spots portend unusual limitation.

We wonder why so many living in the cold of the north, who are able to make the trip, prefer to remain housed up during the winter, when the genial sunshine of this section is broad enough to afford warmth and health to every one.

And now that the route below the snow

WOOL

There would be a "boom" just now in wool if there were enough of the domestic product in the market to supply the demand. There is, perhaps, no branch of agricultural industry that is likely to pay as well for at least the next decade as wool growing. For the coming season high prices are assured. All over the country

rain without any fear ...

CENTRAL BLOCK, LOS ANGELES

line will soon be completed, and, we trust, a lower rate of fare inaugurated, a new era will dawn upon our favored section, where the snow-bound citizen of the Eastern States may make the trip in comfort, view new scenes, and be refreshed and invigorated by the breezes of the grand old Pacific.

manufacturers are contracting for the next clip at very high figures ... are in many places more ... bargains, preferring a ware ... prices later on. With the constantly creasing demand for wool in this ... and the present great inadequacy ... home production, all enterprising ...

Subscribe for SEMI-TROPIC CALIFORNIA, ... per annum.

RIVERSIDE AND ARLINGTON.

THIS enterprising colony has been enjoying a continuous boom for more than a year. Lands have rapidly advanced in value—the reason is apparent. The area in which citrus culture can be successfully cultivated is but limited. Here at a first cost of one hundred dollars per acre land can in three years be made to produce as much per acre annually. In five years from $400 to $500 per acre is the product when planted in grapes for raisins, apricots or oranges—no longer is the Immigrant subjected to cost by experiment but by using the knowledge dearly learned by others he can make no mistake and virtually has a sure thing. This season Slugart & Waite realized $125 an acre for their grapes on the vines and the manufacturer

sure foundations laid for an independent fortune. The climate is the best in the State for pulmonary difficulties, asthma, etc.

Surveys are now being made for the Southern California Pacific R. R. Co., for the line running from San Diego to San Bernardino. It is confidently expected that the route will be located through the entire length of this valley. By all means let intending settlers visit this most successful colony and see the barren waste of 1870 made into the luxurious semi-tropical garden of 1880 by a combination of soil, climate, water, muscle and capital.

In agriculture there are any amount of theories, but there are many more facts; those have to be dug out of the soil; but theories can be spun in an arm-chair.

true, to those whose homes have lain in this sunny land. Every year witnesses a closer fealty, a more clinging attachment, and that is the highest compliment to be paid to any country. And yet, with all this love of our bright homes, we have seen dark, lowering clouds, threatening to settle over its brightness and promise. There are always thorny paths in pioneer life for tender feet, and it is largely those who have trod these new ways; its hopeful treasures, its wonderful beauty, appealed strongly to the æsthetic nature, and made them the last to give up a land of so many attractions. It has long been conceded that for ideal homes, the material was nowhere more perfectly to be found than below the 35th parallel, responding so surely to the hand of taste and culture.

FLUME—RIVERSIDE LAND AND IRRIGATION COMPANY.

expects to realize $100 an acre for the labor of picking and curing—over and above all costs of shipping, packing commissions, etc.

Riverside oranges last year sold in the San Francisco market from $35 to $60 a thousand against all competition. It is estimated that the orange crop this year will realize from $25,000 to $30,000. The Riverside Fruit Packing Co. have this year paid $10,000 for canning fruits, etc. The home crop will not produce less than $3,000 this year.

Here is an opening for capitalists or for men of small means. The water is about all the soil rich and adapted to the most profitable of all farming, the citrus fruits. In less than five years settlers have the

THEN AND NOW.

BY MRS. V. W. WINTON.

THE many attractions and charms of Southern California have been written and sung from the Atlantic to the Pacific these many years, and it has passed into one of the luxuries of eastern life to bring into its possibilities a winter here occasionally, in which to bathe weary, care worn brows in its life giving sunshine and invigorating sea breezes. To the invalid, albeit near the haven of rest, is it the utopia of restless longing, where he can gather strength for the out going forces of life. All this, despite the many croaking disparagements of those to whom Heaven will hardly equal their requirements, is true, and more than

We passed, years ago, in our drives, in process of erection, a simple cottage, quaint in design, and wholly inexpensive, and we said: "Here is growing a new home." In another month we saw that cottage again, and the home was there, the household goods were set in place, the Lares and Penates were enshrined; there were draperies at the windows, and screens for them and the doors. "So purity and order will dwell there," we said, and then we knew that vines, and shrubbery, and bright flowers would soon follow. These are the natural instincts of a pure, refined taste; and when we saw that home again there were draperies of vines fringing the porches and eaves; the German Ivy had clambered everywhere, and Tropæolums and Convolvulus had planned an ambitious campaign to mount skyward, until the rough exterior had become a bright, glowing picture, a rest and a stimulant at once to every beholder. I learned to know the inmates of that cottage, their hopes and their needs; more faith than experimental knowledge, perhaps; and, after a time came shadows and disappointment. The ordinary produce of the farm brought slow and ungrateful returns; freights consumed the profits; the years were not always fully favorable; their deadly warrants; gilt-edged butter failed to bring gilt-edged prices; fowls were clamorous for prolonged vacations, and persisted in taking them when eggs were highest, and chickens grew strangely absent at roll-call; and so the shadows set

tled lower and lower, darkening the hearts of our cottage friends.

The pomological future was slow in its approach, but sure; the orchard was leaf by leaf growing apace, unmindful of the price of corn and potatoes, and uncommunicative returns and unsatisfactory balances. Still shine and shower, dewy mornings, and glowing mountains distilled for them earth's alembic and chemistry, and nature worked silently all their forces for the development of those leafy avenues. Every year drew the arches nearer together, stretching out longingly toward completeness and fruitfulness. Then came the bloom and beautiful promise, enlivening the darkest hour before the dawn, this hope which had spanned the household like a bow of promise, became a fruition,—a surety that in the

future time should come no more days of financial pressure, for out of this abundant return should come full supply for every possible need.

The dwellers in this southern land will know this for no fancy sketch, but an often-told tale, and its duplicates are legion. Now, the disheartening exodus from the old paths is well nigh over, and for those who follow these lies a plain path; the many who went before them, and for those their predecessors, are swept away. Now only vigilance is wanted lest the developing treasures be injured by their natural enemies; an eternal vigilance is always the price of success everywhere and anywhere.

The days of slipshod farming and neglected orchards, which their owners proclaim, with a martyred air, "do n't pay," at

over. No; of course they "do n't pay." We should have our respect, deep as it is for our production of nature, that would "pay" for some people and were treatment. In this respect we all was higher if all were... and neglected orchards, vineyards, a... garden would follow the example of J... nah's gourd, be down and die, rather... once. These slow martyrdoms are so painful to witness, they are crucial tests of the right. We are sadly tempted to enter our thriftless neighbor's gates and these hopeless, stunted growths to... aid... speedier ptisans than nature gives. It is only a painful type of the moral... mental condition of the owner. We never see a well balanced man or woman with any such disgraceful belongings. When we are told that orchards do not pay, we know one

or two things: either the above description is its legitimate label, or there has been planted unprofitable varieties of fruit, and on the wrong soils. In either case a radical change is necessary; this coming season, with its abundant promise of seed time and harvest, should witness such grafting and budding, and thorough overhauling of herds in southern climes as is its sunny... have never looked upon. Most of us want what old Aunt Dinah, in Uncle Tom's Cabin, used to give her kitchen when it reached a like pass, a thorough clearin' up." Every individual neglected... wants a complete cleansing with... and soap suds and any of the popular additions in the way of carbolic acid... baths, etc., that the worst success, all... good. Only get thoroughly done

...and that result will not be reached in a... as far up in the larger branches as... while; then fasten a roll of paper around... trunk of the tree and watch the re...

The early... as well as the earl... catches the worm, or calling south, or... a clever shape of... it comes up, and... name is given...

Some orchards in the northern counties managed have been carefully and fruit... again, after very... east. Never was careful vigilance more the price of liberty than it is of the faithful orchardist. And... so can our very rare staging fruit success... be made permanent. When you... of superior quality and fruitfulness, that is the one to bud or graft from. "A

good eat is always better than a cat of a good kind."

In a small apricot orchard we wot of, there are several trees always bearing an average of 200 lbs. per acre, albeit standing too close together, interlacing their branches, at seven years of age. These are unnamed, but none the less is it a good place for grafts and buds. The fruit resembles closely the Royal, though the record of some orchards go much higher for individual trees and full years. The product of 24 others was sold at the cannery here for $212. These trees stand on less than one-fourth of an acre, and was considered only a fair yield, as the excess of moisture in this county (where no irrigation is practiced) is not considered favorable for either nuts or fruit. We have better crops of both at 10 to 12 inches of rain than above that amount. We saw, in Alameda, one of the few very productive apricot orchards in that vicinity; the variety was the Royal, with 100 Moorparks interspersed; these bore lightly; the remainder of the orchard was injured on the outer rows by a hedge of Eucalyptus, and these apricots being rusnlly in use were dried. The crop, over 150 tons, was sold at $11,000.

The unlimited demand for this fruit from all parts of the world, especially its use so freely in navy and whaling fleets, as an anti-scorbutic, render it one of our most promising industries, both for canning and drying. No disease as yet has appeared, or enemy attacked it seriously, and with intelligent care it will doubtless prove a wonderful gift to Southern California. We on the northern line are talking of planting hedges of Olives, perhaps ten feet apart for wind-brakes. At this distance, we shall get some fruit from our hedge, and by thinning low will secure all the protection desirable, though we are not often liable to severe winds. We still want immunity from them as nearly perfect as possible, and some rank growing trees draw too heavily on the moisture. Many young orchards will be put out here this season, at least as many as can get trees, of apricots, prunes, plums, olives, Bartlett pears, and walnuts. The cinnmeymen of the State we find hardly ready for the large demand for these fruits which this season's experience have proved so salable for canning purposes.

A cow should be as well fed when dry as when giving milk. She should now increase in flesh, so that she may be able to give a greater flow of milk when milking time comes. To feed a dry cow on poor hay, or even think that straw is good enough, is poor policy, and the loss will show itself in the milk pail. Feed the cows well all the time.

W. B. West, of San Joaquin county, has sold, this year, 300 tons of grapes, produced on 20 acres of land, which is over 10 tons to the acre. The two sorts comprised in the sale were the Mission and the Black Prince. It is understood that the average price brought was $37 a ton.

Viticultural.

OUR WINES AND BRANDIES.

EXTRACTS FROM L. J. ROSE'S REPORT TO THE STATE VITICULTURAL COMMISSION.

IT is a pleasing task to review the grape and wine industries of Los Angeles county for 1880.

Crops have never been larger or of better quality, and the demand for the grape by wine makers has been good during the entire season.

There will be more vines planted during the coming season than ever before. There have already been 800,000 cuttings engaged at my place, and the demand for some varieties is in excess of the supply.

It is now a proven fact that we can make the finer qualities of light bodied pure wines; not, of course, with the Mission grape, and the verdict founded on that grape has been a just one, which will we could not make a light wine, and that our wines all had a sherry flavor.

Locality, climate, and other causes have a marked effect on the quality of wines, and all conditions must be favorable to make a wine of the first quality, the variety of the grape used has more influence than any other one condition.

From the Blaue Elbe, Berger, Zinfandel, Charbonean, the finest qualities of light wines are made here.

Soon, too, we shall have a trans-continental railroad, which will relieve us from the necessity of sending our product to San Francisco before it can be sent East. Thus a heavy burden in the way of freights is removed. Cucamonga, the largest vineyard in San Bernardino county, contains 200 acres.

Riverside has many small vineyards, planted generally with Muscat of Alexandria, and Muscatals, and Gordo Blanco, from which a very fine quality of raisins are made.

There are in this county 5,713 acres of vineyard, representing about three hundred owners.

Taking the present year's yield, which is the largest we have ever had, at 15,000 pounds to the acre, it gives 57,130,000 pounds of grapes produced in this county this year; and, taking 15 pounds of grapes for a gallon of wine, this would give the grand total of 3,808,000 gallons of wine.

These figures seem large, yet I have bought this year 12,000,000 pounds of grapes; and some of the vineyards have yielded ten tons, or 20,000 pounds to the acre, so I believe five tons is within the average.

Sweet wines require more than fifteen pounds of grapes to the gallon, and much of both sweet wine and brandy have been made; so I would estimate the product of this county for this year at 2,000,000 gallons of white and red wine, 500,000 gallons of sweet wines, and 300,000 gallons of brandy.

There are several large manufactories for wine making in our county, and all have had all they could do. The more prominent are Dreyfus & Co., Kohler & Frohling, Mr. Bernard, J. DeBarth Shorb, M. Keller, and Stern & Rose. There are very many more who work up their own grapes and, generally, all the vignerons of Anaheim belong to that class.

Probably half of the vineyards of this district are irrigated; and, although grapes can be grown in any part of the district without irrigation, yet with irrigation larger crops are produced, and vineyards retain their fertility and thrift for hundreds of years. Irrigation entails much work, and it may yet be considered an open question which pays best—deep tillage, without irrigation, or irrigation.

Lands without irrigation can be bought very much cheaper, say for one-fourth, and this again forms a factor in the problem of "Which pays best?" It must, however, be confessed that as long as the belief prevails that irrigation is a preventive of the phylloxera, there is a comfortable feeling in having water.

Of course, like the balance of the State, we have thousands of acres which are adapted for the growing of the vine. Men and money are all that are required to make vineyards by the ten thousands, and I doubt whether a better climate or soil can be found, even in this State, for the production of grapes of the best quality. Land, too, can be had cheap enough, say from $10 to $100 an acre—the first without irrigation, the latter with it. Nor would it follow that the cheaper land would be the poorest for grape growing; for the reverse might be the case. Our mountain slopes and our uplands are now the lowest in price, and yet these lands are the lands that will produce grapes of the highest value. The possibilities here are immense. A great future is in store for us, if it is a fact, and I believe it, namely, that Europe will buy our wines.

It may be safely stated that grapes grown for sale to wine-makers, this year, have netted $90 an acre, for the crop was larger and the price good. The average price this year was somewhere near $21 a ton. The wine and brandy made would sell to-day for over a million of dollars.

Much more might be said, but time does not permit me to say more. It has been with difficulty that I have been able to do this much, and I will promise myself the pleasure of again resuming the subject at some future time.

L. J. ROSE,
State Viticultural Commissioner for the
Southern District.

Did you ever stop on the dusty highway of life to remember that there are 7,000 varieties of apples in this country, saying nothing of those found in the boys' pockets?

In southern countries, nearly all the Animals do much better if worn in autumn, so as to have the benefit of the cool, moist weather. Many plants, especially the Pansy, grows in luxuriance during a southern winter.

Sugar Industry.

THE SUGAR BEET.

"IS THERE A NIGGER IN THE WOOD PILE?"
IF THERE IS, WHO WILL GET HIM OUT?

WE have undertaken to get at the bottom of the facts in regard to the sugar beet industry of this county, and we must say that to us, it seems that the bottom is hardly countable.

The facts are about as follows: Messrs. Nadeau & Gennert had about seven hundred acres of sugar beets grown. The samples of green beets grown here upon comparison with the standard sugar beet of Germany, show that those grown in this county are fully up to the standard. The exhibit of beets made by these gentlemen at the Horticultural Fair in October was exceedingly fine, and from the judgment of non professionals were considered first class for sugar making purposes.

Mr. Gennert failed to make sugar at all, with the crude machinery he had erected, but it was no fault of the beets as was afterwards demonstrated by the sugar company at Alvarado, who worked up eight tons of dried beets into a No. 1 quality of sugar; the only trouble being that the percentage of sugar was less than 20 per cent, which is pronounced by E. H. Dyer, Supt. Standard Sugar Company, as poor results obtained from the eight tons.

The samples of dried beets sent from here to Prof. Eugene W. Hilgard, University of California, and to the samples sent to the Standard Sugar Company at Alvarado, are best explained in the following correspondence, which we find in the S. F. Merchant:

UNIVERSITY OF CALIFORNIA, }
BERKELEY, Oct. 4, 1880. }

E. Th. Gennert, Esq., Los Angeles:

DEAR SIR—The machine sliced and dried sun-dried beets sent by you arrived in excellent condition; their fair and fresh taste comparing very favorably with the sample received last year, some of which having been cut too thick were a little mouldy. So far as the keeping quality is concerned your operations have certainly been very successful, and the ease with which the slice can be extracted by maceration ought to render the manufacture of sugar from them easy enough. Their composition was found to be as follows:

Cane Sugar.................................. 51.3
Molature................................... 11.3
Ash.. 5.4
Other organic matters by diffusion..... 31.0

Total.................................. 100

It is easy to see that a material consisting of more than half of sugar, and capable of indefinite preservation, stands on a very different basis both as regards transportation and manufacture from the heavy, bulky and comparatively low value beet from which it is so cheaply produced.

If there be any doubt that beet sugar factories can be made profitable in California, it can hardly be doubtful that the production of dried sugar beets can be made

to pay as good profits to the producer as most other crops, and probably better than a good many now in favor. But it will take a good many more facts than have thus far come before me to convince me that with the enormous advantages afforded by the feasibility of cheap drying beets in this climate, sugar factories running on a sound business and technical basis cannot successfully compete here on the spot with either sugar cane or sorghum.

Very respectfully yours,
EUGENE W. HILGARD.

ALVARADO, Nov. 1, 1880.
Prof. E. W. Hilgard, University of California:

DEAR SIR—The 20th day of September we received about fifty tons of dried beets from Mr. H. Nadeau, of Los Angeles, to be manufactured into sugar. As we were running on our own beets at the time we could not stop to work the whole fifty tons, but manufactured about eight tons into a fair quality of sugar, sufficient to thoroughly test the feasibility of making sugar from sun-dried beets. We found, however, that these dried beets contained a very low percentage of sugar—less than twenty per cent., or on the basis of one ton of dried beets being equal to four in the green state, between four and five per cent.

Mr. Nadeau sent us at the same time some green beets. By polarization they gave about the same result as the dried beets. We made two polarizations with the following results, both taken from two different fields:

Saccharometer 18   Saccharometer 14.6
Polariscope ...... 15.6   Polariscope 14.4
Difference ...... 7.4   Difference 0.2
Quotient 46   Quotient 2

These beets were worked, and the polarizations were made by Mr. Wm. Kullberg, who has charge of the technical department of our sugar works, and has had experience in working dried beets in Europe. * * *

Believing you must have been deceived in some way in regard to the samples sent you, and knowing that from the position you occupy in the State University that your statements in regard to matters of this kind would be recognized as authority, and in case of deception being practiced upon one, would lead enterprising and honest men into error, we have taken pains to procure from Mr. Nadeau samples of his fresh beets as well as those dried by him, and take the liberty to forward the same to you to enable you to make a further test from reliable samples. The samples of green beets are somewhat wilted and dried in consequence of having been so long in reaching this place, consequently will polarize more than if taken fresh from the ground. I give the result of Mr. Kullberg's polarization, carefully made by him, October 30, 1880:

March 14   March ...... 14.1   March 11
Pol ...... 12.1   Pol 12   Pol 9.8
Dif ...... 1.9   Dif ...... 2.1   Dif 1.2
Quo ...... 72.50   Quo 85   Quo 89

Hoping you will favor us with an early reply, we remain,
Respectfully yours,
STANDARD SUGAR MAKING CO.
By E. H. Dyer, Gen. Supt.

UNIVERSITY OF CALIFORNIA, }
COLLEGE OF AGRICULTURE, }
BERKELEY, Nov. 6, 1880. }

E. H. Dyer, Esq., Sup't Standard Sugar Manuf'g Co., Alvarado:

DEAR SIR—Yours of 1st inst., with packages of fresh and dried beets, duly received. The dried beets are now in process of analysis. The fresh beets were polarized immediately after receipt. The results agree substantially with those obtained by Mr. Kullberg, viz.:

March 11   March ...... 12.1   March 11.4
Polarization 12   Polarization ...... 11.2   Polarization 9.4
Purity Quot. ....   Purity Quot. ....   Purity Quot. ....

Except in a higher purity coefficient as an average; but that can easily happen. Except as to the same point, your polarization of beets taken from two different fields, as given on page two of your letter, also agrees; that is, all show a sugar percentage above 12; averaging about 12.4 in the juice. Now since the juice constitutes about 95 per cent. of the fresh beet, this would correspond to a little less than 12 per cent. of sugar in the green beet; and this, at the rate of four to one, accepted by you, would make up about 4.5 per cent. in the absolutely free beets, or 4.2 in those containing 10 per cent. of moisture. A determination of the sugar in a sample of dried beets furnished me by Mr. Nadeau gives 12.1 per cent. of sugar, corroborating, as nearly as possible, the polarizations made and the assumptions of the proportion of four of fresh beets to one of dry. I am at a loss to understand the statement apparently made on page one of your letter that the polarization on page two agrees with the assumption of 20 per cent. of sugar in the dried beets at the rate of 4 to 1. On its face it gives it fully double, or over 40 per cent. Please revise and explain your position on this point. I remark that the dried sample sent by you is much more moist and to the taste much less sweet than the samples furnished by Messrs. Nadeau and Gennert. I am, of course, unable to determine which sample represents the fifty tons most correctly.

Very respectfully,
E. W. HILGARD.

OFFICE STANDARD SUGAR M'F'G CO., }
ALVARADO, Nov. 9, 1880. }

Prof. E. W. Hilgard, University of Cal.

DEAR SIR—Yours of 6th inst., just received, with result of the polarization of the green beets, which agrees substantially with those polarized by Mr. Kullberg, and you pleased to say, "I am at a loss to understand the statement apparently made on page 1st of your letter that the polarization on page 2d agrees with the assumption of 20 per cent. sugar in the dried beets at the rate of 4 to 1. On its face it gives fully double, or over 40 per cent. Please revise and explain your position on this point." This should hardly need any explanation. If the amount of sugar indicated by the polariscope could be obtained in crystallizable sugar from beets, there would no longer be any doubt about the success of this industry. But it is well known to all manufacturers of beet-root sugar and sugar chemists, that the percentage of sugar indicated by the polariscope really obtained by working process depends upon the percentage of salt and other impurities contained in the beet, that prevent crystallization. An application of these well known rules by us and the omission by you, explains the discrepancy.

Respectfully yours,
STANDARD SUGAR MAN'F'G CO.
By E. H. DYER, Gen. Sup't.

A further correspondence between Prof. Hilgard and Supt. Dyer, bordering on personalities but giving no further light on the subject, we omit, only giving the following extracts. Prof. Hilgard, in a letter to Mr. Nadeau, Nov. 8, says:

According to two determinations, the sample brought by you contains 42.0 per cent. of sugar in the airdried condition; or, assuming them to contain 10 per cent. of moisture, 46.6 when perfectly dried.

Not long since I received from the Alvarado Sugar Co., also, a sample of dried beets, said to be those worked by them, and to have yielded only about 20 per cent. of sugar. By my assay, made on a day when a Norther was blowing, the sugar percentage was found to be 23.8, substantially agreeing with their statement.

At the same time they sent two samples of fresh beets obtained from you, as stated. The assay of these gave on an average about 12 per cent. of sugar in the fresh beets; and in this, also, their statement of assay made by them agrees substantially.

It is, of course, impossible for me to say which sample represents correctly your fifty tons. A microscopic examination of your sample, as well as that sent from Alvarado, shows plainly enough a wide difference between the two. About half of the Alvarado sample consists of sheets of a brown tint, tough and not capable of being broken by bending; while all of your sample consists of pieces that can be readily broken, and are white on the fracture; while their surface is covered with small sugar crystals, of which but few are seen on the Alvarado sample.

I should say that slow or imperfect drying or a rain or heavy drizzle on the dried beets before packing might have caused the trouble; but there are other causes that might have caused the same appearance.

As to the question of fact, viz: the true average sugar percentage of your fifty tons lot, 1, of course, can determine nothing. The fresh beets assayed by me would yield, on drying, about such a sample as the one you handed me, if everything were properly conducted.

In a letter from Supt. Dyer to Professor Hilgard, Nov. 18th, he says:

We have made certain tests of his beets and reported the results, which show that the beets contain a very low percentage of extractable sugar. You have stated in your letter to Genrat that they contained one-half sugar. Now to the common mind the inference would be that that amount or nearly so of marketable sugar could be obtained from these dried beets. In your last letter to me you admit that the amount of sugar obtainable or extractable depends

upon the coefficient of purity and the "correctness of manufacture," but omit, or fail to state, in what manner or to what extent it effects the extraction of sugar indicated by the polariscope. * * * *

That portion of your letter to Mr. Nadeau, also to me, in which you insinuate that we did not send you a fair sample of the fifty tons of dried beets, I would, if I could consistently, gladly pass by unnoticed, for if I had not the written evidence before me I would not believe that you would attempt to sustain your erroneous position by such a doubtful mode of defense. * * * * * * *

Now, sir, in conclusion, permit me to say, that I hope you will consider it your duty, as the head of the Department of Agriculture of this State, if you believe, as your letters would seem to infer, that we, either through ignorance or design, are not furnishing Mr. Nadeau reliable information in regard to his beets, that you will investigate this matter to the bottom. Over forty tons of his beets are in the storehouses in the vicinity of our sugar works, and we will afford you, or anyone you may delegate to investigate the matter, every opportunity in our power to do so. Our laboratory and engathouse and all the labor, both skilled and otherwise, in our employ is at your disposal for that purpose. And if you can demonstrate that you can extract within 30 per cent. of what you say these beets contain in good marketable sugar, we will pay you or your representative $100 a day for the time employed, and an additional $1,000 as further compensation. But, if this attempt is made and does not succeed, then we are to be reimbursed for all expenses incurred by us in making the experiment.

Respectfully yours,
STANDARD SUGAR M'F'G CO.,
By E. H. DYER, Gen. Supt.

UNIVERSITY OF CALIFORNIA, }
COLLEGE OF AGRICULTURE, }
BERKELEY, Nov. 24, 1880. }

E. H. Dyer, Alvarado—Sir: Your communication of the 18th inst. is received. You are laboring under a mistake in imagining, that as Professor of Agriculture in the State University, I am under any obligation to determine whether your sample with twenty odd per cent. of sugar, or Mr. Nadeau's with twice that amount, represents that particular fifty-ton lot. You must settle that between yourselves as best you can, and as the public has no interest whatever in the matter I decline to take any part in the question beyond the statement of facts as found by me, and laid down in the letter to Mr. Nadeau, of which you have a copy. That statement contains no insinuation of any kind, although it shows an irreconcilable contradiction in the specimens furnished. From this Mr. Nadeau and yourself must draw your own conclusions.

The general question of the quality of beets grown in California, of the inadvisability of drying them in the open air, and manufacturing sugar therefrom by the proper process, is quite another matter, upon which I have made and am still making, careful investigations. For these and for the conclusions and recommendations based thereon, I hold myself responsible to the proper authorities and to the public.

Respectfully,
EUG. W. HILGARD.

Literature.

WHAT WILL YOU READ?

All hardy plants, such as Pœonias, Hollyhocks, Perennial Phlox, Day Lily, Dicentra, Delphiniums, &c., indeed, all that will endure our winters, should be planted in autumn if possible, to get a good start in the spring.

Keeping food constantly before poultry, as some recommend, is wasteful, as it clogs their appetites, and keeps them scratching when they ought to be sleeping on their roosts.

BUSINESS MEN.

LOS ANGELES is very fortunate in having a reliable class of merchants; men with capital, energy and business push.

It has been our pleasure from time to time to notice the different firms of our city, and we wish briefly to revise a number of them in this issue.

OUR ILLUSTRATIONS.

We reproduce the engravings published during the past year, and at the present will not call attention to the owners.

H. F. COULTER.

Occupies the commodious rooms, No. 30 and 32 Main street, in Baker block, the two rooms are connected by an archway making one of the largest dry goods establishments in the State. By his uniform, kind treatment, straightforward and honorable manner of conducting his business, Mr. Coulter has built up an immense trade since he opened in this city. The ample means and long experience enables him to enter the wholesale markets and buy to suit his trade, and at the lowest prices. "An article well bought is half sold," and having bought well, Mr. Coulter believes in "living and let live" once a customer always a customer, if allowing them the benefit of good goods at uniformly low prices. A stranger will receive the same treatment as a friend, as far as prices and attention are concerned.

Mr. Coulter is also proprietor of the Woolen Mills, and will run the factory to its full capacity, adding a much needed industry to Southern California, making a new market for wool, keeping the money at home it would cost for transportation to the east, its cost of manufacture and shipment back in goods, thus saving the county a large surplus of money that would otherwise be sent away. We commend Mr. Coulter's example to others, and we hope the manufacturing interest of our city will receive the fostering care of our city, and that our men of capital will invest their money in some of the many needed manufactories.

P. J. HILLWORK.

The famous Boston Dollar Store is outdone by our enterprising townsman, Mr. Gillmore, who is proprietor of the Dollar Store, on Spring street, opposite the Court House.

His stock embraces a large and varied list of goods, including the useful and ornamental, the beautiful and essential. Goods that you want every day of the year; goods especially adapted for gifts for the holidays; goods to please the old and delight the young.

If there is anything you want, Gillmore has it; he has everything.

A few years ago, all kinds of goods usually kept in such establishments were sold at high prices, but we are glad to note that Mr. Gillmore has brought the trade to business basis, by using his ample capital in buying from first hands in round lots strictly for cash, and by selling all goods at a low margin of profit.

We would not think of completing our Christmas list of presents, without taking a look through this Bazar of beautiful and elegant goods.

E. MARTIN & CO.

Occupy commodious rooms and cellar in Baker block, where they carry the largest and most complete stock of liquors, wines, cigars, pipes, tobacco and everything to supply the trade of any firm in Southern California. Mr. C. C. Lips is in charge of the house, and is a host within himself. The house will continue to thrive in the future as it has in the past.

This firm is also agents for the wines of "Sunny Slope" vineyards. They make a specialty of supplying families with choice brands of liquors, in addition to the extensive wholesale trade done by the house.

F. GERMAIN.

Baker block, No. 34 Main street, is well located for the General Commission Business, the rooms and basement in this substantial block being well adapted to the safe keeping and curing of all kinds of produce.

Mr. Germain is doing a good work for our farmers by opening an extensive trade with Arizona, having established branch houses at Tucson, Benson and terminus S. P. R. R., in New Mexico. The high prices obtained for our produce in Arizona enables him to pay our farmers a good price for everything they produce, thus encouraging our agriculturist to renewed industry. We believe he buys everything that the farmer produces, and gives them the benefit of the "big prices" he gets in Arizona.

C. W. GIBSON

Came to Los Angeles seven years ago and engaged in the confectionery business. He only remained in the business a short time when he bought out the small soap manufacturing interests, and built the extensive soap factory, corner of Banning street, a business he managed successfully until April 10, 1878, when he started the

AMERICAN CASH STORE

in the adobe building on Spring street, near First. His plan of business was to sell a first class article of groceries for the least possible profit, and to sell strictly for cash. His fair dealing soon brought a host of customers and the business adage that "a nimble penny is better than a slow sixpence" was fully realized and the people soon began to understand that prices will tell. Mr. Gibson soon recognizing the requirements of his increasing business moved into larger rooms in the Masonic Hall block where his business continued to increase until the 1st of December, '79, he was again compelled to look for more commodious quarters.

We now find him in the large and well appointed store

48 AND 50 SPRING STREET,

where he carries a stock of goods worth $50,000, embracing everything usually found in a first class grocery establishment.

Mr. Gibson always recognizes the importance of printer's ink, and knowing he had that which the people must have, and that his plan of selling at a close margin and no doubt was a safe one, he made use of the press in making known the merits of his goods and prices. Soon the American Cash Store came to be a familiar name throughout Los Angeles county and Southern California.

Mr. Gibson's success has induced him to go to San Francisco and open another house on the same plan. His San Francisco house will be a wholesale establishment, and we can recommend him to the trade and vouch for the fact that they will have discovered a new era in close prices in the purchase of their goods when they buy their first bills from Mr. Gibson. Since opening his house in the main quilts, his business so increased as to necessitate the enlarging of his premises, and he now occupies Nos. 203 and 205 Sacramento street. We are sorry to lose Mr. Gibson; yet the loss to Los Angeles of this enterprising citizen is San Francisco's gain.

Mr. Gibson will own and conduct the house here in the same spirit and liberality that has always characterized his business. He is ably assisted by Gustav Hemann, A. C. Dunn, C. A. Peck, Charles Bennett, Charles Baskersville, James Lancaster, Clay Kellogg, N. N. McHurney and Anson Kirchhoff.

In addition to his Los Angeles house he has an agency at Anaheim, under the supervision of Mr. L. W. Evans, a gentleman who thoroughly understands the wants of the people.

J. C. VALDES.

Jake (as he is often called) and we suppose he is thus familiarly spoken of on account of his exceedingly sociable qualities. No newspaper knows him but knows he is always ready to advertise, and once the people have found him through the medium of printer's ink, they are reckoned among his customers forever more. Why? See his advertisement. It says "a penny saved is equal to two earned," and we know that he lives up to his motto, and he who buys once has money left and will buy again.

His Christmas stock is per excellent, and prices within the reach of all.

BRIGHT.

A few months ago we had occasion to refer to our friend, J. C. Bright, of

BRIGHT'S CHEAP STORE

as the man educated to low prices during the dark days in Kansas.

Mr. Bright has just put his experience to the test in this city—by selling everything cheap. Everybody asks how he can do it? To-day he is moving from his cramped quarters into the old City of Paris store, where he proposes to astonish the natives with his low prices. He opens up to-day, go and see for yourselves.

R. B. BOX, 33 SPRING STREET.

Well known as a capitalist and merchant, has succeeded in building up a valuable business by his uniform courtesy to the trade, by selling a superior article at reasonable prices, and one price to all.

His stock embraces everything usually found in a Ladies' and Gent's Furnishing House. If there is something you want in that line and are not sure who keeps it, you

can safely call on Mr. Fox, and he can supply your wants.

It would fill this page to enumerate his
articles, and we pass on to the next, asking
our readers to give Mr. Fox a call when
anything is wanted in his line.

CHRISTMAS GIFT HINTS.

Valdora' for frames and pictures.

Fox's for ladies' and gents' furnishing
goods.

C. W. Gibson's American Cash Store for
groceries, at cash prices.

H. F. Coulter's for your wife a dress, for
your husband a necktie, a "Coulter shirt,"
your sweetheart a cloak, your friend a bolt
of muslin or flannel.

Thursday, to the "opening" at Preuss &
Pironi's drug store. Something new under
the sun. Don't fail. Remember, Thursday, the 23d.

Lan. J. Thompson's for choice butter,
cheese, and anything in the grocery line.

Subscribe for the SEMI-TROPIC, and send
to your friends East, and be sure to take it
yourself.

Heinzeman & Ellis for a nice line of
fancy goods, toilet articles, or a prescription.

To the Queen Store for a fine pair of
shoes or slippers. A pair of slippers always a nice present.

The Dollar Store for everything. You
will be sure to find what you want at Gillmore's.

The Orange Store for gilt edged butter,
choice canned fruits, provisions, and groceries.

E. Martin & Co. for a demijon of fine
liquor, fit for—ye gods!—or a box of wine
—pure "Sunny Slope" wine.

Loiter & Bradley's for a new carpet, a
parlor set, bedroom set, or lace curtains.
In fact, nothing would please the "old
lady" half so well as a nice piece of furniture. Try it.

Tufton & Kennely's for some of their own
imported goods, selected by Mr. Kennely
in Europe, and shipped by them direct to
Los Angeles. They have some of the finest goods in the State.

Harper, Moore & Co. for a new stove,
new tinware, or to have a new tin roof put
on between showers. A new lot of stoves
just received, and marked down low.

Beds of Pansies, Antirrhinum, Asperula,
Datura, Dianthus, Double Daisies, Mirabi-
lis, &c., which are considered as hardy annuals, can often be wintered over with success by strewing a light covering of leaves
or straw on them, and placing a few stones
or sticks to keep the wind from blowing it
off.

All newly planted bulbs, plants, or
shrubs, should have some winter protection
to shield the earth from sudden changes, as
they will not stand the cold weather as well
as old, established plants that have plenty
of root.

Palmer & Co. for the SEMI-TROPIC CALIFOR-
NIA, price $4.00 per annum.

CITRUS FAIR

— OF —

SOUTHERN CALIFORNIA,

TO BE HELD AT THE

HORTICULTURAL PAVILION,

MARCH 14-19, 1881.

RULES AND REGULATIONS.

The Rules and Regulations of the Horticultural Fair of 1880 will govern the actions of the Annual Citrus Fair.

The Pavilion will be opened for the reception and arrangement of articles for
exhibition, Friday, March 11. The exposition will be opened to the public Monday,
at 8 o'clock P. M., and continue open for
five days, from 9 o'clock A. M. to 10 o'clock
P. M. each day.

No entry will be received after 2 o'clock
P. M. of Tuesday, March 15, unless unavoidably detained.

☞ No Entry fee charged.

One half the proceeds of the Fair will
go towards paying the expenses of the
"Traveling Citrus Fair" that is to be made
up from this exposition and sent East.

ADMISSION:

Single admission—day,	$0 25
Single admission—night,	50
Single season ticket,	1 50

Children (under 14), half-price.

If the evenings should be cool, arrangements will be complete for heating the
Pavilion, and making it comfortable.

The Ladies' Benevolent Society will
have charge of the dining-rooms, which is
a guarantee of success in that department.

Applications for space should be made
on or before March 1. Address, Geo. Rice,
Secretary, Los Angeles, Cal.

DEPARTMENT H.

To the individual, locality, or society making the largest and finest
exhibit, ... $100 00

Any county as a county is barred, but each
locality in the county can compete.

At least three entries for competition to
be made.

DEPARTMENT I.

Class 2—Oranges Budded.

A plate of five constitutes an entry. The
same fruit cannot compete for more than one
premium.

Best one variety	$5 00
Best two varieties	7 00
Best four varieties	10 00
Best six varieties	15 00

Class 3—Oranges—Seedlings.

Best one variety	$5 00
Best two varieties	7 00
Best four varieties	10 00
Best six varieties	15 00

Class 4—Oranges—Sweepstakes.

Best variety	$5 00
Best cluster of oranges	10 00

Class 5—Lemons.

Best one variety	$5 00
Best two varieties	7 00
Best four varieties	10 00

Class 6—Limes.

One hundred to constitute an entry.

Size, quality, color, and marketable qualities to decide.

Best exhibit	$10 00

Class 7—Citrons.

Not less than five constitute an entry.

Best exhibit	$5 00
Best preserved citron (home made)	5 00
Best preserved citron (Factory)	S. Medal

DEPARTMENT J.

Class 1—Raisins.

Best and largest display	$25 00
Best box	10 00
Best quarter box	5 00
Best and most attractive package	
for market	Diploma

Class 2—Canned Fruits.

Best peaches (home made)	$5 00
Best peaches (factory)	Diploma
Best apricots (home made)	5 00
Best apricots (factory)	Diploma

Class 3—Miscellaneous.

Best pomegranates (ten)	$5 00
Best strawberries (six boxes)	5 00
Best tomatoes (one peck)	3 00
Best new potatoes (one peck)	3 00

Class 4—Flowers.

Best and finest display	$10 00

Exhibitors must state in every case on
what stock fruit was grown; and it is desirable that it should also be stated whether
irrigated, character of soil, age of tree and
any other conditions affecting quality or
size of fruit.

For further particulars address the Secretary.

Poultry.

ESTABLISHED RULES FOR SUCCESSFUL POULTRY RAISING.

IN raising poultry or stock it should be the aim of every one to keep it healthy and improve it. You can do it very easily by adopting some systematic rules. These may be enumerated up as follows:

1. Construct your chicken house good, and protect from vermin.

2. Provide a dusting and scratching place, where you can bury wheat or corn, and thus induce the fowls to take needful exercise.

3. Provide yourselves with some good healthy chickens, none to be over three or four years old, giving one cock to every twelve hens.

4. Give plenty of fresh air at all times of the year, especially in summer.

5. Give plenty of fresh water daily, and never allow fowls to go thirsty.

6. Feed them systematically, two or three times a day, and scatter the food, so that they can't eat too fast or without proper exercise. Do not feed more than they will eat up clean, or they will get tired of that kind of food.

7. Give them a variety of both dry and cooked food. A mixture of cooked meal and vegetables is an excellent thing for their morning meal.

8. Give soft feed in the morning, and the whole grain at night, except a little wheat or cracked corn placed in the scratching place to give them exercise during the day.

9. Above all things keep the hen-house clean and well ventilated.

10. Do not crowd too many in one house. If you do, look out for disease.

11. Use carbolic powder in the dusting bins occasionally to destroy lice.

12. Wash your roosts and bottoms of laying nests with whitewash once a week in summer and once a month in winter.

13. Let the old and young have as large a range as possible—the larger the better.

14. Don't breed too many kinds of fowls at the same time, unless you are going into the business. Three or four will give you your hands full.

15. Introduce new blood into your stock every year or so, by either buying a cockerel or setting of eggs from some reliable breeder.

16. In buying birds or eggs, go to some reliable breeder who has his reputation at stake. You may have to pay a little more for birds, but you can depend on what you get. Culls are not cheap at any price.

17. Save the best birds for next year's breeding, and send the others to market. In shipping fancy poultry to market send it dressed.

COOK THE FOOD.

Especially through the autumn and winter months, your fowls should be furnished with at least one full meal of cooked food daily. The practice helps to make up the lack of green food, with which free birds can easily supply themselves, through warm weather. Grain or vegetables steamed or boiled, and well seasoned with a little egg food occasionally, are sure to repay all extra cost. No matter whether your poultry is kept for fancy sales, or to furnish eggs and meat for market, don't fail to follow up this plan.

Morning may be the most convenient time for serving this "banquet," and whole grain comes in order for the evening, which the fowls can easily digest through the night. Bright, healthy birds are the only ones that it will pay one to keep, and this method of feeding helps to bring about this result.—*Colorado Farmer.*

CHARCOAL FOR FOWLS.—There is one thing which nature does not supply, and which civilization renders quite necessary to fowls. It is charcoal. Charcoal made of wood does not answer the purpose; it has no taste of food, it is not attractive to fowls, and is seldom eaten. But if any one will put an ear of ripe corn into the fire until the grains are well charred, and then shell off the corn and throw it to the flock, he will see an eagerness developed and a healthy constitution brought about, which will make a decided improvement. All pale combs will become a bright red, the busy song which precedes laying will be heard, and the average yield of eggs greatly increased.

A CORRESPONDENT says that, while on a visit in the fall to a friend, he was surprised to see the number of eggs he daily obtained. He had but sixteen hens, and the product per diem averaged thirteen eggs. He was in the habit of giving, on every alternate day, a teaspoonful and a quarter of cayenne pepper, mixed with soft food, and took care that each hen obtained her share. The experiment of omitting the pepper was tried, and it was found that the number of eggs was reduced each trial to from five to six daily. Our correspondent believes that the moderate use of this stimulant not only increases the number of eggs, but effectually wards off diseases to which chickens are subject.

The Chief of the Bureau of Statistics at Washington reports that the total value of exports of domestic breadstuffs from the United States during October, 1880, was $23,711,488; during October, 1879, $33,048,807; for ten months ending October, 31, 1880, $231,338,030, and for the same period in 1879, $206,085,314.

Why does not some one plant the Pecan tree? A Pecan grove can be found on many Southern farms. The tree is worth culture for its timber alone. The nuts are a staple article of commerce, and always find a ready sale. The tree is hardy, produces a rapid grower and has few enemies. Caterpillars, and dubs with a small boy attachment, are the worst.

The above represents the doorway and office, in the Cosmopolitan Hotel, of the enterprising firm, Messrs. Herdman & Jones, who do an extensive insurance business, representing a line of first class companies.

They also do a general real estate business, buying and selling property. They publish a circular paper, that is circulated by the SEMI-TROPIC throughout the East. If it's insurance you want, or property to buy or sell, we recommend the above-named firm to your consideration.

"OPENING OF A CHESTNUT BURR."

"Any chestnuts 'round here?" asked one of three city boys who met an aged, benevolent looking farmer out in San Gabriel. The old man hesitated.

"You don't want to steal 'em?" he asked. "Oh no, we just wanted to find out."

"Well, there's a few trees back there, but if I thought you wanted to steal them I wouldn't have told you, for the owner is not at home; but you're bright, honest looking boys."

The boys blushed with the pride of conscious goodness.

"When will the owner be back?"

"Well, not before dark, I reckon."

The boys thanked the old man very respectfully, waited till he got out of sight, jumped over the fence and were soon shaking down the burrs. The shaking was easy, but the opening of the burrs was more difficult and unpleasant. At last the boys had a splendid pile of handsome, brown nuts on the ground, and they prepared to put them in the bags they brought with them.

"Please don't take any more trouble," said the benevolent old man, who stood by the fence leaning kindly on the startled boys. "I'm not quite as strong as I once was, and I fear I can't hold in this dog much longer. If you hurry, though, I guess I can keep him here till you get to the railroad track. Down, Tige, sir!"

As the boys looked back from the railroad fence they could see the stooping figure of the old man scraping the rich, brown chestnuts into a two-bushel bag.

THE
AMERICAN CASH STORE.

48 AND 50 SPRING STREET,
LOS ANGELES.

Continues to astonish the Country with its low prices for the best of Goods.

We hold out special inducements in TEAS of our own importation, COFFEES, green and roasted, etc. We roast our own Coffees, and are sure as to what grades we sell, and that it is fresh and as represented in every instance.

C. W. GIBSON, Proprietor.

San Francisco Office, 203 & 205 Sacramento St.

COMPARE PRICES AND JUDGE FOR YOURSELVES!

WE are the only house in Southern California doing strictly and exclusively a Cash Business. We constantly watch the markets, and any lot of good, merchantable goods we find offered at less than regular prices, for cash down, we secure and give our trade the benefit.

We now carry a larger stock and better assortment of goods in our line than ever, and are better shaped to give our customers the most for their money.

CALL AND EXAMINE OUR STOCK OF

STAPLE AND FANCY GROCERIES,
PROVISIONS CROCKERY,
Glassware, Etc.

Our roasted and ground COFFEES are growing in public favor every day. We select all our coffees green, do our own grinding, and sell a CHOICE, PURE, FRESH ARTICLE.

In TEAS we claim to be headquarters. Our stock is large, of all varieties, and we shall continue to crowd prices down as low as possible.

I SELL

SUGAR—

Island	10¼	lbs for $1.00
D.	9¼	"
G C	8¼ "	"
Extra C	8¼ "	"
Granulated	7¼ "	"
Fine crushed	7¼ "	"
Cuba	7¼ "	"
Powdered	7 "	"

COFFEE—

C. R. No. 1	5 "	"
Green, No. 2	5¼ "	"
Rio No. 1	4¼ "	"
Carious	4 "	"
Java	3 "	"

COFFEE ROASTED—

Happy Union.
Mocha and Java, 45c ℔
I X L.
pure Java, 40c ℔
Favorite.
Java & Costa Rica, 35c or 3
Satisfaction.
Choice Costa Rica, 30c or 3¼ "
Value Received
Good Costa Rica, 25c or 4¼ "

TEA—

C. W. G. Teapot, 50c or 4¼ lbs for $2.00
C. W. G. Eng. Breakfast 3 lbs for $2.50
L. J. Tea, ℔
Crown, ℔ 40c
Choice Japan Teas 50c 60c ℔

SOAP—

"IXL," 30 bars	
Chemical Olive	
D. B. Horse Soap	

CANDLES—

All grades, for 30 lb boxes, $1.50 $1.75

CRACKERS—

Soda, ℔	
Extra Soda, 30 ℔	
In 10 ℔ boxes	85c
In 17 ℔ boxes	$1.10
In 74 ℔ boxes	1.40
Butter Crackers, ℔	10c
Oyster Crackers	10c
Nic nacs	15c

STARCH—

Starch, ℔ 10c

SALT FISH—

Halibut fins, ℔	10c
Salmon, ℔	5c
Mackerel, A No. 1, four for	35c
Mackerel, No. 2, six for	35c
Mackerel, kits, No. 1	$2.10
Mackerel, kits, No. 2	1.90

BACON—

Bacon, ℔ 11¼c

FLOUR—

Paradise Mills, ℔ 100 ℔	$2.65
L. A. Capital, ℔ 100 ℔	2.35

The Apiary.

The SEMI-TROPIC was instrumental in shipping bees from Southern California to New Zealand, and opened up an avenue for the sale of fine bees in foreign countries. Every apiarist recognizes the fact that our paper has done a good work for him in creating a demand for his honey and maintaining a fair price for it. If the apiarists will stand by each other, and keep down all frauds, they will not only uphold the dignity of their business, but make it a profitable and pleasant vocation.

We will devote such space to the apiary department of our paper as the demands require, and when the time comes to justify it, we will establish a Bee Journal, in the interest of the apiarist

CHIPS FROM THE HONEY HOUSE.

BY S. G. BARTER.

As no two persons possess the same mental faculties, it could not be supposed that all will adopt the same style of hive or the same method in handling their bees.

To secure a large crop of honey it is necessary, first, to have a good location; second, good season; third, good hives, etc; and fourth, an industrious, watchful bee-keeper.

When symptoms of robbing occur, contract the entrance to all weak colonies, and expose no sweets around the apiary.

The profit of bee-keeping consists in keeping your colonies strong in numbers. When honey is abundant a large apiary will fill up rapidly in the same time and place that a few weak colonies will barely make a living.

Colonies containing drones at this season of the year are either queenless or contain a drone-laying queen. Such stocks should be united with a weak colony, containing a fertile queen.

During January stop all upper ventilation, and confine the heat to the brood chamber, as the rearing of the young will be carried on extensively from this on, if the season is favorable.

Use no moth traps or complicated humbugs. If you use a good frame hive, and keep your colonies strong, you need not fear the moth. Ignorant and negligent bee keepers, with poor hives, are the ones who lose bees by moths.

Avoid opening your hives unnecessarily. Give timely assistance to all that need it. Work quickly; avoid sudden jars. Never fight your bees, but use plenty of smoke.

As Southern California differs materially from other climates, it is to the interest of bee-keepers to learn the proper management of bees in this semi-tropic climate.

No place on the globe can excel Southern California in the production of honey, either in quantity, quality, or increase of bees. The rapid progress that has been made in the last few years is remarkable.

The increase in swarms and the production of honey has been marvelous, to say the least of it, when we take into consideration the great loss of bees this country sustained during the years 1877 and 1879. Yet apiculture is moving steadily on, the floral treasures of Southern California seeming to be adequate to the great demands made upon them.

The principal profit of the apiary is obtained from colonies that are strong in early spring.

Those who have to feed their bees will find that one pound of sealed honey, that can be fed in the frame, is equivalent to three or four pounds of extracted honey or syrup, and takes less labor and causes less robbing. All poor honey should be preserved in the comb for this purpose.

Our prospect for a honey crop in 1881, in Los Angeles city and vicinity, is good.

Markets.

RETAIL GROCERIES, ETC.

BUTTER, Cal choice, ℔	$0 40	@	$0 45
CHEESE	15	@	20
Eastern	30	@	40
LARD, California	10½	@	11
Eastern	15	@	20
FLOUR, extra family, bbl.	6 50	@	7 50
Capital Mills, ℔		@	8 00
Pioneer, ℔ cwt		@	8 00
Superfine do		@	2 70
Graham, 50 ℔ sack		@	1 10
Buckwheat, 10 ℔ sack		@	60
OATMEAL, Cal, 10 ℔ sack		@	60
Eastern, do	5	@	6½
CORN MEAL, ℔	3½	@	
SUGAR, crushed	12	@	
Light brown	8	@	10
COFFEE, green	30	@	40
TEA, fine black	50	@	1 00
Finest Japan	30	@	80
CANDLES, Adamantine	15	@	18
SOAP, California	5½	@	10
RICE	8	@	10
YEAST POWDER, doz.	1 50	@	2 00
CANNED OYSTERS, doz	1 75	@	3 50
SYRUP, S. F. Golden	40	@	60
DRIED APPLES, ℔		@	15
GERMAN PRUNES	12½	@	
FIGS, California		@	10
PEACHES	10	@	20
SILK kerosene	30	@	40
HONEY, comb	12½	@	15
do, No. 2, ...	10	@	12
Extracted	06	@	10
BACON, California	10	@	12½
HAMS, do	12½	@	14
Eastern, ...	16	@	17
POTATOES, cwt	90	@	1 15
ONIONS, cwt		@	2 00
BEANS	1 50	@	2 50
Butter	1 40	@	1 50
Lima	1 00	@	0 00
FRESH BEEF	05½	@	00½
Round steak		@	
Sirloin	10	@	12
Porterhouse	12½	@	
CHICKENS	00½	@	00½
CAL. RAISINS, boxes	2 25	@	2 50
Half boxes	1 25	@	1 35
Quarter boxes	75	@	85

EGGS—Have ruled high for several months and in demand at 40c.

BUTTER—Is also in good demand, for choice only, at 40c.

WALNUTS—Will bring a higher price later in the season, as large quantities have been shipped East, but are now quoted at 8c.

ORANGES—The market has not opened, but prices will be good if shippers are careful in sorting and packing.

GRAPES—Those who are fortunate enough to have a few choice grapes for Christmas can realize a good price. We know of offers in small lots at the price printed.

GARDEN PRODUCE—This trade is left almost entirely to the Chinamen, who continue to run their wagons, and supply the farmer as well as the town people, and at prices that are very reasonable.

WINES AND LIQUORS—This item in the wine business has a tendency to make prices stronger, and prices may be said to have advanced two or three cents on the gallon for new wines.

LOS ANGELES WINES AND LIQUORS

Red wine, No 1, per gallon			$0 50
Red wine, No 2, per gallon			40
White wine, new, per gallon			50
White wine, old, per gallon			75
Port wine, old, per gallon			1 00
Angelica wine, old, per gallon			1 00
Muscat wine, old, per gallon			1 75
Grape brandy, old, per gallon			1 00
Brandy, per gallon			2 50
Aguardiente, per gallon			2 00

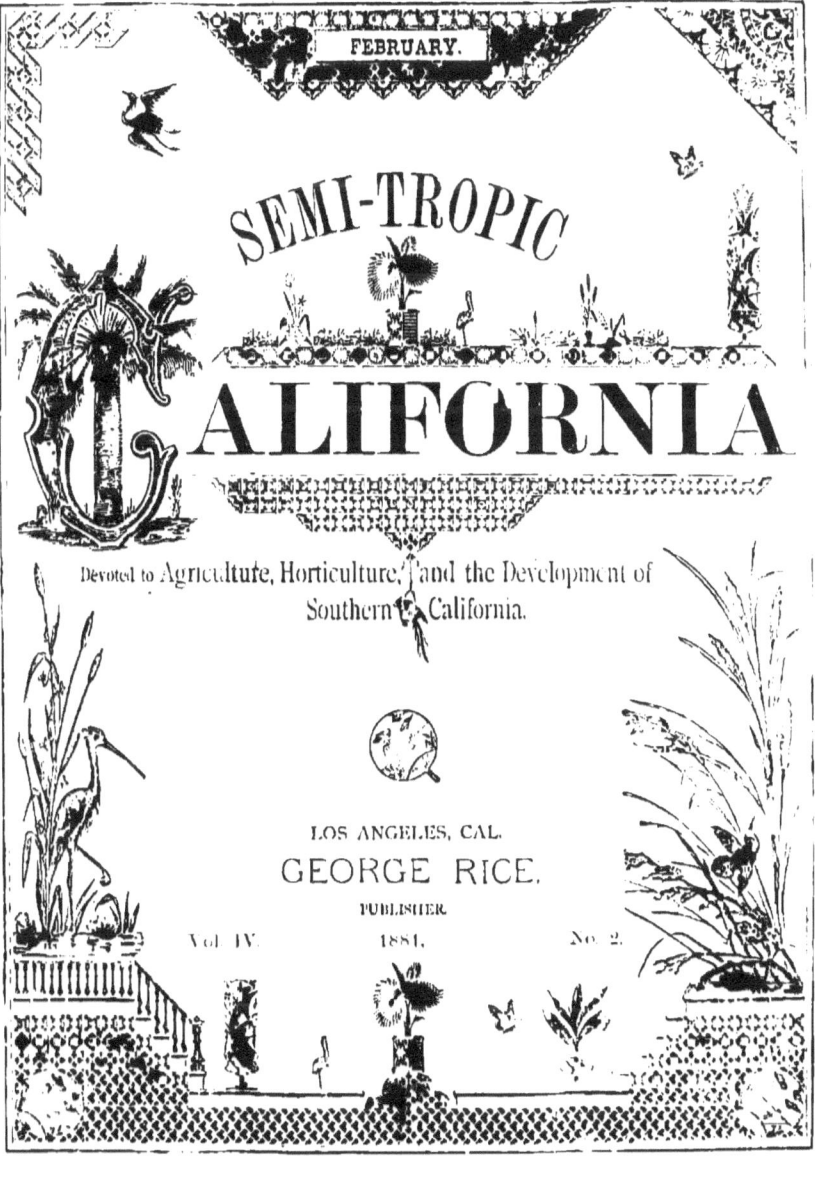

FEBRUARY.

SEMI-TROPIC

CALIFORNIA

Devoted to Agriculture, Horticulture, and the Development of Southern California.

LOS ANGELES, CAL.

GEORGE RICE.

PUBLISHER.

Vol. IV.   1881.   No. 2.

[illegible]

—AND—

SOUTHERN CALIFORNIA HORTICULTURIST.

VOL. IV. LOS ANGELES, CAL., FEBRUARY, 1881 No. 2.

Southern California.

VENTURA COUNTY.

BY S. BRISTOL.

VENTURA County occupies nearly a central position among her sister counties in Southern California, having San Luis Obispo and Santa Barbara on the northwest and Los Angeles and San Diego on the southeast. Her productions and climate are fairly represented by her geographical position—a medium between San Luis and San Diego. Not one of the coast counties can boast a pleasanter climate or a richer soil. Though the youngest and smallest of the coast counties—having been organized only half a dozen years since—already its exports of barley, corn, beans, flax seed, honey, wheat and hogs is very large, taxing to their utmost the capacity of two large wharves and their accompanying warehouses—those of San Buenaventura and Hueneme. Ventura County contains about 250,000 acres of very fine arable land. The soil in general is very deep. In the valley where I live—Santa Clara—it will average fifty feet deep. Facing the ocean as most of the county does, the warm ocean air gives it a happy exemption from frost and snow. Living six miles from the sea, I have never seen a flake of snow fall upon my place; nor have I seen an orange or lemon injured by frost on my place. Very little irrigation is practiced in this county. Three years out of four there is no need of it for the fruits and crops we usually raise, and on the fourth, or dry year, it is usually considered of doubtful utility, being expensive, unhealthy and injurious to the land. The better plan, according to the views of our farmers, is to Summer fallow a portion of the farm every year, and thus preserve the moisture of the previous rainy season for the next year, and then, in case of scarcity of rain, the summer fallowed part will carry them through.

Hitherto Ventura County has been a large producer of barley, corn, hogs and honey, and has helped largely to glut the market with those productions. This year it has fairly entered upon the wheat raising industry. Our crops of Odessa and white Russian wheat have been very large and profitable, averaging 35 bushels per acre. An immense area of these rust-proof varieties will be sown the present winter, and barley and corn will take back seats, and only be called forward when good prices prevail.

To be a little more specific, I will give the production of a farm of 112 acres, farmed the present year by Mr. James Evans. The farm adjoins my own on the north, and was sold by me to his father, Thomas Evans, some dozen years since. Since then it has been in constant cultivation, yielding a crop every year. It has never been manured nor irrigated. Since January 1, 1880, he sowed on this land [illegible] acres of flax, 10 in barley, 30 in bird seed, 20 in Odessa wheat, and the balance—[illegible] acres—is in corn, not yet gathered, and in an orchard, etc. The flax ground turned off from the 50 acres 1,050 centals, or a little over one ton to the acre, and at three cents a pound, brought him $3,[illegible]. The bird seed—30 acres—yielded one ton per acre, and brought him over $40 per ton—$1,200. The Odessa wheat averaged [illegible] bushels, or 30 centals, and brought him $1.50 per cental—$[illegible]. The 10 acres in barley yielded 3 tons per acre, and sold on the ground at $[illegible] per ton, making the cash product of the 100 acres $5,[illegible]. Of course all lands hereabouts do not produce thus bounteously, and yet this land is but little better than the average in Santa Clara Valley.

Ventura County is also an excellent county for fruits, such as the apple, prune, pear, apricot, etc. The apricot is especially at home here. Our seaward exposure seems to suit this fruit right well, as it always leans toward the ocean and stretches out its arms imploringly toward it. Immense orchards of apricots are being planted and projected. Thus, within a month I have learned of a party who has contracted to set out 150 acres in that fruit; another party has bought 220 acres, another 1[illegible], while other parties still are in search of lands in which to plant the same fruit.

Los Angeles rightfully boasts of being the orange Paradise of this State, San Diego that of the olive, and who knows but Ventura will yet become renowned as the apricot county of the State.

Ventura County sends greeting to Los Angeles County, congratulates her on her peerless growth and prosperity, and hopes to become better acquainted and on more intimate terms by and by, when "that railroad" shall reduce a two days' journey to one of only two hours.

SAN BUENAVENTURA, D[illegible] 15, 1880.

EVERY dairyman should bear this in mind: that poor butter or cheese is always the first to feel the effects of a dull market. The best products are always inquired for, even on the poorest market.

ALTA-CALIFORNIA.

ED. SEMI-TROPIC: Northern California with her varied clime, is still prospering, both in her agricultural as well as horticultural interest. Farmers, with their usual [illegible], care but little, unless [illegible] experience better courses are pursued, bringing out a better system of work on [illegible]—studies of the soil, adaptation of [illegible], fruits, and [illegible] implements, doing work in fine order, [illegible] a pleasure to handle, as well as profitable to the owner.

The lateness of the season has given [illegible] to work up a large portion of the [illegible] by the cultivator, and the storms that swept through all the State [illegible] many plows to work, seeding for another harvest. Large quantities of grain are still held back in anticipation of higher [illegible] by those who are able to wait, which [illegible] owing to the demand abroad, [illegible] season to come.

The prospect of our [illegible] natural point of view seems better in [illegible] respects to our [illegible] land. The [illegible] lands that formerly did so well in their [illegible] days are losing their vitality [illegible] with. The [illegible] of the [illegible], washing [illegible] the old land marks, and the [illegible] fine fruits, bigger portions of land [illegible] looked on as a future remittance [illegible] recuperate the loss of olden days.

The ravages of insects in their [illegible] have been, and are still, a study, [illegible] which, many devices are brought [illegible] use to stay their [illegible] many fine orchards in various parts of the State. The grape interest is booming. [illegible] of a large increase [illegible] promising; both raisin and wine outlook [illegible] table. The present season both [illegible] have done well, and our raisin culture [illegible] are furnishing our merchants with fine [illegible], done up in good style, and are [illegible] well. Semi-tropic fruits, cultivated within our borders, have had a [illegible] which [illegible] has given [illegible] valleys, an [illegible] party [illegible] advantage over the other.

It looks as though a new turn of events [illegible] our climatic region is passing over us [illegible] an early [illegible] and our prospects in an [illegible] manner, [illegible] fruit and [illegible] up their leaves in an [illegible] The call of these culture has not [illegible] listening [illegible]; still many like to [illegible] within their own [illegible], if only for private use, which I think will be so far as they will attain in this portion of the State.

G. K.

SEMI-TROPIC
CALIFORNIA.
— AN —
ILLUSTRATED MONTHLY.

Devoted to Agriculture, Horticulture, and the Development of Southern California.

Terms: $1.50 per Annum, in Advance.

Office, Rooms 1 & 56, Baker Block.

Address, - - GEO. RICE, Los Angeles, Cal.

GEORGE RICE, - Editor and Prop'r.

OFFICIAL PAPER
— OF THE —
Southern California Horticultural Soc'y.

J. De Barth Shorb .... President.
H. K. W. Bent .... Vice President
E. F. Spence .... Treasurer.
Geo. Rice .... Secretary.

Directors.

J. F. Clark,   A. B. Clark,
J. H. Shield,   H. K. W. Bent,
C. F. Thom,   J. De Barth Shorb,
      T. C. Fleurange.

Correspondents of the Semi Tropic.

Geo. C. Webb .... San Diego.
Mrs. M. C. Winton .... Santa Barbara.
A. R. Clark .... Downey.
Geo. J. H. Phillips .... Florence.
W. F. A. Bracton .... Petaluma.
Mrs. A. J. Dewey .... Los Angeles.
W. R. Olden .... Anaheim.
Jennie Alce .... Pomona.
Dr. G. R. Bangs .... Pasadena.
Asahel Pease .... Visalia.
Colonel Pope .... Santa Barbara.
Mrs. Flora Kimball .... San Diego.

ADVERTISING RATES.

From this date, and until further notice, our advertising rates will be two dollars per inch each insertion. Advertisements of three inches or over, inserted for six months or longer, a discount of 25 per cent. will be made.

Our Christmas number was appreciated, as the extra large edition was exhausted a few weeks after publication.

The press, not only of Southern California but of the state and the east were enthusiastic in its praise, and we thank them one and all for their kind words.

Our success in this direction will cause us to set at once towards publishing a still larger and finer edition the coming season. In addition to the usual amount of reading matter, written by the ablest agriculturalists and horticulturalists in the state, the usual engravings of dwellings and business blocks we shall publish engravings of our public men, with brief sketches of their lives. We shall also publish engravings of public buildings, churches, plants, etc., etc.

ANNUAL GRAPE NUMBER.

The reception of our grape number last year induces us to enlarge on the experiment this year.

The March issue will be devoted almost entirely to the interests of grape growing and wine-making; will be handsomely illustrated, and well written and compiled. The foremost grape-growers in the State will contribute articles for this issue. We shall issue an extra edition, and parties wanting extra copies should send in their orders now. Single copies, 10c.; three copies, 25c.; fifteen copies for $1. We make these special low rates that persons so disposed can mail them to friends east. We will mail and pay postage without extra charge.

The Citrus Fair to be held in the Pavilion March 14-19 bids fair to be the great exposition of Southern California.

Application for space is being made, and at this time every county in this district, save one, is represented.

Many different localities will make exhibits, and it seems to be understood that a failure to secure space is an acknowledgement of the inferiority of citrus fruits. Spirited, friendly competition will be the order of the day.

Flowers and evergreens will add much to the general appearance of the various departments, and we hope each locality intending to compete for the first place in Southern California as a citrus growing locality, and the $100 premium, will see to it that their several departments are properly decorated. Calla lillies will be in their glory, and will make beautiful decorations combined with other flowers; and then there is a premium for flowers, and it's our guess that it will be along with the $100 premium—"a bird, etc."

Southern California should be represented at the World's Fair in New York, in 1883. We hope we will be allowed a representative in the State Commission. But it is necessary for us to look out for ourselves, and we suggest that the various agricultural, horticultural, and fruit growers' associations in Southern California undertake to make an exhibit that will truly and properly represent our part of the State.

The exhibit showing the commerce of the United States for 1883 is very gratifying. The import and export trade amounts to $1,534,000,000, the excess of exports amounting to $72,000,000. Worthy of special note is the fact that $42,000,000 of coin and bullion have been imported against $33,000,000 exported.

Our suggestion, in our last issue, to celebrate the centennial of Los Angeles by a fitting and appropriate Exposition of her agricultural and material prosperity, has been seconded by the Horticultural Society. Active steps will soon be taken by the Board of Directors, assisted by the public, to make the full Exposition at the Pavilion and on the Pavilion grounds, a grand celebration of the hundredth anniversary of Los Angeles, in which, it is expected, all Southern California will participate.

Two hundred and fifty thousand dollars' worth of California fruit was sold in Chicago last year. $100,000 more than western Indiana sold, and Indiana is considered quite a fruit country.

Bartlett pears, white muscat and Tokay grapes, apricots, nectarines and peaches are the fruits most in demand for shipping. Southern California will be over four hundred miles nearer the east via the southern route, and we must utilize the new markets opening up to us.

The March issue will be our annual grape and wine number, and will be worth the subscription price for one year to every farmer who plants and cultivates the vine, or to the dealer who buys the wine. The illustrations are in the hands of our engravers, and will be especially fine. Don't miss it. If extra copies are wanted, send in your orders early.

The Garden on the Farm.—President McGregor, of the Oxford Farmers' Club—as reported in the Farm and Fireside, of Ohio—says that we run too much to the great staples, and the average farmer has a contempt for eggs, butter, honey, etc.; he looks upon them as small, peddling business. The truck patch will pay in dollars, and more in health. All the interests of the farm depend on health, and the road to health often runs through the truck patch. At a dish of raspberries and cream the farmer forgets his weariness. Apiarists tell us that the egg which under ordinary rearing produces the working bee, if put in a superior cell and fed on the royal jelly, makes a queen. So the diet and surroundings of our children have much to do with their character. Many children have been injured by ginger snaps and painted candy, but to extract of white clover and ripe fruits, never. Many instances are beyond the reach of farmers, but strawberries they can have, and these he believes to be a means of grace. He doubts not that hog and hominy has often been the means of back sliding.

A little five-year-old wants us to write his grandmother back East, who writes about the snow storms and cold weather, to send some snowballs and icicles and send him.

SIERRA MADRE VILLA.

No more attractive and pleasant place can be found than the Sierra Madre Villa at this season of the year. Always beautiful and well kept, it is, during the winter season, simply perfect. The flowers are in their glory, the limes just ripe, the great yellow oranges shining like golden balls, threatening the destruction of the trees in spite of numberless props; rustic seats here and there to rest the weary traveler; and the comfortable parlor, the well-appointed dining-room, and prompt and capable attendants, make this a health resort truly—a place of rest for both mind and body.

There could be no more pleasant and kindly landlord than the one who gives always a cordial welcome to the villa, and it would be difficult to imagine scenes more delightful than the suites which form the visitors' transient homes.

The adjacent mountains afford a fine field for exercise for those who are strong enough and inclined that way. The view from the villa is extensive, embracing the outlying valley and reaching to the sea, near twenty miles away.

And we must not forget the tomato patch, rich with ripening fruit, the long border of rose geraniums, the reservoir of clear, pure water, the cunning little meat shop, the gas manufactory, and, indeed, all the necessary requisites of independent, comfortable, restful life.

The subject of sub-irrigation and drainage is one that is of great importance in all parts of the United States. It has remained for the Asbestine Sub Irrigation Company, of this city, to invent a system that entirely fills the bill, and at the least possible expense. Their system, wherever introduced in the East for drainage, has given entire satisfaction. We call attention to the illustrated article in this issue on the subject, and ask the careful consideration of all interested.

RIVERSIDE CITRUS FAIR.—The Third Annual Exhibition of citrus fruits will be held in Riverside March 9th to 11th, 1881. We urge the fruit growers of Los Angeles to attend and make exhibits. Riverside has taken the lead in this movement, and no sectional jealousy should prevent the citrus growing regions from making exhibits at their Fair. The united efforts of this go-ahead colony are worthy of emulation, and we hope all parts of semi-tropic California will vist this Fair, take their fruits with them, go home well paid for their trouble, and organize a local Fruit Growers' Association. Persons who cannot attend, but wish to make exhibits, can do so by making arrangements at the SEMI-TROPIC office. We will attend to shipping and exhibiting for any and all parties who will deliver their fruit at the depot in Los Angeles.

THE CITRON.

A WORD OF ENCOURAGEMENT.

For many years our orchardists have cultivated the citron, with the desire and belief that some individual or firm would be found capable of utilizing them for commercial purposes. But many seasons passed without any demand; our growers became discouraged, and gradually neglected their trees, some, indeed, unfortunately uprooting them. We are now about to hold forth the olive branch of promise, and a happy moment it is for us; we are authorized to state that a San Francisco firm, Messrs. James, Parizer & Co. have succeeded in preparing California citron, orange and lemon peel in so satisfactory a manner as to compare favorably with the best imported, and no better guaranty can be given than the fact that Messrs. Wm. T. Coleman & Co. have accepted the exclusive agency for the goods of this firm. Now our advice to orchardists is that you plant out and expend considerable time upon Citron, China Lemon, Bitter and Seville oranges, as this firm will purchase all that can be raised at fair prices. This, certainly, is a bright outlook—a good market for products so easily raised and which have hitherto proved so utterly unprofitable.

Far from the snow bound hills of the north the birds come trooping to us, trilling their beautiful melodies, and filling our hearts with a sense of sweet companionship. When the icy north is locked in the still white sleep, as of death, these little feathered flakes of song drift down in myriads to our land of almost perpetual spring. How sweet their cheerful carol! They cheer us, enliven our toil, lighten the hours of leisure, help us to realize constantly that life is bright and beautiful, full of opportunities, and blest with sunshine. And we miss them sadly when they leave us, though our little five-year-old and last year he was tired of the mocker lark, and would be glad when they stopped singing. "And, mama, next summer I guess they'll have a new song learned, won't they?"

The cold wave has swept from Alaska to the Gulf of Mexico, from the Rocky Mountains to the Atlantic, the thermometer in Jacksonville, Fla., marking 20°. We should feel especially favored here in Southern California, where every day has been delightful, the thermometer at no time marking below 50°, and the average temperature of every day ranging from 42 to 60°.

BLACKBERRIES AND ICE CREAM.—Just now, when the mercury is 18° below zero in Indiana, we read of a Hoosier farmer sending sample quarts of fresh blackberries to an editor, with comments, such as "The Snyder is now in its prime; the Kittatiny is loaded with fruit, etc. We do not believe the grangers guilty of any inconsistency, but the editor is somewhat out of season, as well as the fruit.

RIVERSIDE.

The citizens of Riverside are much gratified by the continual appreciation of the value of real property in that pleasant settlement. A continuous influx of men of culture and wealth is daily making itself felt and improvement is the watchword.

The interests of San Bernardino and Los Angeles counties are nearly identical and there is therefore no occasion for jealousy or rivalry. Growers, however, it is to be hoped that an era of good feeling is set to dawn upon all the counties in the "fruit belt" of Southern California, and that the several communities may be drawn together to make common cause for the benefit of our various important industries.

The Riverside raisin crop of last season was not quite up to the average either in quantity or quality. Growers, however, seem to be satisfied with the prospect, and new vineyards are being set out—more than in any previous year. The raisin crop will be the main stay of Riverside for many years to come.

Of the oranges, which hang so plentifully upon the trees of the prominent fruit growers of Riverside, has been scrutinized and published, they could not present a finer or more inviting appearance. There is no smut on the fruit nor scale on the trees, which is a gratifying feature of citrus culture in San Bernardino county.

There is very little disposition among the fruit growers of Riverside to grumble. If any person is discontented with his lot he can speedily sell out at a price which amply compensates him for a labor in the past.

Mr. T. W. Cover, of Riverside, has one of the finest young orchards of citrus trees which we have seen in Southern California. The fruit is all uniform and of a marketable size, being also of the choicest varieties. Mr. Cover has a veritable bonanza in the shape of a fine nursery stock of several thousand trees, totally enjoured by the frost.

In a sheltered nook of the Riverside settlement may be found the beautiful places of Messrs. A. T. Tangred, Codington, Johnson, Wright, Large, Roe and others. A visitor to the colony should examine the fine orchards and vineyards of this locality before leaving.

Arlington and Riverside are practically one and the same, and the former may be styled the child of the latter. Arlington Avenue is one of the finest driveways upon the American continent, and for two miles is lined with the elegant residences of well-to-do citizens from the New England, Middle and Western states.

Every cultivator of a piece of ground should be a reader of our paper. He should support it by writing for it such facts of experiments as would benefit his neighbors, and also enlarge his mind, thus help sustain a paper devoted to his interest and welfare. Will you do it? Commence now.

Semi-Tropical Fruits

THE ORANGE (CITRUS AURANTIUM); ITS ORIGIN AND HISTORY.

BY MRS. A. M. WINTON.

THE exact period at which the orange was introduced into Great Britain is somewhat apocryphal. The date, however, will not differ materially from the introduction into Portugal in the early part of the sixteenth century.

To Sir Walter Ralegh belongs the credit of introducing them into England, carrying thither the seeds which were planted by his nephew, Sir Francis Carew, and from these seeds came the famous trees of Beddington, in Surrey, and which had a historical notoriety in the fifteenth and sixteenth centuries. Their remoteness gives room for question as to their origin; some claiming for them an introduction from Italy, others again from Portugal. These trees at Beddington were grown in open ground, with only winter screens to protect them in inclement weather, though their growth would not indicate a congenial climate, as more than a century after their introduction they had not attained over eighteen feet in height, the trunk only nine inches in diameter, and the head twelve feet in one direction by nine in the other. They had been most carefully guarded by a wall on the north side, and in the seventeenth century surrounded by an enclosure of glass. Whether the confinement was detrimental, or owing to the severe frosts, the following year they all succumbed, the exact cause of which destruction is not known.

There seems, according to the horticultural writers of the sixteenth century, many attempts to acclimate them in boxes carried into the house for the winter, and into the gardens for the summer. John Parkinson, a quaint writer on the subject, observes: "By the warmth of the stove, or such other thing, to give them comfort in the colder time, but no tent or mean provision will preserve them." At the present time better appliances serve the purpose more successfully, as there are numerous fine specimens in both northern France and England, which are very ornamental to the blooming season. In the south of England they are trained like peach trees, and sheltered by straw mats in winter. The fruit thus borne is large and fair. During the wars of the crusaders, oranges were found in Syria, and were considered by them as a part of the natural glories of the Holy Land, though they are not nearly indigenous to the country.

This belief was strengthened by the fables of profane writers, and the descriptions of the golden apples of Hesperides, and the Mosaic accounts in their records were quoted to prove this tree used in the procession described in Leviticus, 23d chapter.

The citron of Josephus, and the Kitron of the Greeks, and the mala medica of the Romans, are supposed possibly to refer to the same fruit, though modern writers dispute it. Traleaia seems the first to have carefully traced this history, and he finds no sufficient data for supposing the orange to have been found in northern Africa, or Syria, or in Media, whence the Romans claim to have obtained their famed Median apples, also speaks of citric acid obtained from lemons. In their travels in India, the Arabians found the sweet orange, known as the so-called China orange of this period, and the bitter, known as the Seville. Marco Paulo does not mention it in his exhaustive account of the wonders of China. Thus it seems probable that we are indebted to the Arabs for our possession of this delicious fruit, and in their unparalleled zeal as propagandists of Mahomedanism, they scattered their acquisitions as widely as their religious belief. Humboldt found the wild orange at Rio Cedoux, laden with excellent fruit, probably the planting of some Indian rancherias, as we cannot claim the orange as indigenous to this continent. The varieties of soils, climate, and conditions under which citrus fruits have been found, have greatly increased their varieties, until, in the early part of this century, there were enumerated 169 varieties, and 43 of the orange, and in the opinion of early writers, the citrus fruits originated in one common stock. The orange in Europe is now mostly confined to the countries lying on the Mediterranean, notably Portugal, Spain, France, Italy, and Greece. They are specialties of the first two countries, the region of the rivers near the coast, and the plains of Andalusia, grow them of great size, and they constitute largely the support of the convents of that region. Among the Moors there are trees supposed to be six or seven hundred years of age, and given an added element of luxury and grandeur to the famous Moorish Court, transplanted and naturalized amid the soft airs of the gracious Sunnland. These trees have begun to decay, encrusted with a peculiar sort of lichen. In France the best orange plantations are principally in Provence, lying eastward of the Rhone; fine groves are also found on the river Var, and in the neighborhood of Nice, and here they reach a fine perfection. Where the Alps descend gradually by successive gradations to the sea, giving shelter from cold winds, the vegetation is very luxuriant, especially the orange. It attains a height of twenty feet, and is unusually graceful, the rapidity of the growth and other conditions give a fine, healthy appearance to the trees, and is apparently one of very few places where no disease attacks them. The fragrance is mentioned as peculiarly powerful here, and the "Odors of Araby, the Blest," are rivalled by these luxuriant groves. The "Sirocco" of Southern Italy is not known in this region around the chain of Apennines, and to its exposure to mild temperature, softened by the vicinity of the Mediterranean, and the wall of mountains to the northward, is supposed due the rare beauty and growth of these attractive orange groves. From the careful study of the history of the orange for centuries, we are forced to the conclusion that it is largely what its climate and conditions make it. A leading English author holds that very high temperature, forcing a large expansion of fruit, renders it coarse, enlarging the oil glands, and thickening the skin; bringing as proof the oranges of St. Michael, in the Azores, and the Malta. The former has equalizing winds on all sides, while the latter has a temperature modified by the contiguous coast of Africa, with its dry, sultry heats.

Somewhat of difference also comes from the soil. St. Michaels has a rich alluvial deposit, while Malta was originally covered with an alkaline crust, to remedy which a surface soil was brought from Sicily. Frequently it is required to trench the ground to remove this under-crust, to prevent the orange growing bitter and less productive. St. Michael's orange has a thin rind, small oil glands, and the pulp very sweet, while the Maltese has all of the opposite qualities. If these suppositions are correct—and their sources should give them some credence—it is evident that there are many locations in Southern California exceptionally adapted to the growth of this fruit successfully, bringing it to its highest perfection. It is also claimed that the essential element is the vicinity of the semi-tropical sea, in comparing oranges so grown to continental ones. That the air is kept perpetually in motion, and so preventing the intense heats which, it is claimed, render the juices disagreeable. A theory, based on much observation and experiment, was advanced at the late meeting of the Santa Barbara Horticultural Society by Mr. Coffin, from Glen Annie. He carefully studied the diseases of citrus fruits in the orchard with Prof. Comstock, and has pursued it for years by himself. Mr. Coffin feels satisfied that the "scale" is not connected with the scale bug, but rather owing to a diseased condition of the leaf. It exudes a gum, which, catching the dust from the atmosphere, causes this deposit, and on trees growing thriftily there is very little of it. He has therefore commenced investigating the roots, and in every case of serious trouble aboveground finds a corresponding appearance of the root. From this he argues some want in the soil, and is strongly impressed with the possibility of it being a want of underdraining, and will carefully experiment in this direction. Trees growing above gravelly subsoil are comparatively free from the trouble. No irrigation is used at Glen Annie, and has not been for years.

Mr. Coffin reports the trees larger for their age and the fruitage heavier than he has found them in any orchard in the country south of us, where irrigation is practical. He does not argue from this that all soils and locations will answer treated in this way, but is satisfied that this county, bordering on the sea coast, with its deep alluvial soil, will never require irrigation. Mr. Bund's experience is of the same character, also Colonel Hayne and others here. Lemons have been raised on the upland in several places with no water from the first, and are flourishing finely. Acapulco limes—a specialty of Santa Barbara County—have been sent to market every month in the year, and have no rival when they reach San Francisco. Mr. Husson, in his recent examination of the fruit interests of Southern California, was unbounded in his admiration of these limes. In size and flavor they are superb, and as they are uninjured by frost in this locality, are abundant bearers. This immunity from destructive frosts gives us a decided advantage in our citrus orchards, especially with the lemon and the lime, which are easily injured by it, and in their earlier years succumb entirely to even light frosts.

EXPERIENCE WITH ALMONDS.

BY GEO. C. SWAN, SAN DIEGO.

SEVEN years with almonds, with bearing trees, does not quite carry out the vision of immense crops pictured to my imagination while reading the glowing accounts, a few years before coming to California. Some persons in this vicinity, disgusted with the small yield, have devoted the space formerly occupied by them to other trees; others have this season reported unsatisfactory returns. Under the new developments by our untiring horticulturists, is it not better to wait further developments before discarding the tree altogether?

The almond is native to the far east and Africa. If not among the trees of the Garden of Eden, it must have been "closely." Frequent mention is made of it in the Old Testament.

Acclimated in Southern Europe, varieties are said to be found upon the Steppes of Russia, and the elevated plains of Mexico, cultivated for its flowers and fruit. From the bitter a delicate oil is made, used by confectioners, and for delicate surgical operations. The fruit is acceptable to the majority; large quantities are imported into the United States and other countries. Great Britain alone receiving 450 tons annually. California cannot afford to give up its cultivation.

In early times it was a royal nut, a luxury for kings, queens, and rulers. Partaken of in moderation, it is a promoter of digestion, and by many considered an indispensable acquisition to the dinner table. We read that when Israel sent his sons a second time into Egypt for corn to keep them alive, among the presents to Joseph almonds are mentioned. In my boyhood days a few were dealt out sparingly to us children; but when Christmas came we were sure of a good supply in our stockings, which may be an excuse for telling how almost came, with socks well filled with them,—socks large enough for Goliah, and Goliahs as numerous as the forest trees in our native State. While the vision has not been fully realized, it is comforting to

know that some of our neighbors have had it fulfilled, and that Elwood Cooper, of Santa Barbara, has many sacks, large enough for socks for any Goliah! his crop said to be 20,000 pounds.

We cultivate Languedoc, Princess Languedoc, Bidwell, Ventura paper shell, Ventura soft-shell, the hard shell, and King's paper shell. With the exception of Bidwell, and a few Languedoc trees, they have not paid expenses. The Languedoc and paper shell in the valley have grown well, and blossomed full, but set very little fruit. These on the hill-side do not grow as freely, neither do they bear any better. The trees are not irrigated; they are pruned and cultivated. The Ventura paper shell and soft shell are seedlings, larger than the Bidwell. They did so well at Ventura, some were ordered, but do no better than the Languedoc. They may in time. The Jordan almond has not been introduced in this section; it might be an acquisition; it is quoted in Chicago, retail at 35c. per pound while soft-shells are 23c. We have not succeeded in obtaining this variety, nor the Valonia. We noticed an account of a very large seedling almond in the northern part of the State, and perhaps upon further trial it may be worthy of cultivation.

The almond being one of a few trees withstanding our long dry seasons, it can be utilized in the waste places; the fruit can be preserved a long time without the waste attending perishable fruits. While the yield may not be as great as some other fruits, perhaps some day, not very far in the future, when the big "bonanzas" are all taken, California will not despise the small things; hence, it may be worth while to find a variety suitable for each locality. Rather than grub them out, it is better to build them to peach or nectarine, in accordance with the best practice in this State and Southern Europe, only having one season, with a large top for future operations. Some trees in this vicinity, budded to peach two years ago, had good crops the past season, with no signs of limbs blowing off from too rapid growth, as reported elsewhere, which might be avoided by budding part of the tree one season and the remainder the next. The affinity of peach for almond is stronger than for plum or apricot; and budded, as we have stated, will in the end be more satisfactory than budded to other fruits.

Our almonds were not ripe as early as usual. We gathered in October this year. We prefer to gather as soon as the husk opens; they become dark if left longer, and require sulphuring. We husk, dry in the sun a few days, then market or put away for future use. We sold here at 18c. per pound for soft shells.

Years ago we used to watch eagerly for the early frost to open the hickory and chestnut burs, to set the coveted nut free, our warm seasons seem to do it just as well, illustrating the well-known law that heat and cold act much alike upon vegetation.

The statements recently published in the

Pacific Rural Press relative to the increase in yield of the Languedoc, fertilized by the paper shell, may revolutionize almond growing, and prove satisfactory to all concerned, the witnesses from different parts of the State agree.

It may not be in accordance with the science of fertilization; the almond belongs to the same genus as the peach, the flowers of which are both staminate and pistillate. The Languedoc may have a super abundance of pistillate which is met by the over supply of staminate in the paper shell, or a lack of one found in the other, which, when brought near to each other, manifests being the same, produce a better fertilization, just as the late Nicholas Longworth produced a seedling strawberry, setting a few berries, required the presence of his gardener's seedling, the McAvoy, to produce an abundance of fruit superior to any then in the country, and which, after 30 years' trial, has not been surpassed for some to this.

But the Languedoc's special recommendation is its lateness, to escape early frosts, while the paper shell is early, earlier than the Bidwell, and the Bidwell earlier than the Languedoc; in fact, the paper shell has so ripe fruit before the Languedoc blossoms; and, while my experience corroborates the testimony given, we think some other cause must be assigned. My Languedocs in the vicinity of the paper shell have produced four fold more this and last season than all other Languedocs in the garden. Should further proof demonstrate this to be a fact, we shall have to fall back upon the remark of the scientist, the late internal correspondent of the Cincinnati Gazette, the Hon. E. D. Mansfield, when the subject of the main upon vegetation was the leading question of the day. The writer asked him if he thought the moon had any such "influence?" Looking through his glasses, with a twinkle in his eye, he replied: "Science is against it, but my wife is the better farmer of the two. Her folks before her were farmers. She and they always succeed by planting and sowing by the phases of the moon!"

Since writing the above, Mr. Cuffin, from Mr. Hollister's, Santa Barbara, has made us a pleasant visit. This topic was introduced. He stated that the Colonel's crop was larger than Mr. Cooper's; that among the Colonel's Languedocs there were some bitter almond trees, and that the Languedocs in that vicinity bore larger crops than the others, which would almost indicate that the presence of another variety is essential to the Languedoc for producing the best results.

The experience in other localities and through several seasons will be necessary, however, to determine this question.

There can be no doubt there is true economy in a kindly considerate treatment by man of the domestic and other animals. The motto of all who have any property in or care over them should unquestionably be, "Humanity is the best policy."

SEMI TROPIC CALIFORNIA'S
Map
OF PORTIONS OF THE COUNTIES OF
Los Angeles,
SAN BERNARDINO
AND
SAN DIEGO,
CAL.

The Apiary.

Why not cultivate honey flowers?

Twenty-five dollars profit per colony on bees. Who can beat it?

Stimulees here are the latest things out, and we would suggest that he who sends his money for the *new Limit* will be *bitten*, and that's worse than to be "stung."

Bee-keepers, attend your monthly meetings; by united action you can accomplish great good. There is work for you to do, and it is time to be at it. Every bee-keeper should be present at the next meeting, and all succeeding meetings.

CHIPS FROM THE HONEY HOUSE.
BY S. D. BARBEE.

Another year, laden with its joys and sorrows, successes and reverses, expectations realized and hopes deferred, has passed away, and again we stand upon the portals of a new year.

Let us, as bee keepers, pause for a moment, and, looking back over the past, examine the results of our labors for the past year.

Have we been successful? If not, what have been the preventing causes? Can we tell just why we have succeeded in some instances and failed in others?

It is easy for any person to tell when their bees are prosperous, and it is just as easy to tell when something is wrong, but it is not so easy to tell what that something is.

It is no longer a matter of doubt that the natural swarming of bees can be controlled, and yet such increase secured as may be desired by artificial means, and at the same time a crop of honey obtained according to the season.

The early swarms are the most profitable; but never be in too much haste to divide your bees. Your rule should be to never cripple the strength of the colony when the old queen is to remain, as she diminishes her laying of eggs according to the number of bees that are on hand to perform the labors of the hive. I prefer to take brood and bees at different intervals from my hives, as they can spare them, and have young, fertile queens to form my new colonies.

Many valuable colonies of bees are ruined by being transferred from one hive to another in a wrong way, or at a wrong time, or by being divided without regard to the principles which should govern the matter in case it successful.

When examining bees at this season of the year, great care should be taken not to expose the brood to a cold temperature sufficient to chill the brood.

Preserve all good combs. That containing drone comb can be used late in the season, or in the upper boxes. Comb is the honey bee's capital to carry on their business.

Equalize your stocks both in the fall and in the spring.

For the next two or three months the bees will be using much honey in the rearing of brood, and frequently a large brood is started, and they will consume so much of their stores that they will destroy a large portion of their brood to save themselves, when a little food given them in time will save them. Examine your bees sufficiently often to know their condition, and give timely assistance to those that need it.

Raise queens the last of February, and in March, if the weather is favorable. A fertile queen at swarming time is equal to a swarm of bees. But the forwardness of the season must be your guide as to time to begin.

We consider it by far the best plan to swarm your bees artificially. Natural swarming is attended with loss of time in watching, and then more or less loss of swarms.

What is termed luck with bees is only another name for careful and skillful management.

We find many of our hives with three and four sheets of brood well filled, from eggs to the hatching bar, on January 6th, 1881.

The prospect here north of the city indicates an early and prosperous year for business. Be ready. Do your work in time. A day lost with bees is forever lost.

ESSAY
READ BY S. D. BARBEE AT THE BEE KEEPER'S CONVENTION, OCT. 41, 1880.

The rapid progress made in apiculture in the last few years is remarkable. The increase in swarms and the production of honey has been marvelous to say the least of it when we take into consideration the great loss of bees that this country sustained in the years 1877 and 1879; yet apiculture is steadily moving on. The floral treasures of Southern California seem to be adequate to the great demands made upon them, and many have come to the conclusion that there is a science in bee keeping that will pay the apiarist, but he will find that success to a great extent very much depends upon his knowledge of that insect, the honey bee, and the natural laws by which they are governed; and, brother bee keepers of Southern California, I now congratulate you of the promise in the near future of a Bee Journal, devoted to the interests of bee keepers in this climate, as the management of bees must necessarily differ in a warm climate to that in a cold and changeable one. And, brother bee-keepers, sustain your Journal; it will do you good, and, by a mutual co-operation, it will promote the interests of bee keeping in Southern California; and since bee keeping here differs materially from other climates, it is to the interest of all to make your Journal a success; and if interested in its welfare, by reasonable patronage, but little can stand in the way of making it one of the best Bee Journals in the world.

The bee keepers of Southern California should subscribe for it, and at the same time write for it, illustrating all the varied features of apiculture in California.

The whole profit of apiculture consists in keeping the colonies strong. When honey is abundant, a large apiary will fill up rapidly in the same place where a few weak colonies will barely make a living. If the means of making bees prosperous and profitable, protect them from wind and wet, extremes of heat and cold, destroy their enemies, and leave them to enjoy a sufficiency of food, accumulated by their own industry, and if any are in want, a timely assistance should be rendered them, and doubt not you will prosper as a bee-keeper. Our knowledge of bee instinct is such at the present time that no important point is longer a subject of controversy; and in the light thrown around the subject, no branch of rural economy can be more liberally regulated, or conducted with such absolute success. The laws which govern these industrious little insects are peculiar to themselves, differing from those which govern everything else, yet they are simple, and easily learned by any close observer. But as a deviation is made from these laws, loss, sure and certain, must follow. To be successful, then, in the practical art, the science on which it is founded must be thoroughly understood. It is easy for any person to tell when their bees are prosperous, and it is just as easy to tell when something is wrong; but it is not so easy to tell what that something is. It is no longer a matter of doubt that the natural swarming of bees can be controlled, and yet such increase by artificial means, secured as may be desired, and at the same time a crop of honey obtained according to the season. The early swarms are most profitable, but never be in too much haste to divide your bees. Your rule in artificial swarming should be, never cripple the strength of the colony where the queen is to remain, as the diminishes her laying according as the number of bees are depended. I prefer to take brood and bees at different times from my hives as they can spare them, and have young and fertile queens to form my new colonies. Many valuable swarms are ruined by being transferred from one hive to another in a wrong way or at a wrong time, or by being divided without regard to the principles which should govern the matter to make it successful.

Yields for Kansas. The Kansas Agricultural Report gives the following as the answer to many questions as to the varieties that produced a full or fair crop in 1872. The answer is given in the order of the quantity borne: Of apples, fifty of the reports name the Rawle's Janet as the most productive; nineteen, the Willow Twig; Winesap and Ben Davis, eighteen each; sixteen, Maiden's Blush; Rambo and Northern Spy, fourteen each. Peaches were almost an entire failure. Pears (in the order named), Bartlett, Duchesse de Angouleme, Seckel, Flemish Beauty, Flora, Wild Goose and Minor.

Semi-Tropic Fruit.

OLIVE CULTURE.

BY ELLWOOD COOPER, SANTA BARBARA.

THE numerous inquiries received from different persons in every part of the country concerning the olive tree, the growth, care, propagation, period of fruit bearing, oil making and pickling, the financial prospect, etc., induces me to make use of your paper as a means of answering the inquiries. I propose, in a series of articles, to give all the knowledge I possess, based upon my experience as well as information obtained from careful reading of the best books that have been published on the subject of propagation.

The common and preferred method is to plant the cuttings, taken from growing trees of round wood, from three quarters of an inch in diameter to one and a half inches, and from fourteen to sixteen inches long. These cuttings should be taken from the trees during the months of December and January, neatly trimmed without bruising, and carefully trenched in loose, sandy soil; a shady place preferred. They should be planted in permanent sites from February 28th to March 20th, depending upon the season. The ground should be well prepared, and sufficiently dry so that there is no mud and the weather warm. In Santa Barbara, near the coast, no irrigation is necessary; but very frequent stirring of the top soil with a hoe or iron rake for a considerable distance around the cuttings is necessary during the spring and summer. About three-fourths of all that are well planted will grow. My plan is to set them twenty feet apart each way, and place them in the ground butt end down and at an angle of about forty-five degrees, the top to the north, barely covered. Mark the place with a stake. By planting them obliquely, the bottom end will be from ten inches to one foot below the surface. In Europe the trees are planted from 27 to 33 feet apart. My reasons for closer planting will be given in a subsequent article.

All trees, as a rule, should be propagated from seeds. The roots are more symmetrical, the trees not so liable to be blown over, and the growth more healthful; but I have not been successful in germinating them; hence, I recommend the cuttings. If the trees are propagated from seeds, budding or grafting is unnecessary. I have seen the statement that it was necessary that the seeds should pass through the stomach of birds before they could be sprouted; also that by soaking in strong lye the sprouting would be assured. I have not seen the result of either experiment and accept the statements with much or less distrust. I presume cuttings can be obtained from any of the Mission orchards in the southern counties.

PRUNING.

The cutting will throw up numerous shoots or sprouts, all of which should be left to grow the first year; any disturbance of the top affects the growth of the roots.

It would be advisable, however, where there are two or more vigorous shoots of about the same size and height from the same cutting, to pinch the tops of all excepting the one to be left for the future tree, so as to throw more force and vigor into that one. In the following spring, when the ground is warm and sufficiently dry, all sprouts excepting the one to be preserved should be carefully removed, cutting them off close to the cutting. The top end of the cutting should also be removed by the aid of a sharp saw. A post should be firmly planted, so that the tree can be well secured, to keep the trunk straight and avoid any disturbance of the roots, and should be kept until the tree is four or five years old. By adopting this method a great deal of time will be saved and better trees assured. The lateral branches should be allowed to grow until the tree is two or three years old; but in every case when any of said branches are rapidly making wood, they should be removed, and not be allowed to rob the trunk.

In the pruning during the first years, have only the one object in view—that is, to force all the woody growth into one main trunk. This being done, the tree will naturally form a beautiful shape. The cultivator must not look at the tree of to-day to to-morrow, but the tree of ten years hence. All branches to the height of four or five and a half feet should be removed, so as to admit of close cultivation by horses. Trees planted at the distance of twenty feet, and well kept, will in ten years touch each other. When this condition is reached they will be in full bearing, and therefore will require constant pruning or cutting back. It is much easier and less expensive to gather the fruit from small trees; besides, if the pruning is intelligently done, it will improve the fruit and secure a greater quantity to the acre than can be produced under any other conditions.

Some orchards in Europe are planted in "threes," that is, three trees in each place, planted in the form of a triangle, and three or four feet apart. This method would require the rows to be thirty-three to thirty-five feet distant, and would give about the same number of trees to the acre as by planting at twenty feet, one tree in each place. It is claimed that by planting in this way no staking is required, the trees protecting one another from the most violent wind storms, the trimming is simplified, and less care and labor required in the cultivation.

FRUIT BEARING.

Trees growing from cuttings, will produce from the fourth year, and sometimes, under the most favorable circumstances, will give a few berries the third year. It is the habit of the tree to overbear, and as a consequence will give but little fruit the year following a heavy crop. This statement is verified by the most reliable books published on the subject in the French, Italian and Spanish languages. There are, however, exceptions to this rule in California. Mr. Davis, who had charge of the San Diego Mission orchard in 1875, assured me that he had gathered from the same tree, two years in succession, over 150 gallons of berries. I have also observed that some trees in my orchards have borne well successive years. The fruit bearing can be controlled by the pruning. The cultivator will not forget that the shoots or branches must be two years old before they will give fruit; hence, partial pruning every year will give the partial crops. My oldest orchard was planted February 21, 1872. At four years I gathered from some of the trees over two gallons of berries, in 1878 over thirty gallons each of a few of the best trees, the orchard then being only six years old. In 1879, the seventh year, the crop was not nearly so large. I had planted several thousand cuttings in the spring of 1873, but these trees did not give at six years a result equal to the first planting. The present crop (1880) is quite good; the old red orchard now being eight years, and I think I do not over estimate when I state that the yield of some of the best and tallest trees will be over forty gallons. Trees large enough to give this quantity of fruit, planted at a distance of twenty feet, will occupy nearly all the ground, and therefore give all the fruit that can be produced on one acre. An orchard bearing uniformly the quantity as above would give the following result; five hundred trees to the acre, at forty gallons each, 4,000 gallons. This would be an enormous crop, unprecedented, and far beyond any statistics given in European publications. The one-fourth of the quantity yearly would be a very profitable crop.

In estimating an orchard, the yield of isolated trees, or trees of great age, occupying considerable areas of ground, must not enter into the basis of calculation of the probable production. The tree mentioned in the San Diego Mission orchard as yielding 150 gallons of berries was more than fifty feet distant from those surrounding it.

My agent, while travelling in Europe through the olive districts, measured a tree growing in the "Alpes Maritimes" that was eight feet in diameter six feet above the ground, and at the ground fifteen feet in diameter. Only a few trees of such size could be grown on one acre.

(Continued.)

Deep ploughing is eschewed in the orange orchards of Australia, for the following reasons. As the roots of the orange tree rarely penetrate to any depth, but almost invariably run near the surface of the ground, its digging or even deep hoeing must be injurious to it to keep the land free from weeds. This is better done by using a steady old horse and a very short toothed harrow—with its teeth not longer than one to one and one-half inches. This is run frequently over the ground, and the surface is kept finely pulverized and open to the night dews and to the fogs. Thus the crumbled surface gets the benefit of the moisture, and is not injured by the cultivator.

Shrubbery.

SEASONABLE NOTES.

BY W. A. T. STRATTON, PETALUMA, CAL.

CYPRESS HEDGES, though highly ornamental and useful, are very dangerous, and should never be grown too near the house. Nor should large cypress trees be allowed closer than twenty feet, because of their combustible character. Hedges and trees, when closely trimmed to keep them in form, are constantly dropping their dead foliage, which accumulates in great quantities on the small twigs and limbs inside, under the outer foliage, and if by chance a spark of fire lights on it, the whole is in a blaze in an instant, and will burn with a rapidity as though coal oil had been drenched over them. A case occurred recently in our city which came near resulting most disastrously. A gentleman had a hedge of Monterey cypress five foot high, six years old, which he had been kept closely cut. Some children started to have a bonfire fully forty feet from the hedge, and a gust of wind carried a twig, blazing, as was supposed by the parents, over into the road, but in an instant a crackling of fire was heard; the green cypress was burning as though a pile of shavings, the blaze fully twenty feet high, giving out a great heat and creating a panic. Water buckets were brought into use, but no one could get close enough to throw any water on, and it seemed as though, from the great rapidity with which it was spreading, the house must burn, and nothing could stop it. In less than three minutes it had run two hundred feet against the wind, when the neighbors came to the rescue. A section was chopped out close to the house, and water thrown on the end just in time to dampen it sufficiently, and the house was saved. I saw the fire, assisted in extinguishing it, and resolved that in the future to never recommend cypress hedges or trees to be grown too near any building. If the dead foliage is regularly removed the danger will be greatly lessened; still, they are a dangerous ornament.

The flower garden, at this time of the year, needs especial study and attention. The planting of bulbous plants, the transplanting of shrubs, manuring and placing the whole in order for the coming season's work, requires more than mere notice. As a rule, we feed our flowers too little, and then we expect too much. Plants have their natures just the same as your children. Nature's reward is perfection, and we must study plant life to know their wants, just as much as we study the laws of animal life to obtain their true value.

Hyacinths and tulips require a very rich, light soil. I as well enrich manure very freely. Dig it in thoroughly and very deep. Always select a spot that is "high and dry" in winter, where no water will stand. Plant them fully four inches deep, and if you have obtained good bulbs you will never regret any extra labor given them. The great bulb country in Europe is Holland.

From here is grown the millions that are annually sold. The ground, or rather sand, that these hyacinths and tulips are grown in was once a part of the ocean; but these energetic Hollanders managed to cover a good many thousand acres of sand, by means of embankments and ditches. The seepage of salt water collects in these many ditches, is pumped out in some places, and in others is run off in the fall of the tide. The country being so low, is naturally very moist, and though the soil is so very sandy that they are compelled to use mulching to keep the wind from blowing the sand away in drifts, they use great quantities of manure, and grow the finest hyacinths and tulips in the world. The secret of their great success is their light soil, a regular bottom moisture, that keeps the bulbs in full growth till perfectly matured, feed in great abundance to nourish them, and, I suspect, also the near proximity of salt water (oftentimes less than two feet from the surface—it will stand in the holes) supplies an element of fuel indispensable. We can grow as fine a hyacinth in California as in any part of the world. Our long summer and genial spring weather gives us a splendid bulb, hard and very firm, and if we will but take care in their growth to keep them growing just as long as they will grow, by irrigation, we can beat even the Dutch. Try it.

Shrubbery is only useful as a scenic effect, and as such, their character, habits, and what we want to produce by planting them, should be closely studied; not must we only look at the little plant of a year or two's growth. What will they be at maturity is the all important point to consider. Patience is a virtue we must cultivate with all the care of a valuable rare exotic. A small plant in many cases is faster than a large one. Yet most persons are only too eager to get the very largest plants, to make a good showing at once. It is an old saying among gardeners that "the best place for a tree to grow is where it first takes root," and will aptly apply. The larger a shrub or tree is when removed, the greater the loss of roots, and as the source of nutrition is in a great measure lost, a severe check in growth is very often the result. In many cases the balance is made by removing a part of the tops and foliage; this may be thus obtained in planting large specimens. But too often this is left undone, or done so very improperly that the subject struggles away in sickly existence.

This brings us to the subject of pruning, one of the most important topics we can write on. When to prune is not always understood any more than how to do it, and we often are the most wretched butchery by would-be practical hands; and as the tree butcher is now at work, we warmly expect these seasonable notes will be of much value.

Young evergreens should be scarcely pruned till they attain strength. A stray lateral may be pinched off, but no more, unless we want to dwarf them. Pruning deciduous always. If a hedge or tree is to

be made a dwarf, prune young and often, but if we want size and strength, wait till greater maturity. Again, pruning in the sap, or during active growth, debilitates, and so reduces the health and longevity of all trees and shrubs by pruning at a time in the year when most at rest.

Roses should be pruned now very carefully. The strong growing sorts may be cut away one half, while the delicate sorts, as the tea, noisette and china roses, should be only thinned out. Yet this rule must not be slavishly followed. Some may be cut very sparsely, while others of the same group would die under such treatment. Last season as had some large standard plants of the well known sort Marie Van Houtt, and as we needed several thousand cuttings to plant of this variety, the parts were all cut very severely. They all died but one, and that one was all summer recuperating. Again, we also had a Sulphur, a very beautiful light salmon, fully as strong a grower as the Marie Van Houtt. It was not equally so much, as only the stumps were left, but it came out just as well as though it had been pruned only sparingly. Caution is therefore a important factor. Each sort must be well understood, as we must pay dear for learning even in doing that nearly all spring laborers are only in the soil and they must be pruned only immediately after it is over going. I shall refer to this interesting topic again. The subject is inexhaustible, and I shall often try to have a term or chat with the readers of the Semi-Tropic, not assuming to know all about it, but simply telling what I know.

THE English Government, from press of business, will soon modify the restrictions upon the importation of American cattle. It has already decided to remove the restrictions upon the importation of sheep.

ARIZONA and New Mexico are the natural home of the cactus, of which there are said to be over 160 varieties. The giant cactus sometimes grows to the height of fifty feet and measures six feet in diameter. Some have no limbs, others have from one to three arms. They seem to stand on the top of the sand, with scarcely any root, and must receive their nutriment largely from the atmosphere. They are capped with a beautiful flower, and later with fruit. The Indians remove the fruit with a long spiked pole, and use it in large quantities.

THE Moquis and Pueblos of Arizona live in houses fashioned after the manner of the Zunis, cultivate the ground, raise flocks and herds, and are self-supporting. Their villages are built on a high plateau, about 60 miles north of the little Colorado river, which runs in the midst of a sandy and apparently sterile plain. Good crops of corn, pumpkins, squash, and other vegetables, and fine peaches are raised around the base of this plateau, on which expensive shrubs fall every year.

SUB-IRRIGATION.

WE invite careful investigation of our system of Sub-irrigation, which is being largely adopted on the Pacific Coast, and can be used to great advantage in any region subject to drouth, for watering orchards, small fruits, vegetables, lawns, etc., and consists in conducting the water in concrete pipes laid below the reach of the plow. At proper distances "plugs" or outlets are set into the upper side of the pipes, through which and nowhere else, the water escapes, and is taken into the soil by capillary attraction.

It saves from three-fourths to nineteen-twentieths of the water used in surface irrigation.

It is under perfect control, and can be applied in any soil—working perfectly on hill sides and undulating land.

The labor of irrigating consists simply in turning a cock to let the water in and to shut it out of the pipes.

Anything which the soil lacks as plant food, (manure, lime, etc.) can be easily,

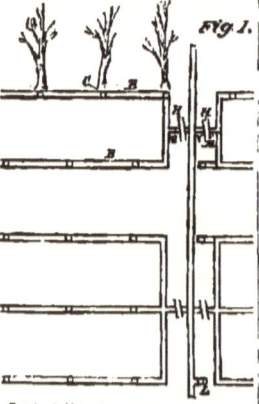

Fig. 1.

Fig. 1. A Main pipe, supplying water from a cistern B—distributing pipes, laid slightly below the surface of the ground, and along a hill from each row of trees, or, these pipes may be laid midway between the rows. **·** P at the pond, a piece of pipe, as shown in Figs. 3 and 4. *H* H stands for outlet, shown in Figs 1. **·** spur from main. **N** V terminus between A and B through B, as in Fig 1.

directly and economically applied as liquid form.

Roots cannot get into the pipes, neither can they suck mud—difficulties never overcome by any other system of sub-irrigation.

The cut on following page illustrates our continuous pipe machine for making and laying in the trench—at one operation concrete pipe for sub-irrigation or drainage.

For drains it makes a superior tile, properly laid for use, for less money than the cost of clay tile at the factory.

Being made continuous, the bottom of the pipe is smooth and solid, so that no sediment can lodge in it, and being composed of cement and sand, is not affected by frost.

To enable the water to enter the pipe, it is perforated on top, or is cut one-half of every ten or twelve inches as it is being made.

The machines are so simple and inexpensive that every farmer can make and lay his own tile with only common farm labor.

Three men can easily make and lay in the trench 1200 feet of two-inch pipe in ten hours.

Pipe from one to five inches caliber is made and laid continuously—larger sizes are made in sections, as shown in cut No. 6. The concrete being fed into the hopper and packed with the tamp (No. 7) between the core and jacket. When filled, the core is

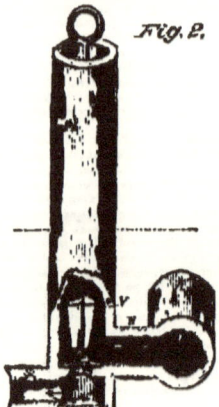

Fig. 2.

Fig. 2. Shows position of hydrant, as set. The plug-valve V being closed, water rises in H in level of water in B correctly upon raising V, water taken direction of arrows, passing into h.

Fig. 3.

Fig. 3. Shows position of Distributing Pipe M. Earth tamped C. the h outlet, set loosely on B, regulating 2 inches above surface of ground, to prevent earth from falling in: plug P and plug H Water passes along B, flows up through the hole at P in P, and falls down on B, out side of P, hence off P, and is taken into the soil by capillary attraction.

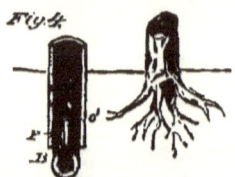

Fig. 4.

Fig. 4. Shows relative position of H, C, P, and the tree—the dotted line representing surface of the ground. The plug P is a tapering piece of wood, tapered to suit, set in the plug h, having through it a tapering hole for passage of water. The reason for making it so is, that anything which can get into the water too readily passes through, and will act by accumulation, close it.

taken out and the jacket off, leaving the pipe as shown in No. 10, and laid after drying about a week, at greatly reduced cost over any other pipe.

For conducting water from springs, a continuous, cement concrete pipe is superior

to any other; because it is cheap, indestructible, as pure and tasteless as granite, reduces friction and the liability to become clogged to a minimum.

ANONSTINE SUB-IRRIGATION CO.,
Los Angeles, Cal.

THE AMERICAN NEWSPAPER ANNUAL, by Messrs. N. W. Ayer & Son, Philadelphia, is as invaluable as our encyclopædia, as our great Webster, and is one of the requisites of every well regulated publishing office, and still more valuable to every large advertiser who advertises judiciously.

The work, in addition to being a complete encyclopædia of the newspaper world, is an ornament in any library. Its elegant paper, typography, press work, and binding make it very attractive as well as useful.

"OUR LITTLE ONES" is the title of a new publication, issued by the Russel Publishing Co., 149 A Tremont St., Boston, Mass., at $1.50 per year. Oliver Optic (Wm. T. Adams) is the editor, a gentleman recognized as the foremost writer of children's literature in the country. It is handsomely illustrated, and brimming full of matter calculated to please those of the tender age of childhood. No family with children can afford to be without a good magazine or paper, and we commend them OUR LITTLE ONES.

A CONTINUOUS CONCRETE PIPE MACHINE!

No joints! No leaks! A greatly reduced cost over any other method. Just the thing for Drain-Tiling. Duly protected by U. S. Patents.

THE AMERICAN COLONY,

LOS ANGELES COUNTY, SOUTHERN CALIFORNIA.

THIS NEW COLONY is now farming and will occupy 10,000 acres of fine farming, fruit and vineyard land, which will be subdivided into five, ten and twenty acre lots, and forty, eighty and one hundred and sixty acre farms. This tract will be sold to colonists at low prices and on easy terms. The prices and terms are given in the Colony Prospectus.

Water is abundant on most of the land for all purposes, and all rights to water are sold with the land. The colony tract lies within the best artesian belt in the valley, and flowing wells are easily obtained. There are upwards of a dozen flowing wells on different parts of the ranch at the present time.

There is wood enough on the colony tract along the river for fuel.

The title to the land is perfect, being United States patent.

In fertility of soil, beauty of location, and advantages of access by rail and water, with good markets for all produce raised, and for salubrity of climate, the tract of land which is to be occupied by the American Colony cannot be surpassed.

Every part of it can be cultivated, and is available for farms, orchards and vineyards, possessing everything required to create here beautiful and profitable homesteads.

The Colony lands will grow to great perfection every product of the northern and semi-tropical climes: such as wheat, barley, oats, corn, tobacco, flax, castor beans, sugar cane and sugar beets, apples, peaches, plums, prunes, pears, apricots, nectarines, quinces, cherries, almonds, olives, oranges, lemons, limes, figs, pomegranates, walnuts, chestnuts, grapes, etc.

Vegetables of all kinds grow luxuriantly and many the year round.

Alfalfa fields are always green. Eight to ten tons of alfalfa are often cut per acre during the season in this valley.

Some of the best corn land in the State is in this colony tract. Corn grown this year on the land yielded 75 to 100 bushels per acre. Wheat does well, and has been grown now three years in succession on the colony tract, producing large crops. The yield this year was from 30 to 35 bushels per acre.

A farm in the American Colony can easily be made to pay for itself before the last payment of the purchase price is due if the place is properly cultivated and managed.

Never, do we believe, was there a better opportunity for parties desiring to secure a good homestead in this delightful valley than is now offered in this colony at reasonable prices. This is one of the chief objects we have in establishing the American Colony—to secure for ourselves and others, at a reasonable expense, homes in a genial and healthful climate, where the choicest fruits of a warm and generous soil can be produced in abundance, and where life can be enjoyed free from the extremes of cold and heat of most other sections of our land. And where, also, we can secure for ourselves in a short time, good schools, churches, and a library, and where good society and the various social organizations will become established; in fact, where all the advantages of a compact and well regulated settlement can be had. We propose no innovation upon the established order of society, but while we hope for healthful

growth and progress in the direction of all that is wise and good, we leave each to enjoy here, as elsewhere, his individual property, as well as his political and religious views.

W. E. WILLMORE, Manager,
Los Angeles, Cal.

THE ladies who have charge of the Orphans' Home, in this city, have made arrangements for a grand carnival, to be given in this city February 24th to 26th. The object is a worthy one, and should receive the hearty co-operation of all our citizens. The entertainment will be very fine, and well worth the admission.

AT an annual meeting of the Sixth District Agricultural Society, held January 4th, the following officers were elected for the ensuing year: President, J. M. ; Sixth, Treasurer, K. F. Speer; Secretary, W. J. Neely; Executive Committee, J. R. Holbrook, F. B. Parrott and J. M. Griffith. The office of General Superintendent was left vacant.

THIS country has a population only one-sixth that of Europe, yet we raise three times as many cows, a third as many cattle, and a fifth as many sheep as are raised all the countries of Europe put together.

A work pretentious against her doings keep away from the bees.

HOW TO TRAIN COLLIES.

[From the Forest and Stream.]

IN reading the various sporting journals of the day, I frequently see articles upon the subject of educating and training setters, pointers, and sporting dogs generally, but none I remember ever seeing anything upon the education and training of my favorite dog, their non-sporting brother, the Scotch collie, who, in his sphere, is as useful and valuable as any member of the canine race. And now, since the success of the collie trials held under the auspices of the Pennsylvania State Agricultural Society, at Philadelphia, in the latter part of September, and as it is more than likely that they will be repeated another year, and that other agricultural societies will follow suit and inaugurate them as one of the attractions of their shows, I think it will not be amiss to give you my ideas in regard to their education and training.

I have owned collies all my life—good, useful, and well trained dogs—and in my walks and drives they are my constant companions. Master Collie is a mischievous and fun loving rascal, and even when well trained this love of mischief will show itself. There is now curled up at my feet one of the handsomest collies in America. She has been shown at several bench shows and has always been placed, and besides is a first-rate worker on stock. She is always under my buggy when I am driving, "except" sometimes I allow two others to follow for a frolic and exercise. Now, here the "except" comes in. If by chance this crow sip a cur on the road the mother collie will be off like a shot; out she goes from under the buggy, passing between the front wheels and horse, throws her head back and gives a sharp, quick bark in two, as much as to say, "Come on Punch and Judy; here's fun for us," and away they all go like a thunderbolt, until the cur is overhauled and tumbled about in the dust. Well, its all over in a jiffy, and they come trotting back, I suppose laughing to themselves. I point my finger at her and say, "Aren't you ashamed of yourself!" Her head goes down, tail between her legs, she smacks her chops, whines, "Yes, but it was so much fun I could not resist the temptation; I'll not do it again—until next time," and next time the same thing is repeated.

For the first six months or so the puppy is allowed to do pretty much as he pleases, as long as he keeps his head out of the cabbage pot, doesn't suck eggs, or worry the pets, for Master Collie is a lively body and is nearly always in some kind of devilry; but even at an earlier age than this the collie may sometimes be seen gathering the chickens in a corner of the lot and maneuvering them as his his does the sheep.

As a general rule we commence their education about the tenth month of the puppy's age; but we sometimes see them younger than this working stock like old stagers. I have one in my eye now that at five months old would go to the pasture field, containing about sixty acres, drive out the cows and bring them home, a distance of over one mile. At six months old she was working sheep and obeying every sign and motion of her master.

The first thing I do is to make the dog love me. I treat him kindly, never kick nor strike him, and never deceive him. I pet him and talk to him until he knows every word I say. There is a great deal, I assure you, in this "love me." When he loves me and understands me I take him into a room and there teach him to follow close to heel, to stop at a whistle, to lie down when told, to go forward by motion of hand, and to either right or left. I always stop my dogs with a whistle, to attract their attention before giving an order by mouth or hand.

When I consider my youngster house-broken, that is, when he obeys my motions and whistle, I take him with sheep—confined in a lane—and allow him to drive them with me, and by motions I keep him moving from one side of the lane to the other—when we are at the end of the lane I say, "Around them," motioning the way up the side, and go with him and show him. When round them I stop him with a whistle, make him lie down, and have him; I then go in front of the sheep and tell him, "Bring them along." If he comes too close to the sheep, I stop him with a whistle, and say, "Keep wider," or "Slower." These lessons I repeat until I consider him nearly perfect in driving up and down the lane. I then commence to teach him to go from where I stand at one end of the lane to the other and bring the sheep to me; this I do by motioning the way and saying, "Far away;" and if he does not go I go with him and show him what to do. When behind the sheep I make him lie down, and I go to the spot where I first gave the order, and from there whistle him to bring them along. When he does this work to my satisfaction I then allow him to the fields to drive the sheep from pasture, and here I repeat all my former lessons to him; I teach him to jump back and forth over a fence, and to bark when told, but never to bite; and when he attempts to use his teeth I punish him. Now as in punishment, as I said at first, I never kick nor strike—I catch the collie around his nose and give him a shake or a light tap on the ear with my hand, a cross word will cower him at once.

There is one thing I never like to do, that is to commence working my puppy on cattle. As a general rule it will not do, as the dog becomes too severe, and it gives trouble to afterward break him of the habit. I commence first on sheep, and when he will work them carefully, I can then allow him to drive other stock.

Now, one other point and I am through. The old adage, "Too many cooks spoil the broth," applies to Master Collie. If you wish your dog thoroughly trained, only one must work him, and that one I insist must be patient, and teach him quietly and gently. If you wish him spoiled and made worthless allow the whole family to work him and you will succeed in this admirably.

COLLIE.

ALFALFA FOR PROFIT.—California farmers might well pay more attention to alfalfa culture. In the fertile mountain valleys, and where water can be procured its productiveness is very great. Sow twenty pounds of good clean seed to the acre. Prepare the ground well before sowing and destroy weeds. If alfalfa stands clean and thick on the ground it makes better fodder. In Los Angeles county seven to nine cuttings are made in one season, or from fifteen to twenty tons per acre, after it is well established. On sheep such land it should last without renewal for ten or twenty years. When hay is cut it should be raked in windrows and bunched the next day, curing it quickly and putting salt through the layers as it is stored in the barn. Alfalfa is the best of food for cattle, but work horses should have some grain and hay in connection with it. There is always one for surplus of well-cured alfalfa though generally it would pay a farmer better to purchase a number of calves and feed it out himself, thus making a double profit.—*Bulletin.*

The Portland, Mr., Beet Sugar Works last year worked 9,000 tons of beets into 900 tons of sugar and molasses, which were sold at $110,000, and a moderate profit was realized. This year they will commence October 10th, and expect to turn out 30,000 pounds of sugar daily. Last year the farmers averaged about $100 per acre for their beets. They hope to do better this year.

Good earth is what all plants need, and when this can be obtained no special manures is needed. The best soil for plants is made from good garden loam, sand and leaf-mould from the woods; one-third of each, well mixed and sifted. A lot of soda piled up, to rot, makes excellent mould to mix with the sand and loam, but I prefer good black leaf mould.

A little bone dust mixed on the surface of the earth will start a quick growth, but it is not often needed. The soil should be loosened up whenever it becomes baked or hard.

SIMPLE AND EFFECTUAL RECIPE FOR MAKING TEA CAKES WITH HONEY.—Take five pounds of flour and three pounds of extracted honey, two eggs, half teacupful (medium size) of butter, half teacupful of sweet cream, and a tablespoonful of baking soda. To the eggs—after being well beaten in a pan—add the honey, and stir well; then the butter, and then add the soda, dissolved in the cream, and stir briskly until it begins to foam; then add the flour, stirring all the time, and flavor to taste. When through, it is, or should be, a thin dough, which roll and cut to honey, and bake as you do soda biscuit. They should be baked one or two days before wanted for use. The older they are the better.

Respectfully submitted to the SEMI-TROPIC by   Mrs. J. W. WILSON,
                      Pasadena, Cal.

SEMI-TROPIC CALIFORNIA, subscription $1.50 per annum.

CITRUS FAIR

—OF—

SOUTHERN CALIFORNIA,

TO BE HELD AT THE

HORTICULTURAL PAVILION,

MARCH 14-19, 1881.

RULES AND REGULATIONS.

The Rules and Regulations of the Horticultural Fair of 1880 will govern the actions of the Annual Citrus Fair.

The Pavilion will be opened for the reception and arrangement of articles for exhibition, Friday, March 11. The exposition will be opened to the public Monday, at 6 o'clock P. M., and continue open for five days, from 8 o'clock A. M. to 10 o'clock P. M. each day.

No entry will be received after 2 o'clock P. M. of Tuesday, March 15, unless unavoidably detained.

☞ No Entry fee charged.

One-half the proceeds of the Fair will go towards paying the expenses of the "Traveling Citrus Fair" that is to be made up from this exposition and sent East.

ADMISSION:

Single admission—day,	$0 25
Single admission—night,	50
Single season ticket,	1 50

Children (under 12), half-price.

If the evenings should be cool, arrangements will be complete for heating the Pavilion, and making it comfortable.

The Ladies' Benevolent Society will have charge of the dining-rooms, which is a guarantee of success in that department.

Applications for space should be made on or before March 1.

DEPARTMENT B.

To the individual, locality, or society making the largest and finest exhibit, ... $100 00

Any county or a county is barred, but each locality in the county can compete.

At least three entries for competition to be made.

DEPARTMENT I.

Class 2—Oranges—Budded.

A plate of five constitutes an entry. The same fruit cannot compete for more than one premium.

Best one variety	$5 00
Best two varieties	7 00
Best four varieties	10 00
Best six varieties	15 00

Class 3—Oranges—Seedlings.

Best one variety	$5 00
Best two varieties	7 00
Best four varieties	10 00
Best six varieties	15 00

Class 4—Oranges—Sweepstakes.

Best variety	$5 00
Best cluster of oranges	10 00

Class 5—Lemons.

Best one variety	$5 00
Best two varieties	7 00
Best four varieties	10 00

Class 6—Limes.

One hundred to constitute an entry.

Size, quality, color, and marketable qualities to decide.

Best exhibit	$10 00

Class 7—Citrons.

Not less than five constitute an entry.

Best exhibit	$3 00
Best preserved citron (home made)	5 00
Best preserved citron (Factory)	S. Medal

DEPARTMENT J.

Class 1—Raisins.

Best and largest display	$25 00
Best box	10 00
Best export box	5 00
Best and most attractive package for market	Diploma

Class 2—Canned Fruits.

Best peaches (home made)	$3 00
Best peaches (factory)	Diploma
Best apricots (home made)	3 00
Best apricots (factory)	Diploma

Class 3—Miscellaneous.

Best Dried Figs	$5 00
Best pomegranates (ten)	3 00
Best strawberries (six boxes)	4 00
Best tomatoes (one peck)	3 00
Best new potatoes (one peck)	3 00

Class 4—Flowers

Best and finest display	$10 00

Exhibitors must state in every case on what stock fruit was grown; and it is desirable that it should also be stated whether irrigated, character of soil, age of tree and any other conditions affecting quality or size of fruit.

For further particulars address the Secretary,

GEO. RICE,
Los Angeles, Cal.

HOW TO MAKE MONEY.

ECONOMY is of itself a great revenue—Cicero. Getting and is more in the saving than in the making. There is no sacrifice which men will not make for money. They will risk life, health, everything—even their souls' peace in this world and the next—for gold. There is no secret about how to make money; it is contained in the world's wisdom as condensed in a few proverbs: "To work hard; to improve small opportunities; to economize; to avoid debt," are the general rules in which is summed up the hoarded experience of centuries.

Economy in buying the necessaries and luxuries of life—the latter are necessary to a limited extent for more perfect happiness. It may be that a suit of clothing is wanted; it should be of good material, well made, and reasonable in price. New York city is the headquarters for the manufacture of clothing. Devlin & Co., New York city, are known as makers of first-class goods, which are always sold at the lowest prices. Every suit is made to order; such always wear better, to say nothing of the fine appearance. We are glad to inform our readers that they can economize by buying their clothing made to order, by calling on B. F. Coulter, the great dry goods merchant, 31 and 32 Baker Block, who is agent for Devlin & Co. Leave your order, and only one price asked, and that the same to everybody—and economize in your clothing bill. Put the money thus saved in bank, unless you have a pair of shoes to buy. If you have, we commend you to the QUEEN SHOE STORE, on Main street, opposite the Court House, Joseph Mesmer, proprietor; or to A. S. McDaniel, on Spring street. Both these gentlemen carry large stocks, and sell number one goods at the lowest cash prices. You must have something to eat, and if a man of family (as most of our readers are), you must have groceries. We give a list (arranged in alphabetical order) of the firms we most heartily endorse, and guarantee you will find each of them square, honest firms, and it will be money in your pocket if you buy your groceries of them. Remember the names and places:

AMERICAN CASH STORE, 48 Spring St.

GRANGER STORE — SEYMOUR & Co.—Main St.

LEN A THOMPSON & Co., 36 Spring St.

Possibly it's drugs or toilet articles you want, or a prescription. The latter is seldom wanted by the readers of the SEMI-TROPIC—they always enjoy good health; it's only the sickly kind that don't read. Anyway, go to either

CENTRAL PHARMACY—Preuss & Bruni—81 Spring street;

HEINZEMAN & ELLIS, 72 Main street.

For dry goods and notions, go to B. F. Coulter, 30 and 32 Main street; Dillon & Kenealy, Main street.

For furniture, carpets, wall paper, curtains, etc., go to

Dotter & Bradley, 80, 82 and 84 Main street.

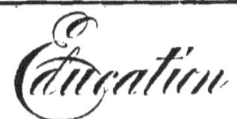

Markets.

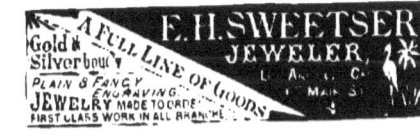

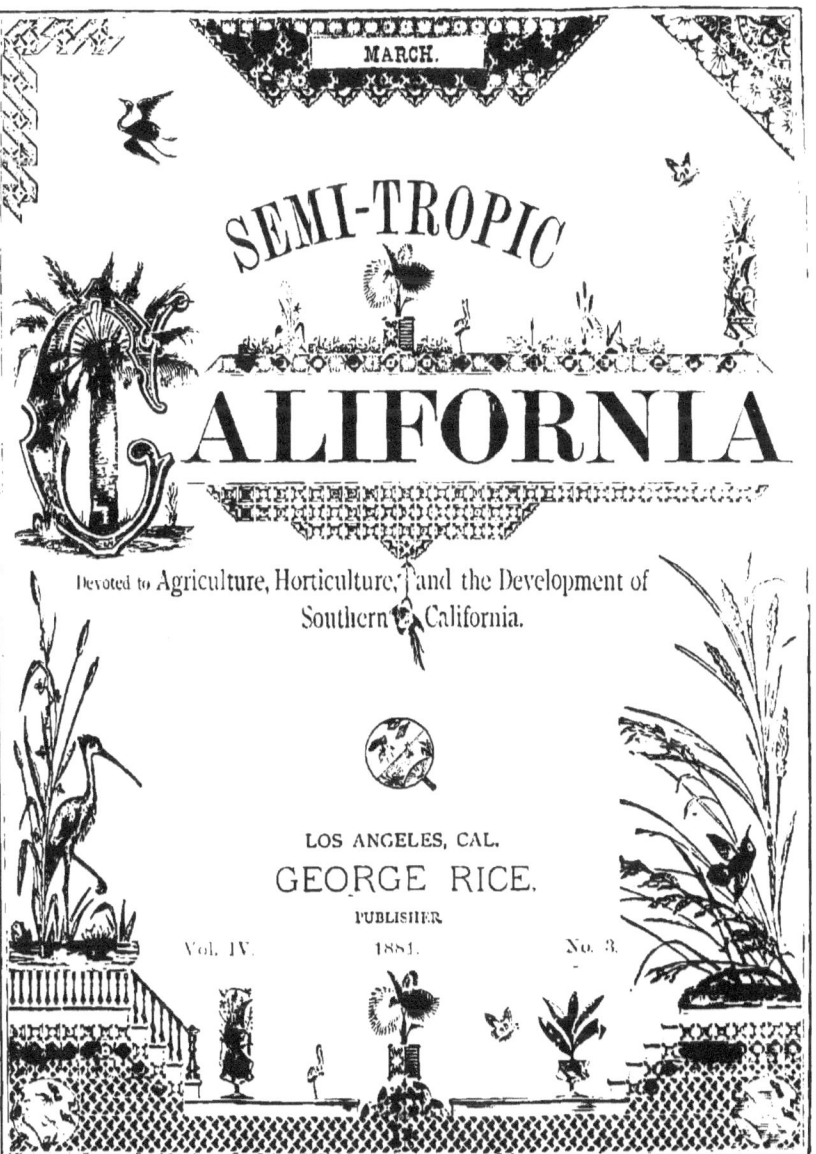

MARCH.

SEMI-TROPIC
CALIFORNIA

Devoted to Agriculture, Horticulture, and the Development of
Southern California.

LOS ANGELES, CAL.

GEORGE RICE,

PUBLISHER

Vol. IV. 1881. No. 3.

—◄ AND ►—

SOUTHERN CALIFORNIA HORTICULTURIST.

Vol. IV.　　　　LOS ANGELES, CAL., MARCH, 1881.　　　　No. 3

NORTH AND SOUTH.

"THE calender of life would be incomplete without the record of a few melancholy days," is what the *Ladies Floral Cabinet*, New York, says in connection with the accompanying beautiful engraving, North and South, and to whom we are indebted for its use.

That *Cabinet* goes on to say: "It is a pathetic sight to see the lovely gardens we have tended with so much care shorn of their splendor, the latest blossoms nipped by frost, and ruin and devastation walking with heavy footsteps over our consecrated places.

"When the Frost-King thus asserts his right to reign, and furnishes the shroud to cover the dead that lie along the line of battle, "discretion is the better part of valor." He who undertakes to fight against such odds will find himself frost-bitten in the encounter, and with a natural instinct the birds hasten to a warmer climate, where flowers bloom and streamlets flow, beyond the reach of ice and snow. Some fly singly, and some in groups, while others migrate in thousands. Even feeble, illwinged birds follow the all-powerful impulse, and traverse vast seas and continents as best they can."

* * * *

"From north to south the tide of emigration flows, thus garlanding the year with flowers and song, bringing about the changeful seasons which clothe the earth with panoramic beauty, and leaving us an outlook into the regions of hope, even when we sit in the shadow of the sepulchre."

A friend who has just arrived in Semi-Tropic California from the cold, bleak East, said, in extatic joy: "Oh! why did I not know of this beautiful land long years

FROM NORTH TO SOUTH.

ago? Why did not some one impress on my mind the reality I now feel and see—a country where

"December is as pleasant as May."

A chorus of voices joined in, and our only regret is that we did not come here sooner.

How fitly our picture represents the cold north, the flight of the birds to a more congenial clime, the land where all is sunshine, where the roses bloom and fill the air with fragrance; where the lucious orange hangs in golden clusters, where the sun shines brightly; where the ocean breeze tempers the atmosphere; where to live is to enjoy life in its fullness.

The real beauties of our south land over all others is the orange, the fruits, without the malaria, the musquito, the extremes of heat and cold. Why not, then, leave the north for the south?

See how the birds leave the cold, bleak land, and migrate in numberless flocks to the land of sunshine. See how truly our picture represents the North and South. The beautiful snow on the one hand, the fragrant flowers on the other; dreary, cold, and cheerless in the north; cheerful, pleasant, joyous in the south. Who would exchange his sunny home in Semi-Tropic California for the old one back in the snow-clad East? Our Citrus Fair, as has been truly said, "will be worth a trip across the continent to see," and it is to be hoped that every citizen who loves this genial land of ours will do his or her duty towards making the coming exposition a true representation of the possibilities of Southern California.

HORTICULTURAL PAVILION will be opened for the reception and arrangements of exhibits Friday, March 10. Editorial reception Tuesday, (12 m) March 14. Formal opening Tuesday evening. Wednesday, grand celebration of opening of the Southern route to the east, and reception of eastern excursionists. Thursday, celebration day. Friday, school day. Saturday, grand gala day and awarding of prizes.

SEMI-TROPIC
CALIFORNIA,
— AN —
ILLUSTRATED MONTHLY.

Devoted to Agriculture, Horticulture, and the Development of Southern California.

Terms: $1.50 per Annum, in Advance.

OFFICE, ROOMS 9 & 10, BAKER BLOCK.

Address,   NEIL RICE, Los Angeles, Cal.

GEORGE RICE, - EDITOR AND PROP'R.

OFFICIAL PAPER
— OF THE —
Southern California Horticultural Soc'y.
OFFICE, ROOM No. 6, BAKER BLOCK.

J. DE BARTH SHORB......... President.
H. K. W. BENT........Vice President.
E. F. SPENCE .... Treasurer.
GEO. RICE...... ....Secretary.
    Directors.
J. F. CRANK,   A. B. CLARK,
J. H. SHIELDS,   H. K. W. BENT,
C. E. THOM,   J. DE BARTH SHORB,
     T. C. SEVERANCE.

Correspondents of the Semi-Tropic.
Geo. C. Swan .... San Diego.
Mrs. N. C. Wilson .... Santa Barbara.
A. R. Clark .... Ventura.
Gen. J. H. Shields .... Florence.
W. F. A. Serution .... Petaluma.
Gov. J. G. Downey .... Los Angeles.
W. R. Olden .... Anaheim.
George Rich .... Sacramento.
Dr. O. H. Conger .... Pasadena.
Andru' Wade .... Pomona.
Ellwood Cooper .... Santa Barbara.
Mrs. Flora Kimball .... San Diego.

GRAPE-GROWING and wine making are to be, if not already, the great industries of Southern California. The grape is a native of our soil, and flourishes in luxuriant growth and luscious fruit. Our vineyards produce, ordinarily, twice as much as the vineyards of any other grape districts in the world. Why, we will not discuss here, but such are the facts.

Our grape crop never fails as it often does in other countries. We have no vine pests or diseases common to other parts of the world, or such as are infesting the vineyards in Northern California.

Growing the vine is easy and pleasant work here compared with the work in the East or Europe, where they are required to train, stake, and tie up their vines every year, at great cost and labor; here the stalk stands alone.

The equability and warmth of the climate, doing away with artificial heat, renders it easy to make wine by fermentation.

All the varieties that are grown in any country can be grown with profit in this.

Our lands are cheap, ranging from ten to one hundred dollars per acre, on which the grape crop will pay for the lands at the end of four years from planting.

Los Angeles county has 5,713 acres in vineyards, owned by about three hundred owners, taking Mr. L. J. Rose's estimate of the wine product of this county, and Mr. Arpad Haraszthy's estimated prices, as we find them in the Viticultural Commission's Report, we find the value of the grape crop to be as follows:

2,080,000 gallons dry wines, at 35c $500,000
500,000 gallons sweet wines, or 60c 300,000
800,000 gals. brandy (in bond), at $1.75 .. 345,000
For raisins and table 15,000
     Total $1,180,000

Of course, this is for the grapes made into marketable wine; but it shows in actual figures what can be done in this county in grape-growing and wine-making.

Mr. Rose states in his report that the grape growers of this county have netted $60 per acre for the crop of grapes sold to the wine makers. We ask if any more lucrative or pleasant pursuit can be followed than the growing of the grape in Southern California?

We estimate the acreage of bramble grapes in this State at 30,000 acres; the wine yield at 10,000,000 gallons; the brandy yield at 800,000 gallons; the raisin grapes and table grapes at $250,000, giving, in cash value, about $3,000,000 to the producers of grapes for 1880.

This is only a beginning of this great industry. This county will, in the next ten years, produce as much as is now produced in the entire State.

Our wines have been received in the wine markets of the world, tested and endorsed as first-class. Our pure grape brandies stand at the head of the list. From a financial point of view, it appears that viticulture in this State, and especially Southern California, is more profitable than any of the usual forms of agriculture.

THE ILLUSTRATED PACIFIC COAST POULTRY BOOK, William Niles, Los Angeles, Cal, publisher, price 50 cents, is a new and practical treatise on the care and management of domestic fowls, adapted especially to the needs of the Pacific Coast, and should be in the hands of every person raising chickens.

CALIFORNIA Roses or flowers of any description excel any others in the United States. Why, then, send East for anything when a superior article, acclimatized and at as low a price, can be had nearer home? W. A. T. Stratton's, Petaluma, (Cal.) catalogue can be had free, and in it a complete list of the choicest of everything for the lawn or garden.

THE STATE VITICULTURAL COMMISSION, with an appropriation of only $4,000, contrary to the usual custom of all commissions which were intrusted with the spending of the public money, report a most satisfactory year's work and a considerable balance still in the treasury. The value of the services rendered to the State by this Commission cannot be estimated in dollars and cents, and the gentlemen who have served as Commissioners can scarce deserve the gratitude of the grape-growers and the public in general on the Pacific Coast. The estimate submitted for the maintenance and furthering the work of the Commission for this year is $10,000, and is very small considering the amount of work and the great good it will accomplish. The bill introduced by our Representative, Mr. Crank, to establish quarantine against infected vines, cuttings, etc., will accomplish what we have long advocated, and is a guarantee to Southern California that we will never be visited by that dread vine pest, the phylloxera. The first annual report of the Commission is the most valuable public document we have had the pleasure of reading, and we only regret the limited number for distribution; the report would be an invaluable help in the hands of every grape-grower.

THE San Francisco *Merchant*, in speaking of the members of the viticultural commission, says: Mr. L. J. Rose lives on his magnificent property near San Gabriel, in Los Angeles county. He owns the largest vineyard in the United States, being some 550 acres in extent. Mr. Rose has done much for various branches of agriculture, and for years has been alike known for his fine race of horses, for his splendid oranges, possessing one of the largest orchards in the State, and for his good wines and brandies. He is eminently a practical man, public spirited, quiet, unobtrusive, very strong in purpose, with excellent administrative abilities, and has a thorough knowledge of the business of raising grapes and the manufacture of wine; a knowledge practically acquired by over twenty years' experimenting. He can use the pen, too, when required, as shown by some three excellent letters recently published on viticultural matters in his section of the country, and which have been since several times reprinted. Mr. Rose is now partner in the wine house of Stern & Rose, whose principal business is in the East.

THE attention of our readers is directed to the advertisement of Bath & Phelps in another column. These gentlemen are acting as agents for the sale of a harrow which we are convinced has no superior. A sample may be seen at the Pavilion during the Citrus Fair.

THIS number of our paper has been delayed, waiting for illustrations that have been snow-bound between New York and here, and even now we have to go to press without the portrait of Mr. L. J. Rose.

Sunny Slope.

[TRADE MARK]

This BEAUTIFUL PICTURE, from a photograph, represents a cluster of roses gathered and arranged by Mr. Rose at his home, and adopted by him as a Trade Mark. It is a fitting emblem of the name Rose, and of the purity of the Sunny Slope wines.

SUNNY SLOPE,

THE HOME OF L. J. ROSE.

SUNNY SLOPE was our destination as we left the city of the Queen of the Angels for a short drive of twelve miles. The day was one of the many beautiful days of February, the sun shining brightly from a cloudless sky, roads always good, and our horse sniffing the invigorating atmosphere, tempered by the cool sea breeze.

Our course was eastward, and led us nearly half the way through the orange groves and vineyards of San Gabriel valley. In the midst of groves and vines sits Sunny Slope, beautiful in this realm of beauty.

A wide avenue, shaded on each side by large orange trees—the "orange avenue," —half a mile in length, leads from the main road to the front door of the comfortable but unpretentious residence of L. J. Rose, proprietor of Sunny Slope.

Upon being informed of the nature and design of our visit, this gentleman gracefully submitted himself to the infliction of what was designed on our part to be an exhaustive interview. His answers to our inquiries were illustrated by the objects of our investigation, and many times did we think, while driving over the estate, with Sheba's queen, "the half was never told."

The nucleus of the now magnificent "Sunny Slope" was founded early in the year 1861 by the purchase of the Courtney tract of 80 acres. In order to secure the water source, Mr. Rose was soon compelled to purchase 2,000 acres of the Rancho Santa Anita, much against his inclinations; but a less amount could not be bought. One hundred and sixty acres at that time constituted in his mind a sufficiently large farm for all purposes of fruit and stock.

But farming forced into so extensive a field, his energies and resources were taxed to their utmost capacity to improve it and make it productive. One thousand two hundred acres, in part now the Sierra Madre Villa property, were sold, and 1,000 acres on the south purchased, making 1,000 acres, which is the present area of Sunny Slope.

This last purchase necessitated a debt, which, with a high rate of interest—2½ per cent. per month—it required the most rigid economy and careful management to carry.

When it is stated that this enterprising gentleman has paid $120,000 interest alone, and most of this amount when rates of interest were high, and the benefits of his improvements were for the most part in the future, it will be readily understood that even such necessary luxuries as coffee, sugar, and many comforts were, for a time, unseen quantities by Mr. Rose and his devoted wife, who worked faithfully by his side with an energy equal to his own. Butter and eggs were "peddled around" to eke out their income, for the general distrust in "fruit farms" made it necessary that their purchases should be made mostly for cash.

There are at present on this estate about 12,000 orange and lemon trees, two-thirds of which are in bearing; 100 acres in other bearing fruit trees; 800 acres now in vineyard, besides 200 acres now being fenced to be planted to vines this year.

This makes, without doubt, the largest vineyard in the world. Two hundred and eighty acres are devoted to raising food for stock. There are 800 acres of pasture land, which is productive wood land.

Sunny Slope maintains a fine stud of thorough breds, many of which are celebrated, chief among them Sweetheart, a two year-old, which won a world-wide fame by trotting a mile in 2:29½, and sold even prior to that for $15,000. For the training and care of this fine stock everything is provided in a most thorough manner. The race track is almost perfect, the barns ample and well constructed, the system of grooming and feeding complete.

Mr. Rose has constructed the most perfect winery it is now possible to produce. Procuring the most approved machinery made he has placed it in the most advantageous position. The grapes are taken from wagons at the top of a hillside and fed into the centrifugal extractor of the juice, whence it runs by gravitation into the vats and stills, and finally into the cellars, without any waste of labor. The fermenting room is 60x180 feet, with vats of a capacity of 240,000 gallons. With this machinery it is possible to work grapes at the rate of ten tons per hour, and to distill 3,000 gallons of brandy in 24 hours. To this add three cellars, 75x140 feet, a cooper shop, and a constant stream of cool spring water, and the present facilities of the distillery are briefly stated. In addition to this immense storage capacity, it is now found necessary to build a mammoth brick cellar, 100x180 feet, and two stories high, which will at once be commenced, to accommodate the immense quantities of wine in pipes hundreds of feet long piled up in great ricks out of doors.

All the principal varieties of wine are made at Sunny Slope—Port, Angelica, Muscatel, Sherry, Cucamonga, Hock and Claret. The finer qualities of hock are Hoya Elben, and of Claret Zinfandel. In these wines a large trade is done in cases as well as in bulk. Brandy has always been a specialty with Mr. Rose, and the quantities of it lying around out doors are so immense that we can only wonder how they will be consumed, yet we are told by the manufacturer that this is only a small quantity comparatively.

Properly belonging to this description, though located in Los Angeles, is a distillery worked by Stearn & H—(who are partners in the wine business), for the purpose of making brandy; and Mr. Rose's ambition in this branch of his business was to manufacture a reliable and uniform article of pure grape brandy. After years of study and chemical experiment he has succeeded; his brandy is as well known as Hennessy & Otard, and over 100,000 gallons have been made at Sunny Slope this year, besides 500,000 gallons of wine.

To manufacture these excessive quantities of liquors, 11,000,000 lbs. of grapes were bought from 120 persons, besides 2,000,000 lbs., the home production. This latter will double each year for several years to come.

Mr. Rose has sold, this winter, 1,250,000 cuttings, and will reach 1,500,000 during the season.

A few ideas of Sunny Slope may be gathered from the above abbreviated description, but, as we remarked in the beginning, to be seen it must be appreciated. To feel the largeness of this wonderfully successful enterprise one must hear the rush of machinery, the clang of the anvil, the rattat of the coopers hammer, the crackle of jets of burning brush, must see the fences building, the busy task of workmen everywhere. It requires a large force during four months to gather the orange and lemon crops, and this is a wonderful sight in Northern eyes. And standing again by the brush fires where the warm air is heavy with evergreen fragrance and profusion of flowers, with cold zone of plum purity, plenty, and peace is every ho home, we are sure that no more appropriate name could have been suggested for this beautiful garden spot than Sunny Slope.

Viticulture.

GRAPE GROWING.

BY L. J. ROSE.

GEO. RICE, ED. SEMI-TROPIC:—I am trying hard to fulfil my promise to you, but I am so very busy with my affairs that it is with difficulty that I can get started.

I have had the desire to give the public such facts as experience has taught me about the planting of the vine, and if it will be of any benefit to any one it will not only be a pleasure but a duty I owe to the many parties who are buying cuttings from me.

HOW TO TAKE CARE OF GRAPE CUTTINGS BEFORE PLANTING.

The best way, whether grape cuttings are to be planted as soon as received or to be kept some time, is to submerge them entirely in water and keep them there for twenty-four hours at least, and as much longer as it is desired to keep them; even if kept submerged for two months it will do no harm, and probably be a benefit. The next best way to keep them is to bury them entirely, or four-fifths their entire length. Care should be taken not to place them in large masses without earth between them, for in that case these cuttings which have no earth in contact with them will mould, and this mold is the forerunner of decay and death. When to be kept for any length of time, then, it would be best to place them in such a manner that earth will come in contact with every part of the cutting which is underground. Then, again, care should be taken to see that the earth is wet, and kept so, for if it is as dry or dryer than the cutting, it will absorb the moisture from the cutting until the point of saturation is equal, whereas if it be kept wet it will give up moisture to the cuttings and keep them in favorable condition for growing.

PREPARING GROUND FOR PLANTING.

The study has ever been with me how to do a given piece of work well enough for success, with the smallest expenditure of labor. I break up my ground say four weeks before planting, using a strong pair of horses for an ordinary double plow, and plow as deep as I can with such a rig. In four weeks, or just before planting, I run the harrow over it and make it as smooth as it can be made. Waiting four weeks gives time for weeds to come up, which are easily destroyed by the harrowing. The ground now being ready for planting, is laid out into squares. We will say a 40-acre tract is to be planted. First, I would lay out a main avenue through the center, and would make it 48 feet wide—or even sixty feet would be no objection—then have a road twenty-four feet wide all around the outside. This will give two pieces of equal size lying on each side of the avenue, and bounded by a twenty-four-feet road on the other three sides. These two squares should be divided into four equal spaces,

extending from the avenue at right angles, and being about twice as long as wide, with roads of eighteen feet width.

Each of the oblong spaces would be about 180 yards wide and 200 yards long. Now, the first base line is ready for planting, beginning at the edge of the avenue and twenty-four feet inside the end line, running parallel with the twenty-four-feet road across the end to within twenty-four feet of the side line or road.

Then the next base line is begun on the avenue 100 yards from the first line, again beginning at the avenue and running *exactly* parallel with the first planting.

This gives two base lines inclusing 100 by say 200 yards. Now, to fill this in an easy matter, provided you are prepared with a line or chain made of the smallest size telegraph wire, the links being six feet long *evenly*, and containing fifty links, with a ring at each end, two feet from the end of the link. Stretching the chain from vine No. 1 in base line No. 1 to vine No. 1 in base line No. 2, will bring the end of each link in the chain even with cuttings No. 1 in both base lines, and every other link in your chain will show you where to plant a cutting, and your base lines being made with exactness all your other work will come out exact, and the rows of your vineyard will all be straight as an arrow in every direction.

WHAT DISTANCE APART SHOULD VINES BE PLANTED?

I believe six feet each way is better than a greater distance for wine. France and Germany plant much closer, and it is contended that a less distance will produce more sugar to the acre, and make better wine. There all labor is performed with spade, hoe and hand; here, all labor should be performed by the plow, cultivator and horse; there, labor is cheap; here, it is high. Six feet apart gives plenty of room to perform this labor by horse power. To plant wider apart will produce larger grapes and larger bunches, and for raisins, where this is desirable, it may be proper. It, too, gives space to dry raisins among the vines, but for wine small grapes are preferred, and per acre there will be a larger yield 6 by 6 than 8 by 8 feet, although to the vine there will be more the greater the distance apart they are planted.

Having planted one square, the planting of the others will only be a repetition of the first, and will be easy sailing.

HOW TO PLANT THE CUTTINGS.

This is usually done by making a hole with a crowbar the depth desired to plant, say from 12 to 15 inches, and a man following and placing cutting. If you are planting without irrigation, then much the best way is to pour a quart of water in each hole, and have some one follow with a crow-bar and immediately close the hole, which is done by forcing the bar down about three inches from the cutting to the full depth of the hole containing it, and working the bar backwards and forwards in the direction of the cutting. In this way the ground is pressed around the cut-

tings the whole length of that portion which is under ground. Upon careful attention to this apparently trifling matter the growth of your cuttings depends, for if the holes are filled or closed at top only, the bottom of the cutting will become mildewed, and decay.

If planting is done by irrigating, while much the better way is to fill up the holes, so much the better, although the first way is good enough if care is exercised; and even when irrigating it is much safer to have a man follow with the crow-bar and probe around each cutting as the water runs, and make sure that each hole is filled with earth.

Much could be said as to how all this is done, how many men can work to advantage, or form a gang; but these are matters soon learned, and would take more time than I now have to devote to this description.

AFTER CARE AND CULTIVATION

Consist in plowing with a single horse, beginning in the centre between two rows of cuttings with a back-furrow, and going backwards and forwards until all the land is plowed up to the cuttings. This requires a careful hand, or else many of the cuttings will be destroyed. If your land is sandy and works easily, and free from clods, this will be all the plowing that will be necessary, and all after stirring of the soil can be done with a cultivator, each time going the cross way from time previous. This will level your ground, and by following it up once a month until July, and again, say in the middle of August, will keep the cuttings growing vigorously, keep your ground, moist with even ten inches of rain-fall during the winter (and irrigation would be of no benefit), and keep your ground free of weeds and looking like a garden. The kind of cultivation is of but little importance; the most simple, durable and cheapest will be the best, for your ground will be in easy condition for working. Stirring the soil in this way, breaking the crust which forms (a condition favorable for evaporation), destroying the weeds while they are small, and keeping the land level, are the things you wish to accomplish.

WILL IT PAY TO RAISE ROOTED VINES?

This depends upon various conditions. If it is found that the season is a very dry one, then planting cuttings in vineyard form will be attended by much loss, a large percentage not growing, without irrigation, whereas, if in nursery, they can be better cared for and watered, even by hauling water from a distance. Again, if rooted vines be planted, even in a very dry season, they will start and grow of such cultivation is practiced as here described. Again, parties not being fully ready with their land to plant this year could root their vines in nursery and be ready for next year, for any season that might come, and gain, say six months in growth, for a rooted vine will make a larger growth than a cutting, although it will not be equal in size to the vine planted in place at once of the same age.

IS IRRIGATION A BENEFIT TO YOUNG VINES?

In ordinary seasons of rain-fall, I think not; but it entails much work and expense for irrigation; for irrigation brings weeds, and each irrigation should be followed by plowing. Young vines require no water for the evaporation from their leaves, there being but few leaves, as the plant is small, is but little; whereas they have 6 feet square of ground for their reservoir to draw from, and that quantity of soil contains enough water, if the water is retained by cultivation, and foreign vegetation, as weeds, prevented from absorbing it, to nourish and maintain the vine in full vigor and largest growth. Irrigation will be beneficial when vines are in full bearing and growth, in keeping them in vigor and health, and in producing each year large crops, although grape vines will flourish and bear for a term of years, and perhaps for a long term (for how long depends on the nature and fertility of the ground), without irrigation. Young vineyards I do not irrigate. Old vineyards I have a desire to, and will more or less as I have water; but winter irrigation I deem more desirable than summer.

Cuttings should have good care, and not be allowed to dry by too long exposure to air; and in a dry winter season should surely be submerged in water for at least a week, for cuttings in such a season will, to an extent, dry on the vine before being removed, thus closing many of their pores, and becoming hard; and it is an advantage any season to so saturate them with water. After planting they should be cut back to say six inches high, which, if the cuttings are short-jointed, will leave about three eyes above ground; the eyes, however, being of less importance than the height above ground, for that portion only of ground will be dried to some extent by sunshine, until growth begins. And it is best not to have them too long, for they will be able to maintain their erect growth if short, whereas, if long, will bend by the weight of the top. They can be raised to any height required from year to year as the plant gains size and strength, and to this way staking becomes unnecessary, and much expense and labor saved. Small sized cuttings will grow better; that is, a greater per cent will grow than thick cuttings. It is a good way to cut off, just before planting, the bottom of the cutting immediately under a bud. Deep planting is a detriment to their starting to grow, for a cutting strikes roots easiest and first from the bottom; and if planted too deep it can not root at all, for it is too far from the influence of air, and choked, or rather, smothered out.

Almost all our lands will grow grapes; in fact, the vine will grow where nothing else will; and lands that will grow brush, weeds and cactus I consider the best grape lands we have.

It must be remembered that in localities where there are many rabbits or hares,

vineyards must be protected from them, for they will eat the young shoots as they sprout, and the vine will die. Squirrels will do the same. In this, like in every thing else, you must be ready before you begin, or your labor will be lost.

I am often asked,

WILL GRAPE-GROWING CONTINUE TO BE PROFITABLE?

My opinion is that, in the long run, it will be. That there will be times in this boom of planting that there will be more grapes than there is a capacity to work up and take care of is almost certain, and prices will go down. The raising of grapes in this favorable climate is the easiest part of the making of wine. The raising of grapes is as easy as the raising of corn; but the making of wine and brandy requires much experience and much capital. Both these will be found if it is profitable; but it will require time. Some years ago, while President of our Agricultural Society, in my address I took the ground in favor of grape vine planting, and predicting that it would become the great interest of this State; yet for a few years following there was an over production. There was more wine than the people were prepared to buy. They had not become accustomed to its purity, and the difference between the pure products and their imitations and adulterations. There is a continued increase of consumption of wine in this country; but the planting of vineyards is increasing much faster, and the home demand will be more than supplied in a short time. When this comes to be the case we must look to European demand; and it is a reasonable supposition that we will have it, for their products are failing, whereas their wants are the same, and ours is now the only country which is likely to produce a surplus.

I have in this article run into the one I wrote before; but there is so much inquiry of me about these various details that, so many wishing information about what kind of land to plant a vineyard on, about growing grapes without irrigation, how to plant, etc., etc., that I thought it best to repeat some things I had written in order to give wider publicity, and by keeping your grape number on hand I can refer them to that and you. There is much more I could say had you the space and I the time; but I will have to defer to some future time. As it is, if my instructions are followed reasonable success is sure.

A NEW enterprise has been inaugurated on Spring Street by Mr. Olds, formerly a resident of Northern California. He proposes to manufacture a spring bed, which for comfort, cleanliness, elasticity and durability we are satisfied has no equal. He has received five highest premiums at fairs held on this Coast and this will supply a demand long felt in this section. The bed has 45 genuine steel springs.

Persons sending their address to the Secretary will receive a copy of the Citrus Fair paper by mail free.

"THE Citrus Fair at Los Angeles will be WORTH A TRIP ACROSS THE CONTINENT TO see," says the San Francisco Bulletin; and we are of the opinion it was correct in the statement.

The inducements to bring out a magnificent exhibit of our citrus fruits are many. Among them we will mention only a few. Three $3 cash premiums, a duty that every farmer or orchardist owes to himself, his neighbor, his county, and Southern California, in the interest of progress and development of his home, to show to the world what he can do in the culture of the orange, lemon, lime, etc., for thousands will read in the newspapers what is here exhibited and inspected by thousands of visitors.

The Pacific Coast Press Association, (numbering over one hundred editors) their wives and friends, are to visit the Exposition on Tuesday noon. Every paper represented by these editors will tell through its columns what they saw at our fair. Their readers, numbering over 100,000 families, will read about us and our capabilities.

The Horticultural Society will print ten to twenty-five thousand papers telling of Southern California, each locality, and each individual's exhibit, about the resources of our soil, the climate, and all of reasons why immigrants should move to Southern California.

An excursion of business men from San Francisco and the northern part of the State, and an excursion from the East over the new Southern route, will visit the Fair. Now is the auspicious time of all others to let the world know what Southern California is doing in citrus culture. Let us do our part in good measure, and our reward will be ample.

Mrs. PARTINGTON says don't take any of the quack nostrums as they are regimental to the human system, but put your trust in Pruin & Pruin's Standard Preparations, which will cure general dilapidation, confess habits, and all comic diseases. They extend lease from a severe attack of tropical fever. They are the ne plus ultra of medicine.

THE freight and truck line of H. Bills, No 7 Market Street is the oldest establishment and most popular in Los Angeles. Visitors to the Citrus Fair will find it to their advantage to have their exhibits and baggage delivered by this line, and all who consider who desire prompt service, careful usage of their goods must call on Bills.

DR. N. H. SAXTON, 118 Main St., is putting up some valuable medical preparations which are deserving of more than a passing notice. His cough, throat, and lung syrup has been used by many in our city with most beneficial results, and his "Hair Producer," composed of harmless ingredients, gives general satisfaction.

Biography.

L. J. ROSE,

THE FOUNDER AND OWNER OF SUNNY SLOPE.

The subject of this sketch was born in Bavaria, May, 1827. When he was twelve years old his father and family emigrated to New Orleans, where his father engaged in the mercantile business. After three years they removed to Monroe county, Illinois, where the young man having received a fair German education, clerked in his father's store, attended public school and finished his education at Shurtleff College, Alton, Illinois.

At twenty-one he became a merchant on his own account, as a member of the firm of Rose & Dunlap, in Quincy, Illinois. At the end of another term of three years the firm removed to Keosauqua, Iowa, where they remained in business seven years. While here Mr. Rose secured what he says is "fully one-half the factor of his success," his faithful, sensible wife. He also bought a farm and indulged, so far as the circumstances of the climate would allow, his passionate fondness for cultivating flowers and fruits of all kinds, especially the rare and beautiful varieties.

But only the very hardiest varieties could withstand those fearful winter storms, the beautiful flowering plants and tender ornamental shrubs succumbed entirely to the cold or were dwarfed and ruined. Summer brought chills and fever (the "fever'n ager" of the South), winter gave lung and winter fevers, and this made a constant experience of "hope deferred."

Finally, in 1858, it was decided on account of failing health to remove to California, and from that time the present proprietor of the largest vineyard in the world has been making history as a rapidist.

This being the year of the Mormon war, it was deemed impossible to proceed via Salt Lake, and after much deliberation it was determined to try the 35th parallel route. So, accompanied by his family, and having nineteen men employed to bring through the finest lot of thoroughbred and graded horses and cattle that had ever started overland to California, he set out on the long and toilsome journey.

They were joined enroute by several families from Missouri and Iowa, so that when they reached Albuquerque their party numbered 200 persons, 30 of whom were men. At this place they secured a guide, and having received many expressions of good will and kindness from the citizens of the town, they resumed their journey over a new and untried road through the wilderness.

Passing through several Indian villages, whose inhabitants were always peaceful, friendly, and sometimes agriculturally employed, their days were filled with the usual incidents of wagon travel, and their evenings were brightened by the ruddy glow of the camp fire, and lightened with song and story. Game was abundant, and the hunt afforded as much satisfaction as the stew.

This rather enthusiastic gentleman, even after the lapse of all these years, waxes eloquent when relating part of his journey, and betrays the honest appreciation and intense love of nature and nature's works, which influenced his choice of occupation for life, and does him infinite credit.

Nearer the Colorado, however, the country became more dry and hot, grass was more stunted, Indians began to prowl around and steal stock; some of the men straggling behind were fired at, and one dangerously wounded. Coming difficulties began to cast their shadows before, and when at last the banks of the Colorado were reached, it was with a feeling that it had been accomplished at great peril.

But just "beyond the Alps lieth Italy," and looking across the shining river they saw the Sierras of their pilgrimage, the Golden State, and thought their goal would soon be reached. They were almost worn out with heat and thirst, many of the cattle having died, and some of the men looking crazy for the want of water. In this demoralized condition the Indians visiting them found the camp completely at their mercy, and the poor wayworn travelers were only too glad that their visitors contented themselves for that time with killing and roasting the fine cattle, and making a feast.

Rafts must now be constructed to convey the emigrants across the river, this being an entirely new route, and this would probably occupy several days' time.

Next day some measures for defense were taken by the somewhat refreshed party, and the visiting Indians, though treated well and presented by Mr. Rose with beads, clothing, blankets, etc., brought by him for that purpose, were held somewhat in check.

They then offered to assist the party in crossing the river, but next morning they did not make their appearance. About noon that day they appeared with a war whoop, and a fight began that lasted till night. One entire family was murdered, and Mr. Brown, Mr. Rose's overseer, killed, besides several men wounded; and the loss of stock was almost total.

Disheartened, the party now took one wagon and ambulance, with two horses, and started at nightfall back over the desolate and perilous road they had hoped never to travel again, leaving their stores and supplies in seven wagons standing on the river bank at the disposal of the Indians. Without a hope of life, but determined to die game, they made their slow way through deep ravines and cañons, where every cactus or shrub was magnified into an Indian, and every noise into an ambush. The yells of the savages could be heard as they discovered the treasures of the abandoned wagons, or wailed over their dead. Late on the succeeding day they met a party who had been traveling in their rear. They all returned together to Albuquerque—ragged, barefoot, thoroughly discouraged, and only surprised that they were still alive.

They were received with open arms by the citizens and every assistance rendered to make them comfortable, and the leader of this disastrous expedition says he never spent so happy and restful three months' time as those following their arrival; though they lived in an adobe, with dirt floor, on chairs or beds, but with hearts full of thanks for life and health.

They were not idle months, however, for soon Mr. Rose was enabled by his own exertions and the additional help of his friend, Judge O'Malveny, to buy the Fonda in Santa Fe, known as the Fonda, being the principal hotel in the Territory. His success in this enterprise, which, when he took control was a losing one, was so gratifying that at the end of two years he felt justified in again turning his face toward California. This time the journey over a well worn road with strong teams and light loads, proved a pleasure trip, and on the 29th of November 1860 the party reached El Monte. Here again Mr. Rose warms up with his subject in describing the beautiful hills and valleys clothed with early verdure as he rode among them for the first time in the warm red light of the setting sun.

He had intended to settle near the Bay; but after a thorough inspection of the country, and an extended visit north to Santa Clara and Sacramento he returned to San Gabriel and cast his lot here, and has never had cause to regret his choice. He has been one of the leading spirits in the development and advancement of his particular locality, and has been called to a prominent place in the horticultural and viticultural interests of the State.

He is a member of the State Agricultural Society, being a director of that Board. He is also one of the Viticultural Commissioners of the State, and contributed largely to the amount of valuable information contained in the Annual Report of that Commission.

Through his instrumentality a bill has been prepared, endorsed by the legislature of the state, and petitions signed recommending Congress to pass a law "To protect the manufacturers of pure grape brandies, by prohibiting its mixture or adulteration by the wholesale dealer; requiring the packages to be sold by the wholesale dealer as they are delivered from the distillery, except under certain specified conditions."

Mr. Rose has been favorably and prominently mentioned as a candidate for Congress, and had he been nominated, it is generally believed, would have been elected by a large majority, irrespective of party.

We believe that the people of Southern California will, at the next election, lay aside politics for the time, and unite as one whole into who is thoroughly identified with the interests of the district, and is a practical, competent, honest man. Mr. Rose is authority on all subjects upon which he expresses an opinion, for his judgments are formed only after thorough investigation and experiment.

No man in the State has given more valuable instruction to the vineyardist, and none has done more to stimulate improvement and growth in this profitable industry of our state than L. J. Rose.

Sunny Slope from the North.
Sunny Slope Wine Building.

SUNNY SLOPE. L. J. ROSE, PROPRIETOR, San Gabriel, Los Angeles County, California.

Wine Making.

ON THE PREPARATION OF SWEET WINES, BUT CHIEFLY MUSCATEL.

BY JOHN J. BLEASDALE, D. D., SECRETARY STATE BOARD OF VIT. COM'RS.

EDITOR "SEMI-TROPIC CALIFORNIA."—
A French gentleman conversant with the sweet wines called Lunel, informed me, a few weeks ago, that he had been shown a sample of Angelica wine at the Baldwin Hotel in this city, which came up to his idea of what such kind of wine should be. I have not seen it; but I infer from our conversation that it had been grown and matured on Mr. Baldwin's property, somewhere in the wine districts of Los Angeles county. From time to time I have met with wines from those districts of the most opposite characters, which convince me that within a comparatively small country there are to be found climates as various as could be found between the north of France and the south of Spain. For instance, some months ago Mr. L. J. Rose, of San Gabriel, sent me some samples of young white wines for analysis, which were truly surprising—a Blauc Elben and a Berger especially. They were very thin, fine, firm, young wines, with plenty of tannin. They kept their color without cloudiness for several days after the bottles were opened. About the same time I was favored with three or four samples of Port and old Sherry, which for richness and fullness of flavor approached the special growths of Spain and Portugal, as nearly as wines well could when prepared from any grapes but those alone in use in the above named countries. These were J. de Barth Shorb's.

I refer to these matters just now because, in addition to the samples of wines referred to, I have seen samples of Muscatel grapes from Los Angeles, which convince me that there must be in those wine districts many localities peculiarly suited by nature for the production of the highest class of Muscatel wine, the liqueur wine which will never want a market so long as there is a lady left in the land.

Now, without disputing the taste of those experts who can go into raptures over dry Frontignan, I would respectfully say that the juice of the Muscatel grape is destined by nature to be made into sweet wine; and so to help in the preparing and management of it, I deferentially submit the following hints and directions, because, in other countries, I have found them to be sufficient and necessary. We are not, however, at present treating of commercial wine, such as must be manufactured on the grand scale, but of an especial product, to be ranked, when perfect, among the works of high art in wine. To this end,

THE GRAPES

Should be as ripe as possible, consistent with soundness, and of the three best

known varieties, viz.: the Muscatel of Alexandria, with long trailing bunches; the Gordo Blanco, with round, large, often greenish, plump berries, and full bunches; and both the dark and white varieties, with small, compact bunches, and round berries. These kinds are used in about the following proportions: one-half Alexandrias; of the rest, half Gordo Blanco and half small bunches.

Every faulty berry must be removed from the bunches, and care taken that there is no spider's web in the bunch, which sometimes is met with in the Gordo Blanco. The stalks should be removed from all but the small kinds, and theirs should be taken out as the crushing goes on.

CRUSHING THE BERRIES AND HANDLING THE MUST.

The grapes stripped from the stalks require to be very thoroughly crushed. The pulp, for such it is in those hard, fleshy grapes, must be freed, as far as possible, from the skins. During this process, or directly afterwards, and before any fermentation sets in, it must be thoroughly and repeatedly aerated; that is to say, every particle of it should be again and again brought in contact with atmospheric air. Nothing yet discovered has reached the perfection with which long treading with the human foot accomplishes this indispensable condition of sweet and full-bodied wines. Oxygen is necessary to the vinous fermentation; and all of it that a must is to have, must be got into it before fermentation commences to any considerable extent. Perhaps the simplest method would be to pump air through the liquid for a considerable time, or force the liquid through a hose with a finely perforated nose on the end.

It is not too much to say that most of the conspicuous defects in California wines are caused by the vineyardists following French or German methods with rich musts, more particularly in the hotter portions of the State. French and German methods are excellent for those countries, but it must be remembered that we here are 17 degrees of latitude nearer the equator than most of the wine districts of France, and can always depend upon a dry autumn and sunny weather. In France it is truly and often stated that every sunny day in vintage time adds considerably to the saccharine matter in the grape, but we must remember that in autumn the weather is often cloudy and dull, while that of this fortunate country is clear and bright. As in Portugal and Spain, so here, if we desire to make wine as free as possible from what we call earthy taste, and the French goût de terroir, the expressed juice must be aerated perfectly. Such being the case with all rich musts, it is yet has a peculiar significance in the instance of the thick pulpy or syrupy musts of the Muscatel of Alexandria. Get air into it by some means, by all means. The fine, rich musts of the Alto Douro are trodden by men at the rate of one man to every one hundred gallons, for more than eighteen hours consecutively, and after a short rest, for six hours more.

The hulls must not be entirely removed; about a quarter should be left in; but in this case a little experience is the safest guide. It must be kept in view that the aim is to make a true wine, not a confection like most of that called Angelica. Tannin is indispensable, and tartaric acid to remove the potash, and malic and other acids to form the bouquet. Tannin is obtained from the skins as the alcohol goes on forming in the process of fermentation, and also the coloring matter for that exquisite gold-yellow, which is to the eye what bouquet and aroma are to the nose and palate.

LENGTH OF FERMENTATION.

A certain latitude is to be allowed for the time required under the varying conditions of temperature at which the fermentation is carried on; but, roughly, it may be stated at between six and nine days. In very hot localities where the fermentation would naturally become tumultuous, five days might well suffice.

About the fifth or sixth day the best course to follow is to distil a little of the must, which can be easily and accurately done in one of Salerun's small stills. This is better than Beaume's instrument. If it show nine (9) of alcohol, stop the violent fermentation by a dose of three per cent. of good wine-brandy of 30 proof at least, and so kill a large portion of the ferment. If this be not enough to stop it, then a little more, and an early wracking, with sulphuring, say within a fortnight. The additional spirit will assist in dissolving tannin and coloring matter from the hulls. At the end of fourteen to twenty days, draw off the young wine into pipes or hogsheads, clean washed with a bath of crude tartar, dissolved in hot water; then sulphured, and when filled left with the bunghole covered with a rag of muslin or a brick to allow a certain amount of gas to escape, and to keep flies and dust out. The young wine may then remain in this state for a few weeks, during which time it will pass through several phases, such as becoming turbid, milky, very sour, tartaric, etc., of which no account need be taken, unless it be to carefully pour in a bottle of brandy so as to remain about the bung hole. At the end of a short time, when each one's observation will form the best guide in his own case, the bung may be driven home, and the wine left at rest.

ANGLING, SO-CALLED BY THE PORTUGUESE.

This strobe is quite indispensable in making fine wines of the Muscatel liqueur character; and I might here properly describe the method of its preparation. For this purpose the richest and best and most saccharine grapes should be selected, carefully freed from any imperfect berries, and stalks, and pressed there and then, perhaps the hands being the best implements on the small scale, and the must at once, before any fermentation can take place, put in open sheet-iron or tin dishes, and evaporated out of doors, where there is no dust flying about, over a fire-place constructed of a few bricks or stones, at a moderate heat, and watched and scummed till absolutely no more scum arises. This is most important. The evaporation should then be continued at a moderate heat till the mass shall have become "sticky" to the fingers, and, when cold, the nearer to thin honey the better. Often a good, rough way to test it is to dip in a bit of chip, and drawing it slowly out observe the length of the thread it brings with it.

There is, however, a point which the person who is watching the evaporation may notice as a guide. He must remember, however, that one essential matter is to avoid any burning of the must; for a taste of the fire greatly injures it. Now, at a certain point, if his fire is just enough to keep evaporation going actively on, the whole contents of his dish will begin to rise up a little, and roll over and over, and look like a mass of gray hair. A few minutes after that appears he should extinguish his fire, and let the matter cool. That having been done, the *sirobi* is put in clean vessels of wood, or, better still, earthware, and five or six per cent. of good proof brandy added to it, to guard against fermentation, and prevent any mouldiness arising. This, then, should be always on hand for the purposes now to be detailed.

USES OF ALCOHOL, AND HOW TO USE IT.

Before all it is prudent to take from two to five gallons of the best and richest must of Muscatel and ferment it in a demijohn as far as ever it will go down, till it becomes, in fact, as dry as possible, and then determine the total amount of alcohol by distillation. Still the tables supplied with Salleron's small stills, whether French or British, do not indicate the *total amount of alcohol* present. To obtain it, the strength indicated by the table must be multiplied by 4, and the product divided by 7, which will give the total quantity. Example: proof strength, 24°; 24×4=96 ÷7=13.714 alcohol. When the total amount has thus been ascertained, care should be taken in adding spirit, in any turn, so that the wine should never much exceed the amount it would have formed naturally if allowed to become perfectly dry wine. Working within the stairs limits with spirit alone, or what is of more consequence with arrobb, the wine will never need to exceed its natural strength; and it will be quite pure wine because it will contain nothing but vinous matter. Wine so prepared would, among other purposes, be available for sacramental uses.

RACKING.

Generally the first racking would take place in this State during the first fine, still weather in March, and again in October.

Now, on each of these occasions, a portion, say one per cent. of strong wine brandy, and one-fourth per cent. of arrobb, is added before the rask is closed down. The one per cent. of brandy is added to the arrobb, and the whole well mixed, and a gallon or two of the wine drawn off and blended with it, and then poured into the

cask and well stirred, or the cask rolled about for some time. Nothing more is needed but to keep the casks constantly full to the bung. At this point it becomes necessary to draw a little on the faith and patience of the cellar master, because, ordinarily, the wine will become milky to look at, sweety-sour to the taste, etc., and in cellar parlance, "kick about a good deal." But it will work all right if the above precautions have been taken.

FINING.

Here the real difficulty with Muscatel wine comes in; for it requires skill to render it "candle bright."

Probably others who have had experience in treating Muscatel have found methods of fining it that satisfy themselves: I can only say what I found to answer both in Portugal and Australia.

The plan was first to take a large *white glass* bottle, the bigger the better, and treat as much as could be conveniently handled in it. The quantity, whatever it may be, is ascertained, as well as the quantity of fining employed. Moreover, the amount of tannin present must be roughly estimated; and this is easily done by filtering a wineglass of the wine, unless it is pretty bright; and then putting into it a teaspoonful of baking soda (the bi-carbonate of soda), stirring it well, and after a few minutes noting the depth of blue-black, or nearly quite black, color. The deeper the tint the more abundant the tannin, and the less fear in using finings. Still, every precaution needs to be taken not to rob it of tannin; and the same applies to all white wines.

The safest plan is to use real isinglass. When soaked in the usual way and quite thin and fine, add first a small quantity of wine, and then about an equal quantity of brandy, partly to fix the isinglass as so not to set too much on the tannin, and yet sweep the impurities with it as it settles. If white of egg or other albuminous substances be used, even greater care is needed. The whites of six perfectly fresh hens' eggs should be ample for 100 gals. wine.

Since the object aimed at fining is to render the wine bright, we should reasonably suppose the readiest way to affect it would be to put it through a filter; but as that cannot be safely done with delicate wines, we make a filter and put it through the wine.

In my experience, and it was considerable in Australia, I found, in the instance of Muscat wines, that the addition of a little finely washed Spanish clay, or very fine white silver sand, thoroughly washed, both accelerates the work of fining, and renders it more effective. The more muddle the temperature of the cellar the better, especially after the finings have been put in.

The above are the principal points, and are respectfully submitted to makers of Muscatel wine.

576 Montgomery St, }
San Francisco, Feb. 7, 1881. }

CITRUS FAIR,
MARCH 14-19.
HORTICULTURAL PAVILION,
LOS ANGELES, CAL.

Open for reception and arrangement of exhibits March 10, and will remain open for the entry of exhibits until 10 o'clock Tuesday, March 15.

At 12 o'clock on Tuesday every exhibit should be in place, as at that time the Press Association of the Pacific Coast — over one hundred editors — will be given a reception at the Pavilion.

Members of the Horticultural Society are appointed a grand committee to aid in decorating the Pavilion, and are requested to meet at the Pavilion Saturday, March 12, for that purpose. Members who will do so are requested to leave word to that effect with the Secretary, Room 3, Baker Block between now and then.

This is a matter of pride, and it is hoped every member will do something. If every one cannot personally help at the Pavilion, at least agree to send flowers, evergreens, etc. Notify us early.

☞ *The ladies are expected to do their part.*

WANTS OF THE CITRUS FAIR. — Wanted, 100 clusters of oranges; wanted, 1,000 to 2,000 oak lilies; wanted, 10,000 roses and flowers; wanted, 100,000 floral decorations; wanted, everybody who is interested in the future welfare and glory of Southern California to supply these wants.

The Pacific Press Association, consisting of about one hundred editors and their wives, will visit our Citrus Fair on Tuesday afternoon, March 15, and it stands us in hand to be ready with our exhibits in place by 12 o'clock that day.

APPLES AND PEARS should form a special feature at the Citrus Fair; thus showing the keeping qualities, and proving that Southern California not only raises the largest and finest apples and pears, but as good keepers as any part of the world.

A CITRUS FAIR. — We learn from the exchange "Semi-Tropic Californian," as the only horticultural journal on the Pacific Coast, that there is to be a "Citrus Fair," held at Los Angeles, California, from the 14th to the 19th of March next. Oranges, lemons, and all other products of the genus citrus are to be exhibited and liberal premiums will be awarded. The cultivation of the genus citrus is the leading industry in that part of California of which Los Angeles is the center, and we have no doubt that the exhibition will be of sufficient interest to attract visitors from all parts of the State. — *American Agriculturist.*

Citrus Fair Paper free to any address.

Subscribe for THE SEMI-TROPIC.

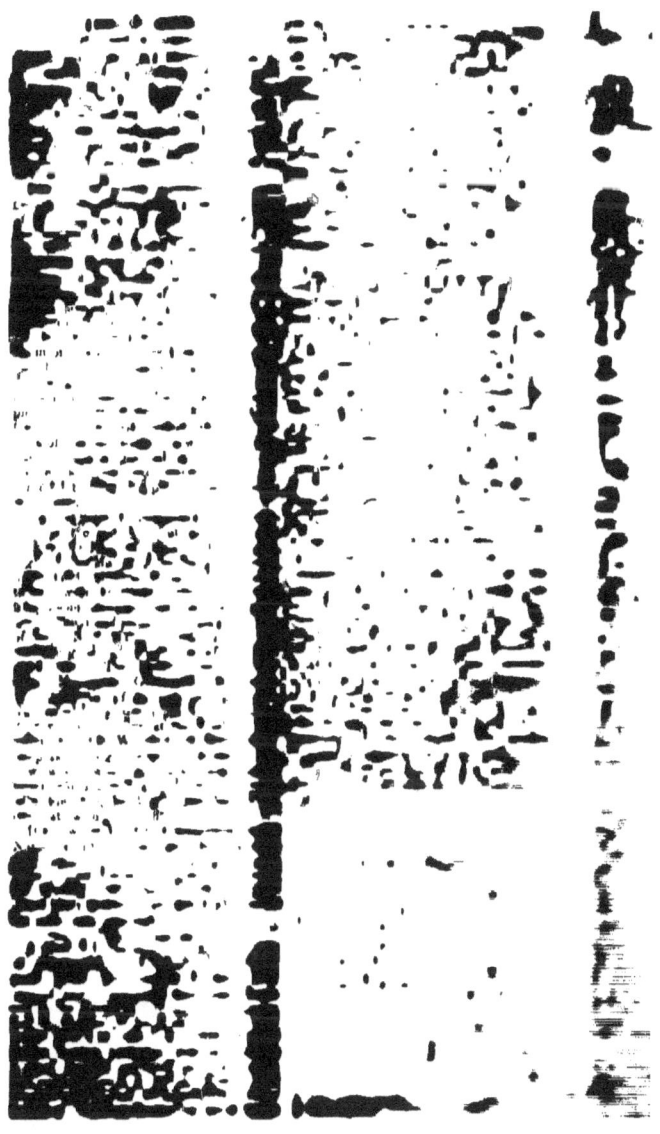

Entomology.

THE PHYLLOXERA OR GRAPEVINE LOUSE.

BY EUGENE W. HILGARD, PROF. OF AGRI-
CULTURE, UNIVERSITY OF CALIFORNIA.

[The following extracts are from the report on the subject by Prof. Hilgard, and will give our readers information as to prevent the introduction of this dread pest into southern California.—EDITOR SEMI-TROPIC.]

The name Phylloxera, meaning leaf witherer, was originally given to a kind of plant louse which infests the European oak. We are now acquainted with sixteen species, of which only one, the *P. vastatrix*, of Planchon, affects the interests of man.

It was first observed in America in 1856, by Asa Fitch, of New York, on the leaves of native vines, and by him named *Pemphigus vitifolii*. * * * *

The Root Rot or "*Pourridie*" of the vines, first mentioned as existing in France about the years 1860-4, was since traced by Planchon to winglose lice, in 1868. But the identity of these root lice with those inhabiting the leaf-galls of certain native American vines, was for some time not even suspected. After attention had been called to their close resemblance, and to the fact that the leaf Gall Louse descended to the root in winter, attempts were made, both in this country and in Europe, to transplant root lice to the leaves, many of which were unsuccessful in consequence of the failure of observers to select suitable varieties of vines. Finally, in 1870-74, Riley conclusively proved the identity of the two types, by effecting the change of habit either way, on vines properly selected. He also showed that the all but universal failure of the European vines, as well as that of certain delicate native varieties in the Mississippi Valley, observed long since, was due to the attacks of the Root Louse.

DESCRIPTION OF THE PHYLLOXERA.

In most respects the Phylloxera resembles the common plant lice (*Aphis*), the main difference being that its wings lie flat, and overlap on the back, instead of being erected roof-fashion; and that the three-jointed antennæ have the terminal joint much the longest. All are quite small, the perfect winged form of the Vine Louse being about one-twentieth of an inch in length. Its peculiar feature is the great variety of forms which it is capable of assuming under different circumstances. Among them we distinguish two chief types, viz.: the leaf-inhabiting one, or Gall Louse, and the root-inhabiting, or Root Louse.

THE GALL LOUSE.

The Gall Louse habitually infests the leaves of certain native grapes in the Eastern States, especially those of the Riverside and Frost Grape (*Vitis riparia* and *cordifolia*). It covers the surface of

† Pronounced as if spelled *fee-lox-ey-rah*, with accent on fox.

the leaf with numerous fleshy swellings, of irregular shape, and often partially of a reddish tint. In them we find a wingless female louse, one twenty-fifth of an inch long.

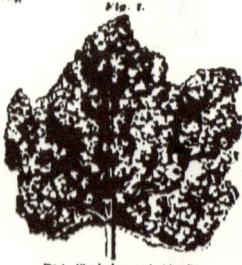

Fig. 1. Vine leaf covered with galls.

When the gall is filled with from two hundred to five hundred eggs, the mother louse dies. The eggs hatch in from six to eight days into active little larvæ, of oval form, which soon leave the gall, go to the upper surface of downy young leaves, and insert their suckers. The latter consist of three to five threads, surrounded by a blunt and hairy sheath. The leaves soon begin to swell below, while a reddish down surrounds the louse above, gradually closing in. On suitable vines the gall forms in a few days, and the grown louse begins to deposit eggs, fills the gall, and dies. The young lice not only attack the leaves, but also cover the tender shoots, and even the tendrils, with swellings.

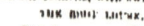

Fig. 2. Section of a gall and egg.

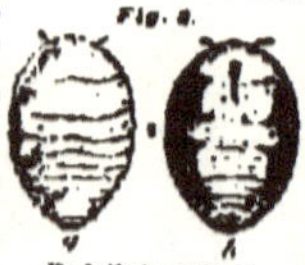

Fig. 3. Mother gall louse.

THE ROOT LOUSE.

Fig. 4. Young larva.

Fig. 5. Mother louse.

The life history of the root inhabiting type of Phylloxera is much more complex than that of the Gall louse.

The newly hatched larvæ of either are alike.

Fig. 6. Adult root-inhabiting larva.

Those of the Root Louse soon acquire

tubercles over their surface; these, however, are irregular, only skin deep, and sometimes absent. As the development progresses, two forms begin to differentiate themselves. One is of a somewhat jointed egg or pear-shape, and resembles the wingless Gall Louse; the other is of an oval form.

Fig. 6.

The former is the mother Root Louse; it remains on the root through life, sucking its juices, locating itself and its colonies by preference in crevices, creases, etc. At maturity, without sexual impregnation, each lays upwards of two hundred and fifty eggs, which, on hatching, again rapidly go through the same round of life.

THE WINGED FORM.

The oval form of the Root Louse larva is destined to become winged.

From the time it has achieved one-third of its growth, the wing pads, or rudimentary wings, are visible. The individuals are more active than those of the wingless form, and are often seen crawling about; finally, in July and August they shed their last skin and take wing. All are females; a supposed male form, with shorter abdomen, proves to be merely a barren female.

The eggs are of two kinds; the larger, about one-fifth of an inch in length, are of the female sex; the others, about two-fifths smaller, hatch into males; the time required being about a fortnight.

The sexual individuals thus produced are again wingless; more than this, they are destitute of sucker, mouth, or alimentary canal being evidently destined exclusively for the reproduction of their species. They are quite active and couple freely.

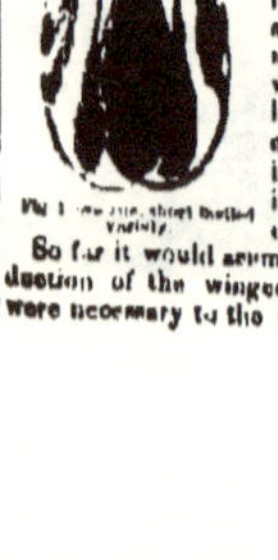

These sexual females lay but one single egg apiece. This solitary egg, which is destined to hibernate, and hatch in spring, produces again the ordinary mother Root Louse, which lays several hundred eggs, and is capable of repeating itself without sexual impregnation, for five or six generations.

So far it would seem as though the production of the winged form at intervals were necessary to the vigor of the species.

[Concluded from page 61.]

the most profitable adaptation to the squash belt, flourish without present or prospective need of irrigation or fertilization. The velvety soil is moistened by capillary ascension, and is probable as deep as the mahogany alluvions of Honduras. Sierra rivers may yet be led to the mesas, to fertilize the arid, naturally rich, but shallower than Honduran soil.

Orange, on the border of the squash belt, sharing in the same sea climate, has settled the once vexed question of making merchantable raisins in the sea climate of the squash belt. Orange put her last year's crop of raisins on the market, which were accepted and paid for, by San Francisco dealers, at the highest quotations for California raisins. Geo. C. Leslie, the great Chicago broker of American and trans-Atlantic fruits, who jobs, among other fruits, half a million boxes of raisins annually, pronounces the raisins made at Orange the best California raisins he has examined, during his present visit to this State. Col. W. W. Hollister and others said that raisins made at Westminster, by Josiah McCoy, are as good as imported layers. Westminster is within the ocean ward half of the squash belt.

VALUE OF SQUASH COMPARED WITH MINES OF PRECIOUS METALS.

The volume of the possible revenues of the squash belt may be compared with that of some prosperous region of mines, rather than with the volume of revenues of an equal agricultural area in the East.

Once a boom, always a boom, will be the squash belt best adapted agricultural boom. But once a boom, not always a boom, is any local bullion boom of mines. The boom of mines is exhausting as flowing. The squash belt boom is renewing as flowing. The yield of the mine is the measure of exhaustion. The yield of the squash belt is the measure of perpetual yield. The squash belt boom will be an ever renewing tidal wave, ages after human reach down present bonanzas is silverless, goldless, and forgotten.

AREA, IN A SENSE, EXPANDS AS BEYOND THE VALUES OF PRODUCTION.

In sheep walks, the squash belt is as a dozen communities. In barley, as an ordinary county. In corn, as an equal slice of Pharaoh's alluvions without his dream of blasted ears (but a reckless till against the cheap climate and cheap corn fields of the Mississippi valley, boulevarded at the rate of less than a penny a mile). In apples, as its equal area in the best quarter of New England. In apricots, as more than its equal area in the choicest apricot vale of Syria. In Turkish prunes, as a stream fertilizing higher than its source. In European or Asiar walnuts, as an equal area of Persian debts. In citrus fruits, a Sorrento here, but not a Sorrento yonder; square miles of perfect success here, square miles in another quarter forbidding success. In beets, as a German Grand Duchy. In alfalfa, for substantial value, as eight times its area of Western Reserve. In alfalfa,

for both substantial value and beauty of year long emerald and monthly blossoming, as a vale of the Tiber, for whose inspiration a Virgil would more than thrice climb Quirinal piled on Aventine. As a region of creameries, the squash belt as so much multiplied Goshen, and as for cheese, a Cheshire. In vineyard, as a State. And, as part of the coming State of New Malaga or West Italy, this vale of Roland assures the majesty of State.

NEW COLONY.

SIERRA MADRE AND SANTA ANITA.

N. C. CARTER, formerly of the Sierra Madre, has bought a large tract of land east and southeast of Sierra Madre Villa, and twelve miles from this city. The location is most desirable, on account of beauty, health and its value as a fruit growing locality. The orange, lemon and lime grow to the greatest perfection; deciduous fruits, all kinds of vegetables as well as cereals, do as well here as in any part of the State. We do not know of any more desirable locality for a home than can be made on this tract of land.

The terms and prices are to be most liberal, and it will only be a short time until the entire tract of 4,000 acres is sold and settled up. In the next issue of the SEMI-TROPIC we will give full details and particulars about this new colony.

Persons desiring information can address N. C. Carter, this city, or call on him at this office, No. 9 Baker Block.

WHAT TO PLANT.—The characteristics of the different grapes as here given. Mission—makes excellent sherry, angelica and port wines, and is a good brandy grape. Malvoise, a port and white wine grape peculiar bearer, not liable to mildew except in very damp ground. Berger, white wine grape, bears heavily, dou't mildew, ripens late. Golden Chasselas and Riesling makes excellent white wine. Zinfandel—a claret grape, Black Hamburg and Rose of Peru—while wine and claret. It may be proper to state here that wine made from the Chasselas, Riesling and Zinfandel grapes attains its greatest perfection when three or four years of age. When it becomes that old it loses no emillion to improve, as does the wine made from other grapes. Even the white wine from the Mission grape becomes excellent when aged, and each succeeding year improves its quality.

A highly respectable young man wants to spend six or eight months in the country, with a respectable farmer's family. References exchanged. Address,

W. S., Postoffice Box 18,
Oakland, Cal.

BRIGHT of the famous Cheap Store is receiving goods direct from the factories and eastern agencies that will open the eyes of all his old customers. Don't buy until you examine his goods and prices. The quality is good, the prices no lower.

THE Kindall mansion on New High St. is a pleasant and convenient hotel for our friends visiting the Citrus Fair.

BRIGHT says he has made an arrangement to put in an immense wholesale stock of goods, separate from the retail department, as soon as he can have another building put on the end of the one now occupied. Will have it complete by 1st of April.

Pork-Packing in the Orange Grove City.

A VALUABLE INDUSTRY IN EAST LOS ANGE-
LES.

THERE has been a notion prevalent that the business of pork-packing cannot be successfully carried on in a climate mild enough to admit of orange culture. Until a very recent period, California imported nearly all her bacon, hams, lard, and other hog products from Chicago and Cincinnati, and few people would have been bold enough ten years ago to predict that Los Angeles Valley could ever compete successfully with these cities, which have so long held a monopoly of this line of trade on the Pacific Coast. But the cold fact is before us that our own city is to-day not only supplying, in a satisfactory manner, the home demand, but also commands the market in Arizona, and shipments are fre-

thirty or forty, soon brought about a desirable change, and now new houses are going up every day, and the old ones rented at high figures. We could detect no offensive odor about the factory, and we believe that the arrangements of the firm are at present so effective that there ought to be no well-founded reasons for complaint.

QUALITY OF THE HOGS MANUFACTURED.

We claim that the bacon and hams cured by this firm are fully equal to the Eastern article and are much cheaper besides. They are free from the heavy, yellow wrapper, weighing three pounds or over, which cannot be eaten, and no *trichina* infests the meats, which cannot be said of the Cincinnati and Chicago article. The bacon furnished by Speedy & Co. is very popular everywhere, and the demand for their lard keeps a hardware establishment busy con-

ing the business of the establishment as far as the iron road extends. It is to be hoped that the city government of Los Angeles will throw no obstacles in the way of this important industry, but will lend a helping hand to this and all similar enterprises tending to build up and enrich our city.

"BETTER pay the cook than the Doctor" is the way the old adage puts it, but unfortunately for the human race not only the doctor but the druggist have become most necessary adjuncts of our civilization. Adjoining the Post Office is located the establishment of Dr. J. B. Frick, Druggist and Apothecary. Owing to the central location and the pure quality of drugs and medicines kept, it has become a favorite purchasing place for those in search of such articles. Prices are very reasonable, and prescriptions carefully compounded.

THE UNIVERSITY OF SOUTHERN CALIFORNIA.

quently made to northern California, and even to Nevada. This desirable state of affairs is due to the enterprise of the

LOS ANGELES PACKING COMPANY,

Who, during the past few years, have built up a trade in the pork packing line which is highly creditable to our city. The establishment of this firm was for a time located on Aliso avenue; but the rapid growth of the business lead to the construction of a large edifice on Hill street, in East Los Angeles, where there is sufficient space to accommodate the wants of a business of such proportions. Up to the time of the erection of the pork packing establishment the quiet and pleasant little suburb of East Los Angeles had been rather depressed, so far as the value of real estate was concerned. Houses were unrented and lots unsalable. But the employés of Messrs. Speedy & Co., numbering some

stantly making cans and caddies. The lard is pure and very white and is put up in an attractive and convenient manner.

WHAT THE BUSINESS OF THE FIRM AMOUNTS TO.

We believe that very few persons in this city have any idea what a large business is carried on by this firm. They have constantly on hand $50,000 worth of goods and at times a stock valued at $100,000, yet they are frequently unable to supply the demand. The firm consists of practical, business men. Mr. Speedy has for several years been a resident of Los Angeles. Mr. Hudsworth comes to us from the upper portion of the State, where he has long been in business. Both are courteous gentlemen, determined to add what they can to the prosperity of Los Angeles. Susan, Wallace & Co., the railroad supply contractors, are also members of the firm, and are extend-

How TO GROW THE ORANGE.—The *Press and Horticulturist*, of Riverside, will commence the publication, early in February, of a series of articles on Citrus Fruit Culture in California, by its editor, L. M. Holt, who was for three years Secretary of the Southern California Horticultural Society, and editor of its publication, the "Horticulturist."

This series will review the whole question from a practical standpoint, and to any one interested in the subject will be worth many times the subscription price of the paper for the year, which is $2.50, or $1.25 for six months in advance. The *Press and Horticulturist* has a well-earned reputation in its particular specialty, and has done and is doing a good work for the State. As back numbers cannot be supplied to any great extent, subscriptions should be forwarded at once.

THE AMERICAN COLONY.

THIS Colony, which is now forming, will occupy 10,000 acres of the Los Cerritos rancho, fronting on San Pedro Bay in Los Angeles county. The location is everything that could be desired for those seeking a home in Southern California. The American Colony tracts possess rich and fertile lands upon which can be grown all the products of the temperate and semi-tropic clime. Good, soft water is abundant, supplied by the river and artesian wells, and the climate is delightful; indeed, it is about as near perfection the year round as it possibly can be.

The Colony lands are subdivided into 5, 10, 20, and 40-acre tracts, which will be sold at low prices and on easy terms as stated in the *Colony Prospectus*.

THE COLONY TOWN PLAT.

The town plat, shown on this page, of the American Colony, contains 350 acres, divided into 140 blocks. The blocks are each 250 feet square. The residence lots are each 62½x125 ft., excepting in the outside tier of blocks where the lots are 125 ft. square. The business lots in the center of the town plat are each 31¼x125 feet.

The streets and avenues will be 80 and 90 ft., and the center avenue 110 ft. wide. The town site is very pleasantly situated on a level mesa or table land fronting on San Pedro Bay, about thirty feet above tidewater, overlooking the harbor and ocean. The view is very beautiful in every direction looking from this place, and the hard, gently sloping sand beach which stretches for miles along the shores of the bay in front of the town site is unsurpassed on the Pacific Coast as a good and safe bathing beach. The water being shallow for a long distance out, with a smooth, sandy bottom, and free from the dreaded under-tow experienced at many places, makes this the very perfection of a place for sea-bathing.

There is everything here that is needed to make it one of the finest seaside summer resorts on the Southern Coast.

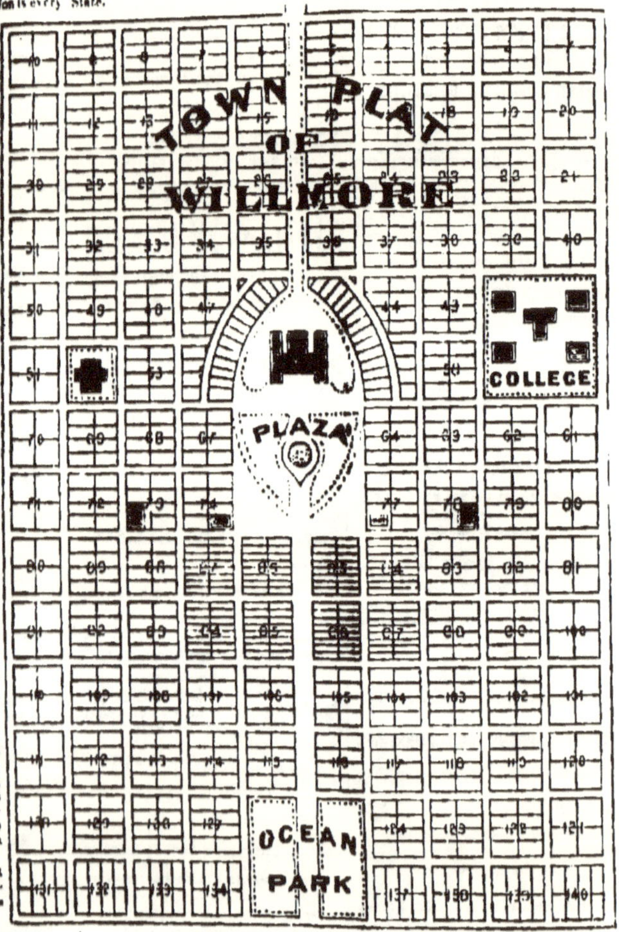

STREETS AND AVENUES.

The streets running east and west are appropriately named after trees that will be planted along each street. The avenues running north and south are named after the States and Territories of the Union.

Both sides of the streets and avenues will be planted with choice shade trees and plants, which, when grown up, will make this one of the most beautiful places in the State.

RESERVED LOTS.

About fifty acres will be reserved in the town of lots and blocks for buildings for the common good, and for a plaza and a park. The lots set apart, as shown on the plat, are for the public school block, 57;

churches in blocks 73 and 76; town hall in block 77; library in block 74; college campus, ten acres; hotel site and villa lots the same, Plaza, ten acres; Ocean Park, ten acres, fronting on the beach. The Park and Plaza will be planted with a variety of shade trees.

AMERICAN COLONY EXCURSION.

The pioneer excursions to the American Colony are now forming in Chicago, St. Louis, Kansas City, and New York. There

TOWN PLAT OF WILLMORE

COLLEGE

PLAZA

OCEAN PARK

will be a series of excursions from the above cities that will leave for Los Angeles each month during the spring, the first of which will start on or about the 10th of March. The route will be over the new Transcontinental Railroad from Kansas City. Arrangements have been made with the several railroad companies for low rates of fare from the above named cities and other points contiguous to the line of roads conveying the excursionists.

The General Eastern Agent of the California Immigration Union, Dr. H. W. Wright, of Kansas, who is now in Chicago, arranging for the above excursions, and all communications addressed to him at the Grand Pacific Hotel will receive prompt attention. He will give full information as regards to expense of trips and also the time of starting of the first excursion.

Parties on the Pacific Coast having friends East who intend coming to Los Angeles, and would like to avail themselves of the advantages of coming out with the above colony excursions, will receive full information of expense, time, etc., upon applying to or addressing

W. E. WILLMORE,
Manager.

Mexican Lime Trees!
Mexican Lime Trees!

NOW IS THE TIME TO MAKE YOUR HEDGES!

About fifty thousand for sale, very low, in lots to suit.

Call on C. WHITE, Attorney-at-law, Room 49 Temple Block.

IT PAYS TO ADVERTISE
IN THE
Semi-Tropic California

Markets.

SEMI-TROPIC CALIFORNIA

DEVOTED TO

AGRICULTURE,

HORTICULTURE,

AND THE DEVELOPMENT OF

SOUTHERN CALIFORNIA

GEORGE RICE, PUBLISHER.

Vol. IV.   No. 4.

LOS ANGELES, CAL.

1881.

MIRROR PRINT, Los Angeles.

—*I AND I*—

SOUTHERN CALIFORNIA HORTICULTURIST.

VOL. IV.   LOS ANGELES, CAL., APRIL, 1881.   No. 4.

HORTICULTURE.

Mr. J. W. Wolfskill has introduced a new variety of rose known as the "Banner" variety, the first blossom of which was exhibited at the Fair. As its name indicates it is beautifully variegated and will prove a valuable addition to our flower gardens.

Prof. A. J. Cooke, of the Michigan University advises farmers who have large apple orchards and are troubled by the ravages of the Codling moth to keep a band of hogs among the trees. The worms apples fall off, are devoured by the hogs, and thus the development of the pest is prevented.

The subject of windbreaks is of so much importance, and at the time alluded to us cannot be spent with more profit than by calling attention to them. We are told that, in the island of Azores, the temperature of which averages higher than Southern California, and from whence England and the United States import the St. Michael orange to the amount of $500,000 annually, and which is esteemed so highly in London market, as to be the leading orange, that walls are built, twenty feet high, of solid stone, to shield the trees from prevailing winds.—Extract from address of Geo. C. Swan at the Riverside Fair.

The best general remedy for scale, is, to keep your trees in vigorous health by thorough fertilization and cultivation. Stir the soil often with the cultivator or hoe; keep down the weeds and grass, and your grove will not require so many remedies to exterminate the insects.—Dr. Geo. W. Davis, of Florida.

Citrus trees require careful pruning to keep the tops open, without exposing naked branches, admitting the sun to free tify the blossoms and gild the fruit, and that the whole tree may be washed clean by descending showers. Clipping the spines promotes fruitfulness and guards against injury to the fruit.—F. Stroegel, at Riverside Fair.

An old fruit grower hands us the following receipt for a superior grafting wax: Take of linseed oil one pint, clear resin six pounds, pure beeswax one pound; melt together slowly, so as not to burn, and stir thoroughly together; pour into a pail of cold water, and when cool enough work white like molasses candy. Make up into rolls six inches long and lay up on a beam in a cool cellar. It will keep perfectly good for many years. When taken out into the garden in a cold day, it will soon be soft enough to handle easily. If the hands are rubbed with a little linseed oil occasionally, the wax will not be troublesome to them.

"The oranges grown in Marysville have a much higher market value than the Los Angeles fruit shipped to this portion of the State. The Marysville orange has a thicker skin, but it is much larger, and more palatable than the fruit from the lower country."

The Sacramento *Record Union* publishes the above nonsense. The few oranges that are grown in sheltered nooks in the Sacramento valley do not differ materially from the Southern California oranges as to size. We presume the *Record Union* formed its opinion of our fruit from a few carloads of worthless windfalls which have been sent from this county to San Francisco during the present season.

A farmer on Lytle creek, San Bernardino County, has an apple tree which bloomed and fruited last winter, the apples being now ripe.

The "Monarch of the West" variety of strawberries has not been superceded by any of the new comers. It still maintains its high character. The fruit is enormous, averaging larger than any variety except the "Sharpless"; nor does it rapidly dwindle in size, as do most kinds, the latter part of the season. Like the "Downing," it does well in nearly all sections. Its flavor is delicious, and it has a most delightful aroma. With the "Downing" it should have a place in every home garden. It is soft for long carriage, and too pale for those markets that demand a hard, high colored berry without regard to flavor.

Mr. Cram, of San Bernardino, will have this year from 100 trees, nearly 100,000 oranges.

ORANGE CULTURE IN FLORIDA.

A correspondent in Florida writing to the Hartford *Times* says in regard to the orange culture of the year:

Many who were almost in dark despair in the spring of 1879 are now in ecstacies of joy over the situation, and fully believe that the time is near at hand when they will have a competence, if not a fortune, from the income from their groves. Among the number is our friend Kit Burnham, who came here from your city four years ago last spring. His means were limited, but he bought some scrubby trees at a large price and set them out, by good management and economy, he has contrived to support his family and keep his trees growing, and added a few to his grove each year. It is a pleasure (though a little humiliating) to acknowledge that he has, un-

der less favorable circumstances, produced the best growth of trees and succeeded in getting the first oranges. He is proud of his success, as he may well be, when he looks out on the golden fruit. You would be surprised to see how the young groves have come out since you were here. The business is now looked upon as a success beyond peradventure, and a big success at that. There are plenty of groves that will yield a net profit of $1,000 per acre this season, and some much more.

James A. Harris stands at the head of the list of orange growers in the State. Some nine or ten years ago he bought a great many wild orange trees. He cut down the large timber and budded the trees without removing them, and they were bearing in three years. Last year he sold his crop for $5,000, and last week he bargained the present crop for the snug sum of $10,000, a good turn for an investment of a few hundred dollars in ten years. This, of course, is an exceptional case, but there is no doubt as to the orange culture being a profitable business.

RIVERSIDE.

The Citrus Fair at Riverside, of which mention is made in another column, was in every respect a grand success. We regret that the people of that flourishing colony were not better represented at our Los Angeles fair, but what specimens were sent compared very favorably with any from other fruit-growing sections.

The Riverside settlement is making astonishing strides forward on the road of prosperity and the people of Los Angeles can feel nothing but the best feelings towards it. The interests of San Bernardino and Los Angeles counties are almost identical, and if we work together the future growth of Southern California will be materially assisted. We admire the energy and enterprise of our neighboring colonists, and trust their present pleasant prosperity may never be blighted.

The great industry of Riverside at present is raisin making, and the quality of the fruit has gained for it a high reputation throughout the United States. The oranges are free from smut, large and juicy, and the lemons and limes have an equally good reputation. The water supply is abundant and the plain for eight miles is in a high state of cultivation.

SEMI-TROPIC
CALIFORNIA,
— AN —
ILLUSTRATED MONTHLY.

Devoted to Agriculture, Horticulture, and the Development of Southern California.

Terms: $1.50 per Annum, in Advance.

Office, Rooms 9 & 10, Baker Block.

Address, - - GEO. RICE, Los Angeles, Cal.

GEORGE RICE, - Editor and Prop'r.

OFFICIAL PAPER
— OF THE —

Southern California Horticultural Soc'y.

OFFICE, ROOM No. 9, BAKER BLOCK.

The annual meeting of the members of the Horticultural Society is called for 11 o'clock A. M., Saturday, April 9th, at the Pavilion. Important business will come before the meeting, besides the election of officers and directors for the ensuing year. It is to be hoped that a full attendance will be present.

The present standing and management of the Society's affairs are in good condition, and if the membership will come out and make proper arrangements for the old indebtedness, the Horticultural Society will be one of the institutions of Southern California of which every citizen will be proud.

Our new title page is certainly suggestive of a semi-tropical country, is very handsome, and is a credit to the designers and engravers. The Moss Engraving Company, New York, take some credit in presenting our readers with so bright and handsome a face, and assures them that steady improvement is our aim. We hope to make the Semi-Tropic second to none in the United States, as a journal devoted to agriculture and horticulture, as it is now the handsomest gotten-up magazine of its kind in the country, and goes to our Eastern friends as a proof of the progress and advantages of Southern California.

The entry list of the Citrus Fair has been published in the local press, and we omit them as our space is limited. We, however, take this occasion to thank all exhibitors for the interest they took in making the Fair a grand success, and hope they will be encouraged to help us in our great Horticultural Fair next Fall.

Wells, Fargo & Co., with their accustomed liberality, which has gained for that corporation the respect and gratitude of shippers in Southern California for many years past, transported, free of charge, at the close of the Citrus Fair, one hundred boxes of fruit to the East, where it will be placed where it can do our section the most good. The Express Company deserves the thanks of every person engaged in horticultural pursuits for its latest generous act, by which our most important industry is benefitted.

What others have said in praise of the Citrus Fair would fill a large octavo volume. The press throughout the State has said the kindest words about our citrus exposition; and it is the unanimous sentiment that the like was never before witnessed in the United States. The Citrus Fair was a grand success, so far as the exhibit itself goes; financially it has fully met the expectation of the management, having paid a liberal premium list, all expenses and left a small balance in the treasury.

CITRUS FAIR FINANCES.

Total receipts from all sources..	$914 10
Expenses—Premiums.....	$414 00
Repairs on Pavilion.....	85 50
Music.....................	235 00
Gas.......................	60 00
Seats.....................	18 00
Freight and express......	21 40
Printing and advertising..	37 60
Help......................	134 00
	$903 50
Balance in treasury ...	$ 5 60

RESOLUTION OF THANKS.

At the close of the Citrus Fair, an informal meeting was held by the leading exhibitors, and among other subjects considered the following resolution was unanimously adopted.

Resolved, That the success of the Los Angeles County Citrus Fair, which has far exceeded our most sanguine expectations, is largely due to the energy, tact, and admirable business management of Mr. Geo. Rice, and that we hereby tender to him our heartfelt acknowledgement for his uniform courtesy to the exhibitors, and for the valuable service he has rendered in so amply illustrating the industrial capacities and achievements of this section of the state.

The people of Anaheim have organized a Viticultural Society, with a view of gaining mutual information on horticultural and viticultural topics and attending to other matters that may come within the province of such a society. Mr. Theo. Reiser has been elected Chairman and B. Melrose, editor of the *Gazette,* Secretary. Success to the new Society.

Land in the vicinity of Sierra Madre Villa is steadily increasing in value. Many purchases of unimproved lands have recently been consummated and improvements are constantly being made.

FAILURE OF FLORIDA ORANGES.

S. F. BULLETIN.

The telegraph reports that the orange groves of Florida have suffered much by recent severe cold. From the accounts given, it is evident that the citrus region of California has never, even in the worst seasons, experienced anything a tenth part as bad. It were the height of cruelty to rejoice over the sad loss of the Florida orange growers, and they will doubtless receive the sympathies of the orange-growers of this State. Nevertheless it is a plain duty to remark that the raisers of citrus fruits in California need not go elsewhere to better their prospects. Neither Australia, nor Italy, nor famed Florida, nor Brazil, can produce a finer orange than the best budded groves of our realm. Protected as the orange districts of this State are by mountain ranges, and separated one from another, there is little prospect that either stress of weather or disease will ever shorten the whole crop. Isolated failures may occur here and there, but it may truthfully be said that the orange crop of California in five years from now will astonish our own citizens. Few men have any conception of the great number of trees not yet in bearing which the semi-tropic counties of California can display.

One of the most trying positions in the Citrus Fair was that of the individual upon whom was imposed the duty of securing men to serve on the several committees appointed to test fruits. Particularly was this the case in the matter of the exhibits of lemons and limes. No one seemed to relish that banquet and it was remarkable how many of our horticulturists had pressing engagements elsewhere, and when at last a man was secured, before the other two could be captured, he had escaped. The only successful expedient was found to corral the unwilling members of the lime committee, as fast as they were found, to the tasting room and, placing a guard over them, complete the search for the remaining truants. Apropos to this we clip the following extract from the report of the Committee on Smelling Oranges at the Riverside Fair:

"Your Committee appointed upon class No. 8 to determine which was the best and second best smelling oranges, put the dissecting knife in the Doctor's hands with strong advice to lance lightly and carefully and be sure and make us have our regular turn. We began, nibbling from our committee, the expansiveness of our friend Hixson, as well as many others who probably absented themselves for fear of the citrus lunch.

"After carefully comparing, contrasting, tasting, hocking, trying, weighing, gaping, wimbering, pandering, testing, gasping, putting our faces into all sorts of expressions, being governed by the case before us, the result was reached, and No. 13 we agreed to consider as the best orange before us, and No. 2 the second best."

Citrus Fair Awards.

PREMIUMS AWARDED AT THE CITRUS FAIR, MARCH 14-19, 1881.

REPORT OF COMMITTEE ON LARGEST AND FINEST DISPLAY.

Your Committee on Largest and Finest Display beg leave to submit the following report:

There were five entries for the $100 premium, as follows: Pasadena, National Ranch Grange, San Gabriel, H. J. Crow, Verdugo Ranch, and Woodhead & Gay, dealers.

The Pasadena exhibit was by far the largest display in the Pavilion, and the fruit was very fine. It consisted of eleven varieties of oranges, four varieties of lemons, limes, citron, raisins, guavas, pears and apples. The mammoth tent of 111 boxes of oranges and lemons, finely packed in boxes ready for shipment to market, was very massive and attracted universal attention. The fruit was very clean and of a fine quality and was tastefully arranged, and the tables were beautifully decorated with flowers.

The National Ranch Grange exhibit was not so large in quantity of fruit, but it contained the most varieties, to-wit: Twenty-one varieties of oranges, seven varieties of lemons, besides the seedlings, also olives, raisins, apples, limes, dried figs and guavas. The fruit was very superior in quality, being clean, very ripe and fine textured in general appearance.

San Gabriel exhibited more artistic taste in arranging its display than any other locality. The pagoda, the sides, roof and spire of which were covered with oranges and lemons, was a design happily conceived and artistically executed.

H. J. Crow made the finest display as an individual, and this exhibit is deserving of special mention, by virtue of the quality of the fruit and the tasty manner in which it was arranged.

The exhibits of Woodhead & Gay was very superior. The fruit was grown at Riverside, San Bernardino, San Gabriel, Orange, Pasadena, Los Angeles and other localities, some samples of oranges coming from Sonora, Mexico. The display represents no locality in particular, but is very creditable as a collection of fine citrus and other fruits.

Your Committee found great difficulty in arriving at its conclusions; some exhibits excelling in one point and others in other points, while all were deserving of credit.

We therefore recommend that the one hundred dollar premium be divided into three parts, and that it be awarded as follows:

First Premium, $50, to Pasadena.

Second Premium, $35, to National Ranch Grange.

Third Premium, $15, to San Gabriel.

The Committee also recommend that a silver medal be awarded to H. J. Crow for the best exhibit by a single individual, and also a silver medal to Woodhead & Gay for a very fine display as dealers.

Respectfully submitted,
N. W. BLANCHARD,
C. F. LOOP,
M. ERB,
J. M. ASHER,
L. M. HOLT.

REPORT OF COMMITTEE ON BUDDED FRUIT.

GEO. RICE, Secretary Board of Directors:

Your Committee on Budded Fruit beg leave to report that, after four very severe tests, in which the oranges were so placed before us that the name of the grower was not known to any of the Committee, we find little, if any, difference between No. 1 specimen, Cover and McCoy, Riverside, Cal., and No. 2 specimen, J. R. Dobbins, San Gabriel, Cal., both being Washington Navel, budded from the same stock. The specimens placed before us led us to award the First Premium to No. 1, Cover & McCoy, Riverside, Cal., while we felt that we might be doing the San Gabriel oranges an injustice, as we consider the difference to be only in time the fruit has been picked. We therefore recommend that Mr. J. R. Dobbins, of San Gabriel, be awarded a special premium of five dollars ($5) for the second best variety of budded fruit.

J. M. ASHER,
S. K. SEWALL,
W. T. CLAPP,
C. H. RICHARDSON,
FRED K. STEPHENS.

DEPARTMENT I, CLASS 2. BUDDED ORANGES.

Best one variety, Cover & McCoy, Riverside	$5 00
Best two varieties, W. T. Clapp, Pasadena	7 00
Best four varieties, H. Muller, San Diego	10 00
Best six varieties, Muller Bros., Pasadena	15 00

CLASS 3, SEEDLING ORANGES.

1st best, D. Gibbons, Plano	
2d best, H. M. Higgins, San Diego	
3d best, T. W. Cover, Riverside	
4th best, Cover & McCoy, Riverside	
5th best, L. Barnes, Duarte	

CLASS 4, SWEETSTANDS.

Best oranges, Cover & McCoy	$5 00
Best cluster of oranges, A. B. Clark	10 00

CLASS 5, LEMONS.

Best one variety, H. J. Holmes, Riverside	$5 00
Best two varieties, G. B. Adams, Pasadena	7 00
Best four varieties, J. W. Wolfskill, Los Angeles	10 00

CLASS 7, CITRONS.

Best exhibit, W. T. Clapp, Pasadena	$3 00
Best preserved citron (home made) S. Richardson	3 00
Best preserved citron (factory) James, Farmer & Co., San Francisco	Silver Medal

DEP'T 2, CLASS 1, RAISINS.

See Report of Committee in another part of this paper.

Best and largest display, Thos. F. Croft, Pasadena	$25 00
Best box, McPherson Bros., Orange	10 00
" quarter-box, Peter Ainsworth, Orange	5 00

CLASS 2, CANNED FRUITS.

Best peaches (factory) Jos. Wallace & Co., Pasadena	Diploma
Best apricots (factory) Jos. Wallace & Co., Pasadena	"
Best apricots (home made) Mrs. M. Rosenbaum, Pasadena	1 00

CLASS 3, MISCELLANEOUS.

Best dried figs, Geo. C. Swan, San Diego	$5 00
Best pomegranates, N. C. Carter, San Gabriel	1 00
Best strawberries, David Townsend, Pasadena	4 00
Best Tomatoes, Wm. S. Young, Duarte	4 00

CLASS 4, FLOWERS.

Best and finest display, Mrs. R. Williams	$10 00

GRAND DISPLAY.

Woodhead & Gay, the enterprising fruit dealers of this city, made one of the largest and finest displays last fall at the Horticultural Fair, and at our Citrus Fair, for which they deserve the gratitude of every fruit grower in Southern California.

This firm was awarded the Society's silver medal (the highest award the Society has ever made), for the largest and finest display of fruit—as dealers. The exhibit made by Messrs. Woodhead & Gay was gathered together by them at great expense from every section of the State, making within itself a grand exposition for comparison, of the progress of the different fruit-growing sections of our country. Their exhibitions are instructive, entertaining, and worthy the close investigation and study they have received, and will continue to receive in the future. An exposition without their exhibit would be, as Mrs. Carr says in an article to the press: "The play of Hamlet with Hamlet left out."

We know the desire of this firm is to stimulate the farmer, and fruit grower too, to cultivation of the choicest and best varieties of fruits. We publicly, and in behalf of the farmers of Southern California, express to Messrs. Woodhead & Gay, our thanks and appreciation of the grand work they have done, and we hope they will continue to do for our fruit growing interests.

Great Citrus Fair.

THE GREAT CITRUS FAIR

A GRAND SHOWING FOR SOUTHERN CALIFORNIA.

THE FINEST DISPLAY OF CITRUS FRUITS EVER MADE IN THE UNITED STATES.

It is now universally admitted that the climate and soil of Southern California is admirably adapted to the culture of citrus fruits, and that fruit growing in general will be the foundation upon which all of our other industries must depend. The water power and fuel incident to extensive manufacturing enterprises is lacking in our State, and the cheap labor of the East is a still greater bar, at present at least, to such development. Grain growing at best, in all portions of the Union, is but an uncertain occupation, and when the California system of cropping is closely followed, wears out the land and renders it unfit for the support of a dense population. In one dry season the profits of years may be swept away, or the unfavorable state of the European market causes the crop to fail to pay the cost of harvesting. Grain growing, bee culture, stock raising, and manufacturing will continue to be leading industries of Southern California, but we claim that horticulture must hereafter take precedence.

Bearing in mind the fact that thousands of citrus trees have come into bearing the present season, and believing that the people of Southern California, and the hundreds of Eastern visitors who are daily arriving on our coast, would like to inspect, in one grand exposition, our progress in semi-tropical fruit culture, the Horticultural Society, immediately after the Fair last October, decided to hold a

CITRUS FAIR

In March which should do justice to our section, enable our several fruit growing localities to inspect each other's progress, and, if possible, induce a desirable class of people to cast their lot with us.

The editor of the SEMI-TROPIC, the Secretary of the society, on the first of the year, took active measures to interest our fruit growers in the project, and with such success that organizations were perfected in most settlements of this county, having for their object a good representation at the Fair.

THE WORK INVOLVED.

Few people have any idea of the work which the managers of an exposition which aimed to really represent the horticultural interests of a great section like Southern California had upon its hands. The expense connected with such an undertaking is also by no means trifling, and glory is too often the only reward which is returned for months of hard labor and large expenditure of coin. The managers, however, desire to thank the exhibitors for their hearty co-operation, both as regards their time and other assistance which was cheerfully given.

THE BENEFITS OF THIS FAIR

Will, we believe, be felt for many years throughout Southern California. The merchants of San Francisco, Chicago, St. Louis, Portland, Oregon, and other points from the North and East, and there were quite a number present, expressed themselves as astonished and delighted at the magnificent exhibit made from what they had heard contemptuously alluded to as the "cow counties." What view the merchants of Los Angeles took of the matter we are not informed, as they did not generally attend, giving as a reason the great rush of business.

THE FORMAL OPENING

Of the Fair took place on Tuesday at 8:30 P. M. The Pacific Press Association was present in a body, and the members were cordially welcomed by the officers of the Association.

The reception address was delivered by President Shorb, who said:

Ladies and Gentlemen of the Press Association: I can well imagine the entire satisfaction of the Omniscient when the eagle was established and dismissed upon his flight, destined one day to become the emblem of that country and people whose institutions and laws were to be so associate with, and to enforce those natural rights and conditions which his love for man ordained and intended him to enjoy.

To the eagle was given a two-fold emblematical mission—the entire bird to represent a nation, and its wing feathers that rise of men who have done more in the great work of freedom, civilization, progress and reform than all the sciences, the steam engine and electric telegraph combined.

To the eagle the wing feather serves only the purpose of raising him to that elevation from which he can more easily observe the movements of his victims, or as to procure spoil and destroy them, while to you, ladies and gentlemen of the press, it is emblematical of that potent instrument which is your hands has served to raise millions of human beings from slavery, degradation, to advance and want to that position of freedom, intelligence and happiness whence self-government follows as a natural consequence.

Recognizing the fact that to all highly civilized communities the press is as much a part and necessary as the piston rod is to the steam engine, and realizing all your protection has done for humanity, our retaining country and State, Southern California extends to you the hand of welcome and friendliness, and trusts that the remembrance of the Citrus Fair at Los Angeles may be a pleasant one to you all, and like the trees from which this exhibition spring, remain ever green in your memories.

MR. TUFTEN'S RESPONSE.

Mr. Tupper, of Fresno, representing the *Pacific Churchman* responded. He eloquently thanked the people of Southern California for the magnificent welcome extended to the Press Association. He said that he had heard that Southern California was a land flowing with milk and honey, but better than all this truth, he and the visiting members of the press had found it a land flowing with hospitality. That the Press Association's visit to Southern California had been one ovation more cordial than which had never attended the journeys even of General Grant. On behalf of the ladies and gentlemen of the Press Association he rendered heart-felt thanks to the ladies and gentlemen of Southern California for their hospitalities, which had far exceeded expectations and other experiences.

MR. SHINN'S ADDRESS.

Mr. Shinn, of the *San Francisco Bulletin*, in response to calls, came forward and stated that the week's visit to Southern California was full of happiness pressed down and running over. Always in full sympathy with Southern California, he never, before his visit, fully knew how to help Southern California. In time, this land of snow-clad peaks and happy vales, would become the home of art, song, music and sculpture. That the many plants flourishing here would learn to thrive without irrigation. That hospitalities had flowed to the Press Association not born in expectation of favor, and in thoughts of us as newspaper men, but in thoughts of us as fellow citizens.

In answer to calls Scipio Craig came upon the stage, whom President Shorb introduced, adding that "you all know Scipio Craig, or ought to." Among the numerous good points made by Mr. Craig none was more heartily received than his prediction that the Press Association had but commenced visiting Southern California; that their future visits would be with such suggested numbers that instead of being, as on the present visit, taken by storm by the hospitable people here, the multitude of the Press Association would take Southern California by storm.

The remarks of all the speakers were received with hearty applause, and the visitors, after an examination of the exhibits, left expressing themselves as highly pleased with the display.

In accompanying articles will be found as minute a description of the exhibits made as our columns will allow. We trust they will prove valuable to our readers who desire to preserve a record of the proceedings of this our first Citrus Fair.

It may be proper here to state that the receipts of the Fair were not as large as had been anticipated by the management. There was no desire or even expectation of making money out of the exhibition, but funds are nevertheless needed to carry on the work of the Society. If, however, the real purpose of building up the material interests of Southern California and assisting our horticulturists in their present era of experiment has in any way been carried out, then have weeks of unremitting toil not been spent in vain. We are glad to state, however, that enough money was taken in to pay all expenses and have a very small amount in the treasury.

The total value of England's imports for 1880 was £409,000,000, an increase of about £40,000,000 over 1879. Living animals were imported to the value of £10,242,363. The number of eggs imported was 747,412,440, worth £3,441,000.

RIVERSIDE CITRUS FAIR.

A SUCCESSFUL EXHIBITION BY THE YOUNG COLONY.

The Citrus Fair held at Riverside the week preceding that held by the Southern California Horticultural Society, was a great success and gave general satisfaction to all visitors. The display was immense, and the hall in which the Fair was held, is by far too small for another such exhibition.

All varieties of the citrus family were well represented, as well as many fruits not of that family, but in season in our semi-tropical climate.

The literary exercises were very interesting, many papers being read on horticultural topics which we shall take pleasure in commenting upon hereafter.

The hospitable people of the settlement gave a hearty welcome to strangers, who, without exception, so far as we can learn, left with pleasant impressions of the thriving colony.

Some of the principal awards were as follows:

Best display of citrus fruits grown by one exhibitor in the counties of San Diego, Los Angeles, Ventura and Santa Barbara, $25.

Premium awarded to S. Richardson, San Gabriel.

Best display of citrus fruits grown by one exhibitor in the counties north of Los Angeles and Santa Barbara, $25.

Premium divided between C. Carrigar Sacramento Co., and John Wolfskill, Solano County.

Best display of citrus fruits grown by one exhibitor in the county of San Bernardino, $25.

Premium awarded to G. W. Garcelon.

Best display of one variety of budded fruit.

First premium ($5), awarded to Cover & McCoy, Riverside.

Second premium ($3), to Edwin Hart.

Best one variety of seedling orange.

First premium awarded to A. J. Twogood.

Second premium awarded to D. C. Twogood.

Best variety of budded orange.

First premium awarded to T. W. Cover on Washington Navel.

Second premium awarded to Messrs. Caldwell and P. D. Cover on St. Michael Paper Rind.

Best seedling orange.

First premium awarded to Mrs. A. L. Eastman.

Second premium to T. W. Cover.

Best display of limes.

First premium awarded to J. W. Wolfskill.

Second premium awarded to P. W. Cover.

Best box of raisins.

First premium awarded to H. L. R. Stiles.

Third premium awarded to E. Caldwell.

A premium of $15 was awarded to Alex Lander Crow for his exhibit of beneficial and injurious insects.

SOUTHERN CALIFORNIA.

GOOD PROSPECT FOR BARLEY.

We have now assurances that the Southern overland railroad will give us grain rates which will enable us to ship all our best barley to Eastern breweries. Some of our commission men have already made large shipments to St. Louis, and if the rates are brought down to $20 per ton to to that point, as has been semi-officially promised, every pound of our best barley will be forwarded to the East for brewing purposes. Large orders are now here for Denver, St. Louis and other Western cities. The effect of finding a profitable market for our best barley will be to materially enhance the value of that which is only good for feed, so that our farmers may confidently look forward to returns from their barley crops such as have not been realized since the days of teams and the Cerro Gordo trade.— L. A. Express.

A box factory is to be erected at Colton, to accommodate the fruit-growers of San Bernardino valley and Riverside.

There is a great demand for tenement houses at Riverside.

According to the Colton Semi-Tropic lumber cannot be furnished fast enough to satisfy persons about to build in San Bernardino Valley.

We understand that the wool clip this year is extraordinarily heavy, and the sheep men are correspondingly happy. Large quantities are coming into the depot for shipment to San Francisco, and it is said to be of extra quality. The first shipments were made this week—twenty bales having been received Wednesday, and sixty on Thursday. Messrs. Rawson, Lewis and Arrivaca are the shippers.—Santa Ana Herald.

PAVILION PARAGRAPHS.

Woodhead & Gay made an elaborate display of budded and seedling oranges from all portions of Southern California, Mexican and California limes, Sicily, Genoa, Lisbon and Eureka lemons, preserved citrons, preserved bitter orange and lemon peel, Riverside raisins, etc. The firm was awarded a diploma for the best display by dealers.

B. J. Crow, of the Verdugo ranch, was awarded first premium for the largest and best display made by an individual. His exhibit consisted of budded and seedling oranges, lemons, limes, apples and pears.

Thos. A. Garey had charge of a very attractive table of fruits from his place, called Sunnyside Plateau, near San Gabriel. No irrigation of the trees has been the rule for the past two years and the clean, bright fruit shows that it came from a place well adapted to its culture.

AGRICULTURE.

Pleuro-pneumonia is raging among the cattle in the Eastern States.

Nebraska suffered severely from protracted droughts last year.

Cows should have access to water at all times, especially cows that give milk. They want to drink often and return to their feed. The best stable, and one in which stock do the best, is one where water is always running in troughs before the cattle. Thus managed, cows may be kept up to a full flow of milk either winter or summer.

Please tell your butter making readers that the best butter makers in our vicinity tell me that get the highest price for their butter, think very highly of cotton-seed meal for feed, in connection with grain. We prefer to use it about as follows: One quart of cotton-seed meal, two of Indian meal, and four of wheat bran as a day's ration for an average cow.

Do not plant any tree deep—cut off top roots and do all you can to encourage surface fibres. Surface manuring is the best way of doing this after the tree is planted. Do not allow anything to grow vigorously around your trees the first year of planting, nor allow the soil to become hard or dry. Let trees branch low and prune a little at transplanting.—Gardener's Monthly.

If one expects to make strawberry culture a success, and at the same time a paying business, seven conditions are essential and necessary:

1   Right kind of soil.
2   Proper preparation of the same.
3   Strong and vigorous plants.
4   Clean and thorough cultivation.
5   Winter protection.
6   Summer packing.
7   Careful picking and handling.

A good authority gives the following statement as the quantity of seed necessary to sow an acre of land:

Wheat, broadcast from a bushel and three pecks to two bushels; a bushel and a half is enough sown in drills.

Barley, two bushels and a half, broadcast; two bushels in drill.

Buckwheat, one bushel.

Corn, in hill, a gallon and a half.

Sorghum, from one to three quarts.

Timothy grass, sown in fall, to be followed by clover in spring, from one and a half to two gallons.

Red clover, to be sown in spring on timothy, one and a half or two gallons. Sown by itself, double the above quantity.

German millet, from three pecks to a bushel.

Red top grass, one and a half to two bushels. A bushel is fourteen pounds by weight.

Kentucky blue grass, same as red top.

Irish potatoes, seven to ten bushels.

Turnips and rutabagas, one pound. (To guard against insects, two pounds would be better.)

Biography.

L. J. ROSE.

THE FOUNDER AND OWNER OF SUNNY SLOPE

THE subject of this sketch was born in Bavaria, May, 1827. When he was twelve years old his father and family emigrated to New Orleans, where his father engaged in the mercantile business. After three years they removed to Monroe county, Illinois, where the young man having received a fair German education, clerked in his father's store, attended public school and finished his education at Shurtleff College, Alton, Illinois.

At twenty-one he became a merchant on his own account, as a member of the firm of Rose & Dunlap, in Quincy, Illinois. At the end of another term of three years the firm removed to Keosauqua, Iowa, where they remained in business seven years. While here Mr. Rose secured what he says is "fully one-half the factor of his success," his faithful, sensible wife. He also bought a farm and indulged, so far as the vicissitudes of the climate would allow, his passionate fondness for cultivating flowers and fruits of all kinds, especially the rare and beautiful varieties.

But only the very hardiest varieties could withstand those fearful winter storms, the beautiful flowering plants and tender ornamental shrubs succumbed entirely to the cold or were dwarfed and ruined. Summer brought chills and fever (the "fever'n ager" of the South), winter gave lung and winter fevers, and life became a constant experience of "hope deferred."

Finally, in 1858, it was decided on account of failing health to remove to California, and from that time the present proprietor of the largest vineyard in the world has been making history at a rapid rate.

This being the year of the Mormon war, it was deemed impossible to proceed via Salt Lake, and after much deliberation and correspondence it was determined to try the 36th parallel route. So, accompanied by his family, and having nineteen men employed to bring through the finest lot of thoroughbred and graded horses and cattle that had ever started overland to California, he set out on the long and toilsome journey.

They were joined enroute by several families from Missouri and Iowa, so that when they reached Albuquerque their party numbered 50 persons, 30 of whom were men. At this place they secured a guide, and having received many expressions of good will and kindness from the citizens of the town, they resumed their journey over a new and untried road through the wilderness.

Passing through several Indian villages, whose inhabitants were always peaceful, friendly, and sometimes agriculturally employed, their days were filled with the usual incidents of wagon travel, and their evenings were brightened by the ruddy glow of the camp fire, and lightened with song and story. Game was abundant, and the hunt afforded as much satisfaction as the stew.

This rather enthusiastic gentleman, even after the lapse of all these years, waxes eloquent when relating part of his journey, and betrays the honest appreciation and intense love of nature and nature's works, which influenced his choice of occupation for life, and does him infinite credit.

Nearer the Colorado, however, the country became more dry and hot, grass was more stunted, Indians began to prowl around and steal stock; some of the men straggling behind were fired at, and one dangerously wounded. Coming difficulties began to cast their shadows before, and when at last the banks of the Colorado were reached, it was with a feeling that it had been accomplished at great peril.

L. J. Rose

But just "beyond the Alps lieth Italy," and looking across the shining river they saw the Sierras of their pilgrimage, the Golden State, and thought their goal would soon be reached. They were almost worn out with heat and thirst, many of the cattle having died, and some of the men being crazy for the want of water. In this demoralized condition the Indians visiting them found the camp completely at their mercy, and the poor wayworn travelers were only too glad that their visitors contented themselves for that time with killing and roasting the fine cattle, and making a feast.

Rafts must now be constructed to convey the emigrants across the river, this being an entirely new route, and this would probably occupy several days' time.

Next day some measures for defense were taken by the somewhat refreshed party, and the visiting Indians, though treated well and presented by Mr. Rose with beads, clothing, blankets, etc., brought by him for that purpose, were held somewhat in check.

They then offered to assist the party in crossing the river, but next morning they did not make their appearance. About noon that day they appeared with a war whoop, and a fight began that lasted till night. One entire family was murdered, and Mr. Brown, Mr. Rose's overseer, killed, besides several men wounded; and the loss of stock was almost total.

Disheartened, the party now took one wagon and ambulance, with two horses, and started at nightfall back over the desolate and perilous road they had hoped never to travel again, leaving their stores and supplies in seven wagons standing on the river bank at the disposal of the Indians. Without a hope of life, but determined to die game, they made their slow way through deep ravines and cañons, where every cactus or shrub was magnified into an Indian, and every noise into an ambush. The yells of the savages could be heard as they discovered the treasures of the abandoned wagons, or wailed over their dead. Late on the succeeding day they met a party who had been traveling in their rear. They all returned together to Albuquerque — ragged, barefoot, thoroughly discouraged, and only surprised that they were still alive.

They were received with open arms by the citizens and every assistance rendered to make them comfortable, and the leader of this disastrous expedition says he never spent so happy and restful three months' time as those following their arrival; though they lived in an adobe, with dirt floor, no chairs or beds, but with hearts full of thanks for life and health.

They were not idle months, however, for soon Mr. Rose was enabled by his own exertions and the additional help of his friend, Judge O'Melveny, to buy the Hotel in Santa Fe, known as the Fonda, being the principal hotel in the Territory. His success in this enterprise, which, when he took control was a losing one, was so gratifying that at the end of two years he felt justified in again turning his face toward California. This time the journey was a well won road with strong teams and light loads, proved a pleasure trip, and on the 29th of November 1860 the party reached El Monte. Here again Mr. Rose warms up with his subject in describing the beautiful hills and valleys clothed with early verdure as he rode among them for the first time in the warm red light of the setting sun. He had intended to settle near the Bay; but after a thorough inspection of the country, and an extended visit north to Santa Clara and Sacramento he returned to San Gabriel and cast his lot here, and has never had cause to regret his choice. He has been one of the leading spirits in the development and advancement of his particular locality, and has been called to a prominent place in the horticultural and viticultural interests of the State.

He is a member of the State Agricultural Society, being a director of that Board. He is also one of the Viticultural Commissioners of the State, and contributed largely to the amount of valuable information contained in the Annual Report of that Commission.

Through his instrumentality a bill has been prepared, endorsed by the legislature of the state, and petitions signed recommending Congress to pass a law "To protect the manufacturers of pure grape brandies, by prohibiting its mixture or adulteration by the wholesale dealer; requiring the packages to be sold by the wholesale dealer as they are delivered from the distillery, except under certain specified conditions."

Mr. Rose has been favorably and prominently mentioned as a candidate for Congress, and had he been nominated, it is generally believed, would have been elected by a large majority, irrespective of party.

We believe that the people of Southern California will, at the next election, lay aside politics for the time, and unite on a candidate who is thoroughly identified with the interests of the district, and is a practical, competent, honest man. Mr. Rose is authority on all subjects upon which he expresses an opinion, for his judgments are formed only after thorough investigation and experiment.

No man in the State has given more valuable instruction to the vineyardist, and none has done more to stimulate improvement and growth in this profitable industry of our state than L. J. Rose.

SAN FERNANDO.

San Fernando is known as a wheat and honey country; but few people are aware that it is well adapted to fruits and early vegetables. The foothills bordering the valley for eight or ten miles, have a soft, rich, easily-worked soil, on which fruits and vegetables mature very early, and thrive with but little water. A poor man can secure one hundred acres of the choicest land almost anywhere along these hills for about one-twentieth the cost of lands in such settlements as Pasadena and River side. The land must be cleared and water developed, but skill and industry will provide a home far cheaper than in our valleys. Some of the earliest fruit and vegetables come to market from the foothills of the San Fernando Valley.

The bee men expect a full crop of honey, if there are no hot, blasting winds later in the season.

SANTA BARBARA.

Santa Barbara, one of the most attractive and delightful towns in the world, to those who enjoy a balmy climate and the advantages of good society, is located on the coast 300 miles south of San Francisco, and 110 miles northwest of Los Angeles. The scenery in the vicinity of the town is very picturesque. The city itself is shut off from cold and disagreeable winds by a high range of mountains, and invalids find the mild, even atmosphere very beneficial, especially in pulmonary diseases. The thermometer averages about 60 degrees Fahrenheit the year round; it seldom reaches 80 degrees even in the hottest weather of summer, and the nights are always cool and comfortable.

The town boasts of one of the best hotels in the State, outside of San Francisco. The Arlington has a large list of regular Eastern visitors who pass their winters in Santa Barbara, and find comfort in the well appointed management of this excellent hotel. There is a fine college building with a large corps of teachers a free library and reading room, several clubs devoted to gentlemanly sports, hot sulphur springs in the vicinity of the town, convenient for invalids suffering from pulmonary diseases, good public schools and churches.

Carpenteria, a settlement bordering the ocean a few miles south of the town, is the real fruit belt of Santa Barbara county. Here all varieties of semi-tropical fruits are grown to perfection, as well as deciduous fruits and vegetables.

Montecito is also a delightful settlement, with unrivalled climate and scenery.

Lompoc is a temperance colony in the northern portion of the county, having about one hundred and fifty families who are making comfortable homes for themselves in a fertile and easily cultivated valley.

The Santa Barbara exhibit at the Citrus Fair occupied very nearly the center of the Pavilion, and was in charge of Mr. Kels Esq., Vice-President of the Santa Barbara Horticultural Society, and Mrs. N. W. Winton, Secretary, whose letters occasionally appear in the SEMI-TROPIC CALIFORNIA. Both as a fruit and floral display it was a success, and deserves a more extended notice than our space will permit.

Col. Hollister, the proprietor of the well known and beautiful ranch which he has named Glen Annie, had a large display of fruits and nuts. Other exhibitors were Messrs. Cooper, Heath, Sutton, Stone, Sullivan, Sexton, Sheffield, Rigby, Bond, Dinsmore and Harper. A. Packard had a curious fruit on exhibition, styled the custard apple, which is said to be very delicious by those who have tested it. The display of flowers by Mrs N. W. Winton was one of the main features of the exhibit.

The first westward bound train over the Southern Trans-continental Railroad arrived in Los Angeles March 21. Visitors from the East are now arriving daily in our city and our hotels, for the time being, are well patronised.

POMONA.

Pomona is distant about thirty miles east of Los Angeles, directly on the railroad. It has a pleasant climate and good water facilities.

Rev. C. F. Loop was the only exhibitor from this settlement, his display consisting of some fine large seedling oranges, grown on one and ten year old trees. This exhibit attracted much attention, and it is conceded that Mr. Loop's seedlings were not excelled by any others exhibited at the Fair.

DUARTE.

A recent visit to this pleasant little settlement satisfied the writer that it is one of the most desirable points in the orange belt of Los Angeles county. Located right under the shadow of the majestic Sierra Madre Range no serious winds, frosts or other climatic evils annoy the inhabitants. The Duarte ranch is situated about seventeen miles due east of Los Angeles and is occupied by forty families. The water supply is good, but might be improved by iron pipes and reservoirs, and treble the amount of land could be brought into cultivation. Messrs. Wilson & Holliday, E. A Wallace, L. Barnes, A. Sandeler, E. Ixas, N. Beardslee, W. Smith, D. Wayne, E. Chappelow, N W Matthewson, and others have well cultivated and pleasant ranches bearing the choicest varieties of semi-tropical and deciduous fruits.

The Duarte exhibit at the Fair was small, but the fruit was fine looking, clean, juicy and sweet. The only entry for tomatoes was by W. S. Young, from the Duarte, and a San Francisco commission merchant present stated that they were the finest he has seen in the State at this season of the year.

GOOD WORDS FOR CALIFORNIA WINES.

The Sun, in an editorial on California wines, concludes that a good California wine is far better than a vast deal of the stuff sold for imported wine, and says "We are, therefore, glad to hear of the progress and prosperity of the vineyards on the Pacific. If California wine-makers go on improving as rapidly in the quality of their product, the phylloxera, already become a pest in their vineyards, will be the only active and efficient enemy against which they will have to contend.

The proprietor of the Daily Commercial in this city, lately issued a fine illustrated edition of his paper, he circulation abroad. It contained a large amount of carefully compiled information concerning Los Angeles city and county.

Cotton-Growing is likely to prove an important industry in Kern county, and we believe it will be a paying crop in Los Angeles. A premium will be offered for the best sample of cotton grown in Southern California exhibited at the Horticultural Fair next fall.

Citrus Fair.

PASADENA.

The exhibit of citrus fruits made by the six-year old settlement of Pasadena, seven miles from Los Angeles, was declared by the committee appointed to examine the exhibits of localities, to be the finest and largest in the Pavilion and the first premium was awarded accordingly. It was a grand display and attracted the attention of every visitor on entering the hall. The fruit was mainly placed on a huge terrace, dubbed "The Wigwam," and was all as bright and clean as twenty-dollar Eagles fresh from Uncle Sam's mint. About 150 boxes of oranges were placed on the terrace and an occasional two of lemons only added greater brilliancy to the golden apples. Two tables were required in addition to properly display the various fruits and the whole formed an exhibit in every respect highly creditable to the flourishing colony.

The floral display was especially fine and delighted our eastern visitors. Mrs. H. Williams was awarded a premium for a very artistic piece of work consisting of a ship decorated with flowers and fitly representing in an allegorical sense the wonderful progress of Pasadena.

The floral exhibit of Mrs Rosenbaum is deserving of especial mention, as it was undoubtedly the largest display in the hall. This lady ought certainly to have been awarded a premium, but through some misunderstanding of the committee she was overlooked. There were some eighty varieties of roses on her table besides other flowers, the whole arranged with much skill.

Mr. James Smith, the energetic owner of St. Kilda, exerted himself to make the exhibit a success and contributed a large number of boxes of fine looking oranges. The same may be said of Mr. Washburn, who, as one of the committee, devoted a large portion of his time in collecting and arranging the display. Messrs. W. T. Clapp, O. H. Conger, Col. Banbury, David Townsend, N. C. Jewett, Muller Bros., J. F. Crank, O. R. Dougherty, J. H. Baker, J. Wallace, R. Williams and many others whose names we have not space to publish deserve the thanks of the horticultural community for their painstaking efforts.

As a place for homes we could produce an unlimited amount of evidence that Pasadena possesses superior advantages, but this fact is due not so much to the fine climate and surroundings as that the people are progressive and enterprising. Pasadena is successful because its fruit-growers take every opportunity to increase their knowledge of the business in which they are engaged and are determined that their success shall be known to the outside world.

A farmer in Hill county, Texas, has rented 600 acres of broom corn the past season, which netted $10,000.

SAN GABRIEL.

San Gabriel was awarded the third premium for the largest and best display made by any locality. No exhibit in the Pavilion was more artistically arranged or attracted more attention than that of the Old Mission; where the Fathers, more than one hundred years ago, selected a site for their temple of worship. San Gabriel is the most romantic and delightful settlement in our county; and its orange groves the pride of Los Angeles. The splendid estates of Messrs. Rose, Titus, Shorb, Baldwin and others are the wonder and admiration of visitors; and the young settlement of Alhambra seems a very Paradise for fruit growers. Great reservoirs, constructed at immense expense, water the country for many miles around, and the railroad almost at the very doors of the settlers, renders communication easy with all portions of the Union.

The climate, free from heavy fogs and winds, is almost perfect; and invalids find there that soft and balmy atmosphere which gives them a new lease of life.

The San Gabriel exhibit was arranged in the shape of a Pagoda, or Chinese temple, covered with oranges, tapering gradually to the top, and wreathed with festoons of flowers. The credit for the work belongs respectively to Messrs. Sewall, Dobbins, Shorb and Carter, who cultivated and arranged the fruit. Some specimens of the celebrated Washington Navel orange from San Gabriel, grown on the place of Mr. J. R. Dobbins were placed on exhibition, and the committee, though obliged to give the first premium to Riverside, awarded to Mr. Dobbins a silver medal for the very fine quality of his fruit.

Messrs. G. D. Adams, E. Pollard, H. Hamilton, A. Phillips, S. Richardson, L. H. Titus and others contributed choice specimens of the citrus family.

San Gabriel Valley ranks at present as the semi-tropical fruit belt *par excellence* of Los Angeles County. The uncultivated tracts of land bordering the mountains are rapidly being surveyed and settled upon; and by a class of people who have the means and ability to properly develop the county. The beautiful winter resort, Sierra Madre Villa, which, since last November, has been crowded with guests from all portions of the world, is but one of many, which in the future will attract wealthy seekers after pleasure. The area of land which will produce really first class oranges, is, on the Pacific Coast, somewhat limited, for while any amount of thick-skinned, small, inferior fruit can be produced in almost every portion of California, south of Humboldt Bay, the oranges which command the highest prices in commercial circles come only from certain favored localities. The equable climate, protection from cold by mountain ranges, rich soil and healthfulness of San Gabriel Valley, give it advantages which can only result in its becoming the favorite resort of those who by reason of health or business desire rural homes.

SEMI-TROPIC CAL., $1.50 per year.

SAN DIEGO COUNTY

San Diego has been termed the City of Bay and Climate. These advantages would be sufficient after the advent of the trans-continental railroad to build up a large and flourishing town, were there nothing more substantial, but the San Diego exhibit at the Citrus Fair convinced everyone that portions of the county are admirably adapted to the culture of semi tropical fruits. The display on the National City table was superb and carefully arranged, thanks to the skill and untiring zeal of the Messrs. Kimball proprietor of the National Ranch, and Mr. J. M. Asher.

San Diego has a great future before it as a commercial port, a fruit-growing section and a resort for invalids. The harbor is perfectly safe in all weather and able to accommodate a large fleet. Great activity exists at present in the city, owing to the railroad building and the good agricultural prospects.

San Diego is settled by people from the Northern and Western States, and no town in California has better society. Good schools, churches and public buildings add much to the attractions of the city. The Bay of San Diego, with the single exception of the Bay of San Francisco, is the only safe port from Puget Sound on the north to the Mexican line on the south. The site of the city, located on a gradually sloping plain, could hardly be improved upon, from a sanitary point of view.

Several years ago Congress passed an act making San Diego the terminus of the 32d parallel railroad, to be constructed by the Texas Pacific Company. The scheme fell through, however, and with it the magnificent hopes of the people for a great commercial city which should rival San Francisco were temporarily crushed. The Directors of the Atchison, Topeka & Santa Fe Railroad have revived this town by organizing a company to construct a road from the Bay to Colton, in San Bernardino county, which will be completed within a year. A large force of men is at present engaged in grading and material in considerable quantities has been shipped from New York to the port.

Among the principal exhibitors from San Diego were Messrs. Kimball, Asher, Higgins, Swan, Clark, Bushyhead, Chase and Harvey. The fruit at the close of the Fair was shipped to Boston, where it will be placed on exhibition.

VENTURA COUNTY.

Ventura is one of the youngest counties in the State, but has resources which in sure its prosperity at no distant day. Its principal valleys are the Santa Clara, Ojai and Sespe and in these may be added the Conejo ranch, near the border of Los Angeles county. Wheat, corn and barley have been the principal products in the past, but fruit-raising promises at no distant day to become a leading industry. The Ojai is one of the most romantic and beautiful valleys in the state, and is a great resort for tourists.

San Buenaventura is the county seat and is a quiet little town, located on the beach. When connected by rail with the outside world it may become of no little commercial importance. It has good churches and schools, many fine residences, a good climate and water facilities unexcelled by any other county in Southern California.

Land is at present offered for sale very cheap in Ventura county, varying in price from $3 to $30 per acre, of course, unimproved.

The exhibit at the Citrus Fair was not large, but made up in quality what quantity lacked. The Camulos ranch sent a very creditable exhibit of oranges, almonds and walnuts; N. W. Blanchard, oranges and guavas; Lyon and Eastlen, budded and seedling oranges and F. S. Buckman, Ojai Valley budded oranges.

The exhibit was in charge of Mr. N. W. Blanchard, who deserves the gratitude of Ventura people for his public-spiritedness in advancing and working for their interest, and he has the thanks of the Horticultural Society for his efforts towards making our first Citrus Fair a success.

ORANGE.

While the exhibit from Orange was made by only a few persons it was deserving of great credit and delighted the observers. Messrs A. B. Clark and Fred'k Stevens (the former a Director of the Horticultural Society) sent a large quantity of fine oranges, which show the superior character of the settlement for the culture of citrus fruits.

Mr. Clark is the owner of the celebrated Yale Orchard, and adopted a plan by which his fruit meets a ready sale at the highest prices. Every orange is wrapped in tissue paper with a printed guarantee of the good quality of the specimen, and by this simple device the value of the fruit is advanced fully twenty-five per cent.

Orange is looming up as a leading raisin producer, and promises at no distant day to put up many thousand boxes of the choicest raisins. Mr. Leslie, a prominent fruit dealer of Chicago, who handles many thousand boxes of raisins weekly, has recently been visiting Orange, and so pleased was he with the location of the settlement that he has purchased a small farm and intends to put it out in trees and vines. He stated to the writer that the raisins exhibited by McPherson Bros. and P. Ainsworth at the Fair, are fully equal to the best imported from Europe, and much superior to any shipped from Southern California. He believes that Southern California will, in a few years, supply with dried fruits, not only the United States, but Canada and Australia. Such testimony is very encouraging, coming as it does, from the head of a firm which for the last ten years has dealt exclusively in dried fruits in one of the largest cities of the United States.

The Orange settlement is located about six miles from Anaheim, two miles from Santa Ana, and thirty-six miles from Los Angeles. The soil and water facilities are good; the churches and schools very good; stables for so young a settlement. There are two general merchandise stores, one hotel and a blacksmith shop. Orange has a station on the railroad about one mile from the center of the settlement, and has thus easy communication with the rest of the world.

The Los Angeles Exhibit at the Citrus Fair.

The leading fruit growers of Los Angeles City were not wholly apathetic in the matter of the Citrus Fair, as was shown by a number of very creditable exhibits. We have many enterprising men in our valley who are determined that Los Angeles shall not suffer in comparison with other fruit growing localities. Foremost among these is Mr. Alex. Craw, who for some years past has had charge of the great Wolfskill Orchard, and is in every respect a practical and experienced horticulturist. Mr. Craw has at great pains and expense made a collection of the insect enemies of the citrus family which he exhibited at the Riverside and Los Angeles Fairs. Our fruit producers will for all time hereafter have a severe and constant battle with these pests and the thanks of the community are due to Mr. Craw for his painstaking efforts.

Unfortunately we have not the Latin titles of the insects at hand and are obliged to give only the common names. The list is as follows:

Acacia scale, rose scale, red scale, apple aphis, white scale, currant scale, walnut scale, brown scale, red spider, leaf eaters, willow scale, arnuscaria scale, codling moth, orange worm, katydid, walnut borer, white ants, green aphis, smooth soft scale, katy did eggs, grape scale, Conke's collection of the scaling moth.

The following enemies of the above insects and friends of the fruit grower, were also exhibited by Mr. Craw:

Soldier bug, lady bug, gray lady bug, lace wing fly, dragon fly, ichneumon bug, devil's horse, spined soldier bug, spotted lady bug.

Mr. Wolfskill, as might be expected, made the largest and finest exhibit from Los Angeles City. The oranges were of a good marketable size, very sweet and of good color. He was awarded the first premium on limes and his lemon display was exceptionally good. A silver medal was also awarded Mr. Wolfskill for finest variety of fruits.

O. G. HISS.

Opposite the Wolfskill exhibit was placed a table arranged by Mr. O. G. Hiss, whose fine ranch on Alameda street is one of the most attractive in town. This gentleman exhibited ten varieties of oranges and ten of lemons. Over the display, with out stretched wings, was placed a large American eagle bearing in its beak the proud ensign, "Southern California." Mr. Hiss exhibited some palm plumes grown on his place which were so fine that the unanimous verdict unanimously awarded him a diploma.

Mr. A. F. Coronel, a native of the city of Mexico, but for many years a resident of Los Angeles, where he has occupied many important official positions, made a beautiful fruit and floral exhibit. The oranges were seedlings but very large and fine. His Mexican limes, some of which were placed on exhibition, are in great demand in San Francisco where he made a large shipments every year.

R. R. BRYANT.

Mr. R. R. Bryant had on exhibition a variety of oranges, lemons and limes from his ranch on Pico street. Mr. Bryant is a practical horticulturist and the fruit sent from his place to market is uniformly fine. Messrs Downey, Hooper, Stein, Matson, Cooper, McDonald, Biggerow, Kercheval, and Stewart were creditably represented on the remaining Los Angeles exhibit.

TUSTIN CITY.

This beautiful and growing settlement in the southern end of the county failed to make as fine a display of the Citrus Fair as had anticipated. We are sorry that the fruit growers could easily have taken some of the leading premiums offered had there been a well directed effort. In no portion of Los Angeles County do citrus fruits attain a larger size or finer flavor, and if the fruit farms continue at the rate they have been increasing for the past ten years, Tustin will ship as much fruit as the season as any other locality in the county.

Tustin would indeed have been amply without representation at the Fair had it not been for the efforts of Messrs Snow and Preble. As it was the fruit exhibited was of fine quality, both oranges and lemons; but the quantity displayed was not large enough to attract the attention of visitors to that degree we had expected prior to the Fair.

The exhibitors of oranges were Messrs Snow and Adams, B. F. Mason, H. W. Jisom, Dr. Wait, S. W. Preble and S. H. Irvin; of lemons, Messrs Snow and Adams and C. W. Wilcox.

We trust that the people of Tustin will not continue to hide their candle under a bushel, but will let their light so shine before the world that their may remove any doubt for their perseverance and energy during the past six years.

A contract has just been agreed upon between the authorities of Florida and a company of capitalists of Philadelphia and the Pacific coast, to plant 1,000 acres in South Florida. If the scheme is carried out, 1,000,000 pounds of the best sugar and in the world will be reclaimed.

William F. Dalrymple, of the famous grain farm in Dakota, says that the bran profit for 1880 was over $140,000. He raised over half a million bushels of wheat on 11,000 acres, and disposed of it in Buffalo at a profit of fifty cents a bushel.

HELLMAN & MASCAREL BLOCK.

THIS elegant business edifice, of which an illustration is herewith given, was constructed at a cost of $100,000 two years and a half ago, by I. W. Hellman, President of the Farmers' and Merchants' Bank, of Los Angeles, and Jose Mascarel, for many years past a resident of Los Angeles. The building fronts on Main street with a side exposure on Commercial street, and is one of the best business locations in the city.

POLASKI & SON.

L. Polaski & Son occupy the first store on Main street in the Hellman & Mascarel Block, commencing from the Commercial street side. The firm under the title of Polaski & Goodwin, commenced business in this city in 1865—sixteen years since. In 1868 Mr. Goodwin withdrew, his place being filled by Mr. L. Polaski, who has since, in connection with his father, carried on the extensive business of the firm.

The establishment ranks among the leading dry goods stores of Southern California, and carries one of the largest stocks in the city. It would be difficult to find anywhere on the coast a more complete assort-

Californians seem to have a pardonable weakness, grace the counters. Mr. Nordlinger has been in business twelve years in Los Angeles and has built up a very satisfactory trade in jewelry. Among the articles in this line which are deserving of respect mention, are his elaborately worked gold rings, watch chains and charms, of which ladies and gentlemen have a most extensive variety to select from. Indeed, no article in the line of fine gold jewelry is missing at the California Jewelry House. Mr. Nordlinger keeps a full stock of sterling silver and plated ware, watches and clocks, spectacles, eyeglasses, etc. Repairing is neatly and promptly done, satisfaction being guaranteed. No other house

HELLMAN AND MASCAREL BLOCK, LOS ANGELES, CAL.

The first story is divided into five large store rooms, all finished in the most elaborate manner, and giving the best opportunity for display possible to the enterprise and merchants of the block.

The second story is occupied by the Supreme Court of California during its semi-annual sessions in this city. The apartments assigned to the use of the Court are superbly finished and very conveniently located. The remainder of the upper story is devoted to business offices. The whole building is very ornamental to Los Angeles, and so durably constructed that centuries may elapse before it will show signs of decay.

ment of gentlemen's furnishing goods, and in other lines the variety and quality of the stock cannot be excelled.

In all departments of the establishment there is nothing lacking to satisfy the most fastidious, and Messrs. Polaski & Son lose no opportunity to advance the material interests of Los Angeles county.

S. NORDLINGER.

The California Jewelry House, 8 Nordlinger, proprietor, occupies the store adjoining that of L. Polaski & Son, and carries the largest stock of jewelry of any establishment south of San Francisco. It is the "Diamond Palace" of Los Angeles, and a full stock of the sparkling gems for which

in Southern California offers so many advantages to customers as the California Jewelry House, No. 60 Main street.

POND & ORR.

Messrs. Pond & Orr, undertakers and dealers in statuary and pictures, occupy the last store in the Hellman & Mascarel Block, adjoining the Commercial Bank. Mr. Pond has been a resident of our city for the past eight years. Mr. Orr joined him in the business four years since. No undertaking establishment on the coast is better fitted to perform the last sad rites for the dead, and the arrangements are as complete as can be found in many of the larger Eastern cities. In front there is a large reception room where bodies are received and prepared for burial. In the rear is an embalming room, where, by a process speedy and perfect, bodies are embalmed and prepared for shipment to all portions of the world. Ponet & Cox are agents for Bronston's Metallic Burial Caskets, admitted by scientific men to be the best in use. A large warehouse is connected with the establishment, and a stock of pictures and statuary very creditable for a young city like Los Angeles fills one department. The Coroner's office is located at the rooms of Ponet & Cox.

W. J. BRODRICK.

Mr. W. J. Brodrick, the agent for a large number of reliable fire and life insurance companies, occupies an office on the Commercial street side of the block. It is needless to say that in case of loss all policies issued by the companies Mr. Brodrick represents, are promptly settled.

R. LEON.

Mr. R. Leon, the popular dealer in cigars and tobacco, is located in the store near the center of the block. Mr. Leon has the most complete stock of the fragrant weed, and all utensils used in connection with it, of any establishment in the city.

UP STAIRS.

We have referred elsewhere to the apartments of the Supreme Court on Commercial street.

Mr. R. Garvey, prominently identified with many mineral and agricultural enterprises in California and Arizona, makes his headquarters at a suite of rooms in the block.

Mr. Hannon, the County Physician, to whom we are indebted for the careful, economical and satisfactory management of the County Hospital, has an office at room ——.

R. M. Widney also occupies a fine suite of rooms in connection with his law office and library. Judge Widney is recognized as one of the ablest counsellors at the bar, and no enterprise is considered complete unless the Judge is among the number to make success assured.

Lima and lemon trees should have about the same care as orange trees. Limes seem to be a failure for a general hedge. Our seasons are a little cool for the best results in orchard form, and only near some other trees, where they receive some protection and are kept from that strong luxuriant growth which invites the attack of a little frost, will they give any satisfaction. Lemon trees seem to be hardier, and the Lisbon and sweet rind varieties, budded into the orange and lemon, give good satisfaction. Seedling lemons are as liable to disease, that seems to affect them through having an excess of water without cultivation, and are as apt to be bitter that I pass them over, only adding that with the exception of pruning according to the habits of growth, the lemon and lime require the same treatment as the orange.—Geo. B. Garretson, at Riverside Fair.

Poultry.

SELECTION OF BIRDS.

A Proper selection of eggs for setting is the first point to be attended to in raising poultry. To get good strong birds, eggs from a two-year-old hen by a one-year old male bird should be chosen, as these yield far more larger chickens than eggs from a very young hen by an older male. The eggs should be regular in shape, and the largest should be chosen, except, of course, when a double yolk is suspected. In dwarf breeds, where the object is to get as small birds as possible, the smaller the eggs the better. The notion that pointed eggs always yield male birds is incorrect; this is only the case when they are from a hen that usually lays round ones, while, similarly, round eggs from a hen that usually lays pointed ones generally yield female birds. Where, however, a hen always lays eggs of one shape, whether pointed or round, the young birds will be of both sexes.

FEEDING YOUNG FOWL.

One point of great importance in feeding young fowls should never be lost sight of. They must be fed often, but never have more at a time than they can take with appetite, since no creature is so dainty as the fowl. Once give them too much food at a time, so that they leave some of it uneaten, and they will rarely partake of it again, unless actually driven by hunger, and then only just enough to prevent starvation. Duckings, it is said, will utterly die rather than touch food to which they have taken a dislike. Plenty of exercise in the open air is a good thing for the young ones, yet even in a very confined space poultry breeding yields excellent results, if conducted with care, zeal and intelligence.

CARE OF ADULTS.

My hen-house is not a model one, but has nests and roosts all in one apartment. I was always troubled in having the fowls roost upon the front of the nests instead of going on the poles, until I made the top of the front board seem circular instead of straight. It is no hindrance for hens going up to lay, but as they are not so apt to be standing long on the edge, they are less liable to learn to eat eggs. To keep poultry free from lice, and their legs clear of scab, I think it a good plan to paint the roosts a few times during winter (before the time for setting eggs for setting commences) with a mixture of sulphur and grease. Dry sulphur may be sifted into a sitting hen's feathers with good effect.—S. L. V., in Country Gentleman.

JUDGING POULTRY FROM WINNER.

Turkey.—The cock bird when young has a smooth black leg with a short spur. Eyes bright and full, and mount supple feet when fresh, the absence of these signs denotes age and staleness; the hen may be judged by the same rules.

Fowls like a turkey; the young cock has a smooth leg and a short spur, when fresh the vent is close and dark

ITEMS.

Santa Barbara and Ventura counties expect to make connection with the railroad system of California before another year.

Los Angeles City is improving in a most satisfactory manner. The new block of Messrs. Mueller & Barker, on Spring street, opposite the postoffice, is nearly completed and will be devoted to the furniture business.

Woodhead & Gay are about to have an extensive addition built on to their establishment.

M. G. Davenport will shortly erect a fine business edifice on the lot adjoining the Cosmopolitan Hotel.

A brick building to be occupied by a French Bakery, is in process of construction on Commercial street. Preparations for the erection of the fine Normal School building have already commenced. Dwelling houses are going up in all portions of the city, and we may look forward for a fairly prosperous season.

The rains which came so opportunely early in March have assured good crops of every kind. The acreage of wheat planted, and the barley crop will be much larger. The farmers of St. Louis, Chicago and Milwaukee, will take all the surplus grain, and good prices may be hoped for. The fruit crop has not been seriously injured by frost, and, from present appearances, the apple, peach, pear and apricot yield will be immense. Buyers will be urgently needed this summer to work up our surplus fruit.

Stock of all kinds will have an abundance of feed, and our dairy interests will receive a fresh impetus.

Mr. D. Bush exhibited rustic chairs and baskets made from California manzanita and maple, for which he has been awarded a diploma.

Mr. J. Begg's collection of native grasses, with some additions, was the same as that exhibited last Fall at the Pavilion.

Messrs. Widney Bro's had a branch of their popular fancy goods establishment at the Pavilion. They offered a fine assortment of abalone shells, gathered from the Los Angeles sea coast, and disposed of many to our Eastern visitors.

The decorating of the Hall was superior to that of any previous year. The pillars were wreathed with cedar, cypress, laurel and oak, with flowers intertwined. Bouquets of flowers were placed in every available spot.

REPORT OF COMMITTEE ON RAISINS

TO THE BOARD OF DIRECTORS OF THE "SOUTHERN CALIFORNIA HORTICULTURAL SOCIETY," HOLDING ITS FIRST FAIR AT LOS ANGELES, MARCH 14-19, 1881.

GENTLEMEN: Your committee in "Department A, Class I, Raisins," after the most minute and careful examination of all the samples presented, respectfully tender the following as their

REPORT:

The production of Raisins in California must, in the near future, become an important factor in the commerce of the Pacific Coast. Wherefore every step in the road of progress toward perfection in this industry is of value to the state.

That most of the arable lands of California are well adapted to grape culture, and that many localities are especially adapted to the production of those peculiar varieties which, alone, make raisins of the first class, no one denies, nor is it questioned, that for half a score of years most commendable efforts have been made, with success, to produce good raisins, and yet we have not reached perfection. To do this is now engaging the best talent on the coast—that we have all the natural facilities for such attainments, every one intelligent upon the subject freely admits. Experience with our peculiar soil and climate, frequent comparison of methods and results and free interchange of ideas on the part of experimenters will complete the entire requirements for an interest of almost unlimited commercial importance.

That we have not, in half a score of years, attained a perfection in the manipulation of the Raisin Grape, that the experience of European raisin growers, through half a score of centuries, has enabled them to attain, is far less a marvel, than the high order of excellence to which we have attained.

Friction of ideas elicits sparks of intelligence; and comparison of tests tends to improve the most advanced thought; and analysis of labor, as well as of facts, elucidates principles and promotes progress. This is not only apology for what some might regard as unnecessary detail in this report.

To make a first class raisin, a grape adapted to that purpose is an absolute sine qua non. Nor is it less important that the producer both knows and faithfully applies the best methods of treating the grape.

It is not the province of your committee to dwell upon, or even refer to the steps necessary to the production of the raisin; yet it is perhaps apropos for us to state the particular points of excellence, which are the basis of our judgment in making awards in the case before us.

Among the essentials, to the raisin of commerce will be found the following:

1. SIZE of berry, which should be large and uniform.

2. BLOOM—Bright, rich, unbroken.

3. COLOR—Bluish and clear, never red, which indicates incipient decomposition.

4. SKIN—Thin, delicate, but strong.

5. PULP—Full, uniform, and clearing freely from the skin—but pulpy.

6. FLAVOR—Rich, vinous, free, aromatic, delicate.

7. SEEDS—Few, small, hard.

8. STEM OF BERRY—Firm, strong, adherent to main stalk.

9. BUNCH—Large, full, compact, adherent.

10. PACKING—Layers only one bunch deep—each bunch isolated as far as possible.

11. BOXES—Uniform in style and of utmost external neatness.

12. COMPACTNESS—Every box should be absolutely full, after proper pressure, and as few stalks as possible in sight.

In the present case our examinations have sought, and our awards have been based upon the highest excellence in the greatest number of the above points.

And we beg to say, in advance, that the raisin growers of California are to-day, in the excellence of their wares, superior to those of any other country.

Under the head,

"BEST AND LARGEST DISPLAY"

There were three entries, numbered respectively—3, 9, 14. Having respect to all the above named qualities, we award the premium to No. 5, exhibited by Thos. F. Craft.

Under this head we beg to call your especial attention to the large and fine display of McPherson Bros. which, if it had equalled in bloom, in size, in uniformity and in solidity of pulp—wherein its inferiority was barely perceptible—it would have been the full peer of the former.

Under the head,

"BEST FIVE BOX"

There were eight entries, numbered respectively—2, 3, 4, 7, 8, 10, 13, 14. We award the premium to No. 13, exhibited (as we afterward learned) by McPherson Bros.

Between this and No. 2, exhibited (as we have since been informed) by Mrs. Jennie C. Carr, the difference was so slight in the aggregate, that to decide with full satisfaction to ourselves, was no easy task.

Had No. 2 been a little less dried, thus avoiding a slight pasty character of pulp, and a little more thoroughly uniform in size, and a little more attentively packed, it would have been entitled to the premium. We earnestly suggest such special award to No. 2 as you may remember due to very superior merit. For the

"BEST QUARTER BOX"

There were three entries, numbered respectively—11, 15, 16. We award the premium to No. 11, exhibited by Peter Aysworth. Each of the others is worthy of especial mention.

In conclusion we beg to call attention to a few defects, leaving any one who chooses to profit thereby.

1. BOXES NOT FULL, which always detracts from commercial value.

2. STEMS OR STALKS—Too large, and allowed to be too prominent after packing.

3. BOXES TOO FULL—so that the pressure of the cover had broken the skin of the berries.

4. INSUFFICIENT CARE in "clipping out" small and shriveled berries previous to packing.

Begging pardon for claiming so long attention by this report, and assuring you that the several exhibits, as a whole, reflect great credit upon the producers, and give enlarged views of our future possibilities in this most important industry, we respectfully tender thanks for the honor you have conferred upon us in calling us to examine this most interesting department.

GEO. LESLIE,
N. W. BLANCHARD, } Com.
O. C. WHEELER.

If everything is favorable citrus trees should be put out early, when the soil has same moisture. When you irrigate, do it thoroughly and well, not rushing the water past your trees, but in small streams running through ditches at least twelve hours—better still, twenty-four hours. Look often through the furrows when the water is flowing, and have the water entirely through. Some furrows will require, from the receptive quality of the soil, more water than others. After irrigation, when the soil is just right, comes cultivation, both to keep weeds down and prevent the soil from baking, as well as a guard against so much evaporation of moisture from the ground. Then comes the all-important question of high or low heading. Somehow, Mr. Chairman, I favor a medium stage, or rather, I never like to see a tree out of proportion. One-third stock and two-thirds of foliage and branches is a good rule to follow. You can gradually raise the stock, if necessary. Cut off any straggling shoots, which may often mar the symmetry. Low budded trees especially are more difficult to manage. Generally they are inclined to branch low. I think the same rule of proportion would be safe. Perhaps one-fourth stock and three-fourths foliage and branches would be the best for budded trees.—G. W. Garcelon, at Riverside Fair.

It is difficult to discover any person who has made a single dollar out of Angora goats except the breeders. There are now the breeders and their victims; the former make the money and the latter lose it. There are many persons to be found who have paid fifty dollars for a pair of goats, or even more, and who have been glad to hasten them upon a friend after a year or two experience with them, and the friend might well have said, "an enemy hath done this," as soon as he had discovered the hollowness of the great delusion. Still one may read now and then of a new victim paying his fifty dollars for experience in this line of business, in which the profits are all on one side.—Rural New Yorker.

SEMI-TROPIC CALIFORNIA, subscription $1.50 per annum.

The new wool and grain house of J. H. Congdon & Co., No. 6 Stewart street, San Francisco, having had over twelve years experience in their particular line of business, offer to the wool growers and farmers in general, superior facilities for handling their products. They do an exclusively commission business, making liberal cash advances, are active, energetic business men, and any consignment made them will receive immediate attention. Secure the highest market prices and prompt remittances. We commend them to the public.

The firm name of Spear, Meade & Co., has become a household word in Southern California, and Mr. Geo. W. Meade & Co., as successors, is a strong firm, whose name is synonymous with honorable dealing in all. We call attention to the card of this firm in another part of this paper, and bespeak them a share of the business in southern California.

C. H. Edwards, the "artistic pressman" in the *Mirror* office, is entitled to great credit for the care and studied efforts in printing the SEMI-TROPIC. The press work of this magazine is hardly excelled by that of any other periodical in the United States, and we are glad to note the fact that it is appreciated by the public.

Whenever an animal exhibits an unnatural appearance, seems stupid, or in any manner seems disinclined to eat or drink, it should be instantly removed to some shed, pen, or stable where it can be properly fed and nursed, for our sick animal will, if not isolated, very soon affect the others.

Miss Longfellow, daughter of the celebrated poet, and Misses Thrant and Horner, of Boston, have been stopping in our city for the past few weeks. They express themselves as highly pleased with our climate and scenery.

The next number of the SEMI-TROPIC will contain several views of San Gabriel, including the Old Mission, we pride ourselves in issuing an elegantly illustrated magazine every month.

A grand ball took place in the galleries on Saturday evening, and many couples "tripped the light, fantastic toe," and a pleasant evening was spent in terpsichorean revels.

The Good Templars spread an ample collation three times a day, which was well patronized.

The City Band furnished excellent music afternoons and evenings.

The outlook has never been so encouraging, and we trust that city and country may enjoy an equal prosperity.

Markets.

EGGS—Have ruled high for several months and in demand at 08c. The market is better supplied, and prices are now quoted at 16c & 18

BUTTER—Is also in good demand, for choice only, at 22½c

ORANGES—The market has ruled dull for poor and inferior, but choice No. 1 fruit has commanded good prices, ranging from $2 to $30 per M. All the choice oranges exhibited at the Citrus Fair ruled readily at fancy prices. Oranges should not be shipped until ripe, and then put up in first-class shape for market.

WINES AND LIQUORS—The boom in the wine business has a tendency to make prices stronger, and prices may be said to have advanced two or three cents on the gallon for new wines.

LOS ANGELES WINES AND LIQUORS.

Red wine, No. 1, per gallon	...... $0 50
Red wine, No. 2, per gallon	 40
White wine, new, per gallon	 50
White wine, old, per gallon	 75
Port wine, old, per gallon	...... 1 00
Angelica wine, old, per gallon	...... 1 00
Sherry wine, old, per gallon	...... 1 75
Champagne, old, per gallon	...... 1 50
Brandy, per gallon	...... 2 50
Aguardiente, per gallon	...... 2 00

SEMI TROPIC CALIFORNIA

DEVOTED TO

AGRICULTURE,

HORTICULTURE,

AND THE DEVELOPMENT OF

SOUTHERN CALIFORNIA

GEORGE RICE, PUBLISHER.

Vol. IV.   No. 5.

LOS ANGELES, CAL.

1881.

MIRROR PRINT, Los Angeles.

· ⊶ AND ⊷ ·

SOUTHERN CALIFORNIA HORTICULTURIST.

VOL. IV. LOS ANGELES, CAL., MAY, 1881. No. 5.

CALIFORNIA ROSES.

Extract from essay read by W. A. Stratton, of Pasadena, before the State Horticultural Society, April 20, 1881.

MY theme is worthy of the inspiration of the gods, not illusory of fantastic splendor or of ethereal glory, but in grandeur of expression to do justice to the noblest emblem of Flora. This is a glorious land of world-wide fame, for the great beauty of our flowers, and pre-eminently ahead of all stands the queen beauty of our roses.

CULTIVATION AND SOILS.

Our roses thrive everywhere alike, on mountain, hill or dale; in adobe, loam or shifting sands. Give them moisture, and Nature smilingly rewards alike in beauteous flowers. Thorough cultivation, however, must be given by those who would have perfection; hence a most liberal supply of food must be yearly given, deep and frequent spading of the ground, and a systematic care in trimming. Ashes and lime are most excellent fertilizers for roses; soot and soap suds are invaluable for all light soils, while for all the nothing excels in value well rotted stable manure. The preparation of green manure for roses should be very thorough. Manure as usually obtained is nearly worthless. After it has passed the first fermentation its most valued nutriment for plants life is lost. It should therefore be obtained absolutely fresh and carefully composted. The operation is simple. First spread the manure on the ground, say twelve inches deep, in any desired form, then cover with sandy loam, wet thoroughly; when another load can be obtained spread it over the last, and cover again with soil, and repeat layer upon layer, soil and manure alternately, always making each layer a little smaller than the last, so that the sides of the pile will be a very little sloping. A regular moisture should be maintained, and in a few months the whole should be carefully worked over. This is plant food, rich in all the elements to grow in perfection; and when liberally applied and spaded thoroughly in, we have the most grand results the world ever produced.

VARIETIES.

I would most gladly leave this interesting portion of my paper to more able and intelligent hands. They are all beautiful, to praise one more than the other is injustice. Each have their beauteous charms, each excel either in color, form or fragrance. To describe the different varieties is no difficult task, but to name them correctly is a serious one. Roses change with climates and soils; this together with the fact that Eastern florists send out many varieties little caring whether they are true to the label or not, has caused such a confusion of names, that I hope this society will recognize the importance of earnest conscientious work, and by the appointment of a special committee on roses, who may settle many of the vexed questions of nomenclature. The labor is an arduous one, yet for the sake of reputation we owe it, and the decision of this Society can alone command the confidence required. I will therefore venture the description of a few choice ones, concisely stating each special point of interest as my experience and I observe, tion may suggest.

La Marque—Well known as one of our most valued sorts, perfectly healthy, but enjoys best a warm position and on its own roots.

Camellia—Another old standard sort of sterling value, flowering best in a somewhat shady, warm position; its magnificent deep yellow buds are often two and one half inches long. Grafted it is a shy bloomer.

Gloire de Dijon—A type admired by many, yet to me its clumsy drooping buds detract from the grace and beauty we most admire; its deep apricot tint is its only attraction; vigorous and healthy under all circumstances.

James Sprunt—A comparatively new rose, one destined to be retained as the best of its color; deep cherry red, delightfully fragrant, robust in habit, free from mildew, it is worthy of all the commendation it receives; does well either on its own roots or Manetta, but on Castilian a failure, its color bleaching badly.

Lamarque—A soft glowing pink of vigorous habit, very free flowering in immense clusters; invitingly yet modestly claims our highest admiration; a shy bloomer on its own roots, but on Castilian in perfection.

Joan d' Arc—A lovely white, delightfully fragrant, vigorous in habit, very free flowering when planted in a warm dry soil, always commands ecstacies of praise. I am aware this rose is improperly named, but as I can find no authority for any other I retain it. I have carefully examined all European and American catalogues worthy of confidence, and am satisfied it is one of those varieties that climate and soil have changed beyond recognition.

Reve d' Or, or *Climbing Safrano*, completes the list of varieties for climbing varieties, of fine habits; rich, deep apricot tinted buds, very fragrant, it enjoys rich, deep culture and abundant moisture.

APRICOTS.

In many localities in California apricots are grown, but in few are they grown in perfection. One of these few is the Santa Clara Valley, especially the lower end of the valley. The apricot, unlike the semi-tropical fruits—the orange and lemon—thrive better near the sea. In the mountains and interior valleys, the heat causes the fruit to ripen before it attains a size sufficient to make it profitable to the fruit drier, but here near the coast, where the ocean breezes render the climate equable, it comes slowly to maturity, is larger, and when ripe more rich and juicy. It is of all the fruits the most free from the ravages of insects. The tree is a hardy, vigorous grower, and within four years commences to bear. We firmly believe those who plant apricot orchards in the coast valleys of Southern California, will reap a richer harvest, and at a much earlier date than those who go farther into the interior and plant oranges, walnuts or grapes. Over two hundred acres have been planted in apricots this year between this place and Santa Maria. Last year twice as many will be planted.—Ventura Signal.

The N. Y. Sun, reviewing California raisin culture, says: At their best, these raisins compare favorably with London layers. The finest of Malaga fruit are of already imported to this country, and on the average they are about equal to plain layers of an inferior quality. Only a few of the higher grades of Malaga fruit are in demand in our market, however, and, therefore, when we say that California raisins are nearly equal to London layers, we merely compare them with the lower grade Malaga raisins. About one fifth of the Spanish raisins are better than any yet produced in California, whose fruit would therefore not be ranked higher than a sixth in quality in Malaga. But the California producers are steadily improving in their process of cultivation, and the objections to their raisins can all be overcome with proper care.

Those of us who have survived thus far through March are now in an agony of anxiety to know what kind of weather Ventura has stored up for April. Enough more of this sort of thing will exhaust even superhuman powers of endurance.—Ventura Signal.

Sounds kind of funny to a Southern Californian.

SEMI-TROPIC
CALIFORNIA,
— AN —
ILLUSTRATED MONTHLY.

Devoted to Agriculture, Horticulture, and the Development of Southern California.

Terms: $1.50 per Annum, in Advance.

OFFICE, Rooms 9 & 10, Baker Block.

Address, ... GEO. RICE, Los Angeles, Cal.

GEORGE RICE,   Editor and Prop'r.

SEMI-TROPIC CALIFORNIA FOR MAY.

Owing to the serious illness of Mr. Geo. Rice, the editor and publisher of this magazine, its management has this month been entrusted to another. Our readers on this ground will excuse any inaccuracies or failure to bring the reading matter up to its usual standpoint. We are glad to say that Mr. Rice's health is gradually improving, and before another month he will resume the editorial chair.

THE OUTLOOK FOR SOUTHERN CALIFORNIA.

It is generally admitted by all who have carefully examined the crops and prospective markets of Southern California, this season, that the prospect has seldom been more encouraging than at present. One of the pleasantest features of the present return of good times is, that there is no present indication of a real estate speculative excitement which might force prices above the means of those who may be inclined to buy. We trust that there will be no exaggerated statements circulated about our section, for we are convinced that such published falsehoods have done much harm in the past, and our people are heartily disgusted with them. Plain facts and official statistics concerning our climate, crops and resources generally, are what is needed, and the healthy immigration which is pour-

ing into our valley may, by such proper methods, be indefinitely increased.

From a recent tour through the country, by inquiries among the farmers, and through reports from our exchanges, we are able to present the following notes concerning the crops.

The fruit yield, unless some unforeseen accident occurs, will generally be good. The orange trees everywhere are loaded with young fruit, and the lemons and limes are fully as promising. The red scale and gum disease have done some damage in certain localities, but the crop will not be damaged to any material extent. Apple, peach, pear and apricot trees are not so overloaded as last year. The fruit promises to be of rather better quality.

In regard to the grape prospect we can do no better than quote the following from the Anaheim *Gazette* of April 23, which will apply to all portions of the county:

There is rejoicing in the land. The season of frost has passed; the vines are growing vigorously, the produce bloom gives promise of a large harvest of tonnage is observable in any of the vineyards; the cut worm is not nearly so common as it was last year. Taken altogether, the season and never began more propitiously to Anaheim, but just as we are tempted to make a calculation as to the result of the grape harvest, their rumors to our mind such wise sayings as "There's many a slip 'twixt the cup and the lip," "Don't count your chickens before they're hatched," etc., etc. We will, therefore, put away our little figures until later in the season, merely remarking that some of the vineyardists with whom we have conversed anticipate any disaster to the crop.

The *Gazette* also gives a list of sixty fruit-growers in the neighborhood of Anaheim, who have put out this season, in the aggregate, 49,000 new vines. This shows that the people in that conservative settlement have an abiding faith in the future of viticulture. Almond trees have surprised their owners this season by bearing very freely. English walnuts promise well. The smaller fruits, as usual, will bear profusely and supply the market to the fullest extent. The farmers this year have found a good market for all the potatoes they can raise and have planted a large area in corn. The barley crop will be short in some localities; in others the outlook was never better. We have seen during the past month fields where the barley headed out three or four inches from the ground, and others right adjoining which were in poor condition. Such are the vagaries of California agriculture. There will probably be a fair crop and the best market for it we have had for many years. The wheat fields of San Fernando are in excellent condition. From other portions of the county we have conflicting statements. Santa Barbara, Ventura and San Luis Obispo report full crops. The hay yield will be large and of excellent quality.

This is a good "grass year," and stock men rejoice accordingly. There is no prevalent disease among stock, and the only trouble is that we have not enough to supply the market. No occupation in

Southern California is more profitable, when undertaken under the right conditions, than stock raising.

The bee men have been disappointed several times during the past six years and look a little dubious this season, notwithstanding the present rather hopeful outlook. There has not as yet been much honey made in this county—for other counties we cannot speak. The white sage will bloom in June, and if there are no discouraging winds, may yield a full supply of the pure article.

The agricultural prospects for the season are therefore on the whole quite satisfactory. The mining interests in this county are being gradually developed, and the long neglected mines of San Bernardino and San Diego counties are about to experience a "boom" which will cause their early and, we trust, satisfactory development.

Before 1883 the track of a competing railroad will connect San Diego, San Francisco and possibly our own valley with the East.

Altogether, as our contemporary, the *Herald* has remarked, the situation could hardly be improved upon, and all we need now is careful legislation and an increase of population to make Southern California one of the most productive countries in the world.

ADVICE TO NEW-COMERS.

Quite a large number of persons from the Eastern States are now in Los Angeles county seeking homes, and it is possible that a few hints, which we have garnered from several years observation in California, may be of some service to them.

During the years 1873, 1874, 1875 and 1876 there was a very large immigration to this county. Many of the newcomers had considerable means, ranging, perhaps, from $5,000 to $50,000 each. Times were, at that time, very prosperous, land was high, and real estate agents, in a figurative sense, were as the stars of the sky in multitude and like the sand of the seashore, innumerable. Our Eastern friends were pleased with the country and concluded to remain and invest. By so doing they acted wisely, and all might have been well had their subsequent course been as judicious. After they had purchased their homes a few were content with modest cottages and plain living. They did not buy every "good thing" that came along, but obtained only those articles which were absolutely necessary, planted their orange trees, deciduous trees and vineyards and waited. The remainder bought about ten times as much land as they could cultivate properly, put up $5,000 or $10,000 houses, and by the time they were finished found their money exhausted. So they ornamented their magnificent residences with mortgages and paid for the luxury at the rate of from fifteen to twenty per cent. per annum. While the money lasted they lived in the most expensive fashion. Their sons dressed in broadcloth and their daughters in silks. Parties and balls, high priced wines, a retinue of servants and occasional trips East made the time pass easily and pleasantly. But there came a change, a dry season, a bank failure, a visitation of the small-pox, imported from China, and money became scarcer than the proverbial hen's teeth, the interest account began to swell, the servants were discharged, and a little later the columns of the *Herald, Express* and other papers began to fill with such notices as these:

MORTGAGE SALE.

EXECUTION No 713.

In the District Court of the County of Los Angeles, State of California,
I. Squeezem, plaintiff,
vs.
H. D. Blower, defendant.

Then followed a description of the property and the order of sale. About that time we began to hear that Los Angeles county was of no account, that the country was going to the dogs and so on *ad infinitum*. But all the while the few that lived in the little humble cottages, and dressed plain and had been quite forgotten in the great boom, held their own, and their orange trees and vineyards began to bear a year or two ago; while, all of a sudden, the railroad opened up fifty new markets in Arizona and New Mexico. The miners wanted Los Angeles fruits, grains and vegetables, paid high prices and could not get enough. The phylloxera killed the French vineyards and the price of California grapes quadrupled. The turn in the tide came, and, although there were comparatively few that were saved, their course will serve as a bright example for those who are now coming. Money is again becoming plentiful, and some, perhaps a little too sanguine, mathematician has reckoned that twenty acres of grapes are worth as much as an investment as $100,000 in Government three-per-cents. However this may be, it is certain that pluck, energy and economy will win every time in Southern California.

PERSONAL.

We acknowledge a pleasant visit from Mr. C. V. Hall, formerly publisher of *Hall's Land Journal*, a magazine which widely advertised Los Angeles county. Mr. Hall occupies a responsible position in the Home Mutual Insurance Company of San Francisco, one of the most reliable fire insurance companies in the United States. Most of our old time citizens remember Mr. Hall and will be glad to hear of his success in business. We hope he will find it convenient to pay frequent visits to the City of the Angels.

THE METHODIST CHURCH.

The Fort Street Methodist Episcopal Church, represented below, is the largest Protestant edifice in Southern California. It was erected in 1875 at the cost of $15,000. It is of Gothic architecture, lighted with gas pendants and heated by a furnace. The church is centrally located. This Society has shown a remarkable growth. Organized in 1867 with seven communicants, they worshipped for eight years in the small brick chapel near by, now used by the Presbyterian Society. It at present numbers 400 communicants, among whom are some of our most wealthy and influential citizens. The 11 o'clock Sabbath morning service finds the church filled to its capacity, having seating accommodation for four or five hundred people.

Fort Street M. E. Church.

The Society has recently been relieved of a debt of $5,000. Rev. E. S. Chase is the present Pastor

IMPROVEMENTS IN LOS ANGELES.

Business of all kinds continues fairly good in our city, and building and other improvements are progressing in a very satisfactory manner. The site selected for the Branch Normal School is universally admitted to be a judicious one, and great credit is due to the enterprising gentleman who have presented the State with a clear title to the property. The construction of the building will give employment to a large number of mechanics and laborers. The materials will of course be supplied here, and our mercantile firms ought to obtain many profitable contracts. The school [...]

will be an important addition to the educational institutions of the city, and we are glad the State has at last seen fit to recognize, even in a small way, the claims of our section.

Few desirable tenement houses are for rent at present, and if the demand continues rents will materially advance. Hardly a day passes but several new families arrive from the East to make their home in the county. Several fine residences are also to be erected in various parts of the city, plans having already been drawn. Deacon Geo. Howe, of Garden Grove, has nearly completed a fine residence on Temple street, costing several thousand dollars. Mrs. H. C. Scott has let the contract for the construction of two tenement houses on the same avenue. Quite a large number of small places have recently changed hands, new comers being the purchasers. The Nichols Place on Pearl street was lately purchased by Prof. Potter for $4,500. Grading has been commenced on the lot belonging to Mr. Davenport on Main street, adjoining the Cosmopolitan Hotel. A fine store building will shortly take the place of the old rookeries which have so long disgraced the city at that point. Mr. Schumacher is building a new [...] on the lot adjoining the fine residence of Messrs. Parker & Mosher.

The Alden Fruit Dryer on the other side of the river will receive fruit promptly on the opening of the season. This year a trust the management will prove satisfactory to our fruit growers. A glove factory, tannery, and a boot and shoe factory and tanning establishment are talked of.

PASADENA IMPROVEMENTS.

Every month we have to chronicle some new improvements at the beautiful colony of Pasadena. At the present time quite a number of new houses are being erected, and the grounds adjoining set out in front [...] ornamental trees and shrubbery. Mr. Hubbard's magnificent house costing $30,000 will be completed in a few weeks. Other parties who are either building residences or are about to build on the Orange Grove Association's tract, are Messrs. Freeman, of Philadelphia, Mr. J. A. Chapman, Mr. Nelms and Mr. Ross, all of whom are to make their home in Pasadena.

Messrs. Painter & Hall will soon have their Monk's tract on the market, and are now busy developing the water. Messrs. Woodbury will dispose of their tract shortly, almost all the land having been already engaged. Mr. Campbell is about to lay out irrigation on five acres of land which he has recently purchased, if the experiment proves successful, others will follow his example.

Our mines offer great inducements for investments and we think that before long capital will find its way into them and the returns from them will surprise many of our old inhabitants.—*Southern Herald*

Horticulture.

COMPETITION WITH MEXICO

A gentleman who has traveled extensively through the Northern States of Mexico informs us that for the most part, at least, our semi-tropical fruit-growers have but little to fear from the orchards of Northern Mexico. At present there are comparatively few trees, and those seedlings, never cultivated and the fruit very pulpy. The frequent drouths render irrigation essential. Until the county water supply is developed, no more trees can be planted. Of course when American capital and enterprise stir up the country, a better showing will be made, but he thinks Southern California oranges will hold their own for a long time yet to come. The orange growers of Europe have never yet failed to find their crops profitable, and it is absurd to suppose that choice Southern California fruit will ever lack a market. Small, sour, inferior oranges are never much in demand, no matter how poorly supplied the country may be with citrus fruits.

PECAN NUTS.

The pecan tree seems to be neglected by our horticulturists, and we know of no good reason why this should be the case. The tree thrives even better in our soil and climate than it does in Texas, from which State large shipments of nuts are annually made, and the growers there consider the crop one of the most profitable. At several points in our county we have seen the trees growing, and we are told that they come to maturity several years sooner than in the South. The pecan belongs to the same family as the hickory, the trees being tall and stately, frequently reaching the height of seventy or eighty feet. They are often used for shade or ornamental trees, and it is said that they usually begin to bear at the age of fifteen or twenty years. Pecans are becoming very popular in the Eastern States, and the trade which was formerly limited to a few thousand bushels has so largely increased that New York city alone takes annually 200,000 bushels. Pecans are now quoted at from eight to eleven cents per pound, with a fair demand.

SILK CULTURE.

An article in a Western magazine gives some interesting items in relation to silk culture at Silkville, Kansas. A wealthy gentleman there had been very successful in silk raising and manufacturing. His silk velvet ribbons took the first premium at the Centennial Exposition, and his accounts were pronounced equal to the best Japanese product. Judging from his statements no employment would be likely to yield greater returns. He says: "If farmers would plant mulberry trees around their farms, that besides the beauty and fruit they would afford—the trees around 100 acres would at the age of eight years

produce enough leaves to raise 1,700 lbs. of cocoons. These cocoons at the lowest price ever known—$1 per lb.—would yield a larger income than perhaps all the other products of the land. And this without costing a single kernel of wheat, or an ear of corn."

This gentleman recommends the simple raising of the cocoons as best, as there are many factories in the country, which wind the cocoons by machinery. Information regarding the care of silk worms and the production of silk may be obtained by writing to the Department of Agriculture, Washington, D. C., for "Special Report No 11."

PASADENA ORANGES IN CONNECTICUT.

The Hartford *Courant* recently acknowledged the receipt of a box of Pasadena oranges, grown by J. R. Clapp, of that place, and, though speaking of them in complimentary terms, thought they were hardly equal to the best Florida oranges. [This item will probably journey through all the Florida journals, from Jacksonville to Lake Worr]. It is a pity that we are not informed as to the exact time that the oranges named were upon their way, and also told something about the packing used, and many other important items without which it were absolutely impossible for any one to decide which of the rival citrus regions produces the choicest fruits. Indeed, it can hardly be done by sending California fruit to the Atlantic States without some previous arrangement for a fair contest, and this would certainly prove interesting. The fruit from the competing sections should be picked on the same day, say on April 1st. Then the thicker skin and better carrying qualities of the California orange would be manifest.

It is also evident that the judgment of travelers who eat the fruit fresh from the trees in each of the many places, must have much to do with the final verdict. This spring, at the Riverside Citrus Fair, a Florida orange grower of repute was present, and made careful examination of the fruit on the trees and in the exhibit. The conclusion was that the California oranges could not be surpassed for size, health, color or flavor in any part of the world, and he added, smiling, "I would rather not put it any stronger, for the sake of the state in which my orange grove is situated, but California is a marvelous region."—*S. F. Bulletin.*

SOILS FOR CITRUS FRUITS.

It is a mistake to suppose that orange, lemon and lime trees will thrive in every kind of soil upon which a variety of other crops may be grown. Many cases have been recorded of persons who have tried unsuccessfully to put out orange orchards in Southern California where nature never intended they should be. Oranges may be produced on heavy clay or adobe lands; they will make a sickly growth on alkali lands, but the fruit is inferior and small

hardly with an exception. The best soils for citrus fruits, in the opinion of nearly all of our leading fruit-growers, are light, deep, gravelly loams, sandy loams, and in some localities reddish clay, which can be easily worked. On soils of an argilaceous character, of moderate depth, to the hard pan or subsoil, the trees do not preserve as vigorous a condition or produce as bright or sweet fruit as on the loamy soils.

THE JAPAN QUINCE.

Of this perfectly hardy shrub we have had six varieties in cultivation for many years. These varieties are very much alike in growth and form of bush, the only difference being in the size, coloration and abundance of their flowers. Their flowers range in color from a light reddish pink to a dark orange red. This fine shrub should be much more planted than it is. It is one of the things that can be readily pruned to any beautiful natural shape or any fanciful shape. It is one of the very best of our shrubby ornamental hedge plants. For this purpose it is permanent and very easily cared for. Six or eight of the best blooming and strong growing varieties planted alternately, or two to four of the most distinct planted a rod of one and then a rod of the other, would be very effective as an ornamental hedge. It is generally increased by a division of the stools, but can be readily grown from cuttings by the summer process. New varieties are obtained from seeds. We have never known it to be injured by insects.

ANAHEIM HORTICULTURAL SOCIETY.

The following is the organization of the new Horticultural and Viticultural Society of Anaheim, as reported by the *Gazette*. It will be observed that all the officials are practical fruit-growers:

President, Theo. Reiser, of Anaheim.

First Vice-President, D. M. Harwood, of Orange.

Second Vice-President, Robert Strong, of Westminster.

Third Vice President, F. A. Korn, of Anaheim.

Secretary, Richard Melrose, of Anaheim.

Finance Committee—F. J. J. Schmidt, John C. Zeyn, E. S. Seaton, all of Anaheim.

To destroy insects on roses, take 3 pounds lime, 3 pounds coarse tobacco, ½ pound sulphur. Slack the lime, and when it is hot and about the consistency of paste add the sulphur, which must be thoroughly mixed with it, then add 3 gallons of water; allow the whole to settle and pour off the liquid. Steep the tobacco in five pailsful of boiling water for twelve hours, add it to add the lime and sulphur water. It is then ready for use and should be used with a syringe.

Too much irrigation and too little cultivation has caused the gum and root disease to make sad inroads on the orange orchards of Mr. Anson Van Leuven in San Bernardino.

HORTICULTURAL NOTES.

THE Italian chestnut is a productive and profitable tree in Southern California and should receive more attention.

RESIDENTS of Florence, in this county, have put out in the neighborhood of 700 acres of grape vines the present season.

NOTHING is gained by buying short, stubby orange trees. Money spent in procuring healthy, vigorous stock, is money well spent.

A SEEDLING orange tree may best be transplanted at the age of four years, although three year old trees do very well. The older the tree the more mutilation to the roots and hence the greater injury.

Two good roses recommended by a Santa Barbara rosarian: Maria Von Houtte, Madame Jean Pernet, Agripina, Madame Rachel, Emperor of Russia, Perle de Jardin, Homer Clare Carnot, Chestnut Hybrid and Archduke Charles.

THERE seems to be no doubt that high land is best adapted to the olive, and the better it is drained, as in the case of rolling and hilly land, especially if the subsoil be heavy, the more satisfactory is the result to be expected.

PROF. BEALS, of Michigan, thinks the reason why apple trees fail of good crops when they blossom fully is to be found in defective pollen or stigmas. If this is so it shows the necessity of planting different sorts near to each other.

THE floral department of the coming Oregon State Fair is 60 by 150 feet in size. It is inclosed by a solid fence ten feet high, and contains a shed 40 by 80 feet, under which house plants are to be set.

CAPT. SEWARD, of Illinois, recommends a mulch of straw around quince trees, with salt scattered around them, as this evaporates dampness, which is what the quince requires. We might say the same of currants, and to those West who have plants of these, but do not get fruit, try it.—Purdy's Record.

MR. KIMBALL, of San Diego, one of the most successful horticulturists in the state, remarked to a person who expressed a fear that too many orange trees may be planted in Southern California: "There are millions of people, who, if oranges cost $1 each, will never eat one; while each of the same million will eat $1 worth of oranges every year if they are sold at one cent each."

THE Grange Store people inform us that they have handled so far this month, chiefly for Arizona and New Mexico trade, about four thousand pounds of butter and over three thousand dozen eggs. As this is only one of the many establishments in our city doing business with the territories, we may infer that the trade of the interior is assuming quite considerable proportions, and that our city and county are reaping a goodly harvest from the mining fields of those parts.—L. A. Express.

IT is an established fact that trees of the deciduous orders require at least from six to ten times more alkalies in the soils upon which they are grown, than the evergreen varieties, which do not shed their leaves. By analysis it was proved that 1,000 parts of the dry leaves of oaks yielded 5½ parts of ashes, of which 24 parts consisted of alkalies, soluble in water; the same quantity of pine leaves gave only 20 parts of ashes, which contained 4.6 parts of soluble salts.

OLIVE trees usually require from seven to ten years to come into abundant bearing; but a correspondent of the New York Times mentions a way the Spaniards have of forcing a much quicker growth. They plant large limbs of trees, often ten feet in length, and two or three inches in diameter, and these, when sunk four or five feet in the ground, and surrounded with two or three feet of clay, take root and begin bearing in a couple of years.

GREEN says in Rural New Yorker: Visiting a large evaporating establishment recently, I inquired what method was found the best for keeping dried fruits from becoming "wormy." "We used to keep them in a dark room," was the reply, "but found that such a place was just the kind desired by the insects, and we lost some small fruits. We have since stored dried raspberries, etc., in very well lighted rooms, leaving as much space as possible between the racks, and the result has been satisfactory."

A MARYLAND peach grower is said to have shipped twenty barrels of peach kernels to Dayton, Ohio, recently, to be used for "chemical purposes." Picture frame makers are said to use the stones in ornamenting the frames they make, and other workers in curiosities in wood find them useful. During the war ingenious soldier boys made various pretty ornaments from peach stones, and doubtless many of these relics are preserved by survivors and others now. Around canning factories, where no other use can be made of them, they have been found to make excellent fuel.

The Congregationalist is indebted to one of its subscribers, Wm. T. Clapp, of Pasadena, in Southern California, for a box of fine oranges which reached us by express, April 4th, in the best order. There was no approach to decay in the entire lot, and we have never tasted fruit of a superior flavor, though it must have traveled more than 3,000 miles by cars, we suppose. If there are a specimen of Mr. Clapp's fruit, it ought to be enough to secure its quick sale anywhere that the packages bear his brand.—Boston Congregationalist.

THE Courant acknowledges the receipt of a box of oranges and lemons from I. H. Clapp, of Pasadena, Southern California. Mr. Clapp is a brother of C. W. Clapp of this city. In the accompanying letter Mr. Clapp writes that the fruits were grown on his farm, which but a few years ago was wild land, and that they were exhibited at the "Citrus Fair" in Pasadena. He writes

enthusiastically of that section and says "I must add that I think this is the land flowing with milk and honey," producing the best fruits, and having the best climate under the sun. We frequently meet and hear from people from Connecticut, in our place and Los Angeles, the last we chanced to meet was Miss Hewitt, formerly stenographer of the Hartford Fire Insurance Company. The oranges are of the Mediterranean Sweet and the Navel kinds, and the lemons are Eurekas." The fruit arrived in good order, and although of fine quality, is not equal in flavor to the finer kinds raised in Florida.—Hartford Courant, April 14th.

As perhaps is well known, almonds are the seeds of the sweet almond tree, and were originally brought from Barbary, but of late years have been extensively grown in southern Europe and the milder climates of Asia. Almonds have recently been cultivated with excellent success in the south and sections of California, and it is very probable that a large portion of the supply for home consumption will ultimately come from that state and its vicinity. Some people consider the nut very indigestible, nevertheless large quantities are annually consumed, both in a raw state and also in fancy cookery and confectionery. The peculiar flavor is very pleasant, and the best qualities are somewhat expensive. Shelled almonds are also largely imported, only the largest and best being used for this purpose, and they command the highest price if they are not in the market, the present quotations being 16 to 18 cents per pound for shelled, and 16 to 18 cents for ordinary grades in the shell. The former pays a duty of ten cents per pound, and the latter six cents per pound.—American Cultivator.

THE Press publishes the following statistics of the fast growing interests of Riverside: Number of acres in orchard, 5,145; seedling orange trees in orchard, 111,657; budded orange trees in orchard, 78,816; bearing orange trees, 2,356; seedling lemon trees in orchard, 2,534; budded lemon trees in orchard, 17,815; bearing lemon trees, 4,832; number of lime trees in orchard, 8,049; olive trees in orchard, 1,975; apricot trees in orchard, 48,015; other deciduous trees in orchard, 14,014; number of Muscat vines in vineyard, 470,000; other varieties in vineyard, 8,636; estimated number of oranges present crop, 816,587; estimated number of lemons present crop, 101,565; estimated number of limes present crop, 70,150; pounds of apricots last crop, 112,425; pounds of peaches last crop, 175,850; pounds of apples last crop, 47,223; pounds of pears last crop, 7,110; pounds of other deciduous fruits last crop, 84,375; number of eucalyptus trees, 18,163; number of Monterey cypress, 12,533; value of buildings erected during 1885 or in process of erection, $44,885; number of boxes of raisins manufactured past season, 13,806; pounds of grapes not made into raisins, 36,800.

THE BEST ORANGE.

The great point for our horticulturists to keep in view is, to produce none but the *best* fruit. The market is at present glutted with small, sour, thick-skinned oranges, and the indications are that hereafter such fruit will not pay to raise. Now, during the past two years fairs have been held at Sacramento, Los Angeles and Riverside, and men long in the fruit business have carefully and critically examined every variety of budded orange produced in California. In every instance where the Washington navel has been entered it has won the laurels over all the competitors, and must be pronounced the best orange at present known. Its merits are that it is very sweet, thin skinned, of good size and shape, and full of juice.

We claim that it will pay every orange-grower in Southern California to procure buds of the Washington navel, even at an increased cost. Those who depend wholly upon the old varieties may have the mortification of finding their fruit less valuable than that of their more sagacious neighbors. We certainly would advocate planting several varieties of orange trees, but would decidedly recommend the Washington navel as a most desirable tree.

Mr. J. H. Dobbins, of San Gabriel, has a stock of 800 trees of the Washington navel variety, and any of our readers who may desire to secure buds, can obtain them by applying early to him. It is unnecessary for us to say that Mr. Dobbins' trees are all in prime condition.

THE MARKET FOR PEACHES.

Our Atlantic coast exchanges come to us daily full of dismal accounts of the almost total failure of the peach crop. The magnitude of the business in this delicious fruit in the States of New Jersey, Delaware and Maryland may be estimated when it is stated that over a million people depend largely upon it for their support. So far as we can learn, the peach orchards of Southern California are backing well, and it is likely that our canning firms and drying establishments will be called upon to supply a portion of the deficiency caused by the great failure in the Eastern States. The price of peaches should rule high this season, and those who have planted large orchards will get returns this year that they had scarcely counted upon.

The Florida *Times and News* says: "Land not fit to live on, but suitable for a grove, sells for from $80 to $300 per acre." California orange land is all fit to live on, and is yet cheap at prices asked.

GIRDLING FOR BARREN TREES.

Not a single tree has ever been injured by girdling, so far as we can learn, even when rings of bark many inches wide, have been taken off, but usually they are about a quarter of an inch wide. The proper season for the operation is June. An Eastern horticulturist says he has induced bearing in trees of Lawrence Pear and Winter Nelis at a very early age, and has some now full of fruit which otherwise would not have shown their quality for many years. A Green Pippin tree, a foot through, which had not borne a peck of fruit in ten years, has been cured of its barren habit by the same simple means. Girdling seems especially applicable to such trees as a check to their tendency to continual growth of wood. To be harmless, the removed bark must be replaced by a new protective covering in the same season.

THE PROFITS OF GRAPE CULTURE.

A vineyard will commence bearing three years after setting out. The yield will be far above expenses of cultivation and harvesting. At five years old a vineyard will yield from four to six tons of fruit per acre. Grapes, last year, sold at the vineyard for from $20 to $30 per ton, according to quality. Old vineyards, say at ten years, will yield from seven to thirteen tons of fruit. There are in California five millions acres of lands which can be obtained at low figures and upon easy terms as to payments, say from $10 to $25 per acre. These lands are located in the foothills of California, both north and south, and are the best grape lands in the State. Many of these lands in the middle and northern portion of California are contiguous to water ditches, for mining purposes. This water could be purchased for irrigation purposes at reasonable rates in many localities, thus making grape culture a certainty. To go into the business requires but a small capital, say from $1,000 to $5,000. Other portions of the foothill regions will grow the vine without irrigation, and the grape of such sections is superior for wine making. A vineyard, after it commences to bear fruit, will continue for fifty years, if properly cultivated. There is no business that will pay so well for the money and labor invested as grape culture—no business equal to it for comfort and health. The vineyardist of the present time has before him the experiments of centuries for guidance of foreign countries, and therefore failure in this State is simply out of the question. The demand for California wines and raisins will increase for many years to come, and the prices will prove remunerative for good articles. What a field is here open to young men of industry and energy, thousands of them.—*Resources.*

Flower plants that succeed well in the shade—Begonias, camellias, ferns, also German and English ivies.

THE NEW FRUIT DRYING ASSOCIATION.

In another column appears the prospectus and announcement of the re-opening of the Alden Fruit Drying Works across the river. The enterprise is now in the hands of some of the leading business men of this city, and will, we believe, give satisfaction in every respect. In the June number we shall publish a full account of the institution and its workings.

Ignorant cultivators frequently weaken the energies of young trees, and cause them to grow up with lean and slender stems by injudiciously trimming off the young shoots. By taking off these shoots the tree is deprived of all the leaves which elaborate the sap for the growing stem which is soon exhibited by its slender increase. In planting the peach, however, of one year's growth these side shoots should be removed, leaving the naked stem, as they are a furred and adventitious growth from the vigor given to a single bud, and the buds formed on the stem are the ones to furnish the top for the current year. The top of the young peach tree should be lopped from three to three and a half feet from the ground on setting. The development of the buds on the stem will then give you a beautiful and healthy head.

A Hartford young man boarded a horse car the other day with a bunch of three roses. One was white, one green, and one of a delicate flesh colored tint. These flowers attracted the attention of the passengers, both ladies and gentlemen. One lady remarked that she had seen the buds of the green rose, and another said she had seen the rose itself, but she had never seen any so perfect and lovely as this one. The flesh colored one was also commented on and praised. Finally the young man volunteered the information that all were white in the morning, and that the coloring was done by putting the stem of one into green ink, and the other into red ink. Although the leaves were beautifully colored, the coloring would not rub off, but it seemed as if nature had done the work. It only required ten minutes to change the color.—*Eastern Exchange.*

The strawberry, among fruits, is more than the rose among flowers. I love it. I have a fondness for the broad leaves that defy the frosty breath of winter, for the pure white blossoms that cheer us first in spring, and for the fruit that breathes the perfume of Paradise. Man may construct steamships and railroads, disembowel the earth for ores, measure the mountains of the moon and make his voice heard across old ocean, but God alone can make a strawberry.—*Downing.*

Whenever a tree is transplanted, many of the roots are injured—a part destroyed. These that remain when set out in a new place are in no condition to feed the plant as it was fed previous to removal. Hence the top must be cut back to restore the equilibrium.

COMPLIMENTS FROM THE OLD BAY STATE

To Gen. Rice, Esq., Secretary Southern California Horticultural Society: Dear Sir: I am desired by the Fruit Committee of the Massachusetts Horticultural Society to return thanks in behalf of the Society, for the large and interesting contribution of citrus fruits and reviews which were received here and exhibited on Saturday, the 9th instant. I do not think we have had such a display of these kinds of fruits since the 11th of April, 1850, when it is recorded that twelve varieties of...

...and Messrs. Ellwanger, Barry, Downing and others, ten years ago last summer, but it was impossible.

Wishing you all success with your journal, and your Society an ever useful career, and extend the cultivation of semi-tropic, I am

Yours respectfully,
ROBERT MANNING, Sec'y M. H. S.
Boston, April 14, 1881

LETTER FROM STATE BOARD OF AGRICULTURE

Mr. Gen. Rice, Editor Semi-Tropic California:—Dear Sir: Your postal received; also sample copy of your valuable journal, which, in my mind, takes the front rank in its particular field for the matter which it champions. The sample is typographically...

LETTER FROM VITICULTURAL AGENCY.

Rice, Esq., ... *Southern California Horticultural Society...*

FULTON WELLS

FULTON SULPHUR WELLS, LOS ANGELES COUNTY.

...rous, lemons, oranges and limes were sent from the garden of Charles W. Dabney, at Fayal, when Mr. Dabney, who was an honorary member of the Society, was United States Consul.

First class Certificates of Merit were awarded by the Committee to Warren Kimball, of National City, for oranges, and B. G. Clark, of San Diego, for raisins. These certificates will be prepared and forwarded in due time.

I have been much interested in the reports of the Citrus Fairs in your magazine. They (the fairs) must have presented a beautiful sight, and I wish I could have seen them. I want very much to visit California, much more than I do to see Europe, but there is little prospect that I shall. I wanted very much to go with Col. Wilder...

...L. J. Rose, deserving of a ... than a ... notice.

Having had a taste of your semi-tropic, I can fully appreciate a good and a ... written article, and one below to a ... might sign that there are a few ... and good ones in your ... noble part. In answer to your postal, am pleased to reply that our Fair commences Monday, Sept 19th, and continues until Saturday, Sept 24th, both inclusive. The action in the dates of holding the District Fairs not yet, but probably will soon be ... received our premium lists, which will be sued during the present month, ... shall forward you same.

Very respectfully,
JAMES P. SMITH, Sec'y
SACRAMENTO, April 19, 1881

Farmer's Department.

FEEDING HORSES.

The horse has the smallest stomach in proportion to his size of any animal. Fifteen or sixteen quarts is its utmost capacity. This space is completely filled by four quarts of oats and the saliva that goes into the stomach with it. Horses are generally over fed and not fed often enough. For a horse with moderate work six or eight quarts of bruised oats and eight or ten pounds of fine hay a day is sufficient. This should be fed in at least three meals, and is better if fed in four.

A horse's digestion is very rapid, and therefore he gets hungry sooner than a man. When he is hungry he is ineffective, and wears out very rapidly. Water kills the stomach, lowers the temperature and dilutes the gastric juice, therefore a horse should not drink immediately before eating. Neither should he be watered immediately after eating, because he will drink too much and force some of the contents of the stomach into the large intestine, which will cause scouring.

Give only a moderate drink of water to a horse. A large drink of cold water before being driven will have a very quieting effect on a nervous horse. A race-horse always runs on an empty stomach. Digestion progresses moderately during exercise, if the exercise is not so violent as to exhaust the powers of the horse. I consider bruised oats or barley worth twenty per cent. more than whole. They are more completely digested. I refer oats to any other grain for horses. Cracked corn is very good under some circumstances, but wouldn't use meal or shorts. The disease called big head is caused by feeding corn.

When a horse comes in hot, I would give a moderate feed immediately. If the horse is too tired to eat would take his feed away. A heated body is a reason against watering, and for feeding, for the system is then just in condition to begin digestion. A horse will not founder if fed moderately when hot. I prefer dry feed unless a horse has some disease of the throat or lungs. I always feed hay from the floor, then the horses do not get particles in their eyes.—*Address before Mass. Farm Club.*

A SANTA CLARA farmer says: A calf at three months old of age is worth $9, at twelve months old, $12, at two years $20 to $25, at three years, a young cow, with a calf at her side, is worth from $35 to $50; then I sell them, as after this age they do not pay so well. Cows bring in $50 per annum in butter and cheese.

A season of universal drought, followed by a winter unprecedented for snow, have shown the present mode of raising stock in Colorado to be a failure. The losses of the past winter in sheep and cattle will foot up a startling total when the truth comes to be told.

BARLEY.

Singular as it may appear the United States import barley very largely from foreign countries. Figures compiled from official sources show that the total imports of this grain from Canada from July to January, 1880, were 7,459,500 bushels. The total imports from Canada during the last ten crop years aggregate 59,829,542 bushels. During the six months ended December 31, 1880, there were imported also from Canada, 233,774 bushels of barley malt, and the imports for nine fiscal years, last past, were 3,510,761 bushels from the same country. Malt is barley which has been made to germinate by moisture and warmth, and afterwards dried, by which the vitality of the seed is destroyed. By this process, a peculiar nitrogenous principle, called diastase, is produced. Although this does not constitute more than 1-500th part of the malt, it serves to effect the conversion of starch of the seed into dextrine and grape sugar. One hundred pounds of barley yield about eighty pounds of malt.

BUTTER MAKING.

A successful Kenosha, Wis., butter-maker gives his method as follows. Our milk, as soon as drawn from the cow, is placed in a double channel pan, with cold water running under the pan till the milk is reduced to 60° temperature; temperature of room 65°; held till it begins to thicken; cream taken off with one-fourth as much milk as cream. Churn in barrel churns until the first appearance of butter-milk; then add one pailful of weak brine, at a temperature of 60°; then churn till it comes to the size of wheat; then add more brine, till the buttermilk is thinned so that it separates easily from the butter. Place the butter upon the worker, work carefully, rinse with water till solid, then add salt—½ ounce to one pound butter—let it stand till the next morning; work over and pack.

It makes an observant resident of this city reel to stop at our green grocers and see their stands loaded with fresh grown California vegetables. In the midst of as fine an agricultural region as the sun shines on, where the earth tickled with a hoe laughs a bounteous harvest of as fine vegetables as grow in the temperate zone; with all that is necessary for their planting, care and cultivation to be had for the labor of preparing them, we import cabbages, celery, lettuce, in fact, nearly every vegetable that will bear transportation from California. We hope that some practical market gardeners will soon discover that there are in Walla Walla city over 4,000 people with tastes and appetites like those possessed by residents of other places of the same size, and that by catering to the palates of this people he can put money in his purse.—*Walla Walla Union.*

MILLIONS of army worms have appeared in the Sacramento Valley.

AGRICULTURAL NOTES.

The Hall brothers, of New Mexico, have sold a ranch and 25,000 head of cattle to a Scotch company for $100,000.

TURUE is a very prolific cow at East Windsor Hill, Ct. April 10, 1877, she gave birth to twins, one male and one female; March 19, 1878, she gave birth to triplets, two males and one female, making five calves in eleven months and three days; July 9, 1879, she gave birth to twins, both males; October 7, 1880, she gave birth to triplets, two males and one female, making ten calves in three years; five months and twenty-one days. The calves have all been of good size, healthy and handsome, and have been raised on the farm.

A New York dealer, in a circular to dairymen, says that the oleomargarine is plenty, good and cheap, and adds that in order to compete with imitation butter and low grade western natural butter, dairymen must—

"Make a full flavored butter, and sell it fresh enough to keep it out of the company of common stock. The milk must be set at a uniformly low temperature and kept there, so as to get all the flavor into the cream. The cream must then be soured enough to draw the flavor, but not stand long enough to get bitter or whey, and the butter after it is come must not have the flavor worked out of it, or washed out of it. To keep up the color in the spring butter, let the strong, easterly light fall on the butter-worker while working it in the morning, and try to get a delicate, natural color. Then with the market supplied with a full-flavored, brittle-grained butter, fresh from the churn, he who runs—may read the difference between it and any imitation whatever."

If I remember right, Dr. Horn somewhere stated that there is no way of expelling bots from a horse. I have been in the habit of giving horses a strong drench of sage, well sweetened, which had the effect of expelling the bots. It was supposed, when I was a boy, that sage was acted as a cathartic, and that the bots were fond of sweet, and would let go to take a sip of tea, and while sipping tea would be carried along the intestinal canal and the horse would be relieved. A few ashes help them along. I write from experience; my guess work about it.—*Correspondence Indiana Farmer.*

FIVE years ago Germany produced but 464,900 tons of beet sugar. In 1880-81 she produced 550,000 tons.

FROSTS have destroyed the peach crop and seriously damaged the wheat fields of Kansas.

An Allegheny livery man has named his stable goat Oleomargarine, because he is a bad butter.

Agriculture.

ALFALFA.

AN INTERESTING COMMUNICATION FROM GEN. SHIELDS.

James L. Fleming Esq., 816 Broad Street, Chicago, Ill. —DEAR SIR: Your letter in one of our prominent citizens (Dr. H. S. Orme) containing inquiries about alfalfa, was handed to me with the request that I give information on the subject. You, I infer from your letter, make the inquiries not in contemplation of a migration to California, but of a trial of alfalfa in the region around Chicago. I will, however, state facts about alfalfa in California, and opinions about it in Illinois.

In order that you may know the origin of what I know about alfalfa, it is mentioned that I at the time when from one to five acres to alfalfa for any one farmer measured the faith in and use for the plant in Los Angeles county, devoted to it fifty acres in a single field; that I followed up the fifty-acre sowing with other sowings; that I have grazed it, mowed it and fed it, green, wilted and dry; that I have fed with it in these various ways, horses, mules, cattle, sheep, Cashmere goats, hogs, dairy cows, chickens, turkeys, geese and ducks. Sometimes a livelier appreciation of alfalfa is shown by wild ducks than comports with domestic economy. During the winter of an exceptionally dry year, myriads of wild ducks made nocturnal raids on the fifty acre field. Their nightly return was but partially checked by occasional shotgun interruptions.

CONCLUSIONS WARRANTED BY EXPERIENCE.

After years of experience with alfalfa and other fodder-plants in California, and extensive experience with fodder-plants other than alfalfa in the East, it is my deliberate opinion that alfalfa is the best of all for fodder. It yields more than other plants, a greater number of crops each year, greater tonnage per mowing, is well adapted to a greater variety of domestic animals, and more readily and beneficially responds to the digestive and assimilative processes.

NUMBER AND TONNAGE OF CROPS.

In Los Angeles county six, seven and even eight mowings of from one to three tons per mowing of alfalfa are annually yielded. These mowings are made from March to November inclusive. There is considerable growth of alfalfa here during December, January and February. The equivalent of one full crop I noted a growth of one foot in thirty days, ending January 31, 1881. Twenty-five days in June would have brought out of the same ground from two and a half to three times the production. During our summer months alfalfa may be mown every month.

NUTRITIVE QUALITIES OF ALFALFA.

The chemist in his laboratory finds the percentage of nutriment in one hundred pounds of alfalfa hay, about equal to the nutriment he finds in one hundred pounds of the best English hay. The horse finds the alfalfa more strengthening and more conducive to the increase of flesh. Horses and mules will do two-thirds full work on alfalfa hay alone. The dairyman finds the flow of milk of his alfalfa fed cows about equal to that resulting from feeding red clover in June. The connoisseur of dairy products detects a betterment of quality by the addition of to the alfalfa ration, a small allowance of hay of some other kind. Sugar beets and even mangel wurzels are added to the alfalfa with advantage to the quality of the butter. The same remarks apply to reed clover as dairy feed. Sheep do well on alfalfa, though better on mixed wild grasses. Angora or Cashmere goats delight in and thrive on alfalfa, but if left to freely choose, will divide attentions between the sweetest alfalfa and the sourest, bitterest, thorniest and dryest miscellany of the chapparral. What is, in this particular, the choice of the goat, is in a less degree the choice, but in a greater degree a part of nature's sanitary regime for the sheep. The hog is about as well suited on alfalfa, green or dry, as on young and growing barley or wheat or on red clover. The Essex and the Berkshire, the more closely built the better after three months old, will thrive as store hogs, and get excellently ready for a sixty days' finishing on grain. However much can you give a hog he will, if permitted, spend hours daily in the alfalfa field, or feeding on alfalfa hay—and contrary to the opinion of some, the hog thrives more on the corn because of the alfalfa, and as all agree, thrives more on the alfalfa because of the corn. To test the comparative availability of the nutritive properties of alfalfa and any other hay, one has only to feed a pig on alfalfa hay and see him thrive, and on any hay except alfalfa or clover, and see him dwindle and perhaps perish.

Poultry, however mark grain or dough they receive, will spend a portion of every day in the neighboring alfalfa field, cramming with alfalfa leaves

COMPARISON OF ALFALFA WITH RED CLOVER.

Alfalfa is a species, or more strictly speaking, a variety within a species of the genus *trifolium*. So are the white and red clovers. Alfalfa is superior to white or to red clover in many respects, and inferior in none, with the single exception that the northern limit of the clovers is at a higher latitude than that of alfalfa. The Chicago inquirer is deeply interested on the subject of the degree of cold which alfalfa can survive. All I can say from personal observation is that I have seen alfalfa come out luxuriantly in May near Salt Lake City, where the roads had passed through a winter in which the mercury fell to ten degrees below zero. I also saw similar illustrations of the capacity of alfalfa to flourish after passing cold snaps of ten degrees below zero east of Salt Lake City, and on the line of the Union Pacific railroad. The second crop of red clover severely salivates. No crop of alfalfa ever salivates. The manger fills up with clover sticks, but there are no alfalfa sticks that a properly allowanced horse will reject. Both clover and alfalfa hay shed leaves, and perhaps about equally. Both are liable to mold in the stack or loft, but here alfalfa is less liable because its stems of less diameter dry out sooner. Neither is it liable to be spoiled by rain here in California for half the year is rainless. Both are so liable in the East, but of the two alfalfa drying sooner, may safely go into the barn earlier to escape the shower, or escape, in a given instance the same shower, the clover hay goes into the barn prematurely and spoils. Alfalfa flourishes in the far South where it is too warm for clover, and prospers throughout a drought that kills clover, root and branches. The longer tap root of the alfalfa makes it proof against drought and the southern sun. The tap root of the alfalfa varies in length according to circumstances, from ten to three feet commonly, to twenty feet rarely. There are well attested cases of the latter length. Alfalfa blasts more rarely than red clover. I have grazed 3,000 sheep, hundreds of cattle and many horses on alfalfa without losing a horse or cow, and not more than a score of sheep by bloat.

OBJECTIONS ABOUT ALFALFA FROM THE COLD.

I fear that your winters are too severe for alfalfa. My doubt should, however, not deter you from making an experiment. Your blanket of snow would afford great protection to alfalfa as it does to your winter wheat. The extreme northern line of alfalfa diverges northwards as the line approaches the Atlantic ocean, because eastward there is more snow as well as a much erratic bending of the isothermal line.

The best localities near Chicago are along the lake shore where water never stands on the surface longer than ten days in winter, nor more than three days in warm weather. Alfalfa, like other plants half dead with cold, will survive longer submersion than when fully alive with warmth. As soon as May has had the last mercury as low as 25° above zero, sow the alfalfa seed. Prepare the ground by frequent harrowings, and then sow and harrow in. The question is not how deep, but how shallow to get in the seed. An inch is too deep by half; one-fourth of an inch is the best; one-eighth will do, and with a guarantee of timely showers the seed might be sown on freshly harrowed soil, and leave rain drops to do the rest. Twenty-five pounds of seed to the acre a little enough, and thirty pounds not too much.

The hay crop is said to be worth more than the cotton crop. A small percentage of increase of the hay crop amounts to millions of dollars. I think it highly probable that if the National Commissioner of Agriculture would go systematically about opening the eyes of the nation's farmers to the merits and possibilities of alfalfa, as were opened centuries ago the eyes of Virgil Columella and other Mediterranean Latins as to its co-ordinate varieties, enough millions would be added to the nation's wealth to pay a century's expense of a dozen institutions a dozen times more extensive than the National Department of Agriculture.   J. H. SHIELDS.

Los Angeles, Cal., May 2, 1881

Southern California.

BEAUTIFUL LOS ANGELES.

The best way to see Los Angeles is to begin in the middle and explore as critically as you please. She is (retiral) fair within, or was when we first saw her. At the Citrus Fair were —— thousand oranges of —— thousand kinds. Our readers may fill up the blanks to suit themselves; we have tried in vain to remember them. Besides these, were figs, and raisins, and olives, and lemons, and almonds, and English walnuts, and other fruits too numerous to taste; and lilies, and verbenas, and roses, and other flowers too multitudinous to look at or smell. But we have no space to describe it. Exploring the suburbs, we roamed through orange, and lemon, and peach and plum orchards. We investigated their mode of culture, and found out their enemies, and we concluded that this business, as well as any other, actually requires mind, and perseverance and economy. But also we were constrained to acknowledge that horticulture has nothing more beautiful than an orange orchard, with its trees laden at the same time with rich foliage, buds and blossoms, and the full, ripe fruit.—*Extract from letter of Bishop Warren to Cal. Christian Advocate.*

PROGRESS IN SOUTHERN CALIFORNIA.

The *Press and Horticulturist* reports that on April 6th the Riverside Land and Irrigating Company sold to S. C. Evans, of Riverside, and Chas. N. Felton, of Oakland, 1200 acres of land in and around Arlington for the sum of £.00 per acre, or a total of $120,000. This sale includes 1200 shares of water stock in the Riverside Canal Company. This land will be placed on the market for sale and scheduled in price from $100 to $200 per acre, according to how much—one share of water stock going with each acre of land.

Let California be up and doing, for she should take a leading part in intercourse with Mexico. Our proximity to her borders, as well as the fact that socially we are in greater sympathy with that country than are our Eastern sisters, gives us advantages which we should not be slow to grasp.— *Anaheim Gazette.*

Mr. J. H. Petit, the fish culturist of San Bernardino, has sold already this season, $9,000 carp, and the season is not fairly opened yet. Three thousand of these were brought to this city, and included three hundred which will spawn this spring.—*Commercial.*

At Pinacante, San Diego county, 136 claims have been recorded; six of these prospects are down 35 feet. The vein contain free-milling ore, and runs north and south in decomposed granite.

San Diego is becoming quite a focus for seal hunting. It is estimated that this industry was worth $100,000 to the place during the past year.

Although a considerable quantity of rain has fallen this winter—enough ordinarily to produce good crops—something has hindered grain in the valley from filling out as it should. The best looking grain may be found north of town. The most accurate estimate that can be made at present, places the barley yield this year at about 125,000 sacks. This may be increased somewhat by favorable weather, or may be decreased by unkind north winds.—*San Bernardino Index.*

When the water resources of the Colton Land and Water Company shall be fully developed to a capacity of 500 inches as they will be in the near future, the Colton tract will simply bloom into a vast and beautiful garden, in the midst of which the picturesque and beautiful town of Colton will stand out in one of the most charming locations in beautiful California.—*Semi-Tropic.*

What would our readers think of us if we suggested to transient visitors to purchase all their fruit and agricultural produce from the northern portion of the State? Yet some fruit-growers of Los Angeles County serve us quite as badly. They patronize up country magazines and papers, published, principally, in the interest of the debris ridden farmers, and decline to do anything for a home paper which strives to be faithful.

"Ask and ye shall receive." Our section has at last received some rather reluctantly bestowed favors by persistently asking for them. Through the determined efforts of our local press and county representatives two years ago we secured sessions of the Supreme Court in Los Angeles. This year in the same manner a branch Normal School has been granted our city. Let us keep on asking.

The hills and valleys of Southern California have turned brown and will remain so until the middle of next October or first of November. Camping parties can go to the beach or mountains without the slightest fear of unpleasant weather, and we learn that several families have already organized for a mammoth excursion.

The demand for the Citrus Fair edition of the Semi Tropic has completely exhausted our supply. The good done by the display to our county, as we stated in our last issue, can never be adequately represented in dollars and cents.

Those of our readers who are entitled to diplomas and medals can get them in a few weeks by calling at this office. The illness of the Secretary has delayed the work.

The *Daily Commercial* of this city has been enlarged and improved with a new dress. We are glad to note these evidences of its prosperity.

Mr. A. B. Moffit, of San Fernando, informs us that the wheat fields of that season never looked better, and a full crop may be expected.

CALIFORNIA ORANGES.

The *Times* acknowledges the receipt of a box of fine oranges from the managers of the Citrus Fair in Los Angeles, California. At a meeting of the Citrus Society it was decided to send one hundred boxes of oranges to editors in different parts of the country! W. P. Large, of this city, who is now in Los Angeles, having the disposition of one box, ordered it sent to the *Times*, and it was sent free of expense by Wells, Fargo & Co. The box arrived safely, and the oranges were greatly enjoyed by the *Times'* force and their families.

Any person, whether of a horticultural turn of mind or not, could not hesitate in recommending the soil and climate of California for orange culture, after eating some of the oranges grown in this State. The fruit is equal in flavor and size to that of Florida or any other orange growing country. If any better oranges can be raised, we want to see and taste them. California is rapidly making for itself a proud name as an agricultural and horticultural State, and now that it is fully proven that such tropical fruit as oranges can be successfully grown there, another feather will be added to her cap. It is useless to send outside of the United States for oranges when one of our own galaxy of States can produce such a delicious sample of this fruit as those sent to this office by the Citrus Society of California.—*Dubuque (Iowa) Times.*

It is not yet too late to do a good work in the way of tree-planting in towns and villages and along country roads. In theory, every real estate owner in the country is supposed to have interest enough in the enhancement of the value of his own property to make the improvements suggested. But these generally go by default for the lack of the stimulus of good examples. A few enterprising citizens, men and women, making a practical demonstration of the way the work can be done, will often stimulate hundreds of others by such an example.

During the last ten years the exports of wine from France have varied between 91,000,000 and 63,000,000 gallons; but it should be added that during the same period the imports have been steadily rising from 2,867,000 to 67,500,000 gallons.

The Los Angeles Woolen Mills are running on full time. Several large orders have lately been received. A Boston gentleman lately ordered 10,000 white blankets to be shipped East over the new line.

El Molino, Col. Kewen's beautiful place at San Gabriel, has recently been sold to Mr. E. L. Mayberry for $36,000.

The Compton cheese factories are making a large quantity of cheese daily, for which they find a ready market.

Work has been commenced on the railroad extension to deep water at Wilmington.

Poultry.

HARD TO BEAT.

Our friend Jillson informs us that he has Plymouth Rock chicks hatched the 29th of December, that weigh over five pounds each, and pullets that are already laying. This shows what may be accomplished with good stock, having good care and proper management. In shipping eggs or fowls Mr. Jillson has had remarkable success in pleasing his customers. When he says his eggs for hatching are fresh laid and from the best of stock, his customers may be sure they are just that kind. By his persistent efforts to improve his birds by purchasing stock and eggs from the most reliable Eastern breeders, is chiefly due the name he has already gained for reliability, and we heartily recommend him to any in need of the varieties he keeps.

HAVE AN INTEREST IN THE WORK.

When a breeder cannot find anything that requires doing, except to regularly feed his birds night and morning, he had better kill and eat them, as they will prove far more profitable in that way, than to keep them, hoping for any satisfactory profit. Each month brings its regular work and duties, which must be attended to, and little things that require attention, all of which tend to insure success. The careful, thorough breeder will have an interest, a love for his work. Do not think that all you have to do is to get the fowls and your object is accomplished. If you do it will not be necessary to say that you will be disappointed. Unless you have an interest for your fowls you will be forgetful of their wants and neglect to give them the proper care. But have the proper interest and love for your fowls, and with the most limited facilities you will derive much pleasure and a good, clear profit.

CHAS. P. JILLSON.

USEFUL HINTS.

No woman knows until she has worn one, what a convenience a clothes pin apron is. To make it, cut a short apron out of a single width of calico, and face it up half the depth with a piece of the same calico, hemmed at the top. Put two perpendicular rows of stitching through the center of this pocket, round off the corners and finish the outside edge with a bias band. Make a stout belt of doubled calico, with a substantial button and button hole.

For cracked hands or hands inclined to feel hard and rough, use raw linseed oil, in which there may be one-sixth of alcohol, perfumed to suit. Or use commoline and cream well mixed and perfumed. Or use alcohol, 4 oz.; glycerine, 4 oz.; castor oil, 4 oz. Shake when about to use, and perfume as you please.

The use of benzine is recommended for the removal of moths and ants from furniture and woolen garments. A small watering-pot, with a fine nozzle sprinkler, is filled with the benzine, which can be bought for forty-five cents a gallon, and the upholstery, carpets or garments to be cleansed are thoroughly sprinkled with the liquid. Furs, flannels, etc. may be subjected to the same process. In a few hours the benzine will dry out and in a day or two the odor will have entirely disappeared, and much sooner if the articles are placed in the open air. Considerable caution is necessary in the use of benzine, as it is highly inflammable. Have no fire, burning light or matches in the room.

When you get chilly all over, and away into your bones, and begin to snuffle and almost struggle for your breath, just begin in time and your tribulations need not last very long. Get some powdered borax, and snuff the dry powder up your nostrils. Get your camphor bottle, smell it frequently, pour some on your handkerchief, and wipe your nose with it whenever needed. Your nose will not get sore, and you will soon wonder what's become of your cold. Begin this treatment in the forenoon and keep up at intervals until you go to bed, and you will sleep as well as you ever did.

Here is a rule for making Boston brown bread, as it is called outside of New England; although like Boston baked beans, it is common throughout New England, and is known as brown bread: Take 4 cupfuls of Indian meal and 4 cupfuls of rye meal (not flour); sift through a coarse wire sieve; add 2 teaspoonfuls of soda, a little salt, 1 cupful of molasses, 1 cupful of sour milk, and water sufficient to make a soft dough. Bake four hours in a moderately heated oven, or what would be better, twenty hours in a brick oven.

It is safe to have a rule for making the simple things in cooking, and so be sure of satisfactory and uniform results. Here is an excellent rule for preparing mustard for the table: Take two tablespoonfuls of mustard, one tablespoonful of flour, mix them well while dry, then take half a cupful of strong vinegar, fill the cup with water, stir the mustard and flour with this, cook it as you would boiled custard; when it is thick enough take from the fire and add one teaspoonful of sugar.

A stout and inexhaustible can be made as follows: Place a quantity of water sufficient for use in a kettle to boil; put in all the alum it will dissolve; when boiling hot, with a brush apply the solution to all cracks, closets, bedsteads, and other places where insects are found. Ants, bed bugs, cock-roaches and creeping things are killed by it, while there is no danger of poisoning the family or injuring the property.

This terrible cramp colic, so often fatal before the dawn, can often be relieved within an hour with a mild emetic, and flannels, wrung in boiling water, applied to the stomach.

To prevent lamp chimneys from cracking place your tumblers, chimneys or vessels, which you desire to keep from cracking, in a pot filled with cold water; add a little cooking salt; allow the mixture to boil well over a fire, and then cool slowly. Glass treated in this way is said not to crack even if exposed to very sudden changes of temperature. Chimneys are said to become very durable by this process, which may also be extended to crockery, stone ware, porcelain, etc. The process is simply one of annealing, and the slower the process, especially the cooling portion of it, the more effective will be the work.

A Cynthia's correspondent gives the following simple remedy for scratches in horses: "Having tried many lotions, etc., only to obtain temporary relief for my horse, I concluded to try a mixture of flowers of sulphur and glycerine, which I mixed into a paste, using sufficient glycerine to give it a glossy appearance, and the results I obtained in a short time were truly wonderful. I apply this paste at night, and in the morning before going out I apply plain glycerine."

Lice are one of the greatest drains upon the vitality of stock, and it is surprising that so many allow their stock to become infested with lousy. Carbolic acid and soft soap, made into a strong ointment, or kerosene and lard are perhaps as good as anything. But the remedy must be applied two or three times thoroughly, to succeed in exterminating them.

Dr. Van Buren, on the subject of burns, remarks that the best course to pursue in case of severe burns is to immediately throw cold water upon the victim or as to prevent the heated clothing from burning deeper into the flesh, and then apply dry ointments of oils. It will be well to bear this simple remedy in mind.

The black walnut was first planted in Contra Costa county, California, in 1846, by some naval officers who had gone ashore for a few days, "trout fishing." They are still growing in front of the residence of Judge Elam Brown, near Lafayette, and average forty-five feet in height. These now growing at the confluence of Lafayette slough with the Sacramento river, were planted by a man by the name of Sharp, in 1848, but are not so thick in the trunk as those at Judge Brown's, though they are quite as tall. From these two groves hundreds of trees have been set out since here, and before twenty years more have passed away, California grown black walnut will form a large part of cabinet maker's stock.

The scales which fly off from iron being worked at forges, from trimmings, filings, or other ferruginous material, if worked into the soil about fruit trees, or the more minute particles spread thinly on the lawn, mixed with the earth of flower beds or in pots, add greatly to the productiveness of the soil. For colored flowers, they heighten the bloom and increase the brilliancy.

Miscellaneous.

TWISTING A CALF'S TAIL.

There is nothing that demands states-manship of a high order so much as the driving of a cow with a young calf to any particular place. Two Galveston colored men undertook a job on this character yesterday, and although they gave the matter their careful attention, the result was very far from satisfactory to anybody except the cow which seemed to enjoy it very much. Sam and Bill were to get a dollar to take the cow and calf and put them in the yard of the owner, Mr Thomas Carlyle, who lives at the South end of Galveston Avenue. After trying in vain to get the cow to understand in what direction they preferred she should go, Sam and Bill called a calm but meeting, at which the following campaign plan was agreed upon: Sam was to take up the calf in his arms and go ahead, while Bill was to hold the cow back by the rope which was fastened to her horns.

"Ef she goes too fast," said Bill, "I'll jest hold her back."

"And ef she don't foller fast enough I'll jest twist de calf's tail, and den she will come right along," said Sam.

Sam took up the calf and went ahead, while Bill, in order to get a real good hold, tied the rope around his wrist. The procession proceeded slowly in the desired direction, and would have reached its destination in safety had not Satan tempted Bill to get off a joke on Sam, so he called out:

"Sam, jes twist de calf's tail."

Sam did so, and the calf bleated as if it was supposed to do to ensure the performance.

The old cow began to trot. She did Sam, holding on to the calf as if he had stolen it. Then the fun began, for every atom in a while the cow would polish the horns on the coat-tails of Sam's pants. Bill could not get his hands out of the rope, and, as he had short legs, he had hard work keeping up with the procession, or rather in not letting go. He ran so fast that the kinks of his wool straightened out. Finally he gasped.

"Sam, let twist dat cow's tail."

Sam's legs moved so rapidly that they looked like the spokes of a buggy, but he called back:

"Bill, don't let go dat rope, de cow a gainin on me."

"Drap de caf," called poo Bill, whose arms was coming out of the socket. "Drap de caf, for I can't keep up wid de cow. Go slow, niggah, or I'll turn de cow loose on you," which, however, was more than he was able to do.

Bill made the next fifty yards on his back, he still most unwillingly retaining his hold on the rope. Fortunately, the cow overtook Sam, and in return for his kind-ness in picking up the calf, she picked him up on his horns and threw him over into Mr. Carlyle's yard. Bill, who was rather tired of chasing the cow, thought he would clamb over and see what Sam was doing.

The cow appeared to understand his wishes in that direction, so she started on a run to help him out, or rather over. She was a little late, but he went about ten feet further into the field than he would have done without her assistance. There was neither of them so badly hurt as they were when old Carlyle came and told them that the contract was that they should put the cow in the yard. Instead of that the cow had put them in the yard, so the dollar belonged to himself as the owner of the cow.

It is thought a lawsuit will grow out of the matter.—Galveston News.

MEXICO'S YANKEE POPULATION.

Mexico is filled with "Yankees," as all people from the United States are called. These "Yankees" embrace engineers, capitalists, tourists, speculators, "drummers" and adventurers. The last named, how-ever, are a disgrace to our nation, as they comprise gamblers, tramps, and other high personages of both sexes who travel in-cognito. This country abounds in vast natural resources, but is almost entirely undeveloped. The gold and silver mines are worked on the same plan as one hun-dred years ago. Sugar is ground, wheat gathered and threshed, cotton spun, paper manufactured, liquors distilled, and cloth and textures of all kinds woven in the most primitive style. In fact, all labor-saving machines and the latest inventions and im-provements of manufacture and agriculture are just being introduced; hence the pro-fuse abundance of the Yankee, who, with his usual foresight and enterprise, sees an immense trade to be developed with his own country.

A GOOD DOG STORY.

While two dogs were playing on a bridge near one of the paper mills at West Fitch-burg, Monday, one of them accidentally fell into the water and was unable to get out on account of the ice. John Hart's dog, remaining on the bridge, looked down at his unfortunate companion, and then ran toward the house of the latter's owner, but before reaching the house stopped and went back, and again looked at the dog struggling in the water. Then he returned almost to the house where the other dog lived, but turned and again sent back to the bridge. Then he ran down and out on the ice, grabbed the dog by the neck and pulled him out of the water. While en-gaged in this humane act the rescued dog was yelping to the best of his ability.

In the manufacture of attar of roses at Ghazepore, Hindostan, the petals of the flowers are put into clay mills, with twice their weight of water, and the product as-signed to the fresh air for a night in open vessels. The attar is skimmed from the exposed pans, and sells at £10 the rupee weight, to make which 20,000 roses are re-quired.

California strawberries are plentiful in the Salt Lake markets.

BULLS.

Among famous bulls fathered upon Irish-men is that one that occurred when an Englishman was chasing his letter (which an Irishman was overlooking) with these words: "I would write more, but a tall paddy is looking over my shoulder and reading all I write." "You lie, you scoun-drel," was instantly thundered in the writer's ear. But this was matched in re-cent years when, in a certain church in Salem, a gentleman falling into a doze, another near him, gently sent into the sleeper's ear an imitative snore. "You lie," said the sleeper, "I didn't." Did an Irish-man ever make a greater blunder than the English lawyer who drew up an indictment in which it was charged that the prisoner at the bar killed a man with a certain wooden instrument called an iron pestle? Or than Peter Harrison, a commentator on the Pentateuch, who in explaining about the tables of stone on which Moses wrote the commandments, said "they were prob-ably made of Scottish wood? Or than a correspondent of the English Royal Society, who talked of an earthquake that had the honor of being noticed by said Society? Or among all the Irish bulls can anything be found to equal that of the Frenchman who complimented a celebrated French actress, somewhat on in years, on the manner in which she had acted Zara, and when the lady said, "To play that part well, one should be young and handsome," he re-plied, "Ah, madam, you are proof to the contrary?" Which certainly intimated that she was neither. Or was there ever a bull more exquisite than that of an English-man, who speaking of his nurse, said: "I hate her, for she changed me for another when I was a baby?"

Two darkies, in South Carolina, had bought a piece of pork, and Sam, having no place to put his share, intrusted the whole to Julius's keeping. Next morning they met, when Julius said, "A most strange thing happened at my house last night, Sam. All mystery to me." "Ah Julius, what was dat?" "Well, Sam, in a minute I went down in de cellar fur to get a piece ob hog for breakfast, and I put my hand down into de brine, an' felt round, but no pork there—all gone—couldn't feel what be went with it; an I turned up the bar'l, an' Sam, sure as preachin', de cats had eat a hole clean from de bottom ob the bar'l, and dragged de pork all out!" Sam was petrified with astonishment, but pres-ently said, "Why didn't de brine run out ob de same?" "Ah," said Julius, "dat's de mystery!"

A San Francisco woman recently sent a letter to a friend in a farming town asking the number of eggs a hen would lay in a day. She knew, she said, that they would lay a dozen or more, but she wishes to learn the exact number, as eggs were very high, and she thought considerable money might be made by keeping a hen.

MOCKING birds are well worthy of special favors from our horticulturists, for, besides being essentially insectivorous, they have the additional merit of being able to render our homesteads cheerful by their unequaled powers of song. The word "unequaled" is here used with consideration, for the Hon. D. Harrington, the English naturalist, speaks of it thus: "The bird fully equals the nightingale in the compass of its song;" and Wilson says, "Its vocal powers are unquestionably superior to those of the nightingale." The nightingale sings only at night, when it has the advantage of stillness, and the cessation of all the noises of the day. Shakespeare says that "if this bird should sing by day when every goose is cackling, she would be thought no better a musician than a wren."

WHAT IS IT?

They were conversing at a private party the other evening, when one of our society belles proposed to solve conundrums. The proposal having been accepted, the young lady commenced as follows: "What can keep us in good health and spirits?" What is it? What is it? asked everybody present. "Well," answered the young lady, "it is the excellent meals served at the famous Mint Restaurant, a Spring street. That is what it is."

DR. HOLLINGSWORTH, whose card appeared last month in the SEMI-TROPIC, has established himself in the new City of Paris building, where he will practice dentistry. The Doctor has probably one of the finest and most complete offices on the Pacific Coast, and having had occasion this month to try his services, we cheerfully recommend him as a skillful and painstaking operator.

MR. FARRELL, a merchant tailor, who has lately established himself in the McDonald Block, on Main street, announces himself in this number of the SEMI-TROPIC. We learn that Mr. Farrell never fails to give satisfaction to his customers, and would recommend any of our readers in need of suits to his store.

AUSTRALIAN roses resemble those of this country in color only, and are among the few antipodal flowers having any odor. Their perfume is very pleasant, if not inhaled too closely or profusely; in the latter case they have a "foxy" smell.

THE man who plants shade trees can have nothing selfish in his nature. He may not live to repose in their cool and welcome shadows, and yet they are a legacy of real value to his children.

Messrs. COMPTON, KERR & WEISS have opened a real estate office in the Pridham building. These gentlemen are well known by our citizens, and offer some first-class bargains in real estate property. They will also rent houses and take charge of property during owner's absence.

Messrs. WIDNEY BROS. pride themselves on having the best selected stock of stationery and fancy goods in Los Angeles. We take pleasure in calling attention to their advertisement elsewhere.

A practical education can be obtained at La Petra College.

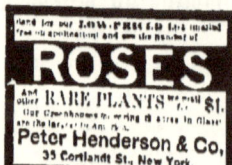

SEMI TROPIC CALIFORNIA

DEVOTED TO

AGRICULTURE,

HORTICULTURE,

AND THE INTERESTS OF

SOUTHERN CALIFORNIA

— — —

GEORGE RICE, PUBLISHER,

— — —

LOS ANGELES, CAL.

1881.

Horticultural Fair and Centennial Exposition Sept 5 to 10, Inclusive.

[illegible]

AND

SOUTHERN CALIFORNIA HORTICULTURIST.

Vol. IV | LOS ANGELES, CAL., JUNE, 1881. | No. 6

PROFITS IN RAISIN CULTURE.

A. H. Westbrook, Riverside, who has 600 vines, not quite one acre (676 vines eight feet apart each way cover an acre) one-half the vines five years old, the balance six years, makes the following report:

97 boxes, 1st class, at $2 per box	$194 00
66 ½ " " at $2.15 "	70 95
100 ¼ " " at $2.35 "	58 75
50 boxes, 2d class, at $1.50 "	75 00
	$398 70

EXPENSES.

Pruning and cultivating vineyard	$10 00
Water for irrigation	5 00
Picking grapes and curing	25 00
Boxes and packing paper	34 80
Packing 205 boxes at 6⅔c per box	13 60
	$88 40

Deducting the expenses from the cash receipts leaves a net balance of $310.25 for the 600 vines, or 51⅗c per vine.

R. H. Henderson, of the same place, has 1,200 vines (nearly two acres) four years old from cuttings, which is one of the finest vineyards in the settlement. He made 450 boxes of raisins:

300 boxes, 1st class, sold at $2	$600 00
150 boxes 2d class, sold at $1.50	225 00
	$825 00

EXPENSES.

Cost of boxes, at 11½c each	$57 75
Packing paper, etc.	15 00
Water for irrigating	10 00
	$82 75

Leaving a profit of $742.25, or 61¾c per vine.

The next statement is that of a small vineyard of 1½ acres, containing 890 vines, six years old, owned by Shugert & Wait, Riverside. The yield was twelve tons of grapes, or about 27 pounds to the vine. The grapes were sold to A. P. Coombs for $20 per ton on the vines, which is $240 for the crop. The expense of taking care of the vineyard and water was $15, which deducted leaves a net profit of $225 to the owners of this little vineyard. Mr. Coombs converted the grapes into raisins, with the following very satisfactory result as his share of the profits:

282 boxes, 1st class, sold at $2	$564 00
100 ½ " " " at $2.15	107 50
200 ¼ " " " at $2.35	117 50
	$789 00

EXPENSES.

Cost of grapes	$240 00
Picking	24 00
Boxes	62 00
Packing paper	12 00
Inspector's fees and teaming	15 75
	$347 75

Expenses deducted leaves Mr. Coombs a profit of $441.25, he performing all the labor of curing and packing. Adding to his profit that of Shugert & Wait's, we obtain the handsome result of $666.25 from 890 six-year-old vines, or nearly 75c per vine, and $500 per acre.

We have printed these statements before, but reprint them for the benefit of our Eastern readers, as we circulate several thousand copies of this edition East.

WHERE SHALL I GO?

I am going to California, but what part of the State must I go to?

The combined judgment of those who have gone before and looked the field over should be evidence enough to convince you, if you have never been in the State. The *Resources of California*, a paper published in San Francisco, says in an extract copied in this number, that Southern California—Los Angeles county—is surpassing any other part of the State, etc. See what ex-Gov. Downey and others say of this county.

We believe every immigrant to this coast will find it to their advantage to come here. Once here they can visit the counties of Santa Barbara, Ventura, Los Angeles, San Bernardino, and San Diego. Visit Riverside, Orange, Pasadena, Anaheim, San Gabriel Valley, San Diego, Santa Barbara, Santa Ana, Duarte, Downey, Westminster and other places and decide for themselves as to the locality they will make their home.

CHANGE OF COVER.—We are compelled to change the color of our cover this month, because the colored paper we had been using could not be had in San Francisco. The large editions of the SEMI-TROPIC exhausted their supply before a new stock could be received from the manufacturers.

EVERY kind of business is well represented in this city. We have 11 shoe-dealers, 17 clothing dealers, 21 dressmakers, 8 drug stores, 18 dry goods, 45 groceries, 8 hardware, 9 harness and saddle, 53 lawyers, 18 meat markets, 31 physicians, 55 saloons, 17 tailors and 13 jewelers.

THE true vineyard belt of this continent is only ten degrees wide. Fertilizers for grape-vines should be ashes, calcined bones and nitrate of potash, which is best of all. The refuse trimmings should be burnt on the ground and the ashes returned to the vines.

WORTH KNOWING.

Ice is manufactured in this city by two companies, and sold at one and two cents per pound.

Gas is sold by the present company at $1.50 per 1,000 feet, but a new company is making contracts at $3 per 1,000.

Water of a good quality is supplied at $2 per month for family use, extra for yard and bath.

Taxes in the city, all told, amount to $3.70 on the hundred; outside of the corporation, $1.50. Taxes are paid on a valuation of from one-half to two-thirds; the former valuation is general in the country.

HOMESTEAD.—California is very liberal and allows the head of a family property to the value of $5,000, which consists of a dwelling-house in which the claimant lives, and the land on which it is situated. A declaration of homestead must be made and filed for record with the County Recorder. In addition to the homestead the following property is exempt from execution: Chairs, tables, desks, books, and to the value of $200, necessary household goods, sewing machine, pictures, drawings, three months' provisions, three cows and calves, four hogs and their pigs, and food for them one month. The farming utensils, two oxen, two horses, two mules and their harness, one cart or wagon, food for stock one month, seed, grain, or vegetables. The tools or implements of a mechanic or artisan, professional libraries, etc., etc. Poultry not exceeding $25 in value. Earnings for thirty days. Every trade or business is amply protected. A homestead really amounts to a cash valuation of $10,000. No State, unless it is Texas, offers such ample provisions for a security against any of the ill winds that frequently leave a family homeless, as does California.

MR. CHAS. R. JOHNSON is the authorized agent for two of the best and most reliable fire insurance companies in the world. The Phenix Insurance Company of Hartford and Home of New York issue joint policies, offering thus a safe and satisfactory plan of insurance. See advertisement elsewhere.

SCHOOL PRIZES. For particulars about the *Mirror Office* — Yarnell, Caystile & Mathes, Proprietors - school prizes, to be competed for at the Horticultural Fair, Sept. 5-10, address the Secretary, or see the July SEMI-TROPIC.

SEMI-TROPIC

CALIFORNIA,

— AN —

ILLUSTRATED MONTHLY.

Devoted to Agriculture, Horticulture, and the Development of Southern California.

Terms: $1.50 per Annum, in Advance.

Office, Rooms 9 & 10, Baker Bros.

Address,   · ·   GEO. RICE, Los Angeles, Cal.

GEORGE RICE,   ·   Editor and Prop'r.

OFFICIAL PAPER

— of the —

Southern California Horticultural Soc'y.

OFFICE, ROOM No. 9, BAKER BLOCK.

J. De Barth Shorb........ President.
H. K. W. Bent........ Vice President.
E. F. Spence........ Treasurer.
Geo. Rice........ Secretary.

Directors

J. F. Clark,   A. B. Clark,
J. H. Shields,   H. K. W. Bent,
C. E. Thom,   J. De Barth Shorb,
       T. C. Severance

Extra copies of this number can be had at any of the news stands in this city, or at this office. Every reader of this notice should send copies of this number to their friends in the East.

For the first time in our life we have been confined to our bed with illness. We had a very close call, but having a strong constitution, and receiving the watchful, tender nursing of a good wife, assisted by the "Jones" prescribed by a skillful physician, we are able to be out after a four weeks' siege. The only consolation we had in being sick, was from the visits of kind friends, and their messages of sympathy. We take this time and opportunity to thank the friends, one and all, for their many kindnesses.

To Mr. J. C. Peabody is due the credit of editing the May issue of this paper. Mr. Peabody is a young man of acknowledged ability, and the numerous compliments paid to the May Semi-Tropic, prove it a popular issue.

Wanted.—At this office, a good, gentle, family horse, one that can make good time, not over eight years old; fifteen hands high, or over. No fancy price.

Money To Loan.—At this office, in sums of $500 and $1,000, on real estate security, at 10 per cent. interest.

Over 2,000 letters of inquiry about Southern California, have been received at this office. We have sent nearly 100,000 copies of the Semi-Tropic East, and their influence has done this section of the State, and especially Los Angeles county, an incalculable amount of good.

The greater part of our space has been devoted to agricultural and horticultural matters; and as an agricultural paper, has received the indorsements of the best agriculturists and horticulturists, not only of this coast, but of the United States.

As an emigration paper, the Semi-Tropic, has always been honest in truly representing Southern California as she is. We would be doing our country an injury by inducing people to come here through misrepresentation, and we shall always tell only what can be substantiated by good evidence.

This number is almost entirely devoted to answering the many questions asked about Southern California, and we hope it will result in great good, as a large edition will be issued for circulation in the East, and will be placed in the principal news-stands, public libraries and hotels in that section, and on the overland trains leaving Omaha and Kansas City for California. Our citizens who would write a long letter to friends East, can do so by mailing this issue to them. Extra copies can be had at any of the news-stands in this city, or at this office.

The Horticultural Fair and Centennial Exposition will be held in the Horticultural Pavilion, this city, September 5th to 10th.

The premium list will be larger than for any previous year.

Preparations are being made on a most liberal scale, for a grand celebration of the one hundredth anniversary of the settlement of Los Angeles city, by an exhibit showing the agricultural and horticultural progress. The programme, while not yet complete, indicates a grand celebration, procession of the trades, mercantile, business societies (civil and military,) citizens, music by several bands, firing salutes, fireworks, etc., etc.

The opening address by Gov. Perkins and Hon. W. G. Le Duc, Commissioner of Agriculture, U. S.

The decorations will excel anything of the kind ever before attempted in the State.

The exhibits will be larger and more extensive than ever before, occupying nearly the entire lower floor and part of the upper.

A large addition is to be built to the Pavilion, for dining and refreshment rooms. The former dining rooms to be used as an art and curiosity department.

Those intending to make exhibits, or interested, should send their address to this Secretary and receive a catalogue and programme free, which will soon be ready to deliver.

A FEW QUESTIONS ANSWERED.

Clergymen.—A lady whose father is a clergyman down East asks if the people would appreciate him, as he is of the "liberal" school? We would say, stay where he is, unless he can draw a large audience and hold them by his eloquence. We have enough preachers, and no demand for poor ones.

Lawyer.—The population of this county is 35,000, and we have fifty three lawyers and more coming on to attend to the business. No room for invalid lawyers nor any others, unless they are "away up" in their profession.

Teacher.—What is true of the two professions above is equally true of yours. We have enough poor teachers, and only Normal graduates need apply. Wages for teaching are good, ranging from $60 to $100 per month. Examinations very rigid and a high standard of qualifications is required to get a certificate.

Business Men.—A number of letters asking about "good openings" for dry goods, groceries and other lines of business. While we would like to see many new business enterprises started, and we have room for many that would pay from the start, we must admit that we don't think it would be advisable to start another dry goods, grocery, furniture, hardware, shoe, clothing or similar business house in this or any other town in Southern California until the county is more fully settled, and wherever there is a demand for such a business enterprise there is always some one on the spot to meet it.

Clerk.—"Soft jobs" are as scarce here as in any eastern town. We say to all who expect to come to California and find an "easy place," don't come.

Consumptives.—If one foot is not already in the grave, if you have not already despaired of living, if you have money to live on, we say come, come at once; one time of the year is as good as another. There is no one that can say this is not the weak lung's sanitarium. From actual statistics, and from actual observation and experience of hundreds, no place in the world can compare with Southern California as a home for consumptives. See in another part of this paper "Our Climate."

What shall we take with us.—All your wearing apparel, bedding, queensware (packed carefully in barrels) and such goods as you can pack in boxes that will be worth more to you here than what you can sell them for with the freight added.

Don't bring any furniture or heavy articles, but sell them. You can buy all kinds of furniture and household articles, agricultural implements, groceries, etc., nearly as cheap here as you can in the East.

Climate.

[Reported since our complete report.]

METEOROLOGICAL SUMMARY at Los Angeles, Cal. for the year ending October 31, 1880, and six months 1881, as indicated at the top of the several columns, obtained from the records of the Signal Service, United States Army.]

DATE.	Humidity, saturation.	Prevailing winds.	Mean barometer.	Mean thermometer.	Maximum. Time.	Minimum. Time.	Range of Ther.	Prevailing direction.	Amount of rain and snow fall in inches.
November... 1879								NE	
December...								NE	
January... 1880								NW	
February...								NE	
March...								W	
April...								SW	
May...								W	
June...								W	
July...								W	
August...								W	
September...								W	
October...								W	
Annual means									
November...								NE	
December...								NE	
January... 1881								NW	
February...								NE	
March...								W	
April...								W	
Means...									

IN response to frequent inquiries asking an explanation of the various scientific terms made use of by meteorologists, we state briefly the salient features, for the convenience of our non-scientific readers.

The expression "mean," as may be observed in the above table, means an average reading of an instrument for a definite period. Say three observations are taken daily. The sum of the three readings of the instrument divided by three, will give as its result, the mean of that instrument for the day; the sum of the daily means for a week, divided by seven, gives the weekly mean. The sum of the daily means for a month, divided by the number of days in the month, gives the monthly mean and the sum of the twelve monthly means, constituting a year when divided by twelve yields, as a result the annual mean.

The expression "barometer" is made use of as a convenient term to express the barometric, bienme indicated by the barometer, or, more strictly, atmospheric pressure. The principle of this instrument is simple. The denser the fluid in a state of equilibrium, the less the height of the vertical column; the less the specific gravity, the higher the column. So then, as mercury is 10,784 times heavier than air, in order to counterpoise, that is, be of equal weight with a column of mercury thirty inches in height, we must have a column of air of the same diameter 10,784 times thirty inches, which would be nearly five miles, if it were composed of layers of the same density throughout. But as we ascend the air becomes constantly lighter, because of its becoming more elastic and the pressure above it decreasing, so that the limit of the atmosphere becomes much greater, and the real height of the air may exceed 200 miles. A barometer consists of

a glass tube about three feet long, either curved at the lower end in the shape of a siphon, or a straight tube resting in a cistern, and filled with mercury. A scale in affixed to a casing enclosing the glass, by which the height of the mercury in the tube can be read. The top of the glass tube is closed, the lower end open. To fill it the tube is upside down. When filled, on being inverted—placed in its proper position—the mercury in the tube sinks, leaving an open space at the top nearly free from air, constituting what is known as the torcellian vacuum. The open end with the mercury exposed is the place where the atmospheric pressure is exerted. The barometer can be likened to an ordinary balance. When, from any cause, a change occurs in the atmosphere, a corresponding change takes place in the height of the column of mercury in the tube. If the pressure of air on the exposed surface of mercury increases, the mercury in the tube rises; if the weight of the air becomes less, the top of the mercury falls. The vacuum at the top of the column of mercury in the glass tube, acts as a sort of regulator, exerting a constant check on the surface of the mercury in the tube. Should air enter the tube, the vacuum is thereby destroyed, the check lessened, and the usefulness of the instrument impaired. The normal height of the column of mercury at the sea level, is about thirty inches. The term barometric or atmospheric pressure, refers to the state of the column of mercury in the tube.

The thermometer is the instrument constructed on the principle of the variation of the volume of a fluid by any change of temperature. Mercury is generally used; alcohol, from its low freezing point, being used for exceedingly low temperatures. The maximum temperature for a day means the highest temperature recorded during a period of a day, week or any definite period. Minimum temperature refers to the lowest thermometric reading of several also for a certain time.

The term relative humidity, or amount of aqueous vapor in the atmosphere, as distinct from actual humidity, is used to express the proportion that the amount of watery vapor in the air bears to a perfectly saturated atmosphere. During dense fogs or drizzling rain the air frequently becomes fully saturated with moisture. This then would represent 100 per cent.; an air only half saturated would be 50 per cent. The readings as reported by the Signal Service observers, therefore, do not give the actual amount of moisture in the air, but only the amount present as proportionate to the amount that the air is capable of detaining without depletion, or a relative percentage of moisture.

To such an extent are these various observations considered by agriculturists and such an important factor in the intelligent conduct of an agricultural enterprise have they become, that it would be well for every farmer to acquaint himself more intimately with the uses of the various instruments employed, as in addition to being an

instructive diversion, it will prove of great pecuniary benefit. A few simple instruments, the study of a good meteorological work and a close attention to the many local signs generally preceding or accompanying any change in the weather, may be the means of saving many a hard day's work and harvest, even in our specially favored semi tropic California.

[The above is furnished us by the U. S. Signal officer, Mr. E. F. Kabel at this point.]

The population of California in 1870 was in round numbers 560,000; in 1880 the census showed 864,000, an increase of about 54 per cent. Upon the same ratio, the population in 1890 will be 1,200,000.

Dr. J. P. WIDNEY, in an article in *Californian*, on "Climatic Studies in Southern California," says: Ours is a climate which can hardly be described. The peculiar charm of it must be felt to be understood. * * * I do not say there is no more perfect climate than this belt affords, but I have never seen one.

Now is the time to come to this State. Lands are cheap, times are good, and there is a disposition to treat the new comer with the greatest kindness and consideration. Inside of two years (and some claim within one year) low rates will be secured from Europe and the East to California. As soon as the great tide of emigration commences to roll in the State, lands will be increased in value, and all the choice locations will be taken up. Already there is a tendency to advance the prices of lands. In the settlements lands have advanced during the last year at least 25 per cent. We advise those who are intending to make Southern California their homes, to do so as soon as possible.

Prof. R. Von Schlagentweit says, "The climate of California resembles in general character that of Italy, but has not its objectionable effect of depriving the people of the disposition and power of energetic mental and physical labor. The dolce far niente, of the Southern Italy is unknown in California." Samuel Bowles wrote, "there is a steady tone in the atmosphere like draughts of Champagne, or the subtle pressure of wine. It invites to labor and makes it possible. Horses can travel more miles here in a day than at the East, and men and women feel impelled to an unusual activity."

C. L. Brace says. "It is the most exhilarating atmosphere in the world."

The London *Spectator* said, editorially, that the climate of California is like that of Greece cooled, and the climate of Tasmania is that of England etherealized, and the two are the nearest perfection in the world

Every subscription from east of the Rocky Mountains, until October 1st for $1.

Manufactories.

SOME INDUSTRIES OF LOS ANGELES CITY.

LOS ANGELES, from an industrial point of view is not far behind other Pacific Coast cities. Our manufacturing institutions at present seem to be well established, in

the company has achieved a most decided success and created a market which is beyond their power to supply. The quality of the hams, bacon, lard, etc., furnished by our packing company is far superior to that manufactured in the East, and is free from all that suspicion of disease which has caused American pork products to be excluded from Europe. How many more important industries might be successfully

labor in preserving the immense crops of fruit and vegetables, organized, last April, a corporation which they style the Southern California Packing Company.

The firm purchased, as a nucleus for their factory, the Alden Drying Works, across the river, and have built an addition nearly doubling their capacity. They have placed the management of the canning department in the hands of Mr. J. J. Groom, a gentleman who has had long experience as manager of the San Jose Fruit Packing companies, and more recently with the Santa Barbara cannery. The selection of Mr. Groom as Superintendent is most fortunate for the company, as he thoroughly understands the business, and will put up the fruit in a manner which cannot be excelled by any other cannery in the United States.

At present, as the fruit season will not open until the first of July, the company have a force of men and boys at work making cans, the number turned out daily being between three and four thousand.

The company proposes to preserve all kinds of fruits and vegetables by canning and evaporation, and to manufacture jams, jellies, marmalades, sauces, pickles, etc. The capacity of the canning department will be about 15,000 cans of fruit daily, and there is no doubt that they will be able to purchase every pound of fruit that our farmers can produce. The apparatus of the establishment is all new and of the most approved pattern. Messrs. Hinckly, Spiers and Hayes, of San Francisco, furnish the boilers and engine.

In the hands the cannery and dryer is at present it is an assured success. The cap-

LOS ANGELES PACKING CO., EAST LOS ANGELES, CAL.

good hands, and all running on full time with plenty of orders ahead. We paid the subject of manufacturing considerable attention last month, both because we believed a short account of what has been done might be interesting to our readers, and also because we believe that many new enterprises in this line may be profitably started.

CITY FOUNDRY.

This most important industry is located at the corner of Main and Second streets, in this city, and is the only foundry which Los Angeles at the present time boasts of. It is in the hands of two practical machinists, Messrs. J. C. Bower and M. C. Baker, who employ a large force of men and are prepared to do iron work of every kind promptly and in a satisfactory manner. We have repeatedly called the attention of our readers to the fact that there is no excuse for anyone residing in this county to send for iron work or agricultural implements to San Francisco, for it has been frequently demonstrated that our local foundry furnishes better and cheaper work in every respect. The illustration on this page will give a very good idea of the capacity and situation of the establishment, which deserves a more extended notice, which we reserve for a future time.

LOS ANGELES PORK PACKING COMPANY.

In the March number of the SEMI TROPIC we gave an extensive account of the important pork packing enterprise carried on in East Los Angeles by Messrs. Speedy, Dodsworth & Co. In this number we present an illustration which will give some idea of the magnitude of their establishment. It will be sufficient for us to say here, as our space is somewhat limited, that

carried on in our city if there were more men with the ability and enterprise of Messrs. Speedy & Co.

SOUTHERN CALIFORNIA PACKING COMPANY.

Probably the manufacturing industry which most generally interests our readers is that which will be inaugurated early next month. Southern California will short-

ly rank as the leading fruit producing section of our State, but until recently has been content to import almost all the canned goods used, while tons of fruit raised in this vicinity lacked a profitable market. Several of our leading citizens, Messrs. Judson, Kittridge and Elliott, seeing the opportunity offered for capital and skilled

ital of the corporation is large, and the corporators are prepared to carry out their project on as large a scale as the fruit growing interests of the Los Angeles and San Bernardino Valleys will warrant.

THE SOAP WORKS.

The Soap Works are located at Nos. 25 and 27 Banning street, and are operated by

BOWER & BAKER, PROPRIETORS, LOS ANGELES, CAL.

Messrs. Forthman and Bergin. The firm manufactures all grades of toilet and washing soaps, and supplies the trade, generally, of Southern California and Arizona.

LOS ANGELES WOOLEN MILLS.

The owners of the Woolen Mills on Pearl street, in the western portion of the city, have built up a demand for their goods which is highly satisfactory. The establishment is in the hands of Messrs. C. L. Torr and B. F. Coulter, of the well-known dry goods store in the Baker Block. The Mills are run to their utmost capacity and are furnishing a very fine grade of woolen goods, which are shipped to all portions of Southern California, Oregon and the East. In a wool-growing country like Southern California the importance of mills to work up the raw product can hardly be over-estimated. Instead of one mill we ought to have half a dozen and we have no doubt that with proper management they would all pay well.

FLOUR MILLS.

Messrs. Lankershim and Van Nuys are the proprietors of the Los Angeles Flour Mills, located at the corner of Commercial and Alameda streets. Both gentlemen are the owners of large wheat farms in the San Fernando valley, which produce many thousands of centals of grain annually. The XXX brand of flour furnished by Lankershim & Co. is very popular and as fine bread can be made with it as by any imported flour.

Messrs. Deming & Palmer, the former gentleman of Los Angeles, the latter of San Francisco, are the proprietors of the Capital Mills, corner of Alameda and San Fernando streets. The mill building was erected last year, the business having previously been conducted in the Aliso Mills, on Aliso avenue.

OTHER MANUFACTORIES.

Beside the above-mentioned manufactories, Los Angeles has a broom factory, a glove factory, several planing mills, several carriage and wagon manufacturing shops, gas works, two ice factories, a first class soda factory on Sainsevain street, artificial stone works in East Los Angeles, car shops at the Union Depot, three or four cigar factories, a fine distillery and a brick yard. Many of our hardware, furniture and plumbing establishments also manufacture on a small scale.

AN INDORSEMENT.

EDITOR SEMI-TROPIC.—Sir: I said to my friends in Nebraska that the SEMI-TROPIC was the most reliable immigration paper that I ever read. After having looked over Southern California I see no reason to change my mind. Truly yours,
O. W. ELWOOD.

IT is estimated that California, with her viticulture, presents an opportunity for the support of 4,000,000 persons to be connected with that industry alone.

WHAT IT COSTS

TO START AN ORANGE ORCHARD OR VINEYARD.

The following figures are from the very best authorities on the subject. The orange orchard figures are by L. M. Holt, with slight changes. Following are the figures for a ten-acre tract.

COST

10 acres of land	$1,000
1,000 trees, budded or seedling	750
Planting and caring for same first season at $25 per acre	250
Caring for orchard second year at $15 per acre	150
Third year $10 per acre	100
Fourth year $20 per acre	200
Fifth year $25 per acre	250
Other expenses incidental to work	550
Total for 5 years	$3,200
Interest on investment	1,000
Total	$4,200

This is the expense account. There will be some receipts. If good budded trees are planted, the third year will give a little fruit; the fourth year still more, and at the end of the fifth year there will be quite a fine crop. In order to be safe in these calculations, we will place the yield and prices at the lowest possible estimate:

Third year crop scattering oranges, a few hundred or thousand—not counted......

Fourth year an average of 50 oranges to the tree—50,000 oranges at $20 per thousand...... $1,000

Fifth year 200 to the tree—200,000 oranges at $20 per thousand.

If these prices are maintained the owner has his investment all back again at the end of five years and is ready to ship oranges in large quantities every year thereafter.

All persons planting orange orchards do not do as well as this and some do better. These figures represent what can be done with good judgment and thorough work. If a man thinks to save by getting cheap and incompetent work, he may succeed in reducing the cost to a few dollars, and the receipts a few hundred dollars or even a few thousand dollars. If he buys a poor tree because he can get it for 20 cents instead of paying the regular market price for a good thrifty tree, he will make another saving in cost of orchard, and in cost of boxes in which to ship the fruit.

COST OF A VINEYARD.

The following figures are by J. de Barth Shorb, President of the California Horticultural Society:

FOR ONE ACRE.

Plowing twice before planting, at $2	$4 00
Harrowing and pulverizing same	...
Cuttings (1200 vines, six feet apart)	5 00
Planting, per acre	1 00
Two plowings after planting	3 00
Cultivation and final pulverization	50
Total cost, end of first year	$15 00

SECOND YEAR.

Pruning, per acre	$1 00
Plowing, twice at $1 50	3 00
Cultivation, twice at 50c.	1 00
Hoeing near the vine	3 00
Total cost, second year	$8 00

THIRD YEAR.

Pruning the vine and removing wood	$2 50
Plowing twice	3 00
Cultivating twice	1 00
Hoeing near vine	1 50
Total cost, third year	$8 00

In the fourth year the expenses of pruning and removing the wood from the vineyard will be increased one dollar more, or to $4.50 per acre; all the other expenses remain the same as during the third year.

Twenty dollars per acre is the estimate covering the entire cost of pruning, cultivating, picking and delivering the grapes at convenient distances from vineyard after the fourth year.

For twenty acres the cost would be:

Land, 20 acres at $50	$1,000 00
Planting and cultivating, 3 years at $8	480 00
Interest on investment	420 00
Total cost	$1,900 00

For profits we refer to other articles in this paper.—[ED.]

CALIFORNIA RAISINS IN NEW YORK.

Geo. W. Meade & Co., commission merchants, San Francisco, shipped sample boxes of our best raisins to their New York agents, with instructions to exhibit them to the leading dealers in the Malaga trade, and get their opinion as to quality, packing, etc. The following is an extract from the letter received in answer to their inquiries:

"The box of California raisins came duly to hand and has excited a great deal of interest and comment among the trade here, to whom we have shown the fruit. It goes without saying that, judging by this sample, California can produce as fine raisins as any in the world, and if our eyes were shut, it would be extremely difficult for one to *distinguish this sample from the finest Spanish Deharis*, though some of our importers claim that the skin is tougher than the imported. The bunches or clusters are even larger than the Malaga, though the fruit is not so blue, and is, of course, not so showy packed. With such fruit as this the question of competition with the Malaga in this market is simply one of price alone."

The S. F. *Bulletin* says: "This is an interesting, encouraging, and in some respects, an unexpected report. It is better than was hoped for. It has a commercial value and might with profit be used to advertise California raisins. It shows clearly that the market is open. The question is merely one of price. Here we have the advantage over all competitors. Our young, healthy vines on new lands can turn out tons of raisins to Europe's centals, and pound for pound at much lower cost. The 'comparatively tougher skin,' will be overcome by some minor change in the sweating system in use here. The color of the fruit will be darkened by using a little more care in gathering them at the proper moment. The brands will be more exact; the labels, if that be needed, made more showy, and in these and similar ways the California raisins kept at the front."

Viticulture.

A Vineyard can be safely estimated as paying 10 per cent. on a valuation of $500 per acre. We know of several vineyards that last year paid 50 per cent. on a valuation of about $1,000 per acre.

We have no hesitation in advising the planting of a vineyard for profit.

Twenty acres properly planted, with the right quality of cuttings, with careful cultivation, will yield a revenue to the owner of $1,000 per year, every year, one with an other, as sure as a note with real estate security will bring 10 per cent. per annum.

Forty acres of land is enough for any man to bustle as a vineyard—twenty acres might be better in fact, and the young men, the middle-aged man, or the old man, with or without a family who can procure twenty acres of this land, and can for two years live upon and cultivate a portion of it as a vineyard, will be better off in a little while, healthier and happier than if he were a clerk, mechanic, laborer or small merchant in this city—and his children will be stronger in every way, and better able to fight the battle of life than they would if raised in this or any other city.

PROFITS IN RAISIN CULTURE.

Dr. O. H. Conger, in an article to the SEMI-TROPIC CALIFORNIA sometime since, said: My vines are of the Muscat variety, and three years from cuttings, and without irrigation from the setting. Former care of the same has not been with the view of raisin-making; hence it is safe to assert that they have lacked the proper attention in some respects that would have been to their advantage. But such as it has been, I am now enabled to present the following as the returns for the crop just marketed: Gross receipts from raisins per acre, $51.76; from grapes per acre, $13; from cuttings, $13.95; total, $88.71. Deducting the sum of $25 per acre for the entire expense of care of vineyard and marketing crop, which includes everything connected with the work, and we have a profit of $63.71.

FACTS ABOUT VINEYARDS.

The editor of the Anaheim *Gazette*, who has had considerable experience in vine growing, has the following in a late issue of his valuable paper: There are few more profitable pursuits than vine-growing; and there is certainly no occupation so pleasant to those who favor an out-door life. One able-bodied, industrious man can, single-handed, cultivate and manage a twenty, or even thirty, acre vineyard up to the time when the vines begin to bear a paying crop. If an immigrant can come here with enough money to purchase thirty or forty acres of land, build a house for himself and family, and a house in this climate need only be a very cheap affair, and

have enough money left on hand to purchase the necessaries of life for three, or at most four years he can at the end of that time have a beautiful and valuable home in one of the best countries in the world, a large income, a propitious future, and be able to enjoy the fruits of his labors —rendered doubly enjoyable by the exertions which their creation called forth. These are hard facts, not fanciful representations. Go and ask any of the owners of the well-kept twenty-acre vineyards in Anaheim what they will take for their home, and, providing they are willing to sell, the price asked would astonish the novice who has given little thought to the income which twenty acres of vigorous bearing vines will annually bring their owner.

THE PROFITS OF GRAPE CULTURE.

A vineyard will commence bearing three years after setting out. The yield will be far above expenses of cultivation and harvesting. At five years old, a vineyard will yield from four to six tons of fruit per acre. Grapes, this year, will sell at the vineyard for from $20 to $30 per ton, according to quality. Old vineyards, say at ten years, will yield from seven to thirteen tons of fruit. There are in California five millions acres of lands which can be obtained at low figures and upon easy terms, as to payments, say from $10 to $25 per acre. These lands are located in the foot-hills of California, both north and south, and are the best grape lands in the State. Many of these lands, in the middle and northern portion of California, are contiguous to water ditches, for mining purposes. This water could be purchased for irrigation purposes at reasonable rates in many localities, thus making grape culture a certainty. To go into the business requires but a small capital, say from $1,000 to $3,000. Other portions of the foot-hill regions will grow the vine without irrigation, and the grape of such sections is superior for wine-making. A vineyard, after it commences to bear fruit, will continue for fifty years, if properly cultivated. There is no business that will pay as well for the money and labor invested, as grape culture—no business equal to it for comfort and health. The vineyardist of the present time has before him the experiments of centuries, for guidance, of foreign countries, and, therefore, failure in this State, is simply out of the question. The demand for California wines and raisins will steadily increase for many years to come, and the prices will prove remunerative for good articles. What a field is here open to young men of industry and energy, thousands of them.

GRAPES.

There were 44,365 barrels, and 36,721 half barrels of imported grapes received at the port of New York during 1873. This does not look like overstocking the market for fresh grapes in this country very soon. Most of these were shipped from Spain.

We say now, as we have often said in these columns, that there is work for men who are full of self-reliance, perseverance and energy. California is not a haven for the lazy, nor a home for the stupid and indifferent. But men also come here with a small amount of ready money, (say $1,000,) and are able and willing to work, and economize as they do in other States, we can safely promise them a great living, and a competence in the near future.

The Sacramento *Bee* only adds another to the long list when it quotes from a letter recently received from Italy, from an intelligent Italian who had long lived in California. He says: "Italy is a fine country —the land of my nativity. Books and travelers say it is the finest in the world. I only had my early memories of it, and believed it even during my many years residence among you. I was all wrong There is no place or climate equal to California. I am home-sick and you need not be surprised to see me any day. Italy and Austria are the best climates of Europe, but do not compare with our own." We will add that we are personally acquainted with two gentlemen who have visited Italy, and they declare unhesitatingly that the boasted climate of that land of song is not to be compared with the climate of California.

Is there is any other country that can offer the immigrant greater advantages than California, we should like to know where it is located. We offer to the immigrant, in the language of another, "a choice of every variety of climate, and land upon mountain tops, hill sides, fertile valleys or broad plains; with a range of productions, embracing the orange, lemon, lime, date, fig, olive, pomegranate, etc.; the apple, peach, pear, prune, plum, nectarine, cherry and the grape—all of which grow to perfection unsurpassed. Of the cereals and vegetables there is not one which conduces to the supply of man's wants and comforts, but can be produced in abundance. While the plants yielding fibre for textile fabrics, the cotton, the flax, hemp, and the ramie plant can be produced in various localities, to supply the wants of the world.

The diffusion of fuller knowledge regarding the climate and other advantages of our State, would undoubtedly cause it to fill up more rapidly with a desirable population. We have a State, within whose borders there is a large area of territory abounding in mineral wealth, a soil fabulously prolific, a climate rivaling that of Greece, and far excelling that of Italy, and a geographical situation unsurpassed by that of any other commercial country. It guarantees to our city the destiny of one of the most important ports in the world It is not exaggeration to say that no State in the Union, possesses to-day a tithe of the advantages, present and prospective, which California offers to all classes of intending emigrants.—*Resources of Cal.*

THE LOS ANGELES CITRUS FAIR

APPRECIATION OF SOUTHERN CALIFORNIA

GEN. SHERMAN ON CALIFORNIA ENTERPRISES

SUMMER IN SOUTHERN CALIFORNIA

THE JOURNEY OF A FLEECE

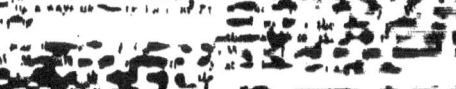

WILLOWDALE.

THE HOME OF N. C. CARTER.

WILLOWDALE the beautiful home of Mr. N. C. Carter, late of the Semi-Tropic California, is delightfully situated in the San Gabriel Valley, about six miles from the Old Mission. Mr. Carter came here from Lowell, Mass. about ten years ago, for his health; his income supposed he would need a resting place in the cemetery in less a year passed, but we are glad to chronicle the fact that he not only lives and has his being, but is a great strong man, the very picture of health. Mr. Carter is one of the most active men of the county, always "among the front," in any public ...

SIERRA MADRE COLONY.

2,500 ACRES OF CHOICE FRUIT LANDS.

This choice body of land, lies along the base of the mountains about 12 miles from this city, and four miles from San Gabriel railroad station.

THE LOCATION

Is one of the most delightful and sightly in the State. From the front doors of the many cottages that will soon be built on this lovely spot the view will be grand beyond description. The Sierra Madre range on the north winds and frost, the valley for miles like a panoramic view, lies before you, the ocean in the distance in plain view, all ...

Mr E. J. Baldwin, from whom the greater part of the Sierra Madre Tract is purchased, the undisputed right to one half of the water in the streams in summer, and all of the surplus winter water. The water right as it stands is perfect, and the supply is judged to be ample for irrigating every acre of land in the tract. Mr. Carter put in a supply reservoir in the cañon, from which the water will be distributed over the tract in pipes. A large force of men are now at work putting the pipes in. He also thinks of constructing receiving reservoirs some, along after the plan of the Alhambra Tract, one for each one or two hundred acres, to be under the control of the people irrigating from it. The plan seems to us an ex-

WILLOWDALE.—RANCH OF N. C. CARTER, SAN GABRIEL, LOS ANGELES CO., CAL.

enterprise, noted for his liberality and good absolute use. Willowdale is highly improved, consisting of vineyard, orange groves, lemons, deciduous fruits of all kinds, alfalfa pasture, carp ponds, etc. It is well watered from large spring that furnish water for the house and for irrigation for which little is required.

Mr. Carter is largely engaged in developing the water and otherwise improving his colony lands, the Sierra Madre tract, of which we have something to say in another column. We understand he will sell Willowdale and move on to his colony tract. When ever Mr. Carter buys Willowdale will have a boon in for the gods.

with for the Semi-Tropic

taken together makes this a most lovely place to have a home. This location as a health resort, a relief for weak lungs can not be excelled, on account of the elevation freeing it from fogs, frosts and harsh wind.

THE SOIL

Is a dark sandy loam, with a slight sprinkle of gravel intermingled with decomposed gypsum, lime and sediment carried down from the mountain a dea for ages, making soil that will be inexhaustible for all time.

THE WATER RIGHT.

Mr. Carter is the absolute owner of the land up the cañon upon which the springs forming the stream rise. He acquires from

cellent one, greatly simplifying the usual methods of supply, and rendering irrigation easy and available at any time. There are numbers of streams which put out from cañons along the base of the mountains, and there are also many springs of cienegas which arise at such an elevation as to be easily available for irrigating the contiguous land. It is probable that a good share of the meas has a body of water underlying it, the source of supply being the accumulations of the mountains.

It remains, then, that

THE THREE ELEMENTS

Which command the finest results in horticulture are here united—good soil, abundance of water and the most favorable cli-

SAN GABRIEL MISSION.—Sierra Madre Mountains in the Distance.—Los Angeles Co., Cal.

First Baptist M. E. Church.

CHURCHES AND SCHOOLS.

No section of the East is better supplied with churches and schools than Southern California. Every locality is well represented by the different denominations, with pulpits supplied with pastors of ability, and above the ordinary talent that supplies the pulpits of the Western States.

Los Angeles has a number of fine church buildings. The above engraving is a front view, from a photo by our popular artists, Messrs. Payne, Stanton & Co. The building cost $18,000, has a membership of 400, with Rev. E. S. Chase as present pastor. In a former issue we published a picture of the Catholic Cathedral, which is the largest church building in Southern California, and cost $85,000.

The principal denominations are represented: Methodist (North and South and German), Catholic (Cathedral) St. Vibiana and Church of Our Lady of Angeles, Episcopal, Presbyterian, Baptist, Congregational, English and German, Christian, and several other organizations.

The school system of the State is second to none in the Union. Ample school fund and a high grade of excellency required of the teachers. A State University and Normal School well maintained and well patronized.

Los Angeles is noted for her excellent public schools, which are well provided over by an able Board of Education and an efficient corps of teachers. We also have the Southern California University, a Methodist Institute in an excellent condition financially, with an able body of teachers in the faculty.

The Catholics have two schools: St. Vincent College, Sisters' School. Miss A. Leland's Academy and Kindergarten, Miss Bougough's select school, and several others.

A Normal school building is to be erected during the present year, at a cost of $50,000, by the State.

Throughout the country splendid school buildings are to be found, and every locality is well provided with schools and churches. The new comer cannot go amiss as far as church and school accommodations are concerned.

Fruit Culture.

BUDS AND SEEDLINGS.

BY AARON FISHER.

These are the terms by which, in common parlance, we designate the two great classes of trees which, in varying proportions constitute our orange orchards. In what do these two classes differ? Primarily, and in general, in this: That whereas the seedling is a natural, simple and unique vegetable structure, developed directly from the seed through processes devised by Creative wisdom, and is therefore perfect, the bud is an artificial and composite organism—the device of human ingenuity and the work of man's hands, and consequently imperfect. [NOTE.—To prevent any misapprehension of these definitions, I explain that by simple, as applied to the seedling tree, I mean uncompounded, consisting of but one sort of wood; and by unique, having a distinct individuality—being unlike any other existing tree. Its opposite I mean made up of unlike materials, so that its exact counterpart cannot be found in Nature.] As an illustration of this distinction take the white thorn bush. Away from it in the air, great two thousand years ago, some long-forgotten fellow mouldered into a heap of good foul-grained year seed from which, in due process of time, was developed a peculiar tree bearing that very thorny little variety of pear now known as the white thorn. Its original seedling tree was unique, unlike any tree that ever will before it. Henceforth this present generation, through a long succession, has gone down to the dust since the roots of that tree utterly perished, but its type is still perpetuated by the kindred processes in budding and grafting, and the fruit of millions of white thorns, pear tree unlike a plot full of nations of the earth. The stocks whether buds, slips or branches, from which these trees derive their succession, are all diverse in material from the superincumbent bud tops or branches, so diverse that large quantities of them consist of the wood of apple, quince, thorn, and various other trees. Each tree is strictly composite, having been made up of two kinds of wood in union or some respects differing from each other—just as in the case of the seedling, every part of the tree has its own distinctive organization, making it in either more or less distinct from every other seedling tree. Set this, when we speak of an orchard of a hundred seedling orange trees, we do not mean it to be understood that the one hundred trees are each a couple of each other, or that their union is in all respects complete, but from it. The greater probability is, not in my theory whence it is that no two of them are in all respects alike or will produce fruits so identical that neither the eye nor the palate can distinguish them. To the allegation that the budded (or grafted) tree, as a tree, has certain superiorities, we have no inclination to gainsaying. The vegetable physiologist is aware of how imperfect and unsatisfactory these superior are. The practical pomologist is equally aware of and rejoices without. Let us then prove distinguish briefly into the character, seat and consequence of these imperfections, and asking the value of nature as will first consider its cause. This is not but is work, and if it is at one or the eye of the investigator in that certain preponderance (or ring) always observable at the point where the union is effected between the stock and the bud or graft. As we have and effects of this union caused, perhaps, by a certain imperfect union by inferring to the broken bone that nature accomplishes in the hand of the surgeon. The fraction of nature's have been carefully brought to its natural collision that is almost contact with each other, have adhered, and by the renovating processes of nature become more or less firmly knitted together. But, however skillfully the work of the surgeon may have been performed, there cannot have been a more or less of displacement and divergence position among the muscles, tendons, nerves, blood vessels and secretory tissues involved in the lacerated parts; and the proprietor of the reconstructed member will, so long as he lives, be made sensible, and often painfully sensible of the difference between the limb thus fashioned by him use and the symmetrical and unerring contour of his other hand's handiwork. A disturbance precisely analogous to that which is undergone in the case of the broken bone must necessarily follow in the case of the mutilated wood, and the results cannot but supervene. Owing to the more or less disjointed condition of the cellular tissues, the sap circulation is obstructed and diminished, and from this failure, as necessary consequences, an enfeebled condition than a dwarfed wood growth, greater susceptibility to injuries of various sorts, and, finally, a briefer period of existence. A rather formidable indictment against the bud, surely. But let us look a little at the other side of the question, and see if something cannot be brought forward in particulars of the bud, if some counterpoise cannot be found to serve as an offset against these mighty objections. I remark, then, in the outset, in attempting a brief defense of the budded (or grafted) tree, what is a very singular and a very interesting circumstance, that all that has ever been said in derogation of it or offered in its praise, rests on one and the same foundation, that ugly, invincible callous joint above alluded to; the explanation of which is that, while the tree, as a tree, is weakened, dwarfed and depreciated, through the influence exerted by that callosity in checking the upward flow of sap, the same agency is equally effective in multiplying, enlarging and appreciating its fruits; so that the real question at issue is in the case is simply one of loss and gain, and may be stated thus: In redeeming the perfect seedling tree, with its imperfect fruit, for the imperfect budded tree with its perfect fruit, is there, in fact, more of gain or loss? For myself, I cannot say I will not pretend to be altogether unprejudiced on this question. It would certainly to stagger if after devoting half a century to the enthusiastic study and practice of growing deciduous fruits and never known an instance of a seedling apple pear, peach or plum tree being planted for the purpose of growing fruit for the market, it should not trouble me to discover a sufficient reason for adopting an entirely different system with the citrus family.

In entering a brief plea, then, for the bud, I will present the following items:

First. Its earlier fruiting. It is well known that the budded (or grafted) tree precedes the seedling in its coming into bearing, by from one to two or several years. The difference in these dates is a matter of no trifling import to the young orchardist, who, with little means at his command, a family to support, and perhaps a mortgage on his farm his little farm, must be anxious to grow before he can settle the question whether he is the owner of his home or not. Add a judicious cultivator to him, a few days since: "If I had had the foresight to set all my grounds with buds instead of seedlings, I should now have money to lend." Halarton, a distinguished Italian writer of great many years in investigating the history of the olive family of fruits, and who has given the world a very exhaustive treatise on the cultivation of the orange, quotes Tusca, a high Spanish authority of the last century, on the same subject, as recommending the practice of grafting, "because the mind of man doth look towards and far from pears to give fruit, and only yields a brief quality." And Italian with this passage so followed by all the best writers." (The writer I have added.)

Second. Its greater productiveness. This is a fact of such evident and modern notoriety; and to them passing awaits one needs but a glance at our budded orange orchards to see its verification in the clusters and richness of 'golden apples' that everywhere deceive the trees beneath the beautiful young buds, whilst of the neighboring seedlings twice or thrice their age and size, only now and then one exhibits even a few scattered specimens. If it be objected that this condition of things will not be likely to enthuse the minority of the trees, I reply that the answer to this question lies wholly in the control of the planter. If, when ready to plant out an orchard he selects his trees with due discrimination, admitting into his collection no variety that has not an established reputation as a fine bearer, he may calculate with certainty that but a very small percentage of them will disappoint his expectations; while, on the other hand, the planter of seedlings but empties his money into the hopper of "the Wheel of Fortune," which, in its revolutions, may grind him out a fair proportion of prizes, but will be equally likely to put him in possession of a large amount of blanks.

Third. The superior quality of its fruit. Whether the theory be founded on fact or fiction, it has been very generally accepted that almost any kind of mutilation inflicted on a fruit tree in its roots, stem or branches, tends to increase the fruit in size, and to give it an enhanced value, whether as a table or a market fruit. Hence, depriving trees of a portion of their roots or their stems of a part or the whole of their bark, violently deflecting or contorting their limbs, ringing them (i. e., taking from them a narrow ring of bark), ligaturing them with wire or small cord, etc., etc., have been in practice for ages, and are at the present time, perhaps more than ever before, relied on for those purposes. Alike with budding and grafting, all these practices have their original conception in the idea that by interrupting the natural, free circulation of the sap, the same becomes more perfectly elaborated and better adapted for the production of fruit than for the growth of wood. That this theory is not well founded, is the opinion of but few. That the largest and finest specimens of our table fruits are grown upon stocks of dwarfish dimensions and habits—as the apple on Paradise stocks, and the pear on quince or thorn—go to corroborate it; so, in a striking manner, does the fact that repeated graftings of the same branch (each succeeding graft being put upon the one last set) effect a continual increase in the *size* of the fruit.

Fourth. The greater *facility* with which buds are planted, pruned, protected from insect enemies and parasitic growths, and their products handled in the time of harvest, all which facts are too self-evident to need anything more than a simple enumeration.

Fifth. The saving, in the case of budded trees, of a large percentage of that serious loss sustained annually in all seedling orchards, through the abrasions and thrashings of their fruits by the agitation (and sometimes *flagellation*) of their high and spreading tops in seasons of high wind. Says the editor of the *Alta Californian*, in his issue of April 13th: "Much of their fruit—in some cases a fourth—is spoiled by striking against thorns during storms." Of these thorns the buds are comparatively (and, at the option of the planter, may be entirely) guiltless. This topic is also too well understood to require any elucidation.

Sixth. The vantage-ground which the fruit of the bud (or *graft*) must always occupy in the markets of the world, by reason of its ascertained superior excellence, and a consequent widespread and well established *reputation*. Reputation presupposes some degree of notoriety. No new variety (and the fruit of every seedling is one, with rare exceptions) can possibly become notorious beyond the limits of a neighborhood, until by means of the bud or graft it is numerously propagated, and thus by the ordinary methods promulgated and disseminated. There are varieties of fruit (once limited, severally, to a single tree) that to-day belt the globe with the shadows of the budded (or grafted) trees that yield them and are accorded a conspicuous place in the markets of two hemispheres. These are the fruits *that sell*, the fruits the world *runs after*, the fruits that well-informed and discreet planters will give the *first* place, the *last* place, and *every* place in their orchards. Seedling fruit, in its *collective* character, can be known, to be sure, but only as an indiscriminate aggregation of multifarious sorts, good, bad and indifferent, the two latter, as a rule, greatly preponderating. Out of the fruit of an individual seedling tree no such thing as notoriety can be predicated. There is not enough of it. But *one tree* produces it. The world can have no knowledge of its existence.

Transactions in the fruit market are apt to take place somewhat after this fashion. A citizen, a lover of good fruit, passing through the market place, and glancing his eye over the contents of a freshly-arrived market wagon, turns up his face and slings out cheerily to the man in charge, "Aha! you have the veritable old St. Michael there, haven't you? The best peel the world ever knew before our day, and scarcely second to any other known variety still. Everybody has known and admired it since the days of Julius Cæsar. Please hand me out a basket." Market man: "They are bearing a pretty high price at the present time, sir, there are so many new fangled sorts in the market, and they are not so plenty as formerly, either." Citizen: "Never mind the price, friend; they always bring an extra price, and it is quite right they should. They pay the purchaser better at almost any price, than the inferior trash the market is always flooded with." A fruiterer next steps up, and directing a very inquisitive look at a certain barrel of fruit, inquires, "What are the large, red apples you have in this barrel here?" Marketman: "They are very fine, large, handsome apples as you see, sir; and they are very good apples, too." Fruiterer: "That may be; but what I was inquiring for is the *name*." Market man: "I have no name for them, I *raised them from seed* in my own orchard, and they are very fine apples." Fruiterer: "*Seedling* apples, and *without a name*. That will do. *My customers always want to know what they buy*. You could not *give* me a *load* of such. They would only rot down in my store."

I have in the beginning of this article spoken of the fruit of the *bud* (taken collectively) as *perfect*; and of the fruit of the *seedling* (taken collectively), *always* imperfect. When I thus characterize the fruit of the bud, I mean that it is *comparatively* perfect—as perfect as human effort has, thus far, been able to make it; for it embraces only *carefully made selections* from *all the best known varieties*. If these selections have been *the best possible*, then our budded fruit is the best possible, in the present condition of things, and when I characterize the fruit of the seedling (collectively) as *imperfect*, I mean that in its composition (or aggregation), there is found much material of a very inferior and worthless character. To be *perfect*, an orange must be of good size, fair form, clear complexion, thin in rind, delicate in fiber, soluble in pulp, abundant in juice, delicious in flavor, agreeable in odor. The great diversity, in all these particulars, that exists in the specimens gathered from a small seedling orchard even, cannot have escaped the notice of an observant orchardist. I have, myself, in the very limited experience I have had in this line of fruit, noted the fact that our seedling oranges vary in their sizes from two or three to five or six inches in diameter; in the thickness of their rinds from one to eight or ten lines; in the number of their seeds from none to more than twenty; and in like manner through all the list of particulars specified above.

Now, there is certainly a choice in oranges. The *best* are fully *as good* as any, and can, I think, be *grown* fully as cheaply as those of less merit, and *marketed* at a much smaller expense. Is it wise then, it may well be asked, to persevere in the *practice of planting seedling orchards?* Much of their product is quite below par, and not a little of it *of less than no value* in the market. Yet, as "dead flies cause the ointment of the apothecary to send forth a stinking savor," so a few bad specimens interspersed among the contents of a package of fruit otherwise faultless, will be sure to send forth an unsavory odor in the market that will "come home to roost" with the grower.

"No cultivated plant has a greater liability to deteriorate; so that seedling oranges are almost always worthless."—*Chambers' Encyclopedia, article "Orange."*

"The seedlings, in some cases, are of excellent quality, but there is no uniformity of size or flavor in an orchard of them.—*Notes on the recent Citrus Fair at Riverside, in Alta California*.

If it be objected by any one that the budded tree is of too *dwarfish a growth*, I only reply to him that a much larger number of buds than of seedlings can be cultivated on the same area, and probably at no greater cost; or should another one declare the bud to be *too short-lived* to suit his notions, I reply *to him* that the chances are much against his living long enough to suffer any harm from this quarter. But, in case the bud should prove short-lived, the question is worth considering whether the *renewal* of a budded orchard as often as once in two or three decades would not well repay the outlay by the superior quality of the fruit grown on young trees.

In what I have now advanced it has been no part of my purpose to malign the seedling *orange*, but only to assign to it its proper place. As an original *parent stock*, by means of which, *through careful crossing*, we can *improve*, *indefinitely*, on the species, its value cannot be overestimated. All the choice varieties at present cultivated as buds have come from this source alone, and that its capabilities are exhausted there is no reason to suppose. That a thorough canvass of the seedling orchards of Southern California might, to-day, reveal several varieties *equal* or even *superior* to the very best now cultivated may be *possible*, that many of *great excellence* would be disclosed is altogether *probable*, and that lemons of *good* size would come to the light is quite *certain*. "The thing that has been, it is that which shall be." St. Michael's, Malta Blood, Mediterranean Sweet, etc., *were all once seedlings*, and this is true of all the fine varieties that now gladden the hearts of men all over the world. The *seedling* orange is the worthy *mother* of all good oranges, and while the lamentable fact cannot be ignored that among her numerous offspring, as among that of Mother Eve, there turn up many worthless vagabonds, I can not attribute the fault so much to Dame Orange as to Dame Nature. The mother pear, the mother apple, and the mothers of all the precious fruits we love and prize so dearly have fallen, alike, under the same misfortune.

In view of the foregoing considerations I can not myself avoid the conclusion that to cultivate seedling oranges *indiscriminately*, is an ill-considered and injudicious practice. Indiscriminately they must be cultivated, or not at all; since before they come into bearing the quality of the fruit cannot be even conjectured. When a seedling tree has fruited, and the fruit has been ascertained to be of a very high order, let it be transferred to the *ubiquitous bud*—and then what becomes of the *seedling* is of little consequence.

If ardent, young amateur fruit growers would put out small *experimental seedling orchards* and devote an occasional leisure hour to caring for it and experimenting with it, they would find the employment full of interest and pleasure, and the fruit of their labors, if not immediately profitable to themselves, might become a precious boon to future generations.

VARIETIES.

"You look so happy that I suppose you have been to the dentist and had that aching tooth pulled," said a Galveston man to a friend with a swollen jaw. "It ain't that that makes me look happy. The tooth aches worse than ever, but I don't feel it." "How is that?" "Well, I feel so jolly because I have just been to the dentist and he was out," and the happy man cut a pigeon wing on the sidewalk.

"What is the meaning of a backbiter?" asked a gentleman at a Sunday school examination. This was a puzzler. It went down the class until it came to a simple urchin, who said, "Perhaps it's a flea."

To the query of a Danbury dentist to an applicant for a new set, as to what sort of teeth she wanted, she said. "Something that won't show dirt."

Business Enterprise.

FRUIT AND PRODUCE SHIPMENTS FROM LOS ANGELES.

WE have often said in the pages of this magazine that enterprise and persistence are sure to win in Southern California. Men who do business strictly upon business principles and show a reasonable amount of business tact and ability will invariably succeed. Messrs. Chas. B. Woodhead and Leslie F. Gay, the former a native of Ohio, the latter of Illinois, commenced business on Aliso avenue, in this city, about four years ago. They were then as now general produce and commission dealers, and although times were very dull for the first two years of the existence of the firm, it steadily gained the confidence of the public and they soon found it necessary to remove to a more eligible location on Spring street. Here they remained for some time, handling green and dried fruits, trees and plants, seeds and bulbs, vegetables, and everything else that shrewd business men can handle profitably on commission. We have frequently heard it observed that the busiest portion of our city seems to be in front of the establishment of Messrs. Woodhead & Gay. But the Arizona, New Mexico and Eastern trade, early the present year waked up the farmers of Los Angeles Valley, and orders poured into the office of the enterprising commission dealers. The capacity of the old store was far from being sufficient, and so about three months ago the foundation of a substantial brick edifice was laid on the lot adjoining, which was speedily completed. The firm already occupies a portion of their new store, which is in every respect convenient and well located.

Mr. Woodhead has lately visited many of the principal Eastern cities with a view of opening up new and better markets for Southern California products. He believes that with some further concessions from the railroad the East will take all we can produce at prices which will compensate growers.

Our farmers hardly realize, we believe, what two energetic men have done to increase the demand for their products. Instead of waiting for trade to hunt them up, they are seeking it and forcing it into our valley. They are causing many blades of grass to grow where none grew before, and in a practical manner are adding much to the wealth of our city and county.

As this number of SEMI-TROPIC CALIFORNIA will circulate largely in the East, we would strongly recommend parties interested in California fruits to address Messrs. Woodhead & Gay, who will take pleasure in promptly and carefully attending to all orders.

It may be proper for us to add that we believe the farmers of this valley can get better prices for their produce when shipped through a reliable firm than when they try to make shipments to distant points on their own account. We learn that merchants of the territories are becoming very distrustful of individual shipments.

WHAT CAN YOU RAISE AND WHAT ARE YOUR SEASONS?

It would be easier to tell what we can not raise. We grow successfully every thing raised in the Mississippi Valley, and a great many things grown in tropical countries. We can raise more and better wheat, corn, potatoes, rye, barley, vegetables, etc., to the acre than they can in the Western States. We can raise more and better fruit; apples, peaches, pears, plums, small fruits, etc., etc., than in any other part of the United States. We can grow oranges, lemons, limes, pomegranates, apricots, guavas, figs, olives, English walnuts, almonds, and many other tropical fruits in perfection. Our grapes are not excelled in the world.

OUR SEASONS.

An old gentleman who came here three years ago from Illinois, remarked to us a few days ago, as we were complimenting our delightful spring: "Why, it's all spring and summer here in California, I've not had any winter since I left the East."

The following is a table showing the time of marketing the leading fruits:

Oranges	Christmas to July.
Lemons	All the year.
Limes	All the year.
Apples	July to November.
Pears	July to November.
Grapes	July 15 to December.
Raisins	October 20 (new).
Peaches	June 15 to Christmas
Apricots	June 15 to September.
Plums and Prunes	June 1 to November.
Cherries	June.
Japanese Persimmons	November.
Guavas	Nearly all the year.
Loquats	May 15 to June 15.
Strawberries	Nearly all the year round
Raspberries	June 15 to September.
Blackberries	June 15 to September.
Currants	May 15 to June 15.
Gooseberries	June.
Watermelons	July to October.
Muskmelons	July to October.

Our thermometer behaves with much more discretion and kindness than the boiling and freezing instruments of the East. We refer the reader to report under head of "Climate," on page 103.

The hottest day last summer, during May, the thermometer registered an average temperature of 82°, with a pleasant ocean breeze to temper the heat and make the day comfortable.

The coldest day last winter was during November, the average temperature, 35°. The month of February, when the cold winds howled and the snows blockaded trade and traffic throughout the East, our average coldest temperature was 43°. A pleasanter month we never experienced.

Who, if they fully understood our climate, seasons and crops, would live in the cold East another winter?

SIERRA MADRE VILLA.

This villa and groves have an altitude of 1,800 feet above the sea and 1,000 feet above San Gabriel Valley, commanding a view of the Pacific Ocean in the distance and a panorama of great extent and loveliness. Six years ago when these mesa lands were first broken for the purpose of planting citrus fruits, many were the forebodings of an extremely hazardous experiment. Now it carries off the palm for the largest, best flavored, earliest and greatest yield. The lessee (Mr. Rhodes) has already shipped to San Francisco 100,000 oranges, (remember from trees only six years old) for which he received the highest market price; also, immense quantities of limes which sold for from $15 to $18 per thousand. I picked in his garden ripe and fine flavored tomatoes from vines planted three years ago, thus showing the salubrity of climate and immunity from frosts. Extensive tracts in the immediate vicinity of Sierra Madre Villa are being surveyed and laid out in twenty acre or larger lots by Mr. N. C. Carter, and will soon be put upon the market with unquestioned water rights at reasonable prices and on liberal terms. Sierra Madre Villa is unequaled by any place in this State as a summer or winter residence, and is a world wide renowned resort for pleasure or health seekers.

THE LEMON.

As a writer in the London *Lancet* remarks, few people know the value of lemonjuice. A piece of lemon bound upon a corn will cure it in a few days; it should be renewed night and morning. A lime or lemon-juice and sugar will always relieve a cough. Most people feel poorly in the spring, but if they would eat a lemon before breakfast every day for a week—with or without sugar, as they like—they would find it better than any medicine. Lemonjuice used according to this recipe will sometimes cure consumption: Put a dozen lemons into cold water and slowly bring to a boil; but slowly until the lemons are soft, then squeeze until all the juice is extracted; add sugar to your taste and drink. In this way use one dozen lemons a day. If they cause pain, or lessen the bowels too much, lessen the quantity, and use only five or six a day until you are better, and then begin a dozen a day. After using five or six dozen, the patient will begin to gain flesh and enjoy food. Until as to the lemons, and still use them very freely for several weeks more. Another use for lemons is for a refreshing drink in summer, or in sickness at any time. Prepare as directed above, and all water and sugar. But in order to have this kept well, after boiling the lemons, squeeze and strain carefully; than to every half pint of juice add one pound of loaf or crushed sugar, boil and stir a few minutes more until the sugar is dissolved, skim carefully and bottle. You will get more juice from the lemons by boiling them, and the preparation keeps better.

BAKER BLOCK, Los Angeles, Cal.

Southern California.

LOS ANGELES COUNTY.

The *Resources of California* in speaking of Southern California says:

This is the richest, most prolific and prosperous county in Southern California. It has every variety of soil and climate to be found in this part of the State. It has been well and thoroughly written up during the last few years—has attracted much attention in the East, and is now receiving a large immigration and consequently is increasing in wealth and population more than any other section of the State.

On the southwest it is bounded by the Pacific Ocean with a coast line of nearly one hundred miles. The larger portion of the county is a parallelogram, being about seventy miles from east to west, and sixty miles from north to south, leaving a triangle in the southeast portion, the northern line of which equals seventy miles and the eastern forty miles. The county, therefore, contains about 5,000 square miles, or 3,000,000 acres.

PRODUCTS.

Corn, barley, potatoes, wheat, rye, beans, castor beans and alfalfa, tobacco, flax, hemp and cotton have been tested and prove a success. Of fruits, the grape, apple, pear, peach, plum, nectarine, cherry, apricot, fig, orange, lemon, lime, walnut and all the small fruits and berries grow luxuriantly and yield largely. This is the great orange section of the State.

Everywhere in Southern California where oranges have matured, we find the Old San Bernardino, Mission San Gabriel and Pasadena orange far superior to all others.

The raising of sheep, cattle, horses and hogs enters largely into the farm husbandry of Los Angeles county. The bee interest is also becoming very important especially along the foot-hills of the San Gabriel range of mountains.

LOS ANGELES VALLEY,

Is the most productive, probably, in the State, and is destined at no distant day to teem with a dense population. It is bounded on the northeast by the foot-hills, dividing this county from San Bernardino and El Monte Valleys; on the southwest by the ocean, and on the northwest by the ocean and the foot hills.

This valley, in a northwesterly and southeasterly direction, is fully fifty miles in length and some twenty miles wide, so that it contains one thousand square miles, or 640,000 acres. Of this land 160,000 acres may be classed as grazing, 160,000 grape and semi-tropical fruit, and 320,000 acres superior corn lands, equally adapted for barley, rye, oats, millet, potatoes, hops, etc. It is estimated that at least 500,000 acres of this land can be irrigated. It lies most favorable for purposes of irrigation, being a level plain with a fall of ten feet per mile in a southerly direction. The water can be deflected on either side from the rivers that flow through it. Many very large ditches are already constructed in this valley leading the water from the rivers, and others are being dug at the present time. The supply of artesian water in this valley is also the most prolific yet discovered in the State, flowing wells being obtained over an immense area at depths ranging from forty to two hundred feet. The soil, as a rule, is a rich sandy loam, easily worked and very productive. There are farms in this valley that have been under constant culture for a century, and the yield is as bountiful to day as when the first crop was planted. Irrigation seems to renew the soil and maintain its fertility. In some portions of the valley there is an excess of alkali, but this can be eliminated by the introduction of beets and other things which require a large amount of potash.

For richness of soil, variety of productions, favorable climate, location, and in many other respects this county is by far the richest county in Southern California, especially in the production of semi-tropical fruits. It is not extravagant to say that there are one million orange trees in orchard form in this county—old and young. The Orange settlement alone, 3x2 miles, contains 135,200.

THE CITY OF LOS ANGELES

Has surprised every one in the rapid progress she has made for the last few years, being now the fourth in the State, ranking next to Sacramento. She is steadily moving on, notwithstanding the hard times—new buildings are going up, new improvements are everywhere visible, and the city is extending in every direction, on the hills and out in the valley.

THE SOUTHERN PACIFIC RAILROAD COMPANY

Have made great improvements in the vicinity of their new depot, in East Los Angeles. This is the great railroad centre of Southern California. The Southern Pacific daily from San Francisco, the Arizona, the Wilmington, the Anaheim and Santa Ana, and the Santa Monica railroads all center here, giving splendid facilities for travelers and freights.

The climate is delightful. The surrounding country forms a landscape of rare beauty.

All the conveniences and opportunities afforded by a city are found here; and current expenses of living, etc., are as moderate in this city as in any other part of California.

Markets.

(Corrected by Leo J. Thompson, Grocer, 36 Spring Street.)

RETAIL GROCERIES, ETC.

BUTTER, Cal. choice, ℔ ℔...	$0 35	@	$0 40
CHEESE...	15	"	20
Eastern...	20	"	25
LARD, California...	12½	"	14
Eastern...	15	"	20
FLOUR, extra family, bbl...			5 90
Capitol Mills, ¼ sack...	2 25	"	3 20
Paucer, ¼ sack...		"	2 90
Lankershim, ½ cwt...		"	3 25
Superfine, do...		"	2 90
Graham, 50 ℔ sack...		"	1 10
Buckwheat, 10 ℔ sack...		"	55
OATMEAL, Cal., 10 ℔ sack...		"	55
Eastern, do...		"	60
CORN MEAL, ℔ 50 ℔ sack...		"	85
SUGAR, w. crushed...	11	"	
Light brown...	9½	"	10
COFFEE, green...	17	"	35
TEA, fine black...	50	"	1 00
Finest Japan...	30	"	80
CANDLES, Adamantine...	15	"	25
SOAP, California...	05	"	10
RICE...	07	"	
YEAST POWDER, doz...	1 50	"	4 00
CANNED OYSTERS, doz...	1 75	"	3 50
SYRUP, S. F. Golden...	80	"	1 00
DRIED APPLES, ℔...	10	"	12½
GERMAN PRUNES...	12½	"	
FIGS, California...	10	"	20
PEACHES...	10	"	20
OILS, kerosene...	20	"	40
HONEY, comb...	12½	"	15
do., No. 2...	10	"	12
Extracted...	06	"	08
BACON, California...	10	"	12½
HAMS, do...	12½	"	14
Eastern...	16	"	17
POTATOES, ctl...	90	"	1 15
ONIONS, ctl...		"	3 50
BEANS...	1 50	"	2 50
Pinter...	1 40	"	1 50
Lima...	1 00	"	6 00
FRESH BEEF...	05	"	08
Round steak...		"	10
Sirloin...	10	"	12
Porterhouse...	12½	"	
CHICKENS...	37½	"	50
CAL. RAISINS, box...	2 25	"	2 50
Half boxes...	1 25	"	1 35
Quarter boxes...	75	"	85

EGGS.—Have ruled high for several months and in demand at 06c. The market is better supplied and prices are now quoted at 16c & 18.

BUTTER.—Is also in good demand, for choice only, at 32½c.

ORANGES.—The market has ruled dull for poor and unripe, best choice No. 1 fruit has commanded good prices, ranging from $22 to $30 per M. All the choice oranges exhibited at the Citrus Fair sold readily at fancy prices. Oranges should not be shipped until ripe, and then put up in first class shape for market.

WINES AND LIQUORS.—The boom in the wine business has a tendency to make prices stronger, and prices may be said to have advanced two or three cents on the new wines.

LOS ANGELES WINES AND LIQUORS.

Red wine, No. 1, per gallon...	$0 50
Red wine, No. 2, per gallon...	40
White wine, new, per gallon...	50
White wine, old, per gallon...	75
Port wine, old, per gallon...	1 00
Angelica wine, old, per gallon...	1 00
Sherry wine, old, per gallon...	1 75
Cucamonga, old, per gallon...	1 00
Brandy, per gallon...	2 50
Aguardiente, per gallon...	2 00

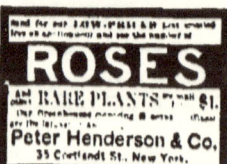

VOL. IV. *JULY.* NO. 7.

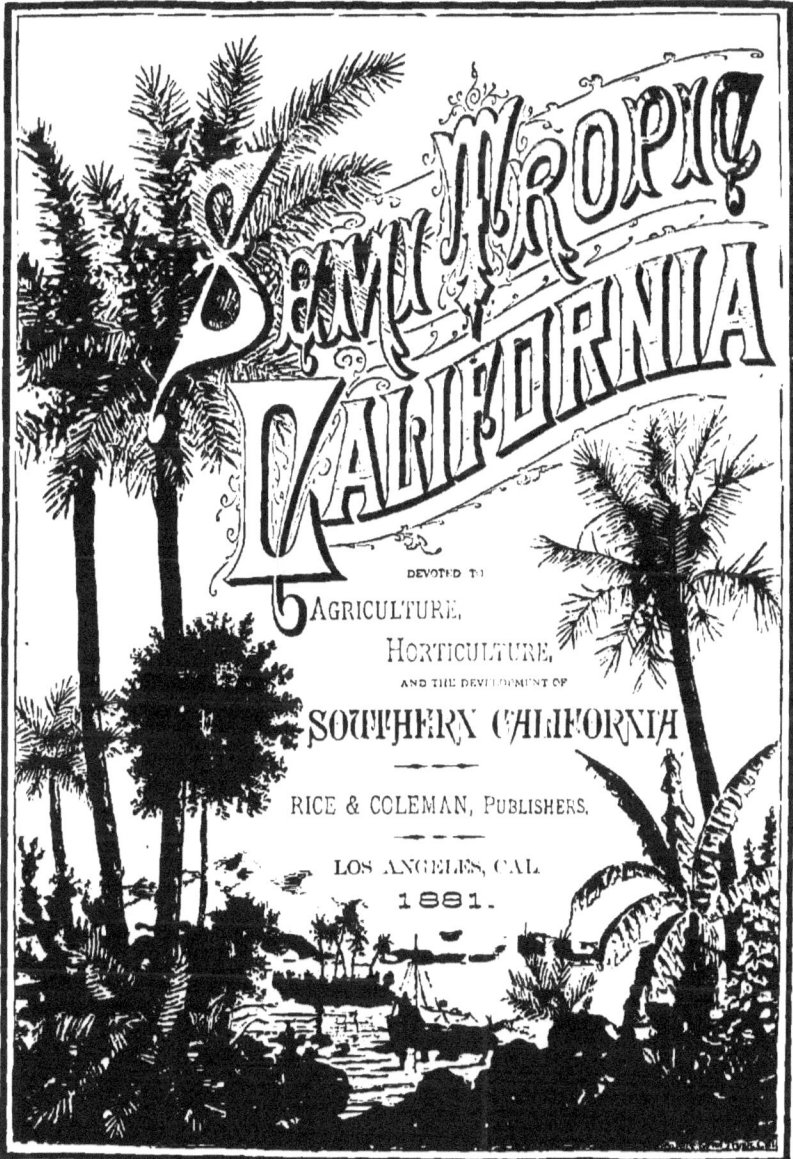

Semi Tropic California

DEVOTED TO

AGRICULTURE,

HORTICULTURE,

AND THE DEVELOPMENT OF

SOUTHERN CALIFORNIA

RICE & COLEMAN, Publishers.

LOS ANGELES, CAL

1881.

Agriculture.

THE GROWTH OF FARMING.

The earliest history with which we are acquainted, sings of the fruits of the field. The ancients had their goddess for every department, and as some particular branch here abundantly, they bowed at the shrine of their propitious benefactress. As we look back through the centuries of the past, we find the profession of farming in its highest state during the time of republican Rome, and note its decline during the the reign of the Cæsars, when the luxuries and vices of their time permeated all classes of society. Broad republican principles, a growing civilization, and a liberal education of the masses, will ever be found going hand in hand with progressive farming. Other professions may prosper and shine with a double luster on the page of history under imperial and kingly rule, but farming, to attain its largest proportions and success, must be fostered by the ennobling hand of liberty. Landlord and tenant may hold their respective positions, but never till the tenant becomes the landlord will the soil bless a prosperous and happy people.

Looking through the dark night of a thousand years which followed the downfall of Rome, we see the gleam of the Celtic sword and the poise of the Teuton lance slowly but surely preparing the way for a better and nobler age. An age that will not be perfect until the iron rule of modern Europe shall disband its standing armies, which are the bone and sinew of the land, and return the members to fields free to the hand that tills them. The very reason why the United States is the leading agricultural nation of the world, lies in the fact of the broad freedom which its citizens enjoy. When the dark cloud of war sweeps over our land, the call to arms is answered by hundreds of thousands ready to do their duty in the field of carnage, but as soon as the treaty of peace is proclaimed the spirit of restlessness prevails until the last tent is folded and the warring thousands who were rivals in war become rivals in the field of husbandry. In truth, we are a nation of farmers in peace, and a nation of soldiers in times of war. No nation can be truly great and prosperous for any length of time where these conditions do not exist. History bears us out in this assertion, and

it is with a certain national pride which we feel that we glance at our own free America with her boundless resources. From ocean to ocean, from the forty ninth parallel to the gulf, we are a nation of workers, and our present wonderful prosperity is all due to the intelligent labor of the active farmer. The trades could not exist, commerce would become a thing of the past, and failures more appalling than were ever known, would appear on every side, should the fields refuse to yield their annual reward. The time has past when farming, in the minds of a few, ranked lower than the professions and trade. The honest rustic is now regarded as the great source of our national strength, a position which his intelligence and success have justly won for him. Farming will be a success in proportion to the intelligence of the masses. Scientific farming alone may not succeed, but science combined with experience and a fair amount of good sense, will always attain a larger success than the unlearned, haphazard system.

Reading, thinking and doing are the three essentials; combine them properly, giving to each the time which its importance demands, and our great plains and valleys will support a degree of prosperity that will command the respect and admiration of all civilized nations.

MIXED FARMING.

More mixed farming, we believe, would bring more coin to the farmers' pocket, and a more lasting prosperity to the country than the all-one thing rule that so generally obtains throughout Southern California. The Eastern farmer who, after his long year of toil, finds one or two hundred dollars added to his bank account, feels satisfied that he has been fairly rewarded for his labor. This amount of money would seem but a small compensation to our farmers. Unless they can raise a large crop of wheat or barley, run in debt for this thing and that, run the risk of a dry season, and carry on a large business, farming has no charms for them. And eight here is where we find failures, if any are to be found.

You never hear of a man with forty or eighty acres, who gives his attention to the different branches of agriculture and horticulture failing. True, it may be that at the end of the year he may not have cleared so much as his more pretentious

neighbor, whose large wheat or barley crop, favored with a good season, has added largely to his exchequer. But how will it be the year following, and the next, should they be dry seasons?

While the small farmer keeps down expenses, lives within his means, improves his few acres, and becomes independent slowly but surely, the larger one goes into debt for teams, provisions, machinery, family mortgages, and at last is sold out and has nothing that he may call his own.

The term gambling can justly be applied to some branches of farming, and especially in California.

Every new branch that is more than ordinarily promising, is taken up with such a furore that it becomes a "boom," and as a rule it eventually proves a failure through over-production.

We refer to the time when everybody became wild over the orange and general citrus culture, and slug up their vineyards to make room for the orange, lemon, lime, etc. Now they are reversing the order of things, and everybody must have a vineyard, even to the neglect of citrus fruits. Some years ago deciduous fruits were by many considered a failure, and unworthy of any attention. Experience, however, has given us a full line of deciduous fruits, save, perhaps, cherries, a few currants and plums, which challenge the world to a comparison. The forty-acre farm properly managed, will have a small vineyard, a deciduous orchard, some citrus trees, a patch of alfalfa, cows, chickens, pigs, and will raise in the field a general variety of products: corn, potatoes, pumpkins, flax, beans, hay, barley, etc. By some this would be considered a sort of puttering, and would be considered beneath their time and attention, but it is a fact, verified by cases near this city, that men who follow this plan will inevitably succeed, and in a short time will become the key to our permanent prosperity.

CAPITAL invested in a farm and managed with skill is more generally rewarded than any other investment a man can make.

THE outlook at the present time is a promising one for a most splendid harvest in 1881. We have not had a note from the croakers for a fortnight.

A MAN of good health, good judgment, frugal habits, industrious and persevering, and with a family to match, may engage in farming at any time and in any place with a prospect of almost certain success.

Horticulture.

THE LOOM OF LIFE.

"All day, all night, I can hear the jar
Of the loom of life, and near and far
It thrills with its deep and muffled sound,
As the tireless wheels go always round.

Busily, ceaselessly, goes the loom,
In the light of day and midnight's gloom,
The wheels are turning early and late,
And the woof is round in the warp of fate.

Click! click! there's a thread of love wove in,
Click! click! another of wrong and sin;
What a checkered thing will this life be
When we see it unrolled in eternity!

Time, with a face like mystery,
And hands as busy as hands can be,
Sits at the loom with its warp outspread,
To catch in its meshes each glancing thread!

When shall this wonderful web be done?
In a thousand years, perhaps, or one,
Or nevermore! Who knoweth? Not you or I,
But the wheels turn on and the shuttles fly.

Ah, sad-eyed weaver, the years are slow!
But each one is nearer the end, I know!
And some day the last thread will be woven in,
God grant it be love instead of sin.

Are we spinners of wool for this life web, say?
Do we furnish the weaver a thread each day?
It were better by far, my friend, to spin
A beautiful thread than a thread of sin.
—Western Rural.

WILL ORANGE CULTURE PAY?

This is a question of great importance to Southern California. The time was when an orange orchard in full bearing was even more sure than a bank in declaring dividends. Dividends not of five or six per cent, but dividends which at once made the fortunate possessor independent. But with this industry the farmer might promises can hardly be realized now. It is useless to disguise the real truth of the matter. Some may wish that we had said nothing on this subject, but why deceive ourselves, our neighbors, and our friends? The truth is what the reading public want, not theories dressed up in fine words and elaborate phrases. When we had but few orchards in bearing the demand gave us good prices, but during the last three seasons there has been very little profit in the business, save to a few of the old orchards which had already established a reputation. These of course received the first attention from dealers, and have continued to be moderately remunerative, while the younger orchards have had the disadvantage of seeking their own markets, and the more successful ones have returned many a ready dollar to the pocket of the grower. In writing about this industry it is but just to speak of the many vicissitudes which have attended it, and it will appear to the intelligent reader at once that the orange has passed through a trying ordeal during the last three years and may still be looked upon with much favor when certain conditions are complied with. To begin our retrospect we will mention the

unusually cold winters of '78-79 and '79-80, which killed thousands of trees in nursery, and besides killing many in orchard form, chilled all more or less, and the result each year was a small crop and much inferior fruit.

Of course man has no power over the elements. He is forced to take the seasons as they come, and to do the best he can with them. We learn from men who have resided here for twenty-five or thirty years that these winters were the exception and not the rule, consequently we have every reason to expect coming seasons to be more favorable to the industry. Again, in the spring of '80 many new orchards came into bearing and the blossoming was very promising, but the summer was cool, frost came just as the fruit was beginning to turn yellow, and the crop of '80-81, though very large, has not brought as much coin into this section as was hoped for. We must say, however, that the growers are in a large degree responsible for this result. Had they gone through their orchards after the fruit had set last spring and thinned out freely, allowing each tree according to age to bear from three to five hundred only, they would have less in number to be sure, but that loss would have been more than balanced by the superior quality of the fruit. So much for one neglect of the grower, and now we will speak of another practice even more injurious to the industry than all others combined, and that is the gathering time. It is a fact that as a rule the orange in Southern California does not ripen before the last of March or the first of April, and we know from actual experience that it improves by hanging on the tree through May, June, and even into July. Now, it is a practice with many to begin picking as early as December, a time when the fruit, although yellow, is not ripe, and is so sour that it is in no degree palatable. This is thrown upon the market, not only upon our home, but upon all the great centers within our reach, and you can easily imagine the result. The fruit is sampled and an unfavorable opinion is formed, a prejudice springs up which the ripe, fine flavored fruit of the proper picking time can hardly overcome. It is to be hoped that the grower's attention will be called to these facts, and that in the future he will look more to thinning out and will not put his oranges upon the market until they are fully ripe.

There are some who carelessly throw their oranges into boxes without the first thought of selecting, and then wonder when their returns come why they received only about half as much as their neighbors, whose fruit on the tree is no better. The fruit on the tree, mind you, no sad was no better, but how of it in the boxes? His neighbor assorted his oranges with great care, put only the finest ones into the boxes, used a wrapping of clean, bright paper around each orange, and not only gave better fruit but put it up in a more attractive manner; who then would wonder at the difference between the returns. You

must often please the eye in order to reach the stomach, and in this age of friendly rivalry in order to be successful we must be original, wide awake, active, ever striving to excel and aiming to lead rather than to be led.

Glancing into the future we have many reasons to be hopeful. Experience is teaching us all a valuable lesson. The fears that prevailed a few years ago regarding putting out orange orchards here, there and everywhere has subsided. Other industries are receiving more attention, less orange planting is going on, and that only in localities which are known to be best adapted to citrus culture. Thus while the demand will increase largely every year, the production will remain about the same, and in a few years the cry of overproduction will not be heard. Another important factor which figures in the consideration is the markets which the new railroads are opening to us. By the Southern Pacific our oranges find their way into Arizona, New Mexico, Texas, El Paso, and the East. In a few months the Atlantic & Pacific will have reached this coast, then we will have a competing line, and a good healthy competition will undoubtedly give us freight rates which will help to stimulate the industry.

In this brief retrospect we believe that we have noticed the more important points bearing upon the subject. The pros and the cons, devoid of all coloring have come under our consideration, and in the final summing up the general verdict will no doubt be favorable to orange culture, when the conditions spoken of in this article receive the attention which their importance demand.

WHAT SHALL BE DONE WITH OUR PRESENT FRUIT CROP?

This question should have been considered earlier in the season, but even now it is not too late to advise a little in the matter. In the first place our commission houses are absorbing large quantities at high prices in their trade with the territories and the east. This demand, however, will accommodate only those living near the shippers or near the lines of railroad reaching to the aforesaid markets.

Again, the canning industry is assuming large proportions and thousands of tons will find ready sale and use in this direction. The new Los Angeles canning factory starting up across the river is preparing to do business on a very large scale and will be a great institution for orchardists in this immediate vicinity. It proposes not only to can but also to run the Alden dryer in order to utilize over-ripe fruits, or such as will not do for canning, but will be perfectly good for drying. The canning factory at Colton will draw largely from Riverside, San Bernardino and other sections in the Colton circuit. Santa Barbara also has its extensive factory, and besides these three large incorporate institutions there are several small individual establishments throughout Southern California, and every settlement, town and hamlet not already supplied should see to it at once that they have a local canning and drying factory. There is money in it, large money; a harvest that begins to yield its returns from the first ripening in the spring until the citrus fruits are ripe in the fall. Many will hesitate through fear of inability to reach the public taste. To them we would cite the success that some private individuals have attained during the experimental times of the industry. It has been our good fortune to test some of the fruit put up by our growers in a quiet way at their homes, and we do not hesitate to say that better goods we never sampled. Cans in large quantities can be had of our local tinners at very reasonable prices, according to size. Two-pound cans we will place at fifty cents per dozen and look for a minute at the profits of the business. To avoid fractions we will put the cost of a two-pound can at four cents, sugar not to exceed one cent, fancy label three cents, total cost eight cents. Now what will your goods wholesale for? A retail dealer of this city tells us that we may figure with absolute certainty on fifteen cents per can as the lowest wholesale price that first class goods will ever reach.

Here, then, you have seven cents for two pounds of fruit and the labor attending the canning. Seven cents for one can, seven dollars for a hundred, seventy dollars per thousand and so on. Who would ask for anything better? Only he who is sitting around for something to turn up to make him rich in a day. Poor fellow, those days with California are past. The territories with their mining excitement may afford you the stimulus which your nature craves. If so, we wish you well, and when you are through dreaming your golden dream and wish to become a hard working humble rustic, return, and we will gladly admit you to our army of workers. Individual canning we would advise only to parties who live remote from the large factories.

While these canneries are moderately liberal in their prices, growers would better sell direct to them, then they have their money in their pocket, and have no more worry or anxiety concerning their crop. All that we have said regarding canning will apply to drying. There is always more or less fruit that is unfit for canning. Such should be dried, none should be allowed to waste; all will be wanted at good prices before next season's crop comes. Numerous drying devices can be had, some of them at a nominal figure, but where money is scarce a little ingenuity and ambition, with two or three dollars worth of lumber, would construct a family dryer that would last a lifetime.

Although our deciduous products are becoming almost too large to contemplate, still the demand absorbs them all and calls for more. California canned and dried fruits are called for from nearly every quarter of the globe. Many orders to our personal knowledge, received here during the past winter, could not be filled at any price. The industry is only in its infancy. This is truly a land of fruits, as each year demonstrates to us more clearly. Nature acts her part nobly, if we do ours half so well the battle is won. Everybody will hold up his head because he is prosperous, every man you meet will have a smiling face and a pleasant word, because he has coin in his pocket, and our very existence will be sweeter, because all around are cheerful and happy.

DECIDUOUS FRUIT BUDDING.

July and August are the proper months in which to bud deciduous trees. The plum generally comes first in order, other varieties follow as the bark, sap and buds are in condition, and the peach comes in at the last.

Any sized tree may be budded, but as a rule only young trees of one year's growth in nursery form are subjected to this operation. The already bearing orchard, however, may be budded with equal propriety, and now is a good time to change a poor fruit for a good one. In budding nursery trees the bud is inserted into the trunk four to six inches from the ground; larger trees receive the bud in the limbs. Buds are taken from branches of this year's growth, and only the largest and finest should be used. The process is so simple that it is hardly worth while to repeat it here, but for fear that some one unacquainted with the business may peruse this article we will speak of it briefly. When the terminal bud is forming on the end of the twigs the tree is ready for budding. Use a budding knife if you have one, if not, a pocket knife will answer. Make a slit in the bark where you wish to place the bud about an inch long, at the top of the slit, cut square across it about half an inch, with the handle of the budding knife carefully raise the lips of the bark thus made and insert the bud, force the bud down to the bottom of the slit, then wind with soft budding twine, or any soft twine that you may have, sufficiently hard to exclude the air. In two or three weeks the string may be removed and everything left until next spring, when the trunk should be cut off a few inches above the bud. And later in the season as the bud progresses the trunk may be trimmed off smoothly down close to the bud. After the bud starts in the spring all other growth should be broken off by the hand so that the full growing force may go to the bud alone. In large trees you pursue the same plan, save it is the limb, instead of the trunk as in the nursery, but the process is the same in every particular.

HORTICULTURAL NOTES.

Deciduous Fruits.—Of course a peach or pear or apricot orchard is not so ruinous to us an orange orchard, nor does it sound as well to write East about, but perhaps there is as much money in it. There is but a comparatively small portion of Southern California that will excel in the culture of citrus fruits, and it is only the superior fruit that will find a profitable market, while there is hardly an acre that will not yield some kind of deciduous fruit in perfection, and there is little danger of the market being glutted in this line.—*Ex.*

Orchard Work.—A gentleman engaged in canning fruit says it pays to pick your fruit carefully and in time; if in right condition one day, the next will be too late to pick. Go over your trees many times. Don't try to pick all at once. If green, you lose weight. The proper condition for apricot, plum, peach and nectarine is when fully matured, but before softening. I've shallow boxes. Shakes make good boxes and are cheap. Above all, hug to the cannery, or send to the market at the earliest possible moment after picking. It is not too late to thin out some fruit. Trees that overbear do not yield marketable fruit.—*Santa Rosa Republican.*

Diverse Industries.—We are glad to hear that some of our prominent farmers are turning their attention to the cultivation of something besides wheat. One gentleman informs us that he has commenced the cultivation of fruit trees on a handsome scale, having planted several thousand pear and apricot trees which are growing finely. The climate of this county is favorable to fruit raising, and, with the exception of cherries and peaches, which would do well on the lowlands bordering the rivers, good profits could be reaped from orchards. The foothills are excellent for grapes, peaches and apples, as is now verified by the presence in our market of excellent fruit. The finer quality of grapes could be cultivated successfully by a little irrigation. Water in abundance can be procured from wells. It is demonstrated by practical grape growers that the raisin grape cannot be successfully cultivated without irrigation sufficient to flood the ground and destroy insects which prey upon vines. Almost any ordinary well will furnish the necessary water for sub-irrigation, which is the only practicable way of irrigating vines.—*Modesto Herald.*

Making Orange Wine.—Finding myself in the midst of a bearing orange orchard in Los Angeles county, and observing large quantities of the fruit on the ground and unmarketable, I concluded to manufacture a few bushels into wine. Procuring an ordinary hand "squeezer," I commenced operations, with the following result: From three bushels of wind shaken oranges I pressed six gallons of juice, which I placed in a keg to undergo fermentation. After the expiration of 30 days I drew it off, bottled it and put it away in a cool place. It is now about 60 days old, and promises to make a very fine wine.

It is not necessary either to wash or pare the fruit. I simply cut the larger ones in two and the end off the smaller ones. From my experience I am satisfied that one man can make 10 gallons per day, or what will make 30 bottles of wine.

There can be no doubt that the most profitable disposition we can make of orange crops is to make them into wine. In doing so the entire crop can be used, large and small.—*Corr. Los Angeles Herald.*

Viticultural.

ADDRESS OF M. M. ESTEE AT THE ST. HELENA VITICULTURAL ASSOCIATION'S ANNUAL RE-UNION.

It is said that a man's disposition, his personal bravery, and devotion to country, is formed, in a larger degree, by his surroundings, where he lives and what he does; that he who lives in constant communion with nature's grandest and most beautiful scenery necessarily is a man of lofty purposes, great conceptions and strong, manly instincts, while he who is bound down in a pursuit in which there is nothing but toil and no pleasure, who only looks out upon the green fields, the hills and rocks and mountains, once in a lifetime, knows nothing of the beauty of the world we live in, the grandeur of its solitudes, or the mute but instinctive lessons which these speechless months teach him. For him existence is the only aim in life; comfort and competence he cannot hope for.

Grape culture is one of the earliest pursuits of civilized man. We read of it in the old testament. Tradition tells us that the grape vine was introduced into Egypt from India. From Egypt it was transferred to Greece, where it flourished during the entire period of the Grecian Republic. A distinguished writer once said: Raising grapes is a pursuit as full of beauty as Alpine landscape; as sweet to the humble toiler as the breath of a prattling child. The rich cuisine of the vine makes springtime upon the summer and gladdens every hour of our existence. Homer himself, speaking of the Greek wines, said they were "luscious, pure and worthy of the gods." From Greece the grape was transplanted to Italy, but not until Rome was civilized. The grape left Greece with its art and civilization. Virgil said: "The arts and sciences and poetry flourish most amid the sunny skies where the grape grows best." In the early history of man the grape was only found among the most civilized people of the world. In Egypt first, then in Greece, then in Italy, then in France, and now in America. Almost all of the Roman writers speak of the kind of wine as the best wine of Italy—the Sweet Falernian. Of this wine the poets sang, while the statesmen and orators prized it. The grapes from which it was made were grown on the Falernian Ager, lying between the Massic hills and the banks of the Vultus. The grapes grew in a volcanic country, among the stones and ashes and debris thrown from the mouth of Mount Vesuvius, and we can almost imagine the men of wealth and learning of these olden times, sitting in their villas, in the suburbs of Herculaneum and Pompeii, over many years ago, drinking this same sweet Falernian, when Vesuvius commenced to send forth its lava and ashes, which covered over a vast extent of territory, including the vineyards and three large and populous cities, the ruins of which have been but recently uncovered. This wine, known as the sweet Falernian, was never allowed to be drunk until it was ten years old. It was of a bright amber color, neither red wine, as we have wine to-day, nor was it white wine. At one time there was a law of the Roman republic prohibiting this wine from being either sold to the market or drunk until it had reached the allotted age of ten years. But when civilization left the Roman world, and the dark ages spread devastation and ignorance over all Europe, grape culture almost ceased. France shared the first signs of recuperation from the barbarism which the turn of the barbarians of that age had scattered over the Eastern continent, and from about the fourteenth century the culture of the grape was transplanted in a larger degree from Italy and Spain to France. For not less than 400 years all that part of France, lying between the Mediterranean and the Rhone, and from the Garonne to the base of the Maritime Alps, has been the home of the grape. The wines made in the Departments of Gironde and Herault are among the most famous of French wines. It not the most famous vintage of the world. For centuries France has exported a vast amount of

wine, until the year 1880, when, according to the "Wine Trade Review," during the first eleven months of that year, she imported 171,549,000 gallons of wine, and exported only 60,181,500 gallons of wine, showing her imports in wine, for the first time in her history, to have been 111,107,500 gallons more than her exports. That during the year 1869 France cultivated 5,447,218 acres in grapes alone; while in 1870, ten years before, there were cultivated in France 5,772,617 acres of land in grapes, showing a diminution of 389,419 acres in ten years. In 1870 France produced 14,433,570,000 gallons of wine, while in 1880 she only produced 7,862,865,000 gallons of wine, almost one-half less. This immense depreciation in the amount of grapes and wine produced in France is attributed to two causes only; first, the wearing out of the soil after a long period of cultivation of the grape, and second, the destructive effects of the phylloxera. For nearly twenty years the grape-growers of France have been fighting this little insect, and while they have discovered that certain knowledge, or incalculable of curious, was an insecticide, yet it appears by a report made by the Count LeMercier, chairman of the principal committee in France, as late as February, 1881, that they could no longer rely upon that as a protection against the destructive effects of the grape; that its effectiveness depended on the character of the soil where it was applied, the manner of its application, the season of the year, and upon so many other doubtful or incidental questions as to the result, that they found but one sure remedy to recommend to the grape growers of France, and that remedy is the introduction into France of the native American vine. In our State, however, where the phylloxera is not so destructive, I feel more disulphide of carbon can be used with success. A brief reference to this report, made by the Count LeMercier, will be found in the "American Wine and Grape Grower," published in New York, March, 1881.

As man in infancy and childhood is the most delicate of all the animal kingdom, and subject to more diseases than any other animal, so the grape is the most delicate of all the vegetable world. It is indeed true, that while man is the marvel of the animal world, the grape is the most wonderful of the vegetable world. Man, unlike all other animals, has the measles, the whooping cough, the small pox, scarlet fever, etc. The rest of the animal world is exempt from these and many other diseases common to humanity. So the grape is subject to diseases unknown to any other fruit bearing trees or vines. It has black knot, crown mould and black mildew; it is attacked by flies, and now it is subject to the great ravager and destroyer of the vine, phylloxera. In France, as I before stated, they have almost given up the hope of destroying the pest, seeking a remedy only in the introduction of vines that are strong enough to withstand the phylloxera, and for this reason the oldest grape growers of France have concluded that the native American vine is the only safe vine to plant upon which to graft the European varieties; and I would recommend every grape grower to try this, if even in a small way.

It would hardly seem necessary for me to tell you, as grape growers, what kind of soil grapes ought to be planted in, or how grapes should be cultivated, or what we should do to avoid the effects of the phylloxera. I may, however, say that no grapes will do well upon any land where the blue rootlets cannot cling to or run around or among either rock, or stone, or gravel, or sand. It is the nature of the root of the vine to seek its warmth and dryness. It will not grow on land with a damp, heavy clay subsoil. It had better be planted upon the cold front of a barren rock than in a pond hole, and it will thrive in the crevice of a rock when it will cling to water and mud, and as the roots of the vine cling to rock and gravel, so the branches necessarily seek nature. Their twigs, like ours, must have air. The roots must have room under the ground; the tendrils must have room to cling to grow above the ground.

Excessive moisture or heat and cold will destroy a grape vine. Excessive moisture or extreme dryness are equally destructive of the vine, and hence it is

that while the grape will grow over a large portion of the earth's surface, yet the most tender and valuable varieties of grapes only flourish over a limited territory. On the Western Continent the European varieties do not flourish well out of doors, except in that little territory lying between the Sierra Nevada Mountains, the Pacific Ocean, Arizona and Oregon. East it is too cold for them. North and south it is either too dry or too wet. The amount of rain that falls in this part of California is about twenty-five inches a year. Of this amount less than one-tenth falls during the period in which the grape is developed and gathered, while in Malaga and the wine growing districts of France from five to eight inches of rain fall during the period in which the grape is making its growth, thus adding an additional peril to the grape which we do not suffer here, namely: the grape rot. Nor is the mean temperature of California as a grape growing country inferior to any other part of the world. The mean temperature this year around is about 83 degrees Fahrenheit, while at Bordeaux it is 57 degrees. At Madeira it is 65. From 60 to 65 degrees mean temperature for the whole year is said to be the best average temperature for the cultivation of the grape. Of course, in summer it is warmer and in winter colder, but we do not have extremes of heat and cold.

In most countries it is considered desirable to have an eastern or southern exposure as the most favorable lands on which to plant a vineyard. Here, if anything, we prefer a western or northern exposure. There is less danger from frost there, because the sun does not strike it so early in the morning. Our climate is warm and dry enough, whatever the exposure may be. The wine grape, it is admitted by nearly all the ablest writers upon the subject, that rolling lands are better than level bottom lands upon which to plant a vineyard. Alluvial soil is not good soil for vines. In Malaga nearly all the vines are grown upon barren and almost sterile hillsides. In many parts of France the soil is exceedingly poor where the grape is grown, the subsoil being a soft rock. Not that they plant the grape in Europe as we do. Whether we are right or wrong, I am not able to determine. In France the average between the rows of vines, where they are planted in rows at all, will not exceed three feet, and between the vines in the rows not more than from one to two feet, while here we never think of planting vines nearer than six feet apart, and I presume the average is about seven feet; and yet French writers think it advantageous to so plant. They say that in Italy and Spain they plant vines farther apart than in France, yet that's near is not nearly as good as French wine. The number of vines do an acre, planted 3 feet apart each way, is 4,840; 4 feet apart, but 2,723 to the acre; 5 feet apart each way, 1,742 to the acre; 6 feet each way, 1,512 to the acre; 7 feet each way, 917 to the acre, while 8 feet each way gives but 680 to the acre. And yet I find that while we have less than 1,000 to the acre, we make from 500 to 600 gallons of wine made on an average from an acre of grapes. In France they usually go beyond 300 to 350, and often do not exceed 200 gallons to the acre. Of course, if we can make 600 or 700 gallons of wine to the acre, and that wine be as good as that made in France, and they can only make some 200 or 300 gallons from the same amount of land from the same cultivation, in that they cannot compete with us, even though their vines were as healthy as ours.

CALIFORNIA'S OLD COMPLAINT

The great trouble in grape culture in California, and in wine making—because the two are closely allied—is that we are too fast a people; we are too anxious to realize upon the investment. We are too poor to wait; we try to produce too many grapes to the acre, and we try to make too much wine from the grapes we have, and, lastly, we try to reduce our wine to money too soon after it is made. This is attributable chiefly to our poverty, in our isolation, to the newness of the business, and to the peculiar characteristics of the American people. We are in a new country, an inexperienced, stirring and thriving people. We cannot wait for the slow process of development, like the Europeans. The future to us is to-morrow, not

Poultry.

CHICKEN CHOLERA.

Commissioner LeDuc has issued a paper from the Department of Agriculture upon chicken cholera, giving the results of some recent experiments made under the direction of the department, by D. Salmon, for the prevention of this very troublesome disease.

Dr. S. says:—For this disease a very cheap and most effective disinfectant, is a solution made by adding three pounds of sulphuric acid to forty gallons of water (or one fourth pound sulphuric acid to three and a half gallons of water,) and mixing evenly by agitation or stirring. This may be supplied to small surfaces with a small watering pot or to larger grounds with a barrel mounted on wheels and arranged like a street sprinkler. In disinfecting poultry houses the manure must be first thoroughly scraped up and removed beyond the reach of the fowls; a slight sprinkling is not sufficient, but the floors, roosts and grounds must be thoroughly saturated with the solution, so that the particle of dust, however small, escapes being wet. It is impossible to thoroughly disinfect if the manure is not removed from the roosting places. Sulphuric acid is very cheap, costing at retail not more than twenty-five cents a pound, and at wholesale but five or six cents; the barrel of disinfecting solution can, therefore, be made for less than a dollar, and should be thoroughly applied. It must be remembered, too, that sulphuric acid is a dangerous drug to handle, as, when undiluted, it destroys clothing and cautures the flesh wherever it touches.

CHARCOAL FOR FOWLS.—The benefit which fowls derive from eating charcoal is acknowledged. The method of putting it before them, however, is not well understood. Pounded charcoal is not in the state in which fowls usually find their food, and consequently is not very anthing to them. Corn burnt on the cob and the refuse, which consists almost entirely of the grains reduced to charcoal and still retaining their perfect shape, if placed before them is greedily eaten by them, and with a marked improvement in their health, as shown by the bright color of their combs and their manner production of a greater average of eggs to the flock than before.

WHAT the good farmer needs more than manual help, is faithfulness and an intelligent interest in pushing work. Where he finds help that can and will give time, he will not part with it at any price; and the hired help feels better satisfied to work for an employer who regards him as something more than a machine to do work. In fact, the more intelligent the farmer, the more willing he usually is to ask (or at least accept) advice.

RECENT shipments of honey from California to Great Britain have been received with great favor.

The Vinicultural Interests

The Vinicultural interests of Southern California stand foremost to-day of any part of the world. We are free from any vine pests whatever; our vines are in a most healthy condition, and a promising outlook for the future. We have frequently made mention in this journal of the importation of vine growing and wine making in Southern California, and we believe that the growing of the vine and the making of wine is the coming great industry of our people. Through the advice of these columns hundreds of acres of vines have been planted the past season, and we are sure no one will have cause to regret the planting of more vines. We claim to champion the interests of the Viticulturist and will leave no stone unturned that will advance their interests. Any information we can give will be done so cheerfully.

ADVERTISERS

Every business man knows that to succeed in his business he must literally patronize printer's ink. He must advertise. But how to advertise is the question that puzzles many. Large advertisers throughout the world who have made the matter a life study, agree that the "true medium to advertise in is the legitimate newspaper, the larger circulation having preference, the attractiveness of the paper standing next, and illustrated papers ranking next. The SEMI-TROPIC CALIFORNIA, Rice & Coleman, publishers, this city, claims the largest circulation of any paper in Southern California, more subscribers in Los Angeles county than any other paper.

It is the handsomest paper published on this coast, and the only one publishing original wood engravings. If you have a business and wish to increase it advertise in the

SEMI-TROPIC CALIFORNIA.

SOUTHERN CALIFORNIA is peculiarly adapted to fruit orchards, to gardens, and small farms, and all she needs to make it team with prosperity is more people of that class of emigrants which has converted the great North west from a wilderness into comfortable homes for its millions of contented people.

THE advertisement of the Capital Bakery and Restaurant of Mr. H. Schumacher appears in this issue. Mr. Schumacher is one of the most popular business men of this city and is well patronized by the public.

Southern California.

SAN DIEGO.

This city has passed through many trying vicissitudes, and at last is about to acquire the standing to which her advantages and resources entitle her. The railroad has become an established fact, and from this on her growth and prosperity will be permanent and lasting. San Diego has ever had our kindest wishes, and it is with great pleasure that we are now able to write of her bright future. The city is, of all other sea-port towns, the most desirable as a place of residence. All that has ever been said as regards her *bay* and *climate*, either in a friendly spirit or sluringly by the various journals of this coast, we most emphatically indorse as true. We became wedded to the place during a residence there some years ago, and although we are not permitted to enjoy her great fortune directly, we feel that indirectly we are greatly benefited.

Whoever seeks a residence in San Diego will find a society much above the general average, all the orthodox religious denominations are represented, and school facilities, though somewhat inadequate in the past, are now taking a decided step forward in the erection of a fine, large school-house and other general improvements in the educational department. The city is lighted with gas, enjoys the telephone, and street railway building is now on the tapis. General activity is manifesting itself in every quarter, and all the conveniences found in the old settled Eastern cities will soon be fully represented in this city by the sea. Its resources which have been grossly misrepresented, probably through ignorance by certain parties, are beyond our present time and space.

In honey it leads the world in quality and quantity; its exports of hides, wool, sheep, hogs, etc., are very large, and in wheat, it is a fact not generally known, that until within two or three years past San Diego county has produced more wheat than all the rest of Southern California. The area of the county is vast and probably much of it not well adapted to general farming, but its productive valleys ranging from twenty thousand acres to one thousand acres, and even down to one hundred acres, can be counted by the score.

The mesas, foot-hills and mountains are valuable in affording good pasturage for large bands of sheep and cattle. Wood and water though not in large quantities, are far from being entirely wanting. The mountains afford some lumber and an abundance of fire wood, while each valley has its stream of water, and artesian wells which have now become a fact near the city, promise to satisfy all demands in the water line.

The tide of travel that way is large, and will increase largely with the connection of the Southern California Railroad at Colton with the Southern Pacific. Railroad building is going on as rapidly as human energy

and money can force it. Two large deep-water ships, besides several smaller craft are now unloading railroad material, and in mid-ocean freighted with steel rails and machinery a small fleet is heading toward San Diego. May the cloud of adversity never again linger over our sister city!

LOS NIETOS.

EDITOR SEMI-TROPIC:—Since my visit a year since to the Los Nietos Valley the status of matters and things in that portion of Los Angeles county has not changed materially.

This section does not claim to grow the semi-tropical fruits to perfection, but is the great corn valley of Southern California and produces some of the finest specimens of deciduous fruits, apples, pears, peaches and apricots to be found in California.

THE GRAPE BOOM

Has reached the Los Nietos Valley, and many thousands of vines have been planted the present season. The vineyards already in bearing appear thrifty and encourage growers to hope that in a few years their grapes will yield a larger profit than their corn fields. Practical men who have been watching the wine market and present grape crop inform us that prices will, in all probability, rule much higher this year than last, so that it is quite likely that the area devoted to vines will continue to expand.

Raisin making, except in the foot-hills bordering the Ranchito settlement, will hardly prove a success in the Los Nietos Valley, as the occasional fogs, so beneficial to the cereals, prevent the grapes from drying as speedily as is desirable. The leading grape growers propose to erect a winery next year, somewhere between Downey and Ranchito, and make both wine and brandy. Mr. J. E. Burke is the prime mover in the matter, and will have the hearty co-operation of his neighbors.

CASTOR OIL.

Dr. Groover, an enterprising gentleman residing at Downey, is putting up a press and will shortly be prepared to manufacture pure castor oil. The bean grows luxuriantly in all portions of the valley, and the new enterprise will encourage the farmers to go extensively into its cultivation.

THE ENGLISH WALNUT.

Few localities in Southern California are so well adapted to the cultivation of the English walnut as Los Nietos Valley. The crop is almost sure, and in from eight to ten years from planting, each tree will average annual profit of from $15 to $20. The walnut belt is even more limited than the orange belt, and growers have no fear of glutting the market.

PROFIT IN FRUIT.

Orchards well cultivated and cared for are very profitable, but a careless system of fruit farming always results disastrously. Many persons who left their trees to take care of themselves, without cultivation, irrigation or pruning, are now bitterly re-

gretting their folly. A gentleman by the name of Quill, who resides near Downey, followed a different course from that of most of his neighbors, and, though only running twenty acres, netted last year from his orchard and vineyard the neat little sum of $1400. Others who have followed his course will do equally well the present season.

THE RANCHITO.

Twelve miles from Los Angeles, is the most progressive portion of Los Nietos valley, at present. The Ranchito (Spanish for little ranch) is a magnificent tract of agricultural land, well watered and adapted to every kind of grain and fruit. I was surprised at the exceedingly thrifty looking farms of this section. The principal owners are Messrs. Tyler, Dunlap, Boyd, Parsons, Burke, Bequette, Tweedy, Standifer, Russell, Phelan, Montgomery and Cate. Every farmer seems well satisfied with his lot, and we are confident that the products of this section will in quality and quantity find no successful rivals in California.

NEW-COMERS.

New new-comers are at present settling in the Los Nietos Valley. The advantages of this section have not been so persistently set forth as some other portions of our county, and consequently the Ranchito and Downey settlements have been overlooked for the past four or five years. Mr. Kendrick recently purchased the Frazee place and is making extensive improvements. Mr. S. Huntly is also improving a tract of 85 acres near Downey. Mr. G. S. Brodie also recently purchased an unimproved farm and proposes to devote it to fruit.

The exports from the Downey depot during the past year considerably exceeded 3,600,000 pounds. Though the fruit crop this year will be short, we believe the present season promises to be a profitable one for the Los Nietos Valley.

J. C. P.

THE DUARTE.

A short time since it was our pleasure to visit this delightfully located settlement, and although we had formed a favorable opinion of the country from the reports of others we must confess that we had our expectations more than realized on our first visit. We were the guest of Mr. O. K. Young, and we are under obligations to him, his sister Mary, Mr. L. Barnes and others for making our visit so enjoyable. Our friend O. K. (a young batch) has our among the fine places on the Duarte. It is in a fine state of cultivation, planted with a choice orchard of orange trees that are already bearing and many choice limited varieties coming on, a select orchard of deciduous fruits, fields for barley, wheat, corn, alfalfa, etc. A neat cottage, before which stands the crowning glory of this pretty home, a grand old live oak, with its evergreen branches spreading over ground enough to afford shade for a Sunday school picnic.

Mr. L. Barnes' place is a fair sample of

what an industrious man can do in a few years. When Mr. Barnes landed in California he had $27, with which he bought a cow worth $27.50, going in debt 50c. The land he now lives on he bought on time, put up a shanty on credit and went to work, worked every minute—worked for his neighbors during the day and on his own ranch at night, and by dint of perseverance, pluck and energy owns one of the pleasantest homes in the county, all paid for and money in bank. We don't know that Mr. Barnes will like for us to tell briefly his private life, but it is one he might well be proud of.

Mr. Wm. C. Young has a place running up to the foothills that with cultivation will in a few years be most beautiful. During the past winter Mr. Young had ripe tomatoes every week from his vines, no frost injuring them in the least. A place so well protected from the frost will be invaluable in the future. Mr. Mitchell adjoins Mr. Young, and has a well protected place from frosts; he is another of your workers, and will in a short time have a beautiful ranch well planted and well tilled.

There are many splendid places on the Duarte that we shall take occasion to speak of in a future issue.

PASADENA NOTES.

Mr. Welnes, an English gentleman, until recently connected with some commercial enterprises in Scotland, has purchased a tract of 30 acres adjoining the beautiful place of Mr. Wm. T. Clapp, in Pasadena. He has ten acres in muscat grapes, between 800 and 900 orange trees, a great variety of deciduous trees, and will proceed to make other improvements. Pasadena has lately attracted several English gentlemen of considerable means, who declare that our flourishing little colony is the most delightful spot they have discovered in their travels.

Under the careful management of Mr. C. C. Brown the tract of the Mutual Orchard Association at Pasadena has wonderfully improved during the past year. The owners of the property will each have a choice homestead when they arrive to take possession, and they certainly made a very wise selection when they placed Mr. Brown in charge. The whole tract has been so carefully cultivated that it will require no irrigation the present year, and the orange and olive plantations show a most healthy growth. The ground is very moist an inch below the surface, showing what careful cultivation can accomplish. Shade and ornamental trees have been planted and the Company intends to shortly put out fifty acres in raisin grapevines.

Messrs. Woodbury Brothers, who recently purchased 2,000 acres of land above Pasadena, have fully developed a fine water supply and planted several hundred acres in vines and trees. In another year we expect to chronicle great progress in that hitherto undeveloped portion of the Sierra Madre foothills.

THE ECONOMY HAY PRESS.

It affords us great pleasure to make a statement about these sterling hay presses from our own personal knowledge and observation. We have been acquainted with Mr. Geo. Ertel, the inventor, patentee and manufacturer, for over seven years. We have visited his manufactory in Quincy, Illinois, quite frequently during that time, have "written it up," from a personal inspection, and all reports to the contrary we can testify that Mr. Ertel's hay press establishment is one among the many extensive manufactories of the beautiful city of Quincy, an honor and credit to Mr. Ertel and to his city.

The buildings of the Economy Hay Press were built with especial reference to the building of these presses. It is a large and commodious brick, fitted up with the most approved machinery, some of it the invention of Mr. Ertel, and made expressly to suit his work. Adjoining the main building is his engine and foundry, the engine being one of the largest from the works of Smith, Hayner & Co., of the same city.

THE ECONOMY HAY PRESS.

The lumber yard attached would be an extensive business alone. Mr. Ertel could find good oak timber for his purposes in his own country, but not being satisfied with it, he searched the country over, and found in the hills of Kentucky timber strong and substantial, which he has shipped by the cargo to his shops. Mr. Ertel has put down in Quincy the largest single lot of lumber ever brought to the city, and all for the building of the Economy Hay Press. We can recommend his press to any one in need of one as a press without a superior in the country.

The Economy Hay Press, of which the above cut is a representation, has not only achieved a well merited precedence over all other hay presses, but it also retains its world wide reputation for pressing hay, etc., more compactly than any other press in the market, hence all kinds of railroad cars may be loaded with full weight of hay. The Economy is operated with but little force, and is sold at so low a price that any farmer can buy it, and more money is made in operating this press than can be

done by any of its competitors, which fact can be fully substantiated in any locality where the Economy has been introduced. Being in use in every State and Territory in the United States and Canada, and having received the first premium over all its numerous competitors in 1880 without exception, the claims of the Economy to superiority remain undisputed. For years of these presses has been turned out daily, but such is the increasing demand that the works will be enlarged to accommodate the accumulation of orders. Parties desiring to purchase a machine for baling hay, straw, etc., would consult their own interests by investigating the merits of this press thoroughly before contracting for any other.

Hundreds of indorsements could be given of the working of these presses, but we give one from this county.

Pleasanton Cal., August 30th, 1879.
Geo. Ernst, Quincy, Ill.—Dear Sir:—I have just finished a 25 days' job pressing hay, have averaged 70 bales per day, and 120 lbs. to the bale, one really press but 8 tons per day, and I have got all the work I can do, while all other hay presses are lying idle here and no work for them but to stand and wait.

Yours respectfully,
H. H. TURNER.

Three men with two horses can press 80 bales of hay in 10 hours, weighing from 150 to 250 lbs. per bale, including moving and making the wire ties as they need them. From 100 to 125 bales can be loaded in a railroad box car, weighing from 10 to 12 tons.

Mr. Ertel can be found or addressed at the U. S. Hotel, in this city, for several weeks to come.

$100 GOLD FOR THE ORPHANS HOME.

We wish it understood that the SEMI-TROPIC CALIFORNIA has a larger circulation than any other publication in Los Angeles county, in Southern California, on the Pacific coast outside of San Francisco, and we have one hundred dollars to back it.

When you hear the cannons near Sept. 1, remember it is the opening of the Horticultural Fair and Centennial Celebration.

J. Goodwin Short

Biography.

J. DE BARTH SHORB

Is a native of Maryland. After leaving Mt. St. Mary's College of Emmitsburg, Maryland, he commenced the study of law with his cousin, W. W. Dallas (nephew of the late George M. Dallas) which he continued for a short time, and then engaged in active business of farming and milling, and was a successful man at the age of twenty-two years. He came to California in 1864, and was soon after appointed assistant Superintendent of the Philadelphia and California Petroleum Company, a corporation of Col. T. A. Scott's creation. The company, after a large expenditure of money in developing the oil interests, proved unsuccessful. Mr. Shorb, having invested in the enterprise, was a heavy loser, whereupon he resigned his position and accepted a civil appointed in the Engineer Corps, United States Army. He was again appointed Superintendent of the Philadelphia and California Petroleum Company, which office he held until they discontinued. He then commenced work in acquiring title to the Temescal grant, known as the San Taleciana placers and developing the water on same. While engaged in this work he married the eldest daughter of the late Hon. B. D. Wilson. Soon after his marriage he engaged in the wine business in company with other parties. In 1876 they extended their business to San Francisco, and soon afterwards established a branch house in New York. They then extended their enterprise to foreign countries, having correspondents in Australia, New Zealand, China, Japan, Central America, England and Scotland. Withdrawing from the firm, he entered into partnership with his father-in-law, which continued until his (Mr. Wilson's) death. He then commenced improvements on his place by cutting up the lands and increasing the vineyards and orange groves, and also in developing the water system. The latter work was all done under Mr. Shorb's supervision, and is without doubt the finest arranged water system to be found in California. Mr. Shorb is President of the Lake Vineyard Land and Water Association, which controls the finest lands in the San Gabriel valley, is President of the Southern California Horticultural Society, is a member of the State Viticultural Commission, and has probably done more than any other one man in the State to advance her agricultural industries. Mr. Shorb has been prominently mentioned as candidate for Congress, and if he would allow his name to be used as such would be elected on any ticket on which he might run, and if in Congress would give Southern California a hard worker in her interest.

It has been ascertained that our wheat crop of last year exceeds by 300,000 tons that of any previous year, and the wine and grape crop more than double in value.

DEAD SHOT TO GOPHERS AND SQUIRRELS.

Dr. Lord and others, of Pasadena, have been experimenting with bi-sulphates of carbon, and have been highly successful in killing squirrels and gophers. To begin with, you provide yourself with a small, straight stick, two thirds as large as the end of your little finger, about one foot long, and at one end attach, by means of a thread or cord, a piece of cotton batting about the size of a small egg. Do not wrap the string over the whole length of the cotton, but only over the upper end, so that the rest will remain free and porous. Having gone thus far, make a funnel out of any moderately stiff paper, about eight inches long, diameter of larger end one and a half inches, insert the aforementioned stick into the funnel and tie a string around the stick, so that the stick will work forth and back in the funnel. The following is the Doctor's mode of administering the poison:

"Put the poison into a bottle with a nozzle just large enough to permit the cotton ball to go in easily. Push the cotton into the nozzle until it is even with the glass. Then tip the bottle up and let the liquid soak down through the cotton. When the cotton is saturated withdraw it from the nozzle, put in the cork, and draw the cotton down half way, more or less, into the paper cone. Then push the cone greatly and carefully into the squirrel or gopher hole as far as possible, put into the hole a mass of earth, a stone or a bunch of grass that nearly fills it. Wait half a minute or more and then cover closely with earth. Stop all the holes that seem to connect with the one you kill. One pound of the refined article will do for fifty or sixty holes, and if done thoroughly nothing that breathes will come out alive."

These parties have experimented largely with this method of extermination, and find that it is more valuable than poisoned wheat or any other preparation found in the market. We hope that our readers will give it a trial and report progress. Mr. S. Jube M. Campbell has left a working model of the funnel and stick at this office, where it can be seen by any who may call.

THAT SUIT.

Where did you get that nobby suit of clothing? Well, sir, knowing that Polaski & Son were noted for keeping the shove suits in the county we called on them and this is the result. What did it cost? Only $16.00. You don't say? That suit looks better than any I saw thinking of getting up at —— for $25. You? We did not ask around, but knew where to go to the fine place, and I advise you to go and see the assortment and low prices at Polaski's. You will find them on the corner of Main and Commercial.

The proprietors of the Los Angeles Business College have decided to take a short vacation and continue during the warm season, resuming their duties again in September. All inquiries respecting the College may be addressed to C. W. La Fetra, Box 920, Los Angeles, Cal.

It is estimated that the total production of wool in the United States for the year 1880 was $240,000,000 pounds, an increase of $11,000,000 over the clip of 1779.

A NECESSITY.

Every man, woman and child must have certain accessories of life, without which life is miserable. The man or woman of good judgment and taste recognizes that in the matter of "what shall we wear on the feet" a necessity, and one that may cost more or less according to the fineness, the style, etc.

Ten things are necessary for every one to take into consideration in buying and purchasing, the quality and the price. The saying that "the best is the cheapest" is especially true when it comes to buying a pair of shoes. The merchant who is a thorough and practical shoemaker knows all about the quality and make of every kind, shoe or slipper, and has the money to go into the market and buy in his good judgment and who sells at a close margin of profit, is the man to buy from. Such a man is A. A. McDonald, the popular Boot and Shoe dealer No. 84 Spring St. Mr. McDonald is prepared to furnish anything in his line from one of the largest works on this coast, at prices that defy competition, in styles to please the most fastidious—in styles of all from the coarse plow shoes to the finest shoe made.

Mr. McDonald makes a specialty of custom made work. Being a practical workman himself, he overlooks the work, seeing that none but good leather is used and every piece of work first class before it leaves the house, guaranteeing all work and making good any failure if it should happen.

During a late pleasure visit to the Francisco Mr. McDonald ran across a large and fine assortment of shoes, etc., which he bought at a remarkably low price and who is he is giving his customers the benefit of it. Remember in examine his stock and prices whether you buy or kind or not it will pay you as well to buy intelligently elsewhere.

FACTS WORTH REMEMBERING.

One thousand shingles, laid four inches to the weather, will cover one hundred square feet of surface, and five pounds of shingle nails will fasten them on.

One fifth more siding and flooring is needed than the number of square feet of surface to be covered, because of the lap in the siding and matching of the floor.

One thousand laths will cover seventy yards of surface, and eleven pounds of lath nails will nail them on.

Eight bushels of good lime, sixteen bushels of sand and one bushel of hair, will make enough good mortar to plaster one hundred square yards.

A cord of stone, three bushels of lime, and a cubic yard of sand will lay one hundred cubic feet of wall.

Five courses of brick will lay one foot in height on a chimney, so bricks in a course will make a flue four inches wide and twelve inches long; and eight bricks in a course will make a flue eight inches wide and sixteen inches long.

The American Newspaper Directory for 1881, published by Geo. P. Rowell & Co., hours the year. It is not ahead of all others, is complete and perfect in every respect. It is invaluable to every large advertiser, every newspaper office and the remaining ones. It has the names of 10,293 newspapers published in the United States. We don't suppose a single paper is omitted. It also shows that the increase since 1881 has been from 9,360 to 10,293, an increase of 40 per cent, while the increase in population has been 30 per cent. There is now a paper for every 6,942 inhabitants.

Subscribe for the Semi-Tropic.

SEMI-TROPIC
CALIFORNIA,
— AN —
ILLUSTRATED MONTHLY.

Devoted to Agriculture, Horticulture, and the Development of Southern California.

Terms: $1.50 per Annum, in Advance.

OFFICE, ROOMS 9 & 10, BAKER BLOCK.

Address, RICE & COLEMAN, Los Angeles, Cal.

GEORGE RICE, | EDITORS AND PROP'RS.
CHAS. COLEMAN, JR., |

OFFICIAL PAPER
— OF THE —
Southern California Horticultural Soc'y.
OFFICE, ROOM No. 9, BAKER BLOCK.
GEO. RICE, Secretary.

We mail every subscriber a copy of the Fair Catalogue as a supplement to this number. Our August issue will contain much valuable information to all exhibitors, and will be mailed free to any address.

THE Horticultural Fair and Centennial Exposition, Sept. 5-19, will excel any previous effort ever made in Southern California. Send for a catalogue, and see the August number of the SEMI-TROPIC for particulars.

THE State Fair at Sacramento will commence September 19th and continue six days. The premium list is large and embraces everything for which premiums could be offered. We ask every person interested in making an exhibit at the State Fair to meet in the Secretary's office at the Pavilion, during our Fair, on Friday at 11 o'clock, to make arrangements for a proper exhibit at the State Fair.

The proprietor of this paper will pay all expenses, and take the exhibits to Sacramento and make the exhibit if the people will furnish the fruit at Los Angeles.

THE sixteenth Industrial Exposition of the Mechanics of San Francisco will open Tuesday, August 2, and continue four weeks. The management have taken active steps to make this exposition excel any previous one. A special effort will be made this year to worthily exhibit the fruits and wines of California. We hope our fruit growers and wine makers of Southern California will be properly represented. The proper exhibit of our fruits and wines at this exposition would be worth hundreds of dollars to this section as an advertisement of what we can and are doing. We would be glad to hear from any parties who will make an exhibit, and if enough can be secured to make a creditable exhibit we will undertake to make arrangements for its proper care and exhibit.

MR. CHAS. COLEMAN, JR., a practical horticulturist and a newspaper man of known ability, has been admitted to a partnership with me in the publication of the SEMI-TROPIC CALIFORNIA. Mr. Coleman will for the most part fill the editorial chair, giving to what we have long desired, time and opportunity to visit every orchard and vineyard, every town and farmer in Southern California, in the interest of this paper and the general welfare of horticultural interests in Southern California.

With the help of a practical, vigorous worker in Mr. Coleman, we propose to make the SEMI-TROPIC CALIFORNIA the paper for the farmer, orchardist, vineyardist, gardener and stock raiser. We ask the hearty co-operation of every friend of agricultural progress in Southern California, and agree to do our part.

GEO. RICE.

THE SEMI-TROPIC CALIFORNIA is now four years old and in a good, healthy condition. It has become a monthly necessity with the people, judging as we do from the large subscription list which it enjoys, and it will be our greatest endeavor to make it second to no other journal of its class published in the United States. It will be run in the general interest of the whole of Southern California, not in the interest of any one particular place or section. It is in no way either directly or indirectly connected with any land scheme or speculation, any more than it is interested in the general settling up of the whole of this southern county. In noticing the general industries, possibilities and probabilities of this section we will hew to the mark, let the splinters fly where they may, believing that the plain, unvarnished truth will win in the end, though it may make some enemies at first. We invite correspondence from every quarter, but in no way will we be responsible for the opinions of our contributors. Our pages are open to friendly inquiry and criticism as regards all subjects coming within the scope of our journal. May we hear early and often from the tillers of the soil.

The Southern California Packing Co. commenced work the 22d ult., everything throughout the entire establishment working like a charm. Each department has an experienced superintendent at its head, and with the ample capital, first class facilities and the choice fruits, vegetables and this establishment will send out to the world canned goods and dried fruits that will not be second to any. The fruit raisers of the county will always find a good market for their best fruits and vegetables, and the gentlemen who have given us this home enterprise deserve the gratitude of every citizen interested in the welfare of Los Angeles county.

THE Centennial of Los Angeles will be duly celebrated on Pavilion hill, with fine works, grander than ever seen in Southern California.

BUSINESS ENTERPRISE.

THE card of Mr. McMenomy, the plumber, appears in this issue. Mr. McMenomy controls the largest share of the plumbing business in this city, and has the best facilities for doing work promptly and cheaply.

Messrs. Fox & Koster, the enterprising merchants on Spring street, have found it necessary to again move into more extensive quarters, and will be found hereafter two doors south of their old stand. Their stock of ladies' and gents' furnishing goods is the largest and finest in Southern California.

J. A. Valder also moves along with Mr. Fox and will occupy the rear rooms in the new and elegant store rooms just built for their use. Mr. Valder will continue to carry a complete stock of pictures, frames, mouldings, etc., and is making preparation to import several noted paintings for exhibition at the coming Fair.

H. Siegel, corner Main and Commercial streets, has succeeded in building up a large trade by his strict attention to business, urbane treatment of his customers, his uniformly low prices, and large stock to select from. He has just received a large stock of white and colored shirts which he is selling at prices lower than ever before offered in this city.

Mr. B. F. Coulter has just returned from the city, where he has bought a full supply of new goods to recruit up his immense stock. Mr. Coulter's method of dealing with each and every customer with strict honesty has made his house a favorite with the public. Everybody begins to understand that when he advertises a reduction he means it, and that every article so announced is marked down just as he or any of his clerks state. No clerk can retain a place in his employ who is known to make any misrepresentations.

RAPHAEL & Co., on Main street, opposite the United States Hotel, whose advertisement appears in another column, carry a full line of painters' and artists' goods. Raphael & Co. make a specialty of painting farm-houses, barns, school-houses, etc., and parties in the country wishing anything in their line would do well to examine their prices and stock before closing a bargain elsewhere. We take pleasure in recommending this firm to the public, because we know from personal knowledge that their work is number one, and that their prices are as low as the times will allow.

CORRECTION.

In our last issue in our article descriptive of the Los Angeles Pork Packing Company, we inadvertently referred to the management as Messrs. Speedy & Co. This was an error, as the firm bearing that title dissolved partnership a year ago. The firm at present consists of M. Ellsworth, E. Speedy and Sisson, Wallace & Co., and is known as the Los Angeles Pork Packing Company.

CORRESPONDENCE.

Owing to the new arrangement this month by which our journal is set off in departments, we are forced to neglect our correspondence in this number. We beg kind indulgence and promise to answer letters of inquiry next month.

HORTICULTURAL FAIR.

CENTENNIAL CELEBRATION

The following is an extract from the Fair catalogue, a copy of which will be sent to any address free on application to the Secretary. The Fair commences September 8th and continues six days.

Department E.

Horticultural.

In this department all fruits, trees, nuts, and other productions must be raised by the person entering them for premiums, and all manufactured articles must be manufactured by the person in whose name they are entered. Special premiums excepted.

Class VI—Northern Fruits.

Best display of California Fruits........$2.00

Best display of fruits grown by one man..$10.00

APPLES.

Best display $15 00
Best twelve varieties 10 00
Best six varieties 5 00
Best three varieties 2 00

PEARS.

Best display 15 00
Best twelve varieties 10 00
Best six varieties 5 00
Best three varieties 2 00

PEACHES.

Best display 15 00
Best twelve varieties 10 00
Best six varieties 5 00
Best three varieties 2 00

PLUMS.

Best exhibit 5 00
Best five varieties 3 00
Best one variety 2 00

FIGS.

Best green figs 3 00
Best display of Japanese persimmons 3 00

SEMI-TROPICAL.

Best exhibit of seedling fruits 10 00

Citrous Fruits.

Best display oranges .... Diploma
Best display lemons .... Diploma
Best display of lemons 5 00

Class VII—Grapes, Raisins, Etc.

Best display of grapes $15 00
Best twelve varieties of table grapes,
   not less than three bunches each 10 00
Best one variety of table grapes, not
   less than three bunches 5 00
Best twelve varieties of white grape, not
   less than three bunches each 10 00
Best one variety of white grape, not less
   than three bunches 5 00

Special Premium by E. F. Spence.

Best and largest cluster of grapes 5 00
Best and cheapest tank or cask for
   wine or brandy for storage .... Diploma
Best exhibit of California raisins,
   crop of 100 .... Silver Medal

Department C.

Miscellaneous.

No essay to exceed 1500 words in length.

Best essay on the use of twenty acres
   of land for family support and
   profit $25 00

The original agricultural and horticultural experiment of the greatest general utility...... Silver Medal

Best arranged and furnished tent of fair visitors $5 00

WIDE KNOW.

Special Premium by GILLMORE. Dollar Store.

Spring Wheat.

Buckbee 3 years old and winter
First Premium ....Baby Buggy, val $10 00

Special Premium by E. H. SWEETZER, Jeweler.

Second premium ....Child's set $10
Third premium ....Child's set $5

Special by the QUEEN SHOE STORE.

Fourth premium, to the youngest baby .... Fair fine shoe

PUBLIC SCHOOLS.

SPECIAL PREMIUM

BY

YARNELL, CAYSTILE & MATHES,

Printers and Binders, Los Angeles.

Premiums Worth $250.00.

Open for competition to the pupils of the schools of Southern California.

Best Original Essay,
   ....Silver Holder, Value $15 00

Best Recitation,
   ....Silver Card Receiver, Value $12 00

Best Song, ...Silver Vase, Value $12 00

Best Industrial Drawing,
   ....Silver Vase, Value $10 00

Rules governing the school exercises will be found in the August number of the SEMI-TROPIC CALIFORNIA. Pupils wishing to compete should notify the Secretary on or before Sept. 3.

NOTE.—During these exercises the floor will be covered with saw-dust, and every precaution taken to secure quiet and order, so that everybody may hear.

Department D.

Agricultural Products.

Class II—Flour and Grain.

Best display and largest variety of grain, $10 00
Best 50 pound sack of flour .... Silver Medal
Best gilt sack corn meal, white. Bronze Medal
Best 25 sack corn meal, yellow Bronze Medal
Best sack of wheat as it ran from
   the threshing machine $5 00
Best sack of barley $5 00
Best sack of rye .... Silver Cup
Best sack of oats .... Silver Vase
Best sample of hops, not less than
   25 pounds .... Silver Cup
Best sample blue grass seed, not
   less than one-half bushel ... Diploma
Best bushel alfalfa seed ...... Silver Medal
Best bushel yellow corn .... Silver Cup
Best bushel white corn .... Silver Vase
Best bushel white corn .... Silver Cup

Special Premium by E. F. SPENCE.

Best and largest six ears of corn $5 00
Best and Largest Ten Premiums $10 00

Class III—Cheese and Butter.

Best display of cheese $10 00
Best Cheese 5 00
Best display of dairy products Silver Medal
Best display of butter in rolls,
   not less than 5 pounds .... Diploma
Best tub or firkin, not less than
   25 pounds, at least 2 mos. old . Diploma

Class VI—Bread, Etc.

Special premium by LANKERSHIM & CO.,
   Millers, Los Angeles.

Best home-made bread from their flour $10 00
Best home-made bread by some
   lady under 12 years of age $5 00

NOTE.—For particulars about bread premium in August Semi-Tropic California.

Department A.

Agricultural Implements. Etc.

Class I—Agricultural Implements.

Note.—Special arrangements will be made for exhibiting a limited amount of Agricultural Implements, Carriages, &c., inside the Pavilion, for which Diplomas will be awarded. See the Secretary, Room 3, Baker Block, to make entries.

Class II—Honey.

Special Premium by HATCH & BARCLAY
   Commission Merchants, all inviting
   main Front Local, A. H. Hook, Agent for
   premiums to be awarded (the Honey
   and Bee Industry), as contained in the
   awards mentioned below. The second
   premiums are offered by the list of
   LOS ANGELES BEE KEEPERS ASSOCIATION.

Best hive Italian bees $5 00
   Second hive Italian bees ....
   American Bee Journal, monthly
Best hive Holy Land bees $5 00
   Second hive Holy Land bees ....
   Bee Gleanings, monthly
Best hive Hybrid bees $5 00
   Second hive Hybrid bees ... Cook's Manual
Best hive Native bees $5 00
   Second hive Native bees ....
   Bee Keepers Magazine
Best hive Cyprian bees, A B C of Bee Culture
   Second hive Cyprian bees ....
Best hive of bees $5 00
Best exhibit of comb honey, not less
   than 5 pounds $5 00
   Second exhibit of comb honey, not less
   than 5 pounds 1 00
Best exhibit extracted honey, not less
   than 5 pounds 1 00
   Second exhibit extracted honey 1 00
Best display of honey 1 00
Best display of honey in jars 1 00
Second display of bees wax 1 00
Best exhibit of bees wax 1 00
Best collection with honey 1 00
Best exhibit from prize stand in honey   1 00
Second exhibit full comb honey 1 00
Best vinegar made of honey 1 00
Best exhibit vinegar made of honey 1 00
Best exhibit of wax flowers ....   Medal
Second exhibit of wax flowers ....   Medal
Best extractor .... Diploma
Best display of implements of apiary .. Diploma

Class VI — Preserves, Pickles, Etc.

Six jars of each required.

Best display of fruit, in glass, six jars Bronze
Best display of jelly .... Silver cake basket
Best jar tomato jelly, in glass ....
Best jar of raspberry jelly, in glass. silver cup
Best jar red currant jelly, in glass ... silver cup
Best jar blackberry jelly, in glass ... Napkin ring
Best jar strawberry jelly, in glass... Silver cup
Best jar apple jelly, in glass .... Silver cup
Best jar plum jelly, in glass ... Napkin ring
Best jar tomato jam, in glass. Napkin ring
Best jar raspberry jam, in glass.. Napkin ring
Best display of preserves, in glass ....
   .... silver spoon holder
Best display of pickles .... Silver cup
Best display of branded peas, box. Silver vase
Best display of cauliflower .... Diploma

Class III — Dried and Pressed Fruits, Nuts, Etc.

Best twelve bottles olive oil .. Silver medal
Best twelve bottles pickled olives. Silver medal
Best display canned fruits .... Diploma
Best display dried fruits ...... Silver Medal
Best ten pounds dried apricots .. Silver cup
Best ten pounds dried peaches .. Silver cup
Best ten pounds dried pears .... Silver cup
Best ten pounds dried plums ..... Napkin ring
Best ten pounds dried apricots .. Silver cup
Best ten pounds dried apricots .. Silver vase
Best 100 pounds dried figs ..... Silver medal
Best exhibition of dried fruit of
   variety .... Silver Medal

Exhibitors of dried fruit must furnish with an statement of the manner of drying and the amount of fruit, from time of picking to present condition. The same rule applies to the exhibitors of olive oil and pickled olives.

CULTIVATED NUTS RAISED BY THE EXHIBITOR.

Best half bushel English walnuts $5 00
Best peck soft shell almonds $3 00
Best peck peanuts $3 00

SUBSCRIBE for the SEMI-TROPIC CALIFORNIA, the only original illustrated journal on the Pacific Coast.

Apiary.

MODERN BEE-KEEPING.

BY PROF. C. F. KROEH, OF THE STEVENS INSTITUTE OF TECHNOLOGY.

I.

It is estimated that three hundred thousand persons are engaged in keeping bees in the United States. The value of the honey produced annually is upwards of ten millions of dollars. The great majority of bee-keepers are farmers having two or three colonies in hollow gums and rough boxes propped up on clam-shells. These

Fig. 1.—BEE PROTECTION.

old fashioned hives they have inherited from their predecessors along with the notion that the bee is a useful little creature which costs nothing and hoards itself, but is excelled in amiability by nearly all the rest of creation. When the time for "robbing" comes, a few still adhere to the barbarous practice of suffocating their old swarms with the vapor of burning brimstone in order to obtain the stores; but most of them wait until after dark, smoke their bees with burning rags, and remove the tops of the hives. Then they cut or break out the honey-comb with clasp-knife or poker, and transfer it, mixed with bee-bread, larvæ, and dead bees, into buckets or tubs. In this condition it is taken to the country store, where they get from six to ten cents a pound.

It is the object of the present series of papers to describe the methods by which we obtain honey that sells at twenty-five cents a pound, and by which the amount of honey per hive has been greatly increased. Millions of dollars would be added to the annual production if these methods were generally understood and adopted. They are not new theory, but are carried out in practice by a few thousand intelligent men who call themselves "apiarists" and make the care of bees their sole occupation. Some of them keep several hundred, and a few over a thousand colonies. Six or seven journals devoted to their interests are published in this country; the most important of which are the *American Bee Journal* at Chicago, *Gleanings in Bee-Culture* at Medina, Ohio, and the *Bee Keeper's Magazine* in New York City. The first has just been changed to a weekly, the other two appear monthly. These papers are full of topics of interest

connected with apiculture, and contain the proceedings of the various conventions held by progressive bee-keepers throughout the country. These facts are mentioned and these sources of information are indicated in order to show that bee-keeping not only furnishes opportunities for industrial enterprise, but also food for reflection. To many it becomes an occupation of absorbing interest, nay, of enthusiasm.

We shall resist our inclination to moralize on the advantage derived from enthusiasm produced by the contemplation of nature, or in fact by anything that rouses men from apathy, and will invite all those desirous of learning, to pay an imaginary visit to our apiary as described in the following paragraphs:

To those who are timid or nervous and have a lurking notion that bees are filled with wrath and poison in about equal proportion, we will lend a pair of rubber gloves and a veil like one of those in the accompanying picture.

Fig. 2.—BEE-HIVE.

The veil on the left is made of black tarlatan, grenadine, or even mosquito net, with two edges sewed together, and a piece of rubber cord at the top, so that it may be slipped over a stiff-brimmed hat. The lower, open end is either tucked in the collar, as in the figure, or better, provided with shirr strings. The veil on the right is made on the same plan, only that a strip of wire cloth, nine inches wide, and about two and a half feet long, is inserted. Those who have used wire cloth much, say that it is bad for the eyes. We prefer a fine black material having a hexagonal mesh.

Beginners should prepare themselves in this way until they have found out by their own experience that bees are quite tractable when properly managed.

They will find that they will not be attacked under ordinary circumstances unless they strike at a bee, make sudden, jerky motions, or jar a hive.

Before starting out, we provide ourselves with a very useful instrument called a smoker, a description of which is subjoined.

A smoker consists essentially of a little bellows communicating with a tin cylinder, surmounted by a conical piece with a hole in the apex. The top is taken off and the cylinder filled with dry rotten wood, peat, or even rags. It is then lighted and the top replaced. The bellows supplies the necessary draught, and we are ready to pour forth volumes of smoke at a moment's notice. When the smoker is put down in an upright position a drop-valve in the piece connecting bellows and cylinder remains open and prevents the fire from going out.

Thus armed we are ready to go into the apiary. The first thing that strikes the visitor is that the hives are down on the ground, that they are all painted white, and that they are all of exactly the same size. A level piece of ground was chosen, cleared, drained, and covered with a layer of saw-dust to keep down the weeds. Then it was laid out so that the hives should stand six feet apart from center to center with their entrances all facing the East. Four half-bricks were put under each hive, and the space underneath was filled with saw-dust. For all these points sufficient reasons will be given later. At present we are anxious to make the acquaintance of the bees as soon as possible.

As we approach more closely we perceive that the apiary is composed of hives like the lower one of Fig. 2.

If we had a trellis and a grapevine on the south side of every hive, as represented in the figure, they would afford a grateful shade in the heat of the day, but ours have not been planted yet.

Let us sit down beside one of these hives and watch the bees as they stream in and out. Listen how much larger and plumper they are when they arrive than when they leave. It is because they come in from the fields with their honey-bags distended. Some are carrying in on their legs little whitish, yellow, greenish, and orange pellets of pollen which they gather in the form of dust from the interior of flowers, roll up into doughy pellets, and stow away in a sort of pouch or basket on their two hindmost legs. Now and then a larger bee comes darting in with a comparatively bass voice that is apt to frighten a beginner until he learns that these are drones, and that they could not sting even if they would, for the simple reason that they are not provided by nature with any aggressive weapon.

As our eyes become accustomed to their rapid motions, we can distinguish the young bees with their yellow fuzz on thorax and abdomen from the veterans returning from the field with ragged wings and bodies worn smooth with much service. Some-limes one of the a shiny bees comes flying about the entrance in a very suspicious manner, and behaving very much like an intruder. It is a robber, a denizen of another hive trying to find some unguarded spot where it may slip in and help itself to honey without the trouble of gathering it from flower to flower. An experienced eye readily recognizes a robber from the fact that its honey-bag is not distended like that of other bees arriving at the hive. As soon as the robber attempts to alight near the entrance, the sentinels on duty repel it at once, taking it by the wings and often stinging it to death. Then our attention is attracted by the peculiar behavior of the bees stationed at the entrance. They are standing with their heads down and their bodies pointing upwards at an angle, while their wings move so rapidly that we can hardly see them. They are ventilating the hive, sending a current of cool, fresh air into it and driving the close air out. Notwithstanding the fact that this hive contains twenty thousand bees, the air in it is quite pure, as analysis has frequently proved. Our architects might take a lesson from the bee. Now and then we see a bee coming out of the hive and carrying a dead larva, a dead bee, a worm of the bee-moth or some other intruder as far from the hive as its strength will permit, for they are neat and tidy both in and around the house.

Such are the facts we may observe on the outside of a hive almost any fair day; but as they have occupied us so long, we must defer opening the hive until our next visit.

A. BRUNSON.   G. WILEY WELLS.

Brunson & Wells,

Attorneys and Counsellors-at-Law.

Nos. 11, 12, 14, 16 and 17 Baker Block.

Will practice in the Supreme Court of this State, and of the United States, and attend to all business before the Departments at Washington, D. C.

V. PONET.   B. F. ORR.

PONET & ORR.

General Furnishing Undertakers.

No. 56 MAIN STREET.

Agents for Raymond's Metallic Burial Cases and Caskets of New York. Undertaker's goods wholesale and retail. Particular attention given to embalming bodies for shipping East.

TEN QUESTIONS AND ANSWERS.

What has brought about this wonderful prosperity which our country now enjoys? Farming.

What has brought our government bonds back from Europe? Farming.

What has brought interest down so low that every legitimate enterprise may work on borrowed capital and grow rich? Farming.

What of all other professions would you recommend to the rising generation? Farming.

What fosters commerce and stimulates manufacturing? Farming.

What has caused the present boom in railroad building? Farming.

What has dispersed our army of tramps? Farming.

What business if wisely conducted will return something more than a living every year? Farming.

What business is conducive to long life, and of all others is least connected with crime, vice, etc.? Farming.

What business, either directly or indirectly, is "the power behind the throne" of all other industries under the sun? Farming.

The Pacific Hotel, at the new depot, has passed into the hands of Mr. E. H. Boyd, formerly of the Mojave Hotel. Mr. Boyd is so well known to the traveling public that it is hardly necessary for us to say that the Pacific will be more popular than ever.

Those who keep hens in favorable localities and who understand their business, find them a paying investment. Their product is not perishable and can wait its time for sale.

Don't fail to carefully read part of the Fair programme on page 127. Notice the large cash premiums offered and make an effort to secure some of them. This Fall's Fair promises to be immense.

H. Bancock & Co. have opened a new manufactory on Los Angeles street, near the White House, which promises to be a valuable addition to our city. Mr. Bancock has been for some time past connected with the great Standard Shirt Co. of San Francisco, and some years in the business of shirt making, etc. on this coast. He will manufacture shirts, ladies' underwear, dusters, etc., employing only white girls. All such enterprises should receive the hearty support of our citizens.

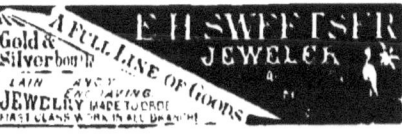

Produce Market.

The following are the prices to farmers wagons:

WHEAT—Local millers indifferent about buying; we quote: No. 1 milling, $1.00@1.10. No. 2, 1@1.10, inferior, fit only for ground feed, 85 @90c

BARLEY—Market strong with ready sales at 78@80c for new, and 85c@86c for old.

CORN—In a small way corn is firm at 75c@80c for large yellow, 80c@85 for small do, 90@95c for white

HAY—Loose on the street, $9, in small bales, $7.75@@25; large bales nominal.

POTATOES—Market fairly supplied at 75@90c

FRUIT—Oranges $1.50@1.75 per box, lemons, $1.50@2.00 per box; apricots, 2½@3½c ⌐ per lb; pears 2@2½c per lb; peaches, 2@2½c per lb.

NUTS—English walnuts, 9@10c per lb, other varieties out of market

HONEY—Very little new honey in the market; old is nominal at 6@7c per lb,

BEESWAX—Not much offering. What comes in finds ready sale at 18@20c per lb.

BUTTER—In good demand at 30@35c per lb. Good butter is of quick sale. Home product fails to supply the demand, and shippers are obliged to draw largely on up country dairies.

EGGS—Good fresh eggs are firm at 20@24c per doz.

POULTRY—Hens, $5.50 per doz.; broilers, $2.50@3.50 per doz.

July 1, 1881.

AMERICAN JUTE.

HOW COMMISSIONER LE DUC HOPES TO SAVE

$10,000,000 A YEAR TO THE COUNTRY.

[Washington Post.]

The Department of Agriculture is happy over the receipt of a magnificent sample of American jute fibre prepared by mechanical process from green stems grown in Virginia. It satisfactorily solves the problem that has engaged the attention of the department for over ten years, and establishes the fact that India jute can be successfully and profitably grown upon American soil. In the language of the Commissioner, Gen. Le Duc, it is "our declaration of independence from India in the matter of jute, and means an annual saving to this country of $10,000,000 and over." The prepared fibre now on exhibition at the Department is pronounced equal in all respects to any foreign fibre. It is largely used in the manufacture of gunny-bags, paper, ropes, carpets, leggings and oil cloths. It will be impossible to glut the market with the fibre, as its use is so diversified and essential.

The plant can be successfully grown in any section south of New York, and, it is believed, further to the north. For several years it has been raised in the Carolinas, Georgia and Virginia. To clean and prepare by hand the fibre for market is a slow and profitless business, and the American laborer in the work could not compete with the women, children and other cheap labor of the East Indies. A machine to do the work was essential to make the cultivation of jute a success on American soil. The Commissioner is satisfied that such a machine has been invented. The inventors and patentees are Martin Dennis and Albert Angell, of Newark, N. J. They intend to operate the machine this season at some point on the James river. The Government of Calcutta has a standing offer of £5,000 reward to the inventor of a successful jute-cleaning machine, and it is believed that the American inventors named will secure the handsome prize.

The Department is distributing a large quantity of jute seed throughout the Southern States. It is planted in the spring and harvested in the fall. The yield of fibre is about 3,500 pounds to the acre, and the market quotation for the prepared article is 12½ cents per pound. Gen. Le Duc is convinced that the acreage of jute-planting this season will be very large, and that the planters will realize handsomely on their crops. For years jute has been to India a great source of wealth, and there is no reason why it should not be an equal source of wealth to the United States. It will suppress the foreign monopoly, annually saving millions of dollars to the country, and at the same time, incite capitalists to establish new manufactories and industries that will give employment to thousands of laborers.

VOL. IV.   *AUGUST*.   NO. 8.

Semi Tropic California

DEVOTED TO

AGRICULTURE,

HORTICULTURE,

AND THE DEVELOPMENT OF

SOUTHERN CALIFORNIA

RICE & COLEMAN, PUBLISHERS.

LOS ANGELES, CAL.

1881.

—⊶ AND ⊷—

SOUTHERN CALIFORNIA HORTICULTURIST.

VOL. IV.   LOS ANGELES, CAL., AUGUST, 1881   No. 8.

Agriculture.

PLANT POTATOES THIS MONTH.

Now is the time to begin to move in the matter of potato planting for the late fall and winter market. In this land of perpetual summer the well-arranged farm may have something to market during every month in the year.

In order to accomplish this end regard must be had to the kind of crop and to the time of year in which it is planted. Of course nobody would think of planting corn so late as this in the season expecting to harvest anything more than a crop of feed. The same might also be said of some other farm products, but there are those which at this time of year may be planted in this southern climate with a certainty of a harvest, and among those we find the indispensable *Solanum tuberosum*. When cool weather comes the children will need thicker shoes and other articles of clothing, a load of potatoes will help very largely in paying for them. Later still the tax collector calls, here again a load of potatoes will help you out. Look ahead, Mr. Farmer, we are talking to you individually, and see what your liabilities will be about holiday time, and if you have not already placed yourself in a position to meet them, take timely warning and be ready and able to meet every bill with a smile and the coin. Our market for this community is not limited to our own towns and cities, but it reaches into the territories and states east of us. Carload shipments are frequently made, and not a day passes but that large quantities are sent forward by the various dealers in mixed car-load lots, that is, with other articles.

To add another factor to the question of demand and supply, we would remark that our home product runs short every year, and that orders for potatoes go up the country to meet the deficiency. This order of things should never exist in a country so well adapted to this culture, as regards both soil and water as ours, especially when the price throughout the year ranges between seventy-five cents and one dollar and a quarter per cental, and often goes to two dollars.

For what better bonanza would an eastern farmer ask? If he could only realize our lowest price back there where it is impossible to grow more than one crop, he would devote his whole farm to raising potatoes, while here where two crops, with two or three months to spare, can be grown

on the same piece of ground, the farmer too often fails to appreciate and to take advantage of his opportunities. New soil of course is best adapted to this culture, next in order comes a deep sandy loam, next a light sand, provided that it has not been cropped to death. Neither is it essentially necessary that the soil should be remarkably rich; that theory has been entirely exploded by practice. A good loamy soil that works easily and carries a fair amount of starch will be found to yield favorable results. Neither is it advisable to use the same piece of land for potatoes from year to year as some do, although by means of manure and other fertilizers they succeed in growing average crops.

It has been established by chemical analysis that whatever we plant extracts those elements from the soil which go to make up the thing produced, and it is reasonable to believe that repeating the same crop for several seasons will eventually exhaust the soil of those ingredients which are essential to the production, and although we do use fertilizers, the yield will be measurably less and inferior in quality. Having selected the piece of ground to be planted, the first thing to be done is to clear it of everything which may lie upon it, then turn on the water and give it a thorough irrigation. The ground should be thoroughly soaked for three or four feet in depth. Remember the more you get into the soil now the less will be required later when the crop is growing, and if this preparatory irrigation has been thorough, only one more irrigation will be needed to mature the crop.

Just as soon as the earth will crumble nicely start the plow and move the soil to the depth of one foot, surely not less than ten inches. Do not follow the vicious practice of trying to turn a furrow far beyond the capacity of your plow; the time spent in properly preparing the ground will be abundantly rewarded in the larger yield of your crop. Having finished plowing, go on with a fine harrow and complete the mellowing process, than with a small plow and one horse run furrows through at four or five inches deep and about three and a half feet apart. Have a man follow you closely, dropping one piece of potato every ten or twelve inches. If you have no help, after plowing two furrows drop them yourself and cover with the plow immediately by turning back the furrow which you threw up. Your last act attending the planting will be to roll the ground. If you have no roller you can easily construct a temporary leveler for the occasion; ground

left in this condition will part with its moisture less readily than ground left in an uneven state.

The choice of seed is not a secondary consideration, for the time of year the Peachblow, because of its slow growth, would not be chosen. The Early Rose or the Early Goodrich would seem best for late summer planting. The former produces a few in the hill, from three to four, but all of large size, while the latter produces considerably more in number but of much less uniformity in size. Both varieties have their favorites in the market and the demand for them is about equally divided, therefore you can safely choose the one that suits your present convenience. The age of the seed used should not be passed lightly by. Potatoes recently dug will not germinate readily, therefore see to it that your seed is at least six months old; a year old is still better, and much to your satisfaction your young vines will be coming through the ground in ten days. Again, there is a difference of opinion whether a potato should be planted whole or in pieces. Both conditions have their advocates, backed up with long arguments and theories, but our experience has taught us that one good eye on a piece of potato is just as good as more.

In evidence we would relate only one experience. Having a large piece of ground to plant and seed, the Early Rose, being three dollars per cental, we cut the potatoes into as many pieces as possible, some potatoes made sixteen or eighteen pieces, hardly any less than eight or ten, and the result was the best crop we ever raised. Again the question of using small potatoes from year to year or large ones for seed is still open and probably will be as long as potatoes are grown. We have tried both, and although we could not notice much if any difference in the crops produced from large or small seed, still we imagine, and it may be wholly imagination, that we would choose large potatoes and would cut them very generously.

Another word, and we are done. Some may ask how late will it be safe to plant. In reply we would say that the inland valleys are two or three weeks earlier than the coast valleys, consequently two answers are required. We have known potatoes to do well planted as late as Sept. 10, in the Reiner locality, but we consider two weeks earlier about the proper time, while for the coast or low ground regions any time before the last week in August

Horticulture.

"WILL ORANGE CULTURE PAY?" REVIEWED.

Editor Semi-Tropic:—Dear Sir: In a friendly way I propose to briefly review your article in the Semi-Tropic for July, on the subject, "Will Orange Culture Pay?" In the main the article is good and comes at an opportune time, as a reminder to our horticulturists to use diligence and care in the manner of assorting and packing their fruit. It is not the size of the fruit so much as the uniformity in size in each package, as I believe the medium sized oranges will outsell in point of bulk the extraordinary sized specimens. The reasons are that out of a given number of oranges, about one-tenth will be a No. 1 in point of size, about three-tenths No. 2, about five-tenths No. 3, and one-tenth unfit for market. Now box No. 1 will be held by the dealer at say $4, No. 2 at $2.50, and No. 3 at $1.50. No. 3 being uniform in size and handsomely packed attract the attention of the eye, and the price the attention of the purse, the consequence being that No. 3 are exhausted long before Nos. 1 and 2. Now if this fruit was put up indiscriminately large and medium and small culls and all the hitherto California style, with some rare exceptions, all would present an undesirable appearance in the markets. A few small inferior oranges in a box of otherwise fine fruit spoils the looks, and a few large ones in a box of second or third rate oranges spoil their looks also. It requires considerable experience and practice to enable a person to assort fruit rapidly, dividing the various sizes in an accurate manner; all the layers should be alike, bottom and top and throughout alike, so the dealer or customer will not become disgusted after getting through with the specimens on the top of the box.

But this, Mr. Editor, is rather following you, so I must begin my review. You say, "Now it is a practice with many to begin picking as early as December," and why not? You say, because the "fruit although yellow is not ripe, and is so sour that it is in no degree palatable." I have heard this argument before, and there is nothing in it. We all know that the very first peaches, apricots and other fruits in the markets are not so luscious as those that come somewhat later in the full season of their kind. Does this prevent us buying when they do arrive in prime condition? Certainly not. A man carries a basket of peaches home to his family. The wife says, "How much did you pay for these peaches?" "Two dollars." "Oh, such a price for such horrid fruit? Don't buy any more until they get riper." Perhaps he will, perhaps he will not. It depends upon his taste, his fancy and his purse. Our oranges are quite golden in December. This Pacific Slope and some the whole United States where oranges are not

grown, will want our golden fruit as soon as possible to ornament their tables, to ornament their Christmas trees with these beautiful apples of the Hesperides. It will require millions to supply this demand, and will relieve our orchards of a considerable percentage of their crop, thus easing the future markets. Although experience does teach us that our oranges improve by hanging on the tree through May, June and even July, it is no reason why we should refuse to supply the demands of the market earlier in the season. To carry your argument to its entirety, we should not ship in December because they are better in February, and not ship in February because they are better in April, and not ship in April because they are simply delicious in June. Keep them till June all of you, orchardists: then your oranges are sweet and palatable, and our customers who get one box will want another and another ad infinitum.

But then, how about the state of the market, how about the glut with our sweet oranges? How about the demoralization of the markets and the inducement to profanity among our commission merchants? No, we will ship our fruit as fast as the markets call for it; if too soon, then there will be no lull and the matter will regulate itself. Our sour oranges have been going to San Francisco for twenty years, and they will go again next December, and our orchardists will be only too glad to have them go.

The argument that our early shipped oranges spoil our future trade because they are sour, does not amount to much. When you say that our December oranges are "in no degree palatable," simply proves that you are not as well informed as you should be. The acid of this fruit after the acid is fully yellow, as we find it in most localities in December, is sprightly and agreeable, and is even preferred by some. The world will soon learn that our fruit improves as the season advances, and will treat us accordingly. A man must have a very sour disposition indeed, who would refuse to buy a box of our luscious May oranges because he had purchased a box in December that were not so luscious.

I differ with you also on the point that "the former bright promises can hardly be realized now." I believe we are but just commencing to plant the orange for profit in this country; we understand the business better than we did a few years ago; we know how, when and where to plant much better than we did; we know more about select and superior varieties propagated by budding, thus enabling us to enter the market in from three to five years as against eight to ten years in the past, and with a superior fruit, a fruit that will please the eye as well as the palate. We are becoming adepts in the modus operandi from the beginning to the end of the business. If to the present time our markets for our supply has been confined to the Pacific Coast, now our market is bounded by the Atlantic Ocean on the East, Canada on the North, and the north-

ern tier of Southern States on the South. And further, we have our eye on Europe. Then we are on the eve of turning our entire crop, if prices are not satisfactory, into orange wine and brandy. At least this is the outlet for our wind falls and culls, and will enable us to sell our fruit for the markets more thoroughly. "It is useless to disguise the real truth of the matter," for the real truth is, the time is but just dawning when the planting of orange trees of the right kinds in the right places will be prosecuted with vigor by hundreds, and it may be thousands, of our intelligent and progressive people.

Your idea of thinning the fruit is of first importance, and he who gives it a fair trial will ever after thin his fruit severely. With the best wishes for the success of your most valuable journal and a hearty good-will for the prosperity of our beautiful California, and the continued embellishment of our lovely lands with orange groves, I am, yours truly, THOS. A. GAREY.

SOME REASONS WHY WE SHOULD ATTEND HORTICULTURAL FAIRS.

If all persons engaged in fruit culture in Southern California placed a proper estimate upon the advantage derived from fairs, your pavilion would not be large enough to hold the crowd seeking admittance.

No matter how many *Great Moral Shows* (usually a pig with one eye or a horse with six legs) are connected with fairs some very important facts obtainable in no other way will be impressed upon the mind, remaining through life. Here, elaborated by nature's forces, air, earth and water, gathered into a small space from a large territory, is presented the best fruits, the best flowers, in fact the best of everything, with the best cultivators of the soil to look after and discuss them.

Combined with the arts and sciences we have Expositions and World's Fairs, where the vast array of all that is useful, valuable and beautiful bewilders the senses. The Centennial at Philadelphia has done more to place our true position before the nations of the world than any other one institution ever inaugurated in this country.

The two faculties, the eye and palate, through which the fruit grower becomes proficient in the shortest time, can be exercised to their fullest extent upon the fruit presented. The novice, who is in doubt about the variety he cultivates, has waited for years to learn the correct name, finds out at a glance the desired information. He can by ocular demonstration select the best variety for his use, and actually learns more in one short hour than he could by years of toil and labor without such a collection to examine.

It is not merely a place to show fruit, but as an educator of aesthetics and in establishing a correct taste it has no equal, so that the slightest difference between two specimens of fruit of almost equal merit can at once be detected. In fairs where wine was made a subject of competition have soon experts who could tell if any foreign substance had been introduced into the wine, and one who was able to tell by tasting the wine, what the soil lacked to produce the best results. It is a tonic to the one who becomes disgusted with the endless vigilance and unsuccessful combats with the enemies subject to all fruit growing, when in the discussions he learns the simple remedies which have produced the line display of beautiful fruit presented to his view. He returns home with new impulses, and at the next Fair will be a strong competitor, and the good done cannot be overestimated. To the hard working man it is a great resting place, where he can take in large draughts of pleasure, enabling him to bear the toils and burdens of the day more readily, and to his wife, who has the same old duties to perform day after day, year after year, it is a perfect "God send." The new sights afford many and many a pleasant theme of thought and conversation for the long days which are to come. It is hardly necessary to say that the man of business who has no moment to spare, requires just such a combination to prevent the overtaxed brain from placing him in an untimely grave.

Entertainments of this kind are not frequent enough, and sometimes so poorly patronized as to be a source of loss to those who tax themselves to their utmost to make them pleasant and profitable. The taking of the eagle of the almighty dollar are fastened upon the souls of so many of our people that they will be consumed body and soul unless more time is taken for just such recreations. Therefore publish it broadcast, that a good time may be expected, that knowledge and pleasure shall go together, thereby giving to fruit culture such an impetus as it has never had before.

Yours truly,
GEO. C. SWAN.

San Diego, Cal.

THE KEEPING QUALITIES OF OUR ORANGES.

NEW YORK, May 26, 1881.

DEAR GEORGE:—The barrel of oranges which you shipped to me on March 25th have arrived here to-day. Owing to delays caused by the recent floods in the west, the fruit has been ninety-one (61) days coming here. Of course I expected to find the oranges all rotten after such an exceptional long journey, but I was agreeably surprised to find that out of the 320 oranges which the barrel contained only 19 were partly decayed. I carefully examined the fruit in the presence of several gentlemen who can testify to the above. The fruit has a very fine flavor, and many of our friends and others to whom I have given some of the oranges, have pronounced them the finest that they have ever tasted. I was myself much surprised to see such fine large fruit. As to the "keeping qualities" of California oranges, I am convinced from this experiment that your fruit can be successfully shipped to all parts of the world.

Your Brother,
HERMAN.

These oranges were exhibited at our Citrus Fair March 18th, by George Muller of Pasadena, and after being on exhibition for more than a week were shipped to his brother in New York, who sends the above letter. It might be said further that the oranges were very poorly packed, they were quit loose in the barrel, wich probably accounts for the few rotten ones. ED.

ORANGES IN MASSACHUSETTS.

A gentleman writing from Massachusetts June 4th, says: "The oranges you gave us in Los Angeles were just splendid; lasted us clear through, and I have some now, to see how long they will keep. The raisins hung to the limbs nearly all the way home, and I think they would all the way if I had not taken them out so many times to show them. They are nearly as fresh as they were the day you gave them to me, which was the 25th of March. When you take into consideration the length of time they have been picked (over two months) and the way I brought them home, in a valise, knocking around everywhere, I think that settles the question about shipping oranges from your valley. Mr. H. kept some of them in a window on Merrimack street over two months, and several persons tested them and pronounced them superior to Florida oranges."

THE APRICOT.

James Lyon, of Artesia, sold from one apricot tree, six years old from the seed, ten dollars worth of fruit this year; said tree, the Early Royal variety, brought him eight dollars last year. Who says that the apricot business will not pay near the coast? It has been held by some that apricot culture would not pay near the ocean, but this report from Artesia, only a few miles inland, and others which have come to our hearing of late, prove that apricots thrive fully as well near the ocean as they do in the inland valleys.

APRICOTS IN VENTURA.

The Ventura Signal says: "In many localities in California apricots are grown, but in few are they grown to perfection. One of these few is the Santa Clara valley. The apricot, unlike the semi tropical fruits—the orange and the lemon, thrives better over the sea. In the mountains and interior valleys, the heat causes the fruit to ripen before it attains a size sufficient to make it profitable to the fruit drier; but here, near the coast, where the ocean breezes render the climate so equitable, it comes slowly to maturity, is larger, and when ripe, more rich and juicy. It is of all the fruits the most free from the ravages of insects. The tree is a hardy, vigorous grower, and within four years commences to bear. We firmly believe those who plant apricot orchards in the coast valleys of Southern California, will reap a rich harvest, and at a much earlier date, than those who go farther into the interior and plant oranges, walnuts or grapes. Over two hundred acres have been planted in apricots this year between this place and Saticoy. Next year twice as many will be planted."

THE BEST PEACHES FOR CANNING.

The Southern California Packing Company, of Los Angeles, have kindly given us a short article to which we would call the attention of those who are now budding, as well as to those who contemplate setting a peach orchard during the coming season. The Superintendent of the canning department, Mr. J. J. Green, is the very best authority on the subject. He has had years of experience in the business, being at one time Superintendent of the Golden Gate and San Jose Packing Companies, and more recently of the Santa Barbara Cannery. This is a matter of very great importance, that you have the proper varieties, no matter for what purpose you intend your fruit: Among cling stones, the White Heath Cling, Lemon Cling and Golden Cling. This last, which is used extensively in the Sacramento Valley, is a very large peach, and is the best. For free stone peaches, the Crawfords, both Early and Late, are considered superior to all others. There may be, however, other peaches, both cling and free, that are nearly as good as the kinds enumerated above, and any peach of good flavor, large size, free flesh, distinct yellow or white color, and not colored differently near the pit, will be good for canning purposes.

CALIFORNIA PEACHES IN NEW YORK.

NEW YORK, July 24—The *Evening Post* says: It was announced last week that the first lot of peaches ever brought from California is in a sound condition had appeared upon the market and were selling at satisfactory rates. It is thought by New York dealers that the season may have something to do with the present success, it being well known that fruits will keep longer in one year than another. It is too soon yet to say whether the importation of peaches will assume the importance of the California pear an plum business; but the trade has proved sufficiently profitable this year to encourage larger purchases next year. The net profits upon a car of peaches, holding 400 crates, is $468, when they arrive in good condition, the cost of the fruit being $884, freight $1,116, allowing $100 for spoiled fruit. Peaches will sell readily at $1 per crate. All the plums now in market are from California and nine tenths of the pears. The business of sending California plums and pears to London is growing rapidly, there being but little danger of spoiling in transit. A box of pears is worth $3 in London. Though the fruit is only fifty cents a box, our merchants do not send the fruit to England, but sell to English shippers in need of freight for the other side. All California fruit which arrives here unfit for sale in the market is bought by canneries, to whom the fruit importer goes when all other customers fail.

Horticulture.

"WILL ORANGE CULTURE PAY?" REVIEWED.

EDITOR SEMI-TROPIC—Dear Sir: In a friendly way I propose to briefly review your article in the SEMI-TROPIC for July, on the subject, "Will Orange Culture Pay?" In the main the article is good and comes at an opportune time, as a reminder to our horticulturists to use diligence and care in the manner of assorting and packing their fruit. It is not the size of the fruit so much as the uniformity in size in each package, as I believe the medium sized oranges will outsell in point of bulk the extraordinary sized specimens. The reasons are that out of a given number of oranges, about one-tenth will be a No. 1 in point of size, about three-tenths No. 2, about five-tenths No. 3, and one-tenth nulls unfit for market. Now box No. 1 will be held by the dealer at say $3, No. 2 at $2.50, and No. 1 at $1.50. No. 3 being uniform in size and handsomely packed attract the attention of the eye, and the price the attention of the purse, the reasons being that No. 3 are exhausted long before Nos. 1 and 2. Now if this fruit was put up indiscriminately large and medium and small culls and all the hitherto California style, with some rare exceptions, all would present an undesirable appearance in the markets. A few small inferior oranges in a box of otherwise fair fruit spoils its looks, and a few large ones in a box of second or third-rate oranges spoil their looks also. It requires considerable experience and practice to enable a person to assort fruit rapidly, dividing the various sizes in an accurate manner; all the buyers should be alike, bottom and top and throughout alike, so the dealer or customer will not become disgusted after getting through with the specimens on the top of the box.

But this, Mr. Editor, is rather following you, as I must begin my review. You say, "Now it is a practice with many to begin picking as early as December," and why not? You say, because the "fruit although yellow is not ripe, and is so sour that it is in no degree palatable." I have heard this argument before, and there is nothing in it. We all know that the very first peaches, apricots and other fruits in the markets are not so luscious as those that come some what later in the full season of their kind. Does this prevent us buying when they do arrive in prime condition? Certainly not. A man carries a basket of peaches home to his family. The wife says, "How much did you pay for these peaches?" "Two dollars." "Oh, such a price for such horrid fruit! Don't buy any more until they get riper." Perhaps he will, perhaps he will not. It depends upon his taste, his fancy and his purse. Our oranges are quite golden in December. This Pacific Slope and soon the whole United States where oranges are not

grown, will want our golden fruit as soon as possible to ornament their tables, to ornament their Christmas trees with these beautiful apples of the Hesperides. It will require millions to supply this demand, and will relieve our orchards of a considerable percentage of their crop, thus easing the future markets. Although experience does teach us that our oranges improve by hanging on the tree through May, June and even July, it is no reason why we should refuse to supply the demands of the market earlier in the season. To carry your argument to its entirety, we should not ship in December because they are better in February, and not ship in February because they are better in April, and not ship in April because they are simply delicious in June. Keep them till June all of you, orchardists; then your oranges are sweet and palatable, and our customers who get one box will want another and another ad infinitum.

But then, how about the state of the market, how about the glut with our sweet oranges? How about the demoralization of the markets and the inducement to profanity among our commission merchants? No, we will ship our fruit as fast as the markets call for it; if too soon, then there will be no lull and the matter will regulate itself. Our sour oranges have been going to San Francisco for twenty years, and they will go again next December, and our orchardists will be only too glad to have them go.

The argument that our early shipped oranges spoil our future trade because they are sour, does not amount to much. When you say that our December oranges are "in no degree palatable," simply proves that you are not as well informed as you should be. The soul of this fruit after the rind is fully yellow, as we find it in most localities in December, is sprightly and agreeable, and is even preferred by some. The world will soon learn that our fruit improves as the season advances, and will treat us accordingly. A man must have a very sour disposition indeed, who would refuse to buy a box of our luscious May oranges because he had purchased a box in December that were not so luscious.

I differ with you also on the point that "the farmer bright promises can hardly be realized now." I believe we are but just commencing to plant the orange for profit in this country; we understand the business better than we did a few years ago; we know how, when and where to plant much better than we did; we know more about select and superior varieties propagated by budding, thus enabling us to enter the market in from three to five years as against eight to ten years in the past, and with a superior fruit, a fruit that will please the eye as well as the palate. We are becoming adepts in the modus operandi from the beginning to the end of this business. It is to the present time our markets for our supply has been confined to the Pacific Coast, now our market is bounded by the Atlantic Ocean on the East, Canada on the North, and the north-

ern tier of Southern States on the South. And further, we have our eye on Europe. Then we are on the eve of turning our entire crop, if prices are not satisfactory, into orange wine and brandy. At least this is the outlet for our wind falls and culls, and will enable us to cull our fruit for the markets more thoroughly. "It is useless to disguise the real truth of the matter," for the real truth is, the time is but just dawning when the planting of orange trees of the right kinds in the right places will be prosecuted with vigor by hundreds, and it may be thousands, of our intelligent and progressive people.

Your idea of thinning the fruit is of first importance, and he who gives it a fair trial will ever after ship his fruit severely. With the best wishes for the success of your most valuable journal and a hearty good-will for the prosperity of our beautiful California, and the continued embellishment of our lovely lands with orange groves, I am, yours truly,   THOS. A. GARRY.

SOME REASONS WHY WE SHOULD ATTEND HORTICULTURAL FAIRS.

If all persons engaged in fruit culture in Southern California placed a proper estimate upon the advantage derived from fairs, your pavilion would not be large enough to hold the crowd seeking admittance.

No matter how many *Great Moral Shows* (usually a pig with one eye or a horse with six legs) are connected with fairs some very important facts obtainable in no other way will be impressed upon the mind, remaining through life. Here, elaborated by nature's forces, air, earth and water, gathered into a small space from a large territory, is presented the best fruits, the best flowers, in fact the best of everything, with the best cultivators of the soil to look after and discuss them.

Combined with the arts and sciences we have Expositions and World's Fairs, where the vast array of all that is useful, valuable and beautiful bewilders the senses. The Centennial at Philadelphia has done more to place our true position before the nations of the world than any other one institution ever inaugurated in this country.

The two faculties, the eye and palate, through which the fruit grower becomes proficient in the shortest time, can be exercised to their fullest extent upon the fruit presented. The novice, who is in doubt about the variety he cultivates, has waited for years to learn the correct name, finds out at a glance the desired information. He can by ocular demonstration select the best variety for his use, and actually learns more in one short hour than he could by years of toil and labor without such a collection to examine.

It is not merely a place to show fruit, but as an educator of aesthetics and in establishing a correct taste it has no equal, so that the slightest difference between two specimens of fruit of almost equal merit can at once be detected. In fairs where wine was made a subject of competition I have seen experts who could tell if any foreign substance had been introduced into the wine, and one who was able to tell by tasting the wine, what the soil lacked to produce the best results. It is a tonic to the one who becomes disgusted with the endless vigilance and unsuccessful combat with the enemies subject to all fruit growing, when in the discussions he learns the simple remedies which have produced the fine display of beautiful fruit presented to his view. He returns home with new impulses, and at the next Fair will be a strong competitor, and the good done cannot be overestimated. To the hard working man it is a great resting place, where he can take in large draughts of pleasure, enabling him to bear the toils and burdens of the day more readily, and to his wife, who has the same old duties to perform day after day, year after year, it is a perfect "God send." The new sights afford many and many a pleasant theme of thought and conversation for the long days which are to come. It is hardly necessary to say that the man of business who has no moment to spare, requires just such a combination to prevent the overtaxed brain from placing him in an untimely grave.

Entertainments of this kind are not frequent enough, and sometimes so poorly patronized as to be a source of loss to those who tax themselves to their utmost to make them pleasant and profitable. The talons of the eagle of the almighty dollar are fastened upon the souls of so many of our people that they will be consumed body and soul unless more time is taken for just such recreations. Therefore publish it broadcast, that a good time may be expected, that knowledge and pleasure shall go together, thereby giving to fruit culture such an impetus as it has never had before.

Yours truly,
GEO. C. SWAN.
San Diego, Cal.

THE KEEPING QUALITIES OF OUR ORANGES.

NEW YORK, May 26, 1881.

DEAR GROOM:—The barrel of oranges which you shipped to me on March 25th have arrived here to-day. Owing to delays caused by the recent floods in the west, the fruit has been sixty-one (61) days coming here. Of course I expected to find the oranges all rotten after such an exceptional long journey, but I was agreeably surprised to find that out of the 320 oranges which the barrel contained only 19 were partly decayed. I carefully examined the fruit in the presence of several gentlemen who can testify to the above. The fruit has a very fine flavor, and many of our friends and others to whom I have given some of the oranges, have pronounced them the finest that they have ever tasted. I was myself much surprised to see such fine large fruit. As to the "keeping qualities" of California oranges, I am convinced from this experiment that your fruit can be suc-

cessfully shipped to all parts of the world.

Your Brother,
HERMAN.

These oranges were exhibited at our Citrus Fair March 18th, by George Muller of Pasadena, and after being on exhibition for more than a week were shipped to his brother in New York, who sends the above letter. It might be said further that the oranges were very poorly packed, they were quit loose in the barrel, which probably accounts for the few rotten ones. ED.

ORANGES IN MASSACHUSETTS.

A gentleman writing from Massachusetts June 4th, says: "The oranges you gave us in Los Angeles were just splendid; lasted us clear through, and I have some now, to see how long they will keep. The clusters hung to the limbs nearly all the way home, and I think they would all the way if I had not taken them out so many times to show them. They are nearly as fresh as they were the day you gave them to me, which was the 26th of March. When you take into consideration the length of time they have been picked (over two months) and the way I brought them home, in a valise, knocking around everywhere, I think that settles the question about shipping oranges from your valley. Mr. H. kept some of them in a window on Merrimack street over two months, and several persons tested them and pronounced them superior to Florida oranges."

THE APRICOT.

James Lynn, of Artesia, sold from one apricot tree, six years old from the seed, ten dollars worth of fruit this year; said tree, the Early Royal variety, brought him eight dollars last year. Who says that the apricot business will not pay near the coast? It has been held by some that apricot culture would not pay near the ocean, but this report from Artesia, only a few miles inland, and others which have come to our hearing of late, prove that apricots thrive fully as well near the ocean as they do in the inland valleys.

APRICOTS IN VENTURA.

The Ventura Signal says: "In many localities in California apricots are grown, but in few are they grown in perfection. One of these few is the Santa Clara valley. The apricot, unlike the semi-tropical fruits—the orange and the lemon, thrives better near the sea. In the mountains and interior valleys, the heat causes the fruit to ripen before it attains a size sufficient to make it profitable to the fruit drier; but here, near the coast, where the ocean breezes render the climate so equitable, it comes slowly to maturity, is larger, and when ripe, more rich and juicy. It is of all the fruits the most free from the ravages of insects. The tree is a hardy, vigorous grower, and within four years commences to bear. We firmly believe those who plant apricot orchards in the coast valleys

of Southern California, will reap a rich harvest, and at a much earlier date, than those who go farther into the interior and plant oranges, walnuts or grapes. Over two hundred acres have been planted in apricots this year between this place and Saticoy. Next year twice as many will be planted?

THE BEST PEACHES FOR CANNING.

The Southern California Packing Company, of Los Angeles, have kindly given us a short article to which we would call the attention of those who are now building, as well as to those who contemplate setting a peach orchard during the coming season. The Superintendent of the canning department, Mr. J. J. Groom, is the very best authority on the subject. He has had years of experience in the business, being at one time Superintendent of the Golden Gate and San Jose Packing Companies, and more recently of the Santa Barbara Cannery. This is a matter of very great importance, that you have the proper varieties, no matter for what purpose you intend your fruit: Among cling stones, the White Heath Cling, Lemon Cling and Golden Cling. This last, which is used extensively in the Sacramento Valley, is a very large peach, and is the best. For free stone peaches, the Crawfords, both Early and Late, are considered superior to all others. There may be, however, other peaches, both cling and free, that are nearly as good as the kinds enumerated above, and any peach of good flavor, large size, firm flesh, distinct yellow or white color, and not colored differently near the pit, will be good for canning purposes.

CALIFORNIA PEACHES IN NEW YORK.

NEW YORK, July 28—The *Evening Post* says: It was announced last week that the first lot of peaches ever brought from California in a sound condition had appeared upon the market and were selling at satisfactory rates. It is thought by New York dealers that the season may have something to do with the present success, it being well known that fruits will keep longer in one year than another. It is too soon yet to say whether the importation of peaches will assume the importance of the California pear an plum business; but the trade has proved sufficiently profitable this year to encourage larger purchases next year. The net profits upon a car of peaches, holding 100 crates, is $140, when they arrive in good condition, the cost of the fruit being $400, freight $1,100, allowing $100 for spoiled fruit. Peaches will sell readily at $5 per crate. All the plums now in market are from California and nine-tenths of the pears. The business of sending California plums and pears to London is growing rapidly, there being but little danger of spoiling in transit. A box of pears is worth $5 in London. Though the fruit is only fifty cents a box, our merchants do not send the fruit to England, but sell to English shippers in need of freight for the other side. All California fruit which arrives here sells for sale in the market is bought by canneries, to whom the fruit importer goes when all other customers fail.

Viticulture.

WINTER IRRIGATION.

"TO COMMUNICATE FORGET NOT."

EDITORS SEMI-TROPIC:—The above injunction, laid by the great Apostle to the Gentiles or his Christian converts, may have a very proper application to men of all professions, trades and occupations whatsoever; since progress in no one of the arts of civilized life can be realized except through the general diffusion of *useful knowledge* therein appertaining, *derived from experience*. The business successes or failures of an isolated individual, however important to himself, are of no consequence to his followmen so long as their antecedent causes remain locked up in his own bosom. But let the key to assured success in any department of human enterprise be discovered by a careful observer (or skillful experimenter, if you please) and by him made public properly, and the entire community is incalculably benefitted thereby. So, on the other hand, if a false theory be entertained by an influential individual regarding some vital question in agriculture, horticulture, or any other of the arts of life, and the community be led to adopt the false conclusions he has drawn from defective premises, wide disaster will be the inevitable consequence. "Evil communications corrupt good manners." What we want is the "boiled down" experience of observant and discriminating men.

At some other time, if his and leisure permit, I may offer to my brethren of the Horticultural denomination a short "lay sermon," based on the text that stands at the head of this article. But the object of the present writing is simply to comply, myself, with the Apostle's injunction by communicating a fact or two which have attracted my attention during the past season.

IN THE VINEYARD.

When I came (from Western Massachusetts) to Southern California, in Nov., '70, I found that I knew, practically, just about as much concerning grape culture as if I had been all my days a next door neighbor to "the man in the moon." But circumstances lay me under the necessity of assuming the management of a small vineyard, on the property my daughter had purchased here. I saw at once the proper place for me was in "the infant class" in the School of Viticulture, where for a season I might "sit upon a bench and say A. B. C." which I accordingly took, and as docile was I for a child of only five and seventy years, that, after a very few lessons, my teachers were willing to trust me alone in the vineyard, with a new, bright pruning-knife in my hand. Apparently I justified their confidence, for in confirmation of my own opinion, previously formed, they pronounced my work "well done." I have been led to entertain a slight suspicion, however, since reading M. Keller's article (in the *Express*) "On Pruning the Vine," that, in my boyish fondness for whittling, I may have relieved the vines of a somewhat larger portion of their wood than a more mature judgment would have dictated, (Note.—The two opposite theories of short and long pruning of the vines are certainly deserving of a very thorough investigation. The fact alleged by M. K. that the poorest clusters of grapes are commonly the product of the eyes nearest the stump and the best the product of those which are most remote, finds a striking analogy in the fact, observed by myself for many years, that apple, pear and plum trees locate the finest specimens in the uppermost branches.)

The next subject, in order of time, that presented itself for consideration, was the *winter irrigating* of the vineyard. Again I sat at the feet of the Gamaliel's of the neighborhood. Having received instruction and become truly wise, as I supposed, I made no delay (after the coming in of Feb.) to hoist the water-gate and turn a flood of "pure snow water, *full of nitre*," upon the vineyard, until I had reason to suppose its thirst to be fully satisfied. Later on I gave studious attention to the matters of plowing, cultivating, hoeing, etc. When the set time was come, the two adjacent vineyards responded with alacrity to nature's summons, and were soon arrayed in the beautiful gala dress of the season. But ours remained dormant, seeming disposed to indulge yet in "a little more slumber," and on they did sleep for ten days yet, while the two other vineyards alluded to, within a stone's throw, and on soils supposed to be perfectly homogeneous, were rejoicing in their spring-time robes. At this respectful (but far from *respectable* distance) it continued to play the laggard throughout the season. Two disastrous consequences resulted: First, the exceptional series of fogs that prevailed in August occasioned the clusters, through their immaturity, to "blast" somewhat extensively; and second, such clusters as did finally mature, owing to the lateness of the season, required thrice the usual amount of attention to convert them into raisins, and when they were thus converted they were only of the reprobate order. The reason of this backwardness of our vineyard perplexed me much, and for weeks I disquieted myself in vain to satisfactorily solve the problem. At length, as I was one day pursuing my reflections on the subject the thought occurred to me (and I think it is the true key to this secret) "It was that pure snow water, *so full of nitre*, with which I drenched the vines in February, that did the mischief." A precisely similar experience, in two vineyards within a mile of us go to confirm me in this theory. At any rate my own convictions of its correctness are so well settled that *nitre or no nitre*, no more *snow water* will find its way into our vineyard through my agency. Further than this, I am persuaded that no irrigation is *ever* needed for our vineyards, unless it be in exceptionally dry seasons.

Another fact which I observed when harvesting our grapes, struck me as being worthy of careful consideration, being of a very practical nature, and possibly very consequential in its bearing on the question of the profitableness of grape growing. It was that the outside, south rows of our vineyard on a wide, unshaded avenue, where it had on one side an unlimited supply of air and sunshine, the clusters were far more numerous, and the berries of much larger size than on any row in the interior of the vineyard, and that wherever *in the interior* of the vineyard an open space had been created about any particular plant, by the removal of one or more of its neighboring vines the same phenomenon was seen. These facts led me to the conclusion that the vine delights in a great amount of free air and sunlight, and whenever restricts them in the enjoyment of these, does so not only to their injury but to his own detriment also. It is my own conviction, settled long ago, that no fruit-bearing trees, bushes or vines can bring either their wood or their fruit to full perfection when so huddled together as to become trespassers on each other's pasture-grounds, and interrupt each other's sunlight. "There are *exceptions* to all general rules," there may possibly be some to this. But as a general rule it is the one I choose to work by; and if it should happen to be one of the things remaining for me to do to set a new vineyard (of any of the *long-wooded* varieties particularly, I would allow no plant to stand nearer its neighbor than ten feet, and would sooner increase than diminish that distance.

ANANIEL FOOTE.

GRAPE CULTURE IN SANTA BARBARA COUNTY.

BY MRS. N. W. WINTON.

It is evident that no maxim embodies a greater truth than the one which touches our experience here, "Knowledge comes, but wisdom lingers." In each new garden and plantation in this section, you will find growing from five to fifty varieties of grapes, and subject to as many different conditions of soil, and culture and training. All these cultivators claim to have especial knowledge, born of the experience of other lands, and they are determined to prove that "We are people, and wisdom shall die with us."

When their neighbors, with years of experience to enforce their knowledge, venture to suggest that the rich bottom lands will not do for many varieties of grapes, that the growth of the vine will be enormous, but that the fruit will mildew, and in many varieties will be very scarce—all of this is no avail. "Come and see my young vineyard for yourself, and you will change your views." "Yes, it looks very fine," but the proof is yet to come. You have a fine hillside for a vineyard. Nothing better. Then your grapes will require no irrigation, are in no danger of frosts, and have a subsoil to hold the moisture. One of the finest as to results which we have seen, is such a one, in which we assisted in the planting seven years ago. It has a southern exposure, lying well to the sun, and is a success in every sense, bearing heavily of the choicest fruit. Another very successful one has the vines planted by the side of small rocks, well up on the mountain side, each cutting being placed there for the warmth and moisture held there by the friendly rocks. Of course, the soil is fine and strong, and gives wonderful growth to the vine. We saw beautiful clusters of muscat grapes on some of these vines the first year, and since that time no finer grapes I ave been brought into market than come from these rocky hillsides, and are raised wholly without irrigation. Among our best grapes in this county are the Black Hamburg, Olivet, Muscat, Santa Blanca, Malaga, Chasselas, Rose of Peru, Iona and Isabella for eastern varieties. The Sweetwater is our earliest grape, but we want an improvement on it if we can find it. The Flaming Tokay is a fine, showy grape, but is coarse and not delicate in flavor.

Our experience in raising fruits without irrigation renders our vineyards more economical, and by carrying them well up on the hillsides we avoid the moisture of the valleys. Our experience differs from that of our northern vineyardists as to soils. Mr. Blowers testifies as to success with vineyards on rich, sandy loam, well underdrained, "but using irrigation and frequent culture." Our vineyards on such soils do better grafted to Eastern varieties, as the Iona and Isabella, which are remarkably free from mildew, even on the richest bottom lands. There are many thousand acres of hillside land just adapted to vineyards, overlooking the city and with a southeast exposure, which will one day be utilized in this direction. The soil is varied but all suitable, some limestone rock of a soft friable nature lies scattered over a portion of it, the ground strong and moist from the underlying subsoil; on some of these elevations unbroken lands show moisture in September, two or three inches from the surface. Of course vines make a fine, healthful growth in such locations, and excellent raisins are made from them. This interest is in its infancy here, but several hints shown at our Horticultural Fair in October showed fine possibilities in that direction. It has been supposed that the range of the thermometer was not high enough here for satisfactory raisin-making, but "nothing succeeds like success." We are rapidly overcoming our reverence for familiar maxim laid down by unprogressive aborigines, and are learning our possibilities in many directions. The fear of overdoing the grape interest in Southern California is one of our exploded theories. It is estimated that the increase of our population in the United States is 1,500,000 annually, and the consumption of fruits and raisins especially will increase in greater ratio. The raisin-producing area is not a large one, even on the Pacific Coast, to which section it must be delegated on this continent. As long as our importation exceeds 32,000,000 lbs, we need have little fear. Added to this is the import of dried currants, nearly 70,000,000 lbs. It will require many times our present area of vineyard to supply our own country, and then we may be prepared by careful experience

to carry the war into the enemy's country. Our skilled labor and the intelligence brought to bear upon the subject, and the wide diffusion of intelligence ought to bring us to the front in this undertaking. We are looking with some interest to the variety shown by Mr. West, of Stockton, wholly seedless. Also those interested in grape culture for raisins have been hoping to hear of the Houseo grapes with their wonderful color, so highly recommended last season. Plants are said to have been grown in the experimental grounds at Berkeley and should be sent out this season in time for planting. We have had no disease as yet to encounter with our vines, and hope to preserve our immunity therefrom. Our vines are trimmed ordinarily from 18 to 24 inches in height, but many beautiful trellises in our home gardens remind one of the terraced slopes of Eastern vineyards. The uniformity of climate and large average of sunshine gives us a grape of exceptional flavor and sweetness. Southern California grapes are known to excel in this peculiarity over those of the northern part of the State.

We have been groping our way for ten years past through a labyrinth of difficulties, learning with neither books nor precedents suited to our wants, and with better power to see our own vailed future. We could only work and wait while the language of the land translates itself for us, and now we have reached the alphabet of Horticulture in Southern California, her day of glory and gladness lies just before her. Let her people be worthy of their holy trust.

PRACTICAL RAISIN MAKING.

In California, artificial heat is commonly resorted to, and is undoubtedly a valuable aid to large growers, of skill and capital. The business is one, however, fitted above all others for the small farmers, being, as it is, one of careful detail, and it seems probable that the California raisins are destined to be supplied from the moderate sized plantations and homesteads. To such farmers, the sun-cure is not only less expensive but much more satisfactory. The curing here is to pick the fruit, when sufficiently ripened—and this point is an important one—on trays of light wood, made about two feet by three feet in size, and holding some twenty pounds of grapes. Great care is taken in handling, both to preserve the bloom and to keep the bunches intact, as a grape broken off the stem during curing becomes valueless, drying away to worthless skin and seeds. The drying trays are exposed to the sun, at an inclination; if possible on a high hill slope, with a southerly aspect, possibly between the vine rows of the vineyard. When half dried, the grapes are turned over—that is to say an empty tray is placed on top of the full one, and they are quickly turned over, leaving the grapes, with the under side up, in the new tray. These trays ought properly to have covers for the night time, that the process might not be so retarded as to

necessitate the use of artificial heat. Grapes dried in a continuously dry atmosphere, with no dampness as of the night dews, make also a higher grade of raisin. After the grapes have been turned, and when sufficiently cured, they are slipped from the trays into larger boxes, every twenty-five pounds of fruit being separated by a sheet of thick paper, and are left in the store-room for a fortnight. These are called sweat-boxes, and the process of sweating is for the purpose of equalizing the moisture, at the end of a fortnight it being found that a medium is established between the very moist and the very dry raisins, and also between the raisins and the stems, the former being now soft and the latter tough instead of brittle. From the sweating box the raisins are boxed for market by means of iron packing frames, having a separable bottom. A handsome layer of raisins is laid in the bottom of the packing frame, five pounds of fruit placed in on top and pressed firmly down. The paper is placed around, the whole slipped into the raisin box proper, and the sides and ends of the iron frame withdrawn. The bottom of the frame is pressed down upon the raisins before it is removed, to crowd them into the box; any hollows in what has become the top layer are filled with large handsome single berries, the paper is folded over, and the box cover nailed on. If the raisins are not to be sun-dried, or if the process is to be hastened, the trays, after being turned as described above, are placed in wagons and taken to a drying room where they can be exposed to strong currents of hot air, continual drafts being obtained, in some cases, by the use of a fan. The indoor process takes only one third of the time required to dry uncovered grapes out of doors, and the cost of the necessary appliances varies very greatly, one outfit, including the drying rooms and a packing house, costing $3,000, which was considered very moderate. It may also be stated that three pounds of ripe grapes make two pounds of raisins. Raisins dried slowly within doors, with no sun exposure at all, or not sufficiently cured, have a finer bloom, or rather, heavier color, and a more delicate flavor, but they do not keep well, and would not do for transportation to cold and moist climates.

The faults of our domestic raisins are of a threefold nature. In the first place they are not evenly cured, some being dried too much and some not enough. This is to be obviated, not so much by the sweat-box, as by going over and carefully sorting them while they are drying, and by grading them properly when they are packed. In the second place, the bloom, flavor and appearance suffer from the night dews and the fact that the drying grapes are not covered from the chill and moisture. Thirdly, the raisins are too small—a fault of the pruning, which is not close enough. If fewer vines to the acre were grown we should have a finer berry, but a vine which bears fifty pounds of fruit cannot supply us with handsome raisins.— W. H. Curtis in F. Call

SAN BERNARDINO.

This is the largest county in the State, having an area nearly as large as that of New Hampshire, Vermont, Connecticut and Rhode Island. Its physical features are much like its sister counties, consisting of mountains, valleys and plains, and with San Diego county shares much of the Colorado desert.

In the mountains we find good pine building lumber in large quantities, and many promising gold and silver mines. The valleys and plains with their hot irrigating streams from the mountains, hundreds of artesian wells, and a number one soil, furnish homes surrounded with fine orchards and vineyards to an active and intelligent population. On the desert are a few fine oases, and several mining camps now being worked at a fair profit. The Mohave, probably the richest camp, promises at present to be a second Tombstone. Returning to the great San Bernardino Valley we find it situated between the Temescal and the San Bernardino ranges of mountains. It is about sixty miles long from west to east, and thirty miles wide from north to south. In this garden spot are just enough hills and buttes to render the landscape beautiful. At the foot of the San Bernardino range, in a matchless climate, we find the city of the same name, the county seat, with a population of 3,000 inhabitants. The city was settled by the Mormons from Salt Lake City, and like its mother city the streets are laid off at right angles, and are broad and clean, skirted with graceful green trees and streams of clear water trickling by to the orange groves below. From the cupola of the Court House, a cut of which we here present you, the city, with its inviting surroundings, presents a beautiful panorama to the eye. The mountains on one hand with their forest of pine and snow clad tops, on the other Colton, with the Southern Pacific railroad passing through to Arizona, and over to the east, five miles beyond, the beautiful settlement of Riverside, with its fine promises and possibilities, turning a little our view to lost in casting a glance toward Los Angeles, sixty miles toward the sea, and at every turn you find something pleasing to the eye and worthy to be admired. The Southern California Railroad from San Diego, the division name of the Atlantic & Pacific and Atchison, Topeka & Santa Fe now building, passes through Riverside, Colton and near or through the city. When this road is completed the fortunate inhabitants of this valley will have a choice of two roads to the east and two to the ocean and San Francisco. Many new comers see this future advantage, and the demand for real estate has increased very largely in consequence.

This section of Southern California is certainly about to take a decided step forward, and the time is not far distant when the major portion of this large valley will be thickly settled by happy, industrious people.

The diversity of soil and the abundant water supply renders every branch of agriculture, horticulture, etc., a possibility. In some of the lower portions of this vast valley corn has been known to yield from seventy-five to eighty bushels per acre, barley and oats in like proportion, and all other soil products bear a prodigious harvest. Alfalfa fields for home, dairy and other purposes, are found on every hand, and turn off from one to two tons per acre at each cutting, and where water is applied after each cutting the same piece may be cut seven or eight times during the year. For feeding purposes it is fully equal to our eastern clover. It is a great milk producing grass and hay, while for hog feed it is very healthful and fattening.

Old San Bernardino, a few miles up the valley, is noted for its early associations. It was settled over a hundred years ago by the Franciscan Friars, who built a fine, large mission church, planted orange and olive orchards, vineyards and palms, and began the good work of civilizing and christianizing the natives. Those early Christian missionaries invariably selected the very choicest locations for their settle-

COURT HOUSE, SAN BERNARDINO COUNTY.

ments, and planted the one variety of grape—the Mission—best suited for all purposes. Their herds of sheep and droves of cattle ranged by the thousand head unrestricted over hill and plain. Their glory has departed, but kind memories still remain, and they, the principal actors, rest in peace while the centuries roll away. Beyond, in the San Gorgonio Pass, Dr. Edgar some years ago sought health, quiet and repose. He found all for which he sought, and more. His vineyard has a national reputation, and as an unpretentious, hospitable entertainer he is known even beyond the seas. In the mountains back of San Bernardino are found the Waterman Hot Springs, noted for the medicinal properties of their water; a short distance from these are the Arrowhead Springs, which are also highly recommended for rheumatism and other diseases. The altitude of these Springs is about six hundred feet above the valley; the prospect is pleasing, hunting is good, and for invalids or those seeking recreation and pleasure the location is to be highly recommended.

The general climate of San Bernardino is much the same as the other Southern counties, save it is dryer owing to its inland position.

Riverside claims to surpass all other locations for lung complaints, and refers to many remarkable cures to substantiate her claims. The unusually dry air which prevails here seems to heal all diseased surfaces, and instead of relaxing it exerts an invigorating influence over the system. The prime atmosphere found upon the mountain sides at a reasonable altitude is certainly to be recommended to those suffering with pulmonary troubles; the mountains for the Summer and the valleys for the Winter season.

This brief review is simply a foretaste of what will appear in our next issue. Next month we propose to go more fully into details and to present our readers with two or three pages of cuts illustrating San Bernardino proper, together with a few fine villas, orange groves and vineyards, and other objects especially interesting to the reader.

———

The entries made, exhibits promised and the general outlook at this writing (six weeks before the opening day) for the Centennial and Horticultural Exposition never looked better. The Pavilion will be crowded with the largest and handsomest exhibit of horticultural and agricultural products ever exhibited on the Pacific Coast.

A STRANGER AMONG US

Among the many recent arrivals in our section we note the visit to Los Angeles and to his relatives here (the family of Shields) Septimus Hypolett Spencer, of the old English and English-Norman families of Spencer of Yorkshire. Knowing that our readers are always pleased to know what intelligent and observing strangers think of our region, we reproduce in a natural way some of the queries, replies and comments suggested, as our friend the Angeleño and our visitor drove through the country:

Visitor—The suburbs of Los Angeles abound in charms, which the greatest cities of less favored climates can neither borrow nor buy. The freshness, thrift and beauty of lawn, shrub, vine and tree here under the summer glare of cloudless skies, rainless from May to November, provoke inquiry. The reply that irrigation procures all this vigor, variety and exhuberance leads to another inquiry, Why does irrigation procure all this profusion and perfection of wood, leaf bloom and fruit here, while in at least many other places the artificial application of water is rather damaging than beneficial?

Angeleño—Irrigation is by no means an unmixed blessing, even in California. Certain varieties of soil here will not tolerate it; most will do. The sea climate everywhere in California is favorable to irrigation. The continental climate occasionally dominant in California, is unfavorable to it. There are usually about four trios of continental or hot days each dry season. The three continental days making each trio come together, but the trios are weeks apart. On these continental days artificially applied water "scalds," and along the trail of the less cautious irrigator, the more tender annuals sometimes prematurely don the sere and yellow leaf. The irrigator must be extra cautious on continental days. On the afternoon of the third day the continental climate retreats and the sea breezes pursue and re-visit every dell, play upon every hill, shake the languor from every leaf and fly onging through every home. The wilted leaf unfolds in the gossamer irrigation of sea vapor, and the damp sea air filtering through the mellowed soil, and passing in its cool, condensing cells, keeps the balm of minute irrigation. The irrigation only continues and enlarges the irrigation begun by sea vapor. And sea vapor continues and graduates artificial irrigation. The plant receives no deleterious shock, but great benefit, because violent change is avoided through the inter-gradation and inter-blending of the natural and artificial processes.

Visitor—I see that many orange trees along the line of our two days' unwonted drive are bending under the weight of two distinct crops of oranges—one a crop of ripe fruit, the other a crop of green fruit.

And a cry of the street fruit vendor is, "Fresh oranges and peaches!"

Angeleño—Los Angeles orange trees habitually wait for the market to unload them. These orange trees are not only as patient as camels under double burdens, but they keep their own fresh growing, the old cargoes fresh, and vigorously prepare bloom buds for still another crop. If you happen to be among the Los Angeles orange groves next spring, you may see on the same tree sound oranges of 1880, ripe oranges of 1881, green oranges of 1882, and the bloom buds for oranges for 1883. You will be apt to select the orange in the third year of its age for your own eating, simply because it is the best.

Visitor—I notice a great change within the last dozen turns of the carriage wheel. The soil, degree of moisture and character of the vegetation are so widely different from what it was a few wheels back, as if one had voyaged from one island to another.

Angeleño—We have entered the artesian belt. Note that bare acre, trodden into deep dust by feeding sheep? Well, that is a rich acre. Last May it was covered with masses of nutritious wild grasses. The sheep have cleaned it as bare as the road. Do you see this bunch of bluish looking weed, diminutive pink flower, and most entire thyme? It is now nearly noon. There was no dew this morning, and yet see how dripping wet this weed is. See the large drops, how they sparkle in the light. I believe this weed is always wet. Taste this branch. You truly say it tastes like a sack of salt. This branch you see is only a yard in diameter. Nothing will eat it. Around it the ground is rich. Corn will grow luxuriantly up to the edge of it. But within this spot nothing will grow but salt or alkali plants. We now come to a surface as hard and bare as the road. No dust bare ground by the feet of feeding sheep. There never was any feed here. This land is too salt to produce even pickle weed. Pickle weed, you perceive, is well named. It is as crisp and salt as tender asparagus is brine. We are approaching better land. See the malva supercedes salt plants; and here it is still better; indeed this is the best of land. See this dense thicket of tall mustard. You now have the infallible test of good and bad land, the salt curse and fertility cure irrigation. It is a lesson merely curious to me, but the hinge of fate to the land buyer. These never absent tests unerringly guide the land. It is who runs may read unless he is a somnambulist. I have known numerous habits to buy land with these signs sticking to it. Sheriffs set up somnambulist land buyers.

Visitor—I notice alfalfa growing luxuriantly in meadows without a weed among it. I see it, tall, well branched, densely leaved and blossomed, and withal of a bright green color, all without irrigation, and without rain for months, as I am credibly informed. I am the more astonished at all this luxuriance and hardihood of alfalfa here, because elsewhere I have known it to

be sown in the spring, flourish the following summer, and in the autumn of the same year die out, root and branch, under the tread of grazing herds.

Angeleño—The weedless alfalfa meadows you see illustrates the despotic and intolerant rule of alfalfa. The complete mastery of alfalfa over weeds in California is the more remarkable because of the extreme fecundity and ferocity of luxuriant weeds, but all the kinds of forms wild growth abruptly stops where alfalfa begins.

Visitor—I thought these bunches of barley hay in the field were spoiled, but I find all underneath a few sun-browned straws is bright, and I am told that hay under the open sky remains bright all summer. What an extensive English alfalfa ranches, and yet a dozen props to the limbs of each tree to help bear the burden of nuts. Here is an oleander tree dazzling one with pink flowers, and yonder is an oleander snow-drift. We made a house pet of an oleander at home four years, without the reward of a bloom. That great forest of eucalyptus, only six years old? Wonderful! How remarkable is every variety of growth."

HOW TO KEEP THE BOYS ON A FARM.

Boys on the farm grow tired of the every day farm work, and even of their homes, unless there is something to relieve the monotony. Farmers make a serious mistake if they fail to make provision for recreation for their children. Give them something they can truly remember their own, and see how soon they become interested therein. Let them have pets, pigeons, poultry, a calf, lamb, or even pigs, with the understanding they may have all the profit they can make from them, and it will be seen that the care and sales will inculcate a business tact, and at the same time engraft on the young and pliant mind a reverence for God's creatures that will be of lasting good through life. Visit a farm house where the children are thus cared for, and note with what cheerful countenances they visit their pets, their own garden plots, their flower beds, after the toil of the day is done, morning to forenoon their enjoyment here tired they were and if you won't realize that it is more blessed to give than receive, read assured you have no soul. Is it any wonder that boys are anxious to leave the farm just as soon as they become old enough to be of assistance, when they have no home attractions, where "home" means toil, toil, no recreation of any kind, not even a sorrow? Farmers, make your homes attractive, furnish the children good reading matter, and see that they enjoy themselves and thus instead of driving the boys away it will be found they have formed pleasant attachments for their homes that will be sufficient inducements to remain.—A'a.

The programme for afternoon and evening during the Centennial and Horticultural Exposition is to excel any entertainments of the kind ever held in the State.

Southern California.

SPADRA AND POMONA.

Editor Semi-Tropic: Spadra and Pomona have not progressed as rapidly during the past few years as some other sections of our county, but now seem in a fair way to prosperity. The land difficulties have nearly all been settled, and it is probable that before long capital will develop the water supply and render both settlements attractive to new comers.

SPADRA.

Mr. A. T. Currier, one of the most enterprising and liberal man of Los Angeles county, has a beautiful home about three miles from the village of Spadra. Here the orange and other semi-tropical fruits seem to grow to perfection, while the grain fields surrounding generally yield an ample harvest. Nearer Spadra is the ranch of Mr. C. T. Wright, which, besides being well adapted to grain and stock, has a fine twenty-acre vineyard loaded with fruit. Between Spadra and Pomona are the thrifty ranches of Messrs. Fryer, devoted to grain and fruit. Jos. Wright, the "Squire" of the little settlement, and Louis Phillips, one of the largest land-owners in the county.

The village of Spadra has an excellent hotel kept by Mr. Metsker, known better as Uncle Jake, a general store owned by A. B. Caldwell, one of the finest school buildings in the county, a railroad station and blacksmith-shop.

The grain crop is not so large as last year, but quite satisfactory to the farmers; the climate is fully equal to that of any other valley sections of the county, and the people seem as a rule to be prosperous and happy.

POMONA.

Pomona has a decidedly encouraging future before it, and in a short time we look for a large and prosperous settlement there. The water supply is being developed, and in a short time there will be an ample supply for many thousand acres. Your correspondent made a pretty thorough inspection of the place and was surprised at the wonderful improvement of the places under cultivation. But little water seems to be actually needed when the land is thoroughly cultivated, and deciduous fruits—apples, pears, apricots, grapes, peaches, and even plums, do exceedingly well. The orange and lemon, when properly cared for, seem to thrive though an exceedingly well. The orange and lemon, when properly cared for, seem to thrive though as elsewhere in our valleys; the nearer they are to the mountains the less danger there is of frost. Pomona has unquestionably a beautiful and healthy location, free from disagreeable winds, and with less fog than we get closer to the coast.

It will pay any person who is interested in horticulture to visit the beautiful fruit farms of this section and see what a little capital and much labor can accomplish in a short time on a seemingly barren plain. Mr. C. K. White is the owner of an eighty-acre tract, which he has planted with deciduous and semi-tropical trees, many of which are now bearing. He is experimenting with olives, and will, we trust, find the culture of this tree both successful and profitable. Dr. Fairchilds, who owns a lot in the center of the town, has a promising little orange orchard, which shows what may be done with this fruit with proper cultivation. The Doctor also has a fine bee-ranch in the mountains, which he assures us will bring a fair crop of honey the present season.

Mr. Jno. White is the owner of ten acres close to the village. His land is devoted to trees and vines, the fruit this year being very fine, his peaches having the flavor of those grown in the mountains. Rev. P. M. Ruth, the Episcopal clergyman of the place, has a beautiful home surrounded with trees and vines. Like others he is a firm believer in the future of Pomona. Mr. S. Gates, formerly of Los Angeles city, has gone into the nursery business on his 15-acre farm, and our friends who wish to buy trees next spring will be pleased to learn that he will have 40,000 budded apricots to dispose of.

Mr. Frank House, formerly connected with the railroad, has one of the prettiest places in the county, Mr. House has brought his place up to a high state of cultivation, sparing neither labor nor expense. The result he may well be proud of. His orange trees are healthy, free from black smut, and in every respect his place is a fine example of what can be done on a small farm in Southern California.

But the time and space will fail me to speak of all the beautiful homes there are in the Pomona settlement. I can only advise my readers to visit and inspect those mentioned as well as many others. Messrs. Loop, Meserve, Palomares, Rodgers, Eno, Garthside, Mills, Bridger, Wade and others have made the desert blossom as the rose, and we trust are about to reap an ample reward for their enterprise and labor.

The village of Pomona has three general stores, postoffice, railroad station, blacksmith-shop, hotel, etc. There are two churches and a fine public school building.

Not far from Pomona is the celebrated China ranch, recently purchased by Mr. Gird of Arizona. Mr. Gird is making great improvements, and it is understood that he will materially aid the people of Pomona in developing their settlement. With the assistance of several capitalists and the superb climate and soil of the San Jose valley the future of Pomona looks very hopeful.　　　　　　　J. C. I.

Men are brave, but a broken hearted wife who carries her loads for years till she finds a man who can truly sympathize with her, or a woman in whom she dare confide, is braver than any man that ever lived, and is a rare jewel in the crown of womanhood.

NOTES FROM SAN FERNANDO.

The wheat yield of San Fernando is about two-thirds as large as last year, but the quality in every respect much better. The total amount of land in wheat is about 40,000 acres. The following are some of the principal owners and amount of acres under cultivation:

Lankershim & Van Nuys	20,000
Maclay	2,000
B. F. Porter	3,000
G. K. Porter	2,500
Jenifer & Burnett	2,000
J. G. Patton	4,000
A. Workman	4,000
Hubbard & Wright	1,100
J. Parsons	500

The honey yield of San Fernando is not a total failure this year, but growers are very much disappointed. Honey proving a doubtful crop the bee men are turning their attention to fruit growing with considerable success. Mr. J. Harps, about three miles from the village of San Fernando, has a very thrifty little orchard which, without irrigation, produces the very finest quality of deciduous and semi-tropical fruits. The McClure Brothers, who own 100 acres about seven miles from San Fernando, are about to put a portion of their splendid canyon into grape vines, to which the land is well adapted. The San Fernando valley will, in time, become a fruit-producing section of no small importance.

Mr. C. R. Rinaldi is the owner of the largest fruit farm in the Valley, having a fine orchard and vineyard. Fruit ripens earlier at Mr. Rinaldi's place than in most portions of the county, and bears very abundantly. This gentleman is a believer in the future of the olive, and has a large plantation of young trees, which average about fifty gallons each. The fruit pickled sells for fifty cents per gallon, and the demand is unlimited. At the old mission of San Fernando close by, is an aged olive tree which the owner says bore 250 gallons last year, an enormous yield. The olive is destined to become a great source of income to those of our horticulturists who are far-seeing enough to plant and properly care for the trees.

FROM LOS ANGELES TO WILMINGTON.

Editor Semi-Tropic: The country between Los Angeles city and Wilmington comprises a variety of good, bad and indifferent land. Where the alkali has not too strongly impregnated the soil crops are generally good, and though not ranking as the best of our semi-tropical fruit land, still oranges, lemons, limes, etc., are produced in some localities of excellent quality.

VERNON DISTRICT.

After leaving the city limits we pass into one of the prettiest and most thriving farming districts in our county, appropriately named Vernon. This section is divided into twenty and forty-acre farms principally devoted to fruit. The soil is generally a deep, sandy loam and very productive, trees attaining full size in half the time required in the East. The deciduous trees and vines seem particularly adapted to Vernon, and a man with twenty acres of land clear of debt can not only secure a good living, but with good management realize a handsome yearly profit. Some of the most thrifty ranches in Vernon are owned respectively by Messrs. Rorick, Entwistle, Fields; Walker, Getchel, Meade, Shattuck, Foote, Richardson, Colby, Kyser, Clapp, McKee and Cargill.

FLORENCE.

Florence district is not in as high a state of cultivation as Vernon, but there are nevertheless many well improved farms. Hay, grain and fruit are the principal products. The hay and grain crops are about half as large as last year, but the quality fully twice as good. Mr. M. P. Cutler, the owner of a nine-acre vineyard, informed us that his grape crop will be a third larger than last year. Mr. Nadeau, one of the principal owners of land in Florence, planted several hundred acres with grape cuttings the present season, nearly all of which are growing vigorously. Mr. Nadeau finds his great eucalyptus grove, planted several years ago one of his most profitable investments and largely supplies the Los Angeles wood market from it. Mr. R. Ranney, another progressive citizen, had an extensive nursery stock on his hands last year, which owing to the demand for trees he sold very profitably. This year he will repeat the experiment, no doubt with similar success.

COMPTON.

The dairy market predominates in Compton, and the cheese factories of Messrs. Harshman and Bullis are the life of the settlement. Large herds of cattle supply an abundance of milk, and Compton cheese now has an established reputation in all parts of the Pacific Coast. The alfalfa fields of Compton are the finest in the county, and the farmers, after feeding their stock, have a considerable surplus of hay to sell at Los Angeles and Wilmington. The water supply is unlimited, artesian wells flowing constantly upon almost every ranch. There are several mercantile establishments, a hall and schoolhouse, lumber yard and railroad depot.

WILMINGTON.

Wilmington is the principal seaport of a vast area of country, and in its immediate vicinity has thousands of acres of the finest agricultural land in the county. The railroad company is at present engaged in extending their track from this town, which has heretofore been their terminus, to San Pedro, a point in some respects more convenient. This alteration will be completed some time this month, but will not, we understand, materially cheapen the cost of transportation, as the lighters will for some time yet be needed between the railroad wharf and the anchorage, for deep water vessels. The people of Wilmington have feared serious injury to their town from the removal of the railroad terminus, but we do not apprehend that much trade will be lost to them, as the adjacent farming land is being rapidly settled up, and the new terminus has no facilities for an extensive settlement. Wilmington boasts of some of the finest private residences in the county, although unfortunately they do not show to advantage from the railroad and harbor. Messrs. Banning, McDonald, Hux by, Alexander, Hinds, Polhemus, Van Valkenberg, and many others have beautiful homes, surrounded with orange groves and vines. There are several substantial mercantile establishments, a drug store, about twenty saloons, blacksmith shops, restaurants, lodging houses, etc. The government has vastly improved the harbor of Wilmington, although the appropriations have been meagre and insufficient. Wilmington ought in time to become a manufacturing center of some importance, as well as the trading point for a rich agricultural district.   H. B. W.

NOTES FROM EL MONTE.

We received some magnificent specimens of deciduous fruits from El Monte last month which show that this, one of the oldest American settlements in the county, has a nearly neglected source of wealth. Corn, potatoes and barley have hitherto been the chief agricultural products of the Monte, but we believe that twenty acres in pear, plum and peach trees will yet prove to be a greater bonanza than grain fields, with their uncertain crops and prices.

Many of the Savannah and El Monte farmers are raising hogs, and the high prices have considerably decreased the stock of hogs in the county. The Arizona markets are our best customers, and every new mining camp started is an additional outlet.

HOW TO PRESERVE THE FERTILITY OF THE SOIL.

W. C. Thompson, State Grange Lecturer, delivered an address before Pescadero Grange, June 26th, in the course of which, as reported in the Redwood City *Times*, he said:

Some soils seem so rich in plant food that they require nothing but proper watering—tillage—to continue fertile for an indefinite period. Such are some of the rich bottom lands of the Western States, and such I consider some of our own adobe and valley lands. Deep and thorough tillage will for a long time produce good crops on such soils; but even on such the prudent farmer will not presume to draw too heavily without resorting to some artificial means to preserve the fertility. And first among these stand manuring. Manures are of benefit, first, by improving the physical condition of the soil; second, by acting as nutrients; and third, by entering the plants as direct nutrition. Were all manures of the latter class, then it might be possible, by analyzing the ash of any crop, to apply as manure just such ingredients as are needed. But unfortunately for this theory many practical difficulties arise. Among others, actual experience has shown that what is efficacious as a manure one year for a certain soil and crop may be of no use the next, and what is of no use this year may prove of the highest use at some future time.

Stable manure stands first in rank of fertilizers, as containing the greatest amount of necessary ingredients. Of commercial manures those are the most valuable which contain most ammonia and phosphoric acid. Hence the value of guano and bone-dust. The true system of manuring is to keep the soil supplied in excess with all three ingredients necessary for plant food. But manuring, although the first and best artificial mode of preserving the fertility of soil, yet to us in this locality it is not possible to manure our hill land. This remedy, then, will only apply to lands easily hauled over. To meet the good farmer will apply his manure liberally and we that the contents of his stables and cow pens does not become a mass of almost worthless rubbish by loss of valuable ingredients before it is applied to the field.

Next to manuring comes rotation of crops. Intelligent agriculturists have classed crops as first, enriching crops, as clover; second, non-exhausting crops, as peas, beans and grain, cut green, third, exhaust ing crops, as grain ripened, beets, potatoes; fourth, very exhausting crops, as flax, tobacco, hemp, hops, etc. A more general classification may be made by noting that shallow-rooted, quick-maturing crops are more exhausting on the soil than deep rooted, slow growing and broad-leaved crops. Hence an intelligent rotation or alternating of crops is of the highest importance. But unfortunately for us, clover, the most enriching of crops, is not available in our soil and climate. Another, and for us a more easily available means of preserving the fertility of our soil, is found in fallowing. A naked fallow consists in letting the land lie uncropped for a year, giving as many plowings during that time as practicable to prevent growth of weeds. A better system of fallowing is to sow buckwheat, peas or some similar crop, plowing it under while green. This plan is excellent where the whole crop is carefully covered by the plow and in a sufficiently moist condition to cause it all to rot. The land is thereby rested and manured at the same time.

One other means of preserving the soil I wish to notice, and then close, namely, cultivate less land and feed more cattle. The advantages of this are three-fold: 1, what land is tilled can be more thoroughly cultivated; 2, more manure will be available to apply where it can be used; 3, the fertility of the hill lands can be preserved by alternate resting as pasture land, and cropping. Considering our soil, climate and locality, this seems to be par excellence the means of preserving our soils from exhaustion, and it is practically and completely within the reach of all our farmers.

SEMI-TROPIC
CALIFORNIA,
— AN —
ILLUSTRATED MONTHLY.

Devoted to Agriculture, Horticulture, and the Development of Southern California.

Terms: $1.50 per Annum, in Advance.

Office, Rooms 9 & 10, Baker Block.

Address - RICE & COLEMAN, Los Angeles, Cal.

GEORGE RICE, } Editors and Proprietors.
CHAS COLEMAN, Jr., }

OFFICIAL PAPER
—OF THE—
Southern California Horticultural Soc'y.
OFFICE, ROOM No. 2, BAKER BLOCK.
GEO. RICE, Secretary.

It seems that our article on orange culture in our July number touched a tender spot in the breast of a few of our more sanguine growers, and by referring to another page of this issue it will be seen that one of our readers has gone for us without gloves and with tomahawk high in air.

Owing to the want of space in their respective departments, "How to Preserve the Fertility of the Soil" was crowded out of Agriculture into Southern California, and "The best Industry for a Poor Man," which should have come under Viticulture, appears in the Poultry department.

The Farmers' and Merchants' Bank has laid upon our table a statement of its condition at the close of business on Thursday, June 30. The showing is very gratifying, and is a standing advertisement of the prosperity of our many industries. Its total assets reach one and a quarter millions. The fact that it owes depositors over seven hundred and fifty thousand dollars, shows that it enjoys the unlimited faith of the business public.

We are pleased to learn that the attack against the Pork Packing Company at East Los Angeles last month was dismissed by the court, owing to the entire want of evidence to sustain the charge. This institution has been doing business among us about four years, and its products have won an enviable reputation near and far. Its hams, bacon, lard and mess pork go into the territories by the car load, and the demand is constantly increasing. Our farmers find a ready market with this company for all the hogs they can produce, and at good round prices.

S. Gates, of Pomona, it is said, has 40,000 young apricot trees in nursery. We believe that most nurseries are short of this fruit. It might be well for holders to note this and bud freely of this fruit, because it is sure to become one of the leading industries.

The codling moth scare reminds us of the time when everybody became wild over the brown scale bug. A little later excitement ran high concerning the red scale, nevertheless our orchards survive, have increased wonderfully, and are yielding abundantly. However, we would not advise a quiet indifference, but would urge our orchardists to an unrelenting warfare against not only the codling moth, but against every species of insect that preys upon our fruit trees until the extermination is complete. While most of our growers are alive to this work there are a few who will sit idly by and allow insects to breed by the wholesale, and send insects of course will find their way into the orchard of the more watchful neighbor. This is all wrong, and we have a way out of the dilemma, by the Board of Supervisors appointing a committee whose business it will be to see that these delinquents apply the proper remedies. Nearly all the leading fruit counties in the State have already made these appointments, and certainly Los Angeles county will be as progressive as they. However, should the Supervisors fail to act favorably in the matter, there is no reason why we should become greatly alarmed, but we should be active ourselves, and should use our influence with our neighbors to be active also. This much as yet exists in only a few places in our county and by using active measures at once its increase and spread is an impossibility, but he is an industrious little fellow, and if you procrastinate, he will revel to your injury. The remedy as follows, is very simple. First scrape off all rough bark, clean out the crevices and crotches, and wash the trees with soft soap, sulphur and water in the following proportions: to one gallon of water add three-quarters of a pound of strong soft soap and a quarter of a pound of sulphur. Instead of this wash, the whale oil soap and sulphur, known as codling moth wash, may be used.

The twenty-eighth annual State Fair will commence on the 13th and end on the 24th of September at Sacramento. An examination of its catalogue shows it to be complete in every department, and the premiums offered are remarkably liberal. We trust that there will be a large individual representation from Southern California, and for ourselves we make the very liberal offer to take a grand collection and exhibit it in a body, not as coming from any one section, but from Southern California as a whole, provided that the people will supply us with said collection. We believe that such an exhibition would be of immense value in advertising the various industries of this southern country. Will our orchardists, vineyardists, farmers, etc., come to the front with their choice productions. Complete arrangements can be made at the Pavilion during Horticultural Fair week, Sept. 5-10, with the editors of this journal.

Gov. Geo. C. Perkins will formally open the Centennial and Horticultural Exposition Monday, Sept. 6.

John Kirk, Danville, Ill., writes:

Is there any chance for a carriage wood-worker to get employment there, or to start a shop on a small scale? There are plenty of carriage shops already here, doing a good business, and no doubt a first class workman would get from $3 to $4 per day.

Do they sell land there on small payments down and monthly installments for the balance? You can make any arrangement you wish about payments provided you pay part down and give security on the land for the balance.

Do you know of a man in your vicinity by the name of Seth Daniels? He is a relative; have not heard from him for years; was in Los Angeles the last we heard from him. No.

ROCK FALLS, ILL., June 22, 1881.

EDITORS SEMI-TROPIC CALIFORNIA:— Some time ago I requested you to send me a copy of your journal. I received the June number, for which accept thanks. * * * * A good many of us here are talking of coming to your country to try our fortunes, and would like to ask you a few questions: 1. What are the chances for any one to go into the fruit business? 2. Best location for fruit raising? 3. People here talk of so much dust out there owing to the long term of dry weather. How is it? 4. Which would you advise a man to buy, improved or unimproved property? 5. What can a man find to do while his trees or vines are coming into bearing?
ROBERT LAWRE.

The above is a copy of only a few of the questions asked, and in reply we would say that the chances for fruit raising are number one and promise to be the best paying business in Southern California. Land can be had with water for from $30 to $100 per acre, or without water for from $15 to $50 per acre. Many are advocating less water than is generally used. Much of our land will grow fruit without water,—we have the proof of this remark to show anybody who will come. In regard to location we would say that there is a difference of opinion. Near the mountains you will probably require more water than on the moist lands, but the fruit in the former location may have a finer flavor. We have some dust, but never mind it. If you were here one season you would be surprised to see how little you noticed the dust. We never think of it. While your young trees and vines are coming into bearing you and your boys can raise potatoes, beans, small corn, etc., between your rows of trees, for the market, and in this way make a part, if not your entire living. As a rule we would advise buying unimproved property.

See the Centennial Guards at the Pavilion during Fair week. The like was never equaled.

THE CODLING MOTH.

This little animal so destructive to fruit trees can be eradicated easily if the farmers give it half the attention that they give to Len. J. Thompson, 36 Spring street. Mr. Thompson watches his chances, and when he sees a bargain he steps into the market and buys and by thus buying cheaply he is able to give better bargains to his customers than any other house in Los Angeles. He also makes a specialty of filling orders from the country, and will guarantee the same satisfaction to those orders as is given to the customer over the counter. The clerks at 36 Spring street are active, courteous and obliging, while Thompson—well, he is here, there and everywhere at the same time, looking after the wants of this one, that one and the other one.

The Centennial Fair and Exposition is now upon us, and parties coming to the aforesaid had better come prepared to lay in a large supply of groceries for the Fall months. Give him a trial and you will stay by him. We know whereof we speak, and don't you forget it.

THE McLellan Bros. appear in our advertising columns with many reliable insurance companies and the Pacific Coast Steamship Company. These gentlemen, by their business tact and integrity, have won the confidence of the public and are worthy of an unlimited patronage. The insurance companies which they represent are among the very best and have justly made an enviable record. For full information as regards the sailing of steamers, freights and fares we would refer you to their finely fitted up rooms over the First National Bank.

The readers of SEMI-TROPIC CALIFORNIA from San Diego, Santa Barbara, San Bernardino, and of our own county, will find a very handsome business edifice nearly opposite the postoffice which they will certainly find it to their advantage to enter and examine. Messrs. Barker & Mueller, the owners, have done much to improve our city, and have opened a first class stock of furniture, carpets, oilcloths, curtains, etc., which can be obtained at the lowest living prices. That the advertisement of these gentlemen appears in SEMI-TROPIC CALIFORNIA will be a sufficient reason for a host of our farmer friends to patronize the establishment, and we cheerfully recommend it to their attention.

Two grand choruses of over one hundred voices each—the American chorus under the directorship of J. B. Ikash, the Spanish chorus under the directorship of Prof. Arevalo—will sing on the grand stage (now being erected) at the Horticultural Fair Sept. 5-10.

THE Pacific Coast Steamship Company and the Southern Pacific Railroad will carry passengers and exhibits to the Fair at greatly reduced rates.

BRIGHT TIMES.

The "hard times" of the East, of which the citizens of the Pacific Coast know comparatively nothing — and which created cheap stores on the "cash or no trade" plan, have changed. One of the most successful merchants during the dark days in the East, was James C. Bright, who has since opened a branch store in this city, at which he is to be found attending to customers, and otherwise conducting his immense trade. His motto is to give the best quality of goods for the least money. His stock of goods are from his eastern establishment, and bought in the great manufacturing centers at the lowest possible prices. Don't take our word for it but visit his store, No. 51 Main St., the old City of Paris stand, and see the goods and quote his prices. Remember his place—James C. Bright's Cheap Store; and remember that he announces his ability to show quality, quantity and prices cheaper than ever known before.

SKILL and CAPITAL combined backed by good judgment will always succeed. The man or woman who has to buy goods from a merchant recognizes the fact that better goods at less prices can be had from the merchants who have the above named requirements. Take for example, a lady who wants a pair of shoes, she knows that A. S. McDonald is a practical shoemaker, a master of his business; that he has ample capital, and a successful business man, therefore she goes to him for her shoes.

Mr. A. S. McDonald, No. 34 Spring street, possesses the above qualifications in an especial degree. During a recent visit to San Francisco he had the good fortune to meet with a large and elegant stock of Boots, Shoes, etc., which was offered to him at a great sacrifice, and having the money in hand he purchased them.

He is now retailing the above stock at wholesale prices, and it will pay everybody to call and examine the goods before purchasing elsewhere, as it is seldom indeed that such an offer presents itself to the people of Los Angeles.

Fine custom made work is a specialty with Mr. McDonald, and having a thorough practical knowledge of the business the public can feel assured that only first class work and good material are allowed to leave the establishment.

THE editors of SEMI-TROPIC CALIFORNIA take pleasure in recommending their farmer friends and others who come to the Fair to the harness and saddlery establishment of Mr. G. W. Peachy, No. 76 Main street. Mr. Peachy is the successor of E. H. Workman, and though comparatively a new comer, has been twenty years in the business on this coast, has attracted a large trade by the excellence of his stock and reasonable prices. Those who are in need of goods in Mr. Peachy's line should call on him, examine his large stock, learn his low prices and receive your full money's worth.

Apiculture.

CHIPS FROM THE HONEY HOUSE.

ARTIFICIAL SWARMING.

To do this successfully queens should be reared and ready to furnish each new swarm with a fertile queen at time of forming such colonies, the time saved in breeding is very important.

TO REAR QUEENS.

Form a nucleus from your strongest stocks, Italians if you have them; select a comb containing capped brood and plenty of eggs and young larvæ, look it over carefully lest the old queen is on it, now cut one-third or one-half the lower part out of this comb, this gives the bees room to build cells on lower edge, a convenient place for the operator to remove them, when forming other nuclei. Place this with its adhering bees in an empty hive, and next to it other comb containing honey and bee-bread, this affords food and protection. Give the nucleus hive at least a quart of bees, and set it on a new stand and confine the bees therein until the next morning. Then contract the entrance so that but one or two bees can pass out at the same time. They will usually build six or ten or more cells on the eighth or ninth day after the nucleus was formed. Then open and with a very thin-bladed knife cut out all the cells but one, and use them immediately in forming other nuclei, by attaching each to a frame of comb and bees taken from an old stock as before described, and placed in an empty hive. In transferring queen cells care must be taken not to expose them to cold or heat, or to injuring the cell. Leave about an inch square of comb at base of cell and insert it among the young brood. Never leave a nucleus hive destitute of young brood after the young queen hatches, as the bees are very apt to abandon the hive when the young queen goes out to meet the drones. Now watch and care for the young queens until they become fertile.

WHEN AND HOW TO SWARM THE BEES.

When your stocks are strong and you are ready to form new colonies, first, cage your young queen, then from a number of old stocks take sufficient frames and bees to form a good colony of bees, close up the new swarm until the next morning, then open it, and on the second or third evening liberate the queen. You can continue in this manner until you have such increase as you desire, but in all your operations use plenty of smoke.

Again, the forwardness of the season must be your guide as to time to form your colonies. You can rear queens early and keep them in readiness; a colony of bees without fertile queen build mostly drone comb. The beekeeper that rears queens for his new colonies must have his hives for the season ready early. His success is not in the number of colonies he can have on hand, it is not bees we want, it is honey. It is not a great number of workers in one field that will secure this, but a large force

in each hive. The apiary should have the cheerful ray of the morning sun. A very good way to check robbing is to place a bunch of grass or wet hay over the entrance to the hive. The bees will find the way to their own hives, but robbers will be caught by the sentinels while passing through the grass. The moth is a scavenger which comes to clean up the wreck of the negligent bee keeper.

S. D. BARBER.

TWELVE FACTS FOR BEGINNERS.

P. A. PIKE.

MR. EDITOR:—I will offer for publication a few facts which every bee-keeper ought to know:

1. That the life of a worker bee, during the working season, is only from six to eight weeks' duration, and that a large majority of them never live to see seven weeks.

2. That a worker bee is from five to six days old before it comes out of the hive for the first time to take an airing, and that it is from fourteen to sixteen days old before it begins to gather either honey or pollen.

3. That all swarms engaged in building comb, when they have not a fertile queen, build only drone comb, and that all the comb in the lower or breeding apartment should be worker or brood comb, except a very small quantity of drone comb, four inches square being amply sufficient.

4. That the more prolific the queen is the more young bees you have, and the more surplus honey will be gathered, other things being equal.

5. That you ought never to cut moldy combs out of the hives, for the reason that you should never allow it to become molded.

6. That you ought never to double swarms or stocks of bees in the Fall, because you ought to attend to that and make them strong during the Summer by taking brood from strong stocks and giving it to the weaker.

7. That a drone laying queen should be taken away and one producing workers put in her place, else the colony will soon come to naught.

8. That as a rule, as soon as an Italian queen shows signs of old age or feebleness, the bees themselves will supersede her.

9. That all colonies should be kept strong in order to be successful.

10. That every hive should contain about two thousand cubic inches in the breeding department.

11. That beginners should be very cautious about increasing the number of their swarms or stock rapidly until they thoroughly understand the business.

12. That the hive itself, if well constructed, is all the bee-house you need in the Summer season.

If I get time I may give you my method of how to get good queen cells, at some future time.

Produce Market.

MARKET REVIEW.

We gather from our exchanges and the telegraph that the crops throughout the world are a fair average with former years. Roses promises a large wheat harvest which will off-set deficiency which may occur in the Mississippi Valley. Present showing is not high enough to advance in price for some time to come unless charters from San Francisco to Europe should decline considerably, a circumstance which is one predicted. In wheat we have a large supply from last year on hand, and the present crop, though not so large as last year's, will add very largely to it. The barley supply is light and prices are well sustained on San Francisco and here. The demand at present is limited owing to unfavorable rates in Arizona. Probably there will be more activity in a few days, however; holders are firm and the market is strong. Fruits of all kinds are in demand at good prices, also dairy and poultry products.

The following are prices paid to farmers' wagons:

WHEAT—No. 1 milling, $1.40 $1.20. No. 2, $—$1.05. inferior, nominal.

BARLEY—Strong with quick sales at 80 to 90c for feed, and $1.00 for brewing.

CORN—No change, worth for large yellow, $1.00, for small do; life a $1.00 for white.

HAY—Higher and of an upward tendency, loose $16.17, small bales, $5.50 to $9.50.

POTATOES—Early Rose $1.00 $1.00, Early Goodrich, 80 to 90c.

FRUIT—Oranges $1.50 $2.00 per box, lemons, $1.50 $2.25 per box, apples per box $1.25 $1.75, peaches $ 6 per $, pears, 5 to 6 per $, grapes $1.75 per $.

HONEY—None coming into market, old honey brings from $.75 per $.

BUTTER—Fresh choice butter bringing at 22½ to 25 per $.

CHEESE—Prices are good 12 to 15c per $ for good and $1.00 $12 for fair.

EGGS—Tendency upward, fresh sold quickly at 25 cents per doz.

POULTRY—Turkeys live per $ 12½ to 15c, live per doz., $5.00 $5.50, young do per doz., $3.00 $4.00 per doz., broilers, $2.50 $3.50 per doz. ducks, $3.50 $4.00.

BALED HAY.

The sale of barley hay depends much upon the condition in which it is baled. About nine-tenths of the hay crop that is shipped from Southern California is now baled by the Economy press. We have been acquainted with Mr. Geo. Ertel, the inventor, patentee and manufacturer, for over seven years. We have visited his manufactory in Quincy, Ill. quite frequently during that time, have "written it up" from a personal inspection, and all reports to the contrary, we can testify that Mr. Ertel's hay press establishment is one of the

among the many extensive manufactories of the beautiful city of Quincy, an honor and credit to Mr. Ertel and to his city.

The Economy Hay Press, of which the accompanying cut is a representation, has not only achieved a well merited precedence over all other hay presses, but it also retains its world-wide reputation for pressing hay, etc., more compactly than any other press in the market, hence all kinds of railroad cars may be loaded with full weight of hay. The Economy is operated with but little force, and is sold at so low a price that any farmer can buy it, and more money is made in operating this

press than can be done by any of its competitors, which fact can be fully substantiated in any locality where the Economy has been introduced. Being in use in every State and Territory in the United States and Canada, and having received the first premium over all its numerous competitors in 1880 without exception, the claims of the Economy to superiority remain undisputed.

Hundreds of endorsements could be given of the working of these presses, but we give only a few names of men who are using the Economy press. H. H. Turner, Florence, has two presses; R. Nadeau, Los Angeles, three; A. T. Cuzner, Spadra, one; M. F. Quinn, El Monte, one; Washburn & Millard, Pasadena, one; J. W. Bailey, San Bernardino, two; and many others have these presses in use in Southern California.

The Economy has the reputation of being the lightest, most easily operated and at far less expense than any other press known in the market. In fact this press is the only one giving profitable investment to its owner and operator. The following letter from Mr. Turner is about what every owner says of this press:

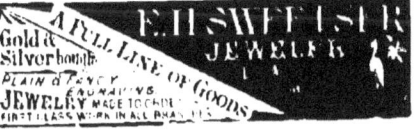

The Poultry Yard.

HOW TO KEEP FOWLS IN GOOD HEALTH.

Give them the field or orchard to run in where they can pick up worms, insects and bugs. Have a dish of lime sitting in or near the hen-house, so the fowls can help themselves as inclination prompts them. If you do this you will never have soft-shelled eggs. Every week, or at the farthest every two weeks, give them a feed of scalded cornmeal with, for fifty fowls, a large tea-spoonful of cayenne pepper and two or three spoonfuls of sulphur. Don't neglect this. If you have peppers of any kind grown on your own place, they will answer the purpose, but you should see that the shell is broken very fine before mixing with the meal. Keep a pan or bucket in a convenient place for them to drink, put into it a piece of blue vitriol as large as an egg, and give them either water or milk. Sometimes a handful of old rusty nails or any old pieces of iron thrown into the water will take the place of the vitriol. Use both if you can.

TO KEEP FOWLS FREE FROM VERMIN.

In the first place never allow hay, straw or anything of the kind to go into the hen-house. Fill your laying boxes one-third full with fresh, fine stove ashes, put in a nest egg and mother hen will complete the work. Occasionally clean the boxes and put in new ashes; if you are raising tobacco rub up a little and sprinkle it in with the ashes. Whitewash your hen house inside and out, also the roosts; for the inside work use crude carbolic acid freely in the whitewash. It is well to go over the roosts and certain parts of the inside every two or three months with this mixture. Once a month it is well to run a little kerosene oil on the roosts just before night, and when the fowls go to roost the heat of their body acting upon the oil will produce an atmosphere which will be sure death to any vermin which may be lurking in their feathers. One pint of oil will be sufficient to saturate the roosts for fifty fowls.

FEEDING FOR EGGS.

The profit of a poultry yard depends to a great extent as to how it is managed. This is true of any business. The idea should be to make every fowl pay as large a profit as possible. There is a great difference in markets, and one should be governed by them, for instance, in one market there is more demand for eggs than fowls. Then it should be the business of the breeder to cater to that trade. As a rule, I think there is more profit in eggs than fowls, unless they are early spring broilers. With proper care and feed, one can increase the number of eggs to a great extent. Hens cannot lay or produce eggs unless their food contains the elements of which the egg is composed. That is, a large share of albuminous or egg-producing elements. In addition to the quantity of albumen required in the organism of the fowl, the laying hen requires an extra amount for ovarian organization, the white of a hen's egg being about 12 per cent of albumen, and this must be furnished in her feed. By making a chemical analysis of the different grains, you will find that wheat contains a larger amount of albumen than any other grain. Therefore it is the grain to make the base for egg-producing food. The other important items are when fowls do not have a large field to range in, to give them once a day, if possible, a feed of chopped meat and more or less green food. Chickens are like the human family in one respect- in that they like a change in food. As a proof, take fowls that have been fed on one kind of grain for some time, and do not seem to have the appetite that you would think they should have, give them a little cooked food, such as a cake made from coarse corn meal and scraps together, or some other grain than that which you have been feeding, and you will see that they will jump for it and eat it in a style that will be satisfactory to the most exacting. While wheat is one of the best feeds for producing eggs, it is one of little value for fattening purposes, compared with corn, as corn contains a great deal of fatty or oily substance, which puts the flesh on fowls in a very short time. Pure water is also a very essential item to the health of fowls; or if you have milk to spare, that is better still, as it not only moistens the food, but also contributes albumen, which goes to the formation of the egg.—*American Stockman.*

THE BEST INDUSTRY FOR POOR MEN.

We know of nothing that promises so large a return for the labor and capital expended as grape-growing. There is no crop that we know anything about that is an sure your after your ten grapes. There is nothing else in agriculture, viticulture or horticulture that will yield so much money in so short a time at so little expense. Forty acres of good vineyard is better than 400 acres of wheat land. The hills are said to be as good as the valleys for grapes, and that land can be had for one-half the price or even less, and consequently a man with very little means can start a vineyard. The third year it will pay. In the meantime any industrious man can earn enough working for others to support a family. After the third year the income will increase rapidly, and in a few years a twenty-acre vineyard will be worth a small fortune. State Commissioner Wetmore gives it as his opinion that a vineyard will yield $100 an acre net profit, for wine purposes. To illustrate this: J. B. West, of San Joaquin, is reported to have sold 300 tons of grapes, produced on only twenty-eight acres, at $27 a ton, equal to nearly six thousand dollars for twenty acres. Does any man want a better chance than this? And he can do still better than that, as we have proof here in our own county, by turning our grapes into raisins. Mr. Flowers, Mr. Briggs and perhaps some others, have cleared over $300 an acre from making raisins. Practical men have abundant confidence in this industry and are enlarging their vineyards year by year. Dr. Glenn, of Colusa county, who is a practical, scientific farmer and close figurer, is reported to have put out a thousand-acre vineyard, referring to which the Stockton *Independent* says: " Dr. Glenn is no amateur experimentalist, but one of the most practical and sagacious of farmers, and would not go into the grape-growing business on so extended a scale unless he could foresee that it would pay. His example on so large a scale will most likely excite a fresh interest in this branch of industry. After all that has been said and done, it is still a matter of astonishment that a field of wealth so inviting, expansive and productive should not be more largely occupied. There is everything to encourage the vine grower in this State. The fact that we have the finest soil and climate, that the crop never fails and needs little irrigation, that the labor is light, cheerful and healthy, and that the reward is greater per acre, is certainly a great inducement. And then, hundreds of people that are unable to do hard work may find this a delightful and profitable employment." And to this we desire to add a few words from the San Jose *Mercury*, as embodying our ideas in behalf of the poor man. That paper concludes an article on the subject: "Here, then, is an inviting field for the overcrowded labor market in all our large towns and cities. Millions of acres of land, especially in the foothill and mountain counties, can be had at from $1 to $12 per acre, that are the best of grape lands. The grain-raising business, while one of the largest and most remunerative industries of the State, requires more land and capital to make it profitable than the average poor laborer can command, but every man who has a particle of energy may own a little vineyard and a snug home."— *Yolo Democrat.*

VOL. IV. *SEPTEMBER.* NO. 9.

DEVOTED TO

AGRICULTURE,

HORTICULTURE,

AND THE DEVELOPMENT OF

SOUTHERN CALIFORNIA

RICE & COLEMAN, PUBLISHERS,

LOS ANGELES, CAL.

1881.

—⊷ AND ⊷—

SOUTHERN CALIFORNIA HORTICULTURIST,

VOL. IV.   LOS ANGELES, CAL., SEPTEMBER, 1881   No. 9.

Agriculture.

MORE BARLEY AND LESS WHEAT.

It is a fact that this county is better adapted to raising barley than wheat. Year after year the farmer has been experimenting with wheat, and it has not proven satisfactory in any particular. There may be years when partial success attends the wheat crop, but these years are so few and far between that it now behooves our farmers to drop experimenting and to sow that which can be relied on for a full crop every year. Until recently the price of our barley depended solely upon the San Francisco market, and it barely paid to raise it, but now we are entirely independent of up-country markets, and barley commands about as high a price here as there. This has been brought about, of course, through the opening up of the Territories east of us, which promise to absorb all the barley that this section can produce from this time forward. Not only will we continue to have our present feeding points to supply, but the Atlantic and Pacific railroad will give us northern Arizona and northern New Mexico with the new towns which will spring up along the way. Without doubt our market, and a good one, is assured for a number of years, and if our farmers will only recognize this fact and bend their energies more to barley, they will find that there is something more connected with their industry than incessant hard labor. Barley may be sown much later in the season than wheat, it will yield nearly double the number of bushels to the acre, it is much less liable to rust, it will stand a dry season while wheat will utterly fail, and to sum it up, you are always sure of a barley crop, but of a wheat crop you are never sure. There is no good reason why this county and the county of San Bernardino should not double their barley yield.

If a choice brewing grain is raised you have the East and Europe at your door bidding for it; railroad freight rates and ocean charters will not always remain where they are now, but even with present rates our prices are such as to justify the farmer paying more largely into this industry. The time of year is drawing near when attention should be turned to the fall and winter sowing. Procrastination should never fall in the way of the farmer; always drive your work and you will see that it will succeed.

If you have any ground that can be dry sown, such as summer-fallow or volunteer,

be sure that it is seeded before the first rain comes, and be so prepared if possible after the rain is over to move into the field with sufficient force and improved machinery to do your work up quickly and well. Too much careless slip shod farming is practiced in the desire to sow a large acreage; better put in a less amount of ground and do it well than run over a large tract in an indifferent manner. It costs just as much to head an acre that yields only ten sacks as it does to head an acre that yields double that amount, the capital invested is just as large on the one acre as the other; therefore the percentage of interest on the bushel is double as much in one case as it is in the other. These facts may seem to some to be beneath their notice, but on a large ranch these items alone would amount to several hundred dollars.

Farming will certainly bear a little close, careful figuring, and the farther the farmer inquires intelligently into all the little minutiae of his business and looks to every avenue of expense and leakage, where he may save here and curtail there, the greater will be his success, and the more satisfactory will be his endeavors.

INDICATIONS OF EARLY RAINS.

It is very seldom that we have had as early as the month of August such unmistakable indications of early fall rains as are noticeable all around us this season. The violent rain-storms and cloud-bursts east and south of us show a disturbed state of the atmosphere over a large extent of country in close sympathy with us in respect to weather matters. These rain-storms have already come so near us as to materially affect our own atmosphere during and succeeding them. Then we have had very little real hot weather, and there has been a noticeable absence of north winds of that drying and poisoning character so common in some former summers. The atmosphere has been charged with an unusual degree of moisture the season through, and for weeks past this moisture has been perceptibly increasing instead of decreasing, as has been the case generally in seasons past. There have been but very few nights this summer in which we have not had more or less dew, and for some weeks past this dew has been rapidly increasing. In the early mornings now the dew is so heavy as to have a decided effect in laying the dust on the roads, and vegetation is visibly enlivened by the dampness. All these signs are favorable for an early and damp fall, though they may not go to

the extent of indicating a wet winter. Farmers have none too much time to get ready for the fall rains, and it will pay them well to employ their time in such preparations.

EUROPEAN CROP REPORTS.

London, Aug. 21.—The volume of reports on the harvest of different countries throughout the world, brought out annually are now being issued. It reports that the wheat crops in France are this year from over a larger area, and indicate a better crop than last year. This year barley is out as good as in 1840, but is fairly good; maize vary ordinary, oats and rye fair. In wheat crops generally the report shows that they are not up to those of last year, but wheat is not much below the average. None of the crops will be very good and none very bad, and acres of the crops are over average. In the Prussian States the crops are fair. The Swiss wheat crop is very poor in quantity, owing to drouth, but in quality it is very fine; oats and barley, good in quantity and quality, but there are small areas sown of the latter. In Belgium wheat is far below the average; barley good, rye and oats fair. All crops in Spain are bad. All cereals in Holland are in good condition. All reports from the United States agree that the crops will be under the average.

THE life of the nation comes from the farm. It is to this source that we must look for our national prosperity. Just in proportion as intelligence and science operate among them, just in proportion will the country assume strength and solidity. It is flatly absurd to say that any nation can be great while its people in the rural districts remain in a condition of ignorance. Such a thing has never occurred in history, and it is fair to assume that such a thing never will occur.

THE success of all business depends upon the prosperity of the farmer. When crops begin to fail and the farmers are holding their grain on hand in order to prepare themselves against emergencies, every department of human industry feels the pressure of the times. Let farmers have abundant crops, and, being a class of people who are not, as a general thing, penurious, their prosperous circumstances lighten the hearts of the miner and the railroad man, the mechanic and the laborer in the rolling mills.

Horticulture.

"OUR HOMESTEAD."

Our old brown homestead reared its walls
From the wayside dust aloof,
Where the apple bough could almost cast
Its fruit upon the roof;
And the cherry tree so near it grew,
That when awake I've lain
In the lonesome nights, I've heard the limbs
As they creaked against the pane;
And those crooked limbs — those orchard trees—
I've seen my little brothers rocked
In their tops by the summer breeze.

The sweetbriar under the window-sill,
Which the early birds made glad,
And the damask rose by the garden fence,
Were all the flowers we had.
I've looked at many a flower since then —
Exotics rich and rare,
That in other eyes were lovelier,
But none to me so fair,
For those roses bright, oh! those roses bright,
I've twined them in my sister's locks
That are laid to the dust from sight.

We had a well, a deep old well,
Where the spring was never dry,
And the cool drops down from the mossy stones
Were falling constantly;
And there never was water half so sweet
Drawn up in the curb by the rude old sweep,
That my father's hand set up,
And that deep old well, oh! that deep old well,
I remember now the flashing sword
Of the bucket as it fell.

Our homestead had an ample hearth,
Where at night we loved to meet;
There my mother's voice was always kind,
And her smile was always sweet;
And there I've sat on my father's knee
And watched his thoughtful brow,
With my childish hand in his raven hair —
That hair is silver now!
But that broad hearth's light, oh! that broad
hearth's light,
And my father's look and my mother's smile,
They are in my heart to night!

—Phœbe Cary

PARASITIC INSECTS AND THEIR REMEDIES.

It seems that the brown scale bug which in former years attacked citrus trees only is now spreading to deciduous trees, and in some sections has become a decided nuisance, if not an actual enemy. However, we are free to confess that we do not share the degree of fear of its presence among our orchards that seems to possess other writers and growers. The reason for this, though, may be found in the fact that effective measures exist, and if they are employed at its first appearance it will not be a difficult task to subdue and exterminate this pest. In the first place, if orchardists would wash and scrub their trees every spring with soft soap and water, using the soap freely, applying it with a soft rag in the hand, reaching high into the limbs and cleaning out the crotches and removing all rough bark or surfaces with a pruning knife, the cry of scale bug, woolly aphis, codling moth and other kindred insects would seldom, if ever, be heard. So much to begin with, and the beginning would be the end if applied once or twice a year. In order to reach the smaller limbs and branches a wash of concentrated lye, say a pound of lye to a pail of water administered by means of a syringe or force pump in the form of a light spray will answer the purpose and will kill every form of insect life. The wash may be even stronger, but it should be applied when the tree is in a dormant state, otherwise it will eat the foliage and tender growth and the tree may suffer permanent injury. Kerosene oil has been used in some instances with marked success; this, too, as a rule should be applied while the tree is at rest, and the high test oil is considered more effectual and less liable to injure the tree than the crude petroleum. One advantage the kerosene has over the lye is that if of the highest test it can be used at any time during the year, but the application should not be made while either trunk or foliage is in any degree moist from dew, fog or other causes. The reason is this: When kerosene strikes a dry surface it at once penetrates, but when it strikes a wet surface the moisture sheds it, as a shingle sheds the rain. Tobacco wash is another remedy which is harmless to the tree and may be applied at any time of year. Two or three pounds of dried tobacco just as it comes from the field, in a kettle of water over a hot fire for a few hours will furnish enough wash if somewhat diluted to spray several trees. Moderately strong soft soap suds may also be used during the growing season, but its action will not be so positive as that of the former remedies. The soap and lye have another virtue besides that of killing the insects: They are active fertilizers, they carry a large percentage of potash; thus while they relieve the tree externally, they administer to its strength and growth internally. There is nothing that will give a bright, healthy, thrifty look to a tree so quickly and so decidedly as a good washing with soft soap or a spraying with concentrated lye. These facts have been established beyond a doubt by careful, practical men, who experiment not for pastime, but that they may know the proper remedies to apply to exterminate the assiduous little enemies that appear in our orchards from time to time.

THE KIND OF TREES TO PLANT.

Editors "Semi-Tropic Cal."—The busy times and endless duties in and about the Cannery prevents me from writing, at this time, as fully as I would like, but will offer a few suggestions to our fruit growers who are looking to the Cannery for a market for their fruits.

The question with fruit growers, at this season of the year, is what kind of trees to plant out during the coming Winter, and what kind of buds to graft. Now, allow me to make a few suggestions, and then will give you the varieties most profitable to plant. First, never go to a nurseryman to find out what kind of trees to plant for profit; but go to some good reliable man that has had experience in the canning and packing of fruits. If you ask the nurseryman what to plant he will, most likely, name over an endless variety of such as he has, and tell you "this is good" and "that is good," and "you want five of this and five of that," as the case may be, according to the number of trees you are going to plant and nine times out of ten, if you follow his advice in selecting an orchard of a hundred trees, you will have twenty or thirty varieties. Then, what is the consequence? you are disappointed in your expectations. When your orchard is grown you have just a little of all varieties, and, of course, a large proportion worthless and the balance in such a small amount that it does not pay you to bother with it; neither is there enough for the fruit buyer to spend his time with it, and so the man with his hundred varieties is disappointed in his orchard and income. Now, I am almost a stranger here, having been here but a few months; but during so short a time I have discovered that there is but a very small proportion of the fruit brought into market that is really desirable. We will take the peaches, they are mostly George the Fourth or Royal George, Old Mexican, and a number of other worthless varieties; and right here let me say a word about bringing them into market:—They are, as a rule, picked in all stages from half grown to over ripe, all the largest and finest are over ripe and so soft that they are all bruised out of shape and entirely worthless for canning or most any other purpose. You say to them, "this fruit is in bad condition; I wish you had handled it more carefully; such as this you ought to have left on the tree for several days, and those you ought to have picked and brought to market last week;" and what is the reply? Why! they will tell you it don't pay to go over their trees so often, and so they just picked them all at once. Now, what is the buyer to do? There is a lot of worthless fruit, so much so from not being handled rightly as the varieties themselves, only one-fourth that can be used by the canner or fruit dealer; and, as a matter of course, the price is set according to condition and quality. What is the consequence? The buyer gets the benefit of all the hard names used in the English language. Never stopping to think that the buyer is not to blame; but that the fault lies with himself. In the first place, he has not a good variety, and in the second place, they were poorly handled and so he goes off dissatisfied, and says growing fruit don't pay; and that he is going to grub up his trees, and so are his neighbors, and he enumerates different kinds of crops and trees that will pay better. For instance, one gentleman says "I am going to grub up my peach trees and put out willow and gum trees;" I said all right (to myself.) If you manage the willow and gum as you do your fruit, you will be just as sick of it, and make just as great a failure as you have on your fruit.

It is just so, a man may have the best business in the world and if not properly managed he will surely make a failure of it. Now, let me tell you, that the poorer your fruit is the more pains you should take in picking and marketing it. There are a few men here that handle their fruit properly; and such men I never have any trouble with.

I look at their fruit, and I say "all right; unload it; make out their weight and hand them their ticket;" and they go away satisfied, pleased with themselves and their orchard and the big price paid them. When you plant out a fruit orchard you plant for profit. For canning the following variation of fruit are the best: Peaches, White Heath Cling, Lemon Cling and Golden Cling. The latter grown in the Sacramento valley. As to the Freestone peach, the early and late Crawford are the standards. Among pears the Bartlett is the most profitable of all others. It is both a good shipping and canning pear, and is about the only one used by canners. Plums, the White Egg and Coe's Gold Drop take the lead; they always command a high price in market. There are only two varieties of apricots that I would recommend for planting, viz; the Large Early and the Peach Apricot. Both are heavy bearers and grow very large, and are raised quite extensively at and near Santa Barbara by Joseph Seaton. There is no need of any one making a mistake at this late day in planting out an orchard. But after it is planted take care of it, and do not let your trees bear too heavily. Thin them out and pick off all the small fruit at an early stage and before it has injured the growth of the larger. Then, above all, pick and market your fruit when it is just right, and you will be pleased with the result, and you will make fruit growing profitable, have no reason to grub up your trees or find fault with the buyer.   J. J. GROOV.

CROPS WITHOUT IRRIGATION.

A writer of experience tells the San Diego *Union* that it is possible to grow large crops there without irrigation. He makes the following statements in the course of his article: "If any one would give us, free of cost, an irrigating stream or an artesian well, and agree to keep it in perfect good order, we would not in this county use either, except for raising vegetables or for household purposes. This may seem a rash assertion, but it is made upon due consideration, after several years familiarity with the best sections of this county, and a careful observation of the soils and products in different seasons, as well as in different modes of cultivation. There are soils that may require some irrigation, such as the very sandy, or that with the top-soil and hard pan close to the surface. But on nine-tenths of the arable land in our county, the soil is sufficiently deep and fine to hold all the moisture necessary for the growth of trees and vines, and even many of the vegetables in common use. All that is needed is the proper cultivation of the top soils.

"Any one who has noticed the failures to raise good corn, potatoes, etc., in this county, has doubtless observed that there was a desperate effort on the part of the crop to do something, and that it fell just as it was nearing maturity. He has also not failed to notice the fact that in almost every case the ground had not been touched since the crop was put in. A visit to the places of John Mitchell, of Fall Brook, or J. P. M. Rainbow, of the Vallecito, will go far toward convincing any one of the value of cultivation. The writer has personal knowledge of the fact that these trees never had a drop of water applied; that the level of the water in the well shows by them, and on the same level with them, is twenty-three feet below the surface. All his other varieties of fruit trees are in as thrifty a condition as his orange trees. Cultivation has done it all. At several places in Fall Brook one can see a fair piece of corn raised in the same way on dry upland, over fifteen feet from water; yet not one piece of it has had one-quarter of the cultivation that in Illinois is absolutely necessary to keep the weeds from killing the corn completely.

"Here is an experiment easily and cheaply tried. Plow a small piece of ground deeply and thoroughly; pulverize well with a harrow; stir the top for three inches every two or three weeks, and oftener if possible. Don't wait for it to bake. Don't decide by appearances that it is loose enough, but *stir it anyhow*. Put corn, potatoes, cabbages, etc., things that can be worked between the rows and both ways. After cultivating take up the good old weapon of your fathers—the hoe—and work around the hills and close to them, too.

"We have no space to discuss the philosophy of it, but it is an uncontrovertible fact that such stirring of the top soil—whether it attracts moisture from the air or from below or does both—keeps the ground just below it moist. On the places at Fall Brook above noticed we have time and again in the Fall—the driest time of the year here—scraped off three inches of the dry top soil and found the earth below damp enough to pack into a ball in the hand, and this in spots twenty-five to thirty feet above the level of the water in the well. If this position be true its advantages are enormous. It opens to our country a future such as few years ago was never dreamed of. It strikes the fetters of sterility from thousands upon thousands of acres, hitherto dreamed worth less except for stock ranges. It makes at once a capitalist of nature and puts vast possibilities into the hands of men who have been sighing for means to develop with windmills and artesian wells.

PROFIT IN FRUIT.

California fruit now practically has the world for a market, without a rival in quality. Car-loads of the fresh fruit are daily started on their journey across the continent, and they reach their destination to find a ready and remunerative market, while our canned and dried fruits are well-known and greatly prized in Europe. This demand for our fruits is not the result of any abnormal and transient condition of the fruit market, but is a gradual development of years, and is destined to increase year by year for at least a decade to come. Probably it is not generally known to the fruit growers of California that although the fruit crop was large in the Eastern States as well as in California last year, all the canned goods in the hands of packers were sold to Eastern dealers within two months after the fruit season was over. With a light fruit crop East this year, the demand for California fruits, and especially canned peaches, plums and apricots is much greater than the supply. There is a special demand for our peaches this year, as the Eastern crop is almost a failure, and the introduction of our peaches will in this way secure and will greatly enlarge the Eastern market for them, so that the supply next year will no doubt prove inadequate and the price, as this year, will rule very high.

It is slowly dawning on the minds of the average California farmer that a few acres devoted to the best varieties of fruit will pay better and prove far more satisfactory than a whole farm given up to wheat and potatoes. Great apprehension was felt lest the market would be overstocked with California fruits, a few years ago, and to-day the demand is greater in proportion to the supply than at any former period, while the actual production is not less than ten fold what it was when the greatest anxiety was expressed and the question most earnestly discussed, lest the fruit market should be glutted and hopelessly overstocked. In some remote interior counties, where no canneries have been established and fruit driers of the best kind are unknown, and where the cost of transportation will not permit the shipment of fresh fruit, there will be a surplus of fruit this year and considerable loss, but all these fruits could be canned and dried with profit, as they will be in the near future, by a little more skill and enterprise. But all fruit raised convenient for shipment to market will find ready buyers this year and for many years to come, and the owners of small orchards of well selected fruits will all be made independent, if prudent and frugal, in the next ten years.—*Resources of California.*

HOWARD & HAMER, foundrymen, corner of Second and Main streets, have just completed a large addition to their building, and with increased quarters and employes they hope to be able to supply the increasing demand for goods in their line. It is not an unusual thing to see the streets about their establishment nearly blocked with teams, each awaiting his turn.

MR. WM. LACY, cashier of the First National Bank, appears in another column with some very staunch Insurance Companies. Mr. Lacy needs no recommendation from us; the mention of his name carries confidence into the business. Geo. H. Bonebrake is acting assistant agent, with office under the Cosmopolitan Hotel.

ONE of the finest displays at the Pavilion during Fair week will be that of Detter & Bradley, the pioneer furniture house of this city, 80, 82 and 84 Main street.

Viticulture.

FILL THE GOBLET AGAIN.

A SONG

Fill the goblet again! for I never before
Felt the glow which now gladdens my heart to its
core,
Let us drink!—who would not?—since, through
life's varied round,
In the goblet alone no deception is found.

I have tried in its turn all that life can supply;
I have back'd in the beam of a dark rolling eye;
I have loved!—who has not?—but what heart can
declare,
That pleasure existed while passion was there?

In the days of my youth, when the heart's in its
spring,
And dreams that affliction can never take wing,
I had friends!—who has not?—but what tongue
will avow
That friends, rosy wine! are so faithful as thou?

The heart of a mistress some boy may estrange,
Friendship shifts with the sunbeam—thou never
canst change;
Thou grow'st old!—who does not?—but on earth
what appears,
Whose virtues, like thine, still increase with its
years?

Yet if blest to the utmost that love can bestow,
Should a rival bow down to our idol below,
We are jealous!—who's not?—thou hast no such
alloy,
For the more that enjoy thee, the more we enjoy.

Then the season of youth and its vanities past,
For refuge we fly to the goblet at last,
There we find—do we not?—in the flow of the
soul,
That truth, as of yore, is confined in the bowl.

When the box of Pandora was open'd on earth,
And Misery's triumph commenced with Mirth,
Hope was left—was she not?—but the goblet we
kiss,
And care not for Hope, who are certain of bliss.

Long life to the grape!—for when summer is
flown,
The age of our nectar shall gladden our own;
We must die—who shall not?—May our sins be
forgiven,
And Hebe shall never be idle in heaven.

—Byron.

THE BEST VARIETY OF GRAPES.

This is still an open question, but it does
seem that by this time experience should
have solved it. For raisin making, unquestionably, the White Muscat and the
Gordo Blanco are the proper varieties. All
are agreed thus far, but for wine and brandy
purposes the discussion waxes warm and
earnest. Some contend that the foreign
varieties only should be used—that the
Mission should be wholly discarded—while
the older and more experienced growers
do not express themselves so emphatically.
This variety has been much decried and
neglected for several years, but now, for its
many good qualities as a grower, a bearer
and a producer of wine and brandy, which
the people are beginning to learn, it is
coming forward as a decided favorite. The
Mission grape is less liable to mildew than
any other known variety in this section,
and while other varieties in the same field
suffer from blight, and mature only a few
scattering grapes here and there, the Mis-

sion will yield prodigiously. As regards
the attacks of noxious insects, and the liability to disease and decay, the Mission is
the last to suffer. True, it makes a strong
wine, but give it age, and it will acquire a
smoothness which will satisfy the most refined taste. That it makes a good brandy
nobody will deny, and for bearing qualities,
what variety, under a similar cultivation,
will yield as heavily from year to year?
The grower can depend on the Mission with
a certainty of a crop every year, and a
slight neglect in cultivation, owing to a remarkable vigor of the vine, does not show
itself so readily as in the foreign varieties.
But while we extol the virtues of this pioneer grape, we do not wish to underrate
some of the tested foreign varieties. Many
varieties are needed in order to meet the
taste of all. If we were to plant a vineyard for wine and brandy, our first choice
would be the Mission; second, Zinfandel;
third, Blaue Elbe, and then, for the sake of
variety, a few other kinds, but the Mission
would make the largest part of the vineyard. There may be a few readers who
will shrug the shoulder at this declaration;
be it even so, the time will come when even
they will wish they had planted more of
the Mission. It is a fact that soil and locality have much to do in establishing the
quality of the grape. The inland valleys
and mountain districts produce less to the
acre than the lower and coast sections, but
the wine in the former location is lighter,
and, for immediate use, is perhaps better
than in the latter section. However, we
have evidence from both localities in favor
of planting largely of the Mission variety.
The principal reasons have already been
stated, namely: a sure and vigorous bearer,
less liable to attacks by noxious insects than
any other variety, resists mildew and blight
better than any other variety, it is the
hardiest vine we have, and, for all purposes,
there is no other variety known that can be
so successfully used in as many ways as
the Mission.

THE BONANZA OF SOUTHERN CALIFORNIA

It is said that a word fitly spoken will
bear repeating, therefore we publish below
a recent editorial from the Los Angeles
Herald:

"What prettier life is there in the world
than that of a man who, in the nearly perfect climate of Los Angeles, buys from
thirty to forty acres of land and makes
himself a vineyard? On the supposition
that his grapes would yield him only $50
an acre net, he would have an income of
from $1,500 to $2,000 a year. But there
is absolutely no exaggeration in putting
the net yield per acre at $75 to $100, and
where the vineyardist also makes his own
wine, at much higher figures. Of course,
there is no income until the third year, and
even then the grape vines are not in full
bearing order, but, once fairly under way,
they live practically forever. There are
vineyards in the San Gabriel Valley which
are quite one hundred years old, and that
are even now prolific bearers. Mr. W. H.

Workman last year netted $200 an acre
from a portion of his vineyard, which is
over sixty years old. Thus the delay and
inconvenience of waiting are well repaid,
in the end. No man, however, should attempt the experiment unless he likes an
open air life, and has money enough to see
the thing through. He should be able to
buy his land and put upon it the necessary
improvements, with an overplus sufficient
to see him through the probationary period.
The inducements held out for Los Angeles
County are, to those who have at least small
means, and to such the return is large if
not immediate. There is nothing like it on
the American continent, or even in France.
The yield of the grape is something to
marvel at, ranging from four to, in some
extreme cases, ten tons to the acre. Last
year grapes sold for from $20 to $25 a ton,
some very choice grapes going as high as
$30 to the ton. Eligible lands for vineyards
can be had anywhere for from $15 to $40
per acre, according to quality and location.
Right here is the genuine bonanza of
Southern California."

CALIFORNIA'S FUTURE WEALTH.

The following is an extract from the ad-
dress of Lloyd Tevis, President of Wells,
Fargo & Company, before the American
Bankers' Convention, at Niagara Falls, New
York, on the 30th inst.:

"It is already evident that in the agricultural capabilities of her soil lie the possibilities of California's greatest wealth.
California is, to-day, not a mining but an
agricultural State. Her wheat crop last
year, after supplying all home demands,
including that of distilling, gave a surplus
for export of not less than 1,400,000 tons—
a surplus worth, even at the low rates that
prevailed on account of the scarcity of
tonnage, $37,500,000, or more than twice
the whole bullion product of the State.
Or, to put it in another way, the wheat
crop of California for 1880 was worth more
than half as much as the bullion product
of the whole United States.

VALUE OF THE VINEYARD AND ORCHARD.

But great as are the possibilities of grain-
growing in California, it is now becoming
apparent that the most valuable of her industries in the future will be that of the
vineyard and orchard. California by its nature
is the France of America; yet, in spite of the
natural adaptation of her soil and climate
to the culture of the grape, wine-making
in California has had many difficulties to
contend with, arising partly from want of
experience as to soils, varieties, modes of
culture and manufacture; partly from the
necessity of developing the proper organization and machinery, and partly from the
time required to gain a reputation and
secure an assured market. It is only within
the last few years that all these difficulties,
inseparable from the naturalization of a
new industry, may be said to have been
overcome. The grape-growers of California
can now sell their grapes as certainly as the
farmer can sell his wheat, and at far more re-

numerative prices. There is an apparently limitless demand for the purpose of supplying you, gentlemen of the Eastern States, with what you deem to be foreign wines, while some California wines are already beginning to make a reputation which it does not pay to disguise under a foreign label. California is now sending to the Atlantic Coast more wine than is imported from France, and it is estimated that the wine crop of last year yielded to the growers nearly $3,500,000. The curing and packing of raisins has only recently commenced, but it is already an assured industry.

MARKET FOR CALIFORNIA WINES AND FRUITS.

What is true of the product of the vine is also true of the product of the orchard. For the finer qualities of fruit, such as will bear long railroad transportation, or are preferred by the canners, there has been developed a market which it seems impossible to glut. In San Francisco, in Alameda and San Jose, are fruit canning establishments, which during the busy season, employ over a thousand hands apiece, and all over the State, wherever there is an important fruit district, this industry is rapidly developing. Orchards of the finer varieties of peaches, plums, pears, nectarines, etc., are being set out in all parts of the State, and in the southern section the culture of semi-tropical fruit is attaining large dimensions. Considerable quantities of fresh fruit, carefully selected and packed, are forwarded by express to Eastern cities, even at the high rates of freight now ruling, and with cheaper railroad communication, or a means of preserving fruit so as to enable it to stand the slower carriage of the regular freight trains (which, it is now said, has been discovered), this business must enormously increase."

CALIFORNIA WINES.

California is the only country in the world that sends to market pure wines, free from admixture of any kind. But now our first-class wine men complain that some are using grape sugar, extracted from corn and vegetables, to doctor inferior wines. Last week we saw a notice that a dealer had received from France extra superior claret, on sale at $1.50 a gallon, and an equally low price in bottles. On tasting we said, "That wine is not from France; no claret of such body and bouquet was ever made in Europe. They haven't the sun to ripen grapes into wine like that." He replied that French labels made it sell to thousands who would not buy it if they thought it was American. Public attention should be called to California claret especially, for its manifest superiority to what is imported. Two French experts differ as to the cause of the body, spirit, and high bouquet of our wines. One attributes it to the richness of our soils and their sunniness. The other says nay; it is their prolonged season without rain or storm, and their everlasting sunshine. It is too much of a good thing; your wines are too strong. But if we had

some of them we could make them first-class by our treatment. They say ours is raw wines. "It needs skillful treatment to adapt it to the popular taste." Our Consul informs us that the falling off of vintage by the phylloxera greatly shortens the wine product, though for every gallon short from the vineyards a gallon and a half is supplied by art. Around Paris alone are seven very large factories making artificial wines to order from rotten apples, damaged dried fruits of all kinds, from beets, and from spoiled molasses; also largely from glucose made from potatoes. Petitions are presented to the government to put a stop to the fraud. The petitioners, who are dealers, assert that not one-third of the wine consumed in Paris is made from grapes. How does that sound to our souls who turn from American grape-juice to patronize what is foreign. Never was planting so active among vinters as it is now. Wine pays, and grapes bring advanced prices. Orders for certain kinds of wine are in excess of supplies, and for every kind the demand promises to be ample at full rates. The French government is prohibiting the use of certain ingredients essential to making these wines, and curtailing the use of other elements less injurious to the health. A late law forbids the mixing of more than half the usual quantity of potassium sulphate in making artificial wines. These restrictions increase the sale of California wines to fortify the artificial.—*Baltimore Sun.*

SURE DEATH TO RABBITS.

Many remedies have been advocated to abate the rabbit nuisance, and all claim some merit, but the following one from the *Rural Press* it seems has proved to be very effective:

"It is believed that a practical extermination of hares and rabbits can be effected in many communities by a concert of well directed efforts. It is reported that in New Zealand and Australia the prevalence of rabbits has been a source of terror to the inhabitants, insomuch that it is made a subject of legislation, and the rural police are instructed to see that the land owners use means of destruction prescribed by law. Phosphorized baits have proved a most efficient agent, for which the following recipe is employed in their preparation:

1 ℔. phosphorus.
2 ℔. dark sugar.
8 gallons water.

Boil, and stir slowly and cautiously 10 minutes; then stir in 180 ℔s. of oats, to remain until saturated. Nearly all kinds of vermin eat it with avidity, and always with fatal results. By its use rabbits are said to be destroyed by the hundreds of thousands.

Being much troubled with hares, rabbits and squirrels amongst my crops, I recently made a test of a similar preparation, as follows:

1 silk phosphorus.
½ ℔ brown sugar.
3 gallons water.

Heated as above, and 20 ℔s wheat ad-

ded. After soaking for half an hour (being kept hot and occasionally stirred), I added enough wheat middlings to absorb the remaining liquid, and, by stirring, gave a coating to the grains of wheat. The preparation was then dried by being spread in the sun upon a flat rock. The rest is a mere trifle.

One-half of this quantity was scattered through the trails along the outskirts of the ranch, several parallel trails being traversed and about a dessert spoonful dropped at the intersection of each cross-trail; also, numerous deposits were made in the squirrel colonies.

The effect was most remarkable. The squirrels have entirely disappeared, and not one hare is now to be seen where previously they could be counted by dozens trooping down from the hills. They will doubtless stray in from neighboring ranches; but I am firmly persuaded if all my neighbors would act together, covering an extended range, using liberal quantities of the poison, and occasionally repeating the treatment, we could rid ourselves of the evil, and turn our profitless hillsides and outlands into vineyards, whose returns would require the owners, and whose verdure would bless the vision of each passing traveler.

D. S. CHASE.
Poway, San Diego Co., Cal., Aug. 8, '81.

ANAHEIM VINEYARDS.

The grapes are fast ripening, and the vintage is expected to begin about the middle of September. Whether the average yield will come up to the phenomenal product of last year is a question that is very hard to answer. Some vineyards will yield much more than last year, others an equal amount, and still others much less. As a rule, the grapes are smaller than last year, but this deficiency is counterbalanced by the fact that the bunches are generally larger. Of one thing we have ample proof —the vineyards of Anaheim are healthier and thriftier than those of either San Gabriel or Los Angeles. In the former place no irrigation, in the latter place too much irrigation. These, we think, are the reasons, succinctly stated, which make the vineyards inferior to those of Anaheim. Here, for two or three years past, the great bulk of irrigation is done in Winter; none of the largest vineyards never receive a drop of water later than March, and this system has been found to give the best results. Our mere pretensions but less sanguine neighbors should profit by our example.—*Anaheim Gazette.*

Our advices from every section point to a large grape crop. The large wineries are already contracting for grapes at about last year's prices, and are preparing, we understand, to do a much larger business this year than ever before. Surely our grape industry is very promising, and this winter will witness a boom in vineyard planting.

MILDEW is a fungus growth, which can be killed by sprinkling the leaves with pulverized sulphur.

Southern California.

1781.}   HISTORICAL.   {1881.

"TO-DAY WILL SOON BE YESTERDAY."

The history of the city of Los Angeles properly belongs to three periods, namely, the period of Mission rule, when the edicts of the Friars were law and everything was subservient to their will; the period of Spanish rule after the independence of Mexico and the downfall of the Mission power; the period of American occupation and the progress which has resulted in building a beautiful, prosperous city. Each period had its separate and distinct work to perform, and that each did its work well is evident when the instruments and advantages of the different periods are properly considered. With the Friars from Mexico came a body of Mexican regulars to act as guards to these zealous missionaries and to perform such other duties as needed their services. This band of regulars was divided among the many Missions established along the coast, and as their term of service expired, most of them being married and having families, their next move was a very important one to them. It was one of the conditions of founding the Missions that a white man could not settle upon the land claimed by the church, consequently, to accommodate the retiring soldiers, who had become enamored of the country it was necessary to establish pueblos or colonies beyond the precincts of these sacred confines.

Every settlement of this kind that was made in conformity with the home government received certain aid and emoluments which enabled it to begin under very favorable auspices. Each retiring public having a family received his regular pay and rations for three years, besides two oxen, two mares, two mules, two goats, two sheep, two cows with one calf, one hog and a donkey were given to each settler, to be paid for in small installments. In order to secure these advantages a number of soldiers at the Mission San Gabriel, whose term of service had expired, petitioned the home government to set aside a portion of land for their use.

This was done by the then Governor of California, Don Felipe de Neve, who, on the 20th of August, 1781, issued an order that the pueblo of Los Angeles should be founded, which was done on the 5th of September of the same year, under the name of Pueblo de Nuestra Señora de Los Angeles.

The soldiers, twelve in number, with their families, making in all forty-six persons of both sexes, began the settlement by laying out a public square in the form of a parallelogram one hundred varas long by seventy-five wide. On three sides of this square and fronting it were located twelve resident lots, one-half of the remaining short side was given to public buildings and the other half was left an open space. Besides this, at a short distance from the

public square, and upon the rich soil near the river, where the waters of the river could be used for irrigating purposes, they laid out thirty fields for general cultivation. These fields contained forty thousand square varas each and were mostly laid out in the form of a square and separated from each other by narrow lanes. They were devoted to vineyards, orchards, corn, barley and wheat raising, together with certain kinds of vegetables, but the principal occupation of the settlers was raising cattle and horses, for the grazing of which they enjoyed the entire surrounding country. The settlers, however, at that time, could not acquire a title to their lands and held them only by virtue of the general law of possession; still justice was in store for them, though somewhat tardy. In 1821 Mexico declared her freedom from Spain, and very radical changes in the general laws were at once instituted, and in 1833 the granting of titles to land came into practical operation. The government of the settlement was a compound of political and military. The chief officer, the Alcalde, was appointed by the Governor, before whom all grievances were tried. In their easy going way the wants of the settlers were few and easily supplied. They had little or no intercourse with the outside world until 1820, when foreign vessels, principally American, began to call at San Pedro and exchange goods for hides and tallow. Some ten years later trade with Arizona, New Mexico and Sonora was brought about through the enterprise of American hunters and trappers. Thus briefly have we glanced over the first fifty years. We began with forty-six souls and a virgin soil, and at the close of the first half century we find a city of six or eight hundred inhabitants, with a goodly number of productive orchards and vineyards, and large bands of cattle and horses roaming over the commons belonging to the settlement. The subsequent history of Los Angeles is too recent and familiar to the general reader to require anything more than a passing notice here. General intercourse with the outside world wrought an entire change over the former tranquility of the settlement. Internal commotion, strife, and often bloodshed, marked the way up to and through the Mexican war times, and even after that period history points us to some very dark, bloodthirsty deeds, in most of which foreigners—that is, other nationalities than Mexicans and Spaniards—were the principal actors. Since the close of the war of 1860-1865 the growth of Los Angeles has been rapid and permanent. Some of the business blocks would do justice even to New York, Boston and other Eastern cities. From the hills back of town where Fremont's cannons dictated terms to the city in 1846 a beautiful panorama meets the view. Among the hills, at their feet and beyond, lies a city of twelve thousand inhabitants. Orchards, vineyards, and beautiful homes stretch away off into the hazy distance. Five lines of railroad with their busy life center at our feet, telegraph lines reach out to every quarter of the globe, indeed the transfor-

mation is complete, and we are lost in contemplating the changes that another hundred years will bring.

SANTA ANA AND TUSTIN.

The southern end of Los Angeles county has made most gratifying progress during the past year. This section depends upon its own merits, and has not had the liberal advertising which other portions of California have so freely indulged in, but every settler, during the past two years, seems to have appointed himself a committee of one to bring out as many of his friends and relations as possible to settle in the beautiful semi-tropic valley. It is a fact that shrewd business men, and not a few of them either, after traveling over all portions of the Pacific Coast have purchased homes near Santa Ana, and since spent thousands of dollars in improvements.

PRESENT STATUS OF SANTA ANA.

Santa Ana is located thirty-four miles from Los Angeles, six miles from Anaheim and about ten miles from the ocean. It is connected with Los Angeles, San Francisco and the East by the Southern Pacific Railroad, which has its southern terminus in the flourishing little town. Outside of the county seats no town in Southern California has a larger trade or a more hopeful future.

FACTS ABOUT FRUIT.

In the immediate vicinity of Santa Ana fruit growing will, probably, be the principal industry. The orange, lemon and lime grow to perfection, and there is seldom frost enough to injure even the tender banana. The soil is, principally, a light sandy loam, easily worked and very productive. Nearly everywhere in this portion of the Santa Ana Valley irrigation, after the first year of setting out an orchard is not only not essential, but is held by many experienced fruit growers to be injurious. Still some fine and productive orchards are regularly irrigated, and a positive rule cannot be laid down, as different grades of soil require different treatment.

WINTER IRRIGATION.

When the winter rains are insufficient, winter irrigation is certainly very advantageous. A thorough soaking at this time will frequently assure crops which might otherwise be uncertain. The fruit having the finest flavor is undoubtedly produced without irrigation; but irrigation increases the size.

THIS SEASON'S FRUIT CROP.

The fruit crop in the vicinity of Santa Ana has not been quite up to the usual standard this year in quantity, although the quality has never been superior. This does not apply to the last orange crop, which was very large and exceedingly fine. Nearly every enterprising farmer put out a vineyard last Spring, and the oldest vineyards in bearing will have a fair average crop the present season.

THE RABBIT PEST.

The greatest pests with which vineyardists in Los Angeles county, who reside on the outskirts of the principal settlements, have to contend with are the rabbits. These mischievous little animals are very fond of the tender shoots of the vine, and speedily destroy a young vineyard. Unquestionably the most effective remedy for this evil is a well constructed lath or shake fence. The expense of this plan is considerable and has deterred many from putting out vineyards. Dr. M. S. Jones, of Santa Ana, has another method which, although it may be known to many of our readers, will do no harm to relate. Taking advantage of the fact that rabbits have a strong aversion to blood, he procures a quantity from the slaughter houses, dilutes it, and thoroughly sprinkles his vineyard each month. The expense is but trifling and the result, in his case, at least, has been highly satisfactory.

TRADE OF SANTA ANA.

The town of Santa Ana commands the trade of a fertile country many miles in area. The merchants are enterprising and liberal, and the continual influx of new comers and new building enterprises inaugurated render trade good for the mercantile community and abundance of labor for mechanics. We do not hesitate to say that no community on the Pacific Coast offers greater advantages to new comers with some capital than Santa Ana.

TUSTIN.

Tustin is, properly, a suburb of Santa Ana, and a very garden spot. Here the semi-tropical orchards have made astonishing progress during the past six years, and the fruit product of the Tustin settlement is already very large. Tustin has been especially blessed by the advent, during the past five years, of a wealthy and enterprising class of settlers who have constructed comfortable and, in many cases, elegant houses; planted the best varieties of trees and vines and given them the best care and cultivation.

PRINCIPAL VARIETIES OF FRUIT.

Tustin is especially adapted to the semi-tropical fruits. Although the San Francisco market was overcrowded with sour and poor oranges last Spring, and the price, consequently, much lowered; the fruit raised in Tustin and the adjoining country was in good demand and commanded a fair price. The lemon and lime escaped, last Winter, the sharp frosts which visited the upper portion of the county, and as the demand for these fruits is continually increasing all these trees which are now in bearing will, probably, find an improving market each year.

THE AREA IN VINES.

In yearly increasing, each new comer putting out from twenty to forty acres. The Muscat seems to be the favorite, although all the leading varieties are well represented. Raisin making is a great success in the neighboring settlement of Orange, but we have not as yet heard of any experiments in Tustin. We have heard of no damage from mildew, and insect pests on the grape are thus far unknown.

THE TUSTIN FRUITS.

The visitors to the Horticultural Fair,

last Fall, will remember the fine display of apples, pears, figs and other deciduous fruits made by the Tustin settlement; all were of the best quality and attracted much attention. A Cannery will be required, within the next five years, for the Tustin and Santa Ana settlements to consume the large fruit surplus which can thus be economically shipped to all portions of the world.

IMPROVEMENTS AT TUSTIN.

The Tustin settlement has had an addition of several families since the first of the year. Mr. N. Vanderlip has purchased twenty acres of fine fruit land and is erecting a large and handsome house. Mr. J. S. Rice has just completed a $3,000 house, and we understand that another new comer, Mr. Vandermuellen, will shortly build. A gentleman from Riverside is also building a cottage and several other parties are contemplating extensive improvements.

THE CITRUS FAIR.

That our tourists and visitors may better appreciate the growth and improvement of the Santa Ana country, the Southern California Horticultural Society contemplate holding a citrus fair at Santa Ana next Spring. If sufficient encouragement is given to the project a new impetus will be given to horticultural pursuits, which will add much to the development of the resources of these young and growing settlements.

THE CAUSE OF CALIFORNIA'S WET AND DRY SEASONS.

BY H. U. BARROWS.

Of course everybody is familiar with the homely phenomenon of the condensation of water at the mouth of the tea-kettle spout, —the simple explanation of which is that the current of air, laden with moisture, passing from a *hot* to a *cold* atmosphere, is chilled, and the humidity or water, in attenuated solution that it carries is suddenly condensed into aggregated and visible drops. In other words, invisible moisture or vapor, by passing *from warm to cold*, becomes visible water. One's breath in cold weather illustrates the same phenomenon.

A reverse current, i. e., from *cold to warm*, produces a contrary result, dissipating instead of condensing the moisture. People talk about timber and cultivating the land, and laying railroad tracks, and commanding, and what not, as being rain-inducers; but the principle above referred to has more to do in determining or governing the rain question than any and all other reasons put together. Whenever the currents of the atmosphere carrying moisture tend towards a cold region from a warm one the inevitable effects will be to retard and chill and condense the floating moisture, and if the humidity is great and the change of temperature sudden, to precipitate it in rain, or hail, or snow. Herein, in a nut shell, is the whole theory of rain

in all countries, in all climates, and in all seasons.

Now if the above theory is true, no argument and no explanation are needed to show that its *concerns* must be true. Heat disperses and dissipates. "Old Salts" tell us that the trade winds of the Pacific blow towards the *southwest* during the six months of the year corresponding to our dry season. Except that for two hundred or three hundred miles off this coast, they are each day *diverted* towards the *southwest*. What is the cause of this diversion? Why, as the sun rises and heats up each day with million-furnace power the sands of the great Colorado Desert, the air over all that vast region becomes rarified and rises, producing a vacuum, which the diverted wind-currents of the Pacific rush in to fill. Whatever humidity they contain is *dissipated or dispersed*, moving as it does, with those currents, from a *cool* region to a warm, i. e., from the ocean to the superheated sands of the desert.

All the facts in the experience of all who live on this coast agree with this theory. We daily see, if we take any notice of the matter, that every morning in summer (or whilst the sun is north of the equator), say from 8 to 11, as the sun over the mountains begins to heat up the desert, the wind begins to rise and gets stronger and stronger, till some time in the afternoon, when our temperature differs very little from that of the ocean itself, because it comes directly from the ocean; and then, as the sun goes down the wind goes down with it, the sands of the desert, cooling quickly (being only superficially heated), after the sun's rays are intermitted, while the ocean does not cool so quickly; and as a result often a breeze blows in the night from the land towards the ocean.

One of the effects of these daily breezes (from a cold to a warm atmosphere) is to gather up all the fog (that we would otherwise be liable to have constantly, as we are near the ocean, and also all the floating clouds and to dissipate them, and thus it is that we have our charming cloudless skies during our long California summers. And what is more to the point than mere sentimentality, especially living as we do in a latitude where the sun, a portion the year, is nearly directly overhead,—these midsummer breezes, coming directly and constantly each day from the ocean, and are thus invigorating instead of debilitating.

Our peculiar situation thus between an ocean and a desert, although it gives us a long, dry summer, by the simple operation of natural laws, also gives us during all that long summer the grateful, bracing breezes that not only make the semi-tropical heat of our locality tolerable, but they in fact help to make our climate one of the finest, if not the finest, in the world.

In winter, as the sun recedes south of the line, it does not heat the desert so fiercely each day, and then we are liable to have wind currents from other directions,—from the warm south to a colder north, and with them rains, as in other parts of the world.

Carp Culture.

THE CARP AND ITS CULTURE.

In the accompanying engraving we reproduce a careful drawing of the mirror carp, *cyprinus carpio speculars*, so-called on account of the large scales which run along the sides of the body. This is one of three races of carp recently introduced into this country, the other two being the scale carp and the leather carp; the one entirely covered with scales, the other having few, or none.

The carp was first introduced into this country from Germany, where it has been cultivated for food for years, and its value has been widely known. The first experiments with this fish in this country were made by our Government, at Washington, and its superior worth was soon evident. From this quarter the fish has found its way into numerous lakes, rivers and ponds throughout the land. But our main desire in calling attention to it, is to show the feasibility of its culture in small ponds on our farms and ranches. Already there are a few carp ponds in this southern country; the seed, of course, came to this coast from Washington, and we know from this that we have the most desirable variety. Mr. Pettit, of San Bernardino, is our pioneer carp man in Southern California, he having begun the culture some two years ago, and is now, we learn, beginning to market fish at good prices. Near Florence we have another pond in the willows, a capital place, and probably another year will see some of the fish in our city markets. Major Tuler, some months ago, put five hundred young fish into one of our city reservoirs, and unless the small boy begins with hook and line too soon, we will shortly have a reservoir full. We learn that another gentleman has recently started a pond just a short distance east of the city, and flatters himself that, in a year or so, he will have a bonanza in partially supplying the city with a fish much superior to that which we generally get from our neighboring waters.

This fish is probably of Asiatic origin, and has been domesticated in China for thousands of years. It is emphatically the farmer's fish, and may safely be claimed to be, among fishes, what chickens are among birds.

Its special merits lie in its sluggishness and the ease with which it is kept in very limited enclosures, its being a vegetable feeder, and its general inoffensiveness. It thrives in shallow ponds, and lives on the succulent roots and leaves of aquatic plants, seeds as they fall into the water, and other similar substances, and may be fed very readily upon corn, grain, bread, root crops —raw or boiled, and, indeed, any vegetable refuse. The carp thrives best in artificial or natural ponds with muddy bottoms, and such as abound in vegetation. In large ponds it may not be necessary to furnish any special food, but in restricted enclosures of less than an acre, they may be fed on the refuse from the kitchen garden; leaves of cabbage, lettuce, turnips, and any kind of boiled grain.

In this climate this fish spawns from April to October; they are very prolific, one fish yielding from 400,000 to 500,000 during a single season. The eggs adhere tenaciously to whatever they touch, and for that reason it is very important that a new pond should be provided with floating weeds for such attachment. The eggs hatch out in a few days, and the young grow very rapidly. They feed voraciously upon the so-called frog spittle, the green alga scum so common in frog ponds; consequently such waters are especially adapted to carp.

As regards the best plants for a carp pond, Professor Baird mentions the ordinary pond weeds (*Pontederia* and *Sagittaria*), splatter dock, or pond lily, and, indeed, any of the kinds that grow in the water, with leaves floating upon the surface, duckweed among the number. Those which produce seed, like the wild rice, are especially desirable, as the fish feed voraciously upon them.

Ponds must not be too deep, as the water will be too cold, and will harbor fewer insects, larvæ, and worms, which form part of the carp's food. A depth of 3 feet is sufficient for the center of the pond. Toward the outlet sluice it may be from 4 to 5 feet, but only for an area of from 200 to 1,000 square feet. In the depths of this "collector," the fish seek their resting place for winter, as also in summer when the water becomes too warm. The outer part of the pond should not be deeper than 1 foot for a distance of 50 to 100 feet.

Toward the center of the pond a cavity is dug 2 feet deeper than the rest of the pond; this also serves the fishes as a resting place in summer and winter. This cavity is called a "kettle." From the entrance of the pond to the other end, where the collector and the outer sluices are situated, two or three ditches, 2 feet in depth and 4 feet in length must be made; these ditches cut the deeper "kettles" transversely as far as the collector. These ditches are intended to carry all the fish into the collector when the pond is being drained. The collector is nothing but a place from 20 to 40 feet in length and breadth, near the outer sluice, and is 1 foot deeper than the rest of the bottom of the pond. This collector must be cleaned out every year, or the fish will become too much soiled by the mud. The inflow of water into a pond should never be direct, as, for instance, a brook falling into it, as this often causes the water to suddenly rise, carrying into the pond injurious

THE MIRROR CARP.

fishes. The inlet sluices from the stream must, of course, be of a strong and practical construction, and they ought to be provided with gratings to prevent other fish from intruding. It will also be found very useful to construct a hatching place, on some flat and sunny spot, near the bank; that is, a so-called cut in the land, measuring 40 to 100 feet in length, and from 30 to 50 feet in breadth, and having a depth of from 18 inches to 5 inches. This cut should be planted with aquatic plants, and ought to be the only place where the carp can ascend from deep water in order to deposit their eggs conveniently on the plants and engage in the spawning process. As soon as this has taken place, the entrance to the cut is closed with a net, so that the eggs cannot be eaten by the fish.

The rules laid down here are, of course, not arbitrary, but are intended to give the reader a general idea of pond construction, which he can modify to suit his convenience.

The culture is attended with so little care that every farmer, who has a pond of water of any considerable size, can soon have it stocked with fish. The reservoirs which are used in many places to collect water

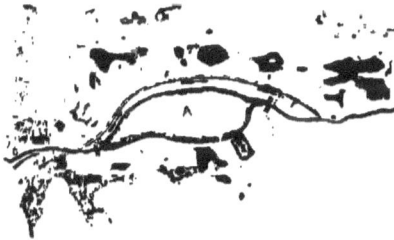

Fig. 1.—Simple Pond.

for irrigating purposes could be very profitably turned to this use without interfering in the least with their irrigating capacity. Sluggish water is better for this fish than a clear, running stream; a muddy bottom, where it can wallow, together with growing grass and weeds around the edges are most desirable. Near most of these country reservoirs we find an alfalfa patch; if a handful were thrown into the pond, the farmer would be surprised to see how soon it would be devoured. The same could be said of refuse apples, peaches, pears and other fruits, also potatoes, melons, turnips, etc., in fact, anything that a hog will eat may be considered good food for the carp. Its growth is very rapid; this years' spawn will be ready for the house table next year, and for the market the year after. It is in its prime when it weighs from three to five pounds, which weight it attains in the second year, but at twenty pounds, its full growth weight, it loses but little of its finness and sweet flavor. It is said that specimens have been taken that weighed even a hundred pounds, but this weight is an exception to the rule. The cut of the first pond, upon examination, will be found to be very simple and easy of construction; this would be well suited for a domestic pond, owing to the small area which it may occupy.

Explanation of Fig. 1.—A is the pond; B is the out, or breeding pond. The dotted line contains the water having a depth of only 5 inches; D is the water of 1½ feet in depth; F F is the outer ditch to prevent an overflow of the pond; G is the inlet sluice, and E is the outlet sluice.

Explanation of Fig. 2.—This is on a little larger scale than pond No. 1. P is a natural pond. It is formed by a dam, D, about seven or eight feet high, crossing a valley, and thus collecting the water of a run flowing there. Before D is a deepening, C, the collector. In the dam, D, there is an outlet leading to another deepening, the so-called outlet collector, O C. The purpose of this collector is to retain fish that may have passed through the outlet when opened. It is provided with a screen or netting, C D. Upon the bottom of the pond, F, is the collector ditch which conducts the fish to C when the water is let out, and thus prevents them from being caught in the mud. R is the run of water, which, to prevent overflow, has to be conducted around the pond in a separate ditch, leaving an inlet at J protected with screens.

We believe that there are many locations in Southern California, which, with but a very small outlay, might be formed into carp ponds, and the rapidity of increase and growth, and the demand and high price paid for the fish as food, would largely repay for all the trouble and expense. That climate is admirably adapted to this culture, and the few who have already gone into the business report favorable progress.

The fountain aquarium, in the Pavilion, will be stocked with carp during Fair week,

Fig. 2.—Larger and More Complicated.

and visitors interested can learn more fully about the business from parties in attendance, who will cheerfully answer any and all questions, to the best of their ability.

Corn syrup can be made from the juice of watermelons. Six gallons of juice will make one gallon of syrup.

The orange crop in Louisiana is reported to be a failure.

The specific virtue of this destroyer of rodents and obnoxious insects has during the last year manifested itself in numerous favorable reports from those who have tried it throughout the State. To those who are as yet unfamiliar with its use and efficacy the following items of testimonial resident of Los Angeles county will doubtless convince the uninformed:

SAN MATEO, August 13, 1881.

Mr. JOHN H. WHEELER, San Francisco—My Dear Sir: I am glad to know that you will give our people an opportunity of seeing your Carbon Bisulphide during the coming Fair. While my personal experience in the use has been limited, yet it has been great enough to convince me that as a means of killing squirrels, gophers, etc. It is unquestionably the best now in use and I believe will be universally adopted. It is more potent than any other poison I know of, and its use is not attended with the same dangers that belong to phosphorus, strychnine, etc., so deadly and unsafe. The distribution of the ordinary poisons is always dangerous, and many destructive fires occasioning the crops that jeopardise to save from the ravages of the squirrels may be traced to the use of phosphorus. I therefore take great pleasure in endorsing your Carbon Bisulphide, and trust it may shortly become, as I believe it will be, universally used by all provident farmers throughout the state. I am, sir, very truly yours,

J. DE BARTH SHORB

In explanation of the bisulphide, it is a heavy volatile liquid which passes into a vapor immediately on exposure to the air. The vapor formed is poisonous to insects and small animals, though not in many unless breathed in strong doses for a long time and that without access to free air. The vapor formed is three times heavier than air (can be poured from one vessel to another) and flows down a squirrel hole like water; then as it continues to expand, as all vapors do, it forces itself into every department of the squirrel, rat or gopher hole, and one breath of the vapor is sufficient to destroy the animal.

The advantages of the poison are summed up as follows: There is no danger in its use such as attends the use of all other poisons; it kills only the animal in the hole, which breathes the vapor, whereas strychnine, phosphorus, etc., is as apt to kill the pet dog, sheep, birds, etc. The animal cannot get away from the vapor nor does it try, but dies immediately and without pain—other poisons may be avoided, and when taken hold by long and hard suffering—with bisulphide all within the hole die and remain there, while other poisons bring them out to create a stench and poison the dog and other pets.

As prepared by John H. Wheeler, the only manufacturer on this Coast, it is put up in convenient packages with complete directions for use. These packages are kept by druggists and keepers of general merchandise. Persons desiring a quantity should address John H. Wheeler, 111 Leidesdorff street, San Francisco.

To rabbits glue your trees and vines, mix a pint of blood with a pail of water and with a sprinkler or hay swab put a little of the mixture on the vines and trunks of your trees. Pure blood is best.

SEMI-TROPIC
CALIFORNIA.
—AN—
ILLUSTRATED MONTHLY.

Devoted to Agriculture, Horticulture, and the Development of Southern California.

Terms: $1.00 per Annum, in Advance.

OFFICE, Rooms 8 & 10, Baker Block

Address, · RICE & COLEMAN, Los Angeles, Cal.

GEORGE RICE, } Editors and Prop'rs.
CHAS. COLEMAN, Jr., }

OFFICIAL PAPER
—OF THE—
Southern California Horticultural Soc'y.
OFFICE, ROOM No. 8, BAKER BLOCK.
GEO. RICE, Secretary.

ANY hints which our former readers will give us, as to new and useful methods connected with farming interests, will be gladly given to our many readers through the columns of this journal. Do not hesitate to send in something of that sort, and rest assured we will give it due and respectful attention.

N. W. GRITCHELL, of Vernon, has placed upon our table a specimen of the Salway peach. It weighs fourteen ounces, and measures 12½ by 13½ in circumference. We believe that this is just a little ahead of all others heard from to date.

OWING to the rush of business in arranging for the coming Fair, we have been forced to defer our visit to San Bernardino until next month; consequently we trust that our readers will bear patiently with us until our next issue, when San Bernardino, fully illustrated, will appear without fail.

IT is our desire that a copy of this issue of the SEMI-TROPIC CALIFORNIA should reach every farmer, orchardist, wine maker, stock raiser and business man in Southern California. With that end in view we have printed an extra large edition of this number. Our next four issues will be large ones, and we request our friends to assist us in increasing our circulation an other thousand.

THERE has been a slight change in the management of the First National Bank. Mr. E. F. Spence, formerly Cashier, becomes President vice J. L. Hollenbeck, who retires to the Directory, and Mr. Wm. Lacy steps into the position of Cashier. The First National has become an indispensable institution, judging from its recent published statement, and merits the fullest confidence of all business classes.

BY the Riverside Press and Horticulturist, we see that the red scale bug has reached Orange and the Santa Ana valley. We are sorry that such is the case; but

that part of our county is not the only one in which this scale has recently been discovered. We learn that it has found its way into East Los Angeles, and the Keller orchard, on Alameda street, this city. Is it not time to wake up in the matter of applying remedies to exterminate it? Why not try high test kerosene oil when the trees are dormant, that is between growths? Better cut down one or two trees, if necessary, and burn them, rather than allow the whole orchard to become infected. We hardly believe, however, that the occasion demands such a radical measure, provided other efficient means are at once employed.

WE had the pleasure of a call from Major Edward Preuss, a Hungarian officer and savant. The Major arrived yesterday from Florida, where he followed, for a number of years, the manufacture of wines from the scuppernong grapes, (*vitis vulpina* or *vitis rotundifolia*), and from the sour and bitter sweet oranges. From papers which he has shown to us, his wines were highly appreciated; he is also the author of the articles "wine" and "manufacture of wines," which were published in the Florida Semi-Tropical. These essays were so highly appreciated that they were copyrighted by the publisher. Major Preuss intends to locate in our county and give his attention to the vine culture. He has been a very extensive traveler, is a walking encyclopedia, and promises us an article on orange wine next month.

WE would call the attention of our readers to a communication from J. J. Groom, in the department of Horticulture, which contains some valuable suggestions to our fruit growers, and especially to those contemplating planting fruit trees this coming winter. Mr. Groom has charge of the canning department and the buying of fruits of the Southern California Canning and Packing Company now in operation in Los Angeles. Mr. Groom has had a large experience, covering a number of years, in canning of fruits and vegetables in several of the most successful canneries in the State and is thoroughly familiar with the best kinds and varieties of fruits to raise for canning and packing, and his advice on this subject is of great value to the orchardist. There is no question but that canning fruits will be one of the most profitable industries of Los Angeles county, and it follows that those who now plant fruit trees of the varieties most suitable for that purpose will reap the best reward for their labor.

The Christmas number of the SEMI-TROPIC CALIFORNIA will be the largest and handsomest illustrated journal ever printed on this coast. The extra large expense will limit the number printed to 10,000 copies, so that persons desiring extra copies should make their wants known in good season. This number will contain ten times the number of engravings in the *Illustrated Herald* and nearly four times as many pages.

THE FAIR.

The management of the Horticultural Society are bending every energy to make the Centennial and Horticultural Exposition to come off Sept. 5–10 the most successful of all their previous efforts. As a source of general good of practical information, recreation and amusement it will be worth to Southern California a value that can not be reckoned in dollars and cents. Every one acknowledges the usefulness of this Society. Its Fairs and magazine have done more than all other agencies to teach the proper things to plant and how to plant and cultivate. The people have come up year after year, and done a noble work and it remains with them to continue it. The Horticultural Fair belongs to the people, is for the people, and with the people it remains to be made a success. Will you do it? The continuation and success of the Society depends on two things—the paying off of the indebtedness and the co-operation of the membership. A proposition is now on foot to accomplish the first, and if carried out the Society will hold its Fair of 1883 in an elegantly finished and furnished and accessible pavilion, out of debt, and a successful future before it.

HORTICULTURAL SOCIETY.

The Board of Directors of the Southern California Horticultural Society, at the meeting held last Saturday found everything progressing in accelerated ratio and with clock-work precision. Several hours were spent in the dispatch of business, most of which related to the great Centennial Exposition to be opened at the Pavilion on Monday, the 5th of September.

It was found that Secretary Rice had so well executed the powers with which the Board had invested him that the superb Fair programme in all its bewildering ramifications will be thoroughly ready for the curtain to rise at the appointed time.

It was resolved by this Board to hold a special meeting of the members of the Society during Fair week, in order to devise some way to raise money with which to redeem the Pavilion and lot. The meeting will be held in the Directors' room of the Pavilion, at 2 o'clock P. M. on Tuesday of Fair week. The time for the redemption of the lot will soon expire. This is the last of the many faithful efforts of the Directors to save the Society's property. Secretary Rice was instructed to notify each member of the time, place and object of the meeting.

A WORD to our readers: If you are in want of anything, from a ten-cent whistle to a thousand-acre ranch, just look our advertising pages through and you will see the name of some firm that can satisfy your wants. We are personally acquainted with nearly all of our advertisers and know them to be first-class, square, honest dealing firms.

NASHUA, N. H., August 10, 1881.

EDITORS SEMI-TROPIC CALIFORNIA:—I beg to send me some number of your paper that has the greatest amount of information regarding the country in it. You will do me a very great favor if you will answer me one or two questions. Am a graduate of the Harvard Medical School, Boston, Mass., in 1880, and want very much to come to California to practice my profession and then also to make me a home. Will you or can you give me any information as to how you would think I might succeed in the city or in some growing town? I don't know how well one might get along as a Dr. in California, but I could bring letters of recommendation from the best surgeons in Boston. Sometime I expect to have enough capital to buy a good piece of land and build thereon. My query, then, is as a Dr. Do you think Southern California offers me a good living, of course other things being equal?

Truly yours,
C. H. H.

Answer.—The medical profession is full in Southern California as in all other quarters; still, as Webster said, "There is room upstairs." If you wish to engage in fruit raising, we know of no other section offering equal advantages.

---

336 Kearny Street,
SAN FRANCISCO, Aug. 20, 1881.

EDITORS SEMI-TROPIC CALIFORNIA:—I take the liberty of addressing this note to you with the request to favor me with any information which it may be in your power to give on the following subject:

A colonization scheme is being organized by some friends of mine, and I have been requested to obtain reliable information with regard to suitable land with available means for irrigation. The object is to find a cheap tract of land with the necessary amount of water suitable for planting and growing a variety of fruit trees and grapevines. The position must not be too near the seaboard.

I presume that portions of Los Angeles as well as San Bernardino counties are equally well adapted for this enterprise; there may be some features in favor of the latter county—I mean further distance from the sea may be cheaper land and easier access to water. Any particulars you can give me will greatly oblige yours very truly,
A. MAJOR.

[Will some of our land owners having land for sale answer the above correspondence, and oblige?—ED.]

HARPER, REYNOLDS & CO., Main street, opposite the Court House, carry the largest line of hardware to be found in the city, and the general verdict is that their prices are as low as is consistent with a living profit. This staunch firm we can recommend with pleasure.

SUCCESS SUCCEEDS.

"Nothing succeeds like success," is as true to-day as it ever was. The man who succeeds in a business, by indefatigable industry and integrity, always enjoys a good trade; from the very fact that he knows all about his business, employs his capital, devotes his time and entire energy in prosecuting that business. If a lady has a pair of shoes to buy she will soon ascertain to buy her shoes from; her husband does the same, and her neighbors and her neighbors' neighbors; and where would they find such a man in Los Angeles? Nearly everybody already knows it's at 34 Spring street, and A. S. McDonald is the man. His stock is complete in every department, bought when prices were at their lowest, with ready cash and good judgment, and it will pay you to see his goods and prices before you buy.

BUSINESS LOCALS.

SEE the Acme Cultivator and Pulverizer at the Pavilion during Fair week.

EXAMINE and taste those fine candies of A. Merriam & Co. at the Pavilion.

FOR fashionable boots and shoes go to the Queen.

T. NOLTE, the merchant tailor, 34 Main street, will make you a good fitting suit of clothes, all the way from $31 up to $65.

WAXGMAN BRO'S, the leading music house in Southern California: see their advertisement elsewhere.

WHEN you find yourself looking for groceries, just drop into Jas. J. Thompson's, 30 Spring street.

THEO. WOLLWEBER, the pioneer apothecary and druggist, would be pleased to have you call at 59 Main street.

IF you want a first-class farm wagon, light or heavy, single or double, call on Hees & Wirsching, 33 and 35 Los Angeles street.

H. GREER, Aliso street, comes out in a full page advertisement on the inside page of front cover. Do not fail to read it; it speaks volumes to the farmers.

THE I X L clothing house, Mr. Welner, Downey Block, carries a full line of clothing, gents' furnishing goods, boots, shoes, hats, caps, etc., which is marked down to bed rock prices. Parties attending the Fair can find bargains by calling at the I X L.

PERRY, WOODWORTH & CO., are the largest lumber dealers south of San Francisco. This firm own and run a line of sailing vessels exclusively for their own use, in bringing lumber from Oregon and other ports. There large planing mill so complete in every department and turns out only first-class work. Fully $300,000 are invested in their business, with a permanently steady increase.

Apiculture.

WILL BEE KEEPING PAY?

Editor Semi-Tropic.— Agreeable to your request, I will contribute to your deservedly popular journal an occasional article on matters pertaining to bee keeping in Southern California. The question is often asked, Will bee keeping pay? I would be inclined to answer both affirmatively and negatively. Affirmatively, if managed with judgment and economy, and negatively, if otherwise. In the present article I will only speak of the preliminary steps in the matter, as I think the success of the business depends as much on these as on anything else, and all that I shall write will be devoted to the sole purpose of making bee keeping a paying business. Those who keep bees for amusement or pastime, can adopt any theory they like, but what must bee men want in Southern California is a systematic course of action which will furnish "grub" and leave something to jingle in the pocket.

If I had known, five years ago, that which I have been forced to learn by "sad experience," I could, to-day, add an extra thousand dollars to the credit of my apiary, and it is the fond hope that some one may profit by my experience, which prompts me to write these lines. I would say, in the first place, start, by all means, with Italian bees. I did so. (I have none to sell.) My first season was a bad one. A neighbor, less than a quarter of a mile distant, had black bees in much better condition than my Italians. He lost half his bees; I lost none. The treatment was the same. The next spring, I increased my bees to double the original number by dividing, and I extracted 360 lbs. of honey for each original stand of bees. I sold the honey in San Francisco at 5 cents per pound, which only netted me about 3½ cents at Pomona, the station I shipped from. I divided, again, in the fall (which I would never do again), and, counting the honey and wax at what I received for it, net, and allowing two dollars per colony for the increase, each original colony paid me a little more than $29 that season. Now, if the next season had been favorable, I would have come out all right, but it proved to be a bad one, and now the mistake of dividing in the fall became apparent, and I lost half of my bees. No one ought to invest all their available cash in an apiary, for bad seasons will come, and they are liable to come in your first year's experience, as it did in mine; and, then, if you should have nothing in reserve, you might mistake the bees and "starve out." And, furthermore, everyone should be able to hold his honey until the price suits him, for when the season affords a good yield of honey, the price is generally low. The honey I sold for 5 cents per pound, as mentioned above, would have sold in the same market, a year later, for 15 cents per pound. The same increase in price need not always be expected, but we have not the least doubt that it will always pay well to hold honey when it is

low. Last year, one of my neighbors sold his honey for 4½ cents per pound. In two months he could have sold it for 6 cents per pound; an increase in value in two months of 33⅓ per cent. In selecting a location for an apiary, we think it advisable, by all means, to select a place having sufficient good land to grow vegetables and fruit, for home use at least, and sufficient feed for a horse, a cow, a few pigs, poultry, etc., all of which will pay well for the care bestowed on them, and will assist greatly in adding to the possessor to avoid "living like a dog."

I recently visited a bee man in a location to which a goat could scarcely climb. In a small bit of dark, rich soil, near the house, he had some fine-looking tobacco plants, well-grown. Near by were potatoes and other vegetables, a banana plant, just fruiting, fig trees, loaded with their tempting fruit, also, strawberries, and the most thoroughly bewitching blackberry patch it has ever been our good luck to fall into. He has no horse, no cow, no pigs, no chickens, and, we believe, not even a cat or dog. And, worse than all, he has no wife to make those nice blackberries into pies. We interrogated him slightly on the subject, and he replied, that when he got married he wished his wife to know, when she got breakfast, where the dinner was to come from. What could we say? We said nothing, but we kept thinking, all the time, that she might get dinner in that blackberry patch. A position in the foot-hills is certainly preferable for an apiary. From such a location bees have access to both the valley and mountain feed. The hills and cañons frequently get late showers, while the valleys miss, and, consequently, they afford late feed when the feed on the valleys is dead and gone. The quality of the honey made in such locations is always superior in flavor and color to that made on the valleys. In fact, much of the honey made exclusively on valley feed, is so dark and ill-flavored as to be unfit for the table, while, even the darkest honey made from mountain feed, has a fine flavor, and, by many, is preferred to the lightest pure, sage honey. Aim to produce only extracted honey. Comb honey will not pay expenses. It can not be shipped with any degree of safety, the demand is weak and uncertain and the amount which can be produced is too small in proportion to the amount of extracted honey which can be produced under the same circumstances. Any bee man who has tried it, will tell you the same, if he will tell the whole truth, and of course no bee man was ever known to tell a lie—at least, hardly ever!

Make up your mind not to sell your honey till you make it. Some of our bee men make hundreds of tons of honey out of gas, printers' ink and paper, thus leading astray, the unsuspecting and saintly San Francisco commission man, who often finds it a difficult matter to find storage for that kind of honey. Prepare for bad seasons, for they will come. Prepare for good seasons, also, and, if you are in readiness when they come, you can revel in sweetness up to your eyes; in fact, you will become so

sweet that everything you touch will stick to you—except your money.

J. F. Steele.

Pomona, Cal.

Produce Market.

MARKET REVIEW.

Since our last issue there has been a divided move in grain all along the line, and prices at this writing are firm and rather on the rise. The rise in wheat in Liverpool is attributed to the fact that shipments from the Atlantic ports have fallen off nearly half, and the unfavorable weather in Great Britain threatens great damage to crops. The rise in Liverpool of course had a favorable effect on our own markets, much to the satisfaction of holders. We are unable, however, to account for the move in barley. Advices from Europe promise a full crop, and Canada reports a large yield of number one quality. The Mississippi Valley is hardly up to the average, and the Pacific Coast, especially California, is a little below the average. In our own county the supply is limited, though probably sufficient to meet all local and home demands. Corn at last, after months of inactivity, has begun to move, in sympathy probably with barley.

The following prices are paid at the farmer's wagon:

WHEAT	$1.50 1.90
BARLEY	1.00 1.10
CORN	80 1.00
POTATOES	80 80
ONIONS	1.50 1.75
BEANS	1.70 2.25
EGGS	25 27
BUTTER	35 40
CHEESE	11½ 14
FRESH FRUIT	
Oranges, per box	1.50 2.00
Lemons, per box	2.00 3.50
Apples, per lb	100
Pears, per lb	1½ 2½
Peaches, per lb	2 3
Plums, per lb	3 4
POULTRY	
Hens, per doz	4.75
Young fowls	3.75
Turkeys, per lb	12½
Geese, each	75

THE CINCHONA RUBBER CURE

Some two years ago an eminent physician of Chicago announced that he had accidentally fallen upon the discovery that the variety of Peruvian Bark known as above, was a positive cure for alcoholism, or dipsomania. For a long time his "discovery" was scouted, but as time passed, and cure after cure was reported, the public became convinced that there was something in it. The Chicago *Tribune* early gave it hearty endorsement, and published the results of its use. A San Francisco journal subsequently gave the experiences of some of its corps, and pronounced the remedy a success. Latterly Eastern papers bore testimony to its great efficacy. As here-tofore prepared the mixture is exceedingly bitter to the taste, but, believing in its virtues, one of our oldest established and most enterprising business houses has succeeded in producing it in a palatable form under the name of Peruvian Bitters, which preserve all its valuable properties and act as a stimulant without its ill effects. It exhilarates a little, but no "thick-headedness" results. A fair trial will satisfy the most skeptical that this is an invaluable remedy, the effects of which are almost miraculous.—*From the Argonaut.*

SAN FRANCISCO NOTES.

In this number of the SEMI-TROPIC CALIFORNIA appear the announcements of a number of San Francisco business houses. To the thousands of readers of the SEMI-TROPIC CALIFORNIA we can only say that the firms represented have been friendly to Southern California in all our ups and downs, and the members of the Horticultural Society, and subscribers to the SEMI-TROPIC, should give them the preference over those who have been indifferent to our interests.

One of the most artistic displays at the Mechanics Fair in San Francisco was that made by the Standard Soap Company. The demand for the soap made by this company is continually increasing, for merit will win every time.

The business card of Messrs. Barclay & Hatch, Commission Merchants, appears elsewhere. Our farmers, generally, have had very pleasant dealings with this firm, which has always been friendly to Southern California.

The card of G. F. Silvester, Seedsman, 317 Washington Street, San Francisco, appears in another column. Mr. Silvester is agent for the Double Cut Improved Spring Pruning Shears, the best instrument of the kind we have seen in use.

The extra dry Eclipse Champagne, manufactured by A. Haraszthy, President of the State Viticultural Commission, has attained a national reputation. It is far superior to most of the imported article, and should be purchased by every lover of fine, sparkling wine.

The card of the Pacific Business College of San Francisco appears in this issue. It is acknowledged to be the leading institution of the kind on the Coast, and offers superior facilities.

The announcement of the Fulton Iron Works, 230 Fremont Street, San Francisco, appears on the last page of our cover. This establishment supplied the machinery for our Cannery, and is prepared to fill all orders with promptness and dispatch.

Messrs. R. J. Trumbull & Co., Sansome Street, San Francisco, are Seedsmen who have gained an enviable reputation for reliability. A fac simile of the Gold Medal received by them from the State Agricultural Fair appears elsewhere.

The electric belts and elastic trusses, manufactured by R. J. Horne, on Market Street, corner of Kearney, are well spoken of by all who have had occasion to use them.

The Curved Pruning Saw, manufactured by the Pacific Saw Co., 17 and 19 Fremont St., San Francisco, is just the thing for our fruit growers. By using it all injurious mutilation of the tree is avoided.

We have had dealings with Sevin Vincent, Seed Dealer, Sansome Street, for the past seven years, and always found him reliable and accommodating.

The advertisement of M. C. Hawley, dealer in Agricultural Implements, appears elsewhere. W. C. Furrey, for many years in the hardware business in this city, and a life member of the Horticultural Society, is Mr. Hawley's agent.

Jackson & Truman, San Francisco, present their compliments to Southern California in another column, where they tell our people some very interesting facts. They have agents in Anaheim, Santa Ana and Colton, besides Jeremiah Rhoades, of Los Angeles. This firm are friends to our section, and glory in our success.

The Poultry Yard.

THE LEGHORNS FOR EGGS.

Without doubt the Leghorns will produce more eggs in a year than any other breed. They are more hardy than the Black Spanish, which is also a number one layer. The young chick feathers out very quickly after getting out of the shell, is active in looking about for worms and insects, and, withal, is very domestic. At four or five months the young pullets will begin to lay, and if given a good warm, comfortable house, and sufficient and proper food, they will lay all winter. Of this breed there are two varieties, differing only in color—the White and the Brown—otherwise, we believe, they are identical, although we have never had the Brown ones under our immediate care. It is characteristic of the Leghorns that they never wish to sit, they are, therefore, called non sitters, consequently it is well to have a few barnyard fowls for sitting purposes. A cross with the Dominique will give good sitters and mothers, and will not lessen the quantity of eggs very largely, though for constant, uninterrupted laying, it is the pure, unmixed Leghorns that we would recommend.

Never keep fowls after they become three years old; either send them to the market or use them for your own table. After that age, in this climate, they are liable to become diseased, and as egg producers they don't begin with young fowls.

Keep your fowls in good health, and they will either be laying eggs or raising chickens the whole time. There is no reason why they should idle away any time, and they will not if they receive proper care and feed.

During the moulting season your fowls need a little tonic. Cayenne pepper and sulphur, in a panful of scalded meal, once a week, will bring them through in fine condition.

What business will return as large a profit on the capital invested as raising eggs at twenty-five cents, our usual price, per dozen?

HOW TO DRIVE A HEN.

When a woman has a hen to drive into the coop, she takes hold of her skirts with both hands, shakes them quietly at the delinquent, and says, "Shoo, there!" The hen takes one look at the object to convince herself that it is a woman, and then stalks majestically into the coop. A man doesn't do that way. He goes out doors and says: "It is singular nobody can drive a hen but me," and picking up a stick of wood, hurls it at the offending biped and counters: "Get in there, you fool." The hen immediately lowers her reason and dashes to the other end of the yard. The man straight way dashes after her. She comes back with her head down, her wings out, and followed by an assortment of stove-wood, fruit cans and clinkers, and a very mad man in the rear. Then she skims under the barn, and over a fence or two, and around the house and back again to the coop, and all the while talking as only an excited hen can talk, and all the while followed by things convenient for handling and a man whose coat is on the raw-jump, and whose hat is on the ground, and whose perspiration has no limit. By this time the other hens have come out to take a hand in the debate and help dodge missiles, and the man says every hen on the place shall be sold in the morning, and puts on his things and goes down the street, and the woman has every one of those hens housed and counted in two minutes.—*Mobile Register.*

CHARCOAL AND ITS USES

Charcoal, laid flat while cold on a burn, causes the pain to abate immediately, by leaving it on for an hour the burn seems almost healed when the burn is superficial. And charcoal is valuable for many other purposes. Tainted meat, when surrounded by it is sweetened; strewn over heaps of decomposed pelts, or over dead animals, it prevents any unpleasant odor. Foul water is purified by it. It is a great disinfectant and sweetens offensive air, if placed in shallow trays around the apartments. It is so very porous that it condenses gases most rapidly. One cubic inch charcoal will absorb nearly one hundred inches of gaseous ammonia. Charcoal forms an unrivaled poultice for malignant wounds and sores, often corroding away dead flesh, reducing it to one-quarter in six hours. In cases of what we call proud flesh it is invaluable. It gives you no unpleasant odor, corrodes no metal, hurts no texture, and is a simple and safe sweetener and disinfectant. A teaspoonful of charcoal in half glass of water, often relieves a sick headache, it absorbs the gases and relieves the distended stomach pressing against the nerves, which extend from the stomach to the head. It often relieves constipation, pain, or heart burn.

The successful farmer does not rely upon a single crop, nor devote his entire attention to the raising of a single article of husbandry. No one can be so excellent a farmer as to run no risk when he plants a crop of its being a failure. Many circumstances, of which he can have not the slightest foreknowledge, may combine to that failure, and while a crop of one article may be so poor as to hardly, if at all, pay for the work of putting it in, another may yield abundantly. Hence the prudent tiller of the soil, however so poor some of the crops may be, will never be without some excellent crops.

VOL. IV. *OCTOBER.* NO. 10.

SEMI TROPIC CALIFORNIA

DEVOTED TO

AGRICULTURE,

HORTICULTURE,

AND THE DEVELOPMENT OF

SOUTHERN CALIFORNIA

CHAS. COLEMAN, JR., PUBLISHER.

LOS ANGELES, CAL.

1881.

MIRROR PRINT, Los Angeles

—⚹ AND ⚹—

SOUTHERN CALIFORNIA HORTICULTURIST.

VOL. IV.   LOS ANGELES, CAL., OCTOBER, 1881.   No. 10.

THE FAIR.

The Fourth Annual Fair of the Southern California Horticultural Society took place this year under unusually favorable auspices. Our farmers and producers generally have been blessed for the past two years with fair crops and good prices, the late eastern connection by rail is stimulating immigration in a most encouraging manner, and our merchants and manufacturers have as much business as they can reasonably expect. The management of the Horticultural Society has a right to claim that this era of prosperity has been largely augmented by its annual fairs. The grand showing made each year of the unsurpassed resources of Southern California has attracted world wide attention and hundreds of visitors have been persuaded to remain in our section and cast their lot with us after an inspection of the wonderful products of this region.

The management of the Fair desire to thank the farmers in all portions of Southern California for their generous co-operation in giving their time and best efforts to the success of the exposition. It is true that some complaint has been made that the fruit growers of Los Angeles city did not exert themselves to the extent they might have, but the entry books of the Society show that the exhibits from the city were not so trifling as many supposed. The county at large, San Bernardino and Santa Barbara counties did themselves ample justice and maintained their already well established pomological reputation.

So far as we can learn the thousands of visitors, and the writer met representatives from all sections, were all highly pleased both with the exposition and management of the Fair. We believe it was as good a representation of the present agricultural and industrial progress of the country as could have been obtained. It has remained for a very few individuals who were willing to receive, and did receive their full share of the benefits of the Fair, without contributing anything of importance to its success, to complain at the management.

The preparation and arrangements of a Fair involve an immense amount of unrecompensed labor. Months must be spent in advertising, and traveling to all portions of the District, and in answering the thousands of letters which come from all quarters. When the Fair opens the benefit of all this advertising and labor must be shared with a host of adventurers who take advantage of the crowds present to draw by side attractions from the attendance at the Fair.

In spite of the annoyance experienced this year from these sources, the Fourth Exposition of the Society was a success from all standpoints, and as one merchant, who has resided here since '53, said to the writer, was worth a million dollars to the town and county. As a very large proportion of the readers of the SEMI-TROPIC were present at the Fair we shall not burden them with a long account of all that took place. We believe that a brief description of the principal exhibits and points of interest, to be found in another part of this paper, will be most satisfactory and if by accident we omit any items of importance our readers will excuse us on the ground that the omission is an unavoidable oversight.

SILK CULTURE.

REPORT OF COMMITTEE—EXHIBIT OF SILK GROWN AT PASADENA, 1881.

By Mrs. Jeanne C. Carr, Vice President of California Silk Growers' Association.

The undersigned Committee on Miscellaneous Exhibits, beg leave to report in addition to the awards marked in the margin of the accompanying list, as follows:

That in view of the immense development of the silk manufactures of the United States, which in 1880 amounted to $32,000,000, and for which all the raw material is obtained in foreign countries, has stimulated the efforts in various States of the Union to promote silk culture wherever climatic conditions are sufficiently favorable.

Again, $1,200,000 worth of silk worm eggs passed through San Francisco last year on their way from China to the markets of France. The raw silk imported by American looms amounted to a total value of $43,432,137, most of this was from China and Japan. To promote the interests of silk culture in California the committee recommend a *Silver Medal* to Mrs. Jeanne C. Carr, for a representative exhibit of silk grown at Pasadena consisting of:

1. Six varieties mulberry for feeding.
2. Cocoons.
3. Silk of two, two and ten cocoons reeled separately.
4. Moths of silkworm, male and female.
5. Eggs just laid.
6. American and foreign silk goods.
7. Charts illustrating culture.
8. Flowers made of cocoons.

We also recommend that the premium list of 1882 should offer encouragement to silk culture by the following specifications:

For best essay on silk culture, $20.

For best exhibit of reeled and manufactured silk grown in this country, including sewing silks, not less than one pound, $10.

For best and largest cocoons, $5.

For best ten mulberry trees from cuttings within the year, $3.

Respectfully submitted,

Wm. H. Lawton, ⎫
W. T. Clapp,   ⎬ Committee.
O. N. Cadwell, ⎭

OUR WINES.

In addition to the awards made for wines exhibited at the Horticultural Fair, the Committee made the following report:

J. De Barth Shorb's Port of 1874, which was not put in competition with the other entries, was a most excellent wine and much superior to the other entries. [Mr. Shorb received the medal for a Port much younger.]

SPARKLING WINE.—Awarded a silver medal.—We cannot too highly recommend the Champagne of Arpad Haraszthy. In our opinion it is destined to take the place of the finest brands of French champagnes.

Robt. S. Baker, ⎫
V. V. Hoover,   ⎬ Committee.
D. T. Freeman, ⎭

BUTTER AT THE FAIR.

No one man showed more enterprise and energy in making an interesting exhibit at our Fair than J. H. Seymour of the Grange store.

The proprietors of the Grange store made a magnificent display of "Gilt-edged Butter," such as they sell over their counters to the thousands of customers who will have no butter unless they get it at the Grange store. They also made an exhibit of butter ready for shipment to Arizona and New Mexico. This butter was packed each roll in a tin can and the cans packed in salt in a heavy strong box. The butter from the Grange always reaches its destination in good order and brings a higher price than any other. Their butter exhibit was changed every day—coming in fresh in the morning—shipped to Arizona, New Mexico, Texas and Old Mexico the next.

The proprietors of this establishment deserve great credit for pushing their trade into the territories and creating a demand for all kinds of produce, for which they pay the very top price.

HORTICULTURAL FAIR.

The Exposition a Grand Success.

THE OPENING DAY.

Monday, September 5th, found a large and well organized band of men at work bringing order out of confusion. The plan adopted by the Society this year of having the agricultural and horticultural exhibits from each section in care of some representative from the same was found to work well, and lifted much responsibility from the regular employés as well as giving much better satisfaction to all parties concerned. In a short time the hall presented the appearance of the court of Pomona and Ceres, and by noon the visitors began to arrive in considerable numbers.

THE CENTENNIAL CELEBRATION

which took place in the afternoon (a creation of Horticultural Fair management) was also a pronounced success. The parade presented one of the most remarkable pageants ever witnessed in Los Angeles. All the military, benevolent and fire organizations turned out in full force, the streets were handsomely decorated and it was universally admitted that a larger crowd never before assembled in the City of the Angels. After the parade Don Juan Toro and Major Horace Bell read interesting historical papers in Spanish and English, respectively, from the platform in front of the Court House.

MONDAY EVENING.

About 6 30 o'clock a dense crowd began to pour into the Pavilion, and by 8 P. M. to use a theatrical term, there was hardly "laughing room" left. At this time Governor Perkins and party, comprising Lieutenant-Governor Mansfield, Secretary of State Burns, General Backus, and Judges Sepulveda and Howard, arrived at the Hall and were escorted to the platform by President Shorb, Directors Bent, Shields and Secretary Rice. The party being seated the "Centennial Chorus," under direction of Mr. J. H. Buck, was sung in a very impressive manner, after which Gov. Perkins made an address, which was appreciated by all who heard it.

EXTRACTS FROM ADDRESS.

Owing to lack of space we are unable to present the whole of the Governor's speech, but give the following extracts, which will give the reader a fair idea of the remainder:

Mr. President, Members of the Horticultural Association, and Ladies and Gentlemen:—In response to your kind invitation I appear before your worthy and honorable association to aid and co-operate with you in paying homage to the shrines of Pomona and Ceres, and to express thanks for their magnificent gifts of fruits and flowers.

     *   *   *   *

Look at the wonderful array of nature's gifts spread before us, amplified and enriched by the efforts of your Association. A few short years ago these valleys, now emparadised in fruits, cereals and flowers, raised their upturned faces to sullen, uninviting barrenness. Surely the ap-

proving smile of heaven is upon us! On every side, in valley, on hill, the happy results of your labor shows forth to gratify both heart and eye. The whole world lies there before us. That fig speaks to us of Syria; that luscious peach recalls to us the fertile land of Persia; Media has gifted us with those citrons; yonder pomegranate bids us remember Africa; these famous apricots have stamped Epirus on our memory; when next the apple, pear or plum gratifies your taste, yield Armenia your thanks, and forget not Pontus when the delicious cherry delights your palate; and, above all, fail not to adore the beneficence and wisdom of Him who has thus blessed this fair land.

     *   *   *   *

The horticultural field of California is exhaustless, it is indeed a promised land. That taste now springing up among us unfolds an appreciation for the beautiful that can and will be greatly enhanced by your efforts.

Let every man learn that in wooing nature he is cultivating the affections; let every man learn the true use and meaning of a home. Improve our homes and you improve our morals. Attachment to our homes is a gem of patriotism.   *   *   * Agriculture and horticulture, however great their pecuniary success, if they do not result in that final triumph, a home, we count a failure. I believe that upon home life and the home culture of the youth of the land, whether in town or country, depend the peace, prosperity and the very life of the nation.

Let us pray for the multiplication of the homes in villages, city and on the farm. * * * Give us such homes in plenty, oh bounteous Heaven. * * * Mid the tumults of a contending world and the fall of thrones and principalities the Republic of America, secure in the hearts of a people from homes like these, shall not perish from the face of the earth!

After the Governor's address the chorus sang "Now the Roll of the lively Drum," President Shorb made a brief address and the large audience quietly dispersed.

THE DECORATION OF THE HALL.

The Pavilion was decorated with unusual taste this year, long wreaths of evergreens being suspended from the center with palm leaves intertwined, and Spanish, Mexican and American flags introduced here and there to advantage. Mr Stengel's magnificent collection of California, Australia and New Zealand ferns was the most interesting feature of the decoration and added much to the appearance of the hall.

THE EXHIBITS.

It will be impossible to do justice in these columns to all the exhibits made by the various sections of Southern California. We shall try to give the most interesting features of each exhibit, commencing outside of Los Angeles county.

RIVERSIDE.

San Bernardino's beautiful colony made a grand display of fruit, principally grapes.

The distance from Los Angeles prevented some of the fruit from arriving in prime condition, but otherwise the display was perfect. The strong soil and abundance of water seem to bring the grape to perfection, and in point of number of varieties placed on exhibition, Riverside far exceeded any other settlement. Mr. A. S. White had a magnificent collection, embracing 41 varieties of the grape, and was awarded a silver medal for this display as well as $10 for the best twelve varieties of white grapes. A six year old vine belonging to Mr. R. H. Henderson was also exhibited, which decidedly seemed to be more grape than vine. It contained nearly 60 pounds originally, but in transit many dropped off. There was also a fine exhibit of pears, apples, oranges, lemons, limes and dried figs, muscat and orange wines. A diploma for the best display of lemons was awarded to G. W. Garcelon, and a silver vase to J. W. Galloway for best box of dried figs. The Riverside exhibit was in every respect very creditable, and the display was carefully inspected by horticulturists from all parts of the State. The magnificent advantages which the colony already enjoys, and which will be still further extended after the advent of the California Southern Railroad, should be known to all. We trust the Riverside people found their stay in Los Angeles as pleasant as our people found the company of their guests, and at the Fifth Annual Fair we hope to see a larger delegation. The exhibit was in charge of Mr. L. M. Holt, editor of the Riverside Press.

SAN BERNARDINO.

San Bernardino Valley was represented by some fine looking cases of dried fruit from the Lugonia Fruit Packing Company, canned goods from the Colton cannery and a display of oranges from Craft's celebrated orchard. The Mojave desert furnished specimens of ore from all the principal mining districts in that newly (in one sense) discovered bonanza; a fine specimen of marble was also on exhibition from the Mojave. A silver medal was awarded to A. S. Spencer for best display of minerals. The thanks of the Society are due to Mr. C. H. Comber for the general exhibit.

SANTA BARBARA.

No one who carefully observed the fine display of fruits on the Santa Barbara table doubted for an instant that there are great horticultural possibilities in store for our northern neighbor. The climate and soil of Santa Barbara county are well adapted to almost every variety of temperate and semi-tropical fruits, but the lack of transportation facilities has discouraged many from engaging in horticultural pursuits. A railroad is needed in Santa Barbara county, and we are pleased to observe that there is every reason to believe that in less than two years the long felt want will be supplied. We believe that the local traffic of Santa Barbara county would, from the first, support a railroad, and in a few years it would be a well paying investment.

One of the most lovely spots on the Pacific Coast is Carpenteria, Santa Barbara county. This district embraces some eight miles along the coast, running a few miles inland, to the lofty Santa Inez range. The picturesque scenery in every direction, including a magnificent view of the blue ocean, the fertile soil and other advantages have rendered the Carpenteria a favorite resort for all in search of the beautiful. Carpenteria furnished one of the finest displays of deciduous fruits in the Pavilion, nearly all gathered from the ranch of that enterprising gentleman, Mr. G. N. Cadwell. His display consisted of sixty-three varieties of seedling apples, eighteen varieties of seedling pears, twenty-four varieties grafted apples, fifteen varieties grafted pears, and a general assortment of other fruits, both green and dried. Mr. Cadwell was awarded $15 for the best display of apples, a silver cup for best ten pounds of dried pears, $5 for the best display of plums, $2 for best one variety of plums, silver cup for best display pears, $10 for best twelve varieties of apples, and $10 for best variety of seedlings. The Santa Barbara cannery had a fine display of canned goods. From the beautiful ranches of Messrs. Cooper, Hollister and others there was a good exhibit of almonds, English walnuts, oranges, lemons, limes, Japanese persimmons, olives, green, olive oil, and claret wine.

A silver medal was awarded to the Santa Barbara cannery, and the same to Elwood Cooper for best 12 bottles olive oil. Col. Hollister was awarded $5 for best half bushel English walnuts.

PASADENA.

Pasadena seems never weary of well doing, and on this special occasion deserves great credit for the most excellent display made. A most worthy example is set by this thriving little settlement to those who think that it is no use to attend fairs, no use to exhibit at fairs, no use to do anything. Since the First Annual Fair of the Southern California Horticultural Society the value of real estate, both improved and unimproved, has advanced fully five-fold in Pasadena. Now while the people of this pleasant little settlement do not generally desire to sell their homes, it is gratifying to know that a cash purchaser can be found nearly every day of the year and an ample return obtained for years of labor.

Perhaps the most interesting and novel feature of the Pasadena exhibit was the display of silk worms and their appurtenances by Mrs. Dr. Carr. This lady had on exhibition several varieties of the mulberry tree upon which the worms feed, also silk worms in every stage of development, cocoons and the raw silk wound from them. The Pasadena table was handsomely decorated and well taken care of. The fruit from numerous exhibitors, and of many varieties, consisted of peaches, pears, apples, figs, green and dried, pomegranates, plums, grapes in great variety, oranges, lemons, limes, crab apples, nectarines, persimmons, Mandarin oranges, citrons, straw-

berries, quinces, blackberries and tomatoes. Also a fine display of beautiful flowers, almonds, English walnuts, corn, hops, jellies, and several varieties of grain. The apple exhibit by Mr. Cooley was particularly fine, also the display of Mr. Jos. Wallace of Ellerslie. The Pasadena Horticultural Society was awarded $25 for the best display of California fruits, W. F. Cooley $10 for the 12 best varieties of apples, G. H. Cooper $5 for best 6 varieties of peaches, Mrs. Carr silver cup for sample of hops, Mrs. Carr silver cup for sample of hops, silver medal for display of silk and silk worms; Mrs. Rosenbaum silver case for best jar guava jelly, silver case, best display cut flowers; I. B. Clapp, silver cup, best 10 pounds apples; J. H. Baker, diploma for best amp for destroying insects. Several other exhibits were adjudged worthy of honorable mention.

ORANGE.

This beautiful settlement, located in the southern end of the county about thirty two miles from Los Angeles, six from Anaheim and three from Santa Ana, was well represented at the Fair. Orange is settled by a thrifty, hard working class of people who are making themselves beautiful homes surrounded by orange groves, orchards and vineyards. The water supply is derived from the Santa Ana river and seems to be ample at present. The climate may be said to be almost perfect, and even a light frost is a rarity in winter. The semi-tropical fruits raised at Orange always commend the highest prices in the San Francisco market and the business of manufacturing is attaining considerable proportions. The most prominent feature of the Orange exhibit was a small pineapple tree in bearing, which first fruited last February. A display of raisins from Mr. W. F. Windheim was very creditable and the table of raisin grapes from Mr. McPherson is also worthy of especial mention. There was also a good general display of oranges, limes, almonds, figs, pomegranates, 18 varieties grapes, apples, bananas, corn, sweet potatoes, watermelons and honey, besides a collection of articles carried from native woods and several bouquets of flowers. McPherson Bros. were awarded $13 for best display of grapes, $5 for best cluster, a medal for raisins, and a diploma for dried currants; A. J. Sanders, two diplomas for fancy wood work. Mr. J. W. Anderson collected and arranged and took care of the exhibit, for which favor the Society desires to return hearty thanks.

TUSTIN CITY.

Thanks to the energy and enterprise of Mr. H. K. Snow and one or two other citizens the display from Tustin was worthy of what may be justly styled one of the brightest gems of Los Angeles county. Tustin is one of the youngest and most progressive portions of our county, and as we noted in an article last month has made most extraordinary progress.

No table in the Pavilion showed a greater range of horticultural and agricultural

products, a fact the more remarkable because the articles were principally collected from the place of but two or three citizens. The display was not only excellent, but it was arranged with great taste, and considering that Tustin is distant from Los Angeles the fruit seemed in good condition.

The finest bunch of bananas we have seen in Southern California this year was exhibited from the ranch of Messrs. Snow and Adams, and from the same place as figs more and potatoes as we desire to see. The same grade of soil produces equally well nearly every variety of fruit and vegetable common in temperate and tropical zones.

The general display consisted of ten varieties of grapes—all fine and large clusters, oranges, lemons, limes, apples, several kinds of raisins, bananas, blackberries, crab apples, figs, watermelons, pears, peaches, quinces, and in the vegetable line potatoes, corn, white beans, big beets, big turnips, besides a good display of flowers.

P. Potts was awarded the special premium of $5 for best and largest six ears of corn.

Snow & Adams were awarded the premium for best bananas, also a diploma for display of oranges, quantity and beauty of arrangement taken into consideration. Also honorable mention for their fine bunch of bananas.

POMONA.

Pomona is rapidly taking rank as one of the leading fruit-producing sections of Los Angeles county. The soil and climate were peculiarly well adapted to horticulture, and we consider it one of the best places in the county for an immigrant as moderate means to settle in. Land is rather cheaper than in some other portions of the front belt, the climate is drier than that of the coast, and we have no doubt that raisin making will be a profitable industry in the future.

Pomona is located about 34 miles east of Los Angeles, the Southern Pacific railroad running directly through the tract. Some local difficulties which hitherto have retarded immigration here just been settled, and improvement from this time on will be steady.

The credit for the excellent display from Pomona at the Fair belongs wholly to Rev. C. F. Loop, who at considerable labor and expense made a collection which did ample justice to his district. If others in every section were willing to show the same enterprise our annual horticultural exhibitions would be grand and complete in every respect.

The display from Pomona consisted of peaches, pears (several varieties, all very fine), grapes, apples, corn, oranges, figs, green and dried, almonds, cactus pears, plums, hazelnuts, and many other articles. An interesting example of the keeping qualities of the Los Angeles orange was shown by a box of the golden fruit packed in February by Mr. Weeks, of Pomona, and being opened on the 1st of September, found to be in perfect condition. Mr. Kincaid was awarded $3 for best 6 varieties of apples, Rev. C. F. Loop $3 for best 6 varieties pears, W. T. Martin diploma for display of broomcorn.

ANAHEIM.

Anaheim was better represented at the Fair this year than at any previous exposition. The display was large, well arranged and a success in every respect. The collection was made by Mr. S. B. Smith and deserves a longer notice than our space will permit. We trust the result of this experiment will encourage the Anaheimers to make an exhibit from their section a regular feature of the succeeding Fairs.

Mr. Geo. B. Hinde, a resident of Placentia District, near Anaheim, made an exceedingly fine display of fruit and vegetables. He was awarded a premium of $10 for best display of fruit grown by one man; also several minor premiums. The general display from Anaheim consisted of ores from Santiago Mining Co., bullion from same, grapes (table and wine), pears, plums, oranges, peaches, apples, strawberries, gooseberries, papayas, bananas, tomatoes, green olives, peanuts, field peas, Japanese persimmons, lichin figs, water-melons, flowers, ten pumpkins—total weight 1,600 pounds, and a bundle of amber cane. An exhibit was also made in the wine department, mechanical department and art department. Hill Bros., Centralia, were awarded $10 for the ten largest pumpkins, S. L. Chilson $3 for best three varieties of peaches, B. Dreyfus silver medal for best display California sherry.

SANTA ANA.

Santa Ana made an excellent showing at the Fair, but we regret that the "swamp" was not better represented. We missed the big pumpkins of former years and other immense specimens of the vegetable kingdom for which the swamp has always carried off the palm. Yet they were not wholly absent, for there were about half a bushel of Irish potatoes of the Early Rose and Bromley varieties, each specimen of which weighed over four pounds. The field in which they grew was not irrigated once this year, the crop depending wholly upon the natural moisture.

The Santa Ana display was in charge of Mr. Robinson of that place, who cared for his charge in a very acceptable manner.

The general display consisted of eighteen varieties of grapes, pears, apples, figs, fine lemon-cling peaches, corn on cob and in sack, oranges and potatoes.

R. J. Bise was awarded $10 for the best twelve varieties of table grapes; Halesworth Bros., $3 for best 1 variety of white grapes. W. F. Halsell, best display potatoes—SEMI-TROPIC CALIFORNIA.

J. F. Berry, display of potatoes—SEMI-TROPIC CALIFORNIA.

SAN GABRIEL.

The glory of San Gabriel lies principally in her orange orchards and vineyards, and a large display of miscellaneous horticul-

tural and agricultural products could hardly be expected at this season of the year. Stern & Rose and J. De Barth Shorb each made a good exhibit of their several brands of wine and brandy, and Mr. Phillips a small collection of fruits, consisting of pomegranates, figs, apples, peaches, grapes and barberries. Mr. S. Richardson also made a creditable display of oranges and other citrus fruits.

The following awards were made to San Gabriel:

Stern & Rose, display of wine and brandies—Silver medal.

J. De Barth Shorb, display of wines and brandies—Silver medal.

J. De Barth Shorb, display of grape and brandy—Silver medal.

Stern & Rose, display of red wine (Zinfandel)—Silver medal.

Stern & Rose, Angelica—Silver medal. S. Richardson, display of citrons—Diploma.

DUARTE.

This pleasant little settlement located in the foothills of the Sierra Madre mountains sent an interesting exhibit to the Fair. The collection was made by Mr. L. Barnes, on whose farm most of the products exhibited were raised. We understand that the water supply of the Duarte is shortly about to be further developed, and we anticipate an increase in the number of beautiful homes in that section.

Peaches, pomegranates, grapes, limes, quinces and watermelons were displayed on the Duarte table—all the fruit of the finest quality and in good condition. A diploma for best display pomegranates was awarded to L. Barnes.

LOS ANGELES CITY.

There was a very large list of entries from Los Angeles, but the fruit exhibit was painfully small. One reason for this was the date at which the Fair was held. Los Angeles is not in the "early fruit" belt.

LOUIS J. STENGLE,

The favorite florist of this city, made a display of tree ferns, flowers and plants of every description which called forth universal admiration. Mr. Stengle may properly be styled an artist in his vocation, and deserves the highest praise for his superb exhibit. We doubt whether any city or town on the Pacific Coast can boast of a landscape gardener or florist superior in ability to Mr. Stengle. The following premiums were awarded: Diploma, silver vase and $35 in coin.

INJURIOUS AND BENEFICIAL INSECTS.

Mr. A. Craw exhibited his elaborate collection of injurious and beneficial insects. Since last spring he has made extensive additions to his list. He was awarded a silver medal.

B. M. Lelong made a similar display of insects.

SUB IRRIGATION.

The Sub-Irrigation Company of Los Angeles made a fine display of fruits and vegetables grown on land sub-irrigated.

Mr. Hamilton, the principal owner of the patent, kindly permitted us to test the fruit, which we found to be of excellent quality. Mr. Hamilton was awarded four diplomas for display of artificial steam work, silver medal for best system of sub-irrigation, SEMI-TROPIC CALIFORNIA for three best mountain watermelons, and honorable mention for several other articles exhibited.

MISCELLANEOUS.

The Southern California Packing Company exhibited canned goods, jams, jellies, marmalades, and dried fruits, all put up in attractive shape and style. The company was awarded a diploma for the best display of factory canned goods. Mrs. G. W. Dye, of La Dow, three miles south of the city, made an elaborate display of jams and jellies, in glass, for which she was awarded nine premiums—all silver ware. Mrs. A. C. Dunn, for a fine display of jellies, was awarded a silver cake basket. Mr. O. H. Bliss displayed a fine collection of fruits from his model farm, on Alameda street. Over his table perched a large Eagle, with outstretched wings, labeled "Southern California." Mr. Bliss was awarded a silver medal for the finest exhibit of pampas plumes.

Vernon District, just outside the city limits, made a creditable display of fruits and flowers. A display of over forty varieties of wheat, in stalks, grown in Los Angeles county, was an interesting feature of the Fair.

THE HONEY AND BEE EXHIBIT.

Although the past season has been one of the most unfavorable for honey making ever experienced in Southern California, the Apiarists seem not to have lost heart, but were present in full force, at the Fair, with a display of honey, bees, and beeswax, collected from Anaheim, Los Angeles, Orange, San Fernando, and other districts. To those interested in apiary the hives of hybrid bees, Holy Land bees, pure Italian bees, and appurtenances of the bee ranch exhibited were very instructive. The bees themselves, many of them were at liberty, seemed to take a good-natured view of the whole matter, and helped themselves liberally to the horticultural supplies in the neighborhood. Honey vinegar and honey cake were two novel features of the bee men's show.

A. S. Hamilton, of Orange, was awarded first premium of $5 for best display comb honey; C. N. Wilson, second premium, $3. The same gentleman was awarded first premium, $5, for best display extracted honey; J. E. Pleasants, second premium, $3. The other premiums offered were, we believe, equitably divided, but our space compels us to defer publishing the list.

This department was under the care and direction of C. N. Wilson, to whom the Society extend thanks.

PAVILION PARAGRAPHS.

A full description of the mechanical, textile fabric, art and miscellaneous departments of the Fair, together with nu-

mium list, would considerably exceed the space allotted to us for our report of the Exposition. Our readers, we trust, will kindly excuse the omission and be content with a few brief notes concerning those departments not relating to agriculture or horticulture.

B. F. Coulter's display of fancy goods, ladies' dress goods and notions, was worthy in every respect of the leading dry goods store of Los Angeles.

Many young couples were observed to stop during their promenade around the Pavilion and carefully inspect the furniture and carpet display made by Dotter & Bradley. This action may have been prompted by disinterested motives, but our suspicions point the other way.

Mr. H. Guise made the largest and most creditable exhibit of agricultural implements in the Pavilion. He deservedly received several prizes.

The Art department this year was equal to that of any preceding Fair. Mr. J. A. Valder, of this city, had a fine collection. Messrs. Payne, Stanton & Co. exhibited specimens of their artistic work in the photographic line. The paintings of Miss Lillie A. Ward of Pasadena received great praise, and several ladies and gentlemen in this city contributed quite liberally to the collection.

Mr. H. Heinsch exhibited a single harness which for beauty and finish we are confident has no superior on this coast. Mr. Heinsch understands his vocation thoroughly; his exhibit was creditable to Los Angeles and well deserved the award of a silver medal made by the committee.

Mr. Day's display of pianos and organs was the only exhibit of musical instruments in the Pavilion. The musical contest which took place Wednesday afternoon was participated in by eight young ladies, all of whom seemed to have genuine musical genius developed by careful training.

There were some twenty-eight entries at the Baby show Friday afternoon. Baby Robertson, Baby Dixby, Baby Lemp, Baby Ingram and Baby Pray were the lucky juveniles, and received the prizes in the order named.

Mr. Lichtenberger's display of buggies, Mr. Gano's iron wagon, the Acme harrow, the incubator exhibited by Mr. Niles, the the Wheeler & Wilson sewing machines exhibited by Mr. Gibhlen, the California windmill exhibited by Mr. S. B. Smith, the display of butter by the Orange Store, Lash's fruit picker, the Zimmerman fruit dryer, the spring bed exhibited by Fuller & Day, and the display of willow ware by Neyburg Bros., all received first premiums.

Miss A. Whitney received the premium offered by the Mirror office for the best recitation, and Miss L. Frick the premium for the best industrial drawing.

Miss Sarah Parkhurst, Miss Dora Barton, Miss Teddie Haines, Mrs. F. E. Browne, Mrs. M. Macy, Mrs. F. L. Marsh and Miss Annie Willing were the winners in the bread contest.

The Eclipse Extra Dry Champagne, manufactured by Arpad, Haraszthy & Co., for sparkling wine—a silver medal.

The exhibit of groceries by I. J. Thompson, of fancy goods by the Widney Bros., of furniture by Sharp & Bloemer, and of boots and shoes by the favorite Queen Boot and Shoe Store, and candy by the Los Angeles Candy Works—all were creditable.

Mr. Jillson had a coop of his favorite fowls, the Plymouth Rocks, on exhibition.

Mr. D. D. Brunk made a handsome exhibit of rustic wood work.

Lankershim & Co.'s exhibit of flour was awarded the first premium.

The ladies were well represented in their department by a fine display of embroidered work, needle work, etc.

The Fair closed Saturday evening, September 10th, with an address by President Shorb, after which those so inclined tripped "the light fantastic toe."

NOTE.—If any exhibitors feel that they have been neglected or slighted in this hurriedly written report of the Fair, they may rest assured the neglect was not intentional. If our attention is called to the matter in time we will see that justice is done in the November number of SEMI-TROPIC CALIFORNIA.

HOT STEAM FOR INSECTS A FAILURE.

Some weeks ago a gentleman of San Jose announced to the public that he had discovered a valuable remedy for the extermination of scale bugs, woolly aphis and other tree insects. This remedy was hot steam to be applied to the foliage with a syringe to the form of a spray, and with him it had proved rather satisfactory. The Santa Clara County Horticultural Commissioners, however, have been experimenting with the remedy recently and report that the steam killed every tree to which they administered it. Furthermore, the temperature of the steam in some cases was as low as 180°, only a few degrees higher than the temperature of the air during some of our warm continental days in summer. If such is the case the fond hopes of another would-be benefactor are blighted, and we must resort to whale oil soap, concentrated lye, kerosene oil, soap washes, etc.

BRANDIED PEACHES.

To every pound of peeled peaches add one gill of white brandy; make a syrup of fine sugar, add only enough water to dissolve it, let it come to a boil, then put the fruit in and let boil five minutes; remove the fruit carefully, then let the syrup boil 15 or 20 minutes longer, until it thickens; add the brandy and take the kettle from the fire; pour the hot syrup over the fruit and seal at once. If, after the peaches have been removed, a reddish liquor oozes from them, drain this off before adding the clear syrup. Put up in glass jars that have been rolled in hot water. The peaches should not be over ripe.

THE KING is the name of a very popular Shoe store at No. 26 Spring street, of which Mr. C. L. Fisher is proprietor. This is almost a new store and the stock is all new. Mr. Fisher brings into the business a ripe experience from a long apprenticeship and ownership in the boot and shoe business. In addition to his fine stock, which he warrants as represented, he has a shop, where all orders are promptly filled. The shop is presided over by an accomplished workman.

MR. BELL, near Florence, has a vineyard of 100 acres planted this year, which is the finest we have ever seen. The cuttings were set out six feet apart and in many places have made such a growth as to lap over between the rows. About seventy per cent. of the cuttings came; his principal loss being from rabbits. Many of them are already bearing, and altogether it is a very remarkable growth.

MR. YORSEN, of Sacramento, State Horticultural Officer, suggests the following sizes for boxes for fruit packing: Plums, 40 pounds, 13x13x9 inches; 20 pounds, 13x9x8 inches; 10 pounds, 13x9x4½ inches; 3 pounds, 13x3x1⅓ inches. Dried fruit, such as peaches, apricots, etc., 50 pounds, 10½x10½x9½ inches; 25 pounds, 10½x10½x4½ inches—all inside measures.

BROWNING (Amicis). It was their first night aboard the steamer. "At last," he said tenderly, "we are all alone, out upon the deep waters of the dark blue sea, and your heart will always beat for me as it has in the past." "My heart is all right," she answered languidly, "but my stomach feels awful."

A warm laid egg takes half a minute longer to boil than a stale one. Raw eggs digest in an hour and thirty minutes; hard boiled and fresh eggs require three hours and one half for digestion, or as long as cheese and mutton. No food of such desirable quality and low cost is within the reach of every farmer, and it behooves each individual to give this important yet neglected subject more thought and attention.—Savannah News.

MR. KOELLE, of Kimler & Frohling, says that his experience has taught him that bees feeding largely on grapes will not produce so many eggs as when given other foods. His theory is that the grapes weaken the system. We are inclined to think that the weakening is owing rather to their molting than to the grapes. In this case an occasional feed of cayenne pepper and sulphur with scalded corn meal, will stimulate them to laying again. What is the experience of others?

As Irish paper advertises, "Fowls for sale (seven hens and cork), all laying."

Our December—Christmas number—will contain 32 pages, and will be full of fine illustrations.

172

SAN BERNARDINO.

Record of a Prosperous Section.

THE RESOURCES AND ADVANTAGES OF OUR SISTER COUNTY

FEW persons in California have any idea of the business activity which now exists in our neighboring county of San Bernardino. At present it is almost impossible to secure comfortable sleeping accommodations at the hotels, and the merchants, mechanics, laborers and other classes have all the business they can attend to. This is in striking contrast with the condition of affairs which existed two years ago, although when the dark shadow which spread over the business communities of the East some eight years ago reached the Pacific Coast, at no time during the period of depression did San Bernardino county suffer to the extent of many other sections of California.

THE IMMEDIATE CAUSES

Of the present "boom" in San Bernardino is the mining excitement on the Mojave Desert and the prospective advantages to be derived from the construction of the California Southern Railroad through the valley. There is by no means at present a speculative excitement in the price of land, but there is a marked and permanent advance in valuations.

THE MOJAVE MINES

Recently discovered are principally located about sixty-five miles from the town of San Bernardino, and unquestionably are very rich. Mr. Waterman, the owner of some celebrated hot springs distant six miles north of San Bernardino, has recently developed a mine in Grapevine District, which is almost fabulously rich. Some of the ore has assayed as high as $5,000 to the ton, although the large vein will average about

COURT HOUSE, SAN BERNARDINO,
ERECTED IN 1874.

its recent discovery we believe to be only a hint of the hidden mineral resources of San Bernardino.

OTHER PROMISING MINES

Are located in Calico Mountain District lately discovered. Very rich ore has been found, and experienced miners say that most of the much vaunted locations in Arizona have no better outlook. One of these mines, the Silver King, has been bonded for $100,000. Providence Mountain District is immensely rich in silver. A sale of four mines has recently been made there for $30,000. The ore at Ivanpah, which is one of the oldest districts is of very high grade, and many thousands of dollars' worth of bullion are annually shipped. The Ore Grande Mining Company regularly employs a force of from 50 to 75 men, and the mines are panning out well; an immense body of ore is in sight. Other prominent mines are those of Dry Lake District, New York, Owl, Black Hawk, Lone Valley, Bear Valley and Blades. Several coal mines have recently been discovered in the Cajon Pass which give great promise. The coal is of excellent quality, and the supply seems inexhaustible. Valuable tin mines exist at Temescal about thirty-five miles south of San Bernardino. Miners are at present prospecting in every direction, and new locations are daily being made.

THE COMING RAILROAD.

The Southern Pacific Railroad, which now extends from California to Texas, passes through San Bernardino county, making its principal station at Colton, three miles from the county seat and six miles from Riverside. A railroad which more directly interests the people of San Bernardino Valley is the California Southern, now in process of construction from the Bay of San Diego. The road is surveyed to the Mojave river, 40 miles north of San Bernardino, passes very close to the town and will give the valley an easy outlet to the sea. The Utah Southern is also being

CRAFTON RETREAT.

$40. Mr. Waterman has refused an offer of half a million dollars for his mine, claiming that the ore in sight is worth at least half that amount. It is a wonderful bonanza, and

extended in the direction of San Bernardino.

TAKING INTO CONSIDERATION

The above favorable condition of affairs both from a mining and transportation standpoint it is certainly not strange that San Bernardino is extraordinarily active. But one of the most gratifying features of the matter is that the agricultural and horticultural resources of the valley are now to be developed to the fullest extent. A great market has opened almost at the very doors of the farmers and their staple products will command the highest prices for many years to come. When we consider the comparatively limited area of arable land in San Bernardino county when compared with the mineral districts it is remarkable that men about to engage in agricultural pursuits do not secure a foothold in a region with such a promising future while there is yet a chance. Let us briefly review San Bernardino Valley from an agricultural and horticultural standpoint.

LANDS, SOIL AND WATER.

The county of San Bernardino contains 23,472 square miles, equal to extent to half the size of the state of New York. The valley embraces an area of about 1,500 square miles of arable land. The soil is ate of several classes, some being adapted to grain raising, some to stock, and by far the largest amount to fruit. In many locations crops thrive without irrigation, but in the matter of water there is no scarcity, for besides the Santa Ana river and a great number of small streams there are over 450 flowing artesian wells, the estimated daily flow of which is 16,153,000 gallons. Abundance of surface water can be found in almost all portions of the valley at a depth varying from 15 feet to 150 feet. It will thus be seen that there is an abundance of water for the present and future necessities of the valley, and even if there were not this abundance, the result would by no means be disastrous, as we are convinced by observation that many orchards and vineyards near San Bernardino will yet be ruined by excessive irrigation and overflow.

Fruit is the principal and undoubtedly most desirable and profitable crop in San Bernardino Valley. The orange groves of Old San Bernardino have long produced annually a bounteous harvest of grapes, apples, and now in every portion of the valley young and thrifty orchards are coming into bearing. Nearly all the fruits are grown in the world that are raised here, and while the local market for the former is overstocked. Nearly all the

A SAN BERNARDINO COUNTY ORANGE ORCHARD

RESIDENCE OF DR. FOX.

varieties of grapes do well, and the present from an exceeding superior...

...chards and vineyards are adapted for the grape and the steady... has greatly stimulated the grape... yards. Both the raisin...

...that from any other variety of fruit. The atmosphere of San Bernardino county is especially adapted for raising oranges which is an important advantage. At... the profits fr... ... raised making... ... range from ... ... per acre, and ... the demand for ...

possess both capital and persistency. Messrs. Anderson Bros. of Temescal inform us that year before last they cleared $4,000 by holding their honey crop one year.

STOCK.

In San Bernardino county there are still numerous herds of cattle, although this industry has greatly fallen off since the passage of the "no fence" law. Mr. J. W. Waters has a fine herd of blooded stock imported by him at great expense. Mr. Waters' enterprise is worth emulating. Sheep raising and wool growing are carried on very extensively.

CLIMATE.

Although the climate of San Bernardino is warm in summer it is by no means unpleasant. The extreme dryness of the atmosphere prevents injury from the temperature and prostration from the sun's rays never occurs. The winter temperature is delightfully mild.

SCENERY.

The mountains in the vicinity of San Bernardino abound in picturesque scenery. Mt. San Bernardino, the highest peak in Southern California (11,000 ft), stands just at the head of the valley. The cañons of the majestic mountain range which guards the valley are favorite summer resorts for pleasure seekers. Camping parties from all portions of the State visit the San Bernardino mountains both for health and pleasure.

THE TOWN

has a population of about 7,500, and as noted elsewhere, is making great progress. It is of American origin, the Spanish element not being as prominent as in most of the larger settlements of Southern California. The streets are nearly all well laid out and lined with shade trees, making the general appearance very pleasant. The Mormon element which first settled on the site of the town is gradually disappearing. Those who remain seem to be an industrious and thrifty class of people.

There are several churches and good public schools, two banks, two hotels, two newspapers—the *Daily Times* and *Weekly Index*—two public halls and numerous business houses referred to elsewhere.

ILLUSTRATIONS.

We are able to present to our readers this month some excellent illustrations of public and private buildings, scenery, etc., in San Bernardino Valley.

No. 1 is a view of the court house, com-

pleted in 1874 at an expense of $60,000. No. 2 is Crafton Retreat, a beautiful place, located 12 miles east of town. Mr. Crafts, the owner, has a tract of some 900 acres, most of which is under cultivation. No. 3 is a view of one of the celebrated orange

STEWART & LINVILLE BLOCK.

orchards of Old San Bernardino. No. 4 the residence of Dr. Fox, located at Colton. No. 5 the Stewart and Linville Block, located on Third street. No. 6 the residence of Mr. F. E. Brown, situated at

RESIDENCE OF FRANK E. BROWN.

Lugonia District, a beautiful and thriving locality. No. 7 residence of Mr. A. H. Hart, located on the Base Line road. No. 8, residence of Mr. J. W. Waters at Old San Bernardino.

The business blocks, private residences and public buildings of San Bernardino are very creditable and speak well for the enterprise of the people. Several handsome residences are now being erected in the Valley by newcomers from the East.

The tide of immigration now setting this way promises to enlarge the city very much and to dot the plain here and there with fine, substantial residences. These residences on the plain will have their accompanying orchards and vineyards, their alfalfa and field crops, and the wealth thus added to the present condition of things will be favorably felt in every industry.

The future of San Bernardino could not be brighter, and if her citizens are just a little vain we will forgive them, because they have every reason to be proud and a perfect right to show to the world that they live in one of the choicest spots on the Pacific Coast.

BUSINESS HOUSES OF SAN BERNARDINO

The town of San Bernardino has many large business houses which command the trade of a considerable area. We desire especially to call the attention of our readers to the live real estate firm of

CONDER & MARSHALL.

Both gentlemen are young, but the town already owes much to them for the benefits derived from their enterprise and ability. They are the leading land agents of this Valley, and have a large list of bargains in real estate. Also mining property for sale. They furnish abstracts both of land, water rights and mining claims. The firm has lately issued an illustrated pamphlet, relating to the resources of the county, which will be mailed to all applicants.

In our advertising columns will be found represented some of the leading business firms of San Bernardino, and we can assure our readers that if they consult these announcements they can depend upon dealing with reliable houses.

J. G. Burt, the successor of M. L. Drew, a cut of whose business house appears among our illustrations, keeps a full stock of hardware and implements of every description.

Hale & Reeves, watchmakers, jewelers and engravers, have a large stock and the best assortment in the Valley. They are agents for several excellent sewing machines.

The Farmers' Exchange Bank lately opened, has superior facilities for the transaction of banking business. Hon. Byron Waters is President, E. W. Morse Cashier, and the directors are some of the leading capitalists of San Bernardino.

The Linville Mill is complete in every respect and one of the leading mills in the Valley.

J. W. Foy, brother of our respected fellow citizen in Los Angeles, has one of the most complete harness and saddle establishments in Southern California. Everything in his line will be promptly attended to.

Hudson & Taylor are the proprietors of a new lumber yard which is well stocked and the most convenient to the business center of the town. Newcomers who are about to build will do well to purchase their supplies of this firm.

S. E. A. Palmer, located about three miles from town, has a large stock of trees for sale in excellent condition and free from insect pests.

Paris & Goodcell is a legal firm, the members of which have long been known in Southern California.

The excellent illustrations of San Bernardino in this number were made from photographs taken by that well known artist, Mr. W. A. Vale.

San Bernardino is shortly to have a first class hotel, which by the way is sadly needed. Mr. Starke is building an addition to his present house which, when completed, will render his establishment the only desirable hotel in the town.

Mr. Henry Fulton, a newspaper man and member of the typographical fraternity for many years in the East, has lately opened a restaurant in San Bernardino which we heartily commend to the traveling public. Mrs. Fulton does the cooking and everything is clean, pleasant and homelike. To the many visitors to San Bernardino who have an abhorrence of Chinese cooking this restaurant will be a great bonanza, and it certainly deserves generous patronage.

STOCK IN SAN BERNARDINO

We lately had the pleasure of inspecting

a portion of the fine Short-horn stock which has been imported to California at immense expense by our enterprising friend, J. W. Waters, Jr., of San Bernardino. We first

RESIDENCE OF A. H. HART, Jr.

RESIDENCE OF J. W. WATERS.

looked at his magnificent three year old bull, yclept Bernardino Wiley 1., which took the first premium as a calf at the Los Angeles Fair some two and a half years since. Next, going to the pasture we found some fifty head of cows, heifers and

calves, all in the best condition and of pure Durham stock. Some of the principal and best breeding families of Eastern stock yards were well represented, such as Multiflorae, Daisys, Admirals, Bredas, Young Marys, etc. It is a fact worth noting that Mr. Waters' stock carried off nearly all the premiums at the Southern District Agricultural Fairs of 1878-79. To those interested in fine stock a visit to Mr. Waters' ranch is a rare treat, and so complete a display of Shorthorn cattle can hardly be found west of the Rockies. The choicest stock imported by Mr. Waters came from the well known J. W. Brown Sons, Berlin, Sangamon county, Ill., and J. C. Hamilton, Jacksonville, Ill.

LUGONIA DISTRICT.

Lugonia is a beautiful little settlement of San Bernardino Valley located about six miles east of the town. Quite a number of pleasant homes have recently been started, and many more will follow before another year has past. The Lugonia Fruit Packing Co. is an institution recently opened by the settlers which will furnish a market for their fruit at their very doors. A diploma for display of dried fruits was awarded to the Company at our late Horticultural Fair.

The soil of Lugonia is a light, sandy loam, well adapted to fruit, the water right excellent, and the price of land reasonable. With such a favorable combination of circumstances the future of Lugonia District is bright and we shall take pleasure in alluding to this thriving little settlement in our succeeding numbers of this magazine.

COLTON.

The principal railroad station in the county. It is built in a substantial manner, and has a height far exceeding it. The Trans-Continental Hotel is first class. The canning factory is doing an immense business, this season's work, 75,000 cans of apricots, 100,000 cans of peaches, and other fruits in proportion. The ably edited Semi-Tropic keeps the town posted on the latest news of the day.

SEMI-TROPIC
CALIFORNIA,
— AN —
ILLUSTRATED MONTHLY.

Devoted to Agriculture, Horticulture, and the Development of Southern California.

Terms: $1.50 per Annum, in Advance.

OFFICE, Rooms 9 & 10, Baker Block.

Address, CHAS. COLEMAN, Jr., Los Angeles, Cal.

CHAS COLEMAN, Jr., Editor and Prop'r.

OFFICIAL PAPER
— OF THE —
Southern California Horticultural Soc'y.
OFFICE, ROOM No. 9, BAKER Block.
GEO. RICE, Secretary.

For nearly two years we have endeavored to fill the editorial chair of the SEMI-TROPIC CALIFORNIA and believe we have done our duty, judging from the generous support of the public. The paying subscription list has been increased until it is thirty times what it was when we assumed control of the paper. We really are a little vain of our success, and are thankful to the public in helping us to make a success of a paper that is truly their own. In stepping down and out we are gratified to have our place filled by so able and practical a gentleman as Mr. Chas. Coleman, Jr., who will hereafter conduct the paper as editor and proprietor. Under his able management we expect to see the SEMI-TROPIC CALIFORNIA grow and flourish, and we bespeak for him the same kind support that has been given us.   GEO. RICE.

With this number we become sole publisher and proprietor of the SEMI-TROPIC CALIFORNIA. We will surely miss the mature judgment and able counsel of our late associate, Mr. Geo. Rice, and fully appreciate the gravity of the position to which we succeed. However, we briefly outline our course in saying that it will be our aim to make this journal practical in every sense of the word, and to that end we have secured the assistance of several of our most experienced growers in agriculture, horticulture, viticulture, and other departments. Besides, we solicit correspondence touching upon any and everything within the scope of this journal, and if our readers will send in their experience, any little minor error of construction will be corrected. Give us the facts, and if the article needs any finishing touches we will add them. Will our readers remember that this is their journal, and assist us to make it second to none of its class? It occupies a distinct field of its own and in no way comes in conflict with the regular daily and weekly newspapers of Southern California; it belongs to the tillers of the soil exclusively, and to them we shall look for the same generous support that has been accorded to our worthy predecessor.   CHAS. COLEMAN, JR.

GARFIELD.

Our martyred President, brave on the field of battle, eloquent in the halls of Congress, promising grand results as President of the United States, and noble and kind in the family circle, has been taken from us. Had he lived until the 19th of November next he would have been fifty years of age, an age ripe with experience which fitted him for the high position to which he had been called. His brief executive life had won to him the highest respect and fullest confidence of all classes, regardless of party. From north to south, from east to west, a feeling of sadness goes forth such as our Nation has never known.

Pure, noble soul, thy work is done, the voice of sympathy comes even from beyond the waters, while thy name finds a home in the hearts of fifty millions of our people. Farewell! friend of the poor and lowly, champion of right and justice! In the years that are yet to come, thy name will be revered by the coming millions, and of all the names that shall appear in our Nation's history none will shine more brightly than that of JAMES A. GARFIELD.

This paper is in no way interested in the sale of any lands, does not and will not receive any commissions on any sales, but we can say that but very few important sales have been made to new comers, but what the advice of this office has been consulted. And we pride ourselves that in no single instance has a purchaser found reason to be dissatisfied with his purchase or our advice. We insert advertisements for the sale of lands, at our regular rates, and know whereof we speak when we say no better medium for such ads. can be found on this coast than in the columns of the SEMI-TROPIC CALIFORNIA.

Should anybody wonder why this number is purely a Fair number, we would say that the demand came from our readers, consequently we have laid away several valuable communications, which will appear next month under their appropriate departments. It is our aim to make this journal practical in every sense of the word, still we would certainly mistake our duty if we allowed the recent Fair to pass with but a brief editorial, when its inception, its maturity and its grand success were due solely to this journal and its indefatigable editors, especially Mr. Rice, Secretary of the Horticultural Society.

The SEMI-TROPIC CALIFORNIA will be sent to any address east of the Rocky Mountains, for one year, upon the receipt of one dollar. This offer does not include premiums, and will remain open only until the first of January, 1882. Parties in Southern California who wish to make their Eastern friends a Christmas present, may take advantage of this offer.

SAVANNAH, Sept. 4, 1881.

MESSRS. RICE & COLEMAN—Gentlemen: You will please send to the address F. W Gibson, Vicksburg, Miss., the SEMI-TROPIC CALIFORNIA, commencing September number. The bill I will settle when in town. The September number is worth the price of the paper. Respectfully,

F. WESLEY GIBSON.

To which we lift our hat, make our most graceful bow and forward our journal.

EVANSVILLE, Ind., Sept. 12, 1881

EDITOR SEMI-TROPIC—Dear Sir: I have just received a sample copy (June number) of the SEMI-TROPIC. Enclosed I send you one dollar, subscription to begin, if you please, with September. There are many things I would like to ask about your country, but for fear of boring you with questions I refrain. I desire to come to California and to go into some sort of agricultural pursuit. I want to be sure, however, that with a capital of about $3,000 I can succeed beyond a peradventure. Will you please explain through your paper—unless you prefer to write—why it is that bees and grapes do not do well together? Can a man have, say 20 to 30 acres and raise bees and cultivate grapes at the same time, or do the bees destroy the grape crop? Does the scale bug really destroy crops of fruit, or is it principally scare? Do tarantulas and rattlesnakes abound there? How is the best plan to avoid buying land likely to be unproductive from alkali? Give some instructions about selecting good farm bad land, and your advice as to the purchase of unimproved or improved farms. Please discuss in your columns the above questions and oblige, yours truly,

J. O. STILLSON.

P. S.—Send copies of June SEMI-TROPIC to A. A. Pearson, Dallas, Texas; C. N. Mollette, Nineveh, Johnson county, Ind.

In reply we would say that with a capital of $3,000 properly handled, backed up with industry, good judgment and a rigid economy, you need not hesitate about moving to this section. For further particulars touching upon this question we would refer you to the essay on bounty acres for family support and profit in another column. Again a glance at our market report will show you what farmers are now receiving for their produce, which at present may be a little above the yearly average. As regards bees and grapes going together we would rather not express an opinion. We do know, however, that vineyardists and orchardists complain of the bees, and when an apiary is located near they make an effort to have it removed. While on the other hand bee men declare that bees do not injure fruit, and are ready to argue the point at any time. The scalebug cry is very largely scare.

The black scale is more a nuisance than an injury. The red scale, however, is considered quite an enemy, though damage up to the present time is very limited, and if early attention is given it, there is little to fear from it. It only exists in a half dozen orchards throughout the whole of Southern California, an area nearly as large as the States of Indiana and Illinois combined. Occasionally you meet with a tarantula or a rattlesnake, but not often. We have resided here over seven years. In that time we have seen one rattlesnake and two or three tarantulas caught by other parties for natural history purposes. You might live here for years and never see either a rattlesnake or a tarantula. There is very little danger of buying alkali land without knowing it. In fact the proportion of alkali land to other land is very small, and you can tell from the kind of vegetation growing upon it and other surroundings whether it contains alkali or not. If you are not more than 35 or 40 years of age and able to work we would advise you to buy unimproved land and improve it to your fancy. Twenty acres would give you all the work that you could do, and with the same economy and industry that characterizes the farmer's life in Indiana, you would experience no difficulty in making a good living from the beginning and money in the near future.

OUR PREMIUMS.

Which One Will You Have?

SUBSCRIBE NOW.

WILL YOU HELP SUSTAIN A PAPER DEVOTED TO YOUR OWN INTERESTS?

Every subscriber who pays one dollar and fifty cents (one year's subscription) in advance for the SEMI-TROPIC CALIFORNIA, will be entitled to either of the following premiums:

1st. OUR MAP OF CALIFORNIA AND NEVADA—corrected up to July, 1880, elegantly engraved and printed and folded in book form, convenient for pocket use. No person should be without a correct map of our State.

2d. OUR DICTIONARY—just from the press, newly revised by Wm. L. Allison on the basis of Webster's Dictionary, with large additions by the editor, from the most eminent modern authorities, including many meanings and words in common use to be found

IN NO OTHER DICTIONARY,

containing over 30,000 words and phrases, comprehensively defined; also abbreviations, useful facts and tables, foreign words and phrases, pronouncing vocabulary of scripture proper names, a list of mythological and classical names, UNITED STATES CENSUS OF 1880, etc., etc.

OVER 300 ILLUSTRATIONS

HOW THE FIRST PREMIUM BREAD WAS MADE.

Take one half a Sacramento yeast cake and dissolve in a little cold water, then

thicken with flour to make a stiff batter, and set for two or three hours to rise, then boil two potatoes, mash while warm and add little salt and butter, and cold water enough to make them blood warm; then add your yeast and thicken with flour to make a batter and let rise till light; then add one pint half of scalded milk and half of water, flour enough to make a stiff batter and let rise over night; in the morning dissolve one small teaspoonful of soda in a little water and add to your sponge with two tablespoonsful of sugar, stirring all thoroughly, flour enough to make it quite stiff; knead it hard and thoroughly, the more the better; let this rise a short time or until light, then break it down and mould into loaves, and put in your pans and let it rise again; when light put into a moderately heated oven and bake one hour. This quantity makes three loaves.

MRS. SARAH PARKHURST.

Los Angeles, Sept. 14th.

THE Horticultural Society offered a premium of $25 for the best essay on "Twenty Acres of Land, for Family Support and Profit," for which there were four contestants, as follows: No. 1, by Gen. R. Houde, No. 2, by Chas. L. Batchelle, No. 3, by Chas. Coleman, Jr.; No. 4, by Thomas S. Garey, all of whom wrote under a nom de plume. The Committee, consisting of Judge Sepulveda, J. D. Lynch and J. J. Ayers, after careful examination, awarded the premium to Chas. Coleman, Jr., of the SEMI-TROPIC CALIFORNIA.—L. A. Commercial.

THE AGRICULTURAL FAIR.

The first week in November will be an eventful one in this city. The District Agricultural Society are bending every nerve and leaving no stone unturned to make this, their second annual Fair, a grand success. Nearly $3,000 will be given in prizes for stock, agricultural products, speed ring and tournaments.

The week will be one of great profit to the stock raiser, farmer, horseman, and to the fun loving public.

During the day the attractions at the Park will be immense, and Southern California will show to the world as she never has done what this stock we are growing, what speed our horses are acquiring, besides tournaments and contests to amuse. In the evenings, at Turn Verein Hall, will be presented interesting and attractive programmes, in addition to the fine display of agricultural products. At this time of the year a splendid exhibit can be made and many exhibits can be secured that were not in season at the time of the Horticultural Exposition.

Don't fail to read the very interesting article on San Bernardino by our traveling correspondent and agent, Mr. J. C. Peabody. The mining industry of that county is promising to become famous, and is rivaled only by its beautiful climate and general husbandry.

TWENTY ACRES FOR FAMILY SUPPORT AND PROFIT.

PRIZE ESSAY BY CHAS. COLEMAN, JR.

[Limit, 1,500 Words.]

For convenience we will suppose that a friend is about to purchase a twenty-acre tract on which to build a home and to make a living, and being unacquainted with this section and its possibilities he comes to us for advice and guidance. His purse contains from three to five thousand, and his family consists of himself, wife and two or three children, all in good or fair health. His preference is for fruit raising instead of a mixed general farming; so we accordingly make a selection as near a railroad, schoolhouse and market as possible, and look to it that the soil is easily worked, is free from alkali and has either water within ten or fifteen feet of the surface, in which case no irrigation is required—or that it has a good water right, either by an artesian well or a running stream. And for this selection we do not propose to pay above forty dollars per acre—probably thirty will buy it.

Six or seven hundred dollars will build him a comfortable, hard finished, little cottage of five rooms, and two hundred dollars will furnish it nicely and buy his first installment of provisions. Two hundred fifty more will supply all necessary outbuildings, such as barn, corral, hen house, pig pen, etc. One good horse with harness, a cow, two dozen fowls, a couple of pigs, a plow, harrow, cultivator, and other incidentals, will absorb two hundred more.

Having become thus far settled in his new home, he is now ready for business, and the season of year will determine somewhat his next move. If it be in midsummer he will irrigate, plow and raise a crop of potatoes and beans for the winter market. If it be late fall or early winter, he will prepare his entire place, save probably an acre for alfalfa, and the same amount for house, barn and garden room, for tree and vineyard planting. The alfalfa patch for many reasons should be as near the barn as convenience will allow, and the family garden will certainly be within a few steps of the kitchen door. Having made these two selections, now the questions arise how much land shall be devoted to vineyard and how much to orchard, and what varieties of fruits shall be chosen. The division of land will be purely a matter of preference and opinion; some would advocate no division, but all grapes, another would advise all pears, while a third might possibly advocate setting the entire to wanting eighteen acres to apricots. However, for a place of this size, intended for a home, a mixture of vineyard and orchard is conceded by our best judges to be far superior to the single fruit plan. Eight acres to vineyard and ten to orchard would probably be a proper division; still the lay of the land, soil and other conditions might demand different proportions. To select the best varieties of grapes and other fruits will not be a difficult task, since experience has shown that for raisins the white muscat,

Sultana and the Gordo Blanco, and for wine and brandy the Mission, Zinfandel, Charbonneau, Blaun Elba and Berger have no superiors. Set six feet apart, the preferable distance on small places, an acre of ground will take twelve hundred vines, and with proper cultivation the third year will witness a few grapes, the fourth quite a crop, and the fifth a fair profit, with an increase in yield from that time forward. The increasing demand for California canned goods and other attending conditions would lead our enterprising friend to plant deciduous fruits almost to the entire exclusion of citrus fruits. Twenty orange trees, half as many lemon and a few lime trees would be the extent of citrus tree planting. The remaining nine and a half acres would be devoted to choice winter apples, such as White Pearmain, Yellow Newtown Pippin, Yellow Bellflower, Smith's Cider and Skinner's Seedlings, best canning varieties of peaches, the Crawfords, Lemon Cling, Heath Cling and Foster, and of pears largely the Bartlett and next winter Nellis, together with a few other fruits and varieties, in order to have some product of the orchard ready for market and the table during every day of the year. Planted twenty feet apart this piece of ground will take something over one thousand trees; the peach trees will bear fairly in two years, the third year will find them loaded; the apple and the pear trees will begin to bear with the third year, the fourth year will bring a few boxes, but it will require five years from setting to see the trees bearing heavily. The planting of the vineyard and orchard, and preparing the garden and alfalfa patch, if accomplished in one season would require the labor of an extra man for a couple of months, at an expense of fifty dollars. The outlings for eight acres of vineyard, twelve hundred per acre, at five dollars per thousand, would cost another fifty; one thousand deciduous trees and fifty other trees, including citrus and ornamental, would absorb at present prices about one hundred and fifty dollars more.

Here ends the outgo of money, unless a fence is desired; which, in this country, owing to existing laws, can be easily dispensed with. However, one feels more at home, and more secure, when his place is surrounded by a good strong fence or a cypress hedge. The alfalfa patch, sown with twenty pounds of seed the first of March, prepared with irrigating ditches, unless water exists near the surface, will yield its first crop of hay the last of June, and if a good, thorough irrigation is at once applied the second crop will be ready for the scythe in five or six weeks. After that it will probably bear two more cuttings before cool weather retards its growth; the following April, however, will see it ready again, and every month thereafter during the summer season, it will yield its ton and a half or two tons of first-class hay. This piece of alfalfa will afford sufficient hay for one horse and two cows, green feed for the poultry and a forkful for the pig pen every day, on which the pig will thrive and keep

fat. The pig pen will keep the kitchen pork barrel full, the two cows will supply milk, cream, and butter for the family, the extra butter, together with the surplus of eggs, will help very largely on the grocery bill, and if one so desired, a good fat chicken might grace the dinner table three days in the week throughout the year. The garden, if taxed to its full capacity, will furnish fresh vegetables every month in the year; and strawberries, blackberries, raspberries and other small fruits which figure largely in the economy of the family support, should have their separate corner near by. The space between the trees for the first two or three years may grow three rows of potatoes, beans, pop-corn or any other low crop, without interfering with the general growth of the orchard. After that time the peach trees will bear, and then only the land among the apple and the pear trees should be used for such purposes. Glancing back and summing up the entire outlay so far, we find that our friend has paid out two thousand three hundred dollars, and if he began with three thousand, after throwing two hundred more into the general expenses he has five hundred dollars left with which to meet any little demands that may present themselves.

By practicing a rigid economy, with this amount of corn on hand, and by following the conditions of cropping, the cows, pigs, poultry, alfalfa and the garden, as advised in this article, a comfortable living is assured from the start, and an independence in the near future.

In five years from driving the first nail, at present prices and a low estimate, the vineyard will pay fifty dollars per acre, and the thousand trees will yield one dollar per tree, giving a gross income of one thousand four hundred dollars per year. This certainly would satisfy any moderate ambition, and if necessary would support a servant in the kitchen, a man on the farm and all the necessary luxuries to make a farmer's home complete.

From the fifth year, however, the yield will increase until the maximum income, probably something over one hundred dollars per acre, will be reached in the tenth year. Even after that the vineyard will improve and will bear more prodigiously in a hundred years from now, while the deciduous fruits, on the other hand, will after a time decay and require resetting.

With this our task is done, but before leaving we wish to say that in writing this article it has been our aim to underestimate rather than to exaggerate. We believe that the ends spoken of may be reached with the conditions mentioned, and if anybody should profit by reading the above, then our pen will have fulfilled the mission for which it was employed.

"Snox," said a Dutchman, "you may say what you please pout pad neighbors; I have had te worst neighbors as never vas. Mine pigs and mine hens come home mit dere ears split, and tudder day two of 'em came home missing."

Produce Market.

MARKET REVIEW.

Since our last there has been a marked advance all along the line. Wheat is strong and promises to rule a few cents before Christmas. Barley has been jumping up five and seven cts per lbs, and is still on the rise. Corn at last has reached $1.60 in San Francisco, with a strong demand. Potatoes are scarce and hard to get, even at quoted prices. Eggs and butter are in demand at advanced prices, and a bare market.

Surely the farmers are having business all their own way at present, and with the high prices prevailing they are making more money than any other class. The average of barley will probably be doubled in this county of this fall's sowing.

The following prices are paid at the farmer's wagon:

WHEAT	$1 25@1 50
BARLEY	1 35@1 40
CORN	1 20@1 50
POTATOES	2 00@2 10
ONIONS	1 35@1 50
BEANS	2 00@1 00
EGGS	35@ 36
BUTTER	37½@42½
HONEY—Extracted	10@ 10
Comb	15@ 18
HAY, per ton	10 00@12 50

FRESH FRUIT—

Oranges, per box	5 00@8 00
Lemons, per box	3 50@4 00
Apples, per box	75@1 25
Pears, per box	1 25@1 50
Peaches, per lb	4@ 5

POULTRY—

Hens, per doz	4 00@4 50
Young roosters	4 50@5 00
Turkeys, per lb	12½@ 14
Geese, each	75
Ducks, per doz	5 00@6 25

The following are the retail grocery prices, as corrected by Geo. J. Thompson, wholesale and retail grocer, 86 Spring street.

EGGS, per doz	$0 55
BUTTER	45
CHEESE—	
California	15
Eastern	20
LARD—	
California	15½
Eastern	18

FLOUR—

Capital Mills, per cwt	
Lumber-dein Mills	2 00
Pioneer	2 05
Graham, 50 lb. sack	2 20
Buckwheat, 10 lb. sack	1 25
Oatmeal, 10 lb. sack	50
Corn Meal, 50 lb. sack	05

SUGARS—

Granulated	
Cube	
Light Brown	

COFFEES—

Java	25
Rio	20
Costa Rica	18

TEAS—

English Breakfast	75@ 90
Finest Japan	40@ 90
Black Oolong	50@ 90

CANDLES—

Adamantine, 8 for	
Patent wax, 6 for	
Paraffine, 6 for	
Lummum, 24 lbs	

SOAP—

Chemical olive, 20 bar box	45@ 65
Borax, 20 bar box	
Magic Bleaching, our own brand	1 40

YEAST POWDER—

Royal, 1 lb cans, full weight	
Dr. Price's, 1 lb cans, full weight	
San Francisco, 1 lb cans, full weight	
best made	75c

CANNED GOODS—

Oysters, 2 lb. cans, doz, standard	
brands	2 75
Salmon, 2½ lb. cans, standard brds	2 00
Lobster, 1 lb. cans, per doz	3 25
Crab, 1 lb. cans, per doz	3 50
Corned beef, 2 lb. cans, per doz	3 00
SYRUP	75c

OILS—

California Kerosene, per gal	35
per gal. case	1 00
Pioneer Kerosene, 5 gal. cans	1 70

RICE | 08

HONEY | 10

POTATOES, etc | 2 50

ONIONS, etc | 1 50

BEANS—

Pink	2 50
White	3 50
Bayo	2 50

LOS ANGELES WINES AND LIQUORS.

RED WINE, No. 1, per gal	$ 75@1 00
" No 2, per gal	40@ 75
WHITE WINE, new, per gal	50@ 50
" old, per gal	75@1 00

PORT WINE, old, per gal	1 25@1 50	
ANGELICA WINE, old, per gal	1 25@1 50	2 00
SHERRY WINE, old, per gal	1 50@1 75	2 05
CUCAMONGA, old, per gal	75@1 00	1 25
BRANDY, per gal	2 50	
AGUARDIENTE, per gal	2 00@2 10	50

LUMBER MARKET.

	Per M.
ROUGH R W and PINE, 1st quality	$27 50
" 2d quality	30 00
SURFACE R W and PINE, 1st quality	40 00
TONGUED & GROOVED RW, 1st qlty	40 00
do Flooring Pine, 1st quality	40 00
" 5th quality	35 00
RUSTIC	42 50
SIDING	35 00
SPLIT POSTS, each	22½
SHINGLES, 7! M	4 60
LATH, 7! M	4 00
SANTA CRUZ LIME, 2! bbl	3 00
PLASTER, 2! bbl	6 00
PORTLAND CEMENT	7 50
ROSEDALE CEMENT	5 00
GOAT HAIR, 2! lb	04
Delivered in yard.	

THE NEW PEACH AT THE FAIR.

The Committee in charge, Messrs. J. B. Clapp, J. S. Mills, S. P. Lukins, are more proud of the new peach which they have the honor of naming than even the premium awarded for best display. The most notable peach on exhibition was a seedling cling propagated by Dr. O. H. Congar, from pits of the Crawford, large, showy, fine flavor, and declared to be superior to even the popular lemon-cling. To the above Committee the Dr. gave the honor of naming his lucky "find," and thereupon Mr. J. S. Mills "struck it" by the apt name of "Pasadena-cling," by which name it is destined to become famous throughout this coast as well as in the East. The Committee consisting of Mr. East, Dr. White and Mr. Gay, of Woodland & Gay, declares this peach to stand far above all others exhibited and think that for its large size and great excellence it will take front rank in its season, especially as a shipping and canning peach.

OUR FLOURING MILLS.

The enterprising firm of Lankershim & Co., the owners of extensive wheat ranches where they grow vast quantities of the finest wheat, the owners of our great mills on Commercial and Alameda street, in all for to their liberal cash premiums given every year to promote the growing of the best quality of grain for making the best manufacture of bread to our market; they have acted themselves, if it were possible, to fear. Their grand exhibition at our Fair was the admiration of all. The great flouring and grain in sacks and barrels, flour, in sacks, the large amount with ample sacks opened for persons to examine them, the upper part in the case was in the display of premium bread made of its flour, was so handy to be admired.

This firm grows the raw wheat, grind and prepare it for market in their large and elegant mills, that will compare in all favorably with the finest establishments of its kind in the United States. Their entire business capacity reduced mills to their capacity, to day and night to meet the demand for their flour.

The enterprise of the world every product of Southern California market and. The capacity of the mills, barrels per annum, a trade in New and Texas, of its products are of finest rate act in.

P. C. S. S. CO.

Goodall, Perkins & Co., Agents,
SAN FRANCISCO.

San Francisco and Los Angeles.

The Popular Steamers

ORIZABA & ANCON.

Carrying Passengers and U. S. Mails.

RATES OF FARE TO LOS ANGELES

From First Class			

Eastern Cities and Principal European Ports,
Apply to

H. McMILLAN, Local Agent,
or D. J. Newby, Master or owner, First Mexican & U. S. Consuls.

AGENTS WANTED

MORFORD & BROWN,

REAL ESTATE AGENTS,

Houses, Orange Groves, Vineyards, Farms and Ranches.

COMMISSION MERCHANTS,

Dealers in Wool, Grain and Live Stock.

Corner Spring and Temple Streets,
Los Angeles, Cal.

SECOND ANNUAL FAIR

— OF THE —

DISTRICT AGRICULTURAL ASSOCIATION, No. 6,

— AT —

Agricultural Park and Turn-Verein Hall,

LOS ANGELES. CAL.

Commencing October 31st and continuing Six Days.

Splendid Camping Accommodations, Low Rates of Fare by Rail and Steamship.

WELLS, FARGO & CO'S EXPRESS will carry all packages of twenty pounds, and under, addressed to the Agricultural Association, FREE.

At the Park A Grand Exhibit of Stock, Horse Racing, Fireman's Tournament, Equestrian Tournament, for Ladies, and other Grand Sports and Amusements.

At Turn-Verein Hall Fine Exhibit of Agricultural and Horticultural Products. Every Evening a Programme of Amusement and interest

A BABY SHOW WEDNESDAY.

SPELLING MATCH —Open to the Pupils of Public Schools

For Catalogue or Information, address,

W. J. Nooly, Secretary.   **F. J. Barrotto,** President

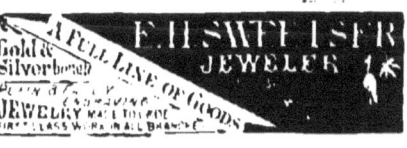

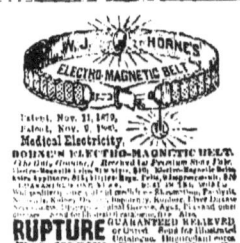

VOL. IV. *NOVEMBER.* NO. 11.

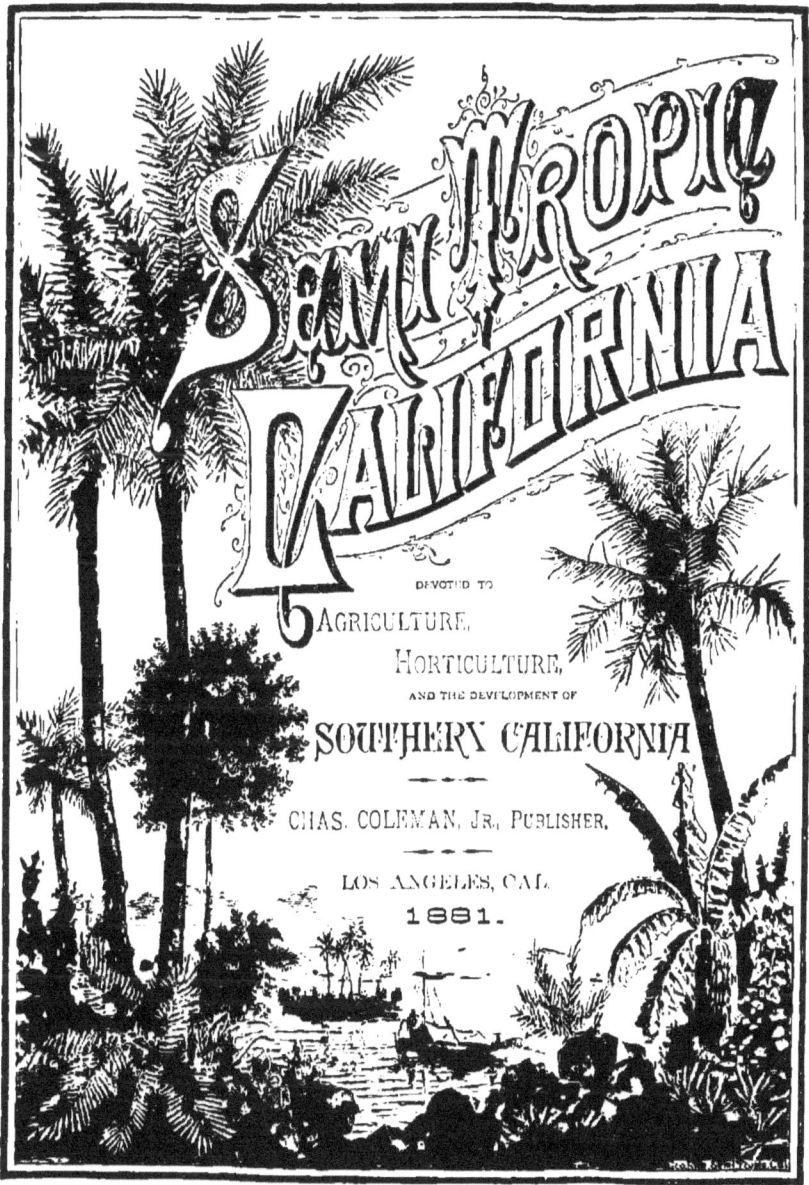

Semi-Tropic California

DEVOTED TO

AGRICULTURE,

HORTICULTURE,

AND THE DEVELOPMENT OF

SOUTHERN CALIFORNIA

CHAS. COLEMAN, JR., PUBLISHER.

LOS ANGELES, CAL.

1881.

MIRROR PRINT, Los Angeles

---AND---

SOUTHERN CALIFORNIA HORTICULTURIST.

Vol. IV.   LOS ANGELES, CAL., NOVEMBER, 1881.   No. 11.

Agriculture.

WORK FOR THIS MONTH.

Although the blending of the months into each other is so softly marked in Southern California, that without an occasional reference to the Almanac, one would hardly realize the month in which he was living, still to a close observer every change of moon brings a change of work. Every wide-awake, intelligent farmer understands that such is the case, still a sort of quiet indifference is so apt to possess some of them, no doubt, a modest reminder that certain things should now receive attention, will serve as a stimulant in the right direction. The summer is gone, and cool nights with scattering clouds remind us that we are nearing another winter with occasional light frosts, rain storms, and a general temperature of fifteen or twenty degrees below that of the summer. Has the poultry such quarters as the above conditions of climate would demand? An air tight, underground hen house may be required for the cold northern latitudes, but not so here. However, the house here should be so constructed that the fowls can roost well up from the ground, the roof should be perfect, and at least part of the house, that on the windward side, should be closely inclosed. Two or three days' labor, a few two-by-four scantling, a half dozen bunches of shakes, two or three pounds of nails, and a few stray boards which we find lying around here and there, will give the poultry a house that will keep them warm, dry and healthy, and without doubt they will more than repay the extra labor and expense in the larger quantity of eggs which they will produce during the winter. Other domestic animals should likewise be given good, warm, comfortable quarters.

It is a cruel and a vicious habit to tie a hard-worked horse to the end of a sixty-foot rope at the close of day to gather what he can within said circumference, and to take the chances of a rainstorm before morning. Interest is so low now, rather than turn stock out to take the chances of the weather, we would almost advise the farmer to go into debt one or two hundred dollars in order to secure these improvements. Very often, however, temporary shelter is only a question of a few days' labor, other requisites being at hand, but the dread to begin loads into procrastination and the next winter's cold falls upon the unprotected stock because of this passive indifference.

In building a barn the farming tools should be given a wing or some large room, and whenever tools are not in actual use they should be found in this room, out of the sun, dew, rains and other changes of the weather. Hundreds of dollars are lost annually by allowing plows, harrows, cultivators, etc., to fall to pieces in the sun. The cost of building a barn would soon be saved in these wastes alone; besides, think of the comfort and convenience which it would afford.

Now, then, suppose we examine the dwelling house; not that we expect to find a large amount of architectural beauty, a thing that would be decidedly out of place in a quiet farm house, but to see if the building will keep out the cold wind and rain this winter. To begin with, the chimney is defective, and when the wind blows from a certain quarter the stove smokes so that everybody is driven from the room. On the first warm day, after the morning house-work is done, investigate that chimney, clean it out, put a few more bricks on the top, carry the top above the peak of the house—don't neglect this; there will be some cold, windy evenings this winter when the family will want to sit around a good, warm fire.

Here and there we see daylight through the roof; a few shingles will remedy that. The hot summer's sun has warped some of the siding and battens out of place, rain will easily find its way through unless a few nails are brought into requisition. So much for buildings, which is altogether too brief, and now for the farm. If you have an orchard, certainly you will stop working the soil in it at once. This should have been said a month or six weeks ago, if deciduous fruits, probably nothing should have been done with the orchard after the first of September. After the summer's growth and frontage sufficient time should be given the trees in which to harden the young growth to withstand the winter's cold, but if the soil is constantly stirred, an effort to grow will be kept up and the first light frost kills the tender, soft growth. In the vineyard after the crop is gathered there is nothing to be done for the present. Apples that are to be kept for a future market should be picked from the tree by hand, and should be handled as carefully as though they were eggs. They may be packed immediately in boxes or barrels or may be put into small piles in a dry cellar, or in the granary or barn. The corn should be husked and cribbed as soon as possible; the pumpkins will require covering of some kind to protect them from frost, and the rich Hubbard squash will find their way into the cellar or granary.

The wheat and the barley farmer will provide himself with the latest improved machinery, will have all tools sharp and in readiness for the first rain. His harness will receive a thorough washing and oiling, he will provide himself with every little incidental which his past experience tells him he will probably need. If a bolt breaks he has one at hand without being obliged to stop the team until a man can go to town and back.

If a buckle breaks or a few stitches give way in the harness his remedy is at hand, and this is the successful farmer. All his summer fallow and other loose land may receive the seed before the first rain comes, thus leaving him to move into the new soil with his full force as soon as the ground is ready for the plow. Speculating on the probabilities of the weather is of little avail in this country; when it rains it rains, but when it clears nobody can say when it will rain again. The latest arrival can prognosticate the weather with as much certainty as the oldest inhabitant. We have this faith, however, in the future, that the acreage sown to grain in Southern California this winter will nearly double last year's acreage, and that next year's harvest will be by far the largest year known in the history of this country.

A FEW OF OUR ADVANTAGES.

California is pre-eminently the State for farmers who have the means to avail themselves of its advantages.

Our soil is above the average.

It can be cultivated far more cheaply than elsewhere, because most of it can be worked with improved farm machinery.

It has not yet become necessary to go into the woods and hew out a farm by severe labor with the axe, as open land is plentiful.

Our climate is so mild that expensive dwelling or outhouses are unnecessary.

Grain will stand for weeks after maturing without shelling out.

Threshing is done in the open field.

The grain having been threshed and sacked may remain on the ground for months without danger of damage from rain.

A man can work comfortably in the open air almost every day in the year. He does not have to lose month after month of the winter season on account of frost and rain.

Almost anything that grows can be raised in California.

Horticulture.

ALICE CARY'S SWEETEST POEM

Of all the beautiful pictures
That hang on Memory's wall,
Is one of a dim old forest
That seemeth the best of all;
Not for its gnarled oaks olden,
Dark with the mistletoe,
Not for the violets golden
That lean from the fragrant hedge,
Coquetting all day with the sunbeams,
And stealing their golden edge;
Not for the robin on the upland
Where the bright red berries rest,
Not the pinks, nor the pale, sweet cowslip
It seemeth to me the best

I once had a little brother
With eyes that were dark and deep—
In the lap of that olden forest
He lieth in peace asleep,
Light as the down of the thistle,
Free as the winds that blow,
We roved there the beautiful Summers—
The Summers of long ago;
But his feet on the hills grew weary,
And one of the Autumn eves
I made for my little brother
A bed of the yellow leaves.

Sweetly his pale arms folded
My neck in a meek embrace,
As the light of immortal beauty
Silently covered his face!
And when the arrows of sunset
Lodged in the tree tops bright,
He fell, in his fair child beauty,
Asleep by the gates of light.
Therefore, of all the pictures
That hang on Memory's wall,
The one of the dim old forest
Seemeth the best of all

PEAR CULTURE.

SAN JOSE, Sept. 25th, 1881.

JOHN R. BRIERLY, ESQ., Los Angeles, Cal.,—Dear Sir: Your kind letter of August 23d, containing an invitation to visit your city, and inclosing a complimentary ticket to your Horticultural and Centennial Fair, came duly to hand. For some days after its receipt I indulged the hope that I might so arrange my business as to be able to avail myself of your kind offer and invitation, but each day seemed to suggest something more important to be attended to the next, until I was obliged to dismiss the idea of seeing your wonderfully productive country until our busy canning season is over. Please accept my sincere thanks for your kind offer and offices. Your interrogatories relating to pear culture I will reply to in the order in which they occur, as follows:

Which stock would you use for orchard, standard or dwarf?

By all means, standard.

The dwarf, outside of a few varieties, under garden culture, has not proved a success. Twenty years ago the columns of the horticultural periodicals in the East were teeming with commendatory articles upon dwarf pear culture, and the catalogues of nurserymen presented a long list of varieties, embracing most of the old tried market sorts and all the new varieties that "promised well," as suitable to dwarf culture. If a sort refused to join the dwarf stock it could be "double worked" and nature circumvented in that way. The California gardeners and so-be orchardists readily embraced the popular doctrines. Large returns awaited the enterprising cultivator of dwarf pears in the near future. "There could be no morus multicaulis in it." It received the endorsement of all the great lights on pear culture, and we planted them, often to the exclusion of standards, when standard could have been obtained. The result has not been satisfactory. Standards have taken the place of dwarfs and the latter are but seldom found in our orchards.

What varieties would you plant, and about what number of each for an orchard of ten acres?

My action would depend upon two considerations. First, the period of maturity of the same variety grown in different localities and seeking the same market; and secondly, the extent and character of the planting in the near vicinity. Setting aside the above considerations, I should plant all Bartletts with the exception of such late varieties as might be required to meet the local demand. Five hundred Bartletts, 15 Winter Nelis, 5 Easter Beurre, 5 Beurre Bosc, 5 White Doyenne, 5 Dana's Hovey, 5 Duyenne du Comice, 3 Seckel, 2 Beurre Clifford, and 5 Beurre Hardy, would make a very suitable selection for ten acres and would give about the right distance for Bartletts. For an orchard made up of large and small growths indiscriminately, thirty feet is not too great a distance for pears.

Would you plant the same varieties with a view of having a market at canneries that you would plant with the intention of shipping to market in this state and the East?

No. Make "varieties" singular. Yes. Canners use the Bartlett only. While this variety is the only canning pear, it is at the same time the most valuable variety for shipping either to markets here or the East. It has a longer period upon the market than any variety that requires marketing direct from the orchard; it is a regular and uniform bearer, and comes early into bearing. The tree is hardy and easily managed in the orchard, and by its lateness in leafing and foliage it often escapes frosts and the ravages of those insects that are so destructive at times to the foliage of those varieties that put forth earlier. It has increased one hundred per cent. in market value within the last three years. The requirements of canners alone give this variety a prominence that no other can over attain, while as a market variety it has no superior.

What distance apart should trees be planted?

This question is partly answered by the response to the second question, but not fully.

The Bartlett, Seckel, Onondaga, Beurre Clairgeau, and other slow growing and dwarfish kinds should be planted nearer together than those varieties that attain a larger growth, and their predominance in an orchard should determine the distance, as regularity should be secured. When the varieties that attain a large size predominate, the distance should not be less than thirty-two feet apart. To secure the best results the trees should be so planted and trained that when they have attained their full size and maturity every part of the outer surface of each tree should in turn be presented to the direct rays of the sun at some period during the day.

What is a fair average yield per tree of an orchard with trees ten years old and upwards?

Three hundred pounds would not be an over estimate.

At what age will trees begin to bear sufficient fruit to pay expenses of cultivation?

So much depends upon soil, varieties and manner of cultivation that a definite answer cannot be given. As a rule, those trees which are the most neglected will bear sooner than those in which a regular and vigorous growth through the whole season is kept up; but such bearing will be at the expense of the future capacity and longevity of the tree, and in accordance with that law of nature which provides for the continuance of species and which asserts itself by hastening the period of maturity as a consequence upon the injury that tends to impair the vigor of the individual, or parent. I think it safe to assume that an orchard composed of the popular varieties will pay the cost of culture the fourth year from planting.

What has been the average price received by the orchardists for pears of good quality the past five years?

Bartletts, Winter Nelis, Doyenne de Alencon, Glout Morceau, Easter Beurre, Beurre Clairgeau, Dana's Hovey, Nelis and some other varieties have averaged about two cents per pound. While the intermediate varieties, embracing Howell, White Doyenne, Duchesse d'Angouleme, Beurre Giro de Rivet, Beurre Bosc, Beurre de Anjou, Beurre Hardy, Onondaga, Shelden, Columbia, Duyenne du Comice, Urbaniste, Vicar of Winkfield, Beurre Diel, Duyenne Boussock and some others, have sold for about one and one half cent per pound to shippers.

It has been asserted and generally believed that the Glout Morceau pear tree was not subject to the attack of the scale bug; but this proven incorrect. There is no variety known to me free from its attack.

The above comprises all the questions requiring specific answers. While I might have been more copious in my replies, yet I regard it but proper that some reasons be given for my conclusions.

With kind regards, I remain, truly your friend,

J O A. BALLOU.

PASADENA CLING.

EDITOR SEMI-TROPIC—Dear Sir: Since the fair held here in September 5th I have been questioned repeatedly, and strongly urged to give my opinion of the new Cling peach grown by Dr. Conger, of Pasadena, and named by the examining committee of the fair the "Pasadena Cling," and pronounced as superior to the Lemon Cling. I saw the report of the committee, and my first impression was to say nothing about it but let it pass and let this plant it that wish to. But there seems to be so many who are anxious to know if it really is as good or better than the Lemon Cling, and to know what I think of it as a canning peach, that I have concluded to give my views of it as a canning peach from my stand point, if you will permit me space in your valuable paper.

First, I will say it is not equal to the Lemon Cling in any respect. Second, it is quite cross-grained. Third, the flesh is red around the pit, which in canning will discolor the syrup and the red part of the flesh will turn to a dark purple, and in fact will discolor the whole peach more or less and give it a dark, muddy appearance after being processed. That alone is enough to condemn it by canners. Fourth, it will be quite an expensive peach to put up, it being so sour. It will take (I put it low) at least two pounds of sugar more to the dozen cans to make it equally as sweet as the Lemon Cling. Now, I happened to be at the fair at the time the peach was examined and compared with the Lemon Cling. In fact, I took the pit from both peaches, and in my opinion it is not to be compared to the Lemon Cling either in fineness of flesh, flavor or color, and still I must acknowledge it is quite a good peach, and canners would put them up provided they could not get the Lemon Cling. But I am satisfied in my own mind that the Lemon Cling will always sell for double the money per pound that the Pasadena Cling will. Then why plant it? Why not plant something that you know is good and always commands the highest price in market? A tree cannot be grown in a day or even a year; but you have to wait four or five years and only to be disappointed at last. Canners usually pay about four cents per pound for Lemon Cling peaches. I have, myself, paid five cents per pound for canning, and glad to get them at that. They and the White Heath peach are the only ones that we can can and ship successfully to the Eastern States and Europe. The Eastern people do not want our free-stone peaches unless in case of a failure in their peach crop.

Now, I have been corresponding with the nurserymen north of here near San José and San Francisco, and I find that they have sold all their stock of Cling peach trees, both the White Heath and Lemon Cling. Now I will say to those desirous of planting peach trees this winter and think they must plant some kind, to take the early and late Crawford, Foster & Smock's late. These are among the best, freestone peaches for canning. Of the latter kinds there are a good many trees still in the hands of the nurserymen.

Respectfully yours,
J. J. Gibson.

P. S. The following was received by Mr. Gibson a day or two after he had written the above:

San José, Cal., Oct. 15, 1881.

Dear Sir: Your favor of 10th at hand I sold my crop of Lemon Cling peaches, about 6½ acres, for $1,100. Some of my neighbors received 1 to 5 cents per foot the cannery. It will take some time before they find a better yellow cling peach that will be so productive and a great in quality, and tree from middle or end.

Jours truly,

LEMONS FOR PROFIT.

This culture is certainly and receiving the attention which its importance demands. Because the seedling are safe bearers inferior fruit, is without a shy bearer and is not a healthy tree, we should not condemn the lemon industry, but look about us for a good variety, a heavy bearer and at the same time a healthy tree. We believe these qualities are found in the Eureka, and possibly in the Lisbon, budded on orange stock. As regards the Eureka we can speak from actual experience, an experience which in every particular has been highly in favor of the variety. Three years ago a certain nursery of three year old orange trees were budded in May to the Eureka lemon, and approved varieties of oranges. Under a good, generous cultivation the buds made two large growths before winter and had fine bushy tops. The winter was frosty, and many of the orange buds were killed, while the lemon buds were not materially damaged. In the following spring setting blossoms were found here and there, and the trees grew so that it was almost impossible to get through the rows to do the fall cultivating. The next spring the buds were ten years old and the orange and five. They were completely loaded with blossoms and young fruit. They were removed and set into orchard form, and now, as we learn from the owner of the orchard, they are producing a profitable crop. The bud was three last spring and the rod six, and this we believe is a fair illustration of what can be done with the Eureka lemon, provided the culture is confined to our inland valleys. From this time forward the bearing capacity of the trees will increase until from six hundred to one thousand will be an average yield. The tree is somewhat dwarfish, a thornless, a hardy, vigorous, healthy grower, and an early and generous bearer. So much for the tree, and now for the fruit.

You go to our markets and call for the best lemon and they will invariably give you the Eureka, a small, oblong lemon, rich in juice, and sweet or slightly bitter, for which you will probably pay double the price of any other variety. Now these are facts, and long span therein, and our only excuse for stating them is that our people may be aroused to a just appreciation of a proper and a profitable lemon culture. But we must not forget that this industry is not intended for all sections. The inland valleys are the proper homes for all branches of citrus culture, while to

the coast valleys we give the palm for development from lemons,

OUR CANNED GOODS

It is estimated that 1,300,000 cans of fruits and vegetables will be packed in this State this year. This amount is much larger than last year's pack and tends to show our orchards and fields are becoming a great source of wealth. There are new canneries being established continually all over the State, while a good many farmers put up fruit of their own. San José alone this year, as stated by daily papers, will put up two million cans. Our canned fruit trade with the East and with foreign countries is constantly increasing in magnitude New York and Chicago are the great Eastern centres of the California canned goods trade, and probably will so continue to be. Thence they are distributed abroad to all lands, as well as to Eastern and Western States.

The shipments by sea are destined to all parts of the world, but the larger share goes to Great Britain. China and Japan take quite a respectable portion, as also the Sandwich Islands. Then our canned goods are shipped to all parts of Mexico, Southern and Central America, to Siberia, and to far distant Australia. In fact, they are beginning to find their way into every port where commerce is known, and when once tried the trade is forever after secured.

With this number will appear the first article of a series on olive culture by Ellwood Cooper, of Santa Barbara.

It is often asked why the olive is not more largely planted, and the usual answer is that it has not had its boom yet. Ellwood Cooper of Santa Barbara, and Frank A. Kimball of San Diego, at present are to have a monopoly of the industry on the Southern coast, and their products are by sale with the imported articles—oil and pickled olives sell fast. These men are annually realizing large returns from their orchards, and we believe that if our readers were better acquainted with the business, that this most healthful of all semi-tropic fruits would come into higher favor.

These articles from the able pen of Mr. Cooper will afford just such information that one needs who contemplates engaging in olive culture. Preserve each number carefully and in a few months you will have a brief though complete treatise from one who stands at the head of this industry.

The Semi Tropic Californian will be sent to any address east of the Rocky Mountains, for one year, upon the receipt of one dollar. This offer does not include premiums, and will remain open only until the first of January, 1882. Parties in southern California who wish to make their Eastern friends a Christmas present, may take advantage of this offer.

Viticulture.

BEST VARIETIES OF GRAPES.

EDITOR OF SEMI-TROPIC:—In your number for September headed "The best varieties of Grapes," you advise the planting of the Mission variety very strongly as the best. May there not be some mistake about this?

It is true the Mission grape is a good grape and has much to recommend it, and perhaps it was fortunate that that was the first grape which was almost exclusively planted, for it makes a great variety of wines, of fair to indifferent quality, and it is healthy and a good bearer. It is doubtful whether any one variety would make such a range of varieties of wine, but it is equally true I think that I could name varieties that would excel it for making any kind of wine or brandy that was ever made from Mission. If it is adapted for anything it is for sweet wines. Yet the Charbonean will make a better port, the Pedros and San Peters will make a better sherry, the Blanc Elben and Charbonean will make a better brandy, Zinfandel and Charbonean will make a better red wine, whether claret or Burgundy, and as to hocks or white wine Blanc Elben, Burger, Zinfandel and many others are far its superior.

As regards the quantity that grapes produce, the Burger, Blanc Elben, or Zinfandel will yield twenty-five per cent. more grapes per acre on any upland adapted for the raising of grapes and will produce at an earlier time—will under favorable circumstances yield something of a crop the second year that will pay for picking. Again, these grapes will do better where there is no irrigation, for they mature earlier.

As regards diseases of the vine we may claim to be free from them yet, for there is nothing which affects the crop materially; except it is mildew and in that the Mission would have the preference, and in low, wet localities the Mission would have the preference. But to plant such low, wet places with grapes will be of very doubtful benefit to the reputation of our wines, in fact, it will be an injury, although for the present it will pay the individual, as he will have larger crops, and as yet there is but little distinction made between the qualities of grapes, for the supply is not yet equal to the demand. But I think I can see the day coming when this will not be, and when grapes grown on our uplands will be the ones that will be in demand.

As regards mildew I have only known one variety, the Burger, which has mildewed on our uplands, and that such a small per cent that it has not been of sufficient importance to take into account, for an acre of Burger, mildew included, yields more wine than any other variety. As regards to other diseases or casualties, I have found as yet nothing to choose between these varieties and the Mission.

If the Mission vine has the pride of place,

why is it that Gen. Naglee who makes brandy a specialty, has grafted all his Mission stock with Charbonean, or why is it that Sonoma and Napa who already have three-fourths of their vineyards in foreign varieties, only plant foreign varieties now, and pay $25 a ton for foreign varieties—such varieties as they believe in—and only $10 for Mission? Of course it will not do to plant all kinds of foreign varieties, for many of them are trash, not one out of ten is desirable, but that a few tried and proven kinds are the superior to the Mission is equally true.

We have our Mission vineyards and they are useful and profitable; not one vine should be destroyed; all are necessary and wanted for sweet wines and brandy, etc., but if we ever expect to make all kinds of wine of the first quality, then we must have more foreign grapes, more Blanc Elben, Zinfandel, Burger, Charbonean. We can make as fine a table wine, as fine hock or claret, as can Sonoma or Napa (there are twenty times as many wines of these kinds used to all other kinds of wine that we make). This I feel I know, that there is no question about it, yet the world will not believe it until we prove it by showing and selling it in competition with Sonoma and Napa counties' products. I am now selling, in a limited way, to private parties in the upper country and San Francisco such table wines, and my wines have by comparison suffered nothing. It is supposed by those and experienced in our climate that being south, ours is a very warm climate. We are here know that this is not true, and they, too, would know differently were they to give the matter thought, for their vintage begins as early as ours and the first fruits in San Francisco market come from the north. As regards strength of the mission wine, it is strong, but that is not the reason why it does not make a good hock or drinkable wine. There is a something else; there is too acidity, no tartaric acid; the taste and aroma are not pleasant; it is coarse, if I may use the expression. Riesling and Blanc Elben are equally strong, but they have finer taste and aroma and the strength does not go to the head. It warms, makes you glow, makes you happy and not dull or headachy. It is a mistake that a wine must be very light in alcoholic strength to be a fine wine, and only our ordinary are light. The finest and highest-proved wines have some strength and the best vintages of Europe are those where they have little rain and warm summers to fully mature their grapes and make sugar. If ever we make wine for Europe, it will have to be a full-bodied wine to please them. Last year I made my wine much lighter than usual. I made wine only carrying per cent alcohol, yet even the complaint comes that it is too light in strength and have to mix it with a stronger wine of the same quality and kind to make it desirable. You say the inland valleys and mountain districts produce less to the acre than the lower coast sections, but the wine of the former location is lighter, etc. In this you are in error, for the reverse is a fact. The

dryer the soil the dryer the atmosphere, and the more heat, the more sugar and the stronger the wine.

L. J. ROSE.

Sunny Slope.

ORANGE WINE.

EDITOR SEMI-TROPIC:—Please excuse my neglect in not complying with my promise in the last month's number of your valuable paper in regard to an article about the manufacture of orange wine. My time was so much occupied with my own private affairs that I could not spare one minute for the *bono publico*, and the "better late than never" will probably satisfy you and the readers of your excellent paper.

I was a resident of the state of Florida for six years, and followed there and in the adjoining Southern States the occupation of wine-making for five years. All my wines, still and effervescing, which I made from the *vitis vulpina* or *vitis rotundifolia* varieties were acknowledged by connoisseurs to be of excellent quality. Encouraged by my success as a wine-maker, I tried to make wine from the sour and bitter sweet oranges, which are indigenous to Florida, and my labors were crowned with success. The first orange wine, which I made from sour oranges at Sanderson, Bakers county, Florida, was sold at Jacksonville, Florida, for three dollars per gallon, and the wine was then only eight months old, and will probably command by this time double the value, as this orange wine cannot be surpassed by any other wines for medical purposes.

In Southern California are a great number of orange groves, the yield of all the trees of the citrus family is very great, the demand for oranges along the Pacific coast is far behind the production, and the exportation of oranges to the East will never be a lucrative business for California, on account of the great distance by rail, as all the Eastern States can procure their oranges at a lesser cost from Florida and Louisiana. But we have to utilize our surplus oranges and can do it only by making wine from them, which diminishes the bulk and can be transported to any part of the country at a greatly reduced price.

I will give to our orange growers a few directions, which are founded upon my own personal experience, how to make wine from the oranges:

The oranges must be perfectly ripe, else the saccharine matter which they contain would not be entirely developed. The oranges are peeled first, then cut in two halves, across and not lengthwise of the cells; the cutting must be done above a tub so as not to lose any juice; both halves are pressed hard by the cutter. A good workman can peel and squeeze 120 oranges in one minute. At the time the tub is full of juice and oranges the whole mass is carried to a press which must be so close that none of the seeds can escape into the must, (the seeds would give the wine a bitter taste). To each gallon of juice of the sour oranges I added two pounds of the best white sugar, to bitter sweets one and one-half pound, and to sweet oranges one pound of the best white sugar, and to each gallon of the mixed juice and sugar one quart of pure water. The whole is put into a barrel and a space of about five gallons capacity is left for the expansion of the wine during fermentation. The orange wine has to undergo the lower fermentation, as by the upper fermentation all the volatile matter and the aroma would escape. The barrel must be closed air-tight and a fermenting tube adjusted. For the first few days the fermentation is very vigorous, and the barrels must be watched closely to prevent their bursting. After a few days the fermentation subsides gradually, the wine has to be raked off and the lees can be filtered. The fermenting tube has to be again adjusted to the new barrel and has to remain till the fermentation ceases entirely. About six weeks after that period the wine has to be raked off a second time, and in a month more will be fit for the market, as no second or "spring" fermentation occurs, as is the case with grape wines.

Orange wine is of an amber color, tastes like dry hock, but retains forever the aroma of the orange.

From the cakes, which I took out of the press, I made vinegar, with an addition of water and molasses, which was sold at twenty-five cents per gallon, wholesale; and from the peels, oil of oranges or an extract of orange could be made, and so every particle of that delicious fruit can be utilized. Twelve hundred sour oranges, and 1,500 bitter sweet or sweet oranges make one barrel of forty-five gallons of wine and ten gallons of vinegar. Yours, etc.,
EDWARD PRESTON.

MISSION GRAPES.

The following are a few extracts from a letter by Governor Downey to the San Francisco *Bulletin*, last November:

"The number of persons in the valley who are prepared with cellars, vats and pipes, is limited, so that owners of small vineyards have to depend upon the sale of their grapes; these small grape-growers have been treated, as a rule, very satisfactorily, and the profits of their little places have been quite large. My own observation has been that the result yielded from $118 to $175 per acre, but exceptional vineyards have yielded far greater returns. When well cultivated and thoroughly irrigated, the results above stated will stimulate the planting of new vineyards to an extent never before contemplated. Our rich alluvial valley will give the greatest yield and the most vigorous, long lived vine, and the Mission grape will prove, at least in Los Angeles county, the most profitable.

Experience is worth something in guiding the beginners, and to them I will state that we have vineyards of the Mission grape seventy and eighty years old that have never ceased to yield their abundant crops without once failing to respond beautifully to the magic touch of the pruning

hook, the plow and the irrigating channels. Water is everything to the vine. It must have it from the heavens or be supplied by the genius of its owner—and those who rely on a paying crop on high and dry soil will be disappointed no matter how much they may run the plow and cultivator. Besides, as a writer from Sonoma stated a short time since, those proprietors on the latter soils will in a short time find their vines giving symptoms of decay and death. Our summers are long, dry and hot, evaporation rapid. There being intervals of rain during this trying period it is evident that moisture must be supplied from other sources than precipitations. In travelling from Mount Shasta to the Southern boundary of our State wherever you find a wild grape vine growing, it will be found that moisture is near the surface. It is natural; for nearly 90 per cent. of the little fruit that has filled the world with delight in water, oxygen and hydrogen; the other 10 per cent. is principally carbon. The bouquet, aroma or volatile oils is in an undefined quantity, and chemists have not yet been able to satisfactorily determine their quantity and quality, so more than they have the mystery of the essential nature of the fermentation. Now, for new beginners, I will advance the idea that we know the Mission grape and have found it useful. So have the Spaniards in the Sherry districts, for it is the same grape. The Portuguese are satisfied with it, and the fortunes of their districts consist in adhering to it. They are not flying off hunting Zinfandel and other varieties. They have a good thing in their sherry and port, and I am thoroughly satisfied; so are some of us, and we desire no change. The beginner can get his cuttings of the Mission grape for nothing. They are vigorous and strong, and with less care than he bestows on an acre of Indian corn he can successfully tend his acre of vineyard.

The reader may wish to know something tangible about the reasonable product of a small vineyard. The wine-makers of Los Angeles have paid this year $22 a ton for grapes. The owner of the Cucamonga vineyard having more vats and pipes than the product of their own vineyard could fill, purchased the grapes of the small proprietors in the surrounding country. These small owners preferred to sell their grapes at Cucamonga at $20 per ton than to haul them to Los Angeles at $22. Among those was Mr. Hillarman, who had a small patch of thirteen acres. These thirteen acres, at $20 per ton, gave him $1,031. This little vineyard was only an incident to his orchard and bee ranch. This profit must be satisfactory. The vineyard is a lifetime estate, requiring no seeding or yearly planting. The requirements are simply to plant, plow and irrigate in season. There is no heartrending runs, no costly machinery, no exhausting trouble about labor, sacks or freight charges. The owner has just to pick his grapes, dump them out of the basket into the wagon bed, put the wagon on the scales, weigh, get his ticket,

and the ticket brings the coin. When the vineyard owner is situated so as to make his wine or his brandy, and do it well, of course the profits are quadrupled.

AMERICAN GRAPE MILDEW

This fungus is best observed on the leaves of the grape, where it makes patches of yellowish brown on the upper side, while a white frost is on the corresponding under side. The smooth leaved varieties show the mildew best, as it is not obscured by the growth of hairs. Farther than a white, powdery appearance, it is not to be determined without the use of the compound microscope. With it the powder resolves itself into small bodies, oval in shape, which are spores, and have been produced in large numbers upon minute branches of the fungus. The threads or filaments of the mildew run in all directions in the tissue of the grape leaf, and fruit also, and rob it of nourishment, out of which to form the spores. The mildew makes its appearance at any date, from June to September, the time depending much upon the character of the weather, a warm, moist spell being most favorable for its development.

Flowers of sulphur sprayed upon the leaves from below by means of a bellows early in the season, as soon as signs of the fungus are seen, is the remedy for grape mildew. Anything that weakens the grape vine, as early and over bearing, will tend to the development of mildew.

WHAT IS WINE MADE OF?

As wine merchants are petitioning the French government to put a stop to the manufacture of artificial wines, the petitioners asserting that not one-third of the wine used in Paris is made of grapes, the many Americans who turn up their noses at the juice of our own grapes will naturally wonder what the spurious French wines are made of. An exchange says that there are a number of large factories near Paris in which wines are made from rotten apples, damaged dried fruits of all kinds, herbs and spoiled molasses. But there are not enough of these materials to make as much wine as is required by foreign trade. Turnip juice has been worked over into wine, and American cider is the basis of millions of bottles of champagne, but good apples and turnips are too costly to be wasted on cheap wines, such as most Americans buy. Some of the temperance societies might find the returns they are after by satisfying public curiosity about what wines are made of.—N. Y. Herald.

Major Tiden will plant Walnut Mission grape vines on his new ranch six miles east of Fulton Wells.

At Downey, Los Angeles county, Dr. Greaves has begun the manufacture of castor oil, and has engaged 2,000 sacks of castor beans. He has already manufactured 125 gallons of the oil, which is said to be pure.

Southern California.

THE STEARNS RANCHOS.

VALUABLE LANDS IN SMALL TRACTS FOR SALE IN LOS ANGELES COUNTY.

The map published on this page showing a portion of Los Angeles and San Bernardino counties will give the reader a very good idea of the location of some of the choicest farming lands in Southern California. The Stearns Ranchos embrace in various tracts 80,000 acres of arable land yet unsold and nearly all uncultivated

on the market is sandy loam, without hard-pan beneath it, very fertile, easily worked and suited to a wide range of agricultural and horticultural products. In places alkali exists, but this may be worked out by proper treatment.

THE PRODUCTS.

Corn, barley, wheat, rye, oats, potatoes, tobacco and jute are very successfully grown on the land embraced by the Stearns Ranchos. The vineyards in bearing on the lands, at present, rank among the best paying property in the State of California. The orange and lemon do well on much of the land. Apple, pear, peach, apricot and

one of our home parts. The experiment has already been tried successfully.

PRICE OF LANDS.

The price and terms of lands in the Stearns Ranchos are very moderate, but for information on this point we refer inquirers to the advertisement of the agents on the last page of our cover. They will take pleasure in answering inquiries, and for results already attained we refer our readers to the well known and flourishing colonies of Anaheim, Westminster, Artesia and the many prosperous homes made comfortable by the various industries which these lands are susceptible.

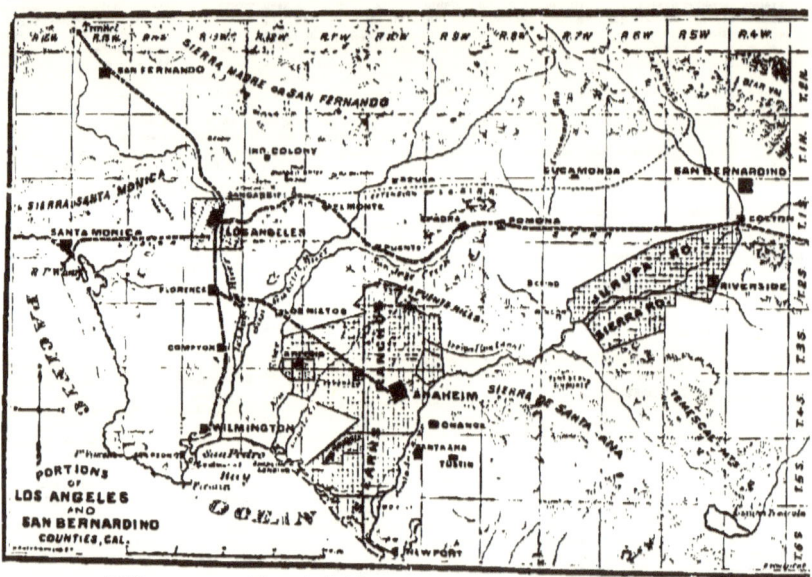

PORTIONS OF LOS ANGELES AND SAN BERNARDINO COUNTIES, CAL.

WATER.

The sine qua non of California is abundant on the Stearns Ranchos at an average depth of from 15 to 20 feet, and there are numerous flowing artesian wells which furnish a never ceasing supply of pure and healthful water. On much of the land abundant crops of grain are produced without irrigation even during years of short rainfall. The Santa Ana river flows through a portion of the tract, and the water supply from this source when properly developed will be practically unlimited.

THE SOIL.

Of most of the tracts of farming land now

plum orchards thrive equally well and pay their owners a handsome profit. Wood for fuel is moderately plentiful, and where it is not, it can easily be grown in sufficient large quantities for home consumption in two or three years. Stock raising is profitable, alfalfa fields furnishing an abundance of feed when there is a scarcity of natural pasturage.

RAIL AND WATER COMMUNICATION.

The Southern Pacific Railroad runs through the tract and steamers call regularly at two points fronting on the lands. Doubtless in a few years nearly all the surplus grain of the southern end of our county will be shipped to Europe directly from

NOTES FROM RIVERSIDE.

This beautiful colony has made most remarkable progress since our last visit some ten months ago. Many new and handsome residences, orchards and vineyards appear on every hand. Land which nine years ago would hardly have brought an annual rental of fifty cents per acre now readily sells for $200 per acre and is difficult to obtain even at this seemingly extravagant figure. At first thought it would seem as if this condition of affairs is due to some speculative excitement, but such is not the case. For fear we may be accused of exaggerating we will not venture to place before our readers a statement of the actual cash receipts of some twenty-acre farms in Riverside. For the present, therefore, we will pass from the consideration of the subject and take a drive down Arlington avenue, the aristocratic thoroughfare of this fine settlement.

THE GREAT IRRIGATING CANAL,

The main artery of the settlement, follows the avenue for some distance and seems to carry an ample supply of the life-giving flood. The main and branch ditches are kept in perfect order, and the irrigating system—that is the method of distributing the water—is one of the best we know of. The soil of Riverside, strong and wonderfully productive as it is, unquestionably needs an abundance of water; cultivation may in a measure supply the place of irrigation, but water is needed in any event, and it is gratifying to know that there is an abundance here.

ELEGANT MANSIONS,

And humble but neat-looking cottages appear on either side of the avenue surrounded with blooming and bearing orange orchards, vines loaded with grapes, flower gardens which are ever in bloom, grass lawns where the amusement-loving portion of the family can rejoice in croquet, tennis and other games, and all beneath a sky of the deepest blue, which is rarely clouded, summer or winter. The rainy season in Riverside is generally rainy only in name, the rainfall being considerably less than that of the coast valleys. Candor, however, compels us to state that Riverside is not exempt from wind. At intervals during autumn and winter northers sweep through the Cajon Pass, and while these visitors are by no means frequent, when a genuine one is in progress, the stranger is generally willing to remain indoors, although the old settlers make nothing of them. The Santa Ana zephyr is not unknown in Los Angeles county, and although scientific men tell us that it is healthy, we prefer to secure our health from some other source.

A RIVERSIDE ORCHARD.

As we pass down the avenue we will stop and take a look at one of these celebrated orchards, and as it happens that we find ourselves in front of the place of our genial friend, Mr. P. W. Cover, we will get him to pilot us round, thus we can see for ourselves whether there is any foundation in the statement that Riverside land is adapted to orange culture. Mr. Cover takes us first to his pet navel orchard, and he has good reason to be proud of it, for this variety of the golden apple has been pronounced the finest of its species at every fair in which it has been placed in competition. The trees are of good shape, and from 500 to 900 oranges are hanging on each tree. The fruit will be ripe about the first of next March, and even at this early date gives promise of being of very good size.

Mr. Cover also has ten acres in limes, his crop will be large and is already contracted for at satisfactory prices by responsible parties. The bushes, or rather trees, were some-

what damaged by frost last winter, but now seem in good condition.

A RAISIN VINEYARD.

Again passing down the avenue we will pause for a few minutes in a ten acre vineyard, where the owner and his sons are industriously gathering bunches of the oval muscat grape and placing them on wooden trays where, exposed to the powerful rays of the sun and dry atmosphere of Riverside, they soon attain the shape and flavor of the well known raisin of commerce. As the proprietor has risen from his labor to greet us we will take the opportunity to briefly interview him

Reporter.—How long have you resided in Riverside, sir?

Proprietor.—About five years.

Rep.—How old is this vineyard?

Prop'r.—It is four years since the cuttings were placed in the ground.

Rep.—Do you irrigate the land frequently?

Prop'r.—I have had the water on it only twice the present season.

Rep.—What is the average weight of the grapes on each vine?

Prop'r.—Between twenty five and thirty pounds.

Rep.—What do you estimate your profit will be the present season?

Prop'r—The older vineyard you examine contains 1,700 vines. The gross proceeds from these last year averaged about ninety cents to the vine. The net proceeds of my ten acre vineyard will average this season something over $850 to the acre.

Enough for the raisin business and we speed onward through the beautiful groves of

ARLINGTON

Where wealthy gentlemen from the great cities of the East are erecting homes in which they may spend the remainder of their lives in a land where the sun shines 355 days in the year, cold and oppressive heat are unknown, and malarial disease—the curse of the older Western states—are unheard of. A few miles further and the orange groves diminish in number and the trees are too young to attract much attention. Still further on men are busily engaged in plowing up new land for new orchards and vineyards, and we return to Riverside village satisfied with one day's observation.

SOUTHERN CALIFORNIA ITEMS.

Pomona is looking up, and advertises for a harness maker, a wagon maker and a tinsmith.

General Stoneman's one-hundred acre Muscat Vineyard has this year yielded an average of seven tons to the acre.

Orange takes the blue ribbon for making the first shipment of new raisins this season. McPherson Bro's made a shipment last week of 1,835 boxes.

A flour mill has been started at Pala, San Diego county, to handle the large wheat crop of that vicinity. It is already in running order.

The work of the California Southern Railroad is finished a short distance beyond Rose's station. Over twenty miles are already laid and the good work goes on at the rate of three quarters of a mile per day.

Colton is about to have a wholesale houses and shoe factory. Parties are now on the ground taking in the situation with an eye to that business. Such a factory is needed in Southern California, and the only wonder is, that it was not here years ago.

Los Angeles county has the lightest tax of the majority of counties in the State. The rate in Calaveras county is $2.80 on the $100; San Bernardino, $1.78; Alameda, $1.40; Sacramento, $1.70; San Luis Obispo, $1.72; Napa, $1.77; Ventura, $1.1; Shasta, $1.5; Trinity, $2.57; Los Angeles, $1.50.

Real estate in Los Angeles City never had a healthier tone than at present. One leading firm consummated sales last week to the amount of eighty thousand dollars. Property is changing hands in a quiet manner, without noise or excitement, and building and general improvements keep pace with the sales.

The Southern California Packing Company has turned out about 8,000 cans of fruit this season. For an experimental year this may be considered a grand success. Their market for these goods is already secured. It or load lots will shortly be shipped East. Next year this Company will probably put up 50,000 cans. The only question is the way it will be, "Can they get the fruit and vegetables?" Their working capacity is almost unlimited.

Mr. L. J. Rose, on Thursday last, crushed the astounding amount of one hundred and nine tons of grapes at his winery at Sunny Slope in addition to what he crushed in the city. This establishment has been running since September 1st, and has crushed from seventy five to one hundred tons per day since that time. Teams loaded with grapes begin to arrive at Sunny Slope at 5 o'clock in the morning and a procession of teams a half mile in length may be seen during the day waiting for a chance to unload at the crushing machine.

Santa Barbara County advertises her first annual Agricultural Fair to be held in the city of Santa Barbara on the 9th, 10th and 11th days of November next. We are pleased to see this move on the part of our sister county. Santa Barbara made a beautiful display at the recent Horticultural Fair held in this city, and now is the time for our citizens to return the compliment.

The State District Agricultural Fair will close in this city on Saturday, November 8th, and the time will be very opportune for the exhibitors here to ship their articles to Santa Barbara in time for the opening day, the following Wednesday, November 9th. This section ought to go up there in force, we owe it to Santa Barbara, to the world, to ourselves. Besides, these friendly exchanges are of great value as the lessons they teach; and as apart at these gatherings will fit you to labor more intelligently in the future.

192

Olive Culture.

HOW AND WHEN TO PLANT.

BY ELLWOOD COOPER, SANTA BARBARA.

The numerous inquiries received from different persons in every part of the country concerning the olive tree; the growth, care, propagation, period of fruit bearing, oil making and pickling, the financial prospect, etc., induces me to make use of your paper as a means of answering the inquiries. I propose, in a series of articles, to give all the knowledge I possess, based upon my experience as well as information obtained from careful reading of the best books that have been published on the subject—"propagation."

The common and preferred method is to plant the cuttings, taken from growing trees of sound wood, from three-quarters of an inch in diameter to one and a half inches, and from fourteen to sixteen inches long. These cuttings should be taken from the trees during the months of December and January, neatly trimmed without bruising, and carefully trenched in loose, sandy soil; a shady place preferred. They should be planted in permanent sites from February 20th to March 20th, depending upon the season. The ground should be well prepared, and sufficiently dry so that there is no mud and the weather warm. In Santa Barbara, near the coast, no irrigation is necessary; but very frequent stirring of the top soil with a hoe or iron rake for a considerable distance around the cuttings is necessary during the spring and summer. About three-fourths of all that are well planted will grow. My plan is to set them twenty feet apart each way, and place them in the ground, butt end down, and at an angle of about forty-five degrees, the top to the north, barely covered. Mark the place with a stake. By planting them obliquely, the bottom end will be from two inches to one foot below the surface. In Europe the trees are planted from 27 to 33 feet apart. My reasons for closer planting will be given in a subsequent article.

All trees, as a rule, should be propagated from seeds. The roots are more symmetrical, the trees not so liable to be blown over, and the growth more healthful; but I have not been successful in germinating them; hence, I recommend the cutting. If the trees are propagated from seeds, budding or grafting is unnecessary. I have seen the statement that it was necessary that the seeds should pass through the stomach of birds before they could be sprouted; also, that by soaking in strong lye the sprouting would be secured. I have not seen the result of either experiment, and accept the statements with more or less distrust. I presume cuttings can be obtained from any of the Mission orchards in the southern counties.

PRUNING.

The cutting will throw up numerous shoots or sprouts, all of which should be left to grow the first year; any disturbance of the top affects the growth of the roots. It would be advisable, however, where there are two or more vigorous shoots of about the same size and height from the same cutting, to pinch the tops of all excepting the one to be left for the future tree, so as to throw more force and vigor into that one. In the following spring, when the ground is warm and sufficiently dry, all sprouts excepting the one to be preserved should be carefully removed, cutting them off close to the cutting. The top end of the cutting should also be removed by the aid of a sharp saw. A post should be firmly planted, so that the tree can be well secured, to keep the trunk straight and avoid any disturbance of the roots, and should be kept until the tree is four or five years old. By adopting this method a great deal of time will be saved and better trees secured. The lateral branches should be allowed to grow until the tree is two or three years old; but in every case when any of said branches are rapidly making wood, they should be removed, and not be allowed to rob the trunk.

In the pruning during the first years, have only the one object in view—that is, to force all the woody growth into one main trunk. This being done, the tree will naturally form a beautiful shape. The cultivator must not look at the tree of to-day or to-morrow, but the tree of ten years hence. All branches to the height of five to six and a half feet should be removed, so as to admit of close cultivation by horses. Trees planted at the distance of twenty feet, and well kept, will in ten years touch each other. When this condition is reached they will be in full bearing, and therefore will require constant pruning or cutting back. It is much easier and less expensive to gather the fruit from small trees; besides, if the pruning is intelligently done, it will improve the fruit and secure a greater quantity to the acre than can be produced under any other conditions.

Some orchards in Europe are planted in "threes;" that is three trees in each place, planted in the form of a triangle, and three or four feet apart. This method would require the rows to be thirty-three to thirty-five feet distant, and would give about the same number of trees to the acre as by planting at twenty feet, one tree in each place. It is claimed that by planting in this way no staking is required, the trees protecting one another from the most violent wind storms; the trimming is simplified, and less care and labor required in the cultivation.

(To be continued)

Harper, Reynolds & Co., our popular hardware dealers, have manufactured 15,000 feet of iron water pipe ranging in diameter from four to thirteen inches, for N. C. Carter, to be used for bringing the water from Santa Anita cañon to the Sierra Madre Tract

Peruvian Bitters is a tonic which strengthens the system, eradicates malaria and may be safely taken by all.

Entomology.

THE CODLING OR APPLE MOTH.

The following extracts are from a valuable work entitled "Insects Injurious to Fruit and Fruit Trees," by Matthew Cooke, Chief Executive Horticultural Officer of the State of California:

It is not necessary for our purpose to detail the amount of damage done the apple, pear and quince crop of central California since 1874, by the insect past known as the *Codlin* or *Apple Moth* (the parent of the apple worm), as unfortunately it is too well known.

FIRST APPEARANCE OF THE MOTH.

The moth generally appears from April 25th to the 15th of May; a few in favorable locations by April 15th. The time at which the eggs arrive at maturity apparently coincides with the end or termination of the pupa or chrysalis state, so that the sexes are ready to unite soon after transformation.

The moths produced by the hibernating larvæ deposit their eggs in the blossom end (or calyx) of the fruit, generally; possibly because they cannot puncture the epidermis (or skin) of the young fruit. Later broods deposit their eggs on any part of the fruit. The eggs are attached to the fruit by a pasty substance. At the time the egg is deposited the skin of the fruit is punctured, making easy entrance for the young larva. It is rare to find more than one egg on any apple, pear or quince, or more than one larva. The larva is hatched in from seven to ten days, and begins to eat eagerly and burrow towards the *carpellary ovarium*, or core containing the seeds.

PROBABLE RATE OF INCREASE OF THESE MOTHS.

Entomologists claim that of the lepidopterous insects, including butterflies and moths, nearly one thousand kinds are known in the United States. That each female lays from two hundred to five hundred eggs. Taking two hundred as the lowest number, twelve female moths in one orchard would produce two thousand four hundred caterpillars; if one-half these were females, they would produce two hundred and forty thousand. In proportion, the third generation would reach twenty-four millions, supposing that no untimely deaths took place.

Most of the books on this subject speak of the codlin moth as going through but one generation in a year. This may be true in colder climates and shorter seasons than ours, but in parts of our favored State there is no question that two or three generations or broods are common. From personal observation, we know that the rule for the Sacramento Valley is three broods each year. This year (1881), on account of the early appearance of the first moths, we shall probably have four broods. These facts explain the exceptional importance of this insect in California.

REMEDIES RECOMMENDED.

From the observations stated, we are led to believe that the destruction of this pest must be consummated while it is in the caterpillar state.

At any time between the first day of November and the first day of March of each season, all the apple, pear and quince trees, in any orchard infested by codlin moth, should be carefully scraped, and all loose bark removed. Procure a cloth made of old sacks or any material convenient, spread on the ground around the tree as far as the scrapings are likely to fall; then commence on the tree as far up as there is any rough loose bark, and scrape it carefully off. Also examine and scrape all crevices in the bark or those formed in the crotches of the tree. Continue scraping until you reach the ground. This done, gather the scrapings carefully off the cloth, so that they can be burned or otherwise destroyed immediately.

In order to destroy any larvæ remaining on the tree, or in the crotches, indents or cracks, also to inaugurate the growth of a new smooth bark, a wash should be applied as recommended in the following rule:

After scraping, the tree should be washed with an alkaline wash made from a soft soap containing at least nine per cent. of potash. This soap, when made, mixed with twenty-five per cent. of its weight with flour of sulphur, then pound of this mixture to each gallon of water used for washing trees. Instead of this wash, the whale oil soap and sulphur mixture known as codlin moth wash, one pound to each gallon of water, or, a mixture containing not less than one pound of commercial concentrated lye to three gallons of water.

Take a common whitewash brush and give the tree a good coat of the solution, or use a garden force-pump of some form, commencing at the top as far up as there are any cracks or crevices in the bark, and wash down to the ground. Repeat the washing in the spring; this will destroy any larvæ or chrysalide left on the tree.

Bands should be placed on trees as follows: Take a piece of common straw wrapping paper, say twenty-four inches long and ten or twelve inches wide, double it lengthwise and put around the tree a few inches above the ground. From experiments made, bands of burlap or old grain sacks torn in strips are preferable. The larva creeping up the tree makes its nest under the band. These bands should be examined every seventh day, the larvæ collected and destroyed. Paper or rags laid on the ground around the tree will answer partly the same purpose, but may not be so easily examined. It is also recommended that some paper or rags should be placed in the crotches of the tree and on the rough branches, so as to entrap any larva coming down the branches looking for a nesting place, and these should be examined as regularly as the bands.

A prominent fruit grower, whose orchard is near to this city (Sacramento), purchased three hundred bands and placed them in his orchard. He employed them to pick fruit off his trees showing signs of larvæ. The hogs followed the men from tree to tree, and ate all fruit thrown down. This operation was often repeated, so that the early broods were nearly destroyed, and a large percentage of the late crops saved. This is an excellent remedy, but expensive. Fruit infested picked off the trees and destroyed, will prove successful to the extent practiced.

IMPORTANT POINTS.

To be successful, use every effort to destroy the spring brood of moths.

Any means taken to destroy the early broods will prevent the late fruit from being lost.

RESIDENCE OF J. A. GRAVES, Los Angeles.

The Natoma Fruit Company, Folsom, Sacramento county, is repaid, washed twice, and handed twenty five hundred pear trees, at an average cost, labor included, of six cents per tree.

Disinfect all boxes returned from market before taking into the orchard.

The female moths deposit their brood of eggs within forty eight hours.

The egg cannot be seen plainly by the unaided eye.

The best time to see the moths at work is at dawn of day, in the months of June and July.

The moth deposits the eggs at night.

Only united action of fruit growers will gain a complete victory over this pest.

There are three broods of the codlin moth at least, each season, in the great central valley of California.

Supposing the moth watered from the winter larvæ on the first day of May, the first brood of the season would reach perfection by the twentieth of June, and the second brood by the twelfth of August.

Biography.

RESIDENCE OF J. A. GRAVES

We have the pleasure this month of presenting to our readers a handsome illustration of the residence of one of the prominent legal lights of Los Angeles—Mr. J. A. Graves. This house, which is finished and nearly perfect as one of the finest in the city, was constructed in 1879, under the supervision of G. Hargill, Esq., one of our pioneer builders. The location, north-east corner of Fort and Third streets, is one of the most pleasant, healthful and convenient in Los Angeles. The size of the house, 32 x 45 feet, and the edifice is built in a most substantial manner, with brick cellar and foundations. Not only is the exterior appearance exceedingly graceful, but we venture the assertion that no residence in this city has more convenient interior arrangements. The surroundings of the house are very pleasant. The lawn in front is beautifully laid out and covered with the choicest plants and shrubs to be obtained.

Mr. Graves is a native of Kentucky but came to California in 1857, when but four years old. His parents are still living in Northern California, in the neighborhood of Santa Rosa. He removed to Los Angeles in 1875, and for some time was connected with the then sitting legal firm of this city, Messrs. Brunson & Eastman. On the completion of the Baker Block he opened an office of his own in that elegantly appointed building, where he has since followed his profession. Two years ago Mr. Graves married the elder daughter of Mr. John M. Griffith of this city. The union has proved a happy one, and a sweet month old girl baby is the pride of their household.

We are glad to record the fact that Mr. Graves has been remarkably fortunate in his business and personal relations in the community. He has acted as agent for the Baker Block since its completion in 1877, and has the satisfaction of seeing Col. Baker's liberal investment at last paying a fair interest.

Mr. Graves and his estimable wife have a host of friends in Southern California who will be glad to hear of his present pleasant circumstances and favorable outlook.

Santa Barbara is gradually filling up again, and rents are firm. There is no excitement nor push, but a steady growth, and business of all kinds is reviving.

SEMI-TROPIC
CALIFORNIA.
— OF —
ILLUSTRATED MONTHLY.

Devoted to Agriculture, Horticulture, and the Development of Southern California.

Terms: $4.50 per annum, in advance.

OFFICE, ROOMS 9 & 10, BAKER BLOCK.

Address CHAS. COLEMAN, JR., Los Angeles, Cal.

CHAS. COLEMAN, Jr.,   Editor and Prop'r

OFFICIAL PAPER
— OF THE —
Southern California Horticultural Soc'y.
OFFICE, ROOM No 1, BAKER BLOCK.
GEO. RICE, Secretary.

Our contributors for this month are worthy of a brief notice from the fact that they rank among the very best on this coast. L. J. Rose, of Sunny Slope fame, gives us a very valuable and interesting article on the varieties of grapes.

This communication is in reply to an article in the August number of this journal advocating the planting more largely of the Mission variety. While he speaks very kindly of the Mission, and acknowledges that it can be put to more purposes than any other single variety, he further argues that to make a certain kind of superior wine he would advocate a certain variety other than the Mission. In other words, the Mission is good in its place, but in order to produce the different classes of superior wines, we must plant certain foreign varieties of grapes.

Major Freis gives us some information concerning the manipulation of orange wine. His experience and success in Florida, of which we have read in publications of that State, may prove to be of great value in this section. J. Q. A. Ballou, the noted pear man of San Jose, and manager and principal stockholder of the San Jose Packing Company, through the courtesy of General John R. Bierly, favors us with his views on pear culture. We would say that he has had one of the finest pear orchards in Santa Clara valley for over twenty years, and his practical knowledge of the cultivation and marketing of pears has probably been larger than that of any other man in this State, while his connection with one of the principal canneries on the coast, has enabled him to determine the present and prospective value of this fruit. J. J. Gnaum, of our own canning factory, has received mention in a former number, and his article on the Peabean cling will be of value in warning our growers that they can not be too careful in selecting varieties.

This is just the kind of information that should go forth. Merit is what we are after in fruit, and these pages are ever open to a free discussion in that direction.

The Bee-keeper's department starts out with the annual address of the President of the Bee-keeper's District Association. The balance of the reading matter, save a few clippings, emanated from the editor's sanctum, and without further comments we pass this number over to your profitable perusal.

Our Holiday number, which will be the January number, instead of the December number as was said in our last issue—will come from the press about two weeks before Christmas, and as an advertising medium for our business firms will be first class. We promise a full 5,000 edition and it may possibly reach 10,000 copies. It will contain, with cover, thirty-six pages, will be handsomely illustrated with new illustrations, and the reading matter will be gotten up with a view to making the number a library of information of South ern California within itself, a book that may be filed away for valuable future reference. This effort will of necessity put us to great expense, and we rely on the good will and favor of our citizens to sustain us with their patronage to the extent that it may be a grand success and that Southern California may go forth to the world in a manner worthy of her greatness.

Mr. W. K. Willmore will start for Kansas City and St. Louis early in November for the purpose of directing immigration to Southern California. We would commend him to the confidence of our Eastern neighbors, believing as we do from a personal acquaintance that he has a just appreciation of the advantages which Southern California offers in comfortable homes and a genial, healthful climate, to those who are contemplating coming to the Pacific Coast. As authorized agent, Mr. Willmore will also further the interest and circulation of the SEMI-TROPIC CALIFORNIA during his visit East.

We call attention to the engraving on another page of this number of the beautiful shorthorn bull belonging to J. W. Waters, Jr., Esq., of San Bernardino. This valuable breed of stock originating in Columbia, England, something over one hundred years since, always a favorite breed with stock raisers, seems to be growing more rapidly in general favor of late years than ever. The distinguishing characteristics of this breed of cattle are roundness, solidity of form, easy keeping, the fine rich flavor of its flesh, to say nothing of its milking properties—several well attested instances of a yield of 15 to 20 lbs. of butter per week being recorded. The great increase in the consumption of meat on this continent and among all the nations of Europe and the growing demand for meats of a better quality, indicate a higher place than ever in the public estimation of this noble breed of cattle.

We consult the best good of our readers in recommending them to now secure this valuable and important information and most interesting reading matter, including a thousand or more of pleasing and instructive engravings and sketches, that can be obtained at trifling expense in the *American Agriculturist*. This is not merely a farm and garden journal, but is very useful to every House-keeper and to every household in Village or Country. It has an entertaining and useful department for the little ones. It is a journal that pays to take and read. Try it, and, our word for it, you will not be disappointed. Its constant, persistent exposures of Humbugs and swindling schemes are worth far more than the cost of the paper. The 41st annual Volume begins January 1, but those subscribing now for 1882 get the rest of this year free. Terms: $1.50 a year; four copies $5 (English or German edition); single copy, 15c.

N. B.—Those desiring can get an extra or double specimen number post-free for 10 cts., by addressing the Publishers, Orange Judd Co., 751 Broadway, New York.

All delinquents and those whose subscription to the SEMI-TROPIC CALIFORNIA expires with this year, in order to secure the holiday number, which is the January number of next year, will need to renew their subscription before Christmas. The holiday number will be too valuable for gratuitous circulation, and it alone will be worth half of the yearly subscription price. Hereafter this journal will not be sent to any address unless payment is made in advance, or arrangement is made with this office for such payment.

The J. Lusk Canning Company, of Oakland, is the largest fruit cannery in the world. The ground floor of their buildings covers seven acres. It is the only cannery growing a great portion of its products on its own grounds. These embrace 700 acres and are within a stone's throw of the factory. On their farm they grow blackberries, raspberries, strawberries, peas, corn, asparagus and tomatoes. Their pack this year will be 200,000 cases against 115,000 last year. Their goods are all sold, as well as those of the canneries preceding.

The Agricultural Fair opens at Turn-verein Hall Monday evening, with appropriate ceremonies. During the week exhibits of stock of all kinds, agricultural implements, firemen's and ladies' tournaments, with exciting races each day. Thursday has been set apart as a school day, and a great crowd will be on the Park grounds on that day. The horticultural display will be made at Turnverein Hall during the week. Each evening will bring forth a new and interesting programme to entertain the crowds that will be in attendance.

The *American Home Journal*, an illustrated monthly published at Columbus, Ohio, is one of our most welcome exchanges. It is printed on a fine quality of paper, is beautifully illustrated, and its pages are full of choice reading for the politician, the business man, the farmer and the fireside. Subscription price, only $1.

OMAHA, Neb., Oct. 10, 1881.

CHAS. COLEMAN, JR., Editor SEMI-TROPIC
—Sir: The October number comes marked
"subscription expired." I do not care to
renew, as I shall be in California before the
year expires; but that I may have the reading of your excellent monthly while in
Omaha, and that others may also, I mail
myself of your offer to send the Semi-
Tropic to one east of the Rocky mountains
for one year, upon the receipt of one dollar.
Herein find Postoffice order for $2, for
two copies to be addressed as follows:—
William L. Adams, Omaha, Nebraska; L.
Bush, Jamestown, Fentress Co., Tenn.

Yours truly,   J. H. KELLUM.

The above letter is but a fair average of
what is received at this office nearly every
day. From these communications we are
led to see that this journal is instrumental
in bringing out many to Southern California,
and that there are thousands in the East
who are seeking reliable information concerning this southern coast. While the
Chamber of Commerce is casting about for
such material to send East would it not be
well to send a few hundred yearly subscriptions to the various reading rooms, hotels
and libraries. We would furnish the same
at a bare margin above cost. The holiday
number alone might be worth the entire investment.

WHO HAS TREES TO SELL?

EDITOR SEMI-TROPIC CALIFORNIA: You
have given us in "Twenty Acres for Family Support and Profit," much valuable information and advice for very little money.
But you do not tell us where and of whom
we can buy reliable trees and grape cuttings. If you reply that the advertising
pages is the place to look for such things,
and not in the above article, I would say I
have often looked them through, as well as
those of the daily papers, without finding a
single blossom. I have no time to ride all
over the country, inquiring here and there
for what I want, when I could read it at
my leisure in your journal. Though this is
not the season to plant trees, I want to
to know now where I can buy them, or at
least see them and know the prices, so that
when my land is in the right condition, or
the rains propitious, I can plant something
that will grow fruit, not seasoned stove-
wood. I know many trees are sold in the
spring in the street, but I object to having
my trees baked or wilted in the hot wind
or sun, or pulled up with all their best
roots broken. I prefer to take them my-
myself or see it done, when I can handle
them properly. You say that the trees and
vines for each twenty-acre farm will cost
$400; surely, it is a business in this county
too large to hide longer under a bushel.
Who wants my $400 in exchange for
apple, pear and apricot trees? In other
words, who has trees to sell?   I. S.

T. E. ROWAN & CO.

This is the firm name of the ablest and
most reliable real estate, general business
and commission agents in the city. Mr.
G. A. Dobinson, one of the firm, came
to Los Angeles six years ago, is a licensed
attorney-at-law, commissioner of deeds for
the State of New York and Arizona Territory, also notary public, and as such attends to Eastern business in the way of
taking depositions.

Mr. T. E. Rowan is a pioneer, having
come to Los Angeles more than twenty
years ago. He has served three terms as
County Treasurer and one term as City
Treasurer, has been under Sheriff for two
years, has been identified with the old firm
of Hellman, Temple & Co., bankers, and
when the F. & M. bank incorporated served
that institution as Teller for five years
under the present able President, I. W.
Hellman, and his knowledge of California
is second to none. They are also agents
for the State Investment and Insurance
Company of California, and the Mutual
Life Insurance Company of New York,
with assets over $90,000,000, and as such do
a large business in this line.

The catalogue bank of Southern California facts, real estate and general business,
which they issue, will be sent to any address free. We can fully recommend this
firm to the confidence of all in every department which they represent, and to
those seeking information regarding real
estate and the thousand and one questions
attending such information, we would say
write for catalogue.

CANDY.

The Los Angeles Candy Factory, A.
Merriam & Co., 31 Spring street, manufacture all kinds of candies, from the common-
est stick to the most fancy creams. These
candies are put up in five and twenty-five
pound boxes and shipped to their customers
all over the Pacific Coast, the territories
and to Texas. Their foreman of the candy
department, it is said by some of our whole-
salers, hasn't an equal on this coast, judging, as they do, from goods received formerly from other factories. In connection
with their factory they also keep an cream
and lunch rooms, which are patronised by
the elite of our city. Pleasant side rooms
for families and ladies, and farmers can get
a lunch here all the way from ten cents up.
Write for price list of candies, and depend
on square, honest dealings.

Chas. P. Jillson, in another part of this
journal, has an advertisement of the choicest
breeds of poultry known, especially for
laying purposes. Mr. Jillson, though not
long in the business, has already built up a
large trade. His orders come from every
section of the southern counties and reach
also to Arizona. His straight forward, honest, square dealing has won him many
friends, and all his customers remain with
him. The White Leghorns and the Black
Spanish are the best layers known; nobody
disputes this fact.

IMPORTANT TO FARMERS

The Los Angeles Pork Packing Company
are now paying farmers San Francisco
prices for their hogs, and have more than
doubled the capacity of their extensive factory. The firm now puts up an average of
100 hogs per day, and the quality of their
goods has created a demand for them in
such an extent that it is utterly impossible
to supply it. The company wish to buy all
the surplus hogs in Southern California,
and farmers will save much inconvenience,
and the freight expense to San Francisco
as well, by dealing with this reliable local
firm.

BUSINESS LOCALS.

Apiculture.

ANNUAL ADDRESS

BY J. E. PLEASANTS, PRESIDENT OF THE DISTRICT BEE KEEPERS' ASSOCIATION OF SOUTHERN CALIFORNIA.

My Friends and Co-Laborers of the Southern California District Bee Keepers' Association:—It gives me great pleasure to welcome you on this occasion, united as we are by a common interest in all that appertains to bee culture, let us greet each other with pleasant smiles and sincere congratulations.

We have come from all parts of the district, not only to have a happy reunion, but also to debate on what will interest us all.

The year of 1881 will be recorded by the California bee keeper as a vital failure in his occupations; but should that discourage him? Should that make him give up a business for which he has been for some time performing himself? and for which perhaps he is peculiarly adapted? No! Perseverance, dexterity and economy will bring us success in almost every legitimate business in which we engage.

Gentlemen, one of the most important subjects for us to discuss is, "Overstocking our range with bees." Can it be done? I say that it can, with bees as well as with animals. I am well aware that during our sage and sumac harvest it would require a large number of colonies to gather all the nectar from the millions of flowers that bloom in our mountains; but as this great flow of nectar does not continue very long it is unwise to have more bees than can go on with brood rearing after the sage, sumac and buckwheat have ceased to bloom, or before they come in bloom. I think that it is admitted by some of our principal apiarists that a given point can be overstocked, and those that are fortunate enough to count their colonies by the hundreds divide them into separate apiaries.

This season of drouth, though very hard on the majority of bee keepers, will, I hope, teach us this—not to push our honey on the market all at once, but to hold for more remunerative prices.

When it comes to the quality of honey, Southern California need not blush to compare her honey with that which is produced in any other part of the world. It is acknowledged in all markets where it has been tried that California honey is unsurpassed. We have the quality, and on an average we have the quantity.

I am now talking to the army of bee keepers of Southern California, among whom we are proud to claim J. S. Harbison, of San Diego, whose fame is world wide as being the largest honey producer in the world. Also, C. J. Fox, of San Diego, who is our vice president of the National Bee-keeper's Association; H. Wilkins, of Ventura, who has made apiculture a study for many years before coming to this state, and in the few years that he has been among us made himself famous by his untiring and

successful efforts to introduce California honey into European markets; Frank Flint, of Santa Barbara; A. W. Hale, of San Bernardino; N. Levering, C. N. Wilson, J. A. Haskel, Capt. Butler, R Hall, J. W. Wilson, of Los Angeles county. Having an army of bee keepers headed by such men whose names I have mentioned, there should be no work wanting. Again then let me urge you to unite. Let us join hands like brothers and stand shoulder to shoulder, for by so doing we encourage each other and gain new strength to overcome obstacles which impede our way to the goal for which we are all striving. Having the best honey in the world, let us put it on the market in a good, neat and suitable package, thereby creating such a demand for our honey that the doleful cry of overstocking the market will be changed to the cheerful inquiry of: How is the demand to be supplied? To me the future prospect of the California bee keeper was never more promising than now. In the near future apiculture will not be a game of chance as it has been in the past. A few good seasons and proper management will enable us to issue from darkness into light, therefore let us

Faint not! but to the steadfast and
Come wealth and honor and renown.

In looking over this assembly I see but few of the fair sex. Why is it so? Are we all bachelors, or still worse, woman-haters? No! Most fervently I hope that neither charge can be laid at our door.

Let us in the future induce as many ladies to attend as we can; also invite them to take part in our discussions. You all are aware that in England the president of the British Bee-keepers Association, Mrs. Burdette Coutts Bartlett, is a lady whose fame is world-wide. While here in the United States one of our best apiarians is also a lady, I am confident that by exerting ourselves we would induce the ladies to grace our conventions.

I have already trespassed upon your valuable time. I thank you for your kind attention, but before closing allow me to say that it is my great desire that peace and harmony may prevail during our convention, and that the time spent here may be both profitable and pleasant, so that when the time comes for each one of us to go our different paths we may have nothing to regret, but that we have to part.

BEE MEN IN COUNCIL.

The County Bee keepers' Association met at the office of C. N. Wilson, president, in this city at 1 o'clock P. M., Oct. 15, the president in the chair. Minutes of previous meeting read and approved.

A resolution was passed by the Association acknowledging the receipt from the Chamber of Commerce of San Francisco, of a memorial to the United States Congress for the passage of an Act to prevent the adulteration of food, and requesting all bee-keepers in this county to use their influence to secure the passage of the Act, and thus prevent the adulteration of honey.

J. W. Wilson offered a resolution to the effect that heretofore dealers in honey practiced an imposition on honey producers by refusing to allow for the weight of tin cans in their honey purchases, and recommending that honey producers hereafter shall be deals with as regards packages containing honey in the same manner as producers of other commodities.

Mrs. Sarah A. Fairchild of Pomona, Mrs. J. E. Pleasants of Anaheim, and Jesse Sutton, an old soldier of the war of 1812, were, on motion of C. N. Wilson, elected honorary members of the Association. Mr. C. N. Wilson also turned that a committee be appointed to take the necessary steps to form a California State Bee-keepers' Association, committee to report at the next meeting of the County Association. The following members compose the committee: C. N. Wilson, J. W. Wilson, N. Levering.

On motion, the Association adjourned to meet at the same place and hour on the third Saturday in November, 1881.

A Boston firm is reported to be doing a large business in making an imitation honey in the comb. The comb is moulded out of paraffine wax, in good imitation of the work of bees; the cells are then filled with simple glucose syrup, flavored doubtless with some genuine honey, and sealed up by passing a hot iron over them. The product is sold for the best clover honey, and much of it is said to be shipped to Europe.

ELECTRICITY IS LIFE.

The electro-therapeutical display by W. J. Horne continues to attract great attention at the State Fair. A careful inspection of it will give one many valuable hints in regard to the preservation of health. In this connection, the Pacific Coast Watchmen, the official organ of the A. O. U. W., says: "Electro therapeutics as a science is growing in favor as one of the best and surest remedial agencies in the treatment of almost all diseases, especially those of a chronic nature, or diminution of the vital forces. Brother W. J. Horne has made this science a life-long study, and by patient and persevering industry has succeeded in making what is known as the electro magnetic medical belt, that is receiving the highest testimonials as one of the greatest curative agents in diseases of the human system. He has lately succeeded to the firm of Horne & West, 108 Market street, and is now the proprietor and manufacturer of this celebrated electric belt. His Electro Magnetic Journal, of twenty eight pages, will be sent to any one wishing to make this a study or avail themselves of the knowledge of enjoying perfect health. In this connection we cannot but regard our esteemed brother, in his researches and inventions, as one of the benefactors of the age."—From the Record Union, Sept. 24, 1881.

Go to J. A. Valdez's, with Fox & Koster, for pictures, mottoes, cards, frames, etc., etc.

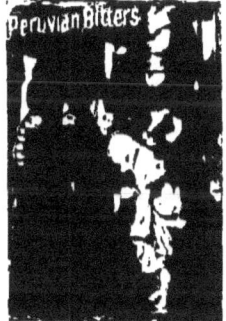

Produce Market.

MARKET REVIEW.

Since our last there has been little change in the market. Prices, however, have been well sustained, while in a few instances they have been a small advance. Barley is probably in greater demand than any other cereal, and the market has an upward tendency.

The following prices are paid at the farmer's wagon:

WHEAT	$1 30@1 50
BARLEY	1 40@1 60
CORN	1 25@1 85
POTATOES	1 00@2 00
ONIONS	1 50@1 75
BEANS	1 00@4 00
EGGS	35@ 50
BUTTER	37½ @42½
HONEY—Extracted	8@@ 10
—Comb	15@ 18
HAY, per ton	10 00@12 50
FRESH FRUIT—	
Oranges, per box	1 50@3 00
Lemons, per box	2 50@4 00
Apples, per box	75@1 25
Pears, per box	1 25@3 50
Peaches, per lb	4@ 5
POULTRY—	
Hens, per doz.	4 00@4 50
Young roosters	4 00@4 25
Turkeys, per lb	12½@c 18
Geese, each	50@ 60
Ducks, per doz.	3 00@3 25

A FEW OF OUR ADVANTAGES.

Land will sell for more next year than it does now. It is constantly increasing in value.

The bulk of arable land is less than one hundred miles from sea. Los Angeles is in the midst of a rich agricultural district, with railroad and steamship connections with every important point on the Pacific Coast.

We have never had any grasshoppers, potato bugs, or disastrous storms.

The people of California are noted for their industry, thrift, intelligence, enterprise, liberality, and general prosperity.

Our school system is second to none in the world.

Church accommodations are ample.

Life and property are as safe as in any State in the Union.

Our laws are intelligent and liberal.

Finally, there scarcely exists a country on the face of the earth where the necessaries, comforts, and even luxuries of life are more certainly attainable or more generally enjoyed than in California.

Poultry.

THE BLACK SPANISH FOWLS

Many persons keep fowls almost entirely for the profit to be obtained from the sale of their eggs. In many respects poultry pays better than any other stock on the farm, as they obtain quite a proportion of their food by their own exertions and as a part of their food consists of insects they become in that respect beneficial to the farmer, besides the profit obtained from their eggs and flesh. The definite cash returns are measured, however, by the number of eggs laid and chickens marketed. For this reason the non-sitters, as they are called, are preferred by many, as their production of eggs is more or less continuous, and can in a measure be calculated beforehand by any judicious and skillful poulterer. Singularly enough, all or nearly all the non-sitting breeds of poultry originated in the south of Europe or on the shores of the Mediterranean.

The most highly-bred variety of this fowl is called the Black Spanish, which was brought to its present perfection by Holland poulterers. There are two varieties of the Black Spanish noticed in the poultry books—the White-Faced and the Red-Faced, or Minorcas. The latter is the heavier fowl, and in some cases appear to be hardier, but the White-Faced lays as large and as many eggs, and having been the result of great skill and care in breeding is the more beautiful variety of the two. As now bred, the White-Faced Black Spanish is a very beautiful bird, the lustrous black color of the plumage contrasting vividly with the scarlet of the very large comb and wattles, and the peculiarly shining white of the ear-lobes and face.

The principal value of the breed is its laying propensity. The eggs are pure white in color and very large. There is no breed of fowls, probably, that will lay more pounds of eggs in a year. With the exception of the moulting season and an occasional cold snap, Black Spanish hens will lay every week during the year. Of course, if eggs are expected in the winter, warm, comfortable quarters, warm drink, and suitable food must be provided, and if this is done very few weeks will pass without more or less eggs from a flock of these fowls.

LIME AND CHARCOAL.

Few breeders really appreciate the value of lime and charcoal. These two articles are almost absolutely necessary in the management of fowls whether bred in the fancier's yard or on the farm. A flock of fowls will soon make even a fair sized yard foul and unhealthy unless frequently spaded up. In many cases this cannot be conveniently done, and recourse must be had to lime and other purifiers to cleanse the premises.

The value of lime in the form of whitewash is well known, and those who use it on the walls, nests, sitting-boxes, floor or anywhere either inside or outside the hen-houses liberally are the ones who keep their flocks healthy and cleanly. For laying hens it is indispensable in some shape for material for egg-shells, though when fowls have their liberty they can procure a good supply of calcareous matter in the soil, but fowls in confinement should be supplied with crushed oyster-shells, old mortar, chalk, broken bits of lime, etc., at all times. Charcoal is valuable in a sanitary point of view in feeding poultry. Pulverized and mixed with the soft feed it aids digestion and assimilation, prevents disease, purifies the contents of the crop and tends to fatten. It should be broken in small pieces about the size of a garden pea and put in troughs or boxes where the fowls could have ready access to it. Charred ears of corn is a good substitute for charcoal and is relished by the fowls. Fed during winter it makes a marked improvement in their health, as is shown by the bright red combs and wattles, and the increase of eggs.—*American Poultry Journal.*

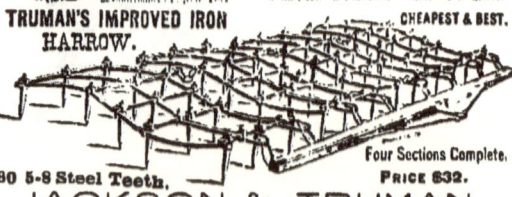

VOL. IV.　　　*DECEMBER.*　　　NO. 12.

SEMI TROPIC CALIFORNIA

DEVOTED TO

AGRICULTURE,

HORTICULTURE,

AND THE DEVELOPMENT OF

SOUTHERN CALIFORNIA

CHAS. COLEMAN, JR., PUBLISHER,

LOS ANGELES, CAL.

1881.

MIRROR PRINT, Los Angeles

—⋈ AND ⋈—

SOUTHERN CALIFORNIA HORTICULTURIST.

Vol. IV. LOS ANGELES, CAL., DECEMBER, 1891. No. 12.

Agriculture.

IS FARMING PROFITABLE?

This question is answered in the affirmative by every rural district, yet the answer comes to us with stronger emphasis from some sections than from others.

In our August number we devoted the whole of this page to an article on potatoes, and advised, as far as we think an editor's right extends, planting largely for the late fall and winter markets. Those who heeded our advice and acted upon it are now receiving $1.75 per cental for their potatoes, and emphatically declare that farming is profitable. Our poultry department has given instruction in the care of fowls, especially for eggs, and those who read it carefully and followed its teachings closely are now marketing eggs at 42 cents per dozen, and they, too, declare that farming is profitable. Those who have an alfalfa patch and two or three good cows are receiving 90 cents a roll for butter—a scant two pounds—and as they vote in the affirmative, their air of satisfaction gives double emphasis to the expression: "farming is profitable." These three branches of the general industry are sufficient to fully illustrate the happy condition of one class of our producers. This may be called small farming in contrast with our large grain and stock ranches, and it is a fact that is daily becoming more patent to us all, that the future wealth of Southern California will eventually be found in our ten and twenty acre homes. There are several causes at work bringing this about. One is, our people are becoming more domestic, another might be found in the fact that the spirit of speculation is being superseded by the more rational spirit of satisfaction bred of honest industry. Again, our large land owners are beginning to realize the fact that there is more money in dividing their large ranches into small tracts and selling at present prices than to use them for pasture lands. It is certainly very gratifying to those who rejoice in the growth and prosperity of this section to notice the promising changes which are now working so harmoniously for the common good and glory of us all. The man who arrives here to-day need not make a mistake. He can draw upon the experience of those who have preceded him ten, twenty and thirty years. In setting an orchard, without being obliged to experiment for the first five years, he at once learns from his neigh-

bor what varieties have been thoroughly tested and found to be best adapted to our soil and climate. The same may be said of vineyard planting, and the possibility of failure will figure as a minus quantity in his case. Along with the orchard and vineyard comes butter, eggs, potatoes, etc., as necessary auxiliaries, and no argument is needed to convince the judicious, industrious man that, with our markets all in his favor, there is no risk but a dead certainty in the profits of small farming.

Again, the man who invests to-day has the advantage of the man who invests a year hence. The earlier he begins his new home the sooner will he be surrounded with all the profits and comforts which a few years will bring. Furthermore, it will cost less to make the start to-day than at any future time. While land is generally reasonable in price now, the tendency is upward, and the rise in some sections will probably double the present price in a few years, an item which would justly figure into the general profits of the new home. In submitting these facts we do so with a desire to start our readers to think, well knowing that the active mind will readily take in the situation, and procrastination will meet with an inglorious defeat at the hands of determined effort.

MANURE, TOOLS AND BOOKS.

The barnyard is of more importance in farm economy than the houseyard, because out of it are the issues of crops. It is there that the manure is made and preserved. Some farmers have no barnyard, and they make very little manure, and save or preserve none. Such farmers must sooner or later go to the wall. The no barnyard system of farming will answer as long as the virgin fertility of the soil is not exhausted, but after that the farmer who forgets his manure pile, or neglects to guard it with a covetous eye, is behind the age. A proper barnyard for the advanced and progressive farmer, is one that is dished—sloping from all sides towards the center—with the bottom cemented, or in some other way made water-tight. The animals are fed under cover, and the yard is for the keeping of the mind and liquid manure that comes from the stock. The litter should be so abundant that the liquid is absorbed by it. To prevent the washing of the manure by rains, a cover for the yard, or that portion devoted to the preservation of manure, should be provided. Such a cover costs only a few dollars, and will pay for itself the first year in a larger quantity and bet-

ter quality of manure. Look out for the manure, and see that none of the valuable material goes to waste.

In riding through the country, I am often surprised at the way that many farmers leave their valuable machinery in the field, just where they left off using it. It does not take many seasons for the best mowing machines to become worthless, if left for a month or so each year exposed to the decaying influences of the rain and sun. I should carry my idea of putting all farm tools under shelter so far as to include wagons of the cheapest and most durable kind, wheelbarrows, and even stoneboats. It costs much less in the long run to have sheds for all these. They are slow, and goes on without any noise, but it does go on nevertheless. To be sure there is some picturesqueness in a reaper standing in the middle of a stubble field with its four red arms pointing towards the four winds of heaven, but it is not true and economical farming. A hay-rack leaning against a tree, with a pig rubbing against it, is a sheet that might inspire an artist, but it is not the best place for either the rack or the pig. If one is more interested in the manufacture of farm implements than the preserving of them, then leave all farm machinery out of doors. I, like many another, sing about methods of doing farm work, leads straight to that conclusion summed up in the three words, "farming don't pay."

The farmer who keeps no accounts must work in the dark. He cannot tell how much his work pays, or whether one part of the farm may not cause a positive outgo, instead of being a source of income. He might know by a few hours spent in book-keeping, that his greatest profit comes from early lambs, or the field of roots, or the dairy, and in that way know what changes to make to increase the income of this farm and diminish the outgo, or both. Accounts should be kept with each field. Only the main points should be entered. It is a mistake to go into all the details, as some have done, putting down each little thing without imposing a burden, and at the same time covering the essentials, we all that should be attempted.—*Cassell's Family Magazine.*

One of the finest displays at the recent Agricultural Fair was the beautiful Jersey butter exhibited by F. J. Barretto, Esq. Mr. Barretto has been getting sixty cents a pound for his butter for the past six weeks. Jerseys are the ones for premium butter.

Horticulture.

LITTLE ENOUGH.

*Each hour of the day there is some demand
On the loving heart and the willing hand,
That for all the blessings they gather, yearn
To make an ample and swift return
'Tis little enough we can do to pay
And yet we're seen as through life we're hedged
That even a little is oft begrudged.*

*If out of our path the thorns are swept,
If out of the raging storms we're kept,
If we're not living, as many may,
To poverty's curse, and poverty's crime,
With grateful thoughts should the heart and mind
The poor, and needy, and helpless feel,
And help them over their way so rough,
And feel that our bounty is little enough.*

*There are griefs the heart will never reveal,
There are wounds that no one on earth can heal,
There is hunger that bread cannot satisfy,
There are lives that Satan has turned awry,
And if to these we can give no aid—
The doomed, the desolate and betrayed—
As recompense for each harsh rebuff,
Our prayers and our tears are little enough.*

*Little enough is it in our power
To give, though we give every day and hour,
As tithe to Him who has led us there
The burdens that others may have to bear,
And if the wealth of the world we lack,
Kind words and smiles we aren't set to back,
And to those who journey a road that's rough,
The best we can give them is little enough.*

—Josephine Pollard.

THE LEMON AND THE PASADENA CLINGS COMPARED.

Editor Semi-Tropic:—I send you the following, in compliance with your request for an article from me:

Yours truly,
John M. Warner.

PASADENA CLING.

Editor "Semi-Tropic", Dear Sir:—

fruits will speedily supplant the present orchards.

If we could handle our fruit as cheaply as the orchardist does in Delaware and New Jersey for instance, viz., 10 to 25 cents per day, we could then almost for a time at least, defy competition. I believe I am bearing out in this statement that but few fruit growers ever think of irrigating their deciduous trees; at least it is never practiced in Pasadena, and yet the prices and critical exactions by our dealers render the culture almost entirely profitless. If peaches and apples will not pay we know the vine will, and it is left for the dealer to decide this matter in the near future.

Respectfully,
O H CONKAR

PRUNING PEACH ORCHARDS.

Different fruit needs different modes of treatment. While the cherry should be kept compact the apple and the peach need a more open top that its fruit may be more highly colored and better flavored by the rays of the sun. The peach that has had fair to the sun in ripening is far superior in flavor and sweetness to the one ripened in the shade. This teaches the propriety of sunshine.

Before commencing operations look over your trees carefully; see what large limbs need removing to balance it properly, and when this is done, shorten in the smaller limbs, thin out the middle, always cutting those limbs that have a tendency to grow crosswise or downward. Let the tree, when your work is done, have a symmetrical, graceful, tidy appearance.

In peach pruning what is termed the "shortening in system" is claimed to have many advantages, but being more labor than many are willing to bestow, it will not probably be practiced generally, although it does possess important advantages. The plan is this: When the tree is first planted let it be cut back to within 2½ feet of the ground; a nice, round head is produced the first year. The second year it is cut back one-half of the last year's growth the third year the same, and so on each succeeding year, of course using judgment in cutting back those limbs that make the most rapid growth shorter than others, so that a proper pause may be maintained. The tree will be healthier; the top being low, the ground is kept cool and the bushes are saved from sun scald and insects and the expense of gathering the fruit much reduced.

This system has many advantages over all others, especially on this event, where the tree makes such a wonderful growth each year. Unless this system is practiced your trees will not only overbear but the load of fruit reaching out on the long limbs will be heavier than the branches can hold, and the result will be broken limbs, scraggly, unsymmetrical and unprofitable trees. This system has the fullest endorsement of all of our leading peach men who have made the subject of pruning a study for any length of time.

ANOTHER RAILROAD FOR LOS ANGELES.

Owing to the gigantic proportions of the horticultural industries of Southern California, the time has come when a market beyond our borders must be reached, and that too with profit to the producers, or our present bright prospects will be turned into gloom. To this end our citizens, feeling that the Southern Pacific and its connections cannot be relied upon for said relief, are calling the attention of the managers of the Atlantic & Pacific and Atchison Topeka & Santa Fe to the large inducements in the way of freights Los Angeles county alone offers to said road should it build into this valley and city

The Herald of this city comes out this morning with a long letter from C T Hopkins, Prest. of the Cal. Ins. Co. of San Francisco, to H C Nutt, Esq., President of the Atlantic & Pacific, and to W B Strong, Esq., President of the Atchison, Topeka & Santa Fe railroads, from which we make the following extracts:

According to the report of the State Board of Equalization of 1880, the agricultural products of Los Angeles county in 1879 (since greatly increased) acres in cultivation, exclusive of grain, hay, vegetables and live stock:

Acres under cultivation (all crops)	130,000
Castor beans—pounds	325,000
Hops	260,000
Tobacco	125,000
Butter	85,000
Cheese	35,000
Wool	2,717,500
Honey	130,000
Wine—gallons	8,019,000
Brandy	85,000
Lemon trees—number	30,150
Orange "	102,500
Olive "	3,000
Apple "	56,000
Pear "	13,343
Fig "	7,725
Plum "	3,125
Peach "	24,575
Quince "	1,000
Grape vines—acres	6,853
Grapes—tons (five tons per acre)	31,173
Miles of irrigating ditches	343
Acres irrigated (orchards, vineyards principally)	33,813
Population of county, about	33,000
" city,	13,000

Now if each of the 272,250 orange and lemon trees, to say nothing of the other fruits, should produce an annual crop of only 500, the aggregate produce would reach 111,125,000 oranges and lemons, equal to 175 in the box or 325,100 boxes, or 23 carloads of 340 boxes each. This would require for their transportation twelve cars daily during the six months, from January 1st to June 30th, of the crop season.

Of course no such crop has yet been grown, because only a small portion of all the trees planted are yet in full bearing, but in three years from now the crop will approximate the above figures.

Take now the grape crop, 31,000 tons. Doubtless the acreage in grapes will in three years reach 25,000 to 30,000 acres, instead of the 6,853 acres reported in 1879, for everyone who can is now planting vineyards with reference to wine and brandy making. But $30 per ton is the average price payable for grapes for these purposes, a low making raisins, say $1 in one case per lb. Yet three grapes will for table use at the rate for 12 years to $1 per pound, something to place and season. If they could be sold at over the East at 10 cents per pound, the demand for them would be universal and practically limitless. If they could be transported by express trains as is now instead of the 3 cents charged by the monopoly to a favored few, and the retailer be satisfied with a profit of 5 cents, the grower could sell at 3 cents, as these were their present rates for wine making. What an impetus this additional price would give to the business! It would increase the product of an acre from $130 to $900 or all table grapes that went East. And if the export were no greater than the present yield, the tonnage movement would require 3,240 cars from Los Angeles county some time between August 1st and December 1st, and before the orange and lemon crop would be ready for packing.

Now as the route of the Atlantic and Pacific and Atchison and Topeka Railroads is the shortest possible between Southern California and the central parts of distribution to the Northern States, as its elevation along the Southern slopes of the Rocky Mountains gives it a cooler climate in summer than the Southern or Texas roads, while it is below the line of the snows which in winter make the central and eastern lines impracticable for ice carriage, the one I wish to impress upon you is that you can, if so disposed, create a much greater tonnage movement in fresh fruits than anything else, and do a much larger business in that specialty than any other railroad can; while at the same time you can populate Southern California with the right kind of people, and go on increasing the business of your roads from year to year more quickly than any other road is likely to do.

President H C Nutt's reply follows, but owing to want of space we merely make extracts, but will add that he proposes to consider our arguments and every inducement Southern California offers to the road, as soon as they can get to it.

After a lapse of two hundred years, science has given us nothing to take the place of Peruvian Bitters. It cures a morbid appetite for stimulants, it attacks excessive love for liquor, while you also receive the full tonic effect of the City mint, which is fully as effective now against malarial diseases as it was in the days of the old Spanish viceroys. Call on your druggist for it. For sale at Horace and & Co's.

We are to an accident of the last moment in going to press, the market report does not appear in this issue.

Viticulture.

HOW TO PLANT A VINEYARD PROPERLY.

The time of year has again arrived when the movement toward setting new vineyards is receiving general attention. The unusual success attending our growers this year will not only lead others to go largely into this industry, but will also be the means of causing present growers to increase their own vine area. To the experienced the setting of a vineyard brings no more anxiety than the planting of any ordinary farm crop, while to others the task is one fraught with uncertainty, some guess work, and no small amount of worry concerning the success of their venture. It is said that the young bird builds as good a nest as her mother built the year before, therefore why should we not be able to equal or even excel our predecessors, when we have inherited the experience which cost them a lifetime?

The ground for a vineyard should be plowed fully fifteen inches deep, if it is the intention to grow without irrigating. Even with irrigating this depth is not too great; still ten or twelve inches would probably answer. If the ground is new, all roots should be grubbed out, carried off and burned; little hillocks here and there should be leveled, and the ground in general should be given an even, smooth surface. Then plow straight trenches, in which the cuttings are to be planted, at least fifteen inches deep, with a two horse plow, as wide apart as you wish to set your vineyard; for wine, not less than six feet nor more than eight; for raisins, probably not less than eight feet nor more than ten. Stretch a rope—or what is better, a wire—across these furrows, and if your rope is knotted or your wire linked every six, eight or ten feet, according to the distance you choose, you are ready for business.

Procure a sharp, narrow spade, and with it dig a cut in the trench as many more inches over fifteen as you desire to plant; then plant the cutting behind the spade, and fasten the loose dirt around the lower end of it with your foot, and, if you like, draw more dirt to it from the sides; afterwards plow the dirt to the cuttings from both sides with a single-horse plow, and you have your cuttings well and expeditiously planted. Be sure that your cuttings are well planted; if not, all your work is in vain. The unwise style of planting is the worst of all. You cannot see what is done at the bottom of the hole; and if you flood it, it will generally rot the end of the cutting, and the callus cannot form there; but some of the upper eyes will send out a few hungry roots, and if it don't die, it were better if it did.

The process for planting rooted vines is the same, save instead of only pushing the spade down once, you would dig a hole of proper dimensions in the bottom of the trench. The question, which is preferable for planting, cuttings or rooted vines? is still open for discussion. Cuttings are much the cheaper, and with proper setting and care, provided they are properly taken from the vines and treated before they are set in vineyard form, from seventy five to ninety per cent. will grow. And if you put out a few hundred or thousand in our nursery form the next year, you will have roots with which to fill out the vacancies. On the other hand rooted vines will cost much more, the labor of planting is considerably more, but all will grow, and probably they will bear a year earlier than the cuttings; still by some it is claimed that there is no gain in time of bearing. Neither do all agree upon the depth that cuttings should be planted. Some contend that fifteen inches is long enough for a cutting, and nine or ten inches in the ground is better than a greater depth. This is probably the correct theory for cold soils, or for lands upon which irrigation is practiced; but for warm, loose soils, or where irrigation is not intended, it would probably be well to increase the length to eighteen or twenty inches. Of course, you would modify the depth of trenches to suit the length of cuttings. If your trench is fully as deep as you wish to plant, so much the better, because the loose soil brought in from the sides will settle closely around the cutting—a point in the operation which is very important, and cannot be too well attended to. Only large, well-matured canes, and those with eyes moderately close together, so that, planting at the above-mentioned depths, two eyes may be above the ground. Some say that one eye above the ground is sufficient; but suppose the upper one should fail to grow, owing to its nearness to the end of the cane, or suppose the rabbits should get one, or the whole tree, in cultivating, should break one off, would you not then appreciate the second? Besides, if you should at any time find two were too many, a strong thumb or a sharp knife would be your remedy. The first two cuttings from the large end of the vine are considered best, but that depends largely upon the length of the vine. Neither an over-rank nor a very small growth of vine is as good to make cuttings from as a medium growth. After cuttings are once made, they should not be exposed to the sun and wind; two or three days' exposure may work them a serious injury. When made, tie them into bunches of fifty or one hundred each, wrap them with moist sacks, or something that will answer the same purpose, and remove them to the ranch on which they are to be planted. Here, with a two-horse plow, prepare a shallow trench, open the packages, and deposit the cuttings lengthwise of the trench, not too many in a place, and cover them with soil four or five inches. If the ground is not too wet, cold and muddy, they could remain in the trench without harm for six weeks, but at the end of ten days or two weeks, if you are ready, they are in first class condition to be taken out of the trench and to be planted. This burying process keeps the cuttings from losing any of their vitality, neither can the ends of the cuttings become dried for an inch or two back, as they do under other treatment, and the eyes are swollen ready to start as soon as they are planted and exposed to the sun and warm air.

WINE OPINION OF L. J. ROSE.

Realizing the value of the opinion of L. J. Rose as regards wine culture, we make the following extract from his report to the Board of State Viticultural Commissioners of December, 1880. Although one year has elapsed since these opinions were written, they are none the less applicable at the present time, and considering their source, we know that they will be read with much interest:

It is a pleasing task to review the grape and wine industries of Los Angeles County for 1880. Crops have never been larger or of a better quality, and the demand for the grape by wine makers has been good, and continued on to the end. All parties concerned are satisfied, and contentment and plenty cheer the vigneron as to the renewed effort for the coming year, which already is full of pleasing prospects. They are casting an agreeable shadow before, through an abundant rain for the season thus far, and the viticulturist is now busy in pruning and saving cuttings for future planting. There will be more vines planted the coming season than ever before.

It is now a proven fact that we, too, can make the finer qualities of light bodied pure wines. In former years Los Angeles had the reputation of being especially adapted for the making of Port, Angelica, Sweet Muscat, and Brandy; but, in the making of light dry wines the county stood last on the coast. The writer never shared in that belief; for, if the Mission grape attained a higher and more perfect maturity, and made a wine of the best quality for which it was adapted, I could not see why other varieties of grapes, which were suited for other kinds of wine, should not, also, when ripened in our genial, pleasant climate, make a wine—a light wine—characterized by a bouquet of the best quality. Of course locality, climate, and other causes have a marked effect on the quality of wine, and all conditions must be favorable to make a wine of the first quality; but I mean to say that the variety has more influence than any one other condition.

Perhaps there is no locality in California which is so little understood as to its climate as Los Angeles and other southern counties. I am often met, when in Stockton, Sacramento, and other places in the State, by the query, "Well, it must be very hot in your county now?" whereas the fact is that our summer heat is much less, and our nights are much cooler, than in the new at either place mentioned. We have but little hot weather, but a more even temperature, warmer winters, and a longer season. As this is the home of the orange, lemon, and other like fruits, the mistake is a natural one, but we excel in raising these, not because we have a greater summer heat, but because we have a warmer winter and a more even temperature for the whole year. It is no longer an experiment whether we can make a light wine of the best quality. It is a fact accomplished—a fact which all viticulturists who have tried our wines admit. I can show wine in quantities which only carries seven per cent of alcohol, and it can be drank with pleasure when one is dry, to quench thirst, and leave no dullness of the mind behind. Of course, this cannot be done with the Mission grape, and the verdict founded on that grape has been a just one, which said that we could not make a light wine, and that all our wines had a sherry flavor. The planting of other varieties of grapes, however, tells a different tale. The planting of Blaue Ellun, Burger, Zinfandel, and Charboneau, changes this verdict, which was based upon wine of every kind and variety made from our grape, viz.: the Mission.

Taking the present year's yield, which is the largest we ever had, at ten thousand pounds to the acre, and allowing five thousand seven hundred acres in bearing, it gives fifty-seven million one hundred and thirty thousand pounds of grapes produced in this county this year; and, taking fifteen pounds of grapes for a gallon of wine, this would give the grand total of three million eight hundred thousand gallons of wine.

These figures seem large, even to me, yet I cannot see how I can make them less. I am in a favorable condition to make estimates, for I have bought the product of many vineyards for several years, and this year have bought over twelve million pounds of grapes. Although five tons to an acre, as an average, may seem large, yet several vineyards which I bought yielded ten tons, and I believe five tons is within the fact.

Probably half the vineyards of this district are irrigated; and, although grapes can be grown in any part of this district without irrigation, yet with irrigation larger crops are produced, and vineyards retain their fertility and thrift for hundreds of years. Irrigation entails much work, and it may yet be considered an open question which pays best—deep tillage, without irrigation, or irrigation. Lands without irrigation can be bought very much cheaper, say for one-fourth, and this again forms a factor in the problem of "Which pays best?" It must, however, be confessed, that as long as the belief prevails that irrigation is a preventive of the phylloxera, there is a comfortable feeling in having water.

Our mountain slopes and our uplands are now the lowest in price, and yet these lands are the lands that will produce grapes of the highest value. The possibilities here are immense. A great future is in store for us.

It may be safely stated that grapes grown for sale to wine makers, this year, have netted ninety dollars an acre, for the crop was large and the price good. The average price this year was somewhere near twenty-one dollars a ton. The wine and brandy made would sell to-day for over a million of dollars.

VINEYARD OBSERVATIONS.

EDITOR "SEMI-TROPIC."—Having recently traveled through a portion of Los Angeles and San Bernardino counties, I have concluded to give you a few notes concerning my observations among the same and promising vineyards of our section. In the first place I have found no one who fears for the future of the grape. The phylloxera which has devastated France and portions of Northern California is not feared by a majority of our viticulturists, mainly for the reason that the irrigating ditches on every hand can be brought into requisition to drive out the pest should it ever appear.

AN OUNCE OF PREVENTION.

However, the phylloxera is to be feared even in our section, and no grape cuttings from Northern California should be admitted until it is certain they have been disinfected. It is surely easier to keep the pest out at present than it will be to exterminate it in the future. The vineyards set out last Spring are nearly all in a healthy condition. The farmer who left his cuttings to the mercy of the voracious rabbit has, however, little to hope for. The destruction of the young vineyards by these creatures must have discouraged many. A good lath fence from ten to four feet in height seems to be the only effective barrier.

LOCATIONS FOR GRAPE CULTURE.

The area in vineyards is extending in an extraordinarily rapid manner. One grape grower in the San Gabriel valley has lately sold over one million cuttings, mostly to new comers. Lands which three years ago were valued from $10 to $15 per acre here, since the grape excitement began, readily sold at from $30 to $50 per acre. Everywhere vineyards are being put out, but the principal demand for cuttings in this section comes from the Santa Ana Valley, Pasadena, Pomona, and the districts South and West of town.

VARIETIES SELECTED.

On the mesa lands and loamy lands freest from fogs the muscat grape seems to be the favorite. On the damp clay lands the muscat mildews in ordinary seasons and is not to be depended upon. For wine making the favorite varieties seem to be the Blaue Ellun, Zinfandel, Burger and Muscat. The Germans of Anaheim, many of whom have resided in the county for twenty years, evinced their confidence in the future of the wine grape by nearly doubling the area of their vineyards. Twenty acres in grapes they have found to be a better investment than two hundred acres in grain.

As for the raisin interest the future is grand, and unquestionably will prove one of the bulwarks of our future prosperity.

PRUNING VINES.

The season of vineyard pruning has now arrived, and some of our vineyardists have already commenced that important work. On the question of the proper time to prune there is a wide difference of opinion. Some of our city vineyardists maintain that it is unsafe to prune till January or

February, so as to make the vine late in putting out blossoms in the spring, so as to avoid an April frost which sometimes tramps along this way in the first half of that month. The same opinion has been advanced by some of the Riverside vineyardists. Gen. Stoneman, on the contrary, stands ready to demonstrate, by his own experience, that in his fine vineyard at Los Robles the latest pruned vines leaf and blossom before those that are pruned earlier in the season. He is prepared to give dates, with facts, to prove all his statements. His theory is, that the vine having all its branches cut off is less susceptible to the stimulating influences of spring than that which has all its branches full of vital forces, that capture the spring forces of growth, and secure a flow of sap with the first breath of spring. According to this theory, late pruning is done after the branches have begun their work of absorbing sap from the parent root, and therefore begins in February. As a result comes premature leaves and blossoms, from vines pruned after the annual ascending sap has well begun its flowing. The sap in its upward flow, finding no vines left to permeate, gives its arrested energy to the immediate production of other vines in which to fulfil its work of growth, which is a law of its nature. He maintains that a whole is greater than a part, and that the fertile influences which the few short branches that are left by the pruner exert on the sources of sap are very small compared with that of a full topped vine in vigorous health. The funeral is a man of large reading and careful observation, and his opinions are entitled to respectful consideration.

In regard to the manner of pruning there are also two theories. One, that the parent vine should be trimmed very slowly, leaving only the short jointed branches in such a manner as to form a crown, from which other branches should spring. These branches are to be few in number with but few buds length on each branch left. This is called short pruning.

Now comes another system, adopted by General Stoneman and others, called "long pruning," which leaves at least five buds on the branches left by the pruner. It is claimed that this length of branch is necessary to bring out the full force of the vine, and the yield of grapes from the same will be very much larger than from the short pruning.

This system is controverted by the advocates of short pruning who contend that short pruning promotes the longevity of the vine and point to the old thrifty vineyards that have been short pruned for one hundred years.

On this point General Stoneman finds by long pruning, that the yield of his vineyard has been greatly increased, but whether the increase will last one hundred years is yet unknown. The grape industry is now so large and important that the most careful experiments should be made and published as to the best methods of pruning - commenced.

Addresses.

ANNUAL ADDRESS BEFORE THE DISTRICT AGRICULTURAL ASSOCIATION No. 6.

AT TURN VEREIN HALL, IN THIS CITY, ON MONDAY NIGHT, OCT. 31, BY F. J. BARRETTO, PRESIDENT OF THE ASSOCIATION.

GENTLEMEN AND LADIES:—It gives me pleasure to meet you this evening. The occasion of this meeting is the opening of the first annual exhibition of the Horticultural Department of Agricultural Association No. 6.

This Association is a State institution, organized under a law passed by the Legislature of 1873, the directors of which hold office under the appointment of the Governor of the State. By this law the purposes for which this Association was created, as also the duties of its directors, are most explicitly defined. The purpose is, for the advancement of the agricultural, horticultural and mechanical interests of this district, comprising the six Southern counties of the State. I, together with my associate directors, have endeavored to the best of our ability to carry out this purpose, and we trust with your co-operation we may establish an institution which will be, for all time, an honor and pride to the people of Southern California. We have for this present fair made every exertion to provide for you an entertainment both instructive and interesting. At the Park our stables and sheds are filled with thoroughbred stock of every description. We have prepared a program of racing, tournaments for the fire companies, together with several other interesting amusements, and from the display you have here before you to-night you will realize that we have in no wise neglected our horticultural department.

I have visited all the fairs in the northern portion of this State, and I am also well acquainted with all the principal fairs of the East, and I am pleased to say, that in my opinion the quality of the stock and produce now on exhibition at the park and in this hall is equalled by but few and excelled by none.

But, my friends, to enable us to make this Association an institution of which we may all be proud, and which will be an everlasting benefit to us, and to our children, and to this whole community, there is one thing absolutely necessary, one thing which we must have or we cannot succeed, and that is your co-operation, your assistance and your help. The directors alone have not the power to carry it to a success, and I am sorry to be compelled to say to you that I fear there is a great lack of interest on the part of the people of your city. The first Agricultural Fair under the direction of this Association was held at the Park last fall, the Horticultural department being then exhibited at the Pavilion under the charge of the Southern California Horticultural Society. Upon that occasion, at the Park we did tolerably

well, being able to pay all our obligations and having a few hundred dollars left in the treasury. But our patrons were not the citizens of Los Angeles; they were mostly strangers. Upon one of our best days, for my own satisfaction, I put a man to canvass and ascertain how many of the persons then present were residents of the city of Los Angeles, and he found less than one hundred persons, or say $30 paid in at the gate. At this rate, in the five days of our exhibition we would have received $250 from the residents of this city, containing, I believe, a population of about 15,000 persons, which would be not quite 1¾ cents apiece in support of an Agricultural Association, and that amount contributed by a city which is located in the very heart of the finest agricultural and horticultural district known to the civilized world. Gentlemen, I cannot take courage from this showing; it does not impress me with the idea that you are interested in the success of Agricultural Associations.

No institution in the world can thrive, or even exist, without the patronage of the public. You all know this. You are all practical business men, and you know that we, as well as yourselves, depend upon the first Agricultural Association you have had among you. When I came here, five years ago, there was the Southern District Agricultural Association, and shortly afterwards the Horticultural Society was organized. The origin of the first of these institutions I know but little of, it having been started, I believe, several years previously; but I did know it during the last three years of its existence, and I can most truthfully say it was a well-conducted institution, managed by able men, who used their best endeavors to maintain an Agricultural Association which would have been a benefit to the county. Of the Horticultural Society it is useless for me to say one word. It is of recent date; you all know of its organization, of the labors of its directors, every one of them good and faithful men. I know well that these gentlemen have done their best to maintain amongst you an institution which, if properly patronized by this city, would have been an ornament, and an untold worker of good throughout the entire breadth of California. But what has been the end of these two Associations? I will tell you what has been their end. For lack of interest taken in them, an apathy which in my opinion is unpardonable, they have been allowed, after a few years of struggling, to die, to become bankrupt—yes, even to be sold out by the Sheriff—and the property which by hard labor they had accumulated has been sacrificed and lost—a stain, a blur, an everlasting, never-fading, indelible blot upon the history sheet of the far famed city of Los Angeles. And, gentlemen and ladies, with this lack of interest still existing, if the directors of this Association will quietly permit it, they, too, will meet the same sad fate. If the city of Los Angeles does not want an Agricultural Association in their midst, there are other

localities in our district, both in and out of this county, that do want it, and who have offered us very tempting inducements to hold our fairs with them. We are now just on the eve of our second exhibition, and should the present state of affairs, or I should say those of last year, still exist, I fear that we shall hereafter be re-impelled to seek a more appreciative community. Do not think that my remarks are prompted by any unkind feeling. Far from it. I will admit that I am disappointed. I consider myself one of you. I have made my home amongst you, and I take an interest in everything affecting the well-being of Los Angeles and its surroundings; but as the President of this Association, I feel it my duty to you, to the Directors and stockholders of this Association, to express to you, frankly and plainly, what in my opinion is the great difficulty. My friends, there is not a city on the face of the earth, with any pretensions whatever of being in an agricultural district, that is not willing and proud to do their part towards the support of their Agricultural Associations. It is so throughout the Eastern States, from Maine to Wisconsin; but I need not take you to Maine or Wisconsin to prove to you the truth of my assertion. Go to the northern part of your own State—go for instance to Stockton and attend the San Joaquin Valley District Fair, and then tell me if I am not stating facts. In Stockton they put up $20,000 every year in premiums and purses, and they draw crowds of people, and outside money is brought in and left there, and their merchants and hotels reap the benefit. But how is this done, you will ask. I will tell you. The San Joaquin Valley District Agricultural Association is no better off than we are; they receive from the State the same as we receive, but their people realize the importance of their Association and the benefits it brings to them and to their city, and they do, each one of them, what he can to assist in the advancement and in the support of this institution. Suppose you walk through the streets of Stockton on one, I think two afternoons during Fair week, and you wont find a store open—not even a barber's shop. And why? Because it is Fair week—it is a holiday, and the merchants, clerks, lawyers, and everybody have gone to the Fair. They don't lose by it; they make their Fair a success, and strangers are attracted to their city, and each spends his money, and their city reaps a rich harvest. Now allow me to ask, have any one of you ever seen a store closed in Los Angeles upon any afternoon during a Fair week? I never have, and if you have, I wish you would tell me of it.

My friends, I have detained you much longer than was my intention, but what I have said I said in good faith, and I hope it may be for the good of the City of Los Angeles, and the prosperity of this Association.

I will conclude by again expressing to you the pleasure I have felt at meeting you this evening, and in having had an opportunity of addressing you, and I trust that I may meet you all at the Park every day, and in this hall every evening during the present week. And should I ever again be called upon to address a Los Angeles audience upon the subject of agriculture, may I then and there have occasion to thank you for the interest you then take in Agricultural Associations, and the liberality you then display towards their support.

ADDRESS BY GOV. DOWNEY.

BEFORE THE ASSOCIATION ON WEDNESDAY EVENING.

If there be a people on the face of the earth that ought to be good, upright, honest, generous and God-loving that people should be the favored citizens of these United States, for a kind and beneficent providence has granted us the choicest of gifts,—a continent from ocean to ocean dedicated to freedom. The eighty years that have transpired of the nineteenth century have witnessed events of more importance to the happiness of mankind than all the ages from the beginning of the world. This progress will not stop. Its advance is irresistible, and it is a proud satisfaction to us to feel and know that future generations will admire and appreciate our efforts.

Since the organization of the District Agricultural Society our progress has been grand, our step has been steady, our march determined and our accomplishments marked and manifest. The progress of all the six counties composing the district has been equally marked, and that happy manifestation of abundance that surrounds our people in Los Angeles is to be seen in them all. Peace and contentment pervade the land, and the patrons of husbandry in their annual cycle come round to exhibit the treasures they have brought forth from mother earth.

This the loved land of the olive and vine,
The land of abundance of health and sunshine.

The retrospect of the year is pleasing, our crops of every kind abundant, with a demand and a value for our products that bring happiness to every fireside; wine and wheat fill our warehouses, tropical and sub-tropical fruits are forever on hand for export.

Our young and growing industries require the fostering care and protection of the Nation, north, south, east and west; and as I view it, there is no people require it so particularly as those of our own district. We feel it because it comes home to us. Our wool, our wine and our brandy have their life through protection. Our vineyards and orange groves would be neglected without it.

The promoters of the agricultural and horticultural societies have generously contributed their money, time and talent to encourage the growth of prosperity among us, and the City of Los Angeles has been in no small degree the beneficiary, therefore her citizens should respond with generous and. Through the efforts of the members of these societies, attention has been

called from abroad to the fact that we have raised the finest stock in the world, and produced the choicest fruits. It would therefore show an ingratitude unpardonable not to appreciate those generous efforts put forth for the general good.

Our Fair Grounds are the finest in the State, our appointments are excellent and ample, and we do not owe one a dollar.

In taking upon ourselves the burden of State Government we started out with an assessment roll, personal and real, of only $50,000,000; in thirty years it has swelled to $760,000,000. We find by looking back to the date of our admission as a State that the great commonwealth of New York shows a roll, personal and real of only $724,000,000 in round numbers; Delaware only $17,000,000; Florida, $22,000,000; Iowa, $21,000,000. And now we have lived to see our own beloved county with her assessment roll amounting to $20,000,000. The following tabulated statement will be the best evidence of the steady progress Los Angeles has made in material wealth since I last had the pleasure of addressing the Society, and the progress of the other five counties has been equally and proportionately marked:

Assessments of Los Angeles County for the past six years:

1876	$14,844,322
1877	15,738,352
1878	16,283,100
1879	16,160,948
1880	18,503,273
1881	20,021,551

We have nominally a State Debt of $3,398,500; but $2,490,000 of this we owe to ourselves, that is, the bonds to that amount are deposited to the credit of our educational system, and we pay interest regularly every year on this, just the same as if we borrowed it from Rothschild and you get your pro rata every year for your school fund.

Now I know there are many who do not think of this, and I feel it will be pleasing for them to know that we, as a State, are practically out of debt.

I have gone into this dry detail of figures because it has been stated that the Southern counties are not rich enough to carry on a State Government on their own account. I have plainly shown you that the County of Los Angeles alone has as big a tax list as the whole State of Iowa, or Florida, or Delaware had in 1850, and they were full fledged States at the time of our admission.

It is pleasing to note that prophecies of the opponents of the new constitution have not been verified. They told you that in case of its adoption capital would flee the State, industries would be paralyzed and that grass would grow in our streets. The contrary, thank God, has been the happy consequence of its passage, for never before in the history of the State did a happier condition of affairs exist.

Some six years ago it was my pleasing duty, as President of the Agricultural Society, to deliver the annual address. At

that period the wine interest, from many reasons not now necessary to recapitulate, was in a depressed condition. The owners of vineyards were despondent, and many were digging up and burning the good old vines their fathers had planted and cultivated with so much care. I had myself great faith in the future of this industry, and I then said:

"Los Angeles is the natural home of the grape, it thrives better, grows larger and sweeter here than anywhere else. The dryness of our climate at the period of maturing and gathering guarantees a crop of excellent quality, free from disease or mildew. One acre of our soil will produce more than anywhere else, and at a less cost, and sweeter and freer from disease. Why not, then, rival France in this great branch of wealth? It will only require the intelligent effort of our people to so make it. I regard this source of our wealth in this district as destined to surpass all others. Its use by our laboring men as an article of diet would destroy a desire for strong drink. Such is the experience of countries where it is used more freely than water or milk. I would say to all our farmers, plant a few acres in grape vines."

It is very pleasing, now that years have elapsed, to see my judgment sustained, my predictions verified, and that our people have multiplied their vineyards many fold. In 1850 our wool clip in the State was, say, 6,000,000 lbs. In 1880 it was 40,000,000 lbs., and of much finer staple. This industry has many advantages. While it brings a large revenue, it does not exhaust our soil, as our grain crops do. We are much indebted to the efforts of C. W. W. Hollister, of Santa Barbara, and to his brother Hubbard, of happy memory, for the improvement of our common or native stock of sheep; also the McConnell Brothers, of Sacramento, and the Pattersons, of Alameda. The efforts of these gentlemen have only had a parallel in success, personal and national, with those of Captain McArthur, of Australia.

I speak of the two industries, wine and wool, because I am familiar with them, and I feel that their success has stimulated all other in this district. Wheat, corn and barley are fast gaining a claim to pre-eminence. Raisins, oranges, nuts and fruits of all kind crowd the avenues of transportation and commerce severely smiles in our cities and hamlets.

Were ever a people so favored as we? The land is dotted with temples of worship, colleges and schools, charity and benevolence bear their monuments on every hand, and now I will conclude by hoping

That man may not curse,
What Heaven has made so glorious.

-o-

Mr. C. H. Rumames would inform poultry raisers that he has the choicest strains of fowls in Southern California. Orders for stock or eggs filled with satisfaction. He was robbed at the Fair.

Dowse's Baking Powder at Lee J. Thompson & Co.'s.

Everybody goes to Fox & Kuster's.

Southern California.

THE LADY OF L——.

BY D. A. Y.

"The home to which,
Could love fulfil its prayers," I'd lead thee, is
A sunny land beyond Sierra's slope,
Where health and happiness abound, and where
No thoughts of winter make the summer short—
That golden land! dear California!
There, in the Valley of San Gabriel,
I know a charming spot—one pleasant year,
Which now seems like a fairy dream—it was
My home. The memories of that time and place
Are perfect, and as full of unalloy'd
Delight as well can be in this mixed world.
Just there from out the valley rises, with
A gentle slope, a mesa, high and wide
And beautiful. Sierra Madre guards
Its rear, and from a cañon picturesque
Pours water clear and plentiful. Before
Us lies a panorama unsurpassed—
Long orchard rows of fragrant orange trees,
And vineyards hung with luscious grapes. Here figs
And olives, live-oaks, peppers graceful, and
The eucalyptus tall. There stately palms,
Bright flowers, and waving plumes of pampas grass.
Beyond, the foot-hills, over which the dark
Blue waves of the Pacific glisten in
The summer sun. In dreamy restfulness
They lie, and seem to say "I bound the goal
Of happiness; here rest, there's naught beyond!"
So here we rest. A cozy cottage, not
A mansion full of care, shall be our home.
"Sweet home!" dear word, and "ours!" Without are all
The beauties Nature can bestow. Within
Shall dwell their bright reflection. Love shall make
It cheerful. Hope shall make it bright. And thoughts
For others' happiness shall multiply
Its light. Our daily cares, and troubles if
They come, we'll liken to those fleeting clouds
Which sink below the mountain's top, and make
The highest peaks, which pierce and rise above
Them, seem but more serene and lofty. So
Our blessings, hid in part, perhaps, by some
Dark clouds, shall yet above them rise and point
Us unto heaven. Or, again, as from
Our vine-clad cottage porch we look across
And see the foot-hills in the west, unconscious
Unconscious of that deep Arroyo which
Would seem, if there our vision stopp'd to be
Impassable—so we will look from one
Height and its hilltop to some other point
Of blessing, little heeding valleys wide
Or gloomy that may lie between.

The beauties of that golden land I have
Not pictured—they are real. May such a home
There be not all a dream!

OUR FLORENCE LETTER

EDITOR "SEMI-TROPIC:"—This much neglected, much overlooked and much abused section is at last coming to the front in a very prosperous and substantial manner. There is no question or a reasonable doubt but that it will become one of the richest vicinities in the whole lower country. Florence has been a great hay-producing section, but as every farmer well knows, there is no profit in hay, and to tell the actual truth of the business, we hardly get paid for our work. It is a good thing to be sure of something better, as *we are sure*. It has been established beyond any doubt, men that came among us six or seven years ago did the experimenting, and established the fact that some things were an entire failure and that others were a grand success. Their failures were a great loss to them at the time, but it was a great benefit to those coming later. Men that come into a new community and spend their money in an enterprise that the profit or loss is not known, they often fail, and are called blind by their less energetic neighbors, who say they often thought he was a strange man, "I knew he would not succeed." "The shower was over, they could then tell to a nicety how much rain had fallen." But if they succeeded, "I could have done the same, and it would have been better for me if I had." It is hard to convince such men that those who did the experimenting should have the credit of being a benefit to the country. They are worth all to a new country. They are the cause of permanent industries and business being established. If it were not for such men this country would now be a sheep pasture and it might as well be ceded back to Mexico, for no enterprising American would live in it. I said at the commencement of this article that this particular locality would, in a short time, become one of the richest in this lower country. The beginning was made by men that experimented with small gains and great losses. The tall, graceful and evergreen eucalyptus grove which is beautiful to behold, was set out in the Spring of 1876 by Mr. R. Nadean. To think that they were planted only five years ago, and now they are seemingly trying to outgrow each other with their lofty heads some seventy-five feet in the air. It is almost incredible to tell but nevertheless true. The proprietor is now cutting some twenty-five cords of wood to the acre which, delivered in Los Angeles brings $8 per cord, or an income of $200 per acre, and as fast as the woodman's axe cuts them down they sprout up from the stump. So it seems that this undertaking is permanent and profitable, and will remain a belt of timber and as a landmark as far as the eye can reach for all time to come. There is eighty acres of this beautiful grove. I will leave it to my readers to say whether or not the person that undertook this enterprise is any benefit to a new country.

The forty acres of land recently sold by Mr. Hull, the present incumbent of our church, will be set out to eucalyptus trees next Spring. Mr. White has the contract for raising the plants, setting out and cultivating for one year. It will be another piece of property that our people can point to with pride, and say that it is profitable to the owner and a thing of beauty to the country. The wood will make many a contented and cheerful fireside.

Mr. Nadean ventured into another enterprise in 1880, on the same grand scale as usual. He planted some eight hundred acres of beets, and built a large sugarie and warehouse, and put in place all necessary machinery and appliances. There were days reaching into months that this man's expenses exceeded one hundred dollars per day for labor in cultivating, slicing and curing the beets. The season arrived for making them into sugar. There was something wrong. Scientific knowledge perhaps was wanting. The growing of beets was a success, but the making of sugar was a failure. The loss was great, but all honor remains with the gentleman that undertook this vast enterprise, for each and every man got the last cent that was due him. The building of the sugarie and warehouse stands paid for and will be put to a profitable use in a year or two. This is an instance where an individual sustained great loss, but at the same time it is a benefit to the country. This same person is going into another vast enterprise, but there is no risk this time; others have succeeded in the same business in the same locality.

There was another person that experimented on a smaller scale in orange trees—ten acres were set out and cultivated for two years. "Jack frost" froze them out. They were good, healthy, five year old trees that were bought at an expense of $1.50 a tree. It was a total loss, but still I consider it a benefit to a country. The same person set out nine acres of Muscat grapes in February, 1876, the roots costing $250 gold coin. His neighbors ridiculed the idea much more than they did the setting out of the orange trees, but this enterprise proved a success beyond all expectation. It was thought irrigation would be necessary, but they have grown luxuriantly without it. The grapes grow large and are free from mildew. They are considered far superior to grapes that are grown in Los Angeles by irrigation—there certainly is more saccharine in them. And right here I wish to say to those that are contemplating setting out vines, that where they are grown without water (irrigation) that the grapes are certainly much sweeter, and from this standpoint they will attract the attention of the Eastern buyer, which we will have the honor to greet by another year. We have one Southern road and will have more. Our route is the shortest to Eastern markets by nearly one thousand miles, and there is no fear but that it will be a cheaper route and will be taken advantage of. We made a good commencement this year in setting out vines. Some seven hundred acres were set out, the most of them succeeding well. We who lived here thought the business was *booming*. Well, it was a good commencement. But this early, when plans of the future are being made but few of which are known in advance, we hear of one vineyard of one thousand acres to be set next winter, and ten and twenty acre vineyards on all sides by different parties, but a few years will elapse before this locality will become one grand, large vineyard, money will be plenty, and our people will be happy.

OMEGA.

The farmers at Artesia find sorghum syrup a very agreeable and economical addition to their bill of fare. The amber cane thrives well in that section, and its culture should be greatly extended.

COUNTY NOTES.

Careless farming is the bane of Southern California. Where the plow, harrow and manure pile are neglected, may be found the poverty-stricken farmer.

A stock company has been formed at Santa Ana for the erection at that place of a fine hotel. Work upon the building will commence immediately, and the building when completed will cost $30,000.

Norwalk and the Artesia settlement seem to have prospered during the past year. Those who took proper care of their places, and carried on their farming on true business principles, were well rewarded for their labor.

Business in Anaheim is improving, and a new hotel is about to be opened, which will do justice to the town. A first class hotel has long been needed at Anaheim, and we have no doubt will be well patronized.

Some thrifty farmers' wives in the neighborhood of Centralia and Artesia inform us that they have netted between $300 and $400 from their poultry during the past year. There is a great demand for improved breeds—Plymouth Rocks, Brown Leghorns, etc.

The people of the southern end of Los Angeles county would greatly appreciate a little attention from the officials of the Agricultural Department at Berkeley. An analysis of the alkali and salty soils, the proper means to eradicate these undesirable factors, and any other information bearing on this topic, would, if practical, be of considerable benefit.

Since exaggerated reports seem to have been circulated concerning the prevalence of injurious winds in the Santa Ana valley, we think it proper to state that after examining numerous orchards in the neighborhood of Santa Ana, Tustin and Orange we can truthfully say that although the trees are heavily loaded with fruit no damage from "Santa Ana's" was perceptible.

The southern settlements of Los Angeles county are gaining in population and wealth in a most extraordinary manner. We doubt if any portion of the Union is progressing so rapidly, and the most gratifying feature of this prosperity is that there seems to be no violation of values. Nature has been prodigal in her gifts to the Santa Ana Valley, and they are just beginning to be appreciated.

The hotel at Orange just opened by J. W. Anderson, Esq., is one of the most homelike and pleasant resorts for tourists we know of in Southern California. The settlement of Orange is prospering wonderfully. Land is changing hands and every month sees a further increase in values. We are glad to be able to state on the best of authority that the items going the rounds of the press concerning the danger from red scale in the settlement is in a manner false. This parasite only appeared in one orchard and is now under control.

Olive Culture.

FRUIT BEARING.

BY ELLWOOD COOPER, SANTA BARBARA.

Trees growing from cuttings, will produce from the fourth year, and sometimes under the most favorable circumstances, will give a few berries the third year. It is the habit of the tree to overbear, and as a consequence will give but little fruit the year following a heavy crop. This statement is verified by the most reliable books published on the subject in the French, Italian and Spanish languages. There are, however, exceptions to this rule in California. Mr. Davis, who had charge of the San Diego Mission orchard in 1875, assures me that he had gathered from the same tree two years in succession, over 150 gallons of berries. I have also observed that some trees in my orchards have borne well successive years. The fruit bearing can be controlled by the pruning. The cultivator will not forget that the shoots or branches must be two years old before they will give fruit; hence, partial pruning every year will give partial crops. My oldest orchard was planted February 21, 1872. At four years I gathered from some of the trees over two gallons of berries; in 1878 over thirty gallons each off a few of the best trees, the orchard then being only six years old. In 1879, the seventh year, the crop was not nearly so large. I had planted several thousand cuttings in the spring of 1873, but these trees did not give as six years a result equal to the first planting. The present crop (1880) is quite good; the oldest orchard now being eight years, and I think I do not over estimate when I state that the yield of some of the best and tallest trees will be over forty gallons. Trees large enough to give this quantity of fruit, planted at a distance of twenty feet, will occupy nearly all the ground, and therefore give all the fruit that can be produced on one acre. An orchard bearing uniformly this quantity as above would give the following result: One hundred trees to the acre, at forty gallons each, 4,000 gallons. This would be an enormous crop, unprecedented, and far beyond any statistics given in European publications. The one-fourth of this quantity yearly would be a very profitable crop.

In estimating an orchard, the yield of isolated trees, or trees of great age, occupying considerable areas of ground, must not enter into the basis of calculation of the probable production. The tree mentioned in the San Diego Mission orchard as yielding 150 gallons of berries was more than fifty feet distant from those surrounding it.

My agent, while traveling in Europe, through the olive districts, measured a tree growing in the "Alpes Maritimes" that was eight feet in diameter, six feet above the ground, and at the ground fifteen feet in diameter. Only a few trees of such size would be grown on one acre.

A. Contance, Professeur des Sciences

Naturelles aux Ecoles de Medecine de la Marine of France, compiled a very exhaustive work on the olive, published in Paris in 1877, from which I copy and translate as follows: "Large olive trees occupy one thousand square feet of ground—that is, require to be distant from each other about 33 feet; will produce every second year 37 gallons of berries, and occasionally as much as 135 to 148 gallons. This tree, nine years old and nine inches in diameter, will produce 10 1-3 gallons. One 12 inches in diameter 24 gallons. The mean promise and number of trees occupying one hectare (two and a half acres) is given as follows. 15 trees 12 inches in diameter, 3 trees 9 inches in diameter, 48 trees 6 inches in diameter, total, 130 trees. Produce of the same, 3000 gallons of berries." This would be equal to 1200 gallons to the acre. Another authority gives 22nd gallons per hectare. Still another gives 2360. All of the above results once in two years. Several authorities quoted by the same author reckon 200 trees to each hectare. This would be 80 trees to the acre, and distant apart 22½ feet. French cultivators give the quantity of oil contained in a given quantity of fruit as one-eighth, and in weight one tenth, that is, eight gallons of berries to one gallon of oil, and about fifty pounds of berries to one gallon of oil. Taking the average quantity of the production as given above, from a mature orchard we have in oil, per tree, two to two and a half gallons every second year. This result is obtained by thorough feeding, about which the berries would yield but little oil.

Olive trees grown from seeds are not so much fruit from the nursery until several years old; grown from cuttings, they bear in Europe as early as they do in California.

The newness and richness of our soil will probably give, the first fifty years, double the best results given to those countries where oil making has been the business for many generations. Our climate is congenial to the habit of the tree; it blooms from the 1st to the 10th of May, and the fruit forms from the 1st to the 10th of June. At this season we have our best weather, free from extremes of either cold or heat. Nowhere in the world are all the conditions so favorable to the perfect fruit bearing of the olive.

FRUIT PICKING.

The olive usually ripens in November in some localities in Eastern countries during favorable years, the fruit passing for ripening as early as October, and for pickling, in September. In Santa Bar-ara the crop of last year (1880), as also that of 1879, was unusually late in ripening, not being ready to pick before the middle of January—a delay of fully two months—the cause no doubt owing to the extraordinary rain fall of these two years.

[To be Continued.]

SEMI-TROPIC
CALIFORNIA,
—AN—
ILLUSTRATED MONTHLY.

Devoted to Agriculture, Horticulture, and the Development of Southern California.

Terms: $1.50 per Annum, in Advance.

OFFICE, ROOMS 9 & 10, BAKER BLOCK.

Address, CHAS. COLEMAN, JR., Los Angeles, Cal.

CHAS COLEMAN, JR.,   EDITOR AND PROP'R.

OFFICIAL PAPER
—OF THE—
Southern California Horticultural Soc'y.
OFFICE, ROOM No. 9, BAKER BLOCK.
CHAS COLEMAN, JR., Secretary.

This number completes volume four of this journal, and to us it will ever be as a closed book, beyond our power to add a single correction. However, we will cherish it as one would an old friend with whom many a happy, toilsome hour has been passed; and as we take up the task of volume five, we will endeavor to profit by our experience with the volume which we now close.

The two very interesting addresses by F. J. Barretto, Esq., and Governor Downey, to be found on another page, will furnish food for reflection. Mr. Barretto justly complains because of the lack of patronage accorded our recent Agricultural Fair, which was truly worthy of a larger and an appreciative attendance. Governor Downey speaks in glowing terms of our country, our State, and our County, and gives reliable statistics which make a very flattering showing as regards the success of our various industries, and the rapidly accumulating wealth of Southern California.

Occasionally we learn that a subscriber has failed to receive some number of this paper, and the question, "Why not?" is sent in to us. Our plea will be found in the fact that we mail the paper with the utmost care, and we are free to say that the trouble must be with the post-office department. Does it look reasonable that we would neglect a subscriber, when we well know that if he cannot receive his paper that he will not continue his subscription? As far as it is within our power we will correct the irregularity, and if anybody who fails to receive his paper will drop us a postal-card, we will mail an extra copy with pleasure.

Just a word for the holiday number, which will appear a week or ten days before Christmas. It will be beautifully illustrated, with mostly new engravings. The edition is guaranteed to be 5,000, and it may reach double that number. It will be full of interesting and valuable reading matter for all classes, our own citizens and

the inquirer not yet arrived; and as an advertising medium this much can be truthfully said in its favor: It reaches more homes in Los Angeles and San Bernardino counties than any other publication. So much for home trade. Further, 500 copies are already engaged by three of our leading firms, to be sent to the different business firms throughout the Territories, and he who seeks trade in that direction would do well to advertise, and send his share of copies away. Many will work on this principle, and the result is certainly apparent to all.

Edwin Baxter, the Attorney who has recently settled in Los Angeles, and opened an office in Baker Block, is not from Washington, D.C., as, by mistake, we stated in our last issue. He came from Grand Haven, the center of the famous fruit belt of Western Michigan, hence his location here. He has, however, for many years, prosecuted claims before the Pension, Auditors' and General Land offices, and other departments at Washington. He has also for some years held the office of Judge of the Probate Court, and is therefore well posted in the matter of wills, settlement of estates, &c.

TO THE LIFE MEMBERS.

You have now received this journal free for four years owing to the following circumstances: It was first started and owned by the Horticultural Society, and by a provision of the constitution of said Society it was furnished to the membership free. At the time L. M. Holt severed his connection with the Society, the ownership passed into the hands of Carter & Rice, who furnished to the membership under contract, for three hundred dollars a year—there being about that number of life and contributing members. Last year Mr. Rice continued to furnish the paper on the same terms, and with this issue, the December number, that contract ceases. The journal passed into my hands some months ago, but I continued to carry out Mr. Rice's contract. Now, then, the position in which I stand might not be considered a pleasant one, since I am proprietor of the journal and also a member of the Board of Directors, and further am Secretary of the Society. However, I would not in any way use my position to force a tax of three hundred dollars per year upon the Society, and if the subject should come before the board in the form of a motion I would certainly vote no or not vote at all. It was my intention to have the subject discussed at the board meeting last Saturday, because some contend that the constitutional provision and the precedents set by the two former contracts should have some weight in deciding the matter, however, other business forced it from my mind, and this number will go to press before another meeting will be held. After this meeting, two of the directors agreed with me that it was a burden which they did not think the Society should bear. As far as I am con-

cerned I shall remain passive, and should the balance of the board decide at the next meeting to continue the journal to the membership I will supply it at lowest rates. But should they take the opposite view, which I in justice to the Society would advocate, I will send a canvasser among you, and I trust you will receive him kindly and will subscribe for a journal which asks for no subsidies and is a power in the land for good in many ways.

Brunt, of the Famous Cheap Store, desires us to tell the people that he is now marking down his entire stock of goods, to reduce them by 1st January, 1882. Any one wishing to get bargains can have them by only calling at the Famous Cheap Store. See his bargains in flannels, cashmeres, dress goods, dress trimmings, shirtings, corsets, handkerchiefs, buttons, suspenders, ladies', men's and misses' hose, ladies', misses' and children's hoods, shawls, blankets, table covers, table linens, towels, napkins, ladies' belts, cords and tassels, ruching and collars, ribbons, silk handkerchiefs, ladies' skirts, linen crash, lace curtains, white bed blankets, white quilts, ladies underwear, men's underwear, a large stock of men's and ladies' hats, ladies dress goods, a very large stock of cashmeres and all other kinds of dress goods, gloves, ties, scarfs, bows, satchels, and a large stock of men's, ladies' and children's boots and shoes. Large lines of all goods kept in his line, and on examination of the goods and prices will be conclusive evidence of the above fact. This is no humbug, as the entire force of clerks, ten in number, have been busy for several days marking goods down to almost cost. Remember, our motto is, "No trouble to show goods, and a great pleasure to sell."

Mr. Lacy has added the Hartford, of Connecticut, to his list of insurance companies. This is the oldest and most reliable company in the United States.

J. S. Mills, of Pasadena, stands ready to contract to set vineyards at the lowest living rates. His experience in this line has been broad, and all his old customers will recommend him in the highest terms.

Mr. Jillson won first premium on everything he had in competition at the recent Agricultural Fair—Plymouth Rocks, Brown Leghorns and W. F. Black Spanish. His foundation stock of P. Rocks were imported from the yards of Mr. C. A. Keefer, Sterling, Illinois; also the beautiful pair of Brown Leghorns he had on exhibition. Mr. Jillson says no breeder in America could send him finer stock than he has received from Mr. Keefer. It speaks for itself. Parties ordering eggs from Mr. Jillson the coming season will get as fine as there is in the State. See advertisement on front cover.

This square-dealing reliable firm of Hatch & Barclay of San Francisco, have removed to No. 10, California street, where they will continue to meet their customers and guarantee satisfaction.

EDITOR SEMI-TROPIC CALIFORNIA:— The highest medical authority asserts that cooked apples, either boiled or baked are the best food for patients in the lever el condition of small pox, typhoid fever and erysipelas. It has been well said that "apples are general favorites." Every eye covets, every hand reaches to them. An apple is a noble fruit, the friend of immortality, and its virtues blush to be tasted Every muse delights in it, as its mythology shows from the garden of Hesperides to the orchard of Plato. A basket of pearmains, golden russets, or any of the choice kinds, standing in sight, shall perfume the scholar's composition as much as it refresh es his genius.

Apples are now considered to contain far more brain food than any other fruit or vegetable, and to be much more nutricious than potatoes, which enter so largely into the component parts of every meal. At present, apples are principally used in the form of puddings, pies, tarts and sauces, and are also eaten raw, in which state they are more wholesome than when mingled with butter, eggs and flour. But they are very delicious when simply baked, and served at every meal; and substituted for pickles and such condiments, they would surely be found beneficial. Sweet baked apples are a most desirable addition at the breakfast and tea table, and are far more healthful, appropriate, and sustaining than half the dishes usually esteemed essential at such times. Served with milk and bread they make the best diet that young children can partake of, and are very satisfying in their nature. Baked apples without meat, are far more substantial food than potatoes can possibly be made, and to us the delicious aroma and flavor are always most appetizing. We would rather go without our daily bread than our daily baked sweet apples.

Yet, although there were such an abundant crop of apples, we presume there are many families who will not use a barrel of them for the table this season, but will devour at least six barrels of potatoes. Let us beg of them to equalize the two a little more, and purchase at least three barrels of apples to five of potatoes. They will find that less flour, eggs, sugar and butter will be consumed in a family when a plentiful supply of apples is stored in the cellar. One of the most celebrated physicians of Philadelphia eats two raw apples every every morning before he retires to rest, and thinks that they not only supply food to his brain, but keep the whole system in a healthy condition. For years I have followed his advice, and am confident that the fruit has been of great service to us.

Business still leads in the real estate boom, and Mr. S. C. Evans, president of the R. L. & I. Co., has his hands full in attending to sales, answering inquiries, etc.

THE "ACME."

The advertisement of which appears on our front cover, and which attracted so much attention at our recent Fairs, furnishes a volume of endorsements in Southern California alone. The following are a few taken at random:

SUNNY SLOPE, Cal ——— 188

Last season I had no single cultivator at work. This year have done all the same work in over 100 acres with one "Acme" three-horse harrow, keeping both heavy and light soil clean and in excellent condition. Have not used a cultivator this season among the trees.

(Signed) MANUEL H. for L. J. Rose, Esq

SAN GABRIEL Mission, Cal, Aug 24 1881

Gents. The "ACME" pulverizing harrow I bought of you last winter does its work well. I think it one of the best, if not the very best, I have ever used.

(Signed) L. H. TITUS.

PASADENA, Los Angeles Co. Cal., April 30th, 1881.

Gents. The "ACME" pure barrow from you is a first class machine, does its work thoroughly, and leaves the ground in first class order. I can go over eight (8) to ten (10) acres per day. It certainly is the best cultivator ever used on the Pacific Coast. Respectfully,

(Signed) ALECK F. MILLS.

ORANGE, Los Angeles Co., Cal., April 16th, 1881.

Gents. I am cultivating seventy acres of orange and lemon orchard. Have used various cultivators. The "ACME" I bought of you has followed the work better and more satisfactory than any other cultivator I ever used. I can recommend it to my neighbors and friends as being the best for general use.

(Signed) R. C. HAYWARD.

COMPOUND OXYGEN TREATMENT.

We take pleasure in commending to the careful attention of our readers the "Compound Oxygen Treatment." This Treatment is becoming very popular as a curative agent, for all diseases of the lungs and other respiratory organs, consisting principally in oxygen inhalation. Dyspepsia, diseases of the liver, and nervous derangement are also cured by this wonderful agent. A New England physician discovered this great remedy for disease after an almost total attack of pneumonia, the result of which did not leave him for months. The dispensers of this treatment have some of the very best testimonials as to its efficacy from those who have used it. Among those who testify to its curative properties are such men as T. S. Arthur, the distinguished author and proprietor of the Home Magazine, and the Hon William H Kelley, member of Congress for Philadelphia. The testimony that comes from persons from all over the land, who have been cured of diseases that were pronounced hopeless, in many instances can be characterized as nothing less than marvellous. It is a source of gratification to be able to recommend a really valuable remedial agent, especially in that terrible disease pulmonary Consumption. Drs. Starkey and Palen are regularly educated physicians, and had much experience and successful practice before adopting this Treatment as a specialty. We call attention to their advertisement in another column.

Apiculture.

THE AMERICAN BEE JOURNAL CORRECTED.

EDITOR SEMI-TROPIC CALIFORNIA:—
The American Bee Journal, published in Chicago, Ill., established in 1861, claiming to be the oldest bee paper in America, and the only weekly paper in the world devoted exclusively to scientific bee culture and the production and sale of pure honey, in the issue of October 12th, 1881, publishes a table concerning the honey production of the United States and Canada for 1881, and the editor calls it "a very interesting table," says "it is very valuable and will be exceedingly useful for reference," and very feelingly alludes to the extra labor and study it has entailed upon the editor, the amount of brain work expended upon such a table, etc.

Now this table may be all the editor of the American Bee Journal claims it is in other States and Territories, as well as Canada, but when the editor puts the number of colonies of bees at 520 for the whole State of California for the fall of 1881, we begin to wonder where and how the extra labor and study, and the expenditure of brain work, comes to play any part as "valuable or interesting." Let us get at facts, and then compare them with the statements of the very much over-worked editor's table.

On the first Monday of March, 1881, the Assessor of Los Angeles county, California, reported 16,811 colonies of bees in the county, and valued them at $41,226, and their owners are paying taxes on that number of colonies. At the same time the Assessor found 535,000 pounds of honey on hand, and the owners of it are paying taxes on that quantity of honey, making a difference of 16,000 colonies of bees between the table and the Los Angeles County Assessor's figures. The total honey product of California, according to the table, is 30,168 pounds, making a difference of 514,832 pounds as between the County Assessor and the editor's calculations. If one remembers that such men as Harbison, Wilkins, Flint, Hale, and others who have long been in the business of bee keeping, are residents of California, and any one of the persons named owning more colonies of bees and producing more honey than is credited to the whole State, and that some of them have shipped honey by the carload from California to Chicago, Ill., the very place where the editor does business and publishes the American Bee Journal, the question naturally occurs, if it would not be a very good thing for the editor to take Horace Greeley's advice and "go west," and save mental wear and tear, get a taste of some of our pure white sage honey, get acquainted with some of the honey producers of California, and interview the County Assessors as to the honey yield of California hereafter.

C. N. WILSON.

WILL BEE-KEEPING PAY?

EDITOR SEMI-TROPIC:—Having spoken in a previous communication of some of the preliminary steps to be taken in establishing an apiary in Southern California we will next speak of the hive to be used. A very slight investigation will convince any one that there is but one kind of hive which can be profitably used here, and that is the moveable frame hive in common use among our apiarists, and claimed to be, I believe, the Langstroth patent. It is as simple in construction as it is possible to make a hive, and in fact I regard it as perfection itself so far as general utility is concerned, as well as its ease of construction and cost of material required to make it. Each complete hive is composed of two boxes of equal dimensions. The same sized frames being used in each box, they will admit of combs being taken from either box and placed in the other, as occasion may require, which will often become necessary in the successful management of an apiary. All the hives in an apiary should be alike and of the same color, whether painted or unpainted, for it will frequently become necessary, especially in dividing, to remove one hive and substitute another, and if the new hive is not of the same general appearance as the one removed the bees often will not enter it. This of course causes more or less fuss and vexation, and might in some instances cause the hive men to feature some of the commandments. Bees not only notice the color but also the location, for few when their hive has been removed during their absence and replaced by another, they will invariably call at the front door, but if the color of these hives is changed they went to regard themselves as lost, and will generally try to enter some other hive, and are sometimes killed, though if they come loaded with honey they are generally received with "open arms" by any colony, just as our fellowman is received when he applies for admission to the family circle, bringing with him plenty of money to add to the general store. I think the most economical material for the body of the hive, and also for bottom boards, is inch rough redwood, the body of the hive to be well whitewashed. For covers use best surface redwood, well seasoned, the top side to be dressed and both sides well painted with Averill patent paint, which is very much better in this climate than lead and oil, as it dries glassy hard and will not "chalk off" when exposed to the weather. I would use no color except white, as white reflects the heat instead of absorbing it, so dark colors will do. By whitewashing or painting white you will escape loss by the melting and dropping of combs in very warm weather. I would not favor painting the body of the hive because that would necessitate the use of surfaced lumber, which is rather expensive, and I believe a hive made of rough lumber and well whitewashed is just as good and very much cheaper. Whitewash, as every one knows, costs comparatively nothing, and can be rapidly applied, and it will put on will last

two years or more. During the present season I lost by melting enough combs to have paid me well for whitewashing every hive in my apiary, my loss being confined merely to unpainted hives which have become quite dark by exposure to the weather and which consequently absorb a great amount of heat. The lumber for the body of the hive should be ripped so as to allow a half inch between the bottom board and the bottom or lower sides of your comb frames, in order that the bees may have plenty of room to pass back and forth. And in addition to this you should allow fully 1 inch for shrinkage in the lumber. If these things be not provided for your frames will soon rest on the bottom of your hives, and this should never be the case. As for the use of comb foundation apiarists are divided in opinion, and probably always will be. I have tried it and do not think its use is profitable, and would advise any one experimenting with it to "go slow," lest they get more money in it than they can get out of it. I am well aware that its advocates tell of some marvelous things which their bees have accomplished working on comb foundation. I can do the same, but I can tell of equally marvelous things which my bees did without touching the comb foundation, which I placed in the hive, thus giving them a chance to manifest their preferences. Some comb foundation men may take exception to this and say my bees do not understand their business. If he thinks so let him visit my apiary without his mask. In fact I have found the Italian bee to be very "sharp," especially so at one end, and I find that on unceremonious occasions he generally introduces himself sharp end foremost.

I would not, however, give much for a bee which will not sting. My hardiest stingers are my best workers, and with my mask on to protect my face, and with my "patent" smoker made of an old coffee pot, I can laugh at their indignation. Let us try to imitate them in perseverance and industry, and when we are robbed half as often as they we will be twice as indignant.

J. F. S.

Pure bee pasturage, although not so bright as it might be, owing to the light crop of honey produced this year, has fair promises for the future. Colonies generally are strong, and next spring will probably find them in good condition for a profitable summer's work. Experience is teaching our bee men how to assist their colonies during an off year, and fewer failures occur in this industry now than formerly.

THE Los Angeles County Bee-keepers' Association will meet at the office of C. N. Wilson, No. 2 Fort street, on the third Saturday of December, 1881, at 1 o'clock p. m. Business of importance will be transacted and officers for the ensuing year elected. Let every member be in attendance.

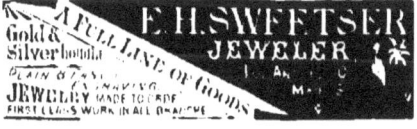

The Poultry Yard.

EGGS IN WINTER.

Mr. B. (in May)—"Hens laying well?"

Mr. C.—"Yes, first rate; all at it, but eggs are so cheap and plenty they don't count for much at this season."

SCENE CHANGES.

Mr. B. (in December)—"How are your hens laying, Mr. C., this cold weather?"

Mr. C.—"Not at all; shut down completely; old hens on a strike, pullets neglecting business shamefully; eggs are way up in price, but I've none to sell. How is it with you?"

Mr. B.—"Well, I don't know; your hens and mine are different."

Mr. C.—"Oh, yes, of course; my hens are scrubs, and yours are"—

Mr. B.—"Hold on; don't get mad because I say my fowls are different from yours. They may not be any better in blood than yours, but I study to make my hens pay for what they eat, and for my time and labor in caring for them. They do it, and largely, by laying eggs when eggs are high-priced; that is, in cold weather. I first give care to their quarters in winter. A warm, sunny place for them, or no eggs; put that down."

Mr. C.—"All right; go on."

Mr. B.—"With a warm house, and dry house, and dry earth to dust in, they are well provided for in that direction. Next, I don't expect hens to lay forever. After a hen has laid eggs for me two winters, she is retired. I have no old hens in my fowl house; nothing but young yearling hens and pullets; they are the ones for winter laying, and mind you, the profitable fowl is the winter layer. I look out for my pullets, too; get them out early, and keep them growing, so they will begin to lay just before cold weather; then they will keep at it till cold weather begins. Again, I keep my hens by themselves, and pullets by themselves; there's a great deal in this. Old birds and young birds do best in pens by themselves. I've found, last, but not least, I feed for eggs. I raise up hay for the layers, give them cabbage to pick at, a little cooked meat daily, crushed bone and oyster and clam shells, a hot morning meal of mashed boiled vegetables, meal and shorts, with a sprinkling of red pepper, all stirred into a hot mixture until a good hot mash is made. Variety of food is what they want. It takes a little of my time to see after them, but it pays, I can tell you, to make hens lay when eggs are forty cents a dozen."

Mr. C.—"Correct. Perhaps mine are past reforming and won't lay, but to-morrow I'll begin on your system, and see if I can't make my fowls lay eggs in cold weather as well as in warm."—*Poultry Bulletin.*

EGGS FOR FOOD.

With all the merits of the earth, eggs have been a favorite food, and yet even now their value is hardly appreciated.

There is no egg of any kind known which can not be used for food. A similarity exists in the construction of all eggs, since the white portion and yolk is present in every specimen. Peculiarities in form, size and color are no tests of the quality or freshness of the eggs of fowls, for every hen has an individuality about her own product; although it is well known that feeding has a decided influence on the flavor and quality of eggs.

The weight of an ordinary fowl's egg is one and a half to two ounces; while that of a duck is two to three ounces; of the seagull and turkey, three to four ounces, and that of the goose four to six ounces. Seventy-four per cent of an egg is water, in which respect it is very similar to fish, lean meat and potatoes. Of the remaining twenty-six per cent about fourteen is nitrogenous and ten per cent is fatty matter. The white of the egg contains no fat, but has more water and albumen than the yolk, while the latter contains all the fat and sulphur. An egg of average size contains about two hundred grains of dry substance, of which nearly sixty per cent is nitrogenous, forty per cent fatty and eleven per cent saline matters. In nitrogenous substances the white of an egg exceeds that of all known food, except peas, cheese and poultry.

J. H. SEAMOUR.   M. D. JOHNSON.   L. M. LA PEIRA.

THE
GRANGE STORE!
CHOICE GROCERIES.

The Freshest and Best of Everything in the Market.

"GILT EDGED" BUTTER A SPECIALTY.

Orders from the interior solicited.

Seymour, Johnson & Co.,
133 Main St., Los Angeles.

NAHUL REES,   ROBERT F. WISCHING.

Rees & Wisching,
Makers and Importers of

Buggies, Farm and Spring Wagons
AND AGRICULTURAL IMPLEMENTS,

Agents for the Newton Wagon and R. M. Osborn & Co.'s Mowers and Reapers.

33 and 35 Los Angeles St.,   Los Angeles, Cal.

A. BRUNSON.   G. WILEY WELLS.

Brunson & Wells,
Attorneys and Counsellors-at-Law,

Nos. 11, 12, 14, 16 and 17 Baker Block.

Will practice in the Supreme Court of this state, and of the United States, and attend to all business before the Departments at Washington, D. C.